THE HEARTBREAKER

THE HEARTBREAKER

Susan Howatch

LITTLE, BROWN

A *Little, Brown* Book

First published in Great Britain in 2003
by Little, Brown

Copyright © Leaftree Ltd 2003

The moral right of the author has been asserted.

All characters in this publication are fictitious and any
resemblance to real persons, living or dead, is purely coincidental.

Extracts from *Mud and Stars*: The Impact of Hospice
Experience on the Church's Ministry of Healing used with
kind permission of OICPC. Extracts from *A Time to Heal: A report*
for the House of Bishops on the Healing Ministry are copyright © The
Archbishops' Council, 2000, and are reproduced by permission.

A CIP catalogue record for this book
is available from the British Library.

HARDBACK ISBN 0 316 86017 4
C FORMAT ISBN 0 316 86018 2

Typeset in Berkeley Book by
Palimpsest Book Production Limited, Polmont, Stirlingshire
Printed and bound in Great Britain by Clays Ltd, St Ives plc

Little, Brown
An imprint of
Time Warner Books UK
Brettenham House
Lancaster Place
London WC2E 7EN

www.TimeWarnerBooks.co.uk

CONTENTS

PART ONE

Setting Out

'Our identity is being forged in the crucible of whatever sufferings turn out to be inextricable from the particular journey of each person . . . into fullness of life.'

Mud and Stars
A report of a working party consisting mainly of doctors, nurses and clergy

CHAPTER ONE

Carta

'But passion needs no recruiting agent. It dominates the head-lines, making fools of the great and the good, breaking hearts, damaging lives . . .'

Godless Morality
Richard Holloway

I

In 1990 I survived a life-crisis. In 1991 I wound up working for a good cause. But never did I foresee that in 1992 my vital companion during the next stage of my journey would be a prostitute. Let's face it, one doesn't normally connect prostitution with church fundraising.

1992 . . . It was that long-ago year when mobile phones still only operated through terrestrial links, that era of technological pre-history before the word 'internet' began to ricochet in earnest around the square mile called the City which forms London's financial district. I had worked there once as a lawyer, but now I had opted for a different lifestyle.

This decision, which I never regretted, led to an invitation to reorganise the business affairs of a City church called St Benet's-by-the-Wall. The people there had supported me following the collapse of my brief marriage and the loss of my job; in fact they had supported me through a time so horrific that I still shuddered to think of it, so when I found myself in a position to repay my debt to St Benet's I seized the opportunity with both hands.

The opportunity arose when the office manager of the St Benet's Healing Centre suddenly died and the Rector was faced with the task of finding someone with financial expertise who was prepared to work for a pittance. I volunteered to work for nothing, and during 1991 I reorganised the office. This inevitably led to a vision of the future in which expensive computers were needed, and once the subject of money arose, the idea of expansion soon surfaced. Immediately all eyes at St Benet's swivelled to the derelict house across the road. The building, a rare City freehold zoned for residential use, was owned by the Church Commissioners, who had been hanging on to it in the forlorn hope that the property market would revive.

At that point the Rector moved fast. Having established that permission to change the use of the building would be forthcoming, he approached the Bishop for help, and the result was that the Church Commissioners agreed to lease the property at a moderate rent to the trustees of the St Benet's Healing Centre on condition that they raised the money to rebuild the interior as offices. The idea was that the Healing Centre's administrative office would occupy the ground floor while the rest of the building could be leased to tenants who would pay our rent and cover the other running costs. In addition, removing the administrative office from the church would give us the chance to remodel the Healing Centre – another major expense.

'Wonderful!' said the Rector. 'Now, how do we raise one and a half million pounds to cover all our costs?'

'Oh, that's peanuts!' I said without stopping to think. 'Five or six million's routine in the fundraising game nowadays.'

A minute later I had been appointed director of the St Benet's Appeal and set squarely on the road that led to Richard Slaney and the seamiest of his many friends.

II

I first met Richard Slaney in 1989 when I began to work for the law firm Curtis, Towers. We were both partners, but while I laboured in the corporate tax department, he was involved with the private clients; he specialised in the making of wills and the administration of estates. Educated at Winchester and Oxford he had a wide circle of well-heeled, influential friends which made him a desirable contact for a fundraiser, and I decided to lose no time in seeking his advice.

I had no experience of fundraising, but I knew that at its most sophisticated level the buck-chaser was expected to combine high-grade diplomatic skills with the hide of a rhinoceros and the chutzpah of a street-trader. Because of the expense we decided against hiring a professional fundraiser to teach me the tricks of the trade, but unfortunately the more I told myself I could cope, the more stressed I began to feel, and soon I was wondering in panic if I had bitten off far more than I could chew.

Then I pulled myself together and called Richard at Curtis, Towers.

III

I met Richard for lunch at Hudson's, an oak-panelled City restaurant where the food was modernised Olde English and the wine list was first-class global. Richard was an oenophile with a weakness for high-calorie puddings. He had never succeeded in giving up smoking and as far as I knew he had never attempted to diet, so it was surprising he looked no more than twenty pounds overweight, but I remembered him telling me that he lived an active life on weekends at his country house in Hampshire. He had an elegant wife, a son reading law up at Oxford and a daughter studying for her A-levels at Cheltenham.

'Carta!' he exclaimed warmly, coming towards me with his hand outstretched. 'How very nice to see you again!'

Despite his excess weight and his smoker's skin, he was attractive. Married men in their late forties were a group I now found wholly resistible, but I could see that other women lucky enough not to have my marital history would be quick to fancy him. He was tall, with black curly hair streaked with silver, dark eyes and a winning smile. His family had come from Ireland, but not recently. An eighteenth-century Slaney had made a fortune serving with the British army in India and had decided to settle in England afterwards – or so Richard always said. There was a rumour that his grandfather had been an immigrant called Slanowicz, but I never thought Richard was the type to lie about his origins – or indeed about any other basic fact of his private life.

5

'First catch your patrons,' he said when I asked for his advice. 'You need a collection of distinguished names on your letterhead to give the cause street-cred and help with the networking – oh, and get a Royal to be patron-in-chief. After that you need first a glossy brochure explaining your aims, second a series of high-profile fundraising events, third a benign journalist giving you publicity in at least one of the broadsheets—'

'Wait, wait, wait – you're describing life on Mars! This is a City church run by people who aren't interested in the glamorous life and don't know any Royals!'

'The Archbishop of Canterbury does – tell him the man you want is Prince Charles. He's the Royal who's interested in alternative medicine.'

'This is complementary medicine,' I said at once. 'It works alongside orthodox medicine and not as an alternative to it. In fact the Rector, Nicholas Darrow, works in partnership with a doctor who has a branch of her National Health practice at the Centre.'

'All the better. Since healing's so trendy nowadays that any charlatan can make a mint out of it, you can't stress the Healing Centre's respectability too strongly. Tell Darrow he's got to collar at least one bishop to be a patron, and get the Archbishop to write a foreword for the brochure.'

I had abandoned my food in order to scribble key words in a notebook. 'The trouble is,' I said, 'I can't just rely on the Church. I've got to plug into the secular world as well to get the money flowing.'

'No problem – everyone's interested in health. The real difficulty here is that you need this money for an office building, and office buildings just don't press the buttons which open chequebooks . . . You say that the Healing Centre itself is to be remodelled?'

'An architect's already drawn up plans.'

'Then here's what you do: you highlight the expanded, redesigned Healing Centre and focus on this church's very important special ministry. People will be intrigued by the idea of a priest and a doctor working together – hype that up, give your boss a high profile . . . What's he like?'

'Lots of charisma but it's subtle. We're not talking about a tel-evangelist wonder-worker here.'

'Just as well, since you need to present him as a man of total integrity.'

'Yes, but Nicholas is far too busy to be a fundraising asset—'

'Never mind, you can always play the Mother Teresa card and present him as totally dedicated, uninterested in worldly matters. How long's he been working in the City?'

'Since 'eighty-one.'

'Then he must surely know a lot of people who have the potential to help. Look, why don't the three of us have a meeting to discuss who should be patrons, who should be marked as potential donors and who should be networked? If Darrow and I have friends in common it'll make your task easier.'

'Fantastic! Richard, I can't tell you how grateful I am—'

'Never say I don't do my best for my friends!'

The discussion of fundraising continued, and it was not until the end of the meal, after I had signalled for the bill, that he said suddenly: 'You've changed. You seem less brash, less driven.'

'I got myself sorted by the St Benet's team after my husband died.' The bill arrived and when I signed it Richard commented: 'I see you're writing your first name with an A at the end. No longer "Carter" as in President Jimmy?'

'No longer a high flyer. So now I don't have to waste energy cultivating a masculine image in order to survive in a man's world.'

'Ah, but is it really possible to live without cultivating an image which enables one to get on in life? We all do it, don't we? We pick the roles we need to play.'

I stared at him. 'But that's the point. We don't have to live like that. I'm through with role playing now — I'm busy being me!'

He gave me his warm, winning smile. But he said nothing – and that was the moment when I should have begun to wonder exactly what went on behind that polished facade of his.

Yet the moment passed. I was too busy plotting my next move as a fundraiser.

IV

I see no need for me to describe in detail my work over the next few months as I launched the Appeal. Suffice it to say that Richard produced a steady stream of friends who were capable of assisting me in some way or other, while his wife Moira gave me tips on fundraising techniques; as a socialite of the ladies-who-lunch variety, she was used to raising money for good causes, and she soon appeared fascinated by the St Benet's Healing Centre. Or maybe she was just fascinated by the Rector. Most women were, but I had never found Nicholas a turn-on even before I had decided that married men in their late forties were best excluded from my bedtime menu. Fortunately Nicholas had never found me a turn-on either, and this mutual non-attraction explained why we were able to work so well together.

I was just wondering uneasily if Moira were about to make a fool of herself over Nicholas, when the reason for her fascination with the Healing Centre finally surfaced. In the March of 1992 she made an appointment to see Nicholas and turned up with her daughter Bridget. A glance at the girl was enough to tell anyone she was anorexic, and with the secret now disclosed Richard was able to talk about his daughter's problems when he and I next met for lunch. I learned that her illness had caused her to drop out of school; hospitalisation had enabled her to gain weight which was soon lost when she returned home; Moira, at her wits' end, saw St Benet's as a last resort.

Bridget refused to see the psychologist who worked at the Centre, but she agreed to talk on a regular basis to Nicholas and also to Val, the doctor. She then started to attend the weekly lunch-time healing service in the church, and Moira even went up with her for the laying-on of hands.

When I mentioned this to Richard I found myself adding: 'Do you feel tempted to join Moira and Bridget at a healing service?'

'Not my scene.'

'Because you're an atheist? I used to be an atheist myself,' I said rapidly, 'but I found it just didn't fit the reality I experienced around the time Kim died, and I couldn't deny my own experience.'

He said nothing.

'Sorry,' I said more rapidly than ever, 'religion isn't everyone's cup of tea. Let's change the subject.'

But he ignored this suggestion. 'I've no objection to Jesus Christ,' he said flatly, 'but that religion his followers founded has no time for someone like me.'

'Someone like you?'

'Someone rich. The Church does nothing but bang on about the poor – it behaves as if it's taken over society's naive belief that money solves everyone's problems!'

'I'm sure Nicholas would tell you that Christ came for everyone, no matter what their financial status.'

'And that explains why Nick's one of the few clergy I can tolerate, but I'm still not willing to get involved in Bridget's healing programme. I know they like to treat the whole family in these cases, but I'm keeping my mouth shut and I've advised Moira to do the same. Our marriage is no one's business but our own.'

Now it was my turn to be silent. Could the subject of the Slaney marriage really be divorced from the mystery of Bridget's illness? I remembered an article I had once read about an anorexia case. The father had been emotionally detached, often absent. In consequence the mother had turned to her children to compensate herself by dominating their lives, and the daughter had used the anorexia as a means to control a situation where she was otherwise powerless. But how typical was this case? Anorexia was a complex illness and almost certainly had more than one cause.

It was not until later that I remembered some words of my mentor Lewis Hall, a retired priest who helped Nicholas at St Benet's. Lewis had said that in dysfunctional families it was often the weakest member who manifested the dis-ease, the weakest member who broke down under the burden of the family's repressed pain. If the Slaney family was dysfunctional, then the parents' marriage became a crucial factor in the problem, and if Richard refused to acknowledge this, he was going to wind up impeding the healing process.

I began to wonder just what he felt he had to hide.

V

I had never heard gossip suggesting that Richard was promiscuous, but I could imagine him having a discreet long-term affair which would spice up his weekday nights in London. I could even imagine Moira condoning it; she might well have her own agenda. But what I found hard to imagine was why such a routine marital arrangement should be causing symptoms of profound sickness in Bridget. I thought there almost certainly had to be something else going on.

I might have speculated far more about the Slaneys if I hadn't been so busy dealing with the aftermath of the Lambeth Palace reception which had launched the Appeal. The first wave of donations had arrived. I was busy plotting fundraising events, nurturing my prize contacts and devising the right strategic approach to various trusts and charities. In fact for a while I lost sight of the Slaneys, and when Richard called one day in September 1992 – that crucial September – to suggest a drink after work, I felt guilty that I had been out of touch.

'I'd love to see you!' I said with enthusiasm, and we agreed to meet at the Savoy.

I then called Eric Tucker to tell him I'd be late home. (I'll get to Eric later.) When he learned that I was having a drink with Richard he pretended to be jealous and I commented that a touch of insecurity never did an attractive man any harm. At once he threatened to be unattractive in future. Had I ever wondered what he would look like with a shaven head and gold earrings?

'Preserve your curls and lobes,' I advised, 'unbutton your shirt to the navel and I promise you I'll be home by eight-thirty to make you feel as secure as a rock star with ten bodyguards.'

But it was to be long after eight-thirty when I returned home from the Savoy.

VI

After meeting in the hotel lobby we moved into the main lounge where a pianist was stroking the keys of the piano, and at first I took the lead in the conversation; I thought Richard would want an update on my fundraising activities, but when I sensed he was merely listening out of courtesy I broke off.

'Sorry!' I said. 'Fundraisers get fixated on money, don't they? Occupational hazard.'

'It was money I wanted to talk to you about.'

I was aware of the pianist playing 'The Windmills of Your Mind' from *The Thomas Crown Affair* for all those people who had been young in the 1960s, but the music seemed to fade as my curiosity accelerated. Richard took another gulp of his Beefeater martini. Then he said: 'I want to make a donation to your Appeal.'

At once I answered: 'That would be more than generous since

you've helped us so much in other ways,' but as I spoke I was wondering automatically how much he would give. A thousand pounds? Five hundred? By this time I had learnt to regard even small amounts with gratitude, but I hardly thought we were talking of a token fifty here.

Meanwhile Richard was saying: 'Last weekend Bridget sat down to Sunday lunch and ate a slice of roast beef, a potato and a Brussels sprout – and there was no vomiting afterwards either. I don't know what Nick Darrow's secret is but he's certainly producing some kind of miracle.'

'Nicholas hates the M-word. He'd just say all healing comes from God.'

'I can't think in that kind of language. All I know is that Bridget's better.' And before I could comment he added: 'I saw Nick today. I'd made up my mind that I had to tell him, face to face, why I'd always refused to be involved in any family therapy, but at the last moment I just chickened out and offered him ten thousand instead.'

I nearly choked on my wine. *'Ten thousand pounds?'*

'Glad you're impressed. Nick wasn't. He just said: "You don't need to buy your way out of talking to me."'

I was speechless.

'Brave, wasn't he?' said Richard amused, seeing how horrified I was that Nicholas should risk the loss of a donation by doling out such an unpalatable response. 'I admired that. In fact I admired it so much that I said: "Let's make that twenty thousand – you've earned it." He then told me he'd say nothing to you for twenty-four hours in case I decided I'd been too impulsive, but I'm sitting here right now with you to say I'm not going to alter my decision.'

'Richard, this is truly magnificent of you—'

'Magnificently crazy, perhaps! God knows what Moira will say.'

'But won't she be pleased?'

'She'll just say I'm still refusing to take part in Bridget's treatment.'

'But it's no good participating if you don't want to! Surely Moira realises that?'

'God knows what Moira realises,' he said with such an abrupt change of mood that I jumped. 'We don't talk at the moment. The whole marriage is totally messed up.'

After a moment I managed to say: 'I'm sorry. It's hell when a marriage goes wrong.'

'Yes, I knew you'd understand that after what you went through with Kim. Maybe that's why I've come clean with you.'

'Have you told anyone else?'

'Good God, no! I don't believe in whingeing about my private life – shut up and get on with it is my motto—' He broke off to down the remainder of his martini and signal the waiter for a refill '—but life's so bloody difficult at the moment that it's becoming almost impossible to get on with anything.'

'But what's gone so wrong?'

'I've fallen in love. I'm out of my mind over a heartbreaker, Carta, and there's no way the disaster can ever come right . . .'

VII

'It's the reason why I can't touch family therapy with a bargepole,' he said. 'If I did, the situation would come out and I'm not prepared to talk about that kind of stuff in front of my daughter, I'm sorry but I'm not.'

I kept my voice calm. 'Why are you so sure the affair has no future?'

'Heartbreakers only wind up breaking hearts.'

'Yes, yes, yes, but—'

'This one's completely unsuitable for me.'

I restrained myself from pointing out that men junked their wives and ran off with unsuitable women every day. Instead I said with concern: 'How long's the affair been going on?'

'Six months. At first I was just entertained. I didn't believe in the falling-in-love syndrome once one was past thirty. Then I woke up one morning and realised I was not only hooked but panting for my next fix.'

'Tell me more about her.'

'I can't disclose any names. Some things should still stay secret if I know what's good for me, so I'll just use the initial G. Age: twenty-nine. Stunningly beautiful. Amazing in bed. Charming, well-educated, likes opera – and sailing. I keep a boat at Hamble, as you know, and when G and I went sailing together recently I don't think I've ever known such happiness.'

'So just what makes her so unsuitable?'

'No interest in a monogamous relationship.'

'Oh God, an elderly adolescent! But maybe once she hits thirty she'll start to grow up . . . What does she do?'

'Works for a company based in the Cayman Islands.'

'Financial services?'

The waiter arrived with our new round of drinks. When we were alone again Richard said: 'There's an office suite near the Stock Exchange, and that's where we meet. Number forty-nine, Austin Friars . . . I always thought the number was significant since I *am* forty-nine – there seemed to be some sort of resonance there which . . . God, listen to me, I'm talking like a New Age nutter! No wonder I feel I'm being such a bloody fool.'

'What's so bloody foolish about wanting to love and be loved?'

There was a pause. Richard looked away as if he had to struggle for self-control, but after a mouthful of the new martini he was able to say levelly: 'Thanks. I needed to hear that. I've been feeling so humiliated.'

'I just wish there was something I could do to help—'

'You've listened, you've sympathised, you've understood – that's all help with a capital H.' On an impulse he added: 'Look, can you have dinner with me? I'd really be grateful for the company – if I go back now to my flat I'll just drink the night away.'

I accepted the invitation and went away to call Eric with the news that I would be late home.

VIII

Richard said no more about either his family or G during our dinner in the Grill Room. Instead we talked about the law, a world which we both knew so well although after my long absence from a high-profile firm I felt I was losing touch with the day-by-day mayhem in the City jungle. After dinner Richard drank brandy and smoked a cigar and announced he felt better.

I was relieved, but later, as my cab headed home towards the City, I found myself reviewing his story of unrewarding love with mounting incredulity. I hardly needed my legal training to tell me that his confession had as many holes in it as a slab of Swiss cheese.

I surveyed the holes.

If the Slaney marriage was so unsatisfactory, why was it surviving in an age when divorce was readily available and carried no stigma? I could accept that Richard and Moira had originally stayed together for the sake of the children, but what was keeping Richard with her now that the children had left childhood behind? I could answer that question by saying: 'Bridget's illness,' but prolonged illness in a family often merely accelerated the dissolution of the marriage as the continuing stress dragged all the buried tensions to the surface. And perhaps this was indeed what had happened; perhaps Bridget's illness had been the trigger that had pushed Richard into a mid-life crisis involving a City glamour-babe twenty years his junior.

But even if that were true, why was self-confident, successful Richard – a most unlikely person to be suffering from low self-esteem – locked into this new relationship which, by his own admission, was humiliating? He was an attractive man. He didn't have to settle for an immature narcissist who puked at the words 'commitment' and 'monogamy'. I could see him trading in Moira for a younger woman; plenty of men his age slithered down this route when the age-factor began to bite, but what I couldn't see was a situation where he messed around with someone who was only going to make him suffer. Maybe his major omission was to tell me he was a masochist, but no, he definitely wasn't enjoying his pain.

I suddenly realised the cab had halted and I was home. I lived in a house on Wallside, one of the handful of houses in the City's vast Barbican estate. The Barbican formed a thirty-eight-acre complex where residential accommodation, offices, schools and the famous Arts Centre were grouped around gardens, lakes and water-falls. My house overlooked the church of St Giles Cripplegate, which rose above the remnants of the City's Roman wall.

Eric was lying on the living-room couch, shirt open to the navel, just as I had requested. When I came in he zapped the TV picture and sprang to his feet to greet me.

'No need to explain what happened,' he said. 'I've already written the outline in my head. Richard confessed his undying love and begged you to run away with him to Ireland where you could both rediscover your Celtic roots in between starting up a business capable of being run on a PC.'

'Is this a horror novel?'

We laughed.

Eric Tucker was my 'cher ami'. Translate that how you like. I was thirty-seven, he was a little older, and having known each other for over two years we now felt very much at ease together so long as we avoided the subject of money. Thanks to my past legal career and my husband's will, I was a rich widow; Eric was a novelist who was hoping that his earnings would cross the five-figure threshold in the current tax year. To supplement his income he worked now and then as a temporary secretary, and it was in this role that he had met me at Curtis, Towers in the spring of 1990.

He too now lived in the Barbican, in one of the studio flats facing the gardens at the bottom of Thomas More House. Writers need a certain degree of solitude, and after my husband Kim died I had felt the need for solitude as well. However, Eric and I still managed to achieve a considerable amount of shared time – which explains why he was lolling around my house at a quarter to eleven that night, fanning himself with my television remote control and amusing me with his fantasy of my future with Richard.

'I wish I could tell you more about this evening,' I said, sinking down on the couch, 'but the core of the conversation was confidential.'

'Bared his soul to you, did he?'

'No comment!'

'I love it when you play the austere lawyer with me, Ms G . . .'

So geared was I to Richard's problems that I even flinched at the sound of the letter G, but this particular G was short for Graham, my maiden name which I had always retained in my professional life.

'So he wines you and dines you at the Savoy,' Eric was saying, still amused. 'Maybe I should be thankful that it was only his soul that he bared!'

'I—'

'Okay, I don't seriously think he's trying to make you, but there's something off-key about Richard Slaney, and it's always annoyed me that I've been unable to figure out what it is.'

15

I stared at him. 'What's making you suspicious?'

'It's that glitzy social manner of the professional extrovert. He's the wrong generation for a cocaine habit, so what's driving him to hype up the gloss? Maybe he's got some very unpleasant secret – and if you put that together with his daughter's illness—'

'Your trouble,' I said severely, 'is that you've got the kind of imagination which can instantly convert good guys into sleazeballs without any evidence. Knock it off!'

'Okay, I accept he's not into incest, but something's got to be going on, Carta. He's a workaholic. He smokes like an industrial furnace. And he drinks too damn fast and too damn much.'

'You mean he's a typical City high flyer.'

'I mean he could be right out there on the edge and teetering on the brink of a crack-up.'

I shook my head. 'No way,' I said firmly. 'Richard's just not the type to have a spectacular nervous breakdown.'

But I felt more worried about him than ever.

X

The news reached me the next morning at the Appeal office. Here I was assisted by a volunteer, a youthful pensioner called Caroline, who held the fort in my absence, typed letters on a vintage electronic typewriter and kept me fuelled with strong coffee. I was just shoring up some details of the reception we were planning to hold at the hall of Richard's City Livery company, when Caroline took a call on the other line.

I saw her expression change. 'Carta, it's Jacqui from Curtis, Towers with some bad news about Richard Slaney.'

Guillotining the conversation I was having with the Livery company's clerk, I punched my way onto the other line. Jacqui, now Richard's PA, had once worked for me, so I knew her well. 'What's happened?' I demanded, wasting no time on preliminaries, and heard her say unsteadily: 'He had a coronary. It was just after he arrived at the office this morning, and—'

'Hang on.' I took a deep breath and listened to my heart banging. Then I demanded: 'Is he dead?'

'No. He's in intensive care at Barts. Carta—'

I started to feel numb as the shock hit me. I had to make a big effort to concentrate on what she was saying.

'—I would have called you with the news anyway, but I do also have an urgent question to ask. I'm trying to cancel his appointments, and I find he's slipped a lunch-date into his desk diary without telling me – there are no details on the computer. Do you by any chance know who "G" is? Could it be someone from the St Benet's Healing Centre?'

I was transfixed. 'When are they supposed to meet?'

'Twelve-forty-five, but there's no restaurant named and no contact number.'

'Leave it with me.' I knew there would be no rendezvous at a restaurant. Richard had said he always met G at an office suite in Austin Friars, and the number of the building was . . . I remembered him mentioning his age, remembered how I had noted he was the same age as Nicholas. Forty-nine was the magic number. Forty-nine, Austin Friars. To Jacqui I added: 'I do know who this person is. I'll make sure the date's cancelled.'

Two hours later I was walking into Austin Friars.

XI

The street was a cul-de-sac in the shape of the letter T, with the crossbar of the T blocked to traffic at both ends; cars could only enter at the bottom of the T by driving under the arch from Old Broad Street, but as a pedestrian I was able to slip into one end of the crossbar. Number forty-nine, I found, was one of the tall, slim Edwardian houses which had somehow survived the Blitz.

In the porch I examined the list of names by the buzzers. The basement, ground floor and first floor formed the offices of a company called Austin Trading International, but although I expected to find other firms occupying the rest of the building, it seemed that the remaining floors were in residential use and I wondered why Richard had talked of an office suite. Obviously he had wanted to mislead me, but what had made him so reluctant to admit that G worked from home? I took a closer look at the names. The fourth-floor slot, the top slot, was marked G. BLAKE.

17

There was no video-entryphone, and although I expected G to use the intercom to check who I was, the front door clicked open as soon as I rang the buzzer. I mentally awarded G bad marks for security. Violent crime is low in London's financial district, but no woman living alone, even in the City, should let someone into her building without first making sure of her visitor's identity.

The building itself had clearly been renovated in recent years for the lift was modern, equipped with a phone for use in emergencies, and the ride was so smooth that there was barely a jolt when the car stopped at the fourth floor.

G was waiting for me. Automatically I stepped out onto the landing, but I never heard the doors whisper shut again and I never heard the lift return to the lobby.

I was absolutely dumbfounded.

And so was he.

CHAPTER TWO

Gavin

'Youth culture is not unaware of sexual love and its implied commitments, but it has a tolerant attitude to what it calls *shagging*. In one significant section of youth culture, many young people shag or have sexual intercourse with each other whenever they feel like it, the way they have a cup of coffee or a hamburger.'

Godless Morality
Richard Holloway

This cool blonde's creamed into my life like a chilled-out meteor. Her legs are luscious and she's got the kind of feet a fetishist would kill for, dainty little numbers wrapped in low-cut, skin-tight black leather. Phwoar! WIKKID, as the teeny-totties croak, the little innocents who have no idea what wickedness really is. I take one look and my eyes are instantly spherical. This babe's mega-shagworthy. In fact she's exactly the kind of babe I dream of shagging when I'm slogging away at pushbutton sex with a load of masculine lard.

But what the hell's she doing here? And where's Richard? And just what the fuck's going on?

'Hullo, Gorgeous!' I say casually. 'Looking for something?'

She turns a ritzy shade of pink. That's probably because I'm wearing nothing except a pair of CK jeans low on the hips with the zip peeled back to reveal an eye-popping portion of sub-navel hair. In contrast she's glossed up in a beige-coloured ball-breaker's business suit and a virgin-white silk shirt. I wonder what she's got on underneath, and at once I'm picturing an onward-and-upward lacy number and a couple of non-silicone knockers that remind the old soaks of champagne glasses – traditional champagne glasses, I mean, not those bloody flutes that get plonked in front of you nowadays in any shithole that calls itself a wine bar.

Ms Shaggable's about to speak, and I'll bet my best Rolex I shan't hear estuary English. We're talking class here. We're talking style.

With an oddly precise inflection she says: 'I'm a friend of Richard Slaney's.'

At once I fling the door wide open. 'Then come on in!' I purr, voice smooth as liquid chocolate. 'Any friend of Richard Slaney's is a friend of mine!'

She takes the plunge and crosses the threshold.

*　*　*

I've recovered from my shock and my eyes have returned to their normal shape after their seconds of being spherical, but I'm more baffled than ever. Can she be Richard's PA? No, she'd have said so. And she's not Moira playing games either. I saw a photo of Moira when I was at Richard's home in Hampshire.

Golden Girl's speaking again. What *is* that precise little inflection she gives to her careful Home Counties accent? There's something foreign there, but I can't identify the country. Fascinating.

'What's the G stand for?' she says, and of course I think of G-spots and G-strings and assume this is some kind of upmarket verbal foreplay, but it turns out she just wants to know my first name.

'Gavin,' I say, and find I'm unable to take the suspense a moment longer. 'Who the hell are you?'

'Carta Graham. I used to be a partner with Richard at Curtis, Towers, but now I'm—'

'—fundraising for that clergy-bloke who's fixing Bridget – yeah, Richard told me about you. Okay, what's going on?'

She looks me straight in the eyes and says: 'He had a coronary this morning.'

'Shit!'

'He's still alive but I don't know what the prognosis is. His PA's promised to—'

I'm too shocked to listen. In fury I yell: 'Those bloody cigarettes! I told him again and again he ought to quit!' But then I get my act together and ask how she knew Richard had a date with me today. It turns out he made an entry in his desk diary which meant nothing to his PA but everything to Ms Shaggable. I feel my

20

eyes go spherical again. This is definitely the day I get slammed by surprises.

'Richard told you about me?' I say incredulously. 'He actually told you?'

'Last night, yes. But he only referred to you as G and he didn't disclose your gender.'

'Ah, I see! Mystery solved. I couldn't imagine Richard coming out of the closet, even for a good friend.' I start to drift across the living-room into the kitchen area. 'Have a seat at the counter,' I say, 'and I'll pour you a glass of wine.' The living-room has no furniture in it except for a swivel chair, the matching footstool and a TV/video on a cart. Sometimes between shifts I like to put my feet up and watch trash.

The babe's saying doubtfully: 'I'd better not stay.'

'Why not? Since Richard won't be here I'm free until my next appointment.'

The penny finally drops with such a crash that her jaw sags. How typical of Richard to tell her everything yet tell her nothing! These closet gays play their cards so close to their chests it's a wonder the cards don't take root there. And what was he doing talking to this gorgeous piece, for God's sake? Of course I realised the last time he took me sailing that he was getting much too emotional, but I never thought he'd do a total freak-out.

Wiping the memory of the sailing trip I refocus on my visitor who's now realised why my living-room's so under-furnished: it's because nothing much ever happens there. 'Yes, I'm in the leisure industry,' I say amused to help her along. 'I give stressed-out City executives some essential relaxation.' Extracting a Waterford crystal wine-glass from the cupboard over the sink I open the refrigerator to take out the Chablis Premier Cru. Orange juice for me, of course. I never drink at work. I'm a top-of-the-market professional, not some pathetic amateur pill-popping in Piccadilly Circus.

When I turn to hand her the drink I see she's looking at me as if I'm a pervy version of Batman who's just about to be sent down for abusing that silly wimp Robin. So the lady's a prig. Tough! Specially as she's also nearly wetting herself because she wants to shag me. I give her a high-wattage smile and casually zip up my jeans.

'Which hospital's Richard at?' I say, gesturing to the stools by the counter, but she won't sit down. She stands stiff as a soldier on the

21

edge of the kitchen area and clasps her glass as if it's a bayonet.

'Barts,' she says, very chilly.

'Great. Hey, did you see in the paper that Barts is threatened with closure? What the fuck does the Government think it's doing?'

Not a muscle of her face moves when I toss the f-word into the conversation. This is one cool, cool babe who fancies herself as ultra-controlled and thinks she's far too smart to end up in the sack with a leisure-worker. Dream on, baby! I'm going to melt that ice even if I have to hire a blowtorch to do it. I'm going to make you steam.

Opening one of the drawers below the kitchen counter I take out a business card. 'If I give you my number,' I say soberly, turning on the class-act, 'could you please let me know how Richard's getting on? I'd be really grateful if you would.' And I give her a serious, appealing look designed to go straight to her tough little heart.

It works. She agrees. Having scribbled on the back of the card I explain: 'Ignore the printed phone number – that just connects to the office at my home in Lambeth, and you'll only get my manager or her secretary. But the number I've written down is the number of this flat. Call me here at five minutes before either eight, noon or four-thirty and I'll always pick up. Those are the times before my shifts begin.'

'Don't you have a mobile?'

I never answer yes to this question. Clients and chicks would give me no peace if I did, and anyway the aging techno-lump which lives mainly in my car doesn't exactly fit my image. I'm waiting for the new wave of mobiles before I update, the digital-satellite-made-in-heaven wonder-toys which the nerd department of *The Times* is always predicting.

'I'm not interested in mobiles,' I lie. 'They weigh too much and die at the wrong moment.'

'But don't you need a mobile for your business?'

'Sweetie, I don't have the kind of business where I'm shitting bricks in case I miss a vital call! I'm available at set hours Monday through Friday, and if a bloke wants to see me he rings the office and makes an appointment – if his credit card pans out, and if he's lucky enough not to go on the waiting list. God, why would I want a mobile? I'm not interested in forming social relationships with these guys – I don't even do escort work! I'm strictly bedroom.'

'In that case,' says Ms Ultra-Cool with all the killer-skills of a leading QC, 'what did you think you were doing when you went sailing with Richard?'

She's blown me away.

Shit, I'm going to shag this piece one day even if it's the last bloody thing I ever do . . .

*   *   *

I hurl back a tough reply. 'Richard's the exception that proves the rule,' I snap, and add before I can stop myself: 'Richard and I are friends. We like each other.'

'He loves you!'

It's clear she's furious about this, but why? Is she in love with him herself and feels conned now that she knows he's gay? I can't work it out. 'Okay, but so what?' I demand. 'And what the hell's it got to do with you anyway?'

'Richard's my friend too!' she snarls back, 'so it's certainly my business if you've put him on the rack!'

'If Richard's on the rack, that's not my fault. Hey, you look so sexy when you're angry and I just love sexy blondes! You busy next weekend?'

She's devastated. She's been thinking I'm gay, camping it up by faking a cod-hetero attraction, but now another big penny drops and she's shocked rigid again. In fact she's so shocked that she fights against believing the truth that's staring her in the face.

Shakily she says: 'You're bisexual?'

'Oh, puh-leeze!'

'You mean—'

'I'm straight as a ruler, sweetheart. Now how about a date?'

But she's pole-axed. All she can say is: 'So Richard's not just in love with a hustler. He's in love with someone who's constitutionally incapable of loving him in return.'

I fake a puke. 'Wow, wheel on the soaring violins and bring out the Kleenex – it's soap-opera time!'

'Why, you—'

'Pussycat, get real – my clients are smart, sophisticated businessmen who know the score. I don't know what kind of crap Richard's been spewing out when pissed on martinis, but don't try and tell me he's the kind of bloke who dies for love!'

23

'He nearly died this morning!'

Shit, she's done it again. What *is* this shredding machine on extra-lush legs? The Attorney-General in drag? Margaret Thatcher's illegitimate daughter?

'You've got him so stressed out,' she storms at me, 'that he's been over-working, over-eating, over-drinking and over-smoking! No wonder he had a coronary! And it was all because of you!'

'Bullshit!' I yell. 'I'm not responsible for his decision to stay in the closet! I'm not responsible for his decision to marry and have kids! I'm not responsible for his successful career and high-powered job! I *ease* the stress, I don't add to it, so don't you try to lay this fucking guilt-trip on me! Just who the hell do you think you are anyway?'

'I'm the friend of Richard Slaney's who's telling you you've got an attitude problem!' Slamming her glass down so violently that wine slops over the rim she stalks off towards the door.

'Hey!' I say quickly. 'You've forgotten my card!'

She tells me what I can do with my card but I shout back: 'Don't you think Richard would want me to be kept informed about how he is?'

That stops her, and in my most reasonable voice I add: 'Look, we both want Richard to get well. It's crazy to quarrel like this. Let me buy you a drink next weekend.'

'I'm busy,' she says, cramming the card into her chic little handbag.

I go fishing. 'Husband?' I murmur sympathetically.

'That's my business.'

'You mean no. If you'd got one you'd say so to slap me down.'

'Sod off!'

'So does the lover live in or out? A sexy chick like you has to have a lover. And where do you live anyway?'

'You'll never know.' She snaps the bag shut and starts the march to the front door again. 'You needn't worry,' she says dryly over her shoulder, and suddenly I identify a Scottish inflection in the way she speaks each word with such unEnglish precision. 'I accept that Richard would want me to keep you informed. I'll call you.'

'Thanks, Frosty-Puss. And thanks for coming to tell me the news. That was good of you and I appreciate it.' I count to five before adding: 'Or did you just come out of curiosity to see who Richard was shagging?'

She storms out and slams the door so hard it nearly drops off its hinges.

Bull's-eye.

* * *

I sit sipping OJ at the counter. I'm upset about Richard. In my head Hugo laughs but I shove him back into the crevice in my mind where he lives. Then I can think of Richard without being interrupted.

Ms Iceball doesn't understand that I'm Richard's friend. She's mentally slagged me off like a mindless moral bigot, but she works for a church, doesn't she, so what can one expect? I hate religion. And as for a clergyman who ponces around pretending to be a healer — that's gross! There ought to be a law against it. Mum took Hugo to a healer and the bastard just grabbed her money and faked miraculous powers. I told Richard that story when he began talking about the St Benet's Healing Centre, but this disclosure was a mistake because he started asking about my family and I never discuss the past with my clients.

But Richard's not like the other clients and that's why I'm sitting here feeling upset. I'm as upset as any friend of Richard's would be, and as Richard's famous for his friends there are going to be a whole lot of upset people out there besides me.

I think of him being a friend.

'I know you don't work on weekends,' he said when he first invited me to go sailing with him, 'but you won't have to work on this occasion, I promise. We'll just be friends.' Hey, pull the other one, mate, I thought to myself, who do you think you're kidding? But he was as good as his word. He only cracked the weekend before last on our sixth trip, but I felt so grateful to him for all the sailing that I didn't mind giving him a freebie. I never normally give freebies, never. When I say you have to pay me to do gay sex that's the literal truth. But I made an exception for Richard because I owed him — and anyway it turned out not to be a freebie after all because he promised me a ten-thousand-pound hit of stocks and shares (which I'll ask him later to convert into cash).

I had to be careful, though, when I announced the good news to Elizabeth. She'd have had a fit if she'd known I'd been seeing Richard at weekends without charging him, and if she were ever to find out that the jackpot fuck had started life as a freebie . . . No, it doesn't bear thinking about. She'd go ballistic.

I glance at my watch. Ten minutes until Iowa Jerry arrives. Then after him there's that bloody Kraut who ought to be terminated – no, wait, if this is Wednesday it's not the Kraut, it's Humpty-Dumpty, the bloke with the stomach. The Kraut comes on Thursdays. I've had plenty of German clients who were no trouble so I'm not being racist, but this particular German makes me wish we'd met in World War Two. Then I could have killed him legally.

I wash up the glass Ms Iceball used and wonder idly how she came to be raising money for a church. It's so weird how smart, cynical Richard likes that church and the people who run its so-called Healing Centre. But then he thinks they're curing Bridget, silly little cow, who's been adding to her father's stress and contributing to that bloody coronary . . .

Okay, forget Richard, it's time to focus on my work. Iowa Jerry has to have American condoms because he doesn't trust the Brits to make them right, the stupid old fart. Must tell that bitch Susanne to order more. I admit I'm finicky about condoms myself, but my finick-iness is based on scientific research, not xenophobic folklore. With gay sex you can't mess around when it comes to condoms. Ignorant little boys who bust out of the closet and hit the scene so hard they bounce think regular condoms are good enough but they're not – not if we're talking high friction in an unforgiving environment. Only the strongest will do. Okay, so there's more to gay fun and games than the highest-risk high jinks, but even with the other routines I don't use just any old fun-rubbish. The condoms have to be top-quality from a top supplier. They have to be not past their sell-by date. They have to be kept away from a heat source when being stored. And water-based lubricants only, please, not oil-based stuff that can rot them. Even the strongest condoms are sensitive little plants and UK condom manufacturers have a quality control scheme to nurture them along. There's even talk of a Pan-European standard, but that'll never work because the French and the Italians will cheat, and meanwhile the best British condoms are as good as anything the Americans can produce even if they haven't been water-tested and air-burst-tested and God-knows-what-else-tested by the FDA.

I'm a condom expert because I want to survive – and don't tell me HIV is a difficult virus to catch! I'm in the bloody front line here, and besides it's not the only STD around, as Dr Filth often reminds me when I go for my check-up. I'm an expert too on sexually transmitted diseases, but whenever I start to feel over-anxious I remind myself that gay sex, as practised by a professional, is probably a lot less risky than other dangerous sports such as motor-racing or hang-gliding. It's the clients who are the problem, not the sex. You only need one nutter going out of control, but Elizabeth screens the clients carefully and I keep my judo skills up to the mark so here too the risk is reduced to a minimum. I do offer minor S&M – the fantasy kind where no skin gets broken and no one passes out – but the major stuff would be senseless to under-take. Much better for the real pervs to be served up to Asherton the Mega-Monster at his Pain-Palace in the heart of Westminster.

I get out the extra-strength American condoms for Iowa Jerry and remember to put his chocolate bar on the bedside table. He always likes chocolate afterwards. I'm very careful to remember little touches like that. It marks me out as a top-grade leisure-worker, performing an essential social service which makes a lot of people feel much happier.

The buzzer goes. It's Jerry. But I'll pretend for a few magic seconds it's Ms Priggy.

Well, it's a nice easy way to get an erection . . .

* * *

The lunch-time shift ends at three, which means the last client reels off around two-fifty and I use the remaining minutes to clear up and prepare for the late shift which begins at four-thirty. Tomorrow it'll take longer to clear up because of that bloody Kraut, but tomorrow's another day.

When I've finished I flop down on my living-room chair, watch an Australian soap opera on TV, eat two bananas and drink a glass of milk. Then I zap the picture and call Elizabeth.

No luck. The private line gets rerouted to the office and that bitch Susanne picks up.

'Where's Elizabeth?' I demand.

'Dunno. Why?'

'Tell her Richard Slaney's had a coronary.'

'You mean when you were doing him?'

'You're joking! You think I'd wait hours to call Elizabeth if he'd passed out in bed? When he didn't show up I called his office and some under-chick said he'd had a coronary and wound up in Barts.'

'You're not supposed to call clients at work!'

'Hey popsicle, you're just the secretary, remember? You don't tell me what I should or shouldn't do!'

'Piss off, pinhead!' says the bitch and hangs up.

I try to do some relaxation exercises but I can't stop thinking of Richard and suddenly my memory gives me such a jolt that I freeze. I've remembered the photos. If he dies and all his things get sorted . . . But he's not going to die, is he? It's the poor who die of coronaries. The rich get the best treatment and live.

I fritter away some time by watching TV again, but I soon find I'm watching the clock instead. Will Ms Priggy call or won't she? She does. At four-twenty-five precisely the bell jangles and I leap up, panting for what'll probably be good news. He must be out of intensive care.

I grab the receiver. 'Yeah?'

'Carta Graham.'

'Great! What's new?' I say, relaxing in anticipation of the progress report, but all she says in that same crisp, efficient voice is:

'He died.'

*   *   *

I'm gutted. I can't believe it. I actually say to her: 'I can't believe it.' But why the big surprise? Do I seriously think there's something out there called God who guarantees that the good blokes survive? Forget it. But I'm still shocked to pieces. Despite all his cigarettes and booze and high-stress lifestyle, I never really thought Richard would die at forty-nine.

Apparently he had another coronary, and even though he had instant medical attention the heart refused to restart.

'How do you know all this?' I blurt out but add quickly: 'I'm not doubting your word. I was just wondering if you were there.'

'I wasn't but Moira was. She called my boss, Nicholas Darrow, the Rector of St Benet's, and he's gone to the hospital to be with her. Well—' She's preparing to end the call '—sorry to be the bearer of bad news—'

'Wait.' I've remembered the photos. 'I need your help. Richard kept some photos in his Mayfair flat and they've got to be junked right away.'

'Photos of you and him?'

'No, just me, but they're not the kind of pics a hetero family man would keep, and since Richard's big obsession was that his kids should never know he was gay—'

'What do you want me to do?'

'Get a set of keys from Moira. Then I can lift the pics as soon as she's gone back to Compton Beeches.'

'But what the hell am I going to say to her?' she demands, but adds before I can reply: 'Maybe I can work something out with Richard's PA.'

I jack up the charm. 'Brilliant! Thanks a million. Can you call me back at six-thirty to tell me if you've fixed it?'

She says she will.

*   *   *

She calls back at six-thirty on the nail. This babe's a real dynamo, and when she's not ball-bustering around playing Mrs Thatcher's illegitimate daughter she's hoovering up messes like a triple-star contract cleaner.

'Gavin Blake?' she barks, reminding me of my headteacher in kindergarten.

'Yes, ma'am. Thank you for calling back,' I say, determined to be well-behaved, but I just sound like one of those poor sods who operate in call centres and gradually get turned into robots. Good morning, thank you for calling London Leisure-Workers, this is Gavin speaking, how may I help you achieve your multiple orgasm today? Thank you, Gavin, this is—

'I've got the keys.'

I wipe the fantasy. 'Congratulations!'

'It turned out he kept a spare set at the office, and when I told his PA I needed to retrieve some papers connected with the Appeal she offered me the keys right away.'

'Cheers. Where's Moira?'

'Staying overnight at the flat. Then she's supposed to go back to Compton Beeches, but I'll have to double-check later to make sure she's gone.'

'So when can I meet you to get the keys?'

'Let's say this time tomorrow. But I'm not handing the keys over. I'm coming with you to the flat.'

29

Wow! How green can a light get? Blowing a kiss into the phone I murmur in a double-cream-suitable-for-pouring voice: 'Can't wait!'

'You'd better behave!' she snaps back. 'The only reason why I'm coming with you is because if I let you get into that flat, I'm responsible for what you do there. How do I know you won't start nicking things?'

What kind of lowlife does she think I am, for God's sake? I bet my upbringing was far classier than hers.

'Maybe we could nick things together,' I say innocently. 'Then we'd be a pair of nickers.'

No laugh. Not even the hint of a gurgle. She's bursting a blood vessel trying to give me no encouragement.

'I'll meet you outside forty-nine Austin Friars at six-thirty tomorrow night,' she says in a voice designed to freeze hell, and hangs up, probably quivering at the thought of a date with someone so depraved. How I'm going to enjoy our first snog! She'll be begging for it in the end, of course. They always do.

Sighing with satisfaction I head home to Elizabeth.

* * *

The shock of Richard's death hits me again that night. I lie awake remembering our six sailing trips and reliving them one by one while in my head Pavarotti sings my favourite aria from *Die Zauberflöte*. Finally I reach the last voyage. Richard and I are sailing down the Solent towards the Needles, the cliffs are stark white, the sea's wine-dark – and suddenly the lost past comes pouring back, recaptured, restored, redeemed. Even Hugo, rooted in that crevice in my mind, is silenced. I feel so special when I remember that moment, so unified, so all-of-a-piece. But does that mean I usually feel a broken-down mess? Course not! I'm highly disciplined, strongly motivated and totally focused on stashing loadsamoney in my Cayman Islands bank account so that I can retire in two years' time and sail away into the golden sunset. Life's great!

'It's a terrible life you lead,' says Richard in my memory, and feeling narked I say: 'So's yours!' but the thought that his lifestyle could be criticised so infuriates him that he gives me this passionate speech about being a pass-for-straight gay. I make no attempt to interrupt. The fact is that as I've long since dropped all my preconceived notions about gays I'm interested in what he has to say. I don't mean I'm a dripping-wet liberal and I don't mean I'm a pro-castration homophobe. I just mean that I've realised all the talk by the activists on both sides of the gay debate has little relation to what really goes on. Homosexuality's much more complex than the two-dimensional propaganda spouted by the fanatics, and the gay activists in particular should try listening to alternative gay views instead of shrieking nonstop about coming out. Here's Richard, letting it all hang loose about his right to be the kind of gay he feels he is.

'I haven't slogged and sweated through a lifetime of keeping quiet about one aspect of myself only to have a bloody activist tell me that coming out will transport me to gay heaven! Gay heaven's the last place I want to be, thanks very much, and these mindless shits who say people like me should be open about their private lives have no right to deprive me of my right to choose what kind of life I want to lead! I *chose* long ago to be silent about my sexual orientation, but I didn't lie to myself about it. I faced what I was and I made a rational decision about what I wanted from life – I wanted marriage and a family, I wanted to be well-respected in my local community, I wanted to get on in my profession, I wanted the kind of things a whole load of other men want, and why should I have my ambitions skewed just because of something I can't help and never wanted? God almighty, no one in their right mind could *want* to have feelings which are the cause of so much misery – and if that's not politically correct, fuck it, I don't care! This is *my* life, to live as I've lived was *my* choice, and if homosexual rights are to mean anything at all they must include the right to pass for straight and pick a mainstream lifestyle!'

In my memory I nod as I listen to him. I don't argue when he stops speaking. He's entitled to his views. There are many homosexualities, just as there are many heterosexualities, and why shouldn't he be allowed to speak up for his particular brand?

'I've lived out my own truth,' he adds, 'and if that means I've never had any kind of deep relationship – if that means I now choose to pay for sex in order to stay in control and avoid a mess – then so be it. The handicapped usually have to pay for sex anyway – and if any activist wants to query my use of the word "handicapped" I'll smash his teeth in! No politically correct bastard's going to deprive me of the freedom to describe my sexuality in any way I please!'

He finally stops talking. He's emotionally exhausted. Taking his hand I grip it tightly and say: 'I think you're bloody brave, Richard,

31

to fly in the face of fashion in order to pursue the truth as you see it.' Of course we both know the fascist activists would call him a coward and spit on him. 'There's a Byron quote I've always liked,' I add before he can reply. 'It goes: "Yet, Freedom! yet, thy banner, torn, but flying, streams like the thunderstorm *against* the wind." You know that one? Byron didn't give a shit for fashionable opinion either and he too lived out his own truth.'

Then Richard breaks down and says he loves me and the whole scene goes off the rails, but I'll never forget how much I admired his guts for defending his right to be a certain kind of gay.

Off the rails, did I say? God, no phrase could begin to metaphor how that scene ended up. It was at the end of our final sailing trip ten days ago, and he didn't just say he loved me. He said he was crazy about me, he'd never been so in love with anyone before, he thought about me day and night. No wonder I gave him a freebie. I was willing to give it because I owed him for the sailing, but my prime intention at that moment was to shut him up before he started saying things he'd really regret. Fat chance. In the end he went totally off his trolley despite all my efforts to stop him. 'I'll give up everything,' he said. 'I'll leave Moira. We'll live together. I can't believe you don't love me,' he said. 'The sex is so great that I just can't believe you're not switched on at the deepest possible level.'

Poor sod, how he blew it! I liked him so much when he was kicking the gay activists in the teeth and being brave as hell. But with those last sentences he caved in, he sold out, he became the stereotype the gay activists whine on about – the bloke who proves he's been only half alive as a non-scene pass-for-straight buried deep in the closet. Yet in Richard's case any attempt to come out would have led him straight to hell. He'd have wrecked his family, dislocated his career, alienated most of his straight friends and invoked the contempt of the homophobes. Worst of all, any affair with me couldn't have lasted more than a week and so the whole move would have been futile. He was right to imply that I'm bloody good at gay sex, but any sexual activity, gay or straight, is a skill which can be acquired – it's a contact sport like rugby or sumo wrestling. The idea that I must have been in love with him deep down or I wouldn't have been able to turn on the high-octane sex was just romantic nonsense.

But I never said this. I didn't jeer, I didn't act smart, and above all I didn't brush him off. I just looked at him and I kept my face grave (because love's a serious matter) and respectful (because I was his friend). I looked at him and he looked back and of course he knew then just how matters stood.

Lightly he said: 'I'm pissed, aren't I? Time for black coffee!' And he laughed, ending the scene gracefully.

Richard had such style.

And now he's dead. No more sailing with him on the wine-dark sea past the stark-white cliffs of the Needles. But I'll always be able to say to myself: I was a friend of Richard Slaney's, a friend he chose to spend non-bedroom time with on weekends, and that friendship puts me in the same league as Carta Graham, who looks down her nose at me and thinks I'm shit. It puts me in the same league as any number of smart people who don't understand that leisure-workers perform a valuable service and make an important contribution to society.

I'm going to go to that funeral.

*　*　*

After such a churned-up night I reckon I need to get to Austin Friars early so that I can have longer for meditation. I always meditate before work. It switches me from one mode of being to another, from the straight mindset to the gay.

I sit cross-legged on the floor and I close my eyes and I listen to myself breathing and then I phase out Gavin Blake Ordinary Bloke and ease in Gavin Blake Superstud. Finally Gavin Blake Ordinary Bloke leaves the body and goes somewhere else so that Gavin Blake Superstud's in control. Once that's happened I get up and play some opera. I've made a special tape of twelve excerpts and I'll play a different one every morning until I decide it's time to make a new tape. Before I start work I have to have a dose of something beautiful, just as most of us like to have our gum numbed before the dentist coseys up to us with his drill. I don't do drugs so I do opera instead.

Top-grade leisure-workers organise their schedules in different ways – we all have to find the method which suits us best. Some blokes just hire themselves out for a whole night, or maybe for an hour at a time in the evening. I couldn't do that, I'd go nuts. I need to have my evenings to myself and if I spend the whole night with a bloke I wind up wanting to castrate him. I'm not saying I never

33

work at night, but my God, I have to be well paid if I do! Elizabeth understands just how I feel, which is why she devised this three-shift schedule, specially designed to cater to City businessmen and prevent me going mental. I never see anyone for too long (unless they book a mega-expensive double-slot) and I get plenty of relaxation between shifts.

Sessions on the early shift are shorter than the ones on the lunch-time and late shifts, but to be fair, the clients aren't demanding. They just need a rush in order to face work. Some City workers get it with coke, some get it with vodka, some get it with double espressos, but my bunch get it with sex. Well, it takes all sorts to make a world.

At ten o'clock I head off to the gym. I work out three times a week and I'd like to do more because I get such a charge out of it, but my trainer says no, I have to avoid it becoming an addiction. No steroids, naturally. Why blokes get into steroid use and abuse beats me. You wind up with shrunken equipment and scrambled brains.

After leaving the gym I stop at Rafferty's for a grade-A breakfast to supplement the grade-C breakfast (C for Cornflakes) I had before leaving home. Today I eat half a grapefruit, eggs, bacon, sausages, mushrooms and wholemeal toast and wash the lot down with a large pot of coffee. I also read *The Times*. I like to follow the fortunes of my clients in the business pages, but of course I read the regular news as well. At the moment all the news seems to begin with an M: Maastricht (as in the treaty which aims to sort out Europe), Major (as in our prime minister, poor sod, who's trying to sort out Maastricht), and Mayhem (as in the Balkans — where else?). The Euro-sceptics are bellyaching away about Maastricht, but person-ally I think anyone under thirty is pro-Europe and can't see what all the fuss is about. I'm all for a United States of Europe — provided we Brits run it, of course. Face it, the Frogs and the Krauts just don't have the track record. I mean, have we forgotten Hitler? Have we forgotten Napoleon? No bloody way, mate, I say, and I'm not even a rabid nationalist, I'm just a sensible bloke with an interest in history.

Back at the flat at last I change the fitted sheet and pillowcases. The last client's going through a phase of putting anti-baldness stuff on his scalp and at least one pillowcase now looks as if it'll defeat every laundry in town. Elizabeth doesn't let me put anything on my head because she says mousse and gel are a sexual turn-off — no client wants to run his fingers through my hair and wind up with gooey hands. But the truth is she needn't worry because I'd never risk putting anything dodgy on my scalp. I even use baby shampoo because I'm so afraid of chemicals triggering a meltdown which leaves me bald as an egg. I watch my hairline like a hawk and every week I check my crown with a mirror. It's a tense moment but so far so good. I'm not getting a transplant, though, even if the stuff drops out in clumps. I've had clients who tried hair transplants and their scalps wound up looking like bug-eaten lawns in a drought.

I've just dumped the dirty linen in the laundry bag when Frosty-Puss calls to confirm we're all set for tonight.

'T'rrific!' I say. 'Hey, how about dinner after we've nabbed the pics?'

'I'm busy.'

'Your bloke keep you on a short leash, does he?'

The line blips out.

* * *

The lunch-time shift's marred by the Kraut, who puts me in a foul mood for the rest of the working day. To cap it all, the last client on the late shift has halitosis. It's so bloody aggravating when clients have bad breath. Why don't their wives tell them they reek? (Most of my clients are married.) In disgust I fling open the living-room window as soon as the client's gone, and as I stand there fumigating my airways I see Ms Shaggable loitering below. She's early. Opportunity knocks.

'Hey Pussycat!' I yell, making her jump. 'I'll be ready in ten minutes – come up and have a glass of wine!'

She looks furious but gives a curt little nod and tries not to rush to the front door. I press the buzzer. Up she comes, and by the time she reaches my landing I'm waiting with my jeans half-unzipped to welcome her. I could see yesterday that my sub-navel strip turned her on.

'Red or white?' I enquire as she walks out of the lift.

'Neither. I came up for one reason and one reason only – to tell you how much I loathe men who call women "pussycat"!'

'How about PussyCarta?'

'Forget the Pussy!'

'You serious?'

35

There's a snuffle. She's trying not to laugh. I think: GOTCHA! and give her an encouraging smile before saying sociably: 'What's your real name anyway? Cartographa?'

'Catriona,' she says severely. 'When I was growing up I got called Catty, Kitty, Kit-Kat and even Pussykins, so you can see why I'm sensitive to nicknames . . . Now can you get moving, please? I didn't come here to listen to you practising chat-up lines.'

'Take a seat – unless you want to come upstairs and watch me dress.'

'How much does that cost?' she says nastily.

'It's free as air, Gorgeous! I don't charge women!'

'Gavin, watch my lips. The name's Carta – C-A-R-T-A. It's not Pussycat, it's not Gorgeous, it's not—'

'Got it, Wonder-Babe. Hang in there while I sharpen up.'

As she looks for something to throw at me I take the stairs two at a time to the floor above. The flat's a duplex and above the living-space there are two bedrooms, one for business, the other for storing a whole range of items relating to my work. In the bathroom I now go through the hygiene routine: mouth-wash, teeth-clean, shower. Then it's dressing-up time: fresh underwear, a clean shirt and my brand new Armani suit – oh, and I stuff my feet into socks plus D&G shoes. Then I comb, fluff and tweak my hair to make sure my very, very slightly receding hairline's concealed. After that comes the clear-up: I cram my discarded jeans into a sports bag which contains my exercise gear plus the clothes I arrived in this morning, and yes, I'm ready to go, the final seconds of the allotted ten minutes are melting away, and it's exit time. Creaming downstairs I glance in the mirror by the front door to check that I'm looking like a million quid, and then I breeze into the living-room area where the blonde's looking very upmarket in my black leather swivel chair.

'Bingo!' I exclaim, flashing her my best smile (since it's not the moment to flash anything else). 'Ready?'

Ms Shaggable tries to look cool, but I know she's melting quite a space for herself in her personal version of Antarctica. It's the combination of me and the Armani suit – the babes go down like ninepins every time.

Can't wait to get to that empty flat in Mayfair . . .

CHAPTER THREE

Carta

'(We) know more about sexuality today. We may be no better at controlling or humanising it, but we do understand how fragile and complex it is, and how mysteriously prone to disorder and disease . . . In spite of the claims made by sexual utopians in the 1960s sex is never value-free, never without its human and emotional consequences.'

Anger, Sex, Doubt and Death
Richard Holloway

I

I want to describe Gavin as he was when we were setting out – setting out, that is, not just to Richard's flat in Mayfair but on our journey through an extraordinary phase of our lives.

When I first saw him he was wearing no clothes except for a pair of tight black designer jeans which were dragged low on the hips and left more than half unzipped. I kept my eye on the zip for too long because I knew instinctively it was safer to stare at that inanimate object than at the muscles of his chest or the body hair tapering down into the crotch. Or maybe I was just in shock after discovering the gender of Richard's lover.

He was tall and slim, perfectly proportioned, effortlessly conveying the impression of physical fitness. His dark hair, cut in a conventional style, was unoiled, unspiked, unpermed and unstreaked. His blue eyes were set wide apart in a flawlessly symmetrical face, and below his prominent cheekbones his mouth was a sensual line above a fine-drawn but unfeminine jaw.

I took note of all these details. I took note of all my mindless but unstoppable physical reactions. Then I dumped my emotions on ice in order to play the lawyer and emerge from the scene with dignity.

But when I saw him again the next day I found I could no longer pretend to myself that a detached approach was easy in the face of such a hyped-up sex appeal. I had to confront the truth in order to have a hope of mastering it, and the truth was that I thought he was devastatingly good-looking, devastatingly attractive, devastatingly sexy – he was all devastation, but in the most aesthetically pleasing way imaginable. I was reminded of films I had seen of American tornados, twisting across the landscape in a thrilling whirl of grace but leaving a trail of smashed homes and broken lives in their wake.

When he went upstairs to change I sank down weak-kneed onto the living-room's one and only chair.

On his return he paused to admire himself in the mirror by the front door, and I saw the narcissism which oozes from so many handsome men, particularly the ones who have a problem relating normally to other people. Why bother to trawl for a relationship when you can adore this stunning reflection in the mirror? I was sure then that he was gay even though he was busy trying to convince me he was straight.

As he finally tore himself away from the mirror I noted he was wearing a beautiful suit, light grey, which shimmered over his long limbs as if the designer had merely waved a magic wand to convert the sketch on the drawing board into a tailor's dream. His close-fitting pale blue shirt, uncluttered by a tie, was the perfect shade to match the unusual grey, and the effect was immensely stylish: modern and sophisticated without being bizarre or louche. I was aware of the nerve-ends tingling in my stomach as the lethal sexual attraction kicked in.

'Ready?' he said, looking straight at me, and as he looked he widened his eyes so that they seemed even brighter and bluer than they already were.

'Sure,' I said at once, managing to sound quite unfazed, but I was wishing that Richard had never kept photos of Gavin in his flat and that I had never committed myself to a scheme to retrieve them.

Outside the building Gavin said: 'No need for a cab. My car's only a couple of minutes away.'

'Where's your parking slot?'

'The Data-Press Building.'

'I bet that costs you plenty!'

'I screw for it four times a year.'

Knowing he wanted me to be disapproving I said in my most neutral voice: 'I suppose you screw for the flat too.'

'No, I own it,' he said without hesitation, and although I was sceptical his car suggested he really did earn big money. It was not an Aston Martin or a Lotus but it was still an impressive boy-toy; I found myself looking at a Jaguar XJ-S Le Mans V12, dark blue with cream upholstery, and I was unable to resist asking how much it cost.

'It was a gift,' he said carelessly, 'but they retail for around forty thousand. You got wheels?'

'A Porsche.'

'Sweetie, you need to update! No one drives a flash krautmobile any more except for Eastenders trying to be Essex men!'

'Bit of a snob, aren't you?'

'Bloody right I am – I'm a Surrey man! Don't you know anything about being brought up in a middle-class ghetto?'

'Why should I?' I retorted. 'I was born in a Glasgow slum and lived in a low-income suburb of Newcastle before I got to Oxford and reinvented myself. Why are you banging on about how classy you are? Am I supposed to be impressed?'

'No, intrigued. Panting to know more.'

'What intrigues me, as a tax lawyer, is how much the Revenue sees of your earnings! Do you have a bent accountant?'

'No need, love,' he said, switching to a south London accent so abruptly that I wondered if the talk about Surrey had been a fantasy. 'I'm a law-abiding leisure-worker and everything I do's legal. My manager takes care of the tax shit.'

'You mean your pimp?'

'I mean the woman I live with. What would I want with a pimp? Pimps are for chicks, not blokes – and particularly not for blokes like me who've got a top section of the leisure market creamed off.' His accent kept veering back towards the Home Counties to make me realise it was the south London accent which was faked. Or was it? He seemed to be experimenting with different personalities to see which one cut the most ice.

As we drove out of the City into the West End he demanded abruptly: 'You been to Richard's flat?'

'Yes, a couple of times when Moira was up in town. Why?'

'Just wondered. I've never seen the Mayfair place but I've been to his home at Compton Beeches – he took me there once after we'd been sailing.' He was trying out yet another identity. This one was non-flamboyant, casual, not unpleasant. The Home Counties accent was still there but it had been flattened and modernised, and deciding I might be able to do business with this personality I asked idly: 'Did he ever take you out on the town during the week?'

'I don't do escort work, I told you that, and I don't do evenings. He had a lunch-time slot on Wednesday and a double-slot on the Friday late-shift.' As if regretting how bleak this sounded he added quickly: 'But I never minded his appointments. I really did like him.'

I thought: you ploughed him under. It took me an enormous effort to sustain the conversation by saying: 'What was it about him that you liked?'

I had expected some facile answer but to my surprise he gave me a weird spiel, shocking in its old-fashioned ideology, about how Richard had 'lived out his own truth' as a closet gay despite his 'handicap'.

'Handicap!' I could hardly believe my ears.

'His word, not mine! He said he had the right to choose what to call his orientation and the right to choose how to live his life!'

But I thought of Moira and the children, impaled on that right to choose, and before I could stop myself I was saying: 'There can be no rights without corresponding responsibilities. Did it never occur to him he could mess up other people's lives as well as his own?'

'Oh wow, Ms Priggy, you're so sexy when you take the moral high ground!'

I ignored this rubbish. 'You've got it wrong,' I said strongly. 'Richard was the very opposite of a man who lived out his own truth. I also think he'd come to realise this but he was frantically trying to push the truth away with all this desperate talk about rights. He should have come out of the closet, and society's to blame for the fact that he felt he couldn't.'

'Oh God, a bleeding-heart liberal!'

'Well, of course I'm not surprised you're a homophobe. You can't acknowledge your real orientation so you despise gays while hamming it up as a straight!'

Gavin just laughed.

'What's so funny?' I demanded in fury.

'You, sweetie! You and your ignorance! Okay, ready for the learning curve? First of all, there's no block of identical people who can be labelled 'gay' and explained according to a single set of rules. Gays are as diverse as us straights, and Richard was a wonderful example of an up-yours individualist who couldn't stand the gay activists ordering him about.'

'Yes, but—'

'The next thing to take on board is that I'm not a homophobe. As I see it, there are shits and there are good guys, and each category has gay and straight people in it.'

'Well, all right, but—'

'And finally I think you should allow the gays to take some responsibility for their actions instead of blaming their rough deal on "society" – whatever that is. If you tell any mixed bunch of people that society's at the root of their problems, you'll always find some who'll develop a poor-little-me victim culture and start whingeing – and I don't know about you but I happen to find moaning minnies bloody unattractive. The great thing about Richard was that he was nobody's victim, he never whinged—'

'—and he went through hell because the strain of living a lie had become too damn much for him!'

Gavin said abruptly in a cut-glass public-school accent: 'The double-life was his choice and it was a choice he was entitled to make. If it turned out to be the wrong choice that's tough, but I'd still defend his right to go to hell in any way he chose.'

We drove on without speaking to Mayfair.

II

Richard's flat was on the first floor of one of those elderly Mayfair houses built in pinkish-red stone. Gavin had trouble parking the car, but when we finally walked away up North Audley Street he said: 'Can we have a truce, Frosty-Puss?'

'Not unless you call me by my correct name.'

'Okay, Catriona.'

'Carta will do.'

'You bet she will! I got lucky!'

I stopped in the middle of the pavement and swung to face him. 'Look,' I said exasperated, 'what's the point of all these heavy passes? You don't need them to get your message across so why do you have to keep ramming it down my throat the whole time?'

'I should be so lucky!'

'Right. That's it. I'm off.'

'Hey, hey, hey – cool it! Don't blame me for your very own Freudian slip!'

'Okay, I'll give you one last chance to shape up.' I felt like a mother struggling with a child determined to misbehave.

Scrabbling in my bag I produced the keys, but when I rang the buzzer to make sure the flat was empty I was suddenly aware of an extreme reluctance to enter the building. Belatedly I asked myself what had happened to my common sense. Perhaps I had been too absorbed by Gavin's proximity to have the obvious streetwise thoughts, but whatever the reason for my mental sluggishness I now realised I was about to give a sex-fixated scumbag the opportunity to assault me.

I was still clutching the keys, still asking myself how I could have been such a fool, when Gavin said behind me: 'You still worrying about me nicking things? Because you needn't. I wouldn't do anything which would have upset Richard. Promise.'

With enormous relief I thought: he sees himself as Richard's friend. He may come on strong but he won't harm me. After all, I was Richard's friend too.

Giving him a brief smile I stepped forward to open the front door of the building.

III

When we reached the flat Gavin was at once fascinated by the contrast between Richard's weird taste in modern art and Moira's preference for conventional furnishings. I could remember Moira telling me which decorator she had used, but Richard had obviously hated the result and imposed his pictures on the place as if with a clenched fist.

'He wanted to take me to exhibitions,' Gavin said, gazing at the nearest painting. 'This makes me wish I'd gone.'

'You mean you like that mess?'

'It's not a mess! The blue-green squares and the yellow triangles are arranged with mathematical precision, but mathematics is a language which doesn't deal with emotions so the colours say everything the shapes leave unsaid. What you have here is the essence of rational, well-ordered Richard infused with all the colourful emotions he had to keep hidden.'

Despite myself I was impressed by this smarty-pants exposition which suggested Mr Gavin Blake was rather more than just a pretty face, but all I said was a sceptical: 'How can you be sure?'

'Lady, I'm not laying down the law, I'm just suggesting why the painting spoke to him . . . Oh my God, look at this bedroom! Moira's run riot in here to compensate for losing the hall to modern art!'

I was careful not to cross the bedroom threshold, but one glance from the doorway was enough to repel me. In the big pink flouncy room beyond, the decorator's 1980s dream had become 1992's nightmare; we were in recession now, not wallowing in conspicuous consumption, and all the coordinating fabrics which swathed the bed and windows seemed stifling.

On the other side of the hall we found Richard's study, designed by the decorator as if for a simple squire hankering for an old-fashioned country life, but Richard had fought back against all the red leather and mahogany by hanging more of his weird paintings.

'This room has to be the one we want,' I said, and Gavin agreed, but the photos still proved difficult to locate. Gavin searched the desk and found nothing. He then checked the chest of drawers and moved the sofabed to make sure nothing was hidden beneath it, but only fluffballs from the thick carpet emerged. At that point I abandoned my role of supervisor and decided to search alongside him.

'What exactly are we looking for?' I demanded. 'How big are these pictures? Would they be in a folder or an album?'

'Probably not an album – too difficult to hide. There are three sets of ten-by-eights, thirty-six photos in all, and each set was in a plain brown envelope when I handed it to him. I'd guess he kept them in those envelopes.'

'But how sure are you that the photos are here and not at Compton Beeches?'

'One hundred per cent. He told me he kept them here to use on the weekdays when we didn't meet.'

'Use?'

'For masturbation.'

I opened the door of the fitted closet. 'So we're looking for hard-core porn.'

'You kidding? The first batch can be passed off as "art" and sold openly in the pseuds' corner of any mainstream bookshop. The second batch can be passed off as fun for the boys and stocked openly in any gay bookshop. And although the third batch contains pics only a sex shop would sell, I'm not photographed with anyone or anything so there's no way the stuff would fall foul of the Act as it's currently enforced.' And he added as easily as if we were talking about the weather: 'My manager says why break the law when it's possible to make so much money legally? That's why I never do parties. One-to-one gay sex between consenting adults is okay. Parties aren't. And I never get mixed up with serious S&M either because that's often legally borderline, and anyway if I get smashed up I can't work. Of course the odds are I wouldn't get smashed up because I know how to fight, but some of these pervs can slip on the handcuffs even while you're condom-stuffing, so you've got to be constantly on the alert.'

'How exhausting it all sounds.' I suddenly noticed the bookcase behind the door. 'Wait a moment,' I said suddenly. 'Even if Richard's kids were in a snooping mood, they wouldn't look twice at Daddy's sailing books, would they? Moira told me neither of them liked sailing.'

'Richard told me that too.' Gavin was already stooping to pull out a large coffee-table book about the history of sailing at Cowes, and as I watched, a brown envelope slid from the pages to the floor.

'Success!' I exclaimed with relief.

'It's only one batch,' he said, but when he grabbed the next book another envelope fell out. Reaching into the empty space created by the removal of both books he then pulled out the third batch which had been hidden behind them.

'Let me do a count to make sure they're all there . . .' He drew out the photos, and although I retreated to the window to wait I was aware of him stealing a glance at me. The next moment I heard him murmur amused: 'Wicked!' but I immediately faked a yawn, glanced at my watch and said: 'Get a move on, can't you?'

'I've just come across this truly amazing pic of my equipment. Want to look?'

'Sweet of you,' I said, adjusting my watchstrap, 'but why should

I be interested in equipment that's sold to all-comers by a pretty-boy too immature to know better?'

'Someone immature wouldn't last two weeks in the kind of world I live in! But thanks for calling me a pretty-boy, angel-tits. It gives me carte blanche to call you any name I like.' Stuffing the photos back in their envelopes he turned aside and paused to pick up the silver-framed photo which stood there. It was a picture of Richard with his children, and the background of a garden suggested it had been taken at Compton Beeches. The two adolescents stood together, slightly apart from him, and as Bridget was plump I knew the photo must have been taken some years ago. It was an excellent picture of Richard. His vitality seemed to rise from the frame and hit me straight between the eyes.

'I want this,' said Gavin suddenly.

I was shocked. 'Well, you can't have it! Nothing leaves this flat except for your vile photos!'

'How do you know they're vile if you refuse to look at them?'

'After your descriptions I don't need to look. Gavin, put that picture down!'

'Moira won't want it!'

'But the kids might, and they've got more right to it than you have!'

He sulked. He sulked beautifully, careful to milk the mood for maximum effect. His handsome mouth tightened. His jaw seemed more elegant than ever as he tilted it. His long dark lashes pointed downwards past his cheekbones as he gazed at the photograph and refused to look at me. But finally he did replace the frame on the chest of drawers.

'You ever consider a career as a dominatrix?'

'Grow up, Blake!' I moved into the hall as smoothly as possible, but my ankles felt flimsy, as if my feet were having trouble connecting with my legs. 'Can't you think of anything but sex?'

'Well, you're not thinking of much else, are you? That's why you refused to see my pics – you were scared shitless they'd turn you on!'

'I absolutely and totally deny—'

'Okay, forget it. What does your bloke do for a living?'

'He's a novelist.'

'A *novelist?* Shit, what kind of neurotic creep are you shacked up with? He's probably bi if not gay!'

'What utter crap!' Turning my back on him in fury I marched –

45

or tried to march – to the front door. I was in such a state, heart pounding, skin sweating, blood roaring, everything below the waist knocked silly by the adrenaline rush, that all I could manage was not a march but a totter, but luckily Gavin was backtracking as if he realised that the revenge he was taking for being deprived of Richard's photo had gone too far.

'Okay, okay!' he said hastily. 'The bloke's as straight as a Mills and Boon hero, but why are you so reluctant to discuss him? Does he drink, do drugs? Is he refusing to marry you? Is your life being blighted by Fear-of-Commitment Phobia?'

I was so shattered by this last question that I dropped my bag, which burst open to shower various objects onto the floor. With a curse I knelt to shovel everything back, and quick as a flash Gavin sank to his knees beside me as he pretended to give me a helping hand.

'It's all right – I can manage – *I can manage*, I tell you—' I was almost screaming.

'Relax, love,' he said amused. 'I'm not going to rape you, although you've as good as begged for it by deliberately dropping your bag to make sure we both ended up together on the floor, but let me ask you again for a date. Monday through Friday I don't do chicks because I need all my energy for work, but weekends I'm neat testosterone, all revved up and ready to go. So how about it?'

I lurched to my feet. 'No way!'

'Ah, come on! Listen, you and I could do things Mr Scribble-Scribble can only write about. You and I—'

'Shut up!' I yelled. I was by this time so infuriated not just with him but with myself for being so mindlessly vulnerable to his smash-and-grab behaviour, that I could hardly get my words out, but I did manage to gasp: 'You're pathetic!'

'No,' he retorted without a second's hesitation, 'I'm not pathetic. I'm a bright, tough bloke who's made a big success of his job, but you'd like me to be pathetic, wouldn't you, because if I was pathetic I wouldn't be churning you up to such an extent that right now you don't know whether to slap my face or beg for a fuck!'

'Wrong!' I shouted. 'I'm in no doubt whatsoever! I'm going to slap your face!'

He laughed. 'Okay, hit me – do it, do it, do it, as they say in the TV cop-soaps! Give me the excuse we both want to get you spread-eagled and ready for mounting in no time flat!'

I wrenched the front door open and blundered out, eyes burning with tears of rage and humiliation, but then I realised I couldn't rush away down the stairs. I had to wait to lock up. I groped for the keys, and as I did so I realised, to my intense relief, that he was switching off the hall light and preparing to leave. So long as I was no longer alone with him in that flat—

'Mounting's a fun word, isn't it?' he was musing lightly, under-lining his control of the scene by making a smooth attempt to steer the conversation onto a civilised pair of rails. 'Sort of Regency – or do I mean eighteenth century? Can't remember when Fielding wrote *Tom Jones*.' Closing the front door he took the keys from my unre-sisting fingers. 'Here,' he said kindly, 'let me lock up for you.'

The moment he turned back to the front door I scuttled down the stairs. Outside in the porch I took great lungfuls of fetid air spiked with diesel fumes as I fought to recover my shattered confi-dence, but when he rejoined me I was still in turmoil.

'Sorry if I upset you back there,' I heard him say as he slipped the keys into the pocket of my jacket. 'Richard wouldn't have liked that, would he? He'd have wanted me to treat you right, and that's what I aim to do in future because I think you're terrific. I'd really like us to be friends.'

All I wanted now was to get away from him so I merely nodded, but at once he added: 'I'm really grateful for your help – and now please let me give you a ride home. That's the least I can do in the circumstances.'

I lost my nerve again. The suave good manners coating the raw sexuality hit me like a bunch of red-hot pokers slamming through loose-packed snow, and in panic I said the first thing that came into my head. 'Oh, you don't want to trail back to the City!' I exclaimed, but as soon as the words left my mouth I knew I'd made a very big mistake.

'So you live in the City, do you?' he said quickly, and I could almost hear him thinking: I'll look her up on the electoral roll.

'I'll get a cab, no problem, don't worry,' I said in a rush, and he shrugged, willing enough to let me go now that he had an easy way of uncovering my address.

'Seeya!' he said buoyantly as we parted, but I could only slump back on the seat as the cab pulled away from the curb.

IV

The house on Wallside was in darkness, a fact which startled me because Eric had promised to have supper waiting. Grabbing the phone I dialled his studio.

'So where are you?' I said aggrieved when he picked up the receiver. 'Where's dinner?'

'Oh, my God! I'll be with you in five minutes.'

Storming to the kitchen I flung some scotch into a glass and began to make myself a low-calorie, vegetarian-cheese sandwich on wholemeal bread. Then I saw the bread was mouldy. With a curse I binned it, swilled some scotch and winkled a couple of biscuits from the packet of Tuc in the store-cupboard.

When Eric arrived I realised he was still mentally and emotionally in his studio where he was reworking a difficult segment of his new novel. 'I've got Marks and Spencer's fish pie,' he was saying from far away in 1940 where he was living with his characters in Norway during the Second World War. 'It won't take a moment to nuke it in the microwave.'

'But you were going to get that low-cal chicken and broccoli dish!'

'Was I?'

'Oh, spare me the Alzheimer's routine!'

'Darling, is something wrong?'

'He finally noticed,' I said to an imaginary audience.

'I'm sorry I lost track of the time, but the commandos were delayed and my hero was almost garotted—'

'Eric, that's fiction – *fiction* – and my problems are for real! I'm totally stressed out after messing around with a tart, and—'

'I've always said you were too obsessed with dieting! If you ate sensibly—'

'Not that kind of tart, you fruity-loop! A tart, a tom, a hooker, a hustler, A PROSTITUTE!'

'Blimey, what were you doing with one of those?'

'Well, I haven't mentioned it before because it was confidential, but – no, forget it. Listen, I'm cross, I'm starving, I'm—'

'I'll take you out. Let's go to Fish Heaven.'

'I don't want fish and chips! Let's go to Searcy's!'

'I can't afford Searcy's.'

'I'll pay.'

Silence. Suddenly all the humour drained out of the conversation and an invisible curtain dropped noiselessly between us. We were two years into our relationship but the money problem had never been solved, even though we often pretended that it had. I always told myself that this problem was the reason why we weren't married; I was too afraid that if Eric was unable to share my money with good grace before we were married he would be most unlikely to do so afterwards, and the marriage would quickly become dislocated.

'God, I'm so sick of you being neurotic about money!' I burst out. 'If *you* were the one who had the cash, this problem wouldn't exist!'

'We've had this conversation before. If you'd only commit yourself by agreeing to marry me, I wouldn't feel so like a kept man whenever you fling money at me!'

'I never fling money at you!'

'You flung Searcy's at me just now when you know damn well I have to go back to office-work next week to pay for my research trip to Norway!'

'Sometimes I think all you're interested in is your writing and I'm just an accessory to keep you amused between chapters! If you feel like a kept man, I feel like a cheap sex-aid!'

Eric plonked down the frozen fish pie. 'Okay, let me try again. Marry me.'

'What?'

'MARRY ME! You say you're over that first marriage, you say you're fully healed from that terrible time you went through with Kim in 1990, but if you were truly recovered you wouldn't have this paralysing fear of commitment. We'd get married and—'

'How can I commit when we haven't solved the money problem?'

'But can't you see? You're using the money problem to avoid—'

'No, I'm not, *no, I'm not*, NO, I'M NOT!'

'Oh yeah? Think about it,' said Eric, and walked out, leaving me alone with my empty whisky glass and the frozen fish pie.

V

A minute later I was calling my best friend Alice Darrow, the Rector's wife. There's nothing so therapeutic as a good moan to one's girlfriend

49

when men are driving one up the wall – as Alice herself said to me before I could even confess I had a problem. I volunteered to be with her in ten minutes. Then I called Lewis Hall, the retired priest who lived with Alice and Nicholas at the Rectory.

'I'm just about to drop in to see Alice,' I said to him. 'Could I please look in on you afterwards? I've got mixed up in a weird way with a prostitute and I've had a row with Eric and I feel I could use a head transplant.'

'My dear,' said Lewis, 'my dull evening has been miraculously transformed.'

I sighed with relief. Then I grabbed my bag, left the house and headed for the St Benet's Rectory, which stood in Egg Street less than quarter of a mile away.

VI

If I had stayed at home that evening I would have moped, wept and drunk too much in an orgy of anxiety and depression, but fortunately I had been saved from all this rubbishy behaviour because my friend Alice needed me. I had to shape up; I had to stop thinking me, me, me and start thinking you, you, you – always a startling philosophy for a former high flyer who had not so long ago thought of no one but herself.

Alice and I were both in our mid-thirties, and although we were in many ways very different, we had one important thing in common: we had both encountered St Benet's by accident when we had been quite outside any formal religion and had had no interest in God. Alice's encounter had taken place in 1988, mine in 1990 at the time of my disastrous marriage to Kim. Now, in 1992, I felt that although Alice's journey and mine were continuing down different paths, they were still running parallel, still cementing our friendship, still making it not only possible but natural for us to reach out and help each other whenever the going got rough.

Alice had married Nicholas last year after a lengthy engagement complicated by his dragged-out divorce, and she was now beginning to worry that she might have a fertility problem. The doctors refused to take her worries seriously, since she hadn't been trying to conceive for long, but what disturbed her more was the question of whether

Nicholas would have time to be an attentive father if a baby showed up. He enjoyed his work too much, and although with the help of his spiritual director he was always battling away not to be a workaholic, it seemed to be a never-ending war in which there were more defeats than victories.

To complicate this stressful situation, Nicholas's first wife Rosalind, who lived only thirty miles away, was always phoning him to talk about their two trouble-prone sons and conjuring up excuses (or so it seemed) to stay closely in touch. Nicholas and Rosalind had been friends since childhood; the marriage might have been dissolved but the friendship was apparently indestructible. Alice had reached the stage where she felt something should be said about Rosalind's persistent intrusiveness, but couldn't quite work out what that something should be.

'. . . so Rosalind phones and says she simply has to talk to Nicholas about Benedict's arrest for drink-driving and would I mind if she and Nicholas met for lunch, and I say: "Oh no, I wouldn't mind at all!" – why are the English so hopeless about complaining? – and of course that's a lie and I'm seething. So I say: "The trouble is he's so busy I doubt if he's got time for lunch," and she says: "Oh no, he's already told me he's doing nothing on his next day off!" And I think: that day off is supposed to be spent with *me*, and I feel so furious that I want to slap her – but of course I never will . . .'

Alice was too nice, that was the problem. I said that if I were her I'd tell Rosalind to piss off and then I'd shake Nicholas till his teeth rattled.

'Oh Carta, you do me so much good!' exclaimed Alice gratefully. 'I don't know what I'd do without your moral support. Have another piece of cake – or would you like a slice of deep-dish apple pie with cream?' A cordon bleu cook with a richly curving figure to bear witness to the irresistible food she produced, Alice was always generous in her hospitality.

'But enough of *my* problems,' she was saying, refilling my plate. 'Tell me about yours . . .'

That's the good thing about being part of a community. People care. People are interested. One never has to endure bad times alone. However, although I did talk to her about how Eric had driven me crazy, I never mentioned Gavin and I was careful not to moan about Eric for too long. That night I was clearly meant to be

51

Alice's listener, and besides, the confidentiality issues meant that Gavin was difficult to discuss.

'. . . and when Eric's working I hardly see him at all,' I said, concluding my brief whinge.

'Welcome to the club!' sighed Alice.

Eventually I left the Rector's flat and went downstairs to the main hall on the ground floor. This was in the handsome Georgian section of the house where Nicholas had his study, I had my office and Lewis occupied a pair of interconnecting rooms known as 'the bedsit', a nicotine-stained, whisky-smelling, dust-laden retreat crammed with Victorian furniture, icons, books, records, tapes, CDs and bound volumes of *The Christian Parapsychologist*. There was no television. On his seventieth birthday Lewis's daughter, who was married to one of the northern bishops, had given him a computer 'to keep his brain active in old age', but this white elephant was consigned to a corner and covered twenty-four hours a day with a disused altar cloth.

Lewis was now seventy-one, a state of affairs which he claimed didn't suit him even though we all knew it gave him an excuse to be as eccentric as he chose. He was chunky in build, neither tall nor short, and had silver hair, sharp black eyes and a foxy look. Apparently in his youth he had sailed close to the ecclesiastical wind, but in his old age he had become something of an older statesman, respected for his traditionalist views.

Nicholas and Alice had both invited him to stay on at the Rectory after their marriage, and although Lewis had said to me more than once that they should be 'left alone to enjoy married life without some senile pensioner cluttering up the landscape', he had so far made no attempt to move out. He and Nicholas went back a long way and were as close as brothers. He had been Nicholas's spiritual director at one time and even now often assumed the role of mentor.

Although Lewis had officially retired he still helped out at the church and still saw a certain number of people for spiritual direction. He was reputed to be better at dealing with men than women, and indeed he always cited his divorce as evidence that he had never been good at long-term relationships with the opposite sex, but for some reason he and I had always got on well. Since Lewis disliked feminism, female high flyers and women who prized their independence, and since I disliked crabby old heterosexuals who

52

were convinced a woman's place was in the home, our friendship was all the more remarkable, but he had been very kind to me after my marriage ended, and very helpful as I had struggled to understand the Christianity of the Christians who had come to my rescue. Lewis dished out certainties. It's all very well for liberal Christians to sneer at clergymen who do this, but when one's starting out on the spiritual journey and making a serious attempt to understand a complicated major religion, one needs certainties in order to find a patch of firm ground to stand on; the sophisticated approach can come later. I had reached the stage where I had dug myself in on a patch of firm ground but had so far been unable to work out how to move on.

The truth was that I was a mere beginner in a situation where an Oxford degree in law did not guarantee enlightenment. I don't mean to imply that the intellectual side of Christianity is irrational. How can it be when it's engaged the best minds of Western Europe for hundreds of years? I merely mean to stress that academic prowess doesn't necessarily produce spiritual wisdom – the ability not just to see the world as it really is but to make sense of it so that one can live in the best possible way.

'I can't make sense of this,' I said to Lewis after I had described the row with Eric and given him a bowdlerised account of my meeting with Gavin. 'I know I love Eric so why can't I make a full commitment to him? And I know Gavin Blake's scum, so why do I have this suicidal urge to swoon into his arms like a pre-feminist airhead?'

'Personally I'm rather partial to pre-feminist airheads.'

'Lewis!'

'I'm sorry, my dear, let me haul myself out of my dotage and address this problem. Can you give me a little more information? How exactly did you meet this man?'

Knowing I could say anything in a one-to-one conversation with a priest, I escaped with relief from the bonds of confidentiality and told him that I had encountered Gavin through Richard. Lewis and Richard had never met, although Lewis had been introduced to both Moira and Bridget at one of the healing services, and he knew Bridget was being treated for anorexia.

When I had completed my story, his comment on Richard's homosexuality was: 'The family was obviously dislocated – it was clear there was a hidden dimension somewhere which was causing trouble.'

'Did Nicholas suspect that Richard was gay?'

'I don't know. Nicholas is bound by confidentiality over Bridget Slaney's case, and it's not one of the cases where I know all the details – nowadays I no longer attend every case-conference.'

'But how could Richard's homosexuality have dislocated the family when he went to such enormous lengths to cover it up?'

'I'd say that if you consistently lie to those closest to you and invest enormous energy in pretending to be what you're not, you're almost begging for dislocated relationships. People, particularly children, pick up falseness on a psychic level and feel not just alienated but frightened and confused. Then even if the unease is never fully brought to consciousness it can manifest itself in ill-health or inappropriate behaviour . . . And talking of dislocated relationships, let's get back to your most immediate problem—'

'Gavin?'

'No, Eric. If your relationship with Eric was right, you wouldn't feel so threatened by this unfortunate young man.'

'*Unfortunate?* That scumbag?'

Lewis never hesitated. 'Carta, I'm sure you want to pursue a Christian course here, so I think the first thing you have to take on board is that it's not up to you to condemn him.'

'That's all very well, but—'

'Don't misunderstand. I'm not condoning his abusive behaviour which left you feeling frightened as well as angry. I'm just reminding you that only God knows the full story about why Gavin behaves as he does, and therefore only God is in a position to pass judgement on him as a person.'

'Okay,' I said, 'okay, I take back the scumbag judgement, but—'

'—but you're still worried by his behaviour.'

'Yes, I am! Supposing he now starts to stalk me? Supposing he turns up at my house?'

'Well, if he does, try not to reward him by giving an emotional reaction – simply be courteous but firm. If, on the other hand, he shows any hint of violence—'

I shuddered. 'I did come to the conclusion that he wouldn't be violent to a friend of Richard's. But I still feel he's dangerous to me.'

'Of course he's dangerous to you! When people are deeply disturbed, they have a capacity to damage those they interact with. They're like the typhoid carrier who moves from job to job and leaves a trail of infected people in his wake.'

'You mean he could make me cheat on Eric, destroy Eric's trust and wreck the relationship.'

'I mean he could undermine and perhaps destroy the whole life you've worked so hard to build for yourself since Kim died in 1990. But perhaps we shouldn't be too surprised by this. Is it really such a coincidence that you, a new Christian, should suddenly find yourself under attack from powers who are using this man to spread disintegration and disruption wherever he goes? And you won't laugh at this suggestion, will you, Carta, because you know how people can be damaged by the powers of darkness, you saw at first hand how your husband was fatally damaged by that evil woman, Mrs Mayfield—'

'Don't talk about her,' I said in a voice I barely recognised as my own, 'don't, don't, don't – if I start to think of how she got away scot-free—'

'Yes, we've reached the core of all your difficulties, haven't we? Mrs Mayfield destroyed Kim and got away with it – and how can you let go of Kim and move on, you say to yourself, when that woman's still evading justice for her role in his death?'

'Well, how can I?' I cried, but then made a huge effort to pull myself together. Levelly I said: 'All right, I know I must allow Kim a certain responsibility for the choices he made, getting mixed up with the occult and a fraudulent healer, but the fact remains that if that woman had never crossed his path he'd probably be alive today and receiving *real* treatment for all his repulsive problems!'

Lewis only said: 'Does Eric understand how strongly you still feel about Mrs Mayfield's escape from justice?'

'We don't talk about it any more, but I don't blame him for opting out. He hates to think I'm still bound up with my marriage to Kim.'

'Do you intend to tell Eric in detail about Gavin?'

'No. Now that Richard's dead the confidentiality issue isn't quite the same as it was, but Eric and I have problems enough at present because I can't make the commitment and agree to set a wedding date. Why risk making things worse?'

Lewis was silent.

'Am I wrong?' I demanded.

'How about asking God instead of me?'

'Well, since I'm not much good at praying—'

'Surely a lawyer like you can draft a couple of simple sentences asking for help!'

I brooded on this challenge for a moment before saying: 'I'd like to say to God: "Please mete out justice to Mrs Mayfield and let me know when you've done it. Then Kim can rest in peace and I can finally get on with my life with Eric."'

'How splendidly concise and pertinent! If only all prayers were that good!'

'But *how* can God mete out justice to that arch-cow Mayfield?' I exclaimed in despair. 'And more important still, how will I ever know he's done it?'

But before Lewis could reply we were interrupted. Footsteps echoed on the marble floor of the hall, there was a knock at the door and the next moment the Rector of St Benet's was entering the room.

VII

'Carta!' exclaimed Nicholas, startled. 'I'm sorry, I didn't realise Lewis had anyone with him.'

'I dropped in to see Alice. She asked me to visit your study and remind you what she looks like.'

As Nicholas smiled warily I saw he was having one of his days when he looked younger than forty-nine, a trick he pulled off easily as he was slim and tall and moved with such a peculiarly self-assured grace. His looks varied. Sometimes, when he was tired and not bothering to project the power of his personality, he looked both middle-aged and nondescript, but at other times he could be so arresting that heads would turn as he walked by. He had pale brown hair and pale skin, and his pale grey eyes could look blue whenever he wore blue jeans and a blue clerical shirt (his favourite office uniform). His pallor, which failed to reflect his excellent health, could be judged either striking or creepy, depending on how far he had turned up the wattage of his charisma. He could so easily have been a shady wonder-worker, using his gifts in the wrong way, but he was meticulous about operating within orthodox frame-works; he used to say the Church of England kept him honest.

'Are you all right, Carta?' I suddenly heard him ask.

'No, but I'll live. I called in to talk to Lewis about a problem connected with Richard Slaney.'

Nicholas instantly became alert. 'Richard Slaney?'

'Yes, I've got myself mixed up with the prostitute he was seeing.'

'But how on earth did you meet him?' said Nicholas amazed, in no doubt at all about Gavin's gender.

VIII

'So you did know Richard's secret!'

'I heard about the homosexuality,' said Nicholas, avoiding all mention of his source although I thought it had to be Moira. 'But nobody mentioned a prostitute.'

'The information was top secret. He'd been seeing this upmarket hustler called Gavin Blake who operates from a flat in Austin Friars. Gavin's straight. Richard was hopelessly in love with him. Bad scene.'

Nicholas sighed. Then he sat down and said: 'I'm very sorry indeed to hear that Richard was in such a painful situation.'

'To make matters worse,' I said acidly, 'I'll tell you that this man Gavin Blake's behaviour's outrageous and I loathed him – which means I'm fighting to deny he's the sexiest piece I've seen in a month of Sundays.'

Both men laughed. 'Well done!' exclaimed Lewis, and Nicholas murmured to him: 'How many other people do we know who could be so honest with themselves?'

'Skip the gloss, Darrow!' I snapped. 'I'm a basket case!'

'The odds are it's Gavin who's the basket case. This sounds like a man who comes on strong to hide a chronic lack of self-esteem.'

'You can't be serious! His ego's monumental!'

'Then why's he renting out his private parts? Would *you* rent out your private parts to a bunch of wealthy lesbian businesswomen?'

I recoiled. 'Well, no, of course not! I mean, no offence to lesbians, but—'

Lewis gave a snort of laughter and at once said guiltily: 'Sorry, my dear, but I always enjoy seeing liberals flounder in the quick-sands of political correctness.'

'My point, Carta,' said Nicholas, 'is that you wouldn't rent out your private parts to anyone, male or female, and that's because your self-esteem is such that you feel you deserve more from life than a career as a sexual punchbag. After all, we're not talking about sex for pleasure here. We're talking about a hard slog built around physical abuse, and if the sex is contrary to the orientation then we're talking of emotional abuse too.'

'Then why's Gavin doing this?'

'That's the big question.' Turning back to the door again he added: 'I must go upstairs to Alice, but come and tell me more about Gavin sometime.'

'I've finished talking about him,' I said. 'I don't even want to think about him any more.'

But I did think about him. As I walked home I thought: what's he doing at this moment? What kind of home did he go back to? How long's he been living with this 'manager' of his, the woman he was so keen to deny was a pimp? And what does 'living with' mean in this context anyway? When he used that phrase did he just mean they shared the house? And if he didn't mean that – if they're lovers – how does she cope with him screwing everything in sight?

The questions slithered around in my mind, coiling and uncoiling themselves like serpents in a pit, and after a while I had the odd feeling he was thinking of me at that moment, just as I was thinking of him – although that was a ridiculous idea since I had no talent for ESP.

When I arrived home the phone was ringing. 'Darling,' Eric said, 'I had to call – I didn't want to go to bed without saying sorry for that stupid quarrel. Look, what exactly happened with that tart you mentioned? You seemed so abnormally upset—'

'No need to worry, he's past history.'

'*He?*'

'We're talking of a rent boy who's been exploiting one of my friends, but I shan't be seeing him again, I promise you . . .'

I sincerely hoped that this wasn't a prime example of wishful thinking.

But it was.

CHAPTER FOUR

Gavin

'What makes the simple act of shaming or blaming people complicated is the knowledge that they each had a specific history, and the more we know about it the easier it becomes to understand why they did what they did.'

Godless Morality
Richard Holloway

I've got Ms Shaggable on the hook! Frosty-Puss is becoming Hotsy-Puss. At Richard's flat I had her steaming so hard that she pretended to drop her bag so that we could be on all fours together scooping up the chick-knacks, but I kept my hands off her because I want to make her boil, not just steam. So I put on a Caring-Nineties-New-Man act, earnestly apologising for my pushy pre-fuck pitch – and okay, maybe I *had* been coming on a shade too strong, but she's still dead keen, that's obvious, so dead keen that she discloses she lives in the City. I always knew I could cut out that bloke of hers with one hand tied behind my back! If he's a typical writer and soaks up the booze he'll have trouble getting the equipment to work, and the odds are he has no idea how to turn in a grade-A performance anyway. Elizabeth says it's sad how so few men do.

After I slip Ms Shaggable into a cab I sink into my XJ-S and breathe: 'Phwoar!' Then I check my face in the mirror. I look good. Everything's looking good. Even my boring H-reg XJ-S looks good, though it's much too has-been for me. The client only sent it my way because he'd hoped to make twenty-five grand selling it at auction and the highest offer he'd received was fifteen-five. So he turned it over to me instead and wrote the whole fiasco off as a tax loss. Thanks to the recession, the luxury car scene's collapsed, and sometimes I long to go out and pick up a Lotus, my dream machine, for peanuts, but even peanuts cost something and I want to put away as much money as possible in my Cayman Islands bank account.

Angling the jaded Jag out of that tight parking space near Richard's flat I head south towards my home.

*   *   *

Home is one of a row of large double-fronted Victorian houses on a main road south of the river and less than half a mile from Lambeth Bridge, which is one of the gateways to that glitzy postal district SW1. But our postal district is SW11, and when Elizabeth bought her house years ago the borough of Lambeth was pretty slummy. Even now it's not exactly SW1, but she's seen the value of the house shoot up during the property boom of the late eighties.

The front garden's been paved to provide three parking spaces, one for my XJ-S, one for her Toyota and one for Tommy's cheapo rattle-bag. The house is divided into three too. There's a basement flat for Tommy, who's Elizabeth's minder, and above this are four floors: raised ground, first, second and third. The main part of the house above Tommy's flat isn't formally divided up but in practice it operates as two duplexes. Elizabeth has the raised ground and first floors while Nigel and I share the second and third.

Nigel's my valet and Elizabeth's housekeeper. He's in charge of all the domestic arrangements and makes sure I'm properly fed, watered and housed, with clean clothes always in the closet. He doesn't cook for Elizabeth, but he shops for her and makes sure the cleaning-dodo doesn't OD on endless cups of tea. Although he and I share the upper floors, he's under strict instructions not to get under my feet, so when he's not busy doing his job he keeps to his room at the top of the house. When he first came I hated him, didn't want him around, thought he was disgusting, but Elizabeth insisted that I'd reached the stage where I needed to have my domestic life taken care of, and she pointed out that Nigel was willing to work for a pittance as he knew he'd have trouble finding a job elsewhere.

Nigel's a sex-offender. I've never asked him for the full story, don't want to know. All I do know is that he used to be a dresser in the theatre but was nabbed by the police after a production involving child actors. When he came out of jail he spent some time hustling in Leicester Square and got picked up, poor sod, by a couple of the Big Boys from Asherton's Pain-Palace, but luckily Asherton discovered he could cook so Nigel escaped from the dungeon to the kitchen. In the end Asherton traded him to Elizabeth in exchange for a black pre-op transexual who had tried to find work at Norah's escort agency and was willing to do anything for money. Norah, who's Elizabeth's business partner, doesn't employ trannies, either transexuals or transvestites. 'It's a question of class, my dear!' she flutes, as if her idea of heaven is to run a brothel staffed by princesses of the blood royal. Silly cow! I often wonder how Elizabeth stands her, but they've been friends for years.

Elizabeth used to run the escort agency at one time, but she's always liked to keep several irons in the fire and when her psychic healing business took off in the eighties she delegated the running of the agency to Norah, her second-in-command. Elizabeth's still got her stake in the company, of course, and after the collapse of her psychic healing business in 1990 she took a hand in running the agency again, although since my career reached the stratosphere she's gone back to delegating everything to Norah. Norah lives across the river in Pimlico, the shadow side of mega-rich Belgravia. She's a lesbian who likes to dress in pink, and her two chihuahuas have jewelled collars. Disgusting.

But luckily I don't have to see much of Norah. Elizabeth does drag me to the Pimlico house for Sunday lunch sometimes, but at least the roast beef's always good. Even the chihuahuas agree on that.

Having parked the XJ-S on its pad in front of the house I spring out, grab my bag from the boot and gaze for a moment at the night sky. There are stars up there somewhere beyond the neon glow and if I were at sea I could pick out the constellations. I freeze, remembering my times at sea with Richard and shuddering as the shock of his death hits me again.

Unfair. Not right. No God. Nothing. The only philosophy worth a shit is 'Eat, drink and be merry for tomorrow we die', and that's why money's all that matters — it's because with money you can live it up before the big wipe-out. I've got a lot of money saved in my Cayman Islands bank account and I'm going to have more. (Isn't it great to have an account in a smart tax haven like the Caymans? I mean, how upmarket can one get?) Then in two years' time I'm buying a boat and sailing off into the sunset — with Elizabeth, of course. She'll be ready to retire then herself. The collapse of her psychic healing business two years ago was really traumatic for her, and if I hadn't been doing so well I think she might have retired at that point, but my success perked her up, gave her an incentive to keep going. She still misses the psychic healing, though. She's made a mint from her leisure industry interests, particularly her 1970s chain of massage parlours (forcibly taken over by foreign pondlife in 1980), but it's the psychic and the occult which really switch her on. It's how she got hooked up with Asherton, who runs a weird pseudo-religious secret society in addition to the S&M group which would make the vice squad's hair curl.

As I get out my keys to open the front door, I wipe the memory of Asherton in case I start having flashbacks, and I focus instead on how brilliant it was when my business took off. I admit I needed Elizabeth to help me in the beginning, but after the first few clients were established my reputation spread at the speed of light all by itself. Then Elizabeth only had to put my career on a well-organised business footing and watch the money roll in. Most leisure-working's done in the West End, but next door in the Square Mile of the City where the streets are paved with gold there are all these rich gay blokes who roost there every day of the working week and are usually much too busy to want to run all kinds of risks out west with God knows who. I offer them absolute discretion and top-class skills in Aids-free upmarket surroundings right on their office doorsteps. Of course they're happy to pay big money! They think I'm terrific value and they're right.

The best thing of all is that I've got control over my life. I'm young, I'm fit, I drive a luxury car, I shop where I like, I shag the sexiest chicks, I look good and feel great because I'm a smoke-free, drug-free zone – apart from alcohol, but I'm smart enough to go easy on the booze. Elizabeth thinks I'm wonderful. I'm never letting her out of my life, never, she's mine for always. My amazing success is all due to her, and now life's fantastic, life's sensational, in fact there's not a single bloody cloud on the horizon.

Opening the front door I walk into the hall and dump my sports bag by the stairs to take up later. The living-room door's ajar and Elizabeth's talking to someone, but I know she hasn't invited guests so I assume she's on the phone.

I glide in, hoping she'll tell me how sexy I'm looking, and my muscles are tightening at the thought of a hot hetero snog after all the boring contact sport today with the sad sacks who can't hack it with women. But nemesis awaits. Maybe I even deserve it for that knee-jerk put-down of the blokes who fuel my bank account, but whether deserved or not, this is where I get my comeuppance. For Elizabeth isn't on the phone. She's entertaining an unexpected guest, and the guest is none other than Mr Mega-Monster himself.

It's Asherton.

* * *

I stop dead. My mind goes blank. No more thoughts about how wonderful it is to have control over my life. All the hairs on the nape of my neck are standing on end and my heart's banging at the double.

Asherton says: 'Good evening, my dear!' and his sugar-and-cyanide voice is silk-smooth. Creamily he adds: 'How attractive you're looking! Isn't he looking attractive, Elizabeth?'

'Ever so attractive,' says Elizabeth placidly, 'but then he always does. Hullo, pet.'

I mumble a greeting.

'I hear you're about to meet a very wealthy gentleman,' says Asherton tenderly, 'and I'm hoping he'll prove to be a suitable candidate for GOLD. You'll make sure you're particularly nice to him, won't you?'

'Yes, sir.'

'There's a double-slot tomorrow afternoon which has unexpect-edly fallen vacant,' says Elizabeth to him. 'I've offered it to Sir Colin but he says the appointment has to be next Tuesday and it has to be in the West End.'

'Ah, one of the cautious ones!'

'It's a bloody nuisance – it means clearing the late shift. If only Sir Colin would take Mr Slaney's double-slot tomorrow at the flat!'

Asherton says idly: 'What happened to Slaney?'

'Dropped dead, dear – and just after he'd promised the boy ten thou in stocks and shares! I was ever so miffed!'

Asherton looks suitably shocked at Richard's lack of consideration. 'My love, refresh my memory: why did you decide Slaney was unsuitable for GOLD?'

'Gavin reported that Slaney had zero interest in religion, and I could see there was virtually no spiritual awareness worth culti-vating. The only thing Slaney worshipped was . . . now, what was it? Something very non-numinous . . . Oh yes, his boat. He liked sailing.'

It suddenly dawns on me that if Richard left a legacy to the St Benet's Healing Centre – an idea which I know had occurred to him – I could be in deep shit. Word travels fast in the City, and wills get to be made public. I start to sweat. I've never told Elizabeth about Richard's connection with St Benet's because she's paranoid about the bloke who runs that place. She says he destroyed her psychic healing business. She says he came close to wrecking her entire life. She says she'll never forgive him, never, she'd like to raze that church of his to the ground, she'd like to fire-bomb the Healing Centre, she'd like to crucify all Christians. Elizabeth can get very worked up if she feels she's been hard done by.

'Gavin?' I suddenly realise Elizabeth's sensed my anxiety. Shit! I'd better get my mental skates on PDQ.

'Gavin, what's the matter? Why are you looking as if you'd forgotten to tell me Slaney was on the road to Damascus?'

In panic I spew out a spiel. 'Oh, he still didn't give a toss for religion! But apparently – and he only admitted this to me last week – he was feeling benign towards the Church of England. His daughter was having problems and his wife had taken her to a clergyman for counselling and the counselling had been sort of, well, successful, know-what-I-mean, so Richard—'

'What clergyman?'

'Uh . . .' I see with horror that I've got to come clean. If I invent an imaginary clergyman at the other end of London and word gets out that Richard's left a hulking great legacy to St Benet's, she'll be so livid with me for lying to her that anything could happen.

'Gavin!'

'Sorry, darling, just trying to work out how to break the news so you don't get upset. You see, it was a City clergyman, a clergyman at one of those Guild churches which have special ministries such as healing—'

'I don't believe I'm hearing this. Are you seriously trying to tell me that Slaney was mixed up with—'

'Oh, Richard was never directly involved with what's-his-face! As I said, it was Moira Slaney who—'

'What was wrong with the girl?'

'Anorexia.'

'That means family therapy. Of course Slaney must have been involved with Darrow!'

'I tell you he wasn't – he refused to go because he was afraid of being outed as a gay! He never even met Darrow, I swear it!' This is a lie, but if I can keep plugging the fact that Moira was the St Benet's fan, I might just possibly survive this braindead dive of mine into deep shit.

The next moment it dawns on me that Asherton's been maintaining the deadest of dead silences, and suddenly I realise that he's just as appalled as Elizabeth – although as far as I know he had no connection with the disaster of 1990 when the Reverend Nicholas Darrow, Rector of St Benet's-by-the-Wall and *bête noire* of the psychic con-trade, managed to close down the healing business which Elizabeth ran under another name out of a house in Fulham.

But before I can ask myself just why Asherton should be so gob-smacked at the thought of Darrow, Elizabeth stands up. Not a muscle of her face moves, but I know that what she minds most at this particular moment is not Richard's tenuous link with St Benet's but the fact that Asherton's seen she's not in control of me.

'It's all right, Ash,' she says quickly. 'I'll deal with this. Gavin just made an honest mistake, that's all – he saw Slaney's connection with St Benet's as minimal so he didn't mention it for fear of upsetting me.'

'Yes, my love. But a church connection could have altered Slaney's religious views. It should have been reported.'

I feel I must try to insist that although Richard had come to respect the St Benet's ministry of healing he was still nowhere near being a religious believer. 'I think—' I begin, but this is where I get zapped.

'You're not supposed to bother your pretty little head with thinking, my dear,' says Asherton, his voice now all cyanide and no sugar. 'Your job is to fuck and do as you're told.'

My tongue seems to have been instantly transformed into wood but I manage to say: 'Yes, sir. I'm very sorry I messed up. It won't happen again, sir, I promise.'

There's a pause. Then Elizabeth relaxes and murmurs hospitably: 'Another drink, Ash?'

'No, thank you, my love. I must be on my way.'

'Gavin,' says Elizabeth, 'show Mr Asherton out, would you?'

I turn on my heel, cross the hall and with unsteady fingers open the front door.

'Close that,' says Asherton behind me.

I close it. My scalp crawls.

'Kneel down.'

I kneel immediately, head bent, and wait for the blow. But it never comes. He's just getting a kick out of making me think I'm about to be walloped.

'That's a good boy!' he croons approvingly. 'I do so like obedience . . . You haven't forgotten how much I like obedience, have you, my dear?'

I'm now having a hard time breathing. I feel him caress my hair and again I wait for the blow, but in the end he only pats my head as if I'm a dog.

'Open the door.'

I stagger to my feet.

'Good night, Gavin,' he purrs as I somehow get the door open again, and without waiting for a reply he walks to the curb where he signals to his chauffeur. The car's parked at the top of the nearest side road in order to avoid the bus lane which runs past the house.

The Rolls glides along, pauses to pick up its owner and melts away towards glitzy SW1 on the other side of Lambeth Bridge.

I'm left feeling shit-scared and subhuman, like a circus animal who's messed up a trick in the ring and can think of nothing but the trainer with the big whip. Wiping the sweat from my forehead I close the door and slump back against the panels.

'Gavin!' calls Elizabeth sharply. 'Come here!'

Obediently I scuttle back into the living-room.

*   *   *

Elizabeth pats the empty space on the couch to signal I should sit beside her, but I'm not taken in by this cosy approach. She's still furious, and in despair I ask myself why I let the idea of Richard leaving a legacy to St Benet's drive me into a confession. He might well have left the place nothing – in which case I'd have been off the hook. And even if the legacy had shown up in the will I could always have marvelled at it and claimed total ignorance of Richard's St Benet's connection.

Looking back I can hardly believe I made such a balls-up, but of course it was Asherton who skewered me. I only have to see him and my brain goes on the blink. He treats me as an animal so automatically I act as if I have an animal's IQ.

I draw breath to embark on a massive apology. 'Elizabeth, I'm

66

really, really sorry I came out with all that shit in front of—'

'Face it, pet, I gave you a helping hand, didn't I? I should have kept my mouth shut when I saw your eyes glaze over at the mention of Slaney's religious interests!'

But I know she's shovelling on the sympathy to screw the whole truth out of me. Then she'll unleash the big blast, but meanwhile I've got the chance to give my story a makeover, and this time I'd better be bloody sure I get it right.

'It's wonderful of you to be so understanding,' I say earnestly, 'but I'm sure you want to know the real reason why I kept quiet about Richard's St Benet's connection. It was because when he mentioned it to me last week he also asked me later on in that same session if I'd go sailing with him. So I think: oh boy, if I tell Elizabeth about Richard and St Benet's she'll axe him from the client list and then my chance of sailing goes down the tubes.'

'Ah, now we're getting somewhere!'

But I daren't relax yet. More earnestly than ever I say: 'Okay, I hate escort work, hate working on weekends, but I figured it would be worth it to get back on board a boat again. Richard said he had one of the new thirty-footers from Hunter with a self-tacking rig and a twin-keel option—'

'Fancy!' says Elizabeth dryly, but she's smiling at me.

'—and so I thought: well, I *will* tell Elizabeth about the St Benet's connection – but not just yet. I thought—'

'You thought: screw Elizabeth, I'll play my own game here!' She's still smiling as she turns up the heat.

But I stay cool. I've provided the missing motive for my decision to withhold information, and the motive has the advantage of being true – more or less. I mean, the truth's just been a bit edited, that's all. Of course I've known about Richard's St Benet's connection for months and I've been sailing with him six times, but I'm hardly likely to trot all that out to Elizabeth, am I? No way!

Meanwhile as all this edited stuff flashes through my mind I'm protesting innocently: 'Elizabeth, I never thought of it as playing my own game! I just didn't want you axing him from the client list before I'd gone sailing!'

But Elizabeth turns up the heat another notch.

'Listen, pet,' she says, and now the smile's vanished. 'You took decisions that weren't yours to take. Slaney was infatuated with you already, and if you'd gone sailing with him he might well have lost it altogether, run amok and ruined your vital reputation for leisure-working discreetly.'

'But—'

'Can you really have forgotten Langley threatening to top himself and Petersen having the nervous breakdown and Perrivale – no, I don't even like to think of Perrivale screaming down the phone that he'd kill me unless I let him see you every day! Slaney was about to become an unacceptable risk, that's the truth of it, and I'd have terminated him just as soon as those stocks and shares were in our hands.'

'But Richard wouldn't have flipped out like the other guys! He was an okay bloke, he wouldn't have harmed me in any way, I was his friend!'

'Oh, grow up, dear! Smart, classy, wealthy, successful men like Richard Slaney don't have leisure-workers for friends! He wanted you for one thing and one thing only, and it would only have been a matter of time before he tried to cut me out and wreck your business in order to have you all to himself. You his friend? Don't make me laugh! If you think he was your friend just because he wanted some fun on his boat, you're deceiving yourself in the biggest possible way!'

I try to keep my face expressionless as she unleashes this big blast, but after her last words I have to struggle to keep focused.

'Now just you listen to me,' says Elizabeth, keeping her voice level but making sure every word comes out rock-hard. 'I accept that you've come clean now about Slaney, but you should have been upfront with me from the start, and if you're ever economical with the truth again like that I'll be bloody angry.'

'Darling, I'll never let you down a second time, I swear I won't—'

'Asherton pays me good money so that you can report on your clients' religious interests. If you keep mum when you should be speaking out, he's going to feel short-changed – and I don't like to think of Asherton being short-changed, dear, I really don't. Short-changing Asherton's not a good idea at all – and as for short-changing *me* by keeping quiet about a client's St Benet's connection—'

'I'm sorry, I'm sorry, I'm sorry—'

'Just remember that if Darrow ever finds out where I am, the whole bloody fiasco of 1990 will be raked up and the police will land on us like a ton of bricks. They may not be able to jail you for leisure-working but they'll smash your business by tipping off the tabloids about the pretty-boy who's got the City sussed, and don't think either that your precious Cayman Islands bank account would survive! The police would drag in the Revenue to make sure you got done for tax evasion!'

It's no big effort to assume the required sober expression. In fact after all the facts I've edited during this conversation, assuming a sober expression is the easiest thing I've had to do for some time. Anyway, since I've heard this scenario before I'm a long way from being in total shock. On the contrary, the next moment my brain's clicking into top gear again as all the neurons skewered by Asherton finally achieve realignment, and I'm realising that this could be my golden chance to find out more about the fiasco of 1990. I'm also realising how important it is for me to seize this chance with both hands because when I get going in a big way with Carta Graham, fundraiser *extraordinaire* for the St Benet's Appeal, it'll be vital to know exactly what risks I'm running. Just how far do I believe Elizabeth's nightmare scenario which she uses to beat me into shape?

My difficulty here has always been the lack of a lever which would coax Elizabeth to open up further about what really happened in 1990. I'll get nowhere by just saying: 'Hey, I need more information to ensure I take St Benet's seriously in future.' Elizabeth's left me in no doubt about how seriously I should take St Benet's and as far as she's concerned there's nothing further I need to know. Where the truth's concerned about the fiasco of 1990, she'll short-change me until she's blue in the face.

Suddenly I have a brainwave. It's the word 'short-change', reminding me of the threat she's just made about Asherton.

Tentatively, very tentatively I say: 'Darling, there's something that's puzzling me. I couldn't help noticing that Asherton was as alarmed as you were when the subject of St Benet's cropped up. Was he somehow involved too in the fiasco of 1990?'

The question works. Shit, she's thinking, that's a complication I don't need, better toss him an explanation that'll shut him up.

Idly, willing to be cosy again after the big blast, she says: 'Get me another glass of sherry, will you, dear? I think it's best if I finally tell you everything.'

She won't, of course.

But I bet she cooks up the helluva story.

* * *

Before I get to Elizabeth's story-cooking in 1992, here's the story she cooked up for me in 1990 after she'd been forced to abandon her business as a psychic healer in Fulham, ditch the alternative identity she'd used there and shut herself up in the Lambeth house until it was safe to emerge for plastic surgery.

Things went wrong (said Elizabeth in 1990) when one of the clients who came to her for healing accused her of being a fraud. Of course the client was mentally ill and of course facing false accusations is an occupational hazard for all healers, even doctors, but Elizabeth was still shocked. She was even more shocked when the nutso client chugged along to the well-known St Benet's Healing Centre and shot his mouth off to the Rector who then took the most unjustifiable step (said Elizabeth) of tipping off the police. Fearing persecution despite her innocence (ran the fairy-tale) she decided she had no choice but to disappear before the wicked police started trampling around investigating her affairs. Even though her businesses were all legitimate (said Elizabeth) the bad publicity would wreck my leisure-working, then heading for the financial stratosphere. So it was better that Mrs Elizabeth Mayfield, psychic healer, should cease to exist in order that Mrs Elizabeth Delamere could continue her law-abiding and blameless career. The big advantage of running two identities in tandem (said Elizabeth) was that if one of them went tits-up the other was always available as a safe haven, but she'd never forgive that villain Darrow at St Benet's for depriving countless suffering people of her exceptional skills as a healer.

Well, even back in 1990 I took this story with a pinch of salt but naturally I wasn't so dumb as to query it. Something serious had without doubt been going on – no one ditches an identity and resorts to major plastic surgery without a strong motivation – but I decided straight away to give her my total support. I loved Elizabeth and I owed her everything. I didn't need to know her goriest secrets because I was going to stay loyal to her whatever she'd done.

So much for 1990.

Today in 1992 I'm as loyal to her as ever, but I'm also older, sharper, tougher and keener to take risks in order to have a fun time. Carta Graham's a risk and shagging her would give me a big buzz, but I'm not stupid and I know I've got to assess this risky behaviour very carefully – which is why I'm now so determined to find out more about what really went on back in 1990 . . .

'Well, dear,' says Elizabeth, taking a dainty little sip from her refilled glass of sweet sherry in September 1992, 'this is what really happened. The fact is that back in 1990 I saw no need to tell you that Asherton was involved. You and I hadn't been working together for long, had we, and although you were doing so well you might still have wound up disappointing me just as Jason and Tony did. Much better, I thought, if you weren't told anything you didn't need to know.'

Jason and Tony were my predecessors who had failed to stay the course and been sacked. I was a case of third time lucky.

'So how was Asherton involved?' I ask, keen to gloss over my fragile status in 1990 and get to the shitty-gritty.

'The trouble centred around a member of GOLD.'

I'm hooked. I'd been assuming Asherton was tied in through his S&M group, not through that weird society of his which specialises in pseuds'-corner religion.

'The member of GOLD who triggered the fiasco,' says Elizabeth, rolling out the information with a theatrical sigh, 'was a man called Betz, B-E-T-Z. He was a naturalised Brit but born a Kraut, and he worked for an investment bank in the City. I'd known him a long time – in fact I was the one who introduced him to Asherton – and in 1990 he was treasurer of GOLD.'

'And what did he get up to?'

'No good, is the short answer, dear. In the late eighties he ran into serious problems in his private life and consulted me not just as a friend but as a healer. In fact he only knew me in my healer's identity, which I ran parallel to my present identity for longer than you've probably imagined. I used to operate out of a room near here in Lambeth before I went upmarket across the river in Fulham . . . But the point I'm making is that Betz only knew me as Elizabeth Mayfield, so when the fiasco blew up in 1990 no one around Betz except Asherton knew I was also Elizabeth Delamere. It was the crucial factor in allowing me to disappear without trace.'

'But if Betz was the treasurer of GOLD, didn't he have access to your Delamere name and address?'

'I told Asherton to keep it from him. As a consultant to GOLD on occult matters I'm paid a fee, of course, but as soon as Betz started signing the cheques I had the fees directed to one of my Mayfield accounts.'

'But mightn't he have heard about the Delamere identity from someone else at GOLD?'

'No, because apart from Asherton the members either knew me as Mrs Mayfield or else they didn't know my surname at all. As the occult consultant I was addressed at meetings simply as Madame Elizabeth . . . But let me go back to Betz. When he consulted me again in the late eighties I soon realised that this time he was too unstable to respond to any therapy I could offer, and after he'd insisted on marrying a thoroughly unsuitable second wife, I could see the fiasco coming. To cut a long story short, I'll just say he had a nervous breakdown and killed himself.'

'Wow – big scandal!' I'm trying to work out whether the severe editing necessary to cut a long story short means that a fiction's beginning, but I think my straining ears can still catch the ring of truth.

'Oh, it was much worse than a mere scandal, dear! By the most malign coincidence, the new second wife – a real bitch if ever there was one – knew someone connected with St Benet's and she complained to bloody Darrow.'

'You mean there really was someone who complained about you?'

'Yes, but it wasn't a nutty client, as I told you in 1990 – it was this interfering bitch.'

'So this naughty totty lit the fuse to the St Benet's keg of dynamite and—'

'*Naughty totty*? You make her sound like a teenage tart! She was a lying, scheming businesswoman who pulled down a six-figure salary, and when she said I was a fraudulent healer who was responsible for her husband's breakdown and suicide, everyone believed her! I can still hardly believe she said such dreadful things about me – I can't tell you how much help I'd given that husband of hers over the years! Was it my fault that in the end she seduced him and cut him off from me so that he went totally out of control?'

I see a dull glow on the horizon and I know it's the truth fading out of sight. Trying to lasso it before it disappears I ask: 'So after Mrs Betz complained to Darrow he tipped off the police, just as you said originally?'

'Well, because of the suicide the coroner was involved and the police were cluttering up the landscape anyway, but they would never have known about me if Darrow hadn't supported the bitch's claim that the fiasco was all my fault. I thought his behaviour was disgraceful, but of course he was biased against me because as a

New Age practitioner I was a rival to him in his own healing business. Jealousy's a very terrible thing,' says Elizabeth righteously, 'and there's nothing more wicked than a jealous Christian priest bent on persecuting the innocent.'

The truth's sunk far below the horizon by this time but I keep up the struggle to keel-haul it back. 'And meanwhile Asherton was shitting bricks because—'

'—because he was terrified that the police would uncover GOLD and use the link with Betz to justify a search of Asherton's house in Westminster. God only knows what *that* would have turned up, but when you think of his SM group . . .'

Elizabeth always refers to Asherton's favourite hobby as 'SM' instead of 'S&M'. She says that's the way it was when she was young, and people today have quite forgotten that the practice isn't sadism-and-masochism but sado-masochism.

'So what you're saying is,' I persist, battling away to keep the truth in view, 'the police would still like to talk to you about the Betz case, and this would be bad news for Asherton as well as you.'

'Yes, dear. You see, innocent though both Asherton and I are in relation to the Betz fiasco, Asherton's even more vulnerable to police nosiness than I am since that SM group generates his video business and we all know hard-core porn can be a bit iffy. But Asherton's only catering to a genuine human need, of course. He's ever so well-meaning when you get to know him.'

The truth's sunk below the horizon again but this time it's fallen into a black hole and it's heading for another galaxy. Mentally reeling in my busted keel-haul rope I take one last pot shot at any truth-fragments which might still be floating around. 'Was Betz a member of the S&M group as well as a member of GOLD?'

'For a short time, yes, but he dropped out. When it came to SM he preferred to be a loner on the prowl.'

'You mean the new wife knew that but married him anyway?'

'Of course not, dear, he kept mum because he thought that marrying the bitch would cure him! But it was quite the wrong therapy, and I told him right from the start it would all end in tears – in fact I even had a psychic premonition about it . . .'

I tune out. I don't believe in psychic premonitions. They're just a way for smart operators like Elizabeth to make their shrewd guesses sound plausible.

This concludes the conversation on Bad-News Betz, but although

I'm sure Elizabeth's done another classy editing job, I believe I really do know more now than I did before.

* * *

I want to run off at once and reassess the risk factor in shagging Frosty-Puss, but I know I have to act cool, implying the new information satisfied my curiosity and isn't of any major importance to me. Making the required effort I tune in again to Elizabeth, who's now saying she's recently had a new psychic premonition, this time in the form of bad vibes about Richard.

'You mean because you felt he was losing it where I was concerned?' I enquire seriously. I've long since learned not to snigger when she goes psychic on me.

'I'm sure the infatuation contributed to my uneasiness, but the premonition embraced more than that. I felt he was going to trigger some big disaster for me, just as Betz did when he married that bitch who hooked herself up with St Benet's . . . But I see now I could have misinterpreted those vibes. Maybe what I was picking up was Slaney's St Benet's connection, and that was reminding me on an unconscious level of the Betz fiasco.'

This is obviously not the moment to ask if I can go to Richard's funeral. She might decide she has a psychic vibe telling her not to let me go. Focusing instead on the explanation I gave her earlier to cover my visit to Richard's flat I change the subject by saying idly: 'I had a wasted trip to Oxford Street tonight – that place is a bloody scrum when there's late-night shopping, and I didn't buy a thing.'

'What a shame! And why, may I ask, did you feel it necessary to wear your brand-new Armani suit for a mere shopping expedition?'

'Hoped I'd get lucky and hit on a babe I can shag this weekend!'

To my relief she smiles. 'You'd better run along and have your supper,' she murmurs indulgently, but when I try to kiss her the smile vanishes. 'No, I'm not feeling too affectionate tonight, dear,' she says, averting her face. 'You were a very silly boy, embarrassing me like that in front of Asherton, and I'm still feeling more than a little put out.'

I trudge upstairs to get fed.

* * *

Nigel the valet-housekeeper's waiting with my dinner. He's about five-seven, thin as a whippet, and he has one of those faces which are all eyes and no chin. His hair's wild. He has it permed and it froths around his head like a black halo. His eyes are a moist green, like grass after heavy rain. His London accent has been ironed into something more neutral: cockney with the corners rubbed off.

'Hi, Gav.'

I grunt.

'Shall I dish up or—'

'Dish.'

He dishes. It's pork casserole with rice and a salad. Delicious. We have an eat-in kitchen in the part of the house we share, and I like to shovel down dinner at the table while reading the *Evening Standard*.

Nigel retires to the living-room to watch TV but returns to serve up the rest of the meal: Eve's pudding with custard. 'Anything else, Gav?'

I finish my single glass of Chateau Neuf du Pape. 'Nah.' That's me adopting a more neutral accent: Surrey with the fringe ironed out.

'Bad day?'

'Elizabeth's pissed off with me at the moment.'

'Oh, that won't last!'

'It seems like it's already lasted a week – I can't believe it only began when I got home this evening. I walk in and who do I find slimeballing around her living-room? Bloody Asherton.'

Nigel recoils. 'What did he want?'

'He was talking to Elizabeth about this rich new client who I've got lined up for next Tuesday, so maybe the financial prospects were under discussion. Anyway, Elizabeth gets angry with me over something and Asherton makes me shit bricks and all I can think afterwards is fucking hell, what a fucking awful day.'

'There's football on Sky Sports tonight – or there's even kick boxing on Eurosport. I could watch with you if you wanted company.'

'Dear old friend . . .' I started calling Nigel that occasionally after he told me he didn't have any old friends because whenever he made a friend he soon got dumped. 'Thanks for the offer, mate,' I say, finally

75

pulling myself together, 'but I think I'll listen to Wagner instead.'

'Oh, that'll cheer you up! You're always better after opera.' He closes the dishwasher. 'Shall I turn this on or do you want to stay longer in here?'

'Turn it on.'

He pushes the button. The machine roars. Nigel and I go our separate ways.

*   *   *

Nigel's right – after a dose of opera I do feel better. On an impulse I pass up Wagner and listen to *Tosca*, currently playing at Covent Garden with Zubin Mehta (always at his best in Puccini) conducting. It's had rave reviews and everyone says Pavarotti's on grade-A form. I've managed to get a ticket for later this month. Can't wait to go.

Can't wait to shag Frosty-Puss either, and now at last I have the chance to do some serious risk-assessing. Carefully I start to pick over Elizabeth's brand-new version of the 1990 mess. I can now follow her example and call it the Betz fiasco after its doomed anti-hero.

Although much of what Elizabeth said was just a variation on her poor-innocent-little-me-going-it-alone-in-the-leisure-industry song (which is pretty gross, considering the kind of money she must have stashed in the Caymans as the result of all her successful ventures) there are a few new nuggets of information nestling among the garbage and I suspect that underneath all the fantasy and the euphemisms the real story goes something like this:

The Betz bloke was a walking disaster who finally triggered police interest, probably as the result of criminal offences relating to his S&M interests. (Why else would a fat-cat banker top himself unless he felt sure both his career and his new marriage had gone down the tubes?) But the criminal S&M activity apparently wasn't related either to Asherton's S&M group or to GOLD. The fact that Betz liked to be a lone wolf when he did his S&M was a lucky break for Elizabeth and Asherton, but they weren't off the hook, far from it, because Betz was so closely connected to them through GOLD on the one hand and the healing scam on the other that any crime he was perverted enough to commit (beating up non-consenting totties?) was going to give the police the excuse to snoop in all the wrong places in order to sort out the case.

But Elizabeth and Asherton had another lucky break, didn't they?

76

Betz dived off the twig. In fact this is so lucky that I'm tempted to think . . . no, I'm not. Asherton's not interested in topping people. He's into pain, not death – death's when all the fun stops. Nigel and I joke sometimes about Asherton making snuff movies for his video business, but we're just resorting to black humour to soothe our nerves. And of course Elizabeth would never kill anyone either, she'd say murder was an unacceptable risk. No, Elizabeth wouldn't have knocked off Betz, especially when she would have known that any kind of dive Betz took from the twig would cause her trouble.

I pause. My interpretation of her newly edited reminiscences seems to be panning out – or is it? I'm sure I'm on the right track in theorising that Betz committed a serious crime connected with his S&M habit – only something really heavy in the background could explain why Elizabeth and Asherton are still so nervy about the events of 1990. But the problem's this: surely after Betz is dead and the coroner's court has produced the suicide verdict, the police would close the case? Why is Elizabeth so convinced that the police would turn back to the Betz fiasco if they found her? Maybe we *are* talking murder here – the file on an unsolved murder always stays open. If Betz was a murderer . . . yes, now everything's certainly adding up. And don't forget that I only have Elizabeth's word that his S&M disaster wasn't connected with Asherton's S&M group. Maybe it was. And maybe both Asherton and Elizabeth became accessories after the fact as they tried to cover up the crime in order to protect themselves.

Well, it's a neat theory, but there's no proof, is there? Yet there's a sense in which this doesn't matter. All that matters is that the Betz fiasco is lying around like an unexploded bomb, and I'd better be bloody careful I don't detonate it when I do my frolic with Frosty-Puss.

Okay, so do I need to put her right out of my mind? Maybe it depends on whether or not she's heard of the Betz fiasco, but as her fundraising's only been going on for a few months the odds are she knows nothing about Darrow closing down a psychic healing business in Fulham in 1990, and there's no reason why she should ever have heard of Betz – he'd have been history long before she joined the St Benet's team. So I reckon I'm as safe as a gold bar in the Bank of England here, but let's be thoroughly sensible about this, let's be as mature as someone nearly thirty should be, let's just take a moment to visualise how this could all go wrong.

But although I exercise my imagination energetically for a while I just can't come up with a doomsday scenario. After all, I'm not going to bring Carta home to meet Elizabeth, am I? And Carta's not going to take me to the church to meet the Rector. And even if we met him in the street by chance I'm hardly likely to say: 'Hey, Rev, I know Elizabeth Mayfield – remember the Betz fiasco?' And we're not going to meet him in the street anyway.

Relaxing at last I lie back on my bed and dream of Frosty-Puss, the ultra-shaggable one, the sort of golden British girl who doesn't normally cross my path. As Elizabeth knows, I've made American tourists my speciality. I pick them up in Covent Garden on weekends, take them to a high-buzz place for a meal and then go back with them to their hotel. The great thing about these American babes is that they're sex-mad – or their therapist has told them they ought to be – and they speak English, more or less, so I can put my brain on autopilot while I enjoy myself. Personally I can't recommend Americans too highly for a weekend shagbender. Saturday night, maybe Sunday – and then off they go to Stratford or Oxford or back to the States with no harm done and no complications. Perfect.

But not as perfect as an interlude with Carta Graham, golden girl of my dreams. I go on thinking about her, and the funny thing is that after a while I feel sure she's thinking about me, even though I don't believe in any of that ESP rubbish and know that in reality I'm just freaking out on wishful thinking. I wonder what her home's like. I wonder if she enjoys living in her world. I used to live in a world like that once, long ago.

'You got lost, didn't you?' murmurs Richard in my ear as I drift into unconsciousness, and at once I fling back a denial, but seconds later I dream I'm sailing across a glittering sea in another galaxy but with no knowledge of how I can ever find my way home.

*   *   *

As soon as I get to Austin Friars the next morning I call Directory Enquiries to see if Carta's number's listed, but it isn't. She could be listed under another name, but probably she just prefers to be ex-directory. I then ask the helpful Telecom totty to give me the number of the St Benet's Appeal office and she turns this up for me with no trouble.

After my meditation I get the coffee going and fix the water jug.

(The first client fancies ice-cubes as sex aids.) Then I glance again at the list of clients and automatically supply the nicknames I've chosen to remind me who's who. Three minutes later the buzzer drones and away we go.

This morning I do the Grunter, who makes more noise than Monica Seles chasing the Wimbledon singles title, the Rimmer, who's ripe for harvesting by the queer-bashers, and Gomorrah, the prima donna who announced at the start of his first session that if I ever mentioned the word S-O-D-O-M he'd piss all over the walls. (Hurriedly I assured him that no one was going to force him either to Gomorrah or be Gomorrahed. The early shift's almost always a buggery-free zone anyway since only the diehards fancy it so soon after breakfast.)

This morning Gomorrah wants to use a condom he's brought back from a trip to Amsterdam. It's bright pink, it's got I LUV U printed on it and it's reeking of synthetic strawberries. I'm glad he's no longer trying to convince me that his favourite routine carries no risk of Aids, but this little latex luvvie's strictly for girls who don't mind getting pregnant. Patiently I explain to him – not for the first time – that it's a house rule that I provide all the condoms, even for oral numbers, in order to ensure the highest possible standard of healthcare. Gomorrah throws a tantrum but finally falls into line.

After he goes I finish the shift by doing the Mandarin, who gets his kicks by watching me go through my repertoire of gay poses. If only all my clients were so undemanding! The Mandarin's an eighty-two-year-old Chinese man with little English and a beatific smile. His son makes the appointments and pays for the sessions. It's wonderful how the Chinese look after their old people.

Since this last appointment involves no physical contact I take my post-shift shower after Gomorrah flounces off, and as soon as the Mandarin's tottered away I shovel down the egg-mayo sandwich Nigel's made this morning at my request, skip the work-out at the gym and streak home in the XJ-S. It's possible to get back in twenty minutes but today it's raining, the traffic's snarled and I make a diversion anyway to the florist in Moor Lane. Stuck in a traffic jam south of the river I decide the moment's come to call Carta on my elderly mobile which becomes a car-phone whenever I bed it down in the Jag.

'It's Gavin Blake,' I say in my most businesslike voice as my pulse rate soars. 'Have you heard yet when the funeral's going to be?'

'Heavens, you're not going to that, are you?'

I nearly take a bite out of the phone. 'I was his friend. I'm entitled.'

There's a pause before she says abruptly: 'I haven't heard anything yet but the notice should be in *The Times* very soon.'

'I need to know now in order to clear a space in my schedule,' I say, keeping my voice dead neutral. 'Please call me as soon as you get the information.' And I blip out just as the traffic eases. Come on strong, back off cool – it never fails to inflame them. She'll now be beside herself wondering when I'm going to come on strong again.

At eleven I arrive home with the flowers I've bought to soften Elizabeth up. Can't stay long, the timing's too tight, but I can take ten minutes.

As I pull up on the paved front garden I spot a tall Barbie-doll figure teetering along in towering heels, black tights, a short black leather skirt, a long black leather jacket and God knows what underneath to keep the silicone mountains in order. She's carrying an umbrella inscribed around the rim with the words: IT'S RAINING WOT A BITCH. She's Elizabeth's secretary, Susanne.

Susanne works from eleven till around seven-thirty because those are the hours which suit Elizabeth, who likes to use the first part of the morning on personal chores such as getting her hair blonded. So Susanne's still at the office when I come home straight from work, and that's when she hands me my schedule for the next day. She also orders condoms and sex aids for me, and she's capable of negotiating fees, although Elizabeth, who loves power, usually handles the haggling. Susanne always treats me like filth. Slag! I can't stand her.

Susanne used to be one of Norah's escort girls but she was no good, partly because she has a tin ear for language and never learnt to drop her Essex rasp, and partly because she's outstandingly charmless. Norah usually employs only well-spoken college graduates, but she thought Susanne (originally known as Sharlene) was bright enough to keep the punters smirking with her repartee. The newcomer was repackaged as 'Suzette', a name supposed to conjure up images of cutesy Parisian popsies, but Ms Charmless said what was wrong with being a Brit, for God's sake, and screw all Frogs, she was going to be 'Susan'. The name 'Susanne' which then emerged was Norah's idea of a compromise.

This kind of behaviour from Ms Charmless eventually generated blasts from appalled clients and in the end Norah sacked Susanne who promptly took her revenge by attempting suicide. It's bad for an upmarket escort agency when one of its totties tries to top herself. Norah's jowls quivered above her pink frilly blouse as she frantically sought advice from Elizabeth. Even the chihuahuas looked anxious.

Elizabeth took charge. She too thought Susanne was bright but recognised that her gift was not for entrancing punters. Susanne was brought to live in the Lambeth house, given just enough therapy to get her functioning again and then sent on various courses to learn typing, a little accounting and some essential IT. Susanne devoured them all and wanted more. Elizabeth promised more on condition that Susanne agreed to work for her, and simultaneously Norah offered Ms Charmless the basement flat of her Pimlico house at a nominal rent. (This was a worthwhile deal for Norah, since Susanne did a lot of paperwork relating to the escort agency without adding to Norah's wages bill.)

At this point Susanne became Ms Upwardly-Mobile, moving into a home of her own and reading books on interior decoration. A cat appeared and was named Alexis after the soap-opera villainess. A framed photo of this animal stood on Susanne's desk at the office, a regular reminder of how greatly I preferred dogs.

As I now arrive home, Susanne unlocks the front door. Naturally it never occurs to her to hold the door open for me – or maybe it does but she slams it anyway. With my arms full of flowers I finally succeed in getting into the hall.

Elizabeth's in the office but on the phone, negotiating a lease on a flat in Battersea. She's told me she's moving into sex therapy groups again. After the healing business was wiped she swore she wouldn't dabble in future in any related areas, but the truth is she just can't resist the chance to do some hands-on reshaping of people's lives – all for the best possible motives, of course, including the desire to open a new bank account. But to give Elizabeth her due, I have to say she's genuinely convinced she's a grade-A healer and psychic. As she's such a tough businesswoman, I think this weakness of hers for paranormal rubbish is all rather touching.

The moment the conversation finishes I glide in to present the bouquet. 'Surprise for you, darling . . .'

Elizabeth's delighted. But that bitch Susanne says: 'Yuk, those lilies

– what a pong!' and stalks out, breasts bobbing furiously beneath her silver-spangled T-shirt. Susanne's breasts are so stuffed with silicone that they remind me of a brace of the balls used in bowls, the summer game the wrinklies play on lawns smooth as green baize.

As soon as I'm alone with Elizabeth I say: 'I want to apologise again for that mess yesterday,' and to my relief Elizabeth benignly waves away the memory as if it's no longer important. I'm forgiven. Now at last I can ask her about the funeral, but first I have to do some skilled manoeuvring.

'Elizabeth, can I just have a word with you about the Kraut?'

'Wasn't he any better yesterday?'

'No, he was worse. He got it all over the bathroom floor and tracked it round the bedroom—'

'Well, at least you don't have carpets to worry about, but I agree he seems to have been a touch thoughtless.'

'A touch – Elizabeth love, you're still not getting it. This bloke's filth – FILTH! – and I want him terminated right away!'

'Better to ease him out gently by raising the price, dear. The clients who pay extra for specialities are usually ever so sensitive, and you don't want to get the reputation for being heartless.'

'That bugger's as sensitive as a bloody tank! But okay, never mind that for now, I want to ask you for a special favour. Can I go to Richard Slaney's funeral? I'd really like to be there as a mark of respect.'

Elizabeth sighs and rolls her eyes upwards in exasperation.

At once I add: 'I'll do overtime to fit in the clients who get cancelled.'

'You know I don't like you working overtime,' says Elizabeth abruptly. 'You know how fussy I am about you not overstraining yourself.'

'I'm overstraining myself dealing with that bloody Kraut!'

'Gavin—'

'Okay, listen, how about this: I'll go on with the Kraut. But you let me go to Richard's funeral.'

Elizabeth picks a lily out of the bouquet and begins to flick the flower to and fro, like an angry cat jerking its tail. 'Now listen, dear,' she says sharply. 'You're confusing two quite separate issues. If you really feel you can't go on with the Kraut, then you don't have to go on with him. I've never insisted that you do anything you don't want to do – that would be counter-productive, since you'd soon start having problems with the equipment. I know you

82

had to be taught a little lesson in the beginning about being obedient, but be honest! I've never made you keep going with anyone you hated, so don't try and strong-arm me now over Slaney's funeral by using the Kraut as a lever.'

'Well, I thought if I offered to make some kind of sacrifice—'

'What are the odds on someone from St Benet's being there?'

Carefully I say: 'I suppose someone might come out of sympathy for Mrs Slaney – a curate, perhaps, or a church volunteer. But since Richard wasn't a believer and had no direct contact with the place I can't see the Rector himself bothering to attend.'

Elizabeth meditates on this but makes no sceptical comment. Instead she remarks: 'I must say, I'm astonished how sentimental you've become about Slaney! I'm beginning to think he's had the most unsettling influence on you.'

'Well, he won't have any influence on me in future, will he? He's dead.'

'Ah, but it's amazing the influence the dead can have on the living, dear. Every psychic knows that . . . Very well, I'm not keen on this, *not keen at all*, but I do see that from a psychological point of view it's best if I allow you to go. You must have the chance to say a formal goodbye because then it'll be easier for you to draw a line under the whole business and move on.'

'Darling, I'm really grateful—'

'But you're not to get into conversation with anyone, you're to leave immediately after the service and you're not to go near anyone who's wearing a clerical collar.'

'Okay, fine, no problem,' I say earnestly, trying not to sag with relief.

Back clunks Susanne with a steaming mug of coffee in her purple-taloned claw. 'Shall I dump those flowers somewhere else before they stifle us, Elizabeth?'

'No, dear, I want to arrange them myself straight away.' Picking up the bouquet she moves out of the room in search of a vase.

Susanne sips her coffee and looks at me with sharp, feral black eyes. 'So you're going to slobber over Slaney's coffin.'

'You've been eavesdropping!'

'So?'

'I don't like eavesdroppers.'

'So?'

'Your speaking-tape's jammed, Barbie-Boobs! Take yourself back to the toy shop to get your head fixed!'

'You talk to me like that because you're jealous!' she spits. 'You're jealous because I've got a proper job now and you're still a rent boy!'

'I'm a big-time leisure-worker earning megabucks and you're an office slag earning a pittance!'

'But I don't have to wake up every weekday morning knowing I've got to shag filth for a living, do I?'

'A top-of-the-range operator doesn't have to shag filth!'

'Oh yeah?' she snarls. 'What about the Kraut?'

'Why, you—'

'Children, children!' says Elizabeth maternally, returning to the room as if she'd anticipated this spat. 'Gavin, run along, pet – we never risk keeping a client waiting, do we? Susanne dear, open the post straight away, please, and let's do as much as we can before lunch.'

I give her a hot snog and head back in triumph to the City.

*   *   *

After the lunch-time shift I check the electoral roll and find Carta lives at Wallside, the classy row of Barbican houses in Monkwell Square. Interesting. She must have money. So what's she doing messing around with a no-hoper who sits around imagining life when he could be out there living it? He probably sponges off her. Disgusting! In fact you could almost say it's my moral duty to rescue her from such a creep.

Richard's double-slot on the late-shift has been split between two occasional clients who happen to be in town: a black American lawyer from Chicago ('Chiccy Dickie') and an Italian clothing magnate ('Mr Meatballs'). They're no trouble but I miss Richard's wit. Well, I miss Richard – period, as my American clients would say.

At six-thirty precisely, as I prepare to leave, Golden Girl calls to tell me the funeral's next Wednesday at three. I thank her profusely, whisper: 'Can't wait to see you in black!' and hang up. But of course I fully intend to see her before then. The weekend's coming up and I've got her address and she's going to have a big surprise . . .

*   *   *

Saturday dawns. Brilliant. I'm up at six, hardly able to wait. Saturday's the one day I get to shag Elizabeth.

When I reach her bedroom with the early morning tea I find her curled and perfumed and wearing her best negligée. Sensational! I rev myself up to deliver a grade-A-triple-starred performance and nearly pass out with excitement. Numerous magic moments slip blissfully away.

Elizabeth's just so wonderful to me. Not only did she teach me how to do sex at stud-star level but she even said that as a very special favour we could keep shagging on a regular basis once my lessons had finished. I'm pretty sure my predecessors, Jason and Tony, never got that far.

However, I'm special, I'm different, I'm the one who's a big success. Elizabeth even takes me on holiday with her. We go to her favourite luxury hotel in Bournemouth and do really weird stuff like play bingo and dance foxtrots.

During our late breakfast in bed on this particular Saturday morning Elizabeth says casually: 'Norah rang last night. She's invited us round for lunch tomorrow.'

'Oh God!'

'I want you to meet the new girl she's taken on.'

'Why?'

'Well, pet, I've been thinking very hard about you as the result of our recent conversations, and I've realised I have very little idea what you might be getting up to at weekends. And that makes me uneasy.'

'Darling, I would *never* have gone sailing with Richard without telling you!'

'I wasn't just thinking of your boat fetish, dear. I was thinking of all those American tourists. It'd be so easy for you to get in a pickle when you go grazing in Covent Garden, and anyway how do I know grazing there's all you do?'

'Elizabeth, if you think I secretly go clubbing to shag teeny-totties, you couldn't be more wrong! I loathe music that's just a headbanger's jerk-off! I'm bored rigid by all those chemically trolleyed teenagers who think they've found the secret of the universe!'

'Yes, dear, I know you're twenty-nine and far above all that kind of nonsense, but that's exactly my point! Now you're nearly thirty you could be unconsciously looking for something a little more *stable* than just a weekend fling, and that's why I've made this lovely arrangement with Norah.'

85

I choke on my toast. 'What lovely arrangement?'

'She'll let you date this really nice upmarket girl – a history graduate who's also an opera fan! No fee to the agency, of course, and the girl will do it with you for free.'

There's so much wrong with this idea that I hardly know where to start my reply but finally I decide honesty's the only possible policy. 'Forget it. Why should any bloke with my looks want to bother with a girl who has to be shared with a bunch of johns?'

Elizabeth sighs as if she can't believe I could be quite so dumb. Then she says: 'I don't think this is quite the moment for fantasy, pet. What other kind of upmarket girl is going to want a steady relationship with you once she finds out what you do for a living? Now wake up, there's a good boy, and face the facts. This girl would know what you do so you wouldn't have all the stress of pretending to be what you're not – and you get quite enough of that sort of stress during the week when you're passing for gay. You could have ever such a nice relationship with her at weekends, and when you do get tired of her you'll be able to have another girl straight away from Norah's stable, no fuss, no mess – and no stressful, undignified trawling around Covent Garden for women who are never around long enough to guess what you do.'

She pauses but when I'm silent she adds kindly: 'Face it, pet, it's the answer, isn't it? All right, I know I'm the one you care about, but if you're to be kept sexually satisfied, it's vital that you link up with someone of your own age. I'm a realist, you see – always was, always will be – and I know I can't expect you to be content with just little old me on Saturday mornings!'

My voice says: 'If we could get together more often—'

'No, don't let's go into all that again, dear, there's no point. You know very well that I've reached the age when I like it once a week, done properly – unless I'm on holiday, that is. Naturally then I have more energy.'

'Yes, but . . . Elizabeth, there's no one else, is there?'

'Don't be silly, who am I supposed to be having it off with? Now be sensible. You know very well how precious you are to me, and that's exactly why I always want the best for you – which in this case means coming to Norah's with me tomorrow to meet the new girl.'

All I can think is that I can't afford to get stroppy. She might change her mind about letting me go to the funeral. So I say nothing, and as Elizabeth relaxes, confident that she's won the argument, she remarks idly: 'I just have this very strong feeling that I must help you into a relationship with a suitable girl before you get into trouble with someone who's entirely wrong . . . In fact I'd definitely call the feeling a psychic premonition.'

I keep my mouth tight shut.

'There's a dangerous girl wandering around out there somewhere,' murmurs Elizabeth, unable to resist giving her crystal-ball act another whirl even though she knows I'm an arch-sceptic. 'A blonde. You've already met her.'

This fails to impress me. Obviously there's always the danger that I might meet a bunny-boiler in Covent Garden, and obviously there are loads of blondes 'out there' in a city of several million people.

'She's older than you,' invents Elizabeth dreamily. 'I can't see her face but I'm sure she's got brains, she's a strong personality. And . . .' She stops.

I somehow keep my expression blank so that there's nothing for her to read. 'And?'

'. . . and she's somehow mixed up with Richard Slaney,' says Elizabeth abruptly, turning her head to see my reaction.

'Ah!' I say without missing a beat as I marvel at her luck in hitting the mark. 'You're thinking of his wife. Richard mentioned once that she was a blonde. But I've never met Moira Slaney.'

'Then it's not Moira Slaney I'm thinking of,' says Elizabeth.

Having offered to make her some more tea, I scramble out of bed and whisk the breakfast tray downstairs.

Funny how creepy all that psychic rubbish can be . . .

*   *   *

Later I go out, crossing Lambeth Bridge into glitzy SW1 as I head for Fortnum & Mason. Here I buy a bottle of vintage Bollinger and have it gift-wrapped before it's popped into a Fortnum's bag. I want Carta to think I'm not just a bloke who picks up booze at the nearest branch of Oddbins. I want her to think I've got style and class.

Back at home I eventually prepare for action. I dress in stone-coloured RL trousers, a creamy shirt and a slickly cut navy-blue jacket which made my bank account creak last month. No tie. A plain belt with only a CK logo on the buckle. And beneath all these maximum impact ogle-items I'm sporting underwear by HB, the designer whose models look as if they might just possibly know what to do with a naked woman if they met one by chance in a bedroom.

Off I drive to the City. As it's Saturday afternoon the parking regulations are suspended, and after abandoning the XJ-S on a yellow line I walk back down Wood Street to the vehicle barrier which guards Monkwell Square. The Wallside houses form the square's northern side.

It's now five o'clock and I'm gambling (a) that the lover lives out, and (b) that they don't get together on a Saturday evening until six at the earliest. (Independent Carta would have other things to do, other people to see.) It won't take long to persuade her to cancel the date, especially if I get lucky and find her lounging around in a skimpy dress, bare-legged and knickerless as she reads about orgasms in some chattermag for chicks.

Finding the right house I give the doorbell a punch, but when the door opens my heart sinks. I'm not face to face with Carta. It's the boyfriend. He's shorter than I am but he's no dwarf. His eyes are chocolate-brown but not soft. His dark, reddish, curly hair needs cutting and styling and yes, *that's* soft. I can't stand moppy hair, there's no excuse for it. He's kind of podgy, obviously never bothering to work out. Soft again. He's wearing mass-produced jeans and a red sweatshirt with no designer logo. Boring. He badly needs to update. He's older than I am, maybe even as much as ten years older, and he's definitely way over the hill.

Without a trace of sexual interest he looks at me and says: 'Yes?'

I add some more facts to my new file. He's straight as a steel stake, not a flicker of any bi undercurrent there, and from that one syllable he's uttered I can tell not only that he's educated but that he's probably from the south of England. He could even be a Surrey boy like me.

'Hi,' I say civilly, one straight bloke to another. 'I'm a friend of Richard Slaney's. Is Carta around?'

From the top of the stairs behind him Carta exclaims, 'Gavin?'

'Carta!' I drawl, very debonair, and glide past her dated old lover into her home.

*   *   *

88

I don't get invited into the living-room straight away, but I realise she has to put on an act for Mr Over-the-Hill. Of course she's secretly thrilled to see me. 'What on earth are you doing here?' she demands as she comes downstairs.

'Delivering a reward for all your help this week!' I say, smiling at her, and hold out the gift-wrapped bottle. Now I'll get invited into the living-room – which I suspect is up the stairs on the first floor. There doesn't seem to be much down here at ground level except a couple of closed doors.

Carta's delighted with the present, of course, but has to pretend she's not. Waving away her fake protest I flash her another smile before turning to Mr Over-the-Hill. 'My name's Gavin Blake,' I say sociably. 'Good to meet you.'

Mr Over ignores me and merely says to Carta: 'You want me to handle this?' but Carta's not going to let him fling me out – oh no! She's going to signal that she's more than glad to see me. *Now* I'll get invited up to the living-room.

'Gavin,' she says crisply, 'this is Eric Tucker. Look, some friends are stopping by at any moment for a drink before they go on to the Arts Centre for a concert, so I can't invite you up to the living-room but—'

'Oh, I'd love to see the living-room!' I exclaim, realising that she's signalling me to override what she's saying. 'Does it look out on the Roman wall?' I get my foot on the first stair.

'Hey, wait a moment!' cries sad old Eric Tucker, getting pathetically territorial, but I'm skimming upstairs before he can stop me.

'Okay, you're welcome to look at the view,' I hear Carta say, cleverly managing to keep the excitement out of her voice. 'I guess you deserve some sort of reward for trekking all the way out here to bring me a present, but after that I'm afraid you'll have to—'

'What an amazing house!' I marvel as I cruise ahead, but in fact the house seems more eccentric than amazing, a sort of mezzanine-with-everything mishmash. Still, the living-room's an impressive spread, a two-level space of about twelve metres which Carta's filled with writhing modern furniture, all curls and curves. The oldest thing in the room is probably the battered teddy bear which is propped up in a display cabinet amidst some bulbous Lalique glass. This bear, who's no doubt an antique picked up for a vast sum at Sotheby's, has an oh-my-God-now-I've-seen-everything look. I immediately want to kidnap him.

Meanwhile my feet have carried me to the huge window and I decide to get rapturous to keep the conversation bowling along.

'What a view!' I breathe, and add as I notice some mass-market prints: 'And look at your pictures!' They're all dire. 'I somehow got the impression the other night that you weren't interested in art.'

'What other night?' demands Sad Eric, sounding as if he's about to combust.

Carta says firmly: 'I'll explain later. Now Gavin, you'll have to excuse us, but—'

The doorbell rings.

'I'll go,' mutters the Sad One, almost too enraged to speak, and disappears downstairs.

Seizing my opportunity I say at once to Carta in a low voice: 'Hey, you're looking great! It's okay, I know you're not really mad at me for stopping by—'

'But I am,' she says, still polite but allowing an edge to creep into her voice. 'I suppose you looked me up on the electoral roll, but all I can say is that I don't want you paying me attention like this and I'd be very grateful if you'd now stop.'

'You mean you'd rather have that chubby heap than me? You can't be serious! He looks like he just fell off the back of a lorry!'

As I speak voices have been ringing out in the hall, and at this point footsteps, lots of them, start to thunder up the stairs. 'Carta darling!' screeches the first visitor as he erupts into the living-room. 'How *are* you, angel?'

Carta has no choice but to turn away but I stay where I am in amazement. These three visitors are all gay and two of them are the in-yer-face type, always gasping to scream about their rights to any media microphone in reach. The first one's what I call a frothy number, but the froth is almost certainly camouflage to disguise the fact that he's articulate, smart and streetwise. These militants are a tough bunch. His in-yer-face chum could be his partner but not necessarily. This bloke's flamboyant too but harder and smoother, probably more of a diplomat. He's flaunting one of those godawful moustaches and displaying a taste in leisurewear so old-fashioned that you almost expect to hear Abba belting in the background. Like Sad Eric he badly needs to update.

But it's gay visitor number three who interests me most, probably because he's such a familiar type in my professional life. He's

Mr Pass-for-Straight. He's tall, dark, not bad-looking in a low-key way, with a friendly face, sensitive and intelligent, the kind of face that makes you think: he looks a nice bloke, I wouldn't mind passing the time of day with him over a lager. His clothes are hopelessly conventional, but at least they don't make you think of Abba. A school choir would be more in keeping – or my mum's favourite, Cliff Richard, crooning about his unimaginably innocent summer holiday.

How do I know Mr Pass-for-Straight's gay when he's looking like every suburban matron's dream of a reliable son-in-law? Because he glances at me and nearly faints beneath the onslaught of the testosterone surge. The other two are vibrating like whacked gongs too, but Mr Pass-for-Straight's the only one who looks like a starving man scenting a square meal.

'Hey!' calls Eric Tucker as he follows his guests into the room and finds them all boggling at me. 'Time to go – you've had your look at the view!'

I'm incensed. Imagine not introducing me to the guests! Imagine humiliating Carta by treating her new acquaintance – a friend of Richard Slaney's no less – as rubbish which had to be put out for the garbage truck! Well, I'm sorry but I'm not standing for that kind of behaviour, no way am I going to stand for it. I'm going to shock that bastard rigid, I'm going to make him want to pass out with embarrassment, I'm going to see he reels as if I'd smashed his teeth in.

Radiantly I smile at the gays. 'Well, hul-*lo*, sailors!' I purr, sashaying towards them as if I've never shagged a woman in my life. 'My name's Gavin Blake and I have a flat in Austin Friars near – wait for it, guys! – *Old Broad Street* which is the kind of address you don't forget when you've got sex on your mind, but here's my card—' I gyrate my hip to ease the wallet from my back pocket '—to drill the memory home. Just call to make an appointment! I take all the major credit cards—'

All hell bursts loose as Sad Eric finally combusts. 'GET OUT, YOU SCUM!' he bawls, but I keep right on.

'—so darlings, if you drop-dead gorgeous guys want to fuck – and I mean *fuck* – F-U-C-K—'

'PISS OFF!' roars Sad Eric, hurling himself at me, but I just laugh and dodge out of his reach.

Golden Girl immediately fears for my safety. 'Eric, don't!' she cries, but at once I call back to reassure her: 'Relax, sweetie, he's past it – I could floor him in no time flat!'

At that point Sad Eric almost froths at the mouth, but before he can hurl himself at me again someone yells: 'WAIT!' and we're all diverted.

It's Mr Pass-for-Straight, making a surprisingly authoritative intervention. 'Cool it,' he says quickly to Sad Eric while grabbing his arm and stepping between us. 'I think Mr Blake will be willing to leave of his own accord now you've demonstrated how deeply he's upset you. No, Carta, leave this to me. Mr Blake, allow me to show you out, please.'

As a parting flourish I fling down my business card on the coffee table, but the gays cringe, horribly embarrassed on behalf of their hosts and hating themselves for longing to jot down my phone number.

'This way,' says Mr Pass-for-Straight to me in a firm voice, and the next moment I'm sweeping triumphantly down the stairs ahead of him.

But by the time I reach the hall I'm feeling uneasy. It was great the way Carta begged that chubby heap not to hit me, but on the other hand she didn't look too keen when I bragged I could floor him. And was I being fair to the gay bystanders when I used them to launch my attack? No, I wasn't. By soliciting so offensively I mocked them in front of their friends. There's a paradox here and it's this: although gay activists campaign for sexual freedom, many of them take a high moral line against leisure-workers. They see them as the subversive shits who help closet gays to stay closeted, and worse than any subversive gay shit is the subversive straight shit who ought to be wiped from the scene and sent back to the straights in instalments. However at least Mr Frothy, Mr Macho-Retro and Mr Pass-for-Straight were spared the ultimate humiliation. As they almost passed out with the desire to shag me, they never guessed I qualified for dismemberment as the lowest of the low.

Which is a fact that Carta knew right from the start. Oh my God! What have I done?

With horror I finally see – as the rage against Sad Eric dies away – that I must have reinforced all her prejudices against me. I made a deliberately disgusting scene *in her house* in front of her friends, and now she can say to herself: 'I was right. He's filth. I never want to see him again.' Fucking hell, what an own goal! I must have been mental, but stay cool, don't panic, even a catastrophe can be put right. I'll just have to bust a gut to push a repentance scenario, and I can start by being extra nice to this bloke Mr Pass who deserved my trashing even less than his boring companions did.

'Hey,' I say to him urgently, 'I behaved like a headbanger back there – please could you tell Carta I'm sorry? Tell your friends I'm sorry as well – and let me tell *you*, one to one, that I'm very sorry indeed I played the leisure-worker from hell. I shouldn't have let myself get needled by that bastard Tucker treating me like shit.' (I think this last remark can be classed as fair comment. And I do need to explain why my brains got scrambled.)

Mr Pass says: 'It's hard to turn the other cheek sometimes.' I can almost hear him panting painfully, but he's exercising such self-control that his hand never even trembles as he pushes back his thinning hair. He's older than I thought he was. Forty, maybe more.

'Well,' he says, opening the front door, 'I'm sure you want to be on your way.'

I do, but I'm determined to send him a message that says SORRY in capital letters. It would help to have him on my side and pleading my cause to Carta.

On another card I scribble down the number of the Austin Friars flat. 'Here, take this,' I say, shoving the card at him. 'I'll give you a freebie as compensation, but don't tell the other blokes, this is just between you and me. Call that handwritten number any day Monday through Friday at four-twenty-five and we'll make a date.'

Mr Pass takes the card gravely and says, bemused, 'I'm not sure why I'm being singled out for special favour.'

'No?' I say. 'I'll tell you why. You called me Mr Blake. You treated me with respect. And more important still, you stopped that brain-dead scene of mine upstairs from getting even worse than it already was. So I owe you, Mr—' I pause.

'Tucker,' he says wryly.

'*Tucker?*'

'Gilbert Tucker, yes, I'm his brother. He's a bit hot-headed some-times, but he's a good chap when you get to know him.'

I just say: 'You're the good one, chum. Look, I mean what I say – it's all free for you, and I guarantee there'll be no risks of any kind.'

Mr Gilbert Tucker looks as if he'd like to believe me but can't.

I probably shan't see him again, but he'll put in a good word with Carta now, I'm sure of it, and that has to rank as a big plus.

The other big plus is that at least Elizabeth will never know I was dishing out a freebie while chasing the St Benet's fundraiser – and by the way, why do I keep doing things which would give Elizabeth a fit?

I know this is a question I need to answer, but I also know this isn't the moment to brood on it. I need to focus on making a digni-fied exit, and after saying a polite goodbye to Gilbert the Good I walk quickly away from the Wallside house and Monkwell Square.

*   *   *

Back in the car I start the task of figuring out why I've acquired this taste for high-risk behaviour, and after a while I dimly realise that I'm feeling negative about Elizabeth. Then I see that in reality I'm not just amazed by her 'lovely arrangement' with Norah about the escort girl. I'm feeling . . . no, not angry. I couldn't be angry with Elizabeth, I owe her everything, she's so wonderful to me. But I feel sort of . . . well, sort of hurt, know-what-I-mean, sort of sad. And that's not just because I don't like being told who to shag on weekends. It's because unless we're on holiday I don't get to shag Elizabeth more than once a week.

Okay, so I'm bloody lucky she wants us to shag at all, I realise that. I know I don't deserve her, I know I was nothing when she picked me out of the gutter and I know I'd go back to being nothing if she kicked me out of the house. But since she's apparently happy for the shag to continue, I don't see why it can't happen more often. I mean, it's not as if she doesn't get good value. Thanks to her, sex is the one thing I do really well, but she's determined to restrict me to Saturday mornings, and I mind, I can't help it, I just do. I feel not only sad but frustrated – and suspicious, okay, I admit it, I admit I'm bothered that she might be having it off with someone else, even though I don't really believe she is. Why did I ask her this morning if there was someone else when the common-sense answer was that there wasn't? I suppose I was in such despair that I lost sight of my common sense and allowed my knee-jerk suspi-cion a free rein.

What makes me believe there's no one else? Well, there's no one around who fits the job description. It certainly isn't Asherton – if he performs with women at all, he's probably only interested in carving patterns on them, and Elizabeth's no masochist. She's not having any kind of lesbo-love-fest with Norah either. They tried that back in the Swinging Sixties, Elizabeth says, but by 1970 they'd decided to be just good friends. Elizabeth has a wide range of acquaintances, but I think she's very careful who she shags. That's because she always has to be the one in control – and yes, let's face it, *this* is what the sex-on-Saturday-mornings-only rule is all about. She keeps me short to keep me on the hook.

So what do I do with this insight? Can't whinge, can't nag, can't sulk, and I certainly can't criticise – how could I after all she's done for me? I mean, what kind of an ungrateful bastard am I, for God's sake? If I love her – and I do – I must accept everything she does. It's the very least I can do after she's been so wonderful to me.

Fair enough, but in that case why am I secretly rebelling? It's something to do with Richard, don't know what, but whatever it is, Richard started it. And though he's not here any more I've now got Carta instead. Which means that whatever it is can't be connected solely with the sailing. Bloody hell, I can't unravel this mystery, it's so peculiar that it's doing my head in. What I know for sure, though, is that if I've got to shag an escort slag I'm going to work all the harder to compensate myself with Golden Girl despite Elizabeth's paranoia about St Benet's.

But I'd better be bloody careful. I'd better not forget just how dangerous rebellion can be.

I glance at my Rolex. I've still got the whole evening ahead of me. Driving over to the West End I prepare to go grazing again in Covent Garden.

Well, Elizabeth didn't explicitly forbid it, did she? And God knows I need some fun before Sunday lunch at Norah's when I get to meet the tart Elizabeth's chosen to be my regular weekend squeeze . . .

* * *

This new filly in Norah's stable isn't bad-looking and she's moderately shaggable but she's what the gays call TTH – Tries Too Hard. I like the babes who play cool and hard to get. More of a challenge.

Also at lunch are three not-so-new fillies, Victoria, Chloë and

Lara, who are all billeted beneath Norah's roof. Norah operates the escort agency out of an office in Kensington, a fact which means her large Pimlico home has the space to house the new girls who need to save money on accommodation while they get started.

I'm surprised today to find that Susanne's been hauled up from the basement flat to join us for Sunday lunch. She chomps the roast beef, looks mutinous and says nothing. Yuk. The chihuahuas have smart new coats from Harrods and look like gentically engineered rats. Double-yuk. I flirt overtly with new girl Serena, covertly with Victoria, Chloë and Lara, and try not to die of boredom.

I wonder what Golden Girl's doing with Sad Eric. I wish to hell I hadn't made such a fuck-up of that scene on Wallside yesterday.

*   *   *

I also wish I'd been smart enough to note the number on Carta's phone when I was at the Wallside house, but I was too busy serving up my gay monster act. I'll call her at the office tomorrow in the hope that Gilbert the Good's told her I'm radiating contrition from every pore – and maybe if he's Gilbert the Best he'll have pointed out to her that my bad behaviour was all Eric's fault anyway.

Monday dawns, and after the early shift I call Carta to deliver my well-rehearsed apology, but some sort of granny-gizmo with a post-menopausal voice tells me that Ms Graham is unavailable. Shit! I call again before the lunch-shift but Ms Graham is still unavailable. I leave my number and request a call back but nothing happens. Shit again! Okay, so she's trying to teach me a lesson, but I'm not going to get depressed because I know she'll eventually be panting to see me again.

In fact even now she could be wetting her knickers at the thought of the funeral . . .

*   *   *

But before the funeral there's a diversion which turns out to have cosmic consequences. On Tuesday afternoon I go to the West End to meet the very rich new client that Elizabeth and Asherton were discussing when I arrived home last Thursday.

His name's Sir Colin Broune, pronounced 'Brown'. Why the dotty spelling? I wonder if it's an affectation put on by a dozy git who's

96

nouveau riche (or as Mum would say, 'common'). But maybe his family came over with the Conqueror and it's a distinguished Frog-name which was originally pronounced 'Broon'. A dip into *Who's Who* reveals that in addition to having some sort of science degree from Cambridge he's fifty-two, unmarried and chairman of RCPP, Royal Chemical and Pharmaceutical Products, a position which my father would have said qualifies Sir Colin to be known as 'a captain of industry'. In other words, we're dealing here with just another stuffed shirt. Should be no problem, although one can never know for sure.

'What makes you think he's mega-rich instead of just rich?' I ask Elizabeth.

'It's always worth checking on the private wealth of someone with a title, dear, so Asherton ran a special check through that bent inspector he knows at the Inland Revenue. It turns out Sir Colin's worth thirty million.'

'Wow! Who told him about me?'

'He wouldn't say. I told him we like to know the name of the referring client as a security measure, but he said: "I'm paying good money. That should be enough."'

'Fancies himself as a tough guy?'

'More likely he just felt grumpy dealing with a woman.'

'Which hotel's he picked?'

She names a five-star modern outfit in Mayfair. I've been there before to meet a nervous first-timer who's distrustful enough to pass up the flat at Austin Friars. No problem.

So at ten minutes to five on Tuesday afternoon I arrive at the hotel and head for the ground-floor men's room where I check my appearance carefully. I'm dressed as a businessman in a charcoal-grey suit, sober tie, blue-and-white striped shirt, black socks and black shoes. The sex gear is stashed in a smart briefcase. I look achingly respectable.

At less than one minute to five I approach a house phone and ask the operator for Sir Colin Broune. The phone rings at five o'clock precisely.

'Good afternoon, sir,' I say after a bass voice has rasped a mono-syllable. 'This is Gavin Blake.'

'Room twelve-o-seven.' He slams down the receiver.

This could be difficult. He sounds in a filthy mood. Leaving the house phones I scan the lobby, but the man I've identified as one

of the hotel security team is passing the time with a girl who's mani-
curing the flower arrangement. I always like to know where the
on-duty gorilla is before I head for the lifts. Some of these blokes
are bent enough to demand a cut of the fee if they don't boot the
leisure-worker straight out into the gutter, so even though I'm
looking so respectable I make very sure he's paying me no attention.

When I reach the twelfth floor I find Sir Colin's waiting for me
with the door ajar.

He's tall, around six-four, and heavily built. That could be tiresome if he expects me to heave him about, but on the other hand
I'd rather he played the beached whale than Jaws in the mating
season. My defensive skills are first-class and I seldom get hurt, but
when someone's big and aggressive and in a foul temper it can be
tough to get the angles right so that the crucial muscles can function in a way that neutralises the danger. It suddenly occurs to me
that I'm not happy with this assignment, and that if things go really
wrong I could be hobbling around at Richard's funeral tomorrow
like someone emerging from the dungeon of Asherton's Pain-Palace.

The man's got the light behind him but even so I realise straight
away he's no beauty. He's got a big fat face and mean little eyes and
a tight-lipped mouth. Balding. Mottled skin. Creased jowls. Whisky-
ish breath.

'Blake?'

'Yes, sir.'

He flings the door wide, turns his back on me and stumps off
past the bathroom to the far end of the room. Here he dumps
himself in a chair at the table by the window and picks up the
evening paper.

Closing the door behind me I go to the bed and unpack the
essential items from my briefcase. Take one step at a time. Focus.
Plenty of condoms in case he fancies some kind of marathon with
plenty of arse-changing. Lashings of lube to make sure neither of
us gets caught short . . . God, I'd kill for some amyl nitrate, but
no, I never do drugs, not even poppers in a sex crisis. I tell myself
I've got the experience, I've got the skills, I'm going to be fine —
but I'd better bloody well watch out for handcuffs because I wouldn't
put it past this bugger to be into S&M.

Very occasionally an S&M perv does slip through the net of
Elizabeth's vetting procedures, and if that happens I'm allowed to
terminate the session right away because he'd know serious S&M

isn't on my menu. In theory I don't have a menu. Clients pay for my time and do what they like, but in practice Elizabeth always slaps on a surcharge for unusual requests and always delivers the stern warning that any violence beyond routine play-acting is as taboo as bare-backing. The trouble in this case, though, is that Elizabeth, dazzled by the thought of the thirty million quid, could have glossed over the screening procedures and told herself: Gavin will cope.

I start to undress, making a sexy production out of it in case he's taking peeps, but the *Evening Standard* never rustles even when I gyrate out of my leather belt and snap it. What's he up to? I find I'm sweating lightly. Time to take deep breaths and listen in my head to my favourite tenor aria from *Zauberflöte*.

Shutting the closet door on my clothes I pause to look at him again, but he's still hidden by the paper. This is seriously weird. He must know I'm stark naked by this time so why doesn't he take a look? Maybe he wants to lure me close to him before trying to land a punch, but if so he's miscalculated – my judo skills mean I could floor this lump of middle-aged blubber with a couple of well-judged flips. But I don't want to get into violence. Unlike Austin Friars this place has no hidden cameras to record who struck the first blow, and if there's a major disaster the hotel security team's going to believe the word of the captain of industry who's rich enough to give the Inland Revenue a corporate orgasm, not the word of an innocent leisure-worker who's only trying to do his job.

Psyching myself up to end this futile anxiety attack, I grab a condom, walk over and make him an offer. I always insist on being the one who puts on the client's condom because then I know it's on properly and my fear of Aids is eased.

Sir Colin's response to my offer is to grunt while continuing to read the *Standard*.

Maybe he's just had a mini-stroke. By this time the blokes are usually gasping and even the most antique equipment's defying gravity . . . But I'm now more sure than ever that this is a perv waiting to pounce.

And suddenly he does pounce, making me jump almost out of my skin. Flinging aside the newspaper he shoots to his feet, biffs the condom out of my hand and yells: 'Get out!' Then he thuds to the bathroom and locks himself in.

This punter's certainly a novelty. I close my mouth, which is hanging open, and pick up the condom. Have to give the client

99

what he wants, of course, but I've never before had a client who threw me out before I'd done my job.

I dress, feeling better. I know now he's not an S&M perv, just a fat man with problems. Maybe he's always like this after a hard day at the office. Or maybe he gets his kicks out of having a leisure-worker present while he reads the *Evening Standard*. Kinky. But not dangerous.

Having repacked the briefcase I write him a class-act note on the telephone pad. It reads: 'Dear Sir Colin: I shall remain available until six o'clock in accordance with the agreement you reached with Mrs Delamere. Should you change your mind and decide that you wish me to return to your room, please call the porters' desk and ask them to let me know you're feeling better. I shall be waiting in the lobby. Yours sincerely, GAVIN BLAKE.'

I put the notepad on the bed so that he sees it as soon as he emerges from the bathroom and then I leave, shutting the door loudly behind me to make sure he knows I've gone.

Downstairs I buy a copy of the *Financial Times* in the lobby shop and settle myself near the jumbo flower arrangement which is still being manicured by the pretty girl. The security man, who's yawning away by a pillar, never gives me a second glance.

After ten minutes I learn that Sir Colin Broune wishes me to know he's feeling better. Back I go to the twelfth floor.

The door's open, so I go in and once more start unpacking the gear and taking off my kit. Sir Colin's no longer reading the *Standard* but he's got his back to me as he stares out of the window. I pause, trying to be imaginative. That's one of the challenges of the job: using one's creative imagination. It's what separates the top-of-the-range leisure-workers from the middle-market drones and the rent boys at the bottom of the pile.

My trousers are still on but I keep them zipped up and pad barefoot to his side.

'I'm sorry if you've had a rough day, sir,' I say gently. 'Life can be difficult sometimes, can't it? Would you like me to fix you a drink?'

Mr Moneybags subsides into the nearest chair like a pricked balloon and slowly starts to weep.

*   *   *

I raid the mini-bar and mix him a whisky. I fetch a wad of Kleenex from the bathroom. Then I kneel down by the side of his chair, sit

100

back on my heels and wait. He has a sip from the glass and blows his nose. I go on waiting but presently I take his hand and hold it.

He likes that. His fingers press against mine. More tears fall but he mops them up doggedly with his free hand. His eyes are bloodshot now. What can it be like to be so plug-ugly, so totally lacking in sex appeal? But at least he's got thirty million quid to cheer him up.

'Did someone die, sir?'

He nods before mumbling: 'A very old friend. Six months ago. Cancer. Bloody awful.'

'I'm very sorry.'

'Everyone says time heals. But it doesn't. I still feel as if it all happened yesterday. I never normally talk of it, but a fortnight ago I met—' He names a client of mine '—and suddenly I did talk to him, don't know why, suppose it was because I knew he was one of us. He said what I needed was someone to help me along, someone absolutely discreet and reliable, and he said he knew this well-educated young chap who knew how to behave, and . . . well, it seemed like some kind of answer, although I've never before consorted with . . . but I felt desperate enough to try anything.'

'I understand. What was your partner's name, sir?'

'Partner! I hate all these modern corruptions of good, solid, old-fashioned words, and the only corruption I hate more than 'partner' is 'gay'. Edward was my friend. We were both homosexual. Why not call a bloody spade a bloody spade?'

'Right, sir.'

'We lived together quietly, with dignity, and never spoke of our friendship in detail to anyone. These bloody activists today with their revolting lack of taste—'

'Yes, beyond the pale, sir, frightful. What was Edward like?'

'Well, he was the best of men in all kinds of ways but his real talent was for horticulture. The garden of my country house is his memorial, and every time I look out of the window I think of him.'

We pause. More tears are shed so I get another clump of Kleenex from the bathroom. When I'm kneeling beside him again I say: 'May I ask, sir, what you and Edward liked to do when he was with you as I'm with you now? I'm not saying I could in any way take his place – that would clearly be impossible – but maybe I can ease the pain by helping you recall happier times.'

The thick hand, mottled with age spots, closes gratefully on mine again, but Sir Colin can't quite bring himself to "call a bloody spade a bloody spade" when describing his sex life, and it takes me a while to realise that he and his Edward never got past the schoolboy stage. Apparently these two men met up at Cambridge and that was it. No infidelity but no development either. It was all just like an old-fashioned heterosexual romance, ripe to be turned into a costume drama by the BBC.

In fact Sir Colin's not too interested in sex. We fish around for a bit and I push the right buttons but after a brief grunt he's happy to forget this interlude and become sociable. This is a bore because he wants me to talk about myself.

'I'm sorry, Sir Colin,' I say, making sure my voice vibrates with rueful charm, 'but I never discuss my private life with clients.'

'But how does a boy like you become involved in a game like this?'

'I was always fond of games, sir.'

He laughs. 'Where were you educated?'

'The University of Life, sir.'

More laughter. This is good. He's feeling much better, but I wish he'd take the hint that I'm not to be grilled about the past.

'There's no need to keep calling me "sir"!' he's exclaiming impatiently. 'You can call me Colin. What are your interests? Do you like music?'

'I like opera.'

He's enchanted. 'Why?'

'Because it's lush, lavish and utterly divorced from real life.'

Unfortunately he's more enchanted than ever by this off-putting reply. 'How original!' he exclaims. 'I like a young man who knows his mind and isn't afraid to speak it. As it happens I'm an opera fan too – you must let me take you to Covent Garden!'

'Colin, I'm sorry but I don't do escort work.'

He's undeterred. 'I'm sure I can come to an arrangement with Mrs Delamere,' he says, and I can hear all those millions thrumming in the background as he speaks, 'but we must meet again soon anyway. I understand you have a flat in Austin Friars.'

I've hooked Mr Moneybags. But I'm not sure I'm happy about that. He's no trouble – I could keep him on the line just by holding his hand – but he's led such a sheltered sexual life that I don't like to think of him falling into the hands of predators. On the other hand, he would hardly have got to be chairman of RCPP if he was a wilting daisy, unable to look after himself. Ironic to think he's such a simple little soul in the bedroom.

We part with a warm handshake and I head home to Lambeth to report my conquest.

*   *   *

Asherton's there waiting, obviously revved up by the thought of all the thrumming millions. If he can recruit Sir Colin for GOLD he'll be in clover, and I find myself wishing, not for the first time, that I knew more about this secret fake-religion society which some of my most affluent clients wind up joining.

Asherton's looking more like a government official than ever, so ordinary that you could pass him in the street without looking at him twice. It's his personality that's not ordinary. It weaves around in his body like a thick worm in a diseased apple.

When I've finished my report he says to me in honeyed tones: 'I must congratulate you, my dear. You've done very well,' and I smile dutifully as my stomach churns.

I really hate that horror-merchant Asherton.

*   *   *

At last I reach Wednesday and my date with Richard's coffin at the church in Compton Beeches. I do the early shift as usual but Elizabeth's cancelled the other two. She's told me that four of the wealthier clients must be fitted in between shifts on Thursday and Friday, but I was prepared for this even though she'd said earlier that she didn't want to risk me getting overstrained. (Obviously I can't be allowed to escape scot-free after my pig-headed plea to attend the funeral.) However Elizabeth softens the overtime blow by telling me she's terminated the Kraut. It's my reward for doing so well with Sir Colin.

The weather's perfect: clear September skies, a warm sun and luxuriously fresh air all combine to raise my spirits once I leave the suburbs behind and head south for Hampshire. Compton Beeches is a picture-book village, the kind you see in commercials for dairy products. In the pub I order a lager and a roast beef sandwich and think how great it is to be out of London.

The barmaid's remembered me. 'You were a friend of Mr Slaney's, weren't you?' she says when I arrive, even though I only appeared here with Richard once, and when I smile and say yes, I was a friend of his, she says how sad it is to think he's gone, he was such a nice man and so well-liked.

After the meal I wander away from the pub past the thatched cottages and head across the green to the church. I like ecclesiastical buildings. Architecture interests me. I thought of being an architect once but Dad said I'd never make a success of it.

I move closer to the church. Richard told me he went to church to set an example and show commitment to the village community. Nothing to do with belief in God. It was all to do with tradition. Richard's family had owned the big house in the village for two hundred years so he had certain standards to keep up. Dad would have admired this. Dad was heavily into the keeping-up-appearances syndrome, the England-expects-every-man-to-do-his-duty syndrome, the pillar-of-the-community syndrome, the support-the-Church-of-England-even-if-you-don't-believe-in-God syndrome, the sailing's-the-only-time-I-feel-happy syndrome – although naturally Dad never said: 'Sailing's the only time I feel happy.' But Hugo and I knew that was how he felt because that was when he relaxed and stopped being such a perfectionist, slaving away in a futile attempt to ensure all his patients lived for ever. Yes, different though Dad and Richard were, they did have a certain mindset in common, and I think Dad would have liked Richard – up to a point. Of course he would have despised him for being gay.

The church isn't open yet, but I walk around the outside and admire the dressed flint of the walls and the square, squat Norman tower which ought to be ugly but isn't. Then I start to read the gravestones, always an interesting way of passing time, but Hugo tries to crawl out of the crevice in my mind and I have to stop. To divert myself I think of Carta. The real problem for me here won't be the clerical underling the Rector of St Benet's sends to the service – the problem's going to be Sad Eric. After last Saturday's scene he's bound to tag along to protect Carta from me. He won't trust the St Benet's limp-wrist to beat me off.

I haven't made up my mind yet which personality I can pull on for Carta, but obviously it must be a serious one, not just because this is a funeral we're attending but because I've got to wipe the memory of my gay monster act. Why don't I pull out all the stops and play the Surrey doctor's son? I'll be so sociably acceptable that she'll realise the Wallside scene was just a temporary blip – and Sad Eric won't be able to do a damn thing except glower with rage.

I suddenly become aware that I'm staring at the north side of the church. The sunshine, hitting the other side of the building, is flooding the nave, and the stained glass above me has caught my attention. I'm in deep shadow but the glass is pulsating with multi-coloured light.

But despite the favourable conditions it's still hard for me to make out the picture when I'm on the outside looking in. I can see some white patches and green blobs at the bottom plus a slew of deep blue at the top but the middle's just a densely worked jumble – apart from a curious little slip of white on one side. All at once I'm overcome with the urge to see this picture properly, and as I move around the church towards the porch I see the clergyman's unlocking the door for the undertakers.

I forget the window as I realise that mourners are starting to arrive. Should I stay outside and wait to display myself to Carta? No, too obvious. Keep her guessing. I still hesitate but at last I walk quickly into the church, take a service sheet and sit down at one end of the next-to-last pew. When Carta arrives I shall see her but the odds are she won't see me. Not at first anyway.

Hordes of people are now streaming in. All Richard's friends are gathering in this little village to say goodbye to him, and I'm with them, I'm not an outsider any more, I belong in this group, I matter. And suddenly I'm thinking: the last word about Richard isn't that he was homosexual. The last word is that he was a great bloke who cared about people in ways which made them care about him.

Swallowing quickly to ease the ache in my throat, I suddenly identify the window I noticed outside and a second later I'm seeing the picture with knock-out clarity. The little white panels at the bottom are all sheep. They're on a green hillside below an azure sky, and in the densely worked middle of the picture is The Bloke. He's togged up in what an ignorant person might think is fancy dress but I know it's the working gear of the Middle East a couple of thousand years ago, just as I know that The Bloke's a bit older than I am and has a name everyone knows, though of course no one now believes all the fairy tales people dreamed up about him after he was dead. The nineteenth-century artist has visualised him as an English gentleman so he looks pretty odd in the Middle Eastern gear, but he's unmistakable: of his many roles he's playing the shepherd with his flock. No, wait, it's more complicated than that. I'd forgotten the slip of white more than halfway up the picture.

105

It's a little sheep. The Bloke's got it on his shoulder, and as I stare at the animal I see it's bedraggled, its fleece flattened, its limbs limp with exhaustion. The little sheep's been rescued. The Bloke couldn't rest till he'd recovered it. The artist has represented in a miracle of coloured glass the story of the sheep which was lost and then found.

The organ begins to play, cutting across my thoughts and switching on overpowering emotions as I stare at the coffin at the head of the nave. It's Hugo's coffin I'm seeing now. Hugo and Richard have fused in my mind. God, why didn't I anticipate – why didn't I realise—

The family are arriving. Moira Slaney's not blonde (as I told Elizabeth when she was on the psychic warpath) but a smart brunette and she still looks like the photo I saw of her during my previous visit to Compton Beeches. But the two kids look very different from the two kids with Richard in that photo which I wanted to lift from the flat in Mayfair. Philip looks as if he's been popping too much E on wild weekends, silly little sod. I started doing drugs when I was homeless and it was the stupidest thing I ever did. All over now, though. I'm drug-free, fighting fit, a big success.

Hugo starts to say I'm still a loser, but I stuff him back in his crevice and start looking around at the other mourners. I seem to have missed Carta's arrival – maybe she came in when I was gaping at the stained-glass window. Or maybe she's just late. The service is starting. I look at my service sheet and see the first hymn's 'He Who Would Valiant Be'. God! That was the hymn we sang in the school chapel on the day Hugo died.

Hugo tries to blitz his way out of the crevice again but I blitz him back and nail him down. Leave me alone, Hugo, *leave me alone*—

Got to pull myself together. I try playing my favourite aria from *Zauberflöte* in my head – and suddenly I escape, I'm sailing past the Needles on a wine-dark sea worthy of Homer, and everything's beautiful, *beautiful*, so absolutely right in a sense no words could ever describe.

Eventually my concentration breaks as the hymn ends and I return to my body, but before we can all sit down someone on the aisle halfway up the nave turns to look at me, as if he's somehow aware of my chaotic emotions. He's tall and middle-aged and for a moment I think he's nondescript, but then I realise I've been misled by his drab brown hair and pale colouring. This bloke oozes charisma. His light eyes would bore a hole through concrete at fifty paces. In fact I'm just thinking that he's boring a hole through me when the woman beside him turns to see what he's looking at, and I suck in my breath as I recognise Carta.

At once she swivels to face the altar, and as the man turns away too but without hurrying, I'm able to take in what he's wearing. I see his black shirt. I see his clerical collar. But this is no limp-wristed church underling I'm staring at. This has to be Carta's boss. This has to be Elizabeth's arch-enemy. This has to be none other than the Rector of St Benet's-by-the-Wall, the Reverend Nicholas Darrow.

*   *   *

Well, I get through the church part of the service somehow, but when everyone clusters around the grave to watch the committal my head's so done in I can't cope – I lean against a gravestone several yards away and concentrate on keeping sane.

Since Carta has an escort who's totally taboo, I've given up the idea of waylaying her, and I know I ought to leave but I don't. Richard's pinning me in place. All I can think is that I want to wait till I'm alone in the churchyard. Then I can go to the grave and say goodbye. Couldn't say goodbye in the church, I was too churned up, and I can't leave without thanking him for those shining hours we spent sailing together, can't leave without saying to him that he made me feel like a real person instead of designer filth tailor-made for the gutter. And I want to promise him I'll sail again one day down the Solent, and when I pass the Needles I'll throw a wreath on the water in memory of him. Okay, so he's dead and can't hear me, okay, so I'm being pathetically sentimental, but that service has really punched my lights out and right now I can't be slick and smart, it's too hard, too painful.

The ceremony around the grave ends and as the crowd begins to break up I see Carta moving away towards the path. She's wearing a black business suit, very slinky and sleek, and I sigh, wishing she was on her own. Belatedly it occurs to me there's no sign of Sad Eric, but of course he'd be quite content to entrust her to Mr Charisma.

Carta catches sight of me and immediately turns her back, but before I can begin to feel upset I get a shock. Mr Charisma's joined Carta and he's looking at me again. Instantly I move away, sheltering behind another tombstone. I don't have to put up with his prurient peeping. Of course Carta's told him I was Richard's leisure-worker

107

and of course he's getting a holier-than-thou charge out of that choice piece of information, but I don't have to lurk around pandering to his curiosity. I see now how unnecessary it was for Elizabeth to order me to keep well away from anyone in a clerical collar. This particular cleric's not going to come near me. He wouldn't contaminate himself by doing such a thing. I'm not just scum to him – I'm a 'sinner', and that means I don't count, I don't matter, I'm just shit waiting to be flushed down the pan.

Well, fuck you too, chum, I think. See if I care.

Plunging into an examination of a huge Victorian tomb, I stare and stare and stare at the stone angels above the obligatory quote from 'In Memoriam'.

'Mr Blake.'

I spin round as fast as if bloody Asherton had stroked the nape of my neck. But it's not Asherton. It's Mr Charisma. His eyes are a steady grey and his face is a mass of hard, sculpted angles. In spite of the collar he doesn't look like a clergyman. He reminds me of those big-time conjurors you see on TV: lots of pzazz mixed with a touch of hypnotism as the magic's delivered *con brio*.

'My name's Nicholas Darrow,' he's saying casually as I'm still wondering where my next breath's coming from. 'Carta pointed you out to me and I thought I'd just come over and offer my sympathy. It's tough to lose a good friend, isn't it? And so hard to say goodbye.'

I'm speechless. I'm immobile. And as I stand there, as gauche as the teenager I was long ago in a world I can't bear to remember, this stranger takes another step forward and firmly holds out his hand.

PART TWO

The Journey

'All of us, carers and cared for, are on a journey whose destination we understand only dimly:

> "We know we are searching for something yet the nature of the thing we seek eludes us. On this strange journey, in this tantalising search, we often feel lonely and bemused, in need of guidance, encouragement, companionship. Not always knowing what we are asking we reach out for the help of others."'

Mud and Stars
A report of a working party consisting mainly of
doctors, nurses and clergy, quoting from
Rediscovering Pastoral Care
by A. V. Campbell

CHAPTER ONE

Carta

'The healing ministry is non-judgemental: those involved in it are encouraged to consider and address their own prejudices and stereotyping to avoid projection of their personal internal codes of behaviour.'

A Time to Heal
A report for the House of Bishops on the Healing Ministry

I

When Richard's coffin was transferred from the church to the grave I lost sight of Gavin, but as soon as the funeral had finished, the mourners began to disperse and I saw him loitering some yards away among the gravestones. Instantly my nerve-ends jangled, just as they had jangled when I had spotted him in church, but this time my stomach lurched as if it were about to liquefy. In panic I turned my back on him, but I remained appalled; in fact I could hardly believe I had been pathetic enough to give such a knee-jerk sexual response.

'What's the matter?' demanded Nicholas at once.

'Gavin. He's still here – I thought he'd gone.' To my relief my voice sounded only mildly harassed, and as Nicholas glanced across the churchyard I felt thankful that he was present. Bridget Slaney had begged him to come, Moira too had added a plea, and finally he had given way, deciding that the funeral should somehow be wedged into his overcrowded schedule.

'Give me a couple of minutes,' I heard him say as he looked at Gavin, 'and then join us.'

'You can't mean you're going to talk to him!'

111

Nicholas raised an eyebrow. 'It's my job. The bereaved need support at funerals.'

'*Bereaved?* But Richard was just a walking chequebook to that man!'

'Then why's he here? No one's paying him to attend.'

'But—'

'Two minutes,' said Nicholas firmly. 'Then join us. Be polite and low-key. If you're angry and snub him he'll stalk you harder than ever.'

I felt like bursting into tears, but this feeble behaviour was not fundamentally because of Gavin's presence and my mindless reaction to it. It was because the service had reminded me of my father who had died the previous year. I had been making a new effort to help him conquer his gambling addiction, but he had died with the problem unsolved, and amidst the grief I had also been aware of relief. 'At least you succeeded in having a reconciliation with him before he died,' my mentor Lewis had said when I had admitted how guilty my relief made me feel, 'and at least his life had altered for the better.' This was true, but Richard's funeral had still stirred up my muddled emotions with the result that I was less capable than ever of dealing with Gavin. I was sure he had been unaffected by the service, just as I was sure he had turned up primarily to make a nuisance of himself.

I was too far away to hear what was said when Nicholas reached his target but I saw Gavin jump as if he'd been shot and spin to face him. I went on watching, certain that Gavin would look in my direction, but he never gave me a glance. Indeed as a conversation began to unfold he no longer even looked at Nicholas. He looked at a nearby tomb, at the ground, at the mourners who were drifting away from the grave, and once or twice he dug a heel into the soft turf in a fidgety gesture, but he made no effort to escape, and in the end, driven on not just by the order from my boss but by my curiosity to know how the monster had been tamed, I began to thread my way in and out among the grassy graves towards him.

II

'Ah, there you are, Carta!' said Nicholas casually. 'We were just discussing the funeral service. Gavin feels Richard would have approved of it.'

Avoiding all comment I said in a laid-back voice which rang repellently false in my ears: 'Hi, Gavin.'

'Hullo, Carta,' he said, very well-behaved, very Home Counties. 'How are you?'

I knew he was playing a carefully chosen role but he was so convincing that I even wondered if I had been paranoid in seeing him as a stalker. Meanwhile Nicholas seemed wholly focused on making small-talk. 'I hear you went sailing with Richard this summer,' he said to Gavin.

'Right. Hey, Carta – I'm really sorry about that scene last weekend! I tried calling your office to apologise but I only got the granny-gizmo.'

'The *what*?'

'I used to know a man who kept a boat at Bosham,' Nicholas pursued, uninterested in granny-gizmos. 'But that was a long time ago. When did you start to sail, Gavin?'

'1969.'

'You must have been very young.'

'My brother was even younger when he started.'

'I had a brother once,' said Nicholas vaguely. 'He was a lot older than me and he's been dead now for some years, but I often think of him – I was thinking of him just now in church, but that's natural, isn't it? Funerals remind us of those we love who are no longer with us.'

There was a dead silence. Gavin was motionless, staring at the ground. His long lashes seemed very dark against the skin which was stretched tightly over his prominent cheekbones, and his mouth was clamped shut in a hard straight line. To my astonishment I realised he was struggling with grief.

'I'm sorry,' I heard Nicholas say. 'Is your brother dead too?'

Gavin nodded, and somehow Nicholas altered the quality of his silence. It was now intensely sympathetic without being in any way cloying or sentimental, and a second later I realised that in this context any word would have been a mistake.

'He was seventeen,' said Gavin flatly to the ground. 'He'd been ill for two years with leukaemia and your God didn't save him.' As an afterthought he added, abruptly jettisoning the Home Counties persona and looking straight at Nicholas: 'Your God's a shit.'

Clamping my mouth shut I prepared to move away, sure that the conversation had ended. But it continued. Nicholas was talking in silences, and in the silence which he designed I felt the emotional space created by his compassion. Gavin could say anything he liked but the emotional space would always be large enough to contain it.

His next words were: 'Why the fuck don't you say something?'

'I wanted you to be ready to hear what I have to say, and it's this: you have a right to be angry. Rage at God as much as you like – he's big enough, he can take it. It's the repressed anger that's dangerous because the road to healing doesn't lie in denying what you feel.'

'I can't rage at God. I don't believe in him.'

'I thought you said just now he was a shit?'

Yet another silence fell, but this one was full of tension. Then Gavin turned his back on Nicholas and gave me a brilliant smile. 'You're looking really cool!' he breathed. 'You ought to wear black every day!'

'Think so?' I murmured, mild as milk. 'Thanks.'

'So am I forgiven for that scene last Saturday?'

'Well—'

'Great! Of course it would never have happened if Eric had treated me with the respect due to a friend of Richard's, but don't worry, you can tell Eric I've decided to be forgiving – almost Christian, in fact!' he added laughing, and suddenly gave Nicholas such an erotic look that I flinched.

But Nicholas betrayed no emotion. In the empty silence which followed, his eyes were luminously clear.

I was just about to ignore my orders and tell Gavin what I thought of his loathsome posturing when there was an interruption. A woman called: 'Nick! I'm so glad you were able to come!' and swinging round I saw that Moira Slaney was hurrying across the churchyard towards us.

III

Realising that Gavin might well have no idea who she was, I said to him urgently: 'It's Moira.'

'Yeah. I've seen a photo.'

'Well, go on – disappear, for God's sake!'

'I was a friend of Richard's! Why shouldn't I get to meet his wife?'

'Moira!' said Nicholas, ignoring this muttered exchange, and moved towards her as she tiptoed over the soft ground.

She was in her mid-forties but looked younger because she was so well-dressed and well-groomed. I admired this talent for capitalising on her assets. Yet she was not my kind of person. There was a class gap between us, and there was also a generation gap even though she was barely ten years my senior. Feminism had passed her by; she seemed to believe that a woman's place was in the home, and although she had never displayed hostility when I had talked of my past career as a partner in Curtis, Towers, I felt she had hardly listened. Unable to conceive of why a woman should want such a life, she was also unable to be interested in it. I had no doubt that she privately pitied me for my childlessness and current lack of a husband.

Since my discovery of Richard's homosexuality I had, of course, tried to reassess her private life but had only found it more baffling than ever. What could have kept her in that marriage? I was unable to decide and Moira herself gave nothing away.

'The service went well, didn't it?' she was exclaiming to Nicholas after their brief embrace. 'Thanks so much for all those helpful suggestions . . . Carta! How nice to see you!'

As I murmured a suitably warm response I noticed that her make-up was intact. No trace of tears there.

'Mrs Slaney,' said Gavin without waiting to be introduced, 'I'm so sorry about Richard. I'm one of his friends from the City. My name's Gavin Blake.'

'Ah yes,' she said, still smiling. 'You're the lover.' And barely pausing to draw breath she added carelessly to him: 'Nicholas and Carta will be coming back to the house – why don't you come with them? After all, you probably knew Richard as well as anyone in that church just now.'

She didn't wait for a reply, and as we all stood staring after her she walked serenely down the churchyard path towards the black Daimler which was waiting to take her home.

IV

The oddest effect of this odd little scene was that it temporarily bonded me with Gavin. Ignoring Nicholas, who appeared unsurprised by

115

Moira's behaviour, we stared at each other in amazement.

'She obviously knew your name,' I said, 'but who mentioned it to her?'

'You mean it wasn't you?'

'Don't be stupid! Richard told me about you in confidence!'

'No doubt Richard himself told her,' said Nicholas.

I said: 'You're joking!' at the exact moment Gavin exclaimed: 'No way!' He added: 'She knew he was gay, of course she did, but he never told her any details about what he got up to,' and I supported this statement by saying: 'When I had dinner with him the night before that first coronary, I definitely got the impression that I was the only person he'd talked to about Gavin.'

Nicholas sighed, magnificently controlling his middle-aged impatience with all this dumb dogmatism from the under-forties. 'I think we have to acknowledge that Richard and Moira were married for over twenty years and she was with him when he died,' he said. 'Is it really so unlikely that he finally confided in her? He'd have been shocked and frightened by the coronary, and there was Moira, signalling by her presence that she still cared what happened to him.'

Reluctantly I saw the logic. 'Okay, fair enough. But why invite Gavin to the house?'

'Obviously she was acknowledging that Gavin was Richard's friend. Gavin, can we offer you a lift to the house, or would you prefer to go in your own car?'

'No need for cars, sir,' said Gavin, very friendly now that Nicholas had confirmed his status. 'The house is just down that lane past the green.'

'How convenient! And by the way, you can call me Nicholas or Nick. I appreciate the respect you're showing but I don't think a post-funeral gathering is a time to stand on ceremony.'

Gavin made no reply as we headed out of the churchyard but in the road beyond he said to me: 'I'm going to ask Moira if I can have that photo of Richard, the one we saw in the flat.'

I was annoyed. 'You can't possibly!'

'Why not?'

'Well, for starters Moira doesn't know you've ever been in that flat. If you go asking her about a photo you couldn't have seen—'

'I'll say Richard took me to the flat once.'

'But you can't demand a gift on the day of the funeral! Can't you see how naff you're being?'

116

'What's so naff about wanting a pic of my friend to remember him by?'

'Talking of Richard,' said Nicholas, overriding this scratchy exchange, 'did he tell you about my church, Gavin? It's St Benet's-by-the-Wall in Egg Street, the Guild church with the Healing Centre in the crypt.'

'Never mentioned it.'

'Oh yes, he did!' I exclaimed, scandalised not only by the lie but by this offensively abrupt response. '"You work for the bloke who's fixing Bridget," you said to me when we first met—'

'The church itself is open from eight in the morning till six at night,' interrupted Nicholas, ignoring Gavin's sudden change of mood, 'except on Thursdays when it's open until eight. In a power-house like the City it's good to have a quiet space where people can meditate or simply be themselves with no one hassling them . . . You became interested in meditation recently, didn't you, Carta?'

I finally remembered I was supposed to be exuding a laid-back courtesy. 'Right,' I said, 'but I came to the conclusion I had no gift for it.'

'Carta's a lawyer,' said Nicholas to Gavin, 'and her special gift for rational analysis isn't easy to integrate with a mystical approach to religion. What would you say your special gift is, Gavin?'

Gavin suddenly flipped out. Like a disruptive child fixated on exploring the boundaries of acceptable behaviour he said: 'Fucking.'

'Oh yes?' said Nicholas politely. 'But you're straight, aren't you? So why are you abusing this talent of yours by misdirecting it?'

'Oh, piss off! God, no wonder my manager told me not to go near anyone in a dog collar today!'

'What unusual advice! Why the dog collar phobia?'

'It's no phobia! She just wanted to save me from being perse-cuted, that's all!'

'Persecuting people isn't actually part of the Christian gospel.'

'Fuck the Christian gospel!' shouted Gavin, and walked on at such a rapid pace that Nicholas and I were soon left behind.

'Sorry, boss,' I muttered. 'If I hadn't put him in a bad mood by calling him naff—'

'That wasn't the remark which yanked his chain. The problem seemed to be me talking about St Benet's . . . This female pimp of his sounds quite a character, doesn't she?'

'He denied she was his pimp.'

117

'Probably didn't want to admit to you he was under some woman's thumb. But do we seriously think he started his very upmarket business all on his own and then advertised in *The Times* for a manager? No, you can bet the manager came first and that she had a handful of useful contacts to get him going.'

'A lady with an eye for the main chance . . . Hold on, Gavin's lingering—'

'Maybe he's managed to solve the baffling social dilemma of how to turn me right off while simultaneously turning you right on. I foresee a dazzling display of apologies, charm and immaculate good manners.'

I groaned. 'If you weren't here I'd run away.'

'Don't you even want to try to be kind to this messed-up kid who's so pathetically proud of his friendship with Richard?'

I was silenced.

Gavin was waiting for us at the start of the lane which led from the village green to Richard's house, and as we drew closer he gave us a rueful smile. 'Sorry I lost it just now,' he said, wide-eyed with sincerity. 'Post-Funeral Stress Syndrome.'

Nicholas merely said: 'It's good of you to apologise . . . How far did you say it was to the house?'

'It's just round the next bend. I was here recently,' said Gavin, and I heard the pride in his voice. 'Moira was away and Richard wanted to show me his home. He showed me all over the house and garden and later we went down to the pub for a drink.'

After a pause Nicholas said gently: 'He was a good man, wasn't he?' and Gavin nodded, averting his face. I tried to answer for him, but I too found the words refused to come. In silence we walked on, and a minute later we reached the gates of Richard's manor house.

I started dredging up the will to be sociable.

V

On our arrival I soon lost sight of Nicholas. Bridget Slaney, still ghost-thin but no longer looking terminal, led him away to some secluded corner where she could pour out her heart to him in peace, and Gavin promptly appointed himself my escort. At first this made me very nervous, so nervous that I spent most of the time refusing to look at him in case my stomach should start to lurch again, but as the minutes passed and he conversed sociably with others I was able to glance at him without fear of behaving like an office fluffette. The truth was he had no time to pay me much attention; he was too busy promoting the fable that he was a salesman who supplied equipment to health clubs.

As usual at a wake, everyone was drinking hard to soothe their nerves after being reminded so forcefully that the gods of money, power and sex, no matter how avidly worshipped, offered no one an escape from the coffin. Moira had extravagantly ordered Krug for the occasion, but after the first half-hour I noticed that the catering staff were pouring non-vintage Moët instead; no doubt she felt that if people were determined to get drunk they might as well do it economically. As I was there not only as a friend of Richard's but as a fundraiser who always needed the chance to meet potential donors, no matter what the occasion, I had taken care to switch to orange juice after one celestial glass of Krug, and now, as everyone became steadily noisier, I paused to congratulate myself on my enormous self-restraint. Glumly I supposed that one really did become more sensible about drink once one was past thirty-five. I even wondered if I would be a teetotaller by the time I was forty, but I cheered myself up by reflecting that this was most unlikely.

Eventually Nicholas resurfaced after his tête-à-tête with Bridget, but at once he was kidnapped by Moira who wanted him to talk to her son. Philip, skulking in a corner, was looking as if his coke dealer had failed to deliver the goods.

I was just feeling sorry for Nicholas, compelled to work overtime when everyone else was seizing the chance to unwind, when to my surprise Moira reappeared and made a beeline for Gavin, who was earnestly discussing the pros and cons of personal trainers with the enraptured wife of an investment banker. Becoming aware of Moira's attention he broke off in mid-sentence, but before he could speak she said: 'Could I have a word with you, please?' and led the way from the room.

I was so startled by this move that after a moment I wandered after them. I told myself I was toilet-hunting, but in fact I was just giving way to an acute curiosity, and feeling vaguely like a detective in a country-house murder mystery I began to prowl around the ground floor.

The party was based in the living-room – 'the drawing-room',

Moira called it – but the socialising had expanded into the conservatory and dining-room as well. By the time I had edged my way through the throng to the hall, Moira and Gavin had disappeared. I checked the dining-room but found it populated only by oldies talking about who was dying, who was dead and who had had the best obituary in *The Times*. Abandoning this bundle of laughs I moved down a passage past a green baize door – a feature which reinforced my fantasy about being a detective in a classic country-house whodunnit – and found myself in a vast kitchen, but this was populated by caterers stuffing empty Krug bottles into crates. Moseying back I found a toilet – or, as Moira would have said, 'a cloakroom' – and paused to use the facilities before returning to the hall to discover another reception room ('morning-room'?), a book-lined study ('library'?) and a modern room, unknown in the 1930s' murder mysteries, which housed a jumbo television plus seating for couch potatoes. This was quite a house, and the sheer size of the ground floor explained how I had managed to miss both Moira and Gavin.

The final area I visited was the billiard-room, and from the window I saw Nicholas and Philip strolling slowly across the lawn to a distant summerhouse. Obviously there was no hope of escape just yet, but when I sank down in a leather chair to recharge my batteries I found myself unable to stop thinking of Eric, who had that morning ordered me to avoid 'that revolting rent boy' at the funeral. I quite understood why Eric should still be seething as the result of last weekend's scene when his brother Gilbert had stopped by at my house with two friends; Gavin, who had bulldozed his way across my threshold minutes earlier, had behaved monstrously and Eric had been humiliated. But the hard truth, which Eric still refused to face, was that he himself had triggered the scene by treating Gavin like garbage. I'd said as much to Eric – and his brother had backed me up – but Eric had just become angrier than ever and as soon as the guests had gone we had had a big row.

Gavin had earlier compounded the mess by disclosing he and I had seen each other without Eric's knowledge. Of course I should have told Eric about that visit to Richard's flat, but I hadn't been able to face the inevitable scene. Big mistake! I now had a far worse scene on my hands, and eventually, in a paroxysm of rage, Eric stormed out.

We spent the next day not speaking to each other, but by nine o'clock on Sunday night I was in such a state after eating a whole pizza and drinking five scotches that I called him with a grovelling apology. He had the decency to grovel back and we were reconciled – or at least we went through the motions of being reconciled. He was still cross enough to be too busy to see me on Monday and Tuesday, but he promised to be at my house on Wednesday when I returned home from the funeral. He even promised to cook dinner. That was when I finally dared to believe that the reconciliation was real and not mere wishful thinking.

I was still moodily contemplating the turgid state of my private life, when three middle-aged males barrelled into the billiard-room and destroyed the oasis of peace I had found there. Rudely recalled to the wake at Compton Beeches, I wondered whether to rejoin the throng in the living-room but decided I needed some more peace to work out what I currently felt about Gavin who, since arriving at the house, had shown himself capable of being thoroughly presentable. Did this make him either more or less dangerous to me? It could be argued that when he was appearing as elegant rough trade (what an oxymoron!) – naked except for designer jeans unzipped almost to the crotch – he was easier to classify as a working woman's fantasy and dismiss, possibly with an amused sigh; there's nothing like a touch of humour to steady a lurching stomach. Far more dangerous, it could be suggested, was the idea of Gavin as a presentable companion, someone who could fit seamlessly into my world as he demanded to be treated as an equal.

While these uneasy thoughts were flickering through my head I had been wandering down a corridor which led away from the billiard-room, and the next moment I spotted a narrow staircase which I identified as 'the backstairs'. Still reluctant to rejoin the party, I decided to extend my search for peace to the floor above.

Up the stairs I glided to the first-floor landing, and although the staircase continued I peeled away from it to explore another corridor. However this only led me to the main staircase where a cluster of female guests were processing unsteadily towards the en-suite facilities of Moira's bedroom. Anxious to avoid further conversation I returned to the backstairs. It was on the floor above that I finally found absolute peace and quiet – or so I thought. But I had taken no more than three steps away from the top stair when I became aware of the noise.

I stopped. My first reaction was that someone was escaping from the emotional aftermath of the funeral by watching a porn video. Then I realised this was no video. This was a live performance and it was taking place behind a closed door no more than twenty feet from where I was now standing.

Instinctively I opened the door nearest to me, slipped into the guest-room beyond and slumped down on the bed.

My mind seemed to be split in two. Half of it knew that the sounds came from Gavin and Moira. The other half refused to believe it. Then I thought how mysterious people were and how little anyone knew about what really went on in other people's lives. But finally my mind snapped together again and I thought: yes, I really believe it's them, and yes, I'm . . . But I couldn't at once think of the word. 'Shocked' and 'horrified' were somehow too banal; they missed the mark and made me sound like a Victorian bigot instead of a late twentieth-century liberal. Dimly I realised the word I wanted was 'stupefied' or even, more violently, 'stunned'. I felt as if I had seen the sun go into an unpredicted eclipse. I did try to get my intellect to sort things out with its usual efficiency, but nothing happened.

I was still grappling with this reaction when I heard a door opening down the corridor and instantly I jumped to my feet to see what was happening. Moira had slipped out and was looking up the corridor away from me. I shrank from sight before she could look down the corridor to check that the coast was clear.

Her voice said: 'You go via the backstairs – I'll use the main staircase,' and the next moment Gavin answered: 'Sure.'

I waited for a full half-minute. Then I hurried downstairs, unbolted a side door into the garden and set off in search of Nicholas.

VI

I soon gave up. My high heels, sinking into the gravel path, made walking awkward, and although I saw Nicholas in the distance he failed to see me. He and Philip were strolling back to the house across the lawn, but they were a long way from where I now stood.

Returning to the house I bumped straight into Gavin.

'So there you are!' he exclaimed as I gasped. 'I thought I'd lost you! Where have you been?'

'Relaxing on the second floor – but unlike you I was on my own!'

'Oh wow!' He was beside himself with delight. 'You mean you couldn't resist following me?'

'I—'

'Well, never mind that now, I want to show you something . . .' He seemed wholly unembarrassed that I had caught him out with another woman. Indeed he was behaving as if he and Moira had done nothing more than chat over a cup of tea. Of course this attitude is common enough in teenage shag-culture where immaturity ensures that fantasies run rife, but Gavin wasn't a teenager. He was far too old to bucket around acting out juvenile distortions of adult relationships, and I found myself looking at him with a new rush of stunned disbelief, but unfortunately he was much too self-absorbed at that moment to notice my expression.

'Look at this!' he was exclaiming as he opened a little pale blue box containing a pair of silver cuff links. 'Richard only bought them from Tiffany's last year so they're not family stuff which has to go to Philip. Cool, aren't they? Oh, and Moira says I can have not just the photo in the flat but the silver frame as well!'

I did try to keep calm but it was impossible. Looking him straight in the eyes I said strongly: 'Screwing your friend's wife on the day of the funeral is disgusting behaviour, and if you just screwed her to get the photo the behaviour's not only disgusting but pathetic as well.' Then I turned my back on him.

Rushing to the hall I sped outside to take refuge in Nicholas's car – only to remember that the car had been left by the church. In confusion I halted, and as I did so, Gavin raced down the steps of the porch in the hottest of hot pursuits.

VII

'What kind of a lawyer do you think you are?' he demanded outraged. 'How can it be right to condemn a man without giving him the chance to defend himself?' And before I could reply he was saying urgently: 'It wasn't like you think. I didn't do it for the photo. I did it because I felt sorry for her.'

Leaning back against a BMW parked nearby I said in a voice acid enough to corrode steel: 'That's sweet. But why should I believe you?'

'Why would I lie?'

'You're always lying! You lied your way through this party!'

'Well, I'm not lying now so just listen, would you? *Listen!* Here's what happened, no editing, no bullshit. Moira says to me: "Richard told me about you before he died – he said you liked to sail and I was pleased for him," she says. "During my marriage I went to hell and back but at the end I just felt glad he'd finally found someone who made him happy, so I want you to have something in memory of him," she says, and she takes me upstairs to Richard's bedroom, and in his dressing-room she fishes out the cuff links.

'Well, of course I thank her, and then I say I think she's one of the bravest women I've met, keeping the marriage going even though Richard wasn't switched on, and I finish up by saying: "I hope you've had lots of lovers because you're a very attractive woman and you don't deserve a husband who was several sandwiches short of a picnic at bedtime." And then . . . well, I'm just thinking how good she looks for her age when suddenly she cries: "Oh my God, you're AC-DC!" – which is such a cute little wrinkly-phrase, I've always thought, and I laugh and say: "Got it!" After all, I have to say that, don't I, because if I'd told her I was straight she'd want to know what I was doing with Richard and I didn't want her to find out I was a leisure-worker.

'So then Moira says: "Do you really find me attractive? I'm a lot older than you," and I say at once: "I really go for older women!" – well, I had to say that, didn't I, it would have been unkind to say anything else, but that kind of eggs her on to say: "I've never been lucky in love, Richard made me feel I never wanted to risk being so hurt again, so I'm sure I always come across to men as cold." And then she starts to cry and say she's wasted the best years of her life, she didn't stay with Richard for the sake of the children, she says, she now sees she stayed because she couldn't bear everyone knowing the truth and pitying her. She says: "When I was growing up, success for a woman meant having a wealthy husband of the right class, producing a son and a daughter and doing the right charity work. So I did all that," says Moira, "but I feel now I'm a failure and I can't bear it because I never fail, never, which was why I was my parents' favourite and why my father was so proud of me." And she cries and cries.

'God, I felt so sorry for her! You won't believe this, but I'm a very soft-hearted bloke where women are concerned, which is why

I could never earn a living doing hetero leisure-work . . . Well anyway, I put my arms round Moira and I say: "You're no failure! You're a heroine and I think you're t'rrific!" And the next moment we're snogging like there's no tomorrow and she's gasping: "Not here, not here!" because there are people around hunting for the ladies' loo, so I say: "How about upstairs?" and away we go – well, what else could I have done? I couldn't have backed out at the last minute, it would have been cruel! And afterwards . . . well, I didn't think she'd mind if I asked for the photo – and I was right. She says: "I'll send it to you, frame and all – what's your address?" But I don't want her getting mixed up with Elizabeth, so—'

'Who?'

'My manager. So I say to Moira—'

'Wait a minute. This manager of yours—'

'Yep?'

'Has she ever called herself Elizabeth Mayfield?'

'Nope. Who's Elizabeth Mayfield? Never mind, don't answer that, I want to finish my story. There's Moira, asking for my address, but I don't want her accessing my home in Lambeth or my business in the City so I say: "I'll buy you a drink at Claridge's – let me call you," and she says forget Claridge's, we can meet at the Mayfair flat, but I shan't do that because I don't want this turning into an affair – and once she thinks things over she won't want that either, she'll realise this was just a one-off to cheer her up. Now, sweetie, be honest – did you rush to judgement or didn't you? And since when has it been – quote – "disgusting" and "pathetic" to be kind to a friend's widow when she's so obviously in need of a boost to her morale?'

With a monumental effort I recalled Nicholas's advice to be polite and low-key and my own determination to remain cool and laid-back. 'Okay,' I said evenly, damp with the strain of staying so calm. 'I rushed to judgement and I apologise. Satisfied?'

'Oh, I wish!' he said, instantly reverting to the role of predator. 'Hey, Frosty-Puss—'

'Carta.'

'—you do realise, don't you, that you needn't be jealous of Moira? *You're* the one who's special!'

'Gavin—'

'No, don't bang on about that chubby heap you keep on tap, he's history. By the way, what does your boss think about you having it off with a bloke without being married?'

The words 'polite', 'low-key', 'cool' and 'laid-back' were now flashing around inside my head like a bunch of laser beams. They formed a winning display but did nothing to lower my blood pressure. 'Eric and I are totally committed to a one-to-one relationship,' I said woodenly, 'and Nicholas has decided this commitment is an acceptable prelude to marriage – and that's not so incompatible with Christian tradition as you might think. Marriage as we know it is a fairly modern institution, and—'

'But what's stopping you from getting married?'

'Well . . .' The laser beams were continuing to flash but more dimly. 'Well, it's absolutely none of your business,' I said, limp with the effort it required not to sound ferocious, 'but I'm recovering from my first marriage.'

'Shit, lady, if poor old Eric can't make you forget your ex, why not pick a man who can?'

I lost it. 'Oh, get real!' I yelled, awash with the relief of casting repression to the winds. 'You can't believe I'm going to take you seriously! Grow up, wise up and get a life, for God's sake – get a proper job, do something that'd make me respect you, take on a project that'd make me think: "Hey, that guy might just possibly be worth knowing!" Because so long as you spend your life playing a hunk of beef up for auction at Smithfield, why on earth should someone like me give you the time of day?'

The front door of the house opened, and Nicholas appeared in the porch.

VIII

'Time to go,' he said to me as he crossed the gravel towards us.

I swallowed, cleared my throat and gave a small cough. 'I'd better say goodbye to Moira.'

'I said goodbye on your behalf – she's retired to her room now.' Glancing at Gavin Nicholas added: 'Coming with us?'

Gavin shook his head and went into one of his beautiful sulks, eyes down, lashes fanning his cheeks, mouth macho-tight, jaw a vision of sculpted elegance. I wanted to hit him.

'Let me give you my card,' said Nicholas, 'to remind you that St Benet's is an oasis where you can be yourself without being hassled,' but Gavin tore the card in two, dropped the pieces and walked back to the house without another word to either of us.

'My fault,' I muttered as Nicholas did his bit for the environment by retrieving the debris. 'I was trying to make him face reality.'

'Always a dangerous course to take with disturbed people!'

'Sorry, boss, you must be thinking I'm a rotten Christian and a dimwit employee, but I just went ballistic, I couldn't stop myself—'

'Dealing with people as damaged as Gavin isn't easy, particularly when they try to push out the boundaries of acceptable behaviour to see how much flak you can take.'

'I did *try* to be polite and low-key—'

'Carta, stop beating yourself up! What exactly happened?'

'I hardly know where to begin.'

We were walking down the drive by this time but departing cars, many no doubt driven by over-the-limit owners, made this a hazardous exercise and we agreed to continue the conversation at the Little Chef pit stop which we had both noticed earlier a mile outside the village. Twenty minutes later I was ordering a vanilla Danish to go with my coffee, but Nicholas, who had almost certainly been too busy with Bridget and Philip to eat anything at the wake, merely looked without interest at the menu before replacing it on its stand. No wonder he was so slim.

Picking up my fork I speared the Danish through its soft centre and said: 'Gavin screwed Moira.'

It took a great deal to dent Nicholas's calm professional persona, but I had dented it. Moreover he was not merely ruffled but aghast. 'Is that what Gavin told you?' he said rapidly. 'Maybe he was fantasising to make you jealous.'

'Nicholas, I heard them,' I said, and told him everything.

IX

'Maybe he's a psychopath,' I said when my story was finished. 'Doesn't he fit the profile? Manipulative, charming, shallow, a habitual liar who leaves a trail of broken relationships in his wake, someone who's unable to feel normal human emotions—'

'But he seemed to be feeling all kinds of normal human emotions when the funeral ended, didn't he? He obviously found the memory of his dead brother hard to handle, and he was close to tears when he recalled how kind Richard had been, inviting him to the house.'

'So you're saying Gavin's just a regular bastard?'

'I'm saying he's just profoundly damaged. That makes him behave like a regular bastard, and can I just make one thing quite clear? You were right to be upset about the incident with Moira.'

'You don't think I was being priggish?'

'There's nothing priggish about being appalled by a man who uses a vulnerable woman to boost his ego.'

'But according to Gavin's story, Moira wanted the sex even more than he did!'

'Yes, but there are two problems with Gavin's story, aren't there? The first is that it may be a fantasy from start to finish, and the second is that even if he spoke the truth the incident was still a disaster.'

'How can you be so sure?'

'Because I know where Moira's at, and let me tell you, without breaching any confidences, that the very last thing she needs right now is a close encounter with a man who intends to treat her as the human equivalent of a Kleenex tissue – use once and dispose.'

I hesitated for a moment before saying: 'Well, I certainly don't want to criticise her, particularly if she's acting out of a deep unhappiness and particularly as Gavin's enough to make any woman plunge into promiscuity. If I found him so sexy, how can I blame Moira for doing the same?'

'Past tense? "Found" not "find"?'

'I couldn't find him attractive now after the way he's behaved, harassing me to pieces one moment and screwing Moira the next! Obviously he's sick, and I don't find sickness sexy. So I can relax.'

'I don't want to sound cynical,' said Nicholas, 'but relaxation would almost certainly be a big mistake. I'm glad Moira's enabled you to see Gavin in a clearer light, but you still need to be on your guard.'

'But how sure are you that he'll surface in my life again? I really tore a strip off him just now, and he obviously doesn't want to come near St Benet's.'

'True, but I've got a feeling neither of us have seen the last of Gavin Blake . . . I must say, I'm intrigued by the way his path's been intersecting with yours.'

'That's just the result of a random chance.'

'Yes, but God works through random chances – they're all part of the creative and redemptive process. I wonder if you've been setting out on a new phase of your spiritual journey.'

'Well, don't ask me – I'm just a beginner Christian with no spiritual gifts whatsoever!'

'My dear Carta—'

'Look, you're making everything much too complicated and the situation's actually very simple: Gavin wants to add me to his babe-list, and he's prepared to stalk me to do it – and if that's of any interest to God whatsoever I'll eat a stack of Appeal brochures!'

'God's interested in everything.'

'Yes, but—'

'I agree Gavin's making a nuisance of himself, but I don't think he's a stalker.'

'Then how do you explain his behaviour?'

'I think he's trying to communicate with you,' said Nicholas, 'and I suspect that what he really wants has nothing to do with sex at all.'

X

I boggled at him. 'But that's crazy! If you could hear how Gavin carries on when he and I are alone—'

'He thinks that's the only way he'll win your attention, but I doubt if he's really interested in *you*, the person behind the image you present. My theory is that you're a symbol to him, and that it's what you symbolise which is so attractive.'

'But what on earth do I symbolise?'

'The world of Richard Slaney. Just think for a moment. You're obviously of special interest to him, and it's unlikely to be just because you're an attractive blonde – for a man like Gavin attractive blondes are a dime a dozen. What's special about you is that you're a friend of Richard's, someone who lives in another world from the world Gavin now inhabits. Richard took Gavin through the looking glass into that world, and although Richard's now dead the link with that world isn't over so long as you're around and Gavin finds ways of staying in touch with you.'

129

I went on staring at him. 'But what am I supposed to do?'

'Maybe you can help him.'

'You're joking.'

'Okay, it's a big "maybe" but the possibility's there. Now, I'm not saying this is going to be easy and I'm certainly not saying it's going to be risk-free—'

'It sounds like one of those insane new sports where people try to kill themselves for the adrenaline buzz.'

'—but if you treat him with as much respect as you'd treat any other friend of Richard's he'll eventually realise he doesn't have to come on like a sex addict to win your attention, and then it might be possible to build some sort of life-saving bridge to him. The big danger, of course, is that if you ever respond to him sexually everything could wind up wrecked, and when I say "everything" I include Gavin himself who'll feel cheated that you couldn't after all lead him into Richard's world but just treated him as a hunk of meat fit only for the world he already occupies.'

I took a deep breath. 'Nicholas, I do appreciate the compliment you're trying to pay me, but I'm not a priest, I'm not a pastoral worker, I'm not—'

'Not your brother's keeper?'

I groaned and covered my face with my hands. 'Why's Christianity so often so difficult?'

'Because life's so often not so easy! But listen, Carta, you're getting intimidated because you're thinking of this as a once-in-a-lifetime project, whereas the truth is it's just an unusual example of something that crops up every day. We're all called to help each other as best we can, that's the truth off it – it's as if we're all cells in one body, we're all connected, and sickness in one cell can't help but affect the healthy cells – the healthy cells can't remain neutral, can't opt out, they've got to stand fast against sickness if they're to survive. And that's why, in the most real sense, I *have* to be my brother's keeper – his health and mine are interdependent.'

I made one last attempt to wriggle off the Christian hook. 'Nicholas, on a purely rational level, how can you be sure I can help Gavin in any way whatsoever?'

'I can't be sure. Maybe I've got it quite wrong and Gavin's been sent to help you.'

Nicholas was clearly off the planet and orbiting in deep space.

Finishing my coffee without further comment I stood up to pay the bill.

XI

We were settling ourselves in the car minutes later when I suddenly said: 'There's something I've forgotten to tell you.'

Nicholas paused, his hand on the ignition key, and looked at me expectantly.

'Gavin's manager. This woman who's involved in vice and who's apparently so nervous of priests she forbids Gavin to talk to anyone in a dog collar. Her name's Elizabeth.'

'Oh yes?' Nicholas started the engine and began to reverse out of the parking space.

'Okay,' I said, 'okay. I know I'm obsessive about Mrs Mayfield, but when Gavin disclosed—'

'Hold it.' Nicholas changed gears and drove back into the parking space. As he switched off the engine he said: 'Did you say the name Mayfield to gauge his reaction?'

I sighed. 'He didn't bat an eyelid. Maybe he only started working for her after she abandoned the healing business in Fulham. Or maybe he just never knew she operated a business using that identity. The police always thought, didn't they, that the reason why she was able to vanish so suddenly and so completely was because she'd developed a parallel identity somewhere else.'

'Did you ask Gavin what his Elizabeth's surname was?'

'No, stupid of me, I was too busy thinking of Mayfield.'

'If we knew the surname I could ask the police to check for previous convictions, but my guess would be she's clean – in fact if she's Mayfield, she'd have to be clean in this other identity or the police would have linked up the fingerprints. Remember Mayfield had a record?'

'Gavin certainly implied to me she was clean. The point came up when he stressed his own work was entirely legal.'

Nicholas mulled this over for a moment before asking: 'How does she avoid a charge of living off his immoral earnings?'

'He doesn't see clients at her house and the money he pays her could be passed off as rent for his Lambeth accommodation. Or maybe, as we're talking of an upmarket business, he pays money into a numbered offshore account.' I paused to martial my thoughts before saying carefully: 'If we compare the two Elizabeths, we can see there are some suggestive coincidences. Number one: Mrs Mayfield had a vice record, and Gavin's Elizabeth – Elizabeth X – is running a male prostitute. Number two: although Mrs Mayfield was jailed on vice charges in the 1960s she retained her Mayfield identity afterwards for her psychic healing practice, probably because she had a reputation in that line, and Kim told me that when he first met her years and years ago she was operating out of a room in Lambeth. The coincidence here is that Lambeth is where Gavin lives with Elizabeth X.'

'Lambeth isn't the most privileged of areas. Can I be tiresome enough to remind you of all the shady ladies called Elizabeth, convicted or otherwise, who have inevitably made it their home?'

'Okay, I know I'm seriously nuts about that vile woman who pretended to heal Kim of all his cosmic psychological problems and made sure he never got the right help until it was too late, but the fact remains that if Mrs Mayfield hadn't peddled that fake healing and encouraged his sexual deviancy by introducing him to that occult society – wait a moment, I was almost forgetting! There's a third coincidence. Nicholas, Mrs Mayfield had City contacts – Kim wasn't the only City high flyer who belonged to that society. So the third coincidence is—'

'—the fact that Elizabeth X must also have had City contacts to launch Gavin. Yes, that's all true, Carta, but there isn't a shred of evidence, is there, to prove the two Elizabeths are one? The earnings from vice, the Lambeth connection and the City contacts could all be random coincidences, and a quite different Elizabeth, based in Lambeth, could have built up (for example) a City catering business, made numerous affluent contacts and decided to sell Gavin in addition to boardroom lunches.'

I offered no argument. I just said: 'Maybe if Gavin stays in touch I can find out more.'

'I was afraid you'd wind up saying that,' said Nicholas.

XII

We sat there in the car park of the Little Chef a mile from Compton Beeches and looked at one another. I was the first to glance away, and as I did so I heard Nicholas say firmly but not unkindly: 'Befriend Gavin if you can. But don't just use him in an obsessive quest to come to terms with the past.'

I found myself unable to reply and eventually Nicholas said: 'I've got a lot of sympathy for you, Carta, where Mrs Mayfield's concerned, but the danger is that by brooding on the past you'll pay insufficient attention to the present. Don't get so locked up in the events of 1990 that you ignore what's happening in 1992 – and I mean what's really happening in 1992. What's really happening isn't Mrs Mayfield making a dramatic return to your life. What's really happening is Gavin, crossing and recrossing your path, and it's Gavin you need to focus on, not that part of yourself which is still welded to the memory of Kim's death. Gavin may never cross your path again, but you can still pray for him, and praying for him is probably much more in line with what God requires of you at this moment than dwelling in frustration on the elusiveness of Mrs Mayfield.'

I thought hard. At last I managed to say: 'I'm sure you're right,' and after a moment I was even able to comment: 'The more obsessed with her I get, the more power she has over me and the more likely I am to behave nuttily – and the last thing you need is a nutty fundraiser ruining the Appeal.'

I sensed Nicholas's relief.

We finally drove away.

XIII

'I'll tell you one topic that never surfaced today,' said Nicholas as we reached the City, 'and that's Richard's proposed donation to St Benet's. Maybe he never told Moira about it.'

'If they were close enough to talk about Gavin during his last hours, I see no reason why Richard wouldn't have mentioned the donation plan,' I objected, 'particularly as the donation was linked with his guilt about not getting involved with family therapy.' But less certainly I asked: 'What's the etiquette on jogging a widow's memory about her husband's promise to give to a good cause?'

'You pray she isn't suffering from amnesia.'

I sighed.

'I could put out a tactful feeler later,' said Nicholas as the car reached the Barbican at last and began to travel east along London Wall, 'but I'd have to pick the right moment and that could well be several weeks away.'

'Even if Moira does know about Richard's promise,' I commented gloomily, 'she might well hesitate on the grounds that it was over-generous.'

'You really think she wouldn't honour the commitment?'

'After what she got up to today, I feel I no longer have any idea what she might do.'

Nicholas was halting the car by the traffic barrier of Monkwell Square. 'We'll discuss it all tomorrow,' he said incisively. 'Meanwhile give my regards to Eric . . . How was that brother of his when you saw him last weekend?'

'I thought he looked tired. Too many visits to those dying Aids patients in the hospice perhaps.'

'I must give him a call.'

We parted, and then setting the day's emotionally exhausting events aside I prepared to relax with Eric over the meal he had promised to cook to welcome me home.

XIV

'Let's hear the bad news first,' said Eric, passing me a glass of Nuits St George. 'How was the sleazeball?'

'He took one look at my bodyguard and decided to spend his time chasing someone else.'

'Honestly? Tell me everything!'

I launched into a blow-by-blow description of what had happened; I thought this was more likely to generate an atmosphere of trust, an essential ingredient in the reconciliation we were still working on after our big row the previous weekend. Even so, I found myself becoming irritated when Eric showed signs of sliding into another snit. I thought that by now he should have been able to set aside the humiliation he had suffered last Saturday, but apparently I had been expecting too much. Or was I dealing here not with humiliation but with simple jealousy? That seemed unlikely. I could see that Gavin was sexy enough to make other men grind their teeth, but what I couldn't see was why an intelligent, sensible man like Eric should sink into such fury over a mere prostitute, no matter how good-looking the prostitute happened to be. It would have been far more typical of Eric if he had just laughed and exclaimed: 'Poor sod, what a loser! Don't tell me you think he's gorgeous!' But that kind of balanced response was definitely not on offer.

When I had finished my story he refilled our glasses, set the bottle down with a thump and said: 'I think Nick's gone crazy. What rubbish to think that Gavin's been put across your path for a purpose! This guy's seriously bad news, and the idea that he could ever be a benign part of your spiritual journey is just sentimental twaddle – and what's worse, it's dangerous sentimental twaddle!'

I kept calm. 'To tell you the truth, I too thought Nicholas was nuts at that point, but—'

'Lewis is the one who's got it right, of course. Gavin Blake's nothing but a metaphysical typhoid-carrier, and you should never under any circumstances see him again!'

'Well, the odds are I never will,' I said, somehow managing to stay cool. 'But don't you think Nicholas was right to say we're all like cells in one body, all called to help one another in the fight against sickness?'

'Of course he was right, but that's not the point at issue here! We're not talking about the principle implied in "I am my brother's keeper" – we're talking of the application of that principle!'

'Sorry?'

'Think of the poor in Calcutta. We're all required to care, but we're *not* all required to be Mother Teresa, giving hands-on help. Most of us are required to care by praying or sending donations or both.'

'Yes, I see, but—'

'Now apply that to the Gavin situation. You can pray for the bastard, of course you can, but the idea that you should give hands-on help is ludicrous! He's definitely one for the psychiatrists!'

I knew it was unwise to argue but I found I had to fight the

135

implication that I was just a dizzy blonde who couldn't cope. 'Maybe God thinks I'm uniquely suited to help Gavin.'

'God wouldn't be so dumb! Why should he use a vulnerable woman to help this psycho?'

'But *am* I so vulnerable? I'm smart, I'm tough, I'm streetwise—'

'Oh, come on, Carta! You're vulnerable because you're obviously fascinated by this totally sick testosterone package who hip-swivels around as if he had WANNA FUCK? tattooed on his chest!'

'Eric, you're losing it. Stop right there.'

'I just want to make it crystal clear that I'm not going to let this rat gnaw our relationship to pieces!'

Making a huge effort I kept my temper. 'Listen,' I said. '*I have no plans to see Gavin again.* Got it? And I'm convinced I gave him a big enough brush-off today to ensure he leaves me alone in future.'

'But he won't.'

'Why not?'

'Because you're there, like Mount Everest. He's got to conquer you. He's committed.'

'Rubbish!'

'It's not rubbish! After his romp with Moira today isn't it obvious he'll stop at nothing? The trouble is women get moronic when they're mixed up with a man like that – all they want to do is swoon into his arms and simper: "Take me!"'

'I don't believe I'm hearing this! Of all the stupid, snotty, sexist garbage I've ever heard—'

'At least I'm giving you some down-to-earth realism, unlike your boss who's been doling out the airy-fairy mysticism like a dud psychic with a crystal ball!'

'I thought you admired Nicholas!'

'Yes, I do, but he's not perfect and like a lot of clerics he can be ruthless in using people to further his spiritual aims. I can just see him being professionally drawn to Gavin – what a sicko, what a challenge! – and I can just see him thinking too that you're the ideal person to lure Gavin into the St Benet's net—'

'You're twisting everything – it's not like that—'

'No? Well, don't tell me Nick can't be ruthless where his ministry of healing's concerned – look how he saddled you with the fundraising! I know you thought it was a call, something which you as a fledgeling Christian could do for God, but ever since you've been buck-chasing you've been overworking, obsessive and prone to be flaky at home. No, you've taken a wrong turn and I'll tell you why you took it: you wanted to boost your ego and cut a dash in the City again! You started to miss everyone telling you how glamorous and successful you were, so you dived into big-time fundraising which nowadays is just as chic and glitzy as any job in PR or the media—'

'You're just furious with the fundraising because it led me in the end to Gavin Blake! Look, I'm calling a halt – I've had a long hard day which has been very stressful emotionally—'

'I bet! Specially losing out to Moira Slaney!'

'God, what a bloody thing to say!'

'But it's true, isn't it?'

'No, it damn well is not! Oh, shut up and leave me alone – stop beating me up like this—'

He walked out.

I burst into tears.

Then I opened another bottle of wine.

XV

Again we struggled to patch up the quarrel but this time the memory of it lay between us like an acrid smell which refused to fade. The following weekend Eric went down to Winchester to see his parents and I didn't volunteer to go with him. I found his mother heavy-going, and besides, I thought it would help the relationship recover if we spent some time apart. Eric evidently came to the same conclusion because as soon as he had finished a stint of office-work to boost his bank account he travelled to Norway to do some research.

One result of his imaginative verbal assault on me after Richard's funeral was that I was now determined to prove that fundraising was exactly what God required me to do at this stage of my life and that Nicholas had been a genius to spot my potential talent. Furiously I toiled away to justify us all, but to my dismay I now encountered nothing but setbacks. I heard no more from Moira about the promised donation, no one else was busy writing cheques, and finally I lost a large donation which I had convinced myself was safely in the bag. The donor pleaded the financial climate – sterling falling through the ERM floor, Lamont devaluing the pound, and the mass tumbling of the currencies as the stock market sank fathoms deep in gloom.

I conceded the severity of the financial climate, but I still felt not only infuriated by the donor's weak-kneed slide out of a commitment but also as crushed as if I'd been rejected by a lover. Fundraising resembles old-fashioned wooing. One courts and flirts and intrigues the potential donor, and a personal relationship is built up which makes it hard for him – in the City it's usually a man – to backtrack. Eventually, if the courtship reaches its desired climax, the donor yields and reaches for his chequebook with the result that ecstasy is achieved on both sides. To be balked of this ultimate satisfaction was both a professional disappointment and a blow to my self-esteem.

The good news was that I received no further word from Gavin. So much for Eric's hysterical prediction. Out of respect for Nicholas, who of course hadn't been ruthless in exploiting me but merely smart enough to pick the best person for the job, I said a quick prayer for Gavin every night. The prayer consisted of the following words addressed silently but briskly to God: 'Please help Gavin Blake get a life. Thanks. Amen.' Guiltily aware that this prayer was so minimalist it could scarcely count, I also made an effort to light a candle for Gavin at St Benet's every morning before I started work.

Meanwhile Eric had decided to extend his visit to Norway, but we were in touch again by phone and the memory of the row was finally losing its jagged edges. This improvement in my private life was just as well because in my professional life things were going from bad to worse. Another potential donor slithered away, my organiser succumbed to cyber-madness and the Healing Centre's trustees quashed my brilliant scheme to get Nicholas on morning television's prime showcase. Then to cap it all Nicholas decided that we still couldn't approach Moira about Richard's promised donation because Bridget had had a relapse and was back in hospital. Nicholas thought that the relapse was probably a temporary setback resulting from Richard's death and that Bridget could be helped again at the Healing Centre later, but I thought Moira might well decide she had had enough of complementary medicine. The entire subject of the Slaney family and the lost donation filled me with gloom.

I did feel better when Eric at last returned from Norway, but soon he allowed the next draft of his book to take him over so completely that I hardly saw him – a state of affairs which made me realise with dread how fragile our reconciliation was. Whipping up my will-power I produced the necessary energy to be endlessly understanding during our occasional meetings, and just as I was about to expire after my umpteenth gala performance as The Great Writer's Loyal Little Helper, my fortunes suddenly revived.

I received a letter from the chief executive officer of an American investment bank based in the City. It read: 'Dear Ms Graham: We are interested in contributing to the St Benet's Appeal as part of our annual donation to charitable causes in and around the City of London. May I invite you to make a presentation to our Charities Committee? If you telephone this office, my secretary would be pleased to set up an appointment. Sincerely . . .'

This is the seductive side of fundraising: the predicted successes may fail to materialise but there's always the chance of a generous donation floating in from an unexpected source. I had already approached this bank by mailshot and had even found the necessary sympathetic third party to promote our cause with the CEO, but nothing had happened. Yet now the CEO was apparently all benevolence! I decided I should try to thank him in person, and although he was away in America when I gave the presentation to his committee, I was able to ask his PA why her boss had chosen to take an interest in St Benet's.

'Ah yes,' she said, 'Jerry thought you might want to know that. He said I was to tell you that he was a friend of Richard Slaney's.'

XVI

I sent a silent prayer of thanks to Richard and felt euphoric. I was sure I had nailed the donation and I thought the amount could be as much as twenty-five thousand pounds, but before I received the letter which confirmed this estimate I was visited by an elderly man who huffed and puffed his way into my office with one of the Appeal brochures tucked under his arm. He was so fat and so bald that I was reminded of the nursery rhyme about Humpty Dumpty.

Having told me his name he explained: 'I'm a partner in JQS

Global, and we've decided we'd like to make a significant donation to your most worthy and interesting good cause . . .' The deep voice with its heavy public-school accent droned richly on. The ideal donor, bursting to write a cheque, had apparently found his way to my office without even receiving so much as a humble mailshot.

'May I ask how you heard about us?' I said, wondering if he was a Christian who had heard of the Appeal through his local church, but he just said simply: 'I was a friend of Richard Slaney's,' and handed me a cheque for fifteen thousand pounds.

XVII

I suppose I knew then. Perhaps I had even known after my chat with that PA. But of course I couldn't believe it. It was easier to say firmly to myself: 'God moves in mysterious ways!' and think how rewarding it was to be a successful fundraiser.

When I told Nicholas he said: 'That's certainly a fascinating development – almost miraculous!' No doubt he too knew then but, like me, couldn't quite bring himself to believe what had happened.

The next day Moira Slaney phoned him to say not only that Bridget would be resuming her visits to the Healing Centre but that Richard's promised twenty thousand pounds would be in our hands as soon as probate was granted on his estate.

XVIII

I was just sitting at my desk and dreaming of the Queen awarding me an OBE (or would it be a CBE?) for special service to the Church of England, when my secretary Caroline looked up from her task of opening the mail and said: 'I don't believe it.'

I forgot the Queen. 'What's happened?'

'We've got another unsolicited donor – and he's sent thirty thousand pounds!' She ran to me with the letter.

The chairman of one of Britain's leading building firms had written: 'Dear Miss Graham: Please find enclosed a cheque which I trust will assist your cause. Should you wonder how I heard of

your Appeal, allow me to tell you that I was a friend of Richard
Slaney's. Yours sincerely . . .'

XIX

At quarter to twelve I left the office and walked the short distance
to my house on Wallside. I still had Gavin's number, scrawled on
the back of the card he had given me. I had consigned it to the
kitchen drawer where I stashed recent newspaper cuttings, business cards from plumbers, Barbican estate circulars and other scraps
of transient information which I would junk when the drawer
became full.

Sitting down at the kitchen counter with my cordless phone I
waited until five minutes to noon exactly. Then I called the number
of the flat in Austin Friars.

He picked up on the second ring.

'You're beginning to interest me,' I said. 'You're beginning to make
me think you might just possibly be worth knowing. If you're free
tonight after work, why don't I buy you a glass of champagne?'

CHAPTER TWO

Gavin

'In particular, people with 'borderline' or antisocial personality disorders, or addictive or impulsive traits . . . [have] a fragmented sense of self and lack of empathy for others, and an egocentric need to gratify their desires or to discharge inner tension . . .'

A Time to Heal
A report for the House of Bishops on the Healing Ministry

The iceberg finally melts. My brand-new career as an undercover fundraiser has ensured I'm no longer filth trading on a connection with Richard Slaney. I'm Richard's white-knight friend who works for a Christian cause. Eat your heart out, Eric Tucker! I'm on the kind of roll where over-the-hill podgy heaps don't stand a chance.

'Name the place!' I say to the melting Ms Catriona Graham when she offers to buy me a glass of champagne.

'The Lord Mayor's Cat between Cornhill and Lombard Street,' she answers, trying to sound businesslike, but her voice can best be described as dulcet. I like that word. It conjures up images of sexy sirens sipping brandy alexanders in between crooning dirtily into snow-white phones.

'The Lord Mayor's Cat?' I say amused. 'That eighties dump past its sell-by date? I'll meet you at One-for-the-Money in Angel Court at six-forty-five!' And I blow a kiss into the receiver before hanging up.

I feel like a superstud. Dammit, I *am* a superstud! But no, I'm better than a superstud because I've got brains as well as balls – and now, thanks to my brilliant battle plan, I've also got Golden Girl undulating on the hook.

But even as I'm freaking out on this genuine non-chemical ecstasy, the phone rings again. This is tricky. Can't ignore it – she'd only call again later.

Gingerly I pick up the receiver. 'Yep?'

'Darling,' she says, 'it's me. I'm calling about next weekend, just as I said I would. Do you know yet whether you'll be free? I could do either Saturday or Sunday . . .' Moira falters, voice wobbling.

Hell. 'Sweetie, I'd love to see you, but this weekend's no good.'

'Well, couldn't we at least talk on the phone?'

'Uh . . . It's kind of complicated because the woman I live with's so jealous.'

'You're sure it's not a man?'

'You're doing my head in! You think I don't know the difference?'

'Oh Gavin darling, please don't joke about this! Listen, I'm not asking you to ditch her, but—'

But that's the long-term aim, of course, the plan that's been evolving in Moira's head ever since the funeral and that chic fuck which should have been a one-off. I should never have agreed to meet her at Richard's flat for a second round, I know that now – well, I knew it at the time, but the trouble was that after I decided to play the white-knight fundraiser it seemed to me I had a kind of moral duty to stay close to Moira to see that she made good on Richard's promise to give twenty thousand quid to St Benet's. I mean, I extended the fucklet for the very best of motives, I really did. I just didn't foresee Moira diving so deeply into a lifestyle where toyboy-on-toast is always dish-of-the-day on the weekend menu.

'I'll call you next week,' I lie firmly, but to my horror I hear a muffled sob. Shit! How could she play her cards so wrong? I thought she was smart and sophisticated, well able to handle a shag-snack on a no-fuss, no-mess basis, but here she is, behaving like a needy housewife who can't get enough of the window-cleaner.

'Gotta go, Gorgeous – talk t'ya later,' I mutter at top speed, and hang up just as the buzzer blares. High noon at Austin Friars and never a dull moment.

I sprint to the entryphone to admit Iowa Jerry. I've got two American clients at the moment who are called Jerry so I tag them by their home states in order to avoid the leisure-worker's nightmare, the unprofessional mix-up. They both have short hair, nice suits and capped teeth, but it's vital to distinguish these two blokes

143

from each other because they like totally different bedroom routines.

Iowa Jerry's a big bore at the moment because he thinks that the donation to St Benet's by his firm's charity committee means I should be giving him a freebie. I'm currently stringing him along by saying it'll take a while to work a freebie into my schedule, but the bloody thing is I know I've got to give him what he wants in order to shut him up. So far he's mellow. He's taken on board the fact that my fundraising has to be top secret – obviously no Christian cause would want to be openly associated with a leisure-worker – and he even enjoyed the cloak-and-dagger business of making sure Richard's name got mentioned. (My signal to Golden Girl.) But if I refuse him the freebie he could get stroppy and complain to Elizabeth, and then I'd be well and truly up shit creek.

While Iowa Jerry's being winched up to my flat the phone goes again. Normally with a client almost on my doorstep I'd ignore the bell, but my life's so complicated at present that I find I have a nervous urge to find out who's calling. Leaving the front door open for Jerry I sprint back to the phone.

'Hullo?'

'Hey, Mr Cool, it's Serena! When do we get to meet up for some more r-&-r?'

Oh my God, it's Norah's slag, the one I'm shagging to make Elizabeth think my weekend sex life's in perfect order! 'Serena sweetie, can't talk now, gotta go, big love—' I slam down the receiver, hoick the cord from the jack and turn to greet my client.

'Jerry!'

'Gavin baby . . .'

The lunch-time shift grinds remorselessly into gear.

*　*　*

By three o'clock I'm exhausted, a state of affairs which makes me worry that I might be getting too stressed out. That's definitely not what I need in order to perform well. I need a well-regulated life, just as an athlete does, and a nice home where I can find security, peace and a woman who tells me I'm wonderful. I'm a very straight-forward bloke really, that's the truth of it, and I'm not cut out for a life in which my stomach muscles go into spasm every time the phone rings, a life where I'm some kind of double agent, a life where one false move could send me on another trip to Asherton's Pain-Palace . . .

But it's best not to think of Asherton.

After my last lunch-time client plods off I'm so knackered I barely have the energy to change the fitted sheet. But I do. I'm not having a nap on soiled cotton polyester. And I wash my mouth out before I collapse. I'm always washing my mouth out to get rid of the taste of condoms and the tang of sweaty skin. Gays hate using condoms for oral numbers, and so many clients try to tell me there's no risk of Aids in this kind of sex, but the truth is there is a risk, it's very small but it does exist and I'm taking absolutely no chances. Sorry, guys, but if you want someone who'll risk all for love, you've come to the wrong person.

But my chief worry is that scientists will discover HIV's present in sweat. Dr Filth says it's impossible to catch HIV from sweat, but what does that wanker really know, especially if the virus is clever at mutating?

The trouble is my clients usually like to be kissed somewhere along the line, and it's difficult to plan satisfactory choreography without any mouth-to-skin contact. And the skin's usually got sweat on it. Naturally I don't do mouth-to-mouth, and that's not just because HIV is blood-borne and my clients are at an age when their gums bleed easily into their saliva – which could then infect any nick in my own mouth, even a nick so tiny that I'm unaware of it. I also don't do mouth-to-mouth because of all the other stuff you can catch. The other stuff might not be life-threatening but it could still put a dent in my career – even the humble head cold can represent a financial loss, and whenever I get a bug I run straight to the doctor to get it nailed right away.

The last time I did this the doctor hit me with such a shot of antibiotics that I passed out (maybe there was more than antibiotics in the syringe) and when I came to he had his fist . . . no, let's forget that, it's too shitty to think about. Where does Elizabeth dredge up all these bloody people from? But it's wonderful the talent she has for spotting bargains in the human basement. Dr Filth, for instance, has good qualifications, but Elizabeth knows too much about him – which is why Dr Filth only charges rock-bottom prices for my regular check-ups and makes sure my blood samples are tested in the best labs.

Having changed the fitted sheet and washed out my mouth I drift into sleep beneath the duvet I keep for naps, but I've hardly been snoozing for ten minutes when the phone starts to ring again. I reconnected it after the last client left.

I want to ignore the noise, but the caller's almost certain to be Elizabeth. Carta, Serena and Moira are all under orders only to call at certain times, and for them three-thirty's taboo.

Opening the drawer in the bedside table where the extension phone lives out of sight of clients I grab the receiver. 'Yeah?'

'Well, take your time!' snaps that bitch Susanne, Ms Bowling-Ball Breasts of 1992. 'I was thinking your last punter had left you tied down to all four bedposts!'

'I was asleep!' I yell, but I'm aware of a soothing wave of relief. Here at last is someone who has no desire to have sex with me, and the reason for the call, though bound to be work-related, is also bound to be trivial. If it was serious Elizabeth would call me herself. 'What's the problem?' I ask, sounding almost chummy.

'Elizabeth wants to check if you've ever heard of a man called Gilbert Tucker.'

I feel as if I'm riding a lift and the cable's just snapped. 'Who?'

'Weird name, isn't it, sounds pervy. *Gilbert Tucker*. Says he's a friend of yours.'

A voice in my head mutters: oh my God. Swinging my legs off the bed I sit tautly on the edge and grip the phone hard enough to bust it as I muse idly: 'Gilbert Tucker. Yeah. Right.'

'Elizabeth wants to know what's going on. She says you don't have friends she doesn't know about.'

'Ah well, this bloke's not a friend, just an acquaintance.' My imagination finally clicks into gear. 'I met him at Richard Slaney's funeral.'

'You weren't supposed to chat to people there!'

'Oh, butt out, Barbie-Boobs! Here, let me talk to Elizabeth—'

'She's not here, and if you call me by that bloody nickname one more time I'll kick you so hard when I next see you that you'll wish you were a tranny on the eve of the op! Now listen, pinhead. I have to check this perv Gilbert because he's calling back at five and we have to make a decision on him – which is why I'm interrupting your snooze. Elizabeth thinks he could be a time-waster because he asked for the cheapest possible slot, and when I told him the price for the wake-up wank—'

'Let me stop you right there,' I interrupt, managing to sound

146

brisk and businesslike in six authoritative syllables. 'This has got to be a wind-up. Give me his number and I'll set him straight.'

'I told you, he's calling back, wouldn't leave a number. Why are you so sure it's a wind-up?'

'He's a social worker. They never have any money.'

'Oh shit! Okay, no need for you to be involved, we'll switch him off right here at the main.'

The call ends but I go on sitting on the edge of the bed. The last thing Elizabeth needs to hear is that I met Gilbert Tucker at the house of Carta Graham, fundraiser for St Benet's, and later gave him a freebie to compensate for a gay-monster act. I've got to get hold of Gil to make sure he keeps his mouth zipped – and what the hell does he think he's doing anyway, contacting my office? After the freebie he himself admitted he could never afford to pay to see me.

Abandoning all hope of another snooze I go downstairs and dig out the phone book. It only covers Central London so if he lives outside that golden perimeter I won't find him, but I don't think he's the suburban type. After he confessed he was a social worker I asked him which area he covered and he said: 'Shoreditch' – which was a plausible enough reply as there's a fair amount of local authority housing north of the City – but his slight hesitation in replying made me doubt he was a social worker. My guess was that he was a doctor, a professional who had to be careful of his reputation. Or he might have been a lawyer, not the usual City fat-cat but one of the dedicated band who work for peanuts to help the disadvantaged.

I reach the list of Tuckers in the phone book. There aren't many Gilberts around nowadays, so provided he's not listed just as 'G. Tucker' he should stand out like a beacon – and he does. Or someone does. 'Rev Gilbert Tucker' is listed as living at St Eadred's Vicarage, Fleetside, EC4, but of course this can't be Mr Pass-for-Straight who has at least two blatantly gay pals.

Or can it?

The Church of England at present is all screaming misogynists and squealing earth mothers as the ordination of women issue comes up for the final debating round in November's General Synod, the dog-collar parliament. I know this because I read *The Times*. I also know, since I'm in touch through my clients with gay views on topical subjects, that there are a few clergymen who are brave enough not just to come out as gays but to oppose the anti-women

147

lobby because they're opposed to all forms of discrimination. This seems like an attractively ballsy stance on the one hand, but pretty damned naive on the other. First there's the outing question: out yourself by all means but don't expect to win any Brownie points later when you're pushing your pet cause. I mean, any gay who opts to be a clergyman (and no one's twisting his arm) is seriously off his trolley if he thinks the huge non-gay majority is ever going to prefer him to a plonker with a wife and two kids.

And second, there's the women priests question itself: if the gay clergy now support women in the hope that more toleration will come their way, they've got their wires crossed, because although the gays' cause and the women's cause may look similar, the similarity's an illusion. Women constitute half the human race, and a woman is a woman is a woman – unless it's some sort of herma-phrodite or an athlete pumped full of the wrong hormones, but there are medical tests available to determine whether these popsies can still be called female. On the other hand, how on earth do you define what's gay? There's no medical test, and although there are lots of theories about what causes homosexuality, no one knows for sure, just as no one knows for sure how many gays there are. How can they be sure when people have such wildly differing ideas about what constitutes a gay? And don't ask the activists. They're the last people who'll give you a straight (excuse the pun) answer.

In some cases there has to be a genetic component to homo-sexuality, that's obvious. But what exactly switches it on? And does it sometimes stay switched off because it's muzzled by cultural condi-tions? And anyway, what about the cases where the genetics factor isn't an issue? I've had clients like Richard, who insisted he was born homosexual, but I've also had heterosexual clients who took it up in the services and got a taste for it, and clients who are happy to be straight but fancy a man a couple of times a year for a treat. Oh, and while we're on the subject of the hard to classify, don't let's forget the pervs who are bored with women and get into same-sex shenanigans for a buzz – they don't really care what they fuck, they're just into holes of any kind. The activists, both gay and straight, would say all these thrusters are gay, exhibiting their inborn immutable orientation. But are they?

The trouble with the activists' claim that homosexual behaviour always springs from an inborn sexual orientation is that it doesn't match the evidence. Mark you, I'm not saying there's no such thing as orientation. Obviously there is. But the point I'm making is that orientation is a lot more shadowy, flexible and mysterious than people think. I mean, we're talking about the human brain which controls the human body, and the human brain's a plastic sort of arrangement, capable of amazing adaptation as well as enormous variety. How else can you explain the non-eunuch celibates who have deliberately chosen to live with no sex at all? If any group can testify to the power of the brain over the sex organs, these weirdos can! And if the brain has the last word here, why shouldn't some straights opt to be gay occasionally if the fancy takes them? And vice versa? The truth is that sexually nothing's impossible and that's why categorising people as either STRAIGHT or GAY is too often just totally unreal.

This rigid concept of orientation, which both gay and straight activists rely upon to keep them in business, is one of the reasons why the activists can't stand people like me. I'm the living proof that they've got their jockstraps in a twist, although it's more than their political lives are worth to admit it. Not only can I testify to the extreme diversity of my clients, but my own working life proves that sexual behaviour can have nothing to do with sexual orientation.

I've never had any doubt that I prefer being straight. I know that if I was offered the choice of a man or a woman I'd always choose the woman – and don't think I'd turn her down if she looked like the back-end of a bus. The back-enders are often absolute furnaces (starved of the opportunity to blaze) and touchingly grateful (never spoilt for choice). Bring on the girls in any shape or form is what I say! Yet the fanatics insist my lifestyle means that deep down I've got to be gay no matter how much I protest that I'm not. But I never protest. Can't be bothered. If people want to think I'm gay, let 'em. I know which way I like my bed to bounce, and that's why I'm relaxed enough in my head to feel mellow towards the gays I like. (Naturally I'm not going to feel mellow towards any bloke, gay or straight, that I don't like.)

Of course some dyed-in-the-wool sexual classifiers would insist I was bisexual, but bisexual means getting equally turned on by both sexes, and that's not where I am at all – as far as I'm concerned, male chests, waists and legs don't even get to first base in the erotica stakes. Still, I appreciate the fact that my clients need to believe I'm turned on. That's why when I'm with a client, whether I like him

149

or not, I act my socks off and try to serve up an erection even if it's not strictly necessary. Well, of course I do, I'm a professional, I take pride in my work.

Which leads me to admit this: despite my orientation, servicing gays isn't a sexual non-event for me. How could it be? Whatever our orientation we all have erogenous zones which could be manipulated successfully by a well-programmed robot. It doesn't really matter who's doing the manipulating. You prefer, of course, that you're not having it off with Godzilla, but if you are you can always close your eyes and dissociate – or at least I can. Mental control like this also helps to prevent orgasm (a serious waste of energy) and enables the body to be unfettered by physical revulsion. Why do I like opera? Because it's noisy enough, when I play it in my head, to drown out all the grunts and groans and squeals and squawks of pushbutton sex, that contact sport which, like rugby football and sumo wrestling, is an acquired skill and nothing to do with sexual orientation at all.

At this point my thoughts turn back to the Reverend Gilbert Tucker, who no doubt thinks sexual orientation is always inborn, immutable and inextricably wedded to sexual behaviour. If he is a clerical gay activist – and I hardly think he'd be bumming around with those two in-yer-face types if he wasn't – I salute him for his guts in coming out yet I groan at the thought of him committing professional suicide in the name of some starry-eyed concept of gayness which doesn't match the reality I know. In fact as I visualise Gil playing Mr Valiant-for-Truth, awash with idealism, I'm groaning so hard that I can only hope the Christians don't crucify him. He's too nice a bloke for such a grisly fate, that's for sure – but now it's time to face the fact that even the nicest bloke should be kept right out of my life if he has St Benet's connections.

I punch out the number of his vicarage.

The bell rings four times. I'm just trying to work out a message for the answerphone when the receiver's picked up and Mr Valiant-for-Truth says: 'Gilbert Tucker.'

'Gil, it's Gavin Blake. Listen, mate, what the hell are you playing at, calling my office?'

He takes a deep breath. 'I decided I did want to see you again after all, and I knew that this time I'd have to go through the proper channels.'

'Yes, yes, yes, but—' Running my fingers through my hair I try

150

to keep cool. 'Okay, let's get a couple of things straight. One: don't tell anyone at the office that I gave you a freebie. And two: for God's sake don't say we met at Carta's house. The story has to be that we met at Richard Slaney's funeral.'

'Who's he?'

'Oh God . . . Right, let's get our heads together on this. Richard Slaney, that's S-L-A-N-E-Y, was a lawyer who worked for Carta's old firm Curtis, Towers. He died of a coronary and his funeral was at Compton Beeches near Andover a few weeks ago.'

'Got it . . . Gavin, it's so good to hear you! I suppose you got my phone number from the book, but what made you so sure I was the Gilbert Tucker living at St Eadred's vicarage?'

'There weren't any other Gilbert Tuckers queueing for my attention, but don't worry, I'm not grassing you up to the Bishop of London. Look, I thought you said you couldn't afford me?'

'I've just inherited a legacy from an aunt.'

'Don't make me laugh! Gil, I don't understand why you want to go down this route, I really don't – you're a nice-looking bloke, you're out, you could get it for free anywhere, so why buy a sliver of my time at a rate you can't afford?'

'You're worth it.'

'I know I am, but—'

'I want to get to know you better.'

'I'm flattered, but as I said after we did the freebie, *I can't have a relationship with you.* If you're booking a slot in the hope that it'll—'

'At least if I book a slot I get to see you again!'

My forehead's damp. I'm pushing a hand against it as I suppress my impatience. 'Okay,' I say flatly, 'let me help you get real here. The truth is that my manager's unlikely to take you on as a client because you don't earn enough.'

'Thanks to my late aunt I'll have a private income.'

'Gil, just *listen*, would you, and stop feeding me these pathetic lies! You can't be a client and I can't be a chum you chat to at weekends!'

'But surely at weekends you can see who you like?'

'Right. That's when I shag women.' I never usually rub a gay's nose in this fact but I can think of no other way to get him to back off.

'Don't be ridiculous!' says Gil laughing. 'Who's telling pathetic lies now?'

This was worse than teaching a mermaid to walk. 'Gil,' I say, making one last effort to reach him, 'you've got to wise up or you'll get hurt, and believe me, that's the last thing I want – I want to think of you tucked up snugly in your vicarage with a nice-natured, church-going soulmate who thinks paying for sex is something that happens on another planet. So why don't you just forget about me and—'

'I'm going to bust a gut to book that slot!' declares the Christian martyr, begging to be thrown to the lions, and hangs up, leaving me feeling not just exasperated but queasy at the thought of him talking to Elizabeth.

*   *   *

I sit brooding on the conversation for a moment before deciding that there's no need for me to go on feeling queasy. Gil will serve up the right story, Elizabeth will turn him off and that'll be that. Gil will mope for a while, but I can't get involved. One of the reasons why I'm so successful at what I do is that I stay detached from my clients' emotional demands. Most of them just want a physical release, but there are always some who almost beg to have their hearts broken. I try to be kind, but I can't afford to get churned up in my line of work, and detachment is the big advantage of screwing across your orientation. Emotions are kept safe in a fire-proof compartment and the clients become just objects which require skilled handling.

Elizabeth explained all that when she converted me to the idea of servicing gays. That was after Norah kicked me out of the escort agency. I didn't do gays when I worked for Norah. My job was to go out with women who were twenty or thirty or even forty years older than I was, and I couldn't stand it. I felt so sorry for them, so humiliated on their behalf, so angry that they should be so desperate. In other words I got emotionally involved, and once I was upset I couldn't shag properly – well, I was a low-grade shagger anyway before Elizabeth trained me.

When I wound up a failure as a hetero-escort, Norah stopped employing males because (she said) she was fed up with temperamental masculine equipment. (Typical lesbian cattiness! Strictly speaking our equipment was none of her business anyway – what makes an escort agency legal is that in theory it's just peddling

152

companionship, and whatever sex takes place is supposedly a private matter between the client and the escort, but that's the kind of legal set-up which can be bent as easily as a stick of chewing gum, particularly when the stick's being chewed by someone like Norah.)

However, she was probably right to get rid of the younger of my two male stablemates. He was straight but a psychopath, all charm and no heart – Norah was lucky he didn't start cutting up the clients. The other bloke was much nicer – a good-hearted bi with not much upstairs – so his sacking made less sense. He was only doing escort work to finance his mother's hip operation, poor sod . . . I must say, one thing the leisure industry's taught me is how diverse human beings are and what a huge, sprawling, exotic, fantastical canvas we're given as a background to our pathetic little efforts to get through life as best we can. If there is a God – which of course there isn't – what a vast painting the old man's working on as he lolls in front of the canvas with a brush in one hand and a can of Australian lager in the other! Forget the pearly gates and the Elysian fields. Heaven's a jumbo art studio with gallons of paint stacked all over everywhere and maybe a music system which plays non-stop opera by Mozart to keep God sane.

I sigh, marvelling that a random thought about my failure as a hetero-escort should have led to this nutso vision of an artist-God sloshing away at a mega-canvas while getting himself trolleyed. Then I stop daydreaming and focus on the job.

The final shift of the week's looming and with it comes the big challenge: for some time now I've been psyching myself up to pitch my fundraising spiel to Mr Moneybags, Sir Colin Broune, in the hope of landing a vast donation to my snow-white Christian cause.

If there really is a God out there who's splashing away drunkenly at that messy painting of his, he should bloody well give me a can from his current crate of Australian lager.

* * *

Okay, it's a risk tapping Colin for money when Asherton wants to recruit him for GOLD, but it's only a slight risk, like that statistic airlines trot out when they want to convince nervous flyers how unlikely it is they'll get killed. The low risk is because Asherton's going for Colin's private wealth but I'm going for a corporate donation, and Colin can certainly afford to shell out to both of us. And

153

he'll keep quiet about my fundraising, no problem, I've built up a good relationship with him over the last few weeks.

I still haven't managed to find out anything about his metaphysical interests, but Elizabeth understands that some clients take longer than others to reveal their private beliefs, and although Asherton's simmering with impatience he knows that too. When I first started recruiting for GOLD I said to Elizabeth: 'Supposing the client doesn't have any beliefs?' But she said everyone believes in something, everyone has a world-view, and even a determination to believe in nothing is itself a belief which can be just as dogmatic as the beliefs of any religious fundamentalist. And as time passed I found that my clients did all believe in something, even if it was just the mystique of the Dow Jones or the magic of the Footsie or, as in Richard's case, the power of sailing to soothe the soul. Nobody was wandering around the City of London with their minds as belief-less as a blank slate, and although not all people had beliefs which made them suitable candidates for GOLD, none of them could be instantly disqualified as a metaphysical write-off.

So I know Colin has to believe in something, and today's the day I hope to find out what it is. We can hardly discuss a Christian cause without getting kind of metaphysical.

Picking the right moment with exquisite care I mention casually, after a natter about winter holidays, that if he's worrying about where to dump his corporate donation this Christmas I know an unusually worthy City cause.

'I'm not a Christian,' says Colin as soon as he realises I'm talking about a church. 'I was trained as a scientist. Religion and science aren't compatible.'

Now it just so happens that this is a subject I know something about. After Hugo died I switched to the science subjects at school so that I could read medicine later at uni, and although science bored me rigid I made it bearable by studying the history of science. This I found fascinating. I can't now remember anything about the science I learned but I can still remember that chunk of history I picked up, and when Colin makes his careless statement that science and religion are incompatible I know I can make him think again. I also realise I've finally uncovered the reason why he's so reluctant to disclose his metaphysical interests: he's old-fashioned enough to think no decent scientist should have any.

'Not compatible?' I say politely. 'Really? Then why did scientists in the old days see nothing weird about being devout Christians?'

'Ah, but that was before Darwin! Nobody could believe in God after reading *The Origin of Species*.'

'But they did, Colin. A lot of clergymen were delighted with that book and thought it totally compatible with their religious faith. And so did a lot of scientists.'

'But after Huxley wiped the floor with Wilberforce in that famous debate—'

'Who said he wiped the floor with him? Did you know there's no written record of that debate and that directly afterwards no one behaved as if Wilberforce had been used as a floor-cloth? Huxley's victory may not be quite so conclusive as you think – have you read any history of science, Colin?'

'I'm a chemist, boy, not a historian, and I didn't come here to be bloody lectured! Massage my left shoulder again, please.'

I sweat away, pounding the blubber so that he shivers in ecstasy. Let no one deny I deserve every penny I earn.

'So what's all this about St Benet's?' says Colin at last, unable to resist his curiosity.

'Well,' I say as he shivers again with blubbery delight beneath my fingers, 'let's put the religious crap aside for the moment and focus on the hard facts here. I'm tipping you off about this place because the word on the grapevine is that it's *the* good cause to be associated with in the City at the moment – a real charity hot ticket. That's because with one donation you nail a lot of high-profile bases: the medical profession, who have sanctioned the church's Healing Centre by allowing a doctor to operate a branch of a National Health practice there; the City livery companies, many of which have also given the Centre support and encouragement; the Royal Family – the president of the Appeal's none other than—'

'What's the money going to be used for?'

I've got this down pat. I've not only written my own summary of the Appeal brochure but I've rewritten it into a spiel designed specifically for Colin and memorised it so that I can spew it out word-perfect, even when I'm stark naked astride him and massaging his shoulders with baby oil. Later I'll give him a brochure from the stack I swiped from the church so that he has something to jog his memory, but right now the pitch is custom-made.

I start to spew on cue but Mr Moneybags, playing the Big Hitter, interrupts me by barking: 'What's in it for you?'

'Nothing!' I declare as a vision of Golden Girl flashes past my eyes. 'Are you implying I'm such a scumbag that I'm incapable of supporting a charity for the best possible reasons?'

'No, of course not, you silly boy! But I can't help wondering—'

'Colin, you're still not getting it. There's no question of *you* doing *me* a favour by arranging a corporate donation here – *I'm* the one who's doing *you* a favour by tipping you off about this big chance to look good and do good by supporting the hottest charity in the City!'

'Yes, but—'

'Look, we're talking complementary medicine here, not alternative medicine, and no one's suggesting science is in any way compromised. Okay, I know so-called "healing" is a playground for conmen, but *that's what makes St Benet's so special*! It's respectable, it's honest, it's sanctioned by the Archbishop of Canterbury! And it's not just run to benefit Christians, it's run to benefit everyone – without charging fees!'

'Sounds most unlikely.'

'That's because it's the real thing, uncorrupted and unperverted!'

'What real thing?'

'Christianity. Healing's the kind of thing Mr Superstar did before the word "Christianity" was invented and the Church clunked into action.'

'Mr Superstar, as you call him, was just one of hundreds of Jewish prophets who wandered around Palestine at that particular time!'

'Yeah, but he's the only one we still talk about, isn't he? And why? He never went to college, never took a management course, never did a doctorate, never wrote a book, never made his first million before he was thirty, never got a PR firm to do an image makeover, never even got married and had two-point-three kids. He just dropped out, bummed around, schmoozed with scumbags, spoke his mind and snuffed it horribly soon afterwards. So why are you and I, two non-believers, still talking about him two thousand years on? Because he was a great spiritual leader who changed the world, that's why – oh, face it, darling, be honest! The Bloke must have had *something*, and this is the something that's alive and well today at St Benet's. You won't look stupid if you support this cause, believe me. You'll look discerning. Wise. Caring . . . which of course, as I know very well, you are.'

There's a long pause while Mr Moneybags reviews my pumped-up performance but in the end he only says gruffly: 'I like to hear you call me "darling".'

I can't believe I'm hearing this. The one word in my entire speech which is totally phoney turns out to be the one word which rings bells for him.

'Where you're concerned I certainly think of myself as caring,' he mutters throatily. 'I care for you very much. And I hope you're starting to care a little for me.'

This speech is clear-cut evidence that 'caring', in the form of an unwise infatuation with a leisure-worker, can seriously damage your brain cells.

'Of course I care for you, Colin,' I say, taking advantage of his prone position and averted face to glance at my watch. I've made my pitch and now I must move on. How much time do I still have to fill? The double-slot's a big yawn when I'm paired with someone who'll never be up to much in bed, but I've been patiently teaching him some basic moves in order to stop myself dying of boredom.

As I guide him into the first of these moves he's in bliss. It's sort of touching to see how little can make this funny old fart happy, and I have one of my moments when I feel I really am performing a valuable public service.

'Gavin.'

I refocus. 'Yeah?'

'If I promise to give the St Benet's Appeal very serious consideration, will you come to the opera with me?'

I've been expecting this response and I've already decided it's worth giving in to him in order to nail the money. 'Well,' I say graciously, although I can't stop my heart sinking at the thought of escort work, 'if this is something you really, really want to do—'

He swears it is. 'I don't mind what I pay,' he adds. 'Money's not important. The important thing is for us to have the chance of extending our friendship beyond the four walls of this room.'

Poor sod. As I said, some clients practically beg to have their hearts broken, but what can I do? I'm not being paid to say: 'Get a life!' or: 'Get therapy!' and I never promise them love or a relationship. So if their hearts get ripped I'm not responsible, am I? I'm not my brother's keeper, for God's sake! And these blokes aren't my brothers anyway. They're just strangers who bring their bodies in for servicing.

'I'll talk to Elizabeth,' I say. 'I'll make it clear I'd like to go to the opera with you.'

Now that he's got my consent Colin allows himself to get grumpy.

'Can't think why you let that woman interfere so much in your life! Why can't you look after your business interests yourself?'

'They're too complicated.'

'Then why have such a complicated life? Why not let me make it simpler? I could set you up in your own flat and make sure you find a decent job!'

I want to run for cover but I take care to look overwhelmed by his generosity. 'That's really good of you, Colin, but I couldn't possibly live off you like that! It's a question of principle.'

'*Principle?*' He levers himself up onto one elbow and stares at me. 'You lead this deeply immoral life, seeing God knows how many men every week, and you talk to me about *principles*? I'm offering you love and a decent life. Are you seriously trying to tell me that the life you currently lead is morally preferable?'

I'm winded by this ethics fanatic who's just stepped out of the closet. 'Colin, I didn't mean to imply—'

'Everyone should seek to lead a moral life in order to help their fellow men and contribute to social stability! The desire to live morally isn't confined to the major religions, you know!'

'Of course not!'

'And I'm not one of those scientists who think asking metaphysical questions is a waste of time – it's *religion* that's the waste of time, but so long as one's not in the laboratory one can and should ask oneself questions about the value and meaning of life!'

'Absolutely!'

'And please note that *I'm not talking about religion*! I'm talking about having an inquiring mind and a passion for truth!'

'Right!' Funny how these violently anti-religious people can't call their religious interests religious. They remind me of gays too terrified of being ridiculed to do anything but call themselves straight.

But I've certainly hit the jackpot with Colin today – I've made a successful pitch for St Benet's and I've uncovered the information Asherton wants. It doesn't matter that Colin, with his high view of morality, is obviously unsuited to GOLD. All that matters is that I've done my job, and now all I've got to worry about is how to jack up the amount when he begins to talk about the donation. Of course he's bound to try to get away with giving next to nothing . . .

*   *   *

As soon as Colin leaves I prepare for my dynamite date with Golden Girl. Thank God I wore one of my Armani suits to work today! (Colin likes me to start my striptease sleaze dressed to kill.) In no time flat I'm telling myself I'm looking great, but I must stop the confidence-boosting routine and hit that wine bar before Carta does. I don't want her snaffled by some City hit-and-run villain on the make.

One-for-the-Money is part of a chain of wine bars designed for the under-thirties, which means it's large and lavish with a ballsy buzz. I shagged the owner of the chain for a while earlier in the year and he told the manager at the branch near Austin Friars that Mr Gavin Blake was always to get the red-carpet treatment whenever he showed up. So tonight I say to the boss-man: 'Hey Darren! I got lucky with a blonde class-act – how about a corner table upstairs?' because I know he keeps the upstairs corners free till seven for favoured customers. He sends a waitperson off to check there's a RESERVED sign on the best table, and I loaf around waiting, eyeing the female legs crossed at various angles as their owners chatter on barstools or chirp on chairs.

In glides Carta, looking very wary. I'd forgotten she's a little older than I am and might well think this hyper-today swill-joint's beneath her, but after I escort her upstairs to the special table she soon starts to unwind.

A fawning waitperson takes her order for a couple of glasses of champagne.

*   *   *

'Shall we get down to business?' she says, cutting short the small-talk about City watering holes after we've had our first swig from the glasses. She's sitting slightly sideways in order to cross her legs, and her ankles are so exquisite that I'd like to slip a gold anklet around each one – after kissing each toe and running my tongue along the sole of each slim little foot. I'm not normally into feet but for the first time I can see the attractions of a career as a chiropodist.

'Gavin, are you listening? I'm saying I want the truth here! Have you been fundraising for St Benet's?'

I snap to attention. 'Yes, ma'am!'

'Prove it. Name the three recent donors who all claimed to be friends of Richard's.'

'Sorry, ma'am, but I never reveal the names of my clients. Let me

159

tell you the exact sums instead.' I reel off the figures and add smoothly to seal my triumph: 'Oh, and don't let's forget Moira! She's promised you she'll come across with the twenty thousand, hasn't she?'

Carta looks gobsmacked but finally manages to say in an awed voice: 'So it's true. You really have been raking in thousands and thousands of pounds for us.'

'Yes, ma'am.' This is my golden moment and I'm savouring it. I've sweated and slaved and shagged for this moment when Carta has no choice but to look at me with respect. I'm no longer a slime-ball. I'm a successful fundraiser. I count. I matter.

Carta's certainly looking at me now with respect but she's still shattered. In an urgent, earnest voice she asks: 'But why did you do it? I mean, I accept that you wanted to impress me but that can't be the whole answer – why should you go to such enormous trouble when all that's at stake is a bout of recreational sex with a woman who's never given you the green light?'

I take another swig of the Froggy-Fizz. As a matter of fact I'm not a big champagne fan, and after the kind of day I've just had I'd have preferred to down a lager, but I don't want her to think I'm yobbish. 'Well, to be honest,' I say, looking her straight in the eyes, 'I thought I owed you something. I've been bloody offensive, I know, coming on too strong and making a nuisance of myself, so I wanted to show you I do have my acceptable side. I thought if I did that we might manage to be friends. Platonic friends, I mean. Obviously. Of course I realise Eric's got the prior claim.'

She looks at me and I look at her and she goes on looking at me and I go on looking at her. I'd like to say this is a romantic gazing on both sides, but it's not. It's the intent stare of two street-wise people locked in a verbal wrestling match.

At last she says: 'There could be some grain of truth in all that, but the ending was pure fantasy. Try again.'

'Forget it, sweetie, just unscramble your brains and beam in on this: the money I've sent your way so far is just an appetiser and I've got one hell of a main course now cooking in the oven!'

Her eyes widen. 'But in that case I've just got to understand your motivation!' she cries. 'Don't you see? How do I know you won't turn around and sell your story to the tabloids?'

'Wow, brilliant – what a fundraising coup! Can't you just see the headlines? "CHURCH BOOSTED BY SIN: 'I SHAG FOR GOD,' SAYS CITY SUPERSTUD"!'

'Gavin!'

'Oh come on, Frosty-Puss, don't be so dumb! I don't want that kind of publicity any more than you do – I'd never work in this town again!'

She sees the logic of this but she's still worried. 'All right,' she says, getting her act together, 'I do trust you not to sabotage us, but I've just got to have a conference about this with Nicholas. Don't get angry – I think what you've done's terrific, but every fundraiser should consult the boss if the situation's in any way unusual.'

I nod gravely, thinking how attractive she is when she's earnest. I like her nose. It's dead straight, perfectly shaped. And her mouth isn't just a hole designed for oral sex. It's delicate, the upper lip narrow, the lower lip fuller, more curvy. Her teeth are very clean, very even. I like her teeth. I'd like to run my tongue over them and—

'Gavin?'

'Yes, Carta. Of course I understand – you've got to take time out to consult. When can I see you again to get an update on the situation?' We're two businesspeople now, discussing an important project. The conversation's acquired class, style, gravitas.

'I'll call you,' she says, and downs some more champagne.

'Before you rush off,' I say, hoping to spin out the date a little longer, 'how's that nice bloke I met at your house, the one who turned out to be Eric's brother?'

'Gil? I haven't actually seen him since that weekend. His work keeps him very busy.'

Innocently I ask what he does and she offers up his CV as a turbulent priest: the Church authorities had put him in a place where they thought he'd cause the minimum trouble as a gay activist, but he'd promptly raised St Eadred's Fleetside from the dead by deciding it would have a special ministry to Aids victims, a move guaranteed to give his work a high profile. Carta chats on, but I soon get tired of hearing about Gilbert Tucker, plaster-cast saint, who's nowhere near as interesting as the Mr Valiant-for-Truth who's panting to be my client.

'Got a partner, has he?' I enquire blandly.

'He did have one but they broke up eighteen months ago and Gil's determined that he's going to be celibate till he finds another Mr Right . . . It's very hard to be a gay clergyman.'

'I bet! Personally I think that if you work for an organisation and take their pay cheques you should stick to their rules or quit.'

161

'The situation's more complicated than you think,' she says quickly, more serious than ever now and dripping with that kind of moist-eyed sentimental liberalism that always manages to transform me from a tolerant bloke into a butt-kicking bastard. 'There's no bar to homosexuals becoming clergymen, but they're supposed to be celibate. Well, in the old days they *were* celibate, but nowadays when we live in such a very different culture—'

'If they did it in the old days they can do it now – or are they on some kind of decaying evolutionary trip the scientists don't know about?'

'Okay, sneer away! But let me just make it clear that Gil's totally opposed to promiscuity. He's in favour of long-term monogamous relationships, and he's campaigning for gays to be allowed to have a sanctified contract on a par with marriage so that they have something good to aim for, just as straights do.'

'Oh, puh-leeze! Has it never occurred to you and the saintly Mr Tucker and all the other wet liberals who want to slobber over gays that a whole load of these blokes have no desire whatsoever to ape hetero relationships? They want to carve out their own special gay ones – and that needn't include anything long-term or monogamous at all!'

'And has it never occurred to *you*,' storms Carta, zipping into her role of the Shredder, 'that people who pay for gay sex aren't exactly the dead norm of the homosexual community? How much do you really know about homosexuals, Gavin Blake?'

'More than you'd ever want to know, that's for sure! But I admire the idealistic Mr Tucker's commitment to do without sex. Nice to know there's at least one gay out there who's not balling around begging for buggery.'

She's truly shocked by my relentless political incorrectness. These bleeding-heart liberals are amazing! Do they really have no idea that political correctness is the fashionable fascism peddled by the new thought-police, the I-believe-in-free-speech-and-if-you-don't-agree-with-me-I'll-kill-you loonies?

'*Gavin!*'

'Look, dream-crumpet. I've actually got a lot of sympathy for gays, specially the good blokes like Gilbert Tucker. But my sympathy has its limits and I refuse – *refuse* – to view them through rose-tinted spectacles. They're just ordinary human beings like us straights and they get into messes and do shitty things just as we

162

do. I mean, would *you* make it a point of honour always to view straights through rose-tints? Of course you wouldn't! It's a question of truth, isn't it – or at least it should be, but what does political correctness know of truth? Fuck all!'

But she can't take this. Funny how today's liberals have so efficiently developed the art of preserving a closed mind that they now seem more bigoted than any conservative.

'What do you know of truth?' she flashes back, all the shredder blades whirling at full speed. 'Your whole life's a lie!'

'How can it be,' I flash back, 'when I'm busting a gut working for a Christian cause?'

Brilliant! I've decked her. This time, thanks to St Benet's, I've managed to smash the shredding machine.

Draining her glass she says flatly: 'I'll call you once I've talked to Nicholas,' and she scoops some money from her bag to hurl upon the table.

I give her my special smile, the one which never fails to make the chicks cheep. 'Thanks for the drink, sweetheart!' I purr, but she just rolls her eyes in exasperation and stalks off without looking back.

*　*　*

I'm not at all unhappy with this conversation despite the verbal punch-ups. The important thing is that she's overcome with admiration for my fundraising. She'll be back in touch, just as she promised, and sooner rather than later. I'm a real person to her now, not just testosterone sludge in designer clothes, and we're the kind of friends who have meetings and important business discussions and even debates on fashionable issues. In other words I'm the sort of person a golden girl would go to bed with, and I'm on course to hit the jackpot.

'More champagne?' says the waitperson, batting its eyelashes at me, but I flick it away and leave. I'm not a big fan of wine bars. Too full of slags of both sexes, and now I'm nearly thirty I'm bored with slags. Which reminds me: can I really be bothered to see escort girl Serena tomorrow night? Yes, I must. If I don't, Elizabeth will start getting suspicious about what I might be getting up to, and as I sweat at the thought of Elizabeth making more clever guesses about a mysterious blonde, I'm reminded of something that happened on the day of the funeral: Carta's weird, ESP-like nailing of the word 'Elizabeth', uttered by me without a second thought, to 'Elizabeth Mayfield', Elizabeth's long-running healer's identity which she junked after the Betz fiasco. How I survived Carta's knock-out response, I'll never know. Thank God I'm a good actor and bloody quick on the draw.

As I pad back to my car I puzzle over this incident again but can only reach the same conclusion I did before. My explanation runs like this: (1) the Betz fiasco is still talked about at St Benet's, and new employee Carta soon hears all about wicked Elizabeth Mayfield, the psychic healer who showed how healing should never be done. (2) Carta reasons that my Elizabeth must also be wicked since she's managing a successful leisure-worker. Therefore (3) my Elizabeth and Elizabeth Mayfield (Carta deduces in the wildest of wild deductions) could well be one and the same person.

I don't think this explanation's the last word in plausibility – unless I start believing in ESP – and I feel I've got to be missing big chunks of information which would show why Carta's behaving like someone with an *idée fixe*. Does Carta automatically think: Mayfield! whenever anyone mentions the word 'Elizabeth'? If so she's more nuts than Pavlov's mutt. Weird.

I want to get to the bottom of this mystery but I can't. Too dangerous. I'm safe at the moment – there's no way Carta could prove my Elizabeth was the wicked lady in the Betz fiasco – and I've got to stay safe by keeping right away from the subject.

My thoughts move on to another potentially dangerous subject as I get into my car and drive out of the garage. I'm remembering Gil Tucker with his lethal St Benet's connections, and I know I've got to make sure he doesn't get taken on as a client. Susanne said she'd switch him off, but she might choose to annoy me by letting him scrape into the wake-up slot after all. And talking of people annoying me, how do I present to Elizabeth Colin's invitation to the opera? As I hate escort work I can't appear too keen or Elizabeth'll smell a rat.

What a life! I loved every second of that time with Carta, but working undercover for St Benet's doesn't exactly guarantee a stress-free existence.

Back in Lambeth at last I open the front door and immediately hear Elizabeth's voice in the living-room. With a shudder I think Asherton's visiting again, but no, she's just talking on the phone.

'. . . oh, here he is now, dear – hang on!' She waves the receiver at me. 'It's Serena!'

I take care to hurry to the phone. 'Serena? I was just thinking of you! Dinner tomorrow night?'

'Mmmm! Where?'

I'm in such a plugged-out state after my complicated day that I can't think of a single restaurant in the West End. 'I'll surprise you!' I say gallantly. 'Pick you up at seven, Gorgeous – big love—' I drop the phone back in its cradle and stoop to kiss Elizabeth. 'Darling! Sorry I'm back late.'

'Where were you?'

I trot out an explanation about bumping into the One-for-the-Money CEO in the street and getting offered a drink at the new branch, but Elizabeth says severely I should have checked with her first. 'Clients should pay if they want to socialise with you,' she says. 'Oh, and talking of clients—' She names the Grunter and says he's dropped out of Tuesday's eight o'clock slot. Then she adds: 'I'm thinking of offering it to this social worker, Gilbert Tucker.'

'Oh, forget him, darling, he's just a time-waster!'

'But is he? And what's all this about you meeting him at Richard Slaney's funeral? I gave you strict instructions not to talk to anyone there!'

'Well, I wouldn't have done but this bloke Gilbert spoke to me. He said he recognised me because some client (he wouldn't say who) had shown him a bunch of my pics and he wanted to introduce himself.'

'But he must move in moneyed circles if he was at the Slaney funeral and knows one of your clients! Maybe he has a private income.'

'No, no – you should have seen his clothes!'

'Just because he wasn't wearing an Armani suit doesn't mean he couldn't afford a wake-up slot! How old is he? I suppose as his name's Gilbert he must be around sixty or more.'

'Yeah, totally over the hill.'

'What's he look like?'

'Short, bald, spectacles, paunch.'

'Well, obviously there's no long-distance mileage in it for us if he wouldn't look good on video, but we could still use him next week as a one-off.'

'True, but—'

Elizabeth suddenly swivels to face me. 'Why don't you want to do this man?'

'Well—'

'Are you keeping something back from me?'

'Elizabeth, you know I'd never—'

'What the hell really happened at Richard Slaney's funeral?'

'Nothing! I told you!'

'You didn't tell me about this man Tucker!'

'That was only because I felt guilty that I'd talked to someone despite your instructions!'

Elizabeth stares at me. 'I think you've become rather slippery lately, Gavin, and I don't like that at all. Jason and Tony both became slippery when they started failing to make the grade, and I don't want you going the same way as Jason and Tony.'

I'm shocked to be compared with my predecessors, the blokes who got fired. I've always been told I'm in a different league from those two. In panic I blurt out: 'Darling, I'll do whatever you want, I swear I will.'

'Then you'll see Gilbert Tucker at eight o'clock on Tuesday morning – and don't you forget to switch on the bloody cameras! I want to see for myself what this man looks like.'

Disaster. 'Fine, no problem,' I mutter, heart sinking as fast as a boulder hurtling down a cliff.

Elizabeth relaxes. She pats her immaculately dyed golden hair which is swept up into a topknot today and allowed to trail elegantly at the sides in tendrils. Her eyes, flounced up by false lashes, are a pale baby-blue.

'All right, pet,' she says, smiling at me. 'Run along upstairs and have your supper.'

Without another word I do as I'm told.

* * *

Nigel has a beef casserole waiting and he serves it with a baked potato and green salad, but I'm too shell-shocked to eat much. Staring down into my lager I wonder when I should confess to Elizabeth that Gil isn't a wrinkled creep of sixty-plus but a nice-looking bloke of around forty.

Nigel looks in to see if I'm ready for dessert. 'You okay, mate? Some tosser upset you?'

'Nah, life's just a bit complicated right now, that's all.' I never tell Nigel too much. It's very tempting to confide sometimes, but

166

it's safer not to. Then I don't have to worry about him.

'Want to watch telly with me tonight?' he's saying hopefully, but I shake my head and he drifts away.

*　*　*

By midnight I've reasoned myself into a better frame of mind. My trump card, I soon realise, is that I've obtained the crucial information for Asherton about Colin's religious interests, and once Elizabeth knows that, she'll forgive me for being 'slippery' over Gil Tucker. So what I've got to do is withhold this trump card until I have to confess I lied about Gil's age and appearance. When do I do the big confession? Best to leave it as long as possible to give Elizabeth time to cool down, so . . . yes, I see how to do this. Colin's next appointment is on Tuesday, the day Gil gets the wake-up slot, and I can claim that *this* is the day when Colin comes clean about his religious interests. It'll all dovetail, I'm sure of it. Happy ending.

At that point I hope I may be able to sleep but no, my thoughts are still racing around producing insomnia. I'm thinking of Carta now, rerunning every word of our conversation. How I wish I was taking Carta out tomorrow night instead of Serena, that college-educated tramp who's dumb enough to think escort work's a dead easy way to earn a buck. Just wait till Norah propositions you, jingle-bells, after softening you up with all this free accommodation, free health club vouchers, free manicures and free kisses from those spooky chihuahuas! If you flunk it at payback time, Norah will sack you and withhold as much of your earnings as she can, and if you object she'll just say: 'Sue me!' and mail your nude glamour-pics to Mum and Dad in Goring, that arch-respectable seaside town they've picked for their retirement. But if you go down the payback route what have you got to look forward to? Money? Sure, but not as much as you've been led to think, and meanwhile it'll be all Sapphic frolics in between the shags with the old men and the pervy foreigners and the drunken businessmen and the sickos who don't give a shit. And after a while it'll become a bit stressful, not much, just a bit, so you'll start boosting your alcohol intake and doing a line of coke every now and then, but very soon the drink will escalate and the coke lines will multiply and gradually your prized bank account will get a moth-eaten look until in the end you're in debt with a dud liver and a duff nose and you'll

167

have a nervous breakdown because no escort agency will take you on and you can't face selling out of your pants on the street. Believe me, Serena sweet pea, the leisure industry's not for wimps and you haven't got what it takes! Stop trying to hit back at Mum and Dad in Boring Goring and get yourself out of Norah's world PDQ . . .

At last I manage to sink into a stupor which has a good chance of ending in unconsciousness, and as the images begin to flicker surreally before my eyes I see the shepherd in fancy dress looking out over the Needles. But the little sheep's not tucked up on his shoulder. I think: where's that little lost sheep that was found? And the next moment I realise I'm covered in white fleece. Then I hear Asherton whisper as he fingers his long knife: 'Time for your shearing, my dear!' and as it dawns on me that he wants to take off not just my fleece but every inch of my skin, the world ends and the sun blacks out and I yell and yell and yell for the help that's never going to come . . .

* * *

A thousand miles away Nigel urges: 'Gav, wake up!'

I sit bolt upright, sweating and gasping. 'I was being skinned by Asherton—'

'It was a dream, mate, only a dream. Asherton doesn't do snuff movies . . .'

I realise I've been yelling loud enough to bring Nigel down from the attic but I'm too traumatised to be embarrassed. Shuddering from head to toe I grab his hand and whisper: 'Dear old friend.'

Then a very strange conversation takes place. Later I dismiss it as a conundrum, but I don't forget what was said. I think I do but I don't.

It starts with Nigel saying: 'Gav, you know I'd do anything for you, don't you? I mean that. I love you.'

I think automatically: yeah, yeah. But I'm so shaken up that I say something else. I mumble: 'Thought you only went for kids.'

'That had to stop. I faced up to it in the end. In the programme I was on in prison the psychiatrist called it "coming out of denial".'

'Didn't think those programmes cured kiddie-fiddlers.'

'You don't get cured but you can get healed, like an alcoholic who makes it in AA. But I had to come out of denial, see, before any of that could happen. I used to say I was doing nothing bad,

168

but finally I was able to stand up before the group and say: "I'm a paedophile and what I did was wrong."'

'Cool.'

'No, just truthful. It's the truth that heals, you see, not the lies you tell yourself to keep going. Denial's like a jail, keeping you locked up in a bad place.'

'Uh-huh.' I decide it's time to get him out of my bedroom. 'Okay, leave off now, Nige, there's a good bloke – I can see you're some kind of hero, but I can't take 'Thought for the Day' in the middle of the night.'

Nigel patters obediently away.

*　　*　　*

Four hours later I'm celebrating Saturday by arriving in Elizabeth's bedroom with the early morning tea. I'm nervous in case she's still displeased with me, but after I've apologised again she says I'm forgiven.

'You do love me, don't you?' my voice says.

'Of course I do, pet! You're very handsome, very sexy and wonderfully amusing and clever,' says Elizabeth indulgently, kissing the tip of my nose. 'Now let's do something really fun today! I feel in the mood for—'

She tells me what she wants.

Setting aside all my worries I focus my whole being on pleasing her.

*　　*　　*

When I bring her breakfast in bed, she's propped up on the pillows and reading *Hello!* magazine. One of the celebrities interviewed consulted her when she had her psychic healing business in Fulham. As I pour out the coffee she idly recalls his sexual problems.

'. . . oh, and by the way,' she adds after laughing at the memories, 'talking of men in the sex-for-beginners class, how did you get on with Mr Moneybags yesterday?'

Casually, very casually I start to butter some toast for her. 'Fine,' I say, 'but he's got it into his head that he has to take me to the opera . . . Marmalade or honey?'

'Marmalade today, I think, dear . . . Well, he'll have to think

169

again. I won't have you overstrained by doing escort work unless it's essential, as I said to Asherton only the other day.'

I do a quick think. It's no good pushing the opera further at the moment or she'll get suspicious. What I have to do is start lukewarm and then become keener when I find out what opera's on offer.

'As a matter of fact,' Elizabeth's saying, still thinking of her mega-pervy chum, 'I'm rather worried about Asherton.'

I'm startled. 'Why?'

'The GOLD rituals are getting iffy. He's importing too much SM – quite against my advice, I may add – and I think there could be a real danger that GOLD might decay into something the vice squad would want to mop up. Such a shame! It's always been a lovely little earner without being iffy at all.'

'Are you going to fight with Asherton on this?'

'One doesn't fight with Asherton, pet. That's not a good idea. One can state one's views as firmly as one wants, of course, but if he takes no notice one simply melts away and follows the example of that sensible gentleman in the Bible.'

'Sensible—'

'Pilate, dear. The hand-washer. I'm thinking of washing my hands by resigning as GOLD's consultant on the occult.'

'But you adore GOLD! You invented it – it's the jewel in your crown!'

'Yes, dear, but I don't adore the vice squad and I simply haven't got where I am by being sentimental. I'll tell Asherton my business interests are expanding and I no longer have time to give GOLD the attention it needs.'

I suddenly see where this proposal's going. 'Does that mean I can give up recruiting?'

'Yes, but we'll have to work up to that gradually so that Asherton doesn't get miffed.'

'But how would you get me off the hook?'

'I'd say you've become so successful that it's silly for you to go on doing piecework.'

My heart gives a great thump of excitement. 'You mean I can retire?'

'From piecework, yes. Now that you're so experienced I'm quite sure you could make big money – even bigger than you make now – as a film star. The other day I was watching that tape you made with what's-his-name, the young Swiss bloke, and I said to Tommy:

170

"We could make more money in this field," I said, "than just running our little export business with these poor-quality tapes." With state-of-the-art video cameras it's easy to make high-quality products, and if I could link up with the right producer to achieve the best marketing opportunities—'

'But why can't we both just retire and—'

'Always grasp golden opportunities, dear! It's the key to making lots of money, and we can't be happy without lots of money, can we? And besides, this would be so different from your present filmed piecework. This is the movie business we're talking about now! This is *art*!'

The phone rings.

'Hullo?' enquires Elizabeth, taking the call, and then she exclaims: 'Oh, it's you! Talk of the Devil.' Covering up the mouthpiece she says quickly to me: 'Asherton, wanting to know how you got on with Mr Moneybags yesterday.' And she adds to him: 'As far as I know there's nothing new but I haven't yet heard the details. Let me check.' Turning to me again she murmurs: 'I suppose there's no little crumb of comfort you can give him?'

Zapped by Elizabeth's porn-film pipe dream, my brain starts to flicker like a faulty light bulb as I once more skim over my options. Should I backtrack on my decision to keep my trump card about Colin's religious interests up my sleeve till next Tuesday? I could use Asherton's help here to pressure Elizabeth into letting me go to the opera. Got to go to the opera to trigger Colin's donation to St Benet's. Mustn't let Elizabeth know I'm keen to go or she'll smell a rat. But on the other hand I still need my trump card to neutralise the mess I'm in over Gil Tucker. On yet another hand I can probably talk my way out of the Tucker mess without a trump card now that Elizabeth's forgiven me. No, wait a moment, since I've kept quiet so far about Colin's religious interests I've already implied to Elizabeth that there's nothing to report – and oh my God, I was totally forgetting that the news I have about Colin means he's of no interest to GOLD anyway – which in turn means Asherton won't give a shit about whether I go to the opera or not. So no, I must keep on keeping my mouth shut – everything has to wait till Tuesday just as I planned, everything, the opera, the trump card, Gil – I can't cope with another scenario now, my metaphorical jockstrap's in such a twist that I'm practically a eunuch.

'What's the matter?' demands Elizabeth.

Shit, I've blown it! Okay, don't panic, keep calm—

'Ash, I'll call you back,' says Elizabeth abruptly and hangs up. 'All right, dear,' she says to me, 'talk. But it'd better be good.'

'Darling, I'm sorry! I just didn't want to give you bad news last night when you were mad at me about Gilbert Tucker, but the truth is Colin's a write-off, not GOLD material at all.'

'Why?'

'He's a strict moralist, hates Christianity and worships science instead – he banged on and on about his passion for truth and his inquiring mind.' I'm on a real knife-edge here as our reconciliation teeters on the brink of the tubes.

Elizabeth stares at me. Then she grabs the phone again and taps out Asherton's number.

'Ash? You're in business, dear. Sir Colin's a seeker with a thoroughly religious temperament and a closed mind about Christianity. What could be more perfect? I'd say he was tailor-made for GOLD . . .'

* * *

I'm still pop-eyed when she hangs up, but I freeze in anticipation of a major slap. No need. She just laughs and kisses me. 'Silly boy!' she says fondly. 'You have trouble spotting the religious temperament, don't you?'

This is true. I've had previous clients who seemed to me to be totally unsuitable yet were pounced on greedily by Asherton. But I really did think that Colin, railing away against religion hard enough to burst a blood vessel, was right out of the GOLD ballpark.

'It's science he worships!' I protest. 'Surely—'

'A very inadequate religion, pet, because it was never designed to be a religion in the first place. The ancient system of religious thought which I've adapted for GOLD is far more suitable for a religious seeker . . . Now, go and run my bath for me, would you, there's a pet, because Asherton's coming over for a blow-by-blow account and he's definitely not someone I want to see when I'm wearing only my negligée.'

I stagger to the bathroom in a daze.

* * *

172

Later when I'm dressed I go downstairs and find Elizabeth in the hall with Tommy, her minder, who lives in the basement flat. Long ago when Norah moved into the Pimlico house and wanted to feel safe from all the nasty men who might try to get in, Elizabeth cast around among the locksmiths and selected well-qualified Tommy. Simultaneously, with her talent for spotting potential even among sewer-rats, she saw endless uses for him. They were never lovers, since Tommy has no sexual interest in females, but he still performs some husband-functions. He fixes things that go wrong in the Lambeth house. He washes Elizabeth's car and waxes it. He mows the little lawn in the back garden. Elizabeth feels he's a useful sewer-rat to have around.

And he has other functions. He installed and now maintains the hidden cameras at the Austin Friars flat. He edits the marketable videos, and when Elizabeth took her mild-porn, medium-porn and dead raunchy photos of me, it was he who turned them into glossy ten-by-eights. He's in charge of replicating the videos which are mailed to our subscribers in the Third World. Tommy made some valuable international contacts back in the seventies when he worked for a major firm of locksmiths at various embassies. Foreign workers like to kill their homesickness with heavy doses of the Western porn that's either banned or hard to get in their own countries.

As I come down the stairs and see him talking to Elizabeth he gives me a wave. 'Hi, Gav,' he says casually, but I just grunt. I hate seeing Tommy nowadays. When I first arrived on the scene he was jealous of me for getting so much attention from Elizabeth, but once Elizabeth had instructed me in gay sex to a commercial level she put away her sex aids and ordered Tommy to give me the required hands-on experience. Tommy automatically threw a tantrum but soon decided it would be more fun to do as he was told. Meanwhile I wasn't arguing – I just wanted to get competent enough to earn a decent living and please Elizabeth, who'd so magically rescued me from the hash I'd made of working for Norah's escort agency. Tommy and I started practising. I got competent. Can't say more than that, it was too horrible.

Tommy's in his forties, thickset, dark, hairy, with a weakness for studded denim. Pathetically macho, he reads magazines on guns whenever he isn't sweating over hard-core porn. He ought to be terminated – and I say that not because he's gay but because he's scum of the worst kind, just as bad as anything hetero.

'I was asking Tommy for the videos of your session with Sir Colin yesterday,' Elizabeth's saying, 'but he hasn't yet picked them up from Austin Friars. Can you pop over and get them, Tommy dear? As it's Saturday there'll be no traffic and it won't take you long.'

The shit-for-brains filth slouches off just as the bell rings and I open the door.

'Good morning, my dear!' says Asherton, all smarmy charm, and snakes forward over the threshold into my home.

*   *   *

'But of course Gavin must go to the opera!' says Asherton twenty minutes later.

We're drinking coffee in the living-room. Elizabeth and Asherton are sitting facing each other in the white leather armchairs while I'm perching on the matching footstool at Elizabeth's side. There's a CD playing softly in the background as if we need to be tranquillised with Muzak, and some ancient American warbler's droning about how he left his heart in San Francisco. Elizabeth adores all that mulch. I suppose it reminds her of her youth.

'I don't want my boy overworked by doing escort duty,' she's saying toughly, but adds: 'He'd need compensation.'

'Of course!' says Asherton, very soothing. 'But surely Sir Colin will be all too ready to pay?'

'I think we'd need some compensation from you too, dear! After all, this'll be a big boost for GOLD, won't it?'

They haggle away, enjoying themselves.

'Well, as Gavin likes opera,' says Elizabeth at last, 'I'll be content with that sum from you, but if Sir Colin wants more escort duty, I'll want more money.'

'Let's cross that bridge when we come to it,' says Asherton, and they loll back satisfied in their armchairs.

'Gavin pet,' says Elizabeth, 'pour Mr Asherton some more coffee.'

'Thank you, my dear,' says Asherton to me, and as the coffee streams into his cup, he remarks to Elizabeth: 'I must say, the thought of Sir Colin's quite whetted my appetite! Are there any other exciting new clients?'

'Gracious me!' exclaims Elizabeth. 'How greedy can you get? A new client did come our way this week, as it happens, but he's got no long-term potential. Poor Mr Tucker's only a social worker, so he's hardly in our financial league.'

Asherton's spoon pauses over the cream-streaked mess in his cup. 'Wasn't there someone called Tucker,' he says, 'who was mixed up in the Betz fiasco?'

'This is a different Tucker,' Elizabeth answers at once. 'This man's Gilbert. The Tucker in the Betz fiasco was Eric, and he was involved with that blonde bitch of a second wife Betz had, the woman who called herself Carta Graham.'

Coffee jerks out of my cup and runs all the way down my sweat-shirt to my jeans.

*   *   *

By some miracle neither Asherton nor Elizabeth pays any attention to this giveaway that I've been zonked. Elizabeth's watching Asherton, and although she must be aware that I'm trying to mop up a spill she's obviously assuming I've just had a routine accident.

It's only when I'm able to draw breath again that I realise how startled Asherton is. That's why he and Elizabeth, immersed in their dialogue, are paying me no attention.

Swinging to face me he demands: 'Is Gilbert Tucker fortyish, tall, dark and good-looking?'

Disaster. All I can think is that I daren't lie again about Gil's appearance or I'll really be up shit creek when Elizabeth sees the tapes of the Tuesday wake-up slot.

Swallowing quickly I mutter to her: 'I'll explain everything later,' and before she can comment I'm saying to Asherton: 'Yes, sir.'

'Well, well, well!' says Asherton with a little smile, and bright-eyed he takes a sip of his coffee.

Meanwhile Elizabeth's grasped my iniquity but she's not going to interrogate me in front of Asherton. Instead she looks straight at him and says: 'You've met this man?'

'I have indeed. Do you remember Bonzo, who was so good at recruiting chickens for me?' (Asherton's not, of course, referring to birds but to the victims in his S&M games, the poor sods who end up in cages in his dungeon.)

'You mean that steroid-junkie who got Aids and popped his clogs? But what's Bonzo got to do with Gilbert Tucker?'

'Well, when I first went to see Bonzo in his Aids hospice he spoke very highly of Mr Tucker, who specialised in visiting people there. Then on a later occasion, just as I was holding Bonzo's hand and wondering how long it would be before The End—' Asherton sighs, perhaps genuinely moved by this creepy picture he's painting '—this Mr Tucker arrives at the bedside and introduces himself to me. He was a very attractive man, which is one reason why I remember him, but there was also another reason why I remember him so well.' As Asherton pauses for full dramatic effect all the hairs stand on end at the nape of my neck. 'Mr Gilbert Tucker,' he purrs, 'is a clergyman in the City with a Guild church not too far from St Benet's-by-the-Wall.'

Instantly I say to Elizabeth: 'I never suspected. He gave nothing away.'

Elizabeth ignores me. She just says to Asherton: 'All right, I'll take care of this. I'll cancel the Tuesday appointment.'

'But my dear, I'm not sure I want that at all!'

'Too bad! I'm not having my boy mixed up with anyone who knows that man Darrow!'

'Aren't you being a touch paranoid? Do you seriously think we need to be afraid of Mr Tucker, a gay clergyman who's been so very, very unwise as to fall for our beautiful boy?'

Sweat starts to prickle on my back.

Elizabeth says: 'I'm not sure what you think's in it for you, Ash, but I'm not doing blackmail.'

'Who said anything about blackmail? You've told me he has no money! But he'd be wonderful fodder for GOLD.'

There's a pause while I feverishly try to work out what 'fodder' means in this context, but at last Elizabeth says: 'He'd know Darrow's the specialist in fighting organisations like GOLD. He'd run to him straight away.'

'Not after I'd finished with him.'

Elizabeth says after a pause: 'If you want to use my boy to hook this fish you'll have to bloody pay.'

'My dear!' says Asherton fondly. 'Did you seriously think that I wouldn't?' He glances at me as if I were no more than a trained animal. 'All right, my lovely – off you go. I want to talk further to Elizabeth about GOLD.'

Elizabeth says roughly, pressing a hand down on my shoulder to ensure I remain seated: 'You don't order my boy about in my house. I give the orders here.'

176

'My dear, forgive me! I'm so excited by the thought of the divine Gilbert that I was quite carried away!'

'Gavin,' says Elizabeth colourlessly, 'wait upstairs in your sitting-room.'

I spring to my feet, muscles aching after being clenched so hard for so long, but I'm feeling nauseous. My head aches and my mouth's dry.

Stumbling upstairs I try to prepare myself for the big scene with Elizabeth.

*   *   *

Nigel's out. On Saturday mornings he takes Elizabeth's car and drives to Austin Friars where he restocks the liquor cupboard and the fridge, cleans the flat and picks up Friday's dirty linen for the laundry service which calls at the Lambeth house. Tommy does the linen pick-up Monday through Thursday when he collects the day's tapes and checks the video equipment. I used to do all the housewife stuff myself, but the more successful I became the more Elizabeth rewarded me by delegating the chores elsewhere and nowadays Nigel's weekend time off doesn't begin until Saturday lunchtime.

So I'm alone as I sit in my living-room upstairs and try to get my brain to work. I feel as if everything's suddenly veered right out of control, and it's not a good feeling. In fact I soon work out that the only way to kill the nausea is to throw up, so I go to the lavatory and stick my finger down my throat. At least I can control my stomach contents even if I can't control anything else.

Meanwhile Asherton's still downstairs, probably viewing the latest instalment of the Colin tapes. I wouldn't have thought there was anything there to amuse Asherton, but I suppose he can't resist the chance to gloat over the big fish while he dreams of GOLD's future bank balance – if he isn't too busy dreaming of Gil Tucker.

I start to feel sick again despite the barf-binge, so I divert myself by marvelling at the coincidence of Carta having a leading role in the Betz fiasco. But I come to the conclusion it's not such a coincidence after all. We're all connected to the City, that tight little area at the heart of sprawling metropolitan London, we're all simmering in the same Square Mile stockpot, and 'coincidence' is just the word which means our lines of connection have suddenly snapped tight.

The only real coincidence here is Asherton knowing Gil, but no, even that's not such a surprise when you think about it. Asherton's in vice, a world where Aids is a big risk, and there can't be many clergymen in London who specialise in Aids sufferers. Yes, we're all connecting, we're all starting to form some kind of horrifying pattern, but does this mean there's a malign designer who's trying to hijack the canvas belonging to the old man with the paintbrush in the sky? Not necessarily. The old man could have just made a balls-up, the way painters do sometimes – but for God's sake, mate, have another lager and bust a brush to put the bloody thing right PDQ . . .

Fat chance. And I'm going mental, imagining anyone's in control of this scene. Shit, what am I going to say to Elizabeth about Gil? Just what the fuck am I going to say?

* * *

'I know it sounds crazy,' I say, 'but he was such a nice bloke and I didn't think he needed all the aggro of being mixed up with me. Besides, it was obvious he had no money and I just couldn't believe you'd want to take him on, even for video sales, when his credit was going to run dry in double-quick time.'

Elizabeth decides to keep calm. Austerely she says: 'I make the decision, not you, about whether or not someone gets taken on as a client.'

'I know, and I'm sorry I've been so off the wall – maybe I was knocked off balance by that funeral.'

'That reminds me, why was Tucker there? What was his connection with Slaney?'

I sweat to be both creative and plausible. 'He gave me the impression he was more connected with Moira than with Richard. He talked about being involved with one of her charity projects, and when he said he was a social worker, it seemed natural that he should be helping her.'

'Why didn't he tell you he was a clergyman?'

'Oh, that's easy to figure! He'd seen my pics, as I told you, and he fancied me enough to make an approach. Of course he wasn't going to admit to being a clergyman!'

Elizabeth has no trouble believing this but she's still bothered by the thought of Gil's job. 'I remember you saying it was Mrs Slaney rather than her husband who was involved with St Benet's,' she says. 'Is there a chance, do you think, that she met Tucker through Nicholas Darrow?'

'Maybe she met Darrow through Tucker. I just don't know. All I do know is that Tucker never mentioned either Darrow or St Benet's and there's nothing to indicate the two blokes are more than just professional acquaintances.'

Elizabeth sighs, relaxing a fraction. 'Well, I'd still prefer you not to see Tucker again, but for the moment I've got to play along with Asherton. I don't want him guessing at this stage that I want to wash my hands of GOLD, but I think he's a fool to mess with someone who must know Darrow – and an even bigger fool to think he can get any mileage out of a bent clergyman! That kind of stuff's so dated now, but he was always fixated on the writings of—' She mentions a name which sounds like Alice Tecroli '—and I can see there's no hope he'll change . . . Is Tucker really such a dreamboat, pet?'

'Maybe he's got some kind of gay allure that I missed.'

'I suppose he must have, or Asherton wouldn't be in such a bloody stupid flutter. All right, dear, let's just get this deal sewn up. You'll see Tucker on Tuesday as arranged, but tell him you can go on seeing him – say you can get him a big discount. Film every session, of course, to keep Asherton drooling.'

'But what's going to happen to Gil when—'

'No need for you to worry about that, pet. You won't be there. Just concentrate on building the sex relationship so that a top-notch duet gets taped. If I give him big discounts on his sessions I want to be sure I get the money back in video sales.'

'I just hate the thought of—'

'Now Gavin, I hope you're not going to get as sentimental about Mr Tucker as you were about Mr Slaney! No more nonsense, please, about him being too nice to be involved with you, and most important of all, *no more lies*. I shall be very angry indeed if you start lying to me again, but you're not going to disappoint me as Jason and Tony did, are you, pet? I really can rely on you, can't I, to be honest with me in future?'

In a rush I say: 'Of course you can, darling, I swear it, no need for you to worry at all.'

She gives my hair a quick stroke and leaves me in a room which suddenly seems coffin-cold.

* * *

179

As far as I can see there's no way I can warn Gil and emerge in one piece. If he now backs off it'll be obvious that I've grassed. At least he's not being recruited as a chicken for that S&M group, but I wish I knew more about what Asherton's planning.

At this point I suddenly realise that in her annoyance with Asherton Elizabeth's let slip a clue. She mentioned a name which sounded like Alice Tecroli and talked of 'using a bent clergyman'.

My brain finally wakes up. The name's actually Aleister Crowley, he lived most of his life in the early twentieth century and he specialised in creepy religion. I know this because Elizabeth's got one of his books on the shelves in her bedroom where she keeps what she calls her 'literary erotica'. I looked at the book once and found it neither literary nor erotic, but it's probably unputdown-able if you're into pseud's-corner twaddle.

I now realise that when Elizabeth was talking of Crowley and a 'bent clergyman' she was almost certainly referring to Satanism and the black mass. I want to laugh out loud but I don't. That's because I know that if Asherton's involved in this kind of guff, the black mass wouldn't be played for laughs.

However, the good news here is that I can now stop worrying about Gil because I'm sure the worst thing that's going to happen to him is that he'll be pressured into celebrating this braindead Satanic rite. That's humiliating for a clergyman, of course, but it's not physically painful, and afterwards Asherton'll shut him up by using the same pressure which he'll use to get him to perform: he'll threaten to send Tommy's edited version of the Tucker tapes to the Bishop of London or whoever's responsible for Gil. Okay, that's not exactly a dream scenario, but at least it's survivable.

Having reached this conclusion I find I'm free to worry about someone else, and my thoughts turn automatically to Colin. I'm not worried about Colin himself. He's a heavyweight hitter and if he doesn't like GOLD he'll slug his way out, but I'm worried about me. Now that Elizabeth knows I've been through a bout of economy with the truth – and now that her St Benet's paranoia's in full flow – I'd be dumb to continue to soak clients for the Appeal. Thank God Colin's donation is the only one in the pipeline at the moment! Maybe I should even turn that off, but no, how can I backtrack on Mr Moneybags now that I've boasted to Carta about the vast amount of cash to come? I've just succeeded in proving to her that I'm a man she has to take seriously. I can't mess everything up by getting cold feet!

But if Elizabeth finds out I'll not only wind up multiple-fucked, cattle-prodded and pulped at the Pain-Palace but I'll lose her, she'll ditch me just as she ditched Jason and Tony, and how would I ever survive if I didn't have Elizabeth to love me? I'd start doing drugs again, I'd slide right back into the gutter, I'd get Aids, I'd—

Shit, all this stress is driving me mental.

I decide I need some music to calm me down, but just as I'm reaching for a CD the stress kicks in again as I remember that I've got to take Serena out tonight.

I think: if I was living in Carta's world I could cancel this date with Serena.

But I live in a world where I can't even choose my girlfriends any more, a world where I'm getting increasingly stressed out and scared shitless, a world where the woman I need to love me now suggests I should stave off retirement in order to make porn movies. How could Elizabeth believe I'd ever want to do that? I want to retire from all this crap as soon as I can! Bloody hell, I'm not in the leisure business because I can't bear to give it up – I'm just in it so that I can make enough money to be free . . .

But meanwhile I'm not only locked up but Elizabeth's talking of increasing my jail sentence.

*　　*　　*

Well, we all get down now and then. That's natural, isn't it? But the successes of this world recover from any bout of minor depression pretty damn quickly, which is why by lunch-time I'm pouring out a glass of wine and reminding myself how lucky I am with my six-figure income and my expensive car and my valet and my Armani suits and all my fans who want to crown me Stunner-Stud of the year.

Life's terrific! I'm fine. One or two problems, sure, but I'll take care of them, and I'll soon succeed in talking Elizabeth out of all that porn-movie nonsense.

I have dinner with Serena, and it's no great hardship to take her along to Austin Friars afterwards for the required shag. The next day's Sunday and she wants a rerun but I make an excuse to opt out. I say I'm going down to the country to see an old friend, and she's too naive to realise I don't have any old friends now. They're all on another planet with Carta. Don't have any new friends either, just shag-fodder I don't want to keep in touch with. I mean, what's the real reason why I haven't updated my clunker of a mobile phone? I don't use it in my work, apart from the occasional calls to the office from my car, and I don't have a social life. At least, not the kind of social life people on Carta's planet have.

I think about that planet. Then I decide to take a look at my old patch there. I can't land on it, but I can glide by in my spaceship. I do this sometimes on a Sunday. Maybe once every four months.

So off I drive to Surrey where I roam around the woodsy lanes. I used to drive past the house where I grew up but I don't do that any more. My parents no longer live there. My mother remarried after my father died. I saw his death notice in *The Times* and later the notice of her remarriage. Later still I checked the phone directory. Her new husband wasn't listed, but even though she'd moved out of the area I knew she'd still make that pilgrimage to Hugo's grave on the anniversary of his death. I used to have this fantasy that we'd meet in the churchyard, each carrying flowers . . . But of course I'd never go there on that day, never, because I know she wouldn't want to see me.

Hugo, who lives in the crevice at the back of my mind, now dances out and starts yelling that I should have been the one to die of leukaemia. He does that sometimes. I usually let him spew out the rage and exhaust himself. Then I can stuff him back in the crevice without a fight.

Back in London I keep Hugo in the crevice by watching telly with Nigel. Nigel's a great telly-companion, never talking too much – except when he tries to tell me his love is totally unconditional and requires no response. (What bullshit!) Anyway he shuts up when I tell him there's no such thing as unconditional love, and we sit peacefully side by side on the sofa as we watch the drivel the channels put out. I'm in charge of the zapper. I zap and zap but Nigel never complains.

Up I get next morning for a new working week. Off I go across London to the City, park the car – shit, I'll have to screw for that space soon! – and trail under the arch into Austin Friars. Maybe it's because I've been meeting clergymen recently, but I find myself staring at the Dutch church there as if I'm seeing it for the first time.

Imagine the Dutch, who contrive to keep Amsterdam the sex capital of Europe, not only having time for Christianity but even keeping a church in a foreign city – and in the financial district, where Mammon rules supreme! And suddenly as I remember the stained-glass window in Richard's church, I'm reminded that The Bloke in fancy dress with the little sheep tucked up on his shoulder doesn't just exist in a pretty stained-glass picture in a village. He's commemorated amidst the sex shops of Amsterdam and the money-factories of London. It's almost as if he's still out there hacking it amidst all the scum and the filth, but of course that's just senti-mental nonsense. He's dead. He's gone. He's history.

But I keep thinking of that stupid little sheep, prancing down the wrong path and getting hopelessly lost. If The Bloke had been a different kind of shepherd . . . But he wasn't, was he? That's the point. He went back. He searched till he'd found the silly animal, and he even carried the little bugger all the way home. Did shep-herds still do that kind of heroic number today? No way! Given the current moral climate the shepherd would probably just say to the farmer: 'Sorry, mate, I'm missing one, can you write it off as a tax loss?' and the farmer would say with a yawn: 'Hell, why not?' and the little sheep would die. No one today would care about some-thing of such minimal value, and The Bloke wasn't around any more to do the job himself. I mean, if he was around there'd be a sign, a hint that something extraordinary was flitting about, but there's nothing, is there? Least of all in a quiet backwater like Austin—

My God, look who's waiting outside my building! She's togged out in a brown suit, very autumnal, very chic. The blonde hair's immaculate, the legs are as dazzling as ever, the feet still make me want to tear off her tights and practise chiropody.

'Carta!' I shout – or I try to shout but I'm so amazed I only achieve a croak.

She glides towards me. 'I'm here to deliver a message from my boss,' she says smoothly with an austere little smile. 'Could you come to a meeting later today at St Benet's? We want to talk to you about all this fantastic fundraising you've been doing for us, and Nicholas said he did so hope you'd allow him to say thanks in person . . .'

CHAPTER THREE

Carta

'Clergy and laity may find themselves caught between con-
flicting ethical principles, which could involve issues of public
interest or private conscience . . . Even after conscientious and
prayerful consideration of the ethical issues involved, some
dilemmas cannot be resolved easily or wholly satisfactorily.'

A Time to Heal
A report for the House of Bishops on the Healing Ministry

I

As soon as I left Gavin at that dreary yoof-boozer on Friday night
I hefted my mobile phone out of my briefcase and called Nicholas.
'Here's some news to make your hair stand on end,' I said. 'Gavin
Blake's screwing for St Benet's. Prostitution's boosting the Appeal.'

Nicholas said dryly without a second's hesitation: 'Nice to know
you've already got the headlines written for the tabloids. How soon
can you get here?'

'Give me ten minutes,' I told him, and began to hurry west from
the bar in Angel Court.

II

'Tell me exactly what happened,' said Nicholas as soon as I was
seated in his study on the ground floor of the Rectory. Lewis had
joined us from his bedsit across the hall, and upstairs in the Rector's
flat Alice was probably turning the oven down low, praying dinner
wouldn't be ruined and wondering why she hadn't married someone
who had a normal nine-to-five job.

'But the knock-out news,' I said, bringing my report to a climax, 'is that the money so far's just an appetiser and there's a huge donation in the pipeline.'

There was an appalled silence before Nicholas said: 'A tall story designed to impress you?'

'It impressed me all right, but I don't think he was storytelling. There's nothing fictitious about the three donations we've already had – or about Moira making good on Richard's promise.'

'Nicholas,' said Lewis, 'we can't possibly take money derived from prostitution.'

I heard myself say: 'I don't think the situation's that simple,' and Nicholas added: 'Neither do I. Obviously we're going to have a big problem with the discernment issue.'

I had been around clergymen long enough now to be familiar with their professional language. Nicholas and Lewis, working in the ministry of healing and deliverance, often referred to 'discernment', which was an abbreviation of the phrase 'the charism of the discernment of spirits'. What this meant, in everyday language, was the gift of weighing up the evidence correctly when deciding whether a situation was pregnant with good possibilities or weighted with bad ones – or, to call a religious spade a religious spade, whether the situation was from God or not from God. (I was shy of using the word 'Devil' even though I knew the word was a valid symbol for the worst kind of evil, something which was very real indeed.)

If a situation was from God the result would be peace, joy, healing, renewal and any number of other life-enhancing benefits. If the situation was not from God, the consequences didn't bear thinking about. This sounds simple but unfortunately the situations requiring 'the exercise of the charism of discernment' were usually so complex that trying to work out whether they were inherently good or bad was immensely difficult, capable of flooring even those with long experience in perceiving 'the work of the Spirit' (religious shorthand for God's current activity in the world). I had already figured that 'the discernment issue' in Gavin's case was likely to drive us all nuts, and Nicholas, seemingly in agreement with me, now sidestepped the temptation to debate the matter at that moment. Instead he said: 'We have to discuss this with Robin and Val – I'll set up a meeting for tomorrow afternoon.'

I opened my mouth to state the obvious but Lewis beat me to it. 'Nicholas, tomorrow's Saturday and Saturday's your day off. Take Alice out somewhere, for heaven's sake, and try to relax for a few hours!'

'But this is an emergency! I'll make it up to Alice on Sunday, but we've got to have this meeting tomorrow.'

Lewis and I looked at each other but realised an argument would be futile.

III

'But I've invited Gil Tucker to lunch tomorrow!' Alice exclaimed when she heard the news. 'You did say you wanted to see him!'

'Yes, but we'll have to cancel. Could you call him to fix another date?'

I saw Alice sigh and I sensed her exasperation. Wondering when workaholic Nicholas would be able to fit another date into his over-crowded schedule, I decided it was lucky Gil was in no need of urgent pastoral care.

IV

'I've been dynamic and planned a surprise for tomorrow!' said Eric, who was waiting for me when I arrived home. 'I thought it would be fun to see some country things like woods and hills and fields, so I've made a reservation for lunch at – what's the matter?'

'I hate to say this, but Nicholas is arranging a big meeting at the Rectory and I have to be there.'

'But tomorrow's Saturday.'

'I know, I know, but an unexpected dimension's surfaced in relation to the fundraising, and—'

'What kind of dimension?'

'I can't say. It's confidential.'

'Are you seeing someone else?'

'*What?*'

'Well, I'm taking such a back seat in your life at the moment that you can't blame me for imagining the worst! What's Gavin Blake doing these days?'

'Still screwing, no doubt, but he's not screwing me.'

The phone rang. With relief I pounced on the receiver. 'Hullo?'

'Carta, it's Moira Slaney. Listen, I think I'm going mad and you're the one person who might keep me sane. Can I drop in and see you tomorrow at around ten?'

'Sure. I've got a lunch-time meeting, but—'

'I'll be gone long before lunch.' She thanked me and rang off.

'Who was that?' demanded Eric.

'Moira, wanting to see me, God knows why, forget her. Look, why are you depressed enough to fantasise about being two-timed? How's the book?'

Eric abruptly subsided on the sofa beside me. 'Beached like a dead whale. I've even been thinking of going back to Norway – if I was there, where my characters were messing around in 1940, the book might relaunch.'

'So why don't you go? Are your cards maxed out?'

'No, but I don't want to build up a big debt.'

'I could give you a loan—'

'No thanks! Why are you so keen to get rid of me?'

'Oh, for God's sake!'

'You've been seeing that hustler again, haven't you?'

Rejecting the impulse to lie yet exasperated by this paranoid badgering, I said shortly: 'Yes, but it was on business. There's a St Benet's connection.'

'Tell me the whole story.'

'I can't.'

'You don't trust me to keep my mouth shut? Well, thanks for the overwhelming vote of confidence!'

'Eric, wait—'

'No, I'm not sitting around here watching you being fixated on Gavin Blake! Give me a call sometime when he's finished trashing you, and maybe – *maybe* – if I'm not too busy with the book, I'll stop by and sweep up the pieces!'

'Eric!' I shouted, but the door slammed and although I nearly ran after him I thought: no.

The truth was that my view of Gavin had undergone a profound shift and I wasn't willing to put up with Eric's uncharacteristically neurotic behaviour any longer. I did feel deeply upset, but most of all I felt angry with him for not giving me support when I needed it.

I started thinking again about Gavin . . .

V

'I decided I just couldn't talk to Nick about this,' said Moira the next morning as we sat looking out through the huge window of my living-room to the church of St Giles Cripplegate. I had poured the coffee and set out some biscuits, but I was feeling very uneasy, not just because she was almost vibrating with tension but because I was sure the subject of Gavin was going to surface – although why she should want to confide in me, when we knew each other so imperfectly, I couldn't imagine.

'. . . and then I realised the person I had to see was you,' she was saying rapidly, well on her way to confirming my worst fears. 'After all, you're the one who knows him.'

Moira was wearing a very smart navy-blue suit and her hair looked as if she had just stepped out of a Knightsbridge salon, but her eyes were bloodshot, hinting at a recent bout of tears or alcohol abuse or both. I noticed that her neck was beginning to assume the crepe-like texture of middle age.

'I'm talking about Gavin Blake,' she added as I kept my face neutral to conceal my knowledge of their affair, and before I could comment she burst out: 'I'm mad about him. We've been seeing each other, but now I think he's trying to ditch me and I can't bear it . . .' She dissolved into tears.

Knowing this extreme frankness to a mere acquaintance could only be the result of emotional agony, I struggled hard to make the right moves. 'Moira . . .' I put an arm awkwardly around her shoulders as I knelt beside her chair.

'I'm sorry . . .' The tears had by this time hardened into sobs and she could barely speak.

I had an inspiration. 'Let me get you some Kleenex,' I said quickly, remembering my own time of being *in extremis* back in 1990. The St Benet's team had passed me God knows how many tissues as I had grappled with the aftermath of my disastrous marriage.

Moira finally managed to mop herself up. Then came the drama of a quick glance in the mirror which revealed the cosmetics disaster, and after I had provided some make-up remover pads for the necessary repairs I asked her if she wanted to switch from coffee to tea. Many were the cups of tea I had drunk at the Rectory in 1990.

'No, for God's sake keep pouring the coffee,' said Moira, making a brave attempt to sound tough, but the next moment she was giving a dry sob and clenching her fists to maintain her self-control. After I had refilled her coffee cup she said: 'Carta, believe it or not, I didn't come here to sob on your shoulder – I came for information. You've been to that flat in Austin Friars, haven't you? Gavin said you went there to tell him about Richard's coronary – and he also said he lives there with a woman, but I've been wondering if he lives there with another man. I believe him when he says he sells gym equipment to health clubs, but as far as his private life's concerned—'

'He doesn't live with another man.'

She sagged with relief. 'Thank God. I didn't want to doubt him, but since he's bisexual—'

'He's not bisexual. He's straight.' I was beginning to feel capable of strangling Gavin with my bare hands.

Moira stared at me. 'Then what was he doing with Richard?'

'Having gay sex.' I took a deep breath as I realised I could no longer avoid the big dénouement. 'Look, Gavin doesn't sell equipment to health clubs. He doesn't live at the Austin Friars flat either. That's just where he works. He lives in Lambeth with a woman called Elizabeth who's his manager.'

'Manager? But what does she manage? And what does he do at Austin Friars?'

'Has sex with gays for money.'

There was a terrible pause before she stammered: 'Do you mean – are you saying he's a—' She broke off and looked away as her mouth started to tremble.

'I'm sorry,' I said, knowing she would never forgive me for being the bearer of such humiliating news, 'but if you came here for vital information, information which will help you make the right decision about what to do next, then I'd be doing you no favours if I lied. Please forgive me if I've mishandled this—'

'God, what a bloody fool you must think I am!' She began to grope her way across the room to the door.

'No, I do understand, I promise! He's so attractive—'

'And I'm so pathetic. I despise myself.' She was moving rapidly down the stairs to the front door.

Realising there was nothing more I could do for her I waited until she had left the house. Then I immediately called Nicholas.

VI

'I'll leave straight away,' said Nicholas.

'But how will you explain—'

'I'll say I've been meaning to call on her for some time – which is true.'

'I don't want her to think I've betrayed her confidence—'

'Leave that to me. You've done the right thing,' he said, and was gone.

I hung up feeling more furious than ever with Gavin, but beyond the fury was fear as I saw how easy it would be to be trashed by him. Of course Nicholas had been right to be sceptical when I had declared after the funeral that I no longer found Gavin attractive. I had realised as soon as I'd seen him at the yoof-boozer that the logic-defying sexual frisson was still there, still waiting for the chance to boot me disastrously off-course.

Forcing myself to set aside the memory of Moira's agony, I began to review the cool, balanced comments I intended to make about Gavin at the Rectory meeting.

VII

The major players in the St Benet's team were due to discuss the case over lunch, but it was one-thirty before Nicholas surfaced at the Rectory after his visit to Moira. Alice had just taken the decision not to delay lunch any longer, and when we all heard the welcome sound of the front door opening she was removing a casserole from the oven.

'Moira's all right,' said Nicholas to me as I hurried out to the hall to intercept him. 'Your name never came up because as soon as she saw me she broke down and told me about Gavin. Her best friend's with her now, but I'll phone her this evening to make sure she's not alone . . . Is everyone here?'

'Champing at the bit.'

Switching from one crisis to the next with an ease born of long practice, he led the way into the main kitchen on the ground floor where his colleagues were already sitting around the large table. As

190

this was to be a business meeting we were not in the Rector's flat, and as soon as Nicholas had taken over the task of dishing out the casserole Alice slipped away upstairs.

'Lewis,' said Nicholas, sitting down in his chair at last, 'would you say grace, please?'

Instantly we were immersed in the familiar, soothing routine: the grace, recalling us to the presence of God; the communal meal, emphasising the Christian tradition of hospitality; the sense of shared goals and ideals which reminded us we were working together not primarily for ourselves but for the God who had called us all, in our different ways, into the Church's traditional ministry of healing. After the distress of the scene with Moira, I finally started to feel more centred.

'Here's what I plan to do,' said Nicholas once Lewis had completed the grace. 'I'm now going to summarise the problem we have at the moment with our fundraising. Then we'll keep silent till the end of this main course while we all think carefully about the complex issues involved. And finally I'll say a prayer for God's guidance and we'll start the discussion. Any questions? Okay, here we go . . .'

VIII

There were five of us present.

Nicholas, out of uniform and wearing the casual clothes he favoured at weekends, was sitting at the head of the table. I sat on his right, and on my right Lewis was busy enjoying one of his favourite pastimes: consuming Alice's cooking. Unlike Nicholas Lewis almost always wore his clerical stock and collar, even on weekends, and today he was wearing them with a tweed jacket and a pair of grey flannel trousers which looked as if they had been bought in the 1950s.

Across the table from me sat Val Fredericks, the doctor who was Nicholas's partner under the Acorn Apostolate, the scheme that enabled a doctor and a priest to work together to heal the sick. Val belonged to a National Health practice based just outside the City, and she was in charge of the branch which operated at the Healing Centre. In a bold salute to weekend leisurewear she was sporting pink denim dungarees, a fluffy blue sweater and large round earrings, each of which supported a complicated pendant of silver and turquoise.

Next to her and opposite Lewis sat Robin, the Healing Centre's psychologist who specialised in counselling. Older than Val though younger than Nicholas, he was in his mid-forties, married with four children. He had an eccentric taste in clothes, and today he was wearing a violet shirt beneath a lime-green sweater while his trousers were pale blue, matching his eyes which were mild yet alert behind his glasses.

Nicholas now embarked on his briefing, and later, after making coffee, he said the introductory prayer which began by stressing that we should listen to one another patiently and respect one another's views. He then asked for God's guidance. At that point we all said a firm 'amen' and looked as if we were reluctant to gauge the temperature of the water by dipping our toes in it, but within seconds Val was exclaiming: 'What a case!' and there was laughter, breaking the tension.

'Where do we begin?' said Robin as the cheeseboard and fruit bowl began to circulate, and Nicholas answered: 'Let me first state the basic principle, which is this: we can't condone prostitution. We can't condone a lifestyle in which the body is split off from the mind and soul and systematically treated without respect – we can't condone, in other words, a way of life which is so contrary to the integration of body, mind and spirit as exemplified by Our Lord Jesus Christ. But, on the other hand, we shouldn't overlook the famous saying which urges us to find a way of going along with the sinner without going along with the sin – we mustn't be so ready to reject the prostitution that the prostitute gets lost in the shuffle.'

'And the discernment issue?' said Lewis as sighs were heaved at the challenge we were being set.

'In my opinion that particular problem's unsolvable at this stage because we don't have sufficient information; we can argue that Gavin represents a booby trap designed by the Devil to blow St Benet's sky-high, and we can argue that this is God moving in his famous Mysterious Way, but we've no way of knowing which argument is right. So let's leave the discernment issue for the moment and focus instead on the three gifts we've already received – this is the first specific issue we have to discuss. Carta, in your opinion is there any way we can return these donations?'

'Not unless we breach Gavin's confidence, send the donors into an embarrassed rage and break all the fundraising rules about not asking donors about their motives.'

'People give for a wide variety of reasons under the guise of altruism,' commented Robin helpfully, 'and plenty of those reasons would look dubious if they were held up for close inspection.'

'But a line has to be drawn somewhere between what we can and can't accept,' objected Val. 'For instance, we couldn't take money from the Mafia.'

Lewis exclaimed: 'Exactly! We can't accept tainted money, and if ever a batch of money was tainted, this batch from Gavin's clients is! How can we be sure it's not only the fruits of immorality but the fruits of illegality as well?'

'Homosexual acts between two consenting adults in private aren't against the law,' I said at once. 'If more than two adults are present an offence is committed but Gavin told me he never did parties.'

Lewis asked: 'But surely the Austin Friars set-up's illegal?'

'Not necessarily. He may well be in breach of the lease but the trouble would be proving it. The flat wouldn't be a brothel within the meaning of the Act. There's no pimp on the premises. As far as I can gather business is done by credit card over the phone by using a number unconnected with the flat, so there'd be no big sums of money lying around to indicate prostitution. For tax purposes Gavin probably claims to be a masseur, and if he receives clients (who make no complaints) for activities which aren't illegal, nobody in authority's going to get excited.'

'The clients are hardly going to complain, are they?' pointed out Val at once. 'He could blackmail them.'

Nicholas turned to me. 'How do we know Gavin's not a black-mailer, Carta?'

'Because we know he's a big success,' I said promptly, 'and he couldn't possibly have achieved that success if his clients believed he wasn't to be trusted.'

'Very well,' said Lewis, 'but even if there's been no blackmail in the sense of extorting money, how do we know there hasn't been blackmail in the sense of exerting psychological pressure to make these donations?'

Nicholas said swiftly: 'Exerting psychological pressure to achieve a certain end can well be legal. It's called advertising – or even fundraising. Let's keep the focus on behaviour we know to be illegal as we try to figure out how tainted this money is.'

193

'I'm sure Gavin's not engaged in illegal activity,' I said in my firmest voice. 'He's okay on the buggery and the gross indecency—'

'Dear God!' muttered Lewis.

'—and he's okay on the prostitution so long as he doesn't combine it with an illegal activity such as soliciting on the street.'

'The trouble is,' mused Robin to the others, 'that although Carta's probably right in saying there's nothing illegal going on here, we can't know that for sure. Prostitution's so often linked to organised crime.'

Nicholas said evenly: 'Carta, it's not as if Gavin's a lone operator. He's apparently part of a well-organised set-up, and this manager of his, Elizabeth, may well have links with criminals.'

'But the fact remains,' I said, trying hard to be patient, 'that Gavin's not breaking the law by providing sex for these donors.'

'There might be a drugs angle,' said Val suddenly. 'How do we know he's not pushing cocaine to these City high flyers?'

'City high flyers don't need to go to a prostitute in order to get cocaine,' I answered shortly, and Nicholas remarked: 'I don't think Gavin's into the drugs scene at all. I saw no sign of it when I met him, and according to Carta he prides himself on worshipping regularly at his health club.'

'Well, if illegal activity isn't tainting this money,' said Robin, 'do we now debate the moral issue?'

'Not just yet – we'll leave the general debate about morality, ethics and everything but the kitchen sink until we've finished taking a look at the specific issues of the case,' Nicholas said, steering us along with a firm hand. 'We're still dealing with the first issue – the money we've already received. Further comments, anyone?'

'I'd just like to hammer home two points to underline my opinion that we shouldn't return the money,' I said. 'One: when we accepted these gifts we had no idea Gavin was involved so we can always say we acted in good faith. And two: we accepted the gifts from men who wouldn't want their connection with Gavin to be known and would probably be deeply upset if they knew we knew about it. Do we really want to go around upsetting vulnerable people?'

'Let's run with that for a moment,' said Nicholas before anyone else could speak. 'If we can't return this money without causing difficulty to others, does that let us off the hook and justify a decision to do nothing?'

Everyone immediately began to talk at once.

Of course we all had different views.

'Okay, let me sum up,' said Nicholas after all the opinions had been batted around. 'Carta thinks the potential damage to others if we try to return the money lets us off the hook of being obliged to return it, Val thinks we're not quite off the hook and the possibility of a return should still be explored, Robin thinks we should stop worrying about the hook and concentrate on the prospect of spurned donors bad-mouthing us with dire results for the Appeal, and Lewis thinks—'

'Lewis thinks,' said Lewis, 'that we should concentrate on doing what's right, not on what's going to make everyone feel most comfortable. The truth is that morally this money is quite unacceptable and the donations must be returned.'

Nicholas held up his hand to quell my wail of protest. 'Lewis, if we do return the money, what's Carta going to say in the letter which accompanies the cheque?'

'Crikey!' said Robin, drawing on some ancient well of schoolboy slang. 'Yes, that question alone is enough to stop a moralist dead in his tracks.'

'It doesn't stop me,' said Lewis. 'Let me ask you a question of my own: why is no one facing the fact that the tabloids could crucify us if we take this money?'

'But of course we're facing it!' said Val irritated. 'The reason why we're all here in the middle of a precious weekend is to face the possibility of meltdown!'

'Then why aren't we discussing whether the press's inevitable response to this moral issue would be justified?'

'Can I just say something?' I intervened as the acrimony threatened to expand. 'There may be no moral issue here at all. Gavin may simply have said to his clients: "Hey, if you're looking for a top City project to support, I can give you a useful tip," and the donors, following up this suggestion, may have decided to give to the Appeal purely on its merits as a charitable cause which fits their requirements. And if that's the way it happened, how can we say their donations are immoral? People often hear about charity projects by word of mouth. Are we to start distinguishing between respectable mouths and non-respectable mouths? Or enquiring whether the tip was given in the bedroom or the boardroom?'

But Lewis refused to back down. 'Isn't it much more likely that Gavin picked three clients who were infatuated with him and then promised them free time in bed if they contributed to the Appeal?'

Val said tartly: 'Lewis, if you're really so keen on returning the money, I suggest you answer the question Nick's just posed: what's Carta going to say in the covering letter?'

'The covering letter shouldn't come from Carta,' said Lewis promptly. 'Nicholas should write it and say: "Dear Mr X: For reasons which, because of the confidentiality of the confessional, I am unable to disclose, I very much regret to inform you that I cannot accept your extremely kind and generous donation, which I return herewith. I sincerely apologise if my gesture should seem to you both ungracious and unwarranted, but I feel sure you will understand that a priest must at all times obey his conscience, even if this results in a decision which is not to his material advantage. Yours in Christ, etcetera, etcetera—'

'But the donors will assume Gavin's talked!' I cried. 'You'd be putting him right up excrement creek!'

'That's probably just where he deserves to be,' said Lewis crisply. 'Aren't we at risk here of establishing co-dependency – of not only condoning Gavin's way of life but actually making it desirable for him to go on?'

'Carta,' said Nicholas before I could speak, 'take a couple of deep breaths. You may not agree with Lewis, but we have to discuss all the angles here in order to reach the correct decision about how we should proceed.'

'Right.' With extreme reluctance I remembered his prayer that we should respect one another's views.

'Let me just summarise where we've got to,' said Nicholas, swiftly moving on. 'We've established, thanks to Lewis, that it would be possible to return the money if I were to write a letter along the lines he suggests, but thanks to Carta we've also established that no immoral pressure need have been exercised by Gavin in order to produce the donations. Comments, anyone?'

'The tabloids will join with me in never believing Gavin didn't exert pressure of some kind,' said Lewis acidly. 'Think, everyone, *think*! We're talking about a man who's been receiving money from these donors for sexual services. Do we really believe these hot tips about St Benet's were given by Gavin over anything so innocent as a cup of tea?'

'I must say, Lewis,' remarked Robin mildly, 'I don't know why you're quite so sceptical about the role of a cup of tea here. I'd say the fundraising approach almost had to be post-coital.'

Everyone began to argue about possible post-coital activity in sex-for-money transactions.

'Stop!' ordered our maestro, eventually seizing control. 'Cut the prurient speculation – leave that to the *News of the World*!' And as we all fell silent he added: 'Lewis was right to remind us of the context in which these donations were generated, but unless we hear more about the fundraising from Gavin himself we're still essentially in the dark.'

'So where do we go next?' demanded Val.

'Let's move on to the second specific issue of this case – having considered the past let's take a look at the future. Do we or do we not accept any further donations generated by Gavin? Remember that this time we won't be able to claim later that we accepted them in good faith.'

The discussion lurched on, like a troubled ship, into still deeper uncharted waters.

X

'I think we should accept no more money whatsoever from Gavin's clients,' said Lewis predictably.

'I agree,' said Val, trying not to look surprised at finding herself at one with Lewis. As if to distinguish her views from his she added: 'It would be as if we're knowingly profiting from Gavin's exploitation of gays.'

'You just say that because Gavin's straight,' I commented, trying unsuccessfully not to sound irritated. 'Would you be so quick off the mark if he was gay?'

'Hold it,' said Nicholas, intervening incisively again. 'Let's get one thing quite clear. The issue here's prostitution, not homosexuality, so we can save the gay debate for another day. Robin, let's hear from you, please, on the subject of accepting future donations.'

Robin said he felt it did make a difference that we now knew where the donations were coming from. 'But I think we should talk to Gavin,' he added, 'and find out much more about what the donation-generating context really is. For instance, I'd like to know why he's doing this and what it all means to him.'

'I agree more information's essential,' said Nicholas. 'Certainly the discernment issue's unsolvable without it – and while we're on the knotty subject of whether or not this situation's from God, let me just issue a word of warning: we must all take great care not to be prejudiced against Gavin because of the way he earns his living. Don't forget that God can act through a prostitute – God can act through anyone anywhere, and that's why we can't ignore the possibility, fantastic though it may seem, that Gavin's fundraising's the work of the Holy Spirit. So if you feel your legs twitching in a knee-jerk reaction to Gavin's less attractive behaviour, take a moment to remember that he's a human being made in the image of God, just as we all are, and as such is entitled to be treated with respect. In fact let's take a moment to think about that.'

We thought about it. Or to be accurate, I thought: how horribly hard it is to be a Christian! As I tried not to think of Gavin trashing Moira, I struggled to concentrate on his astonishing achievements as a fundraiser.

'And having reminded ourselves that we need to be fair to Gavin,' said Nicholas, 'let's also remind ourselves not to be sentimental. We're told to love our neighbour, but that doesn't mean being soppy about him while wearing rose-tinted spectacles – love should be a great deal tougher and more realistic than that, and I suspect Gavin will require us to be very tough and realistic indeed. This man's big trouble. Not only does he break hearts as easily as a chef breaks eggs but he's capable of doing an enormous amount of damage to St Benet's if we get this wrong and he buckets beyond our control. So the big question we have to ask ourselves, as Robin implied a moment ago, is what makes Gavin tick? If we can understand that, we not only have a better chance of surviving him but a better insight into whether these donations should be seen as the work of the Spirit . . . Robin, let's hear your views as a therapist.'

'Strictly speaking I can't have a view,' said Robin, 'as I've never met this man, but if you want some theorising mingled with one or two imaginative guesses . . .'

We settled down to listen to his opinion.

'I'll start by stating the obvious,' said Robin. 'Gavin's almost certainly suffering from low self-esteem. Prostitutes are a diverse bunch, but this characteristic crops up regularly right across the spectrum.

'Now, people with low self-esteem have trouble coping with a normal life, so coping with an abnormal life like prostitution is usually very difficult indeed, and that's why I find it so interesting that Gavin appears to be thriving. Nick and Carta have mentioned a drug-free, keep-fit lifestyle, and that suggests to me that Gavin's well looked after, even cosseted, in his private life by someone who's giving him the motivation to keep going. I think this manager of his – what did you say her name was, Nick?'

'Elizabeth,' I said before Nicholas could answer.

'I think Elizabeth must be playing a significant role in his private life as well as his business life, and I'd guess she'd have to be older than him, perhaps considerably older, in order to wield this amount of power and influence over how he operates. At this point Freud rears his venerable head and we all think—'

'MOTHER!' said Val, amused.

'Exactly, and this prompts me to speculate about Gavin's background. Nick's told us that Gavin had a brother who died in his teens of leukaemia, and this fact must represent a major trauma. Maybe the mother was so absorbed in her sick son that Gavin was neglected, made to feel of no importance. Maybe Gavin suffered from survivor's guilt. And where was the father while all this was going on? Where was Gavin's role model? But before we blame all Gavin's troubles on his parents, let me say that the parents' behaviour might well have been as good as it could have been under very adverse circumstances. I'm sure we've all met examples of what Winnicott calls "good enough" parents who have several children, all exemplary except for one who's hell on wheels. But bearing in mind the current presence in Gavin's life of a masterful older woman, I'd guess his relationship with his mother was off-centre and his relationship with his father was defective.'

'But how can he think Elizabeth cares for him when she organises his life as a prostitute?' I protested.

'His poor self-esteem would make him overwhelmed with gratitude that any woman could want to take a serious interest in him.'

'But how *can* he have poor self-esteem when he's bursting with sexual confidence?'

'Yes, we know he has no trouble getting people to go to bed with him,' said Nicholas before Robin could reply, 'but does he have a single worthwhile relationship?'

'My guess is that Gavin specialises in the one-night stand,' agreed Robin. 'And even if he had an affair, I think you'd find he'd always be the one to end it because he would unconsciously be so afraid of rejection. The enduring interest of his manager would seem miraculous to him, so miraculous that he would shut his mind against the fact that she could only offer him a grossly distorted relationship.'

Lewis said unexpectedly: 'What about the possibility of sexual abuse when he was young?'

'It's just that: only a possibility. Highly sexualised behaviour can certainly be seen in sexually abused children, but it's not uncommon in adults brutalised by the sex industry.'

'What do you make of this business of screwing in defiance of his orientation?' asked Val. 'Is he, in fact, straight? Or is he just doing what comes naturally?'

'Prostitution's hardly doing what comes naturally!'

'Val's reminding us,' said Lewis, 'that male homosexuals are often extremely promiscuous.'

'I was doing no such thing! Honestly, Lewis, your homophobia—'

'I'm not homophobic! I'm just committed to the unvarnished truth even if it means being politically incorrect!'

'May I remind everyone that homosexuality itself isn't the topic under discussion?' said Nicholas, effortlessly aborting the diversion. 'Robin, your opinion on Gavin's orientation, please.'

'He could well be as straight as he says he is. It would make it easier for him to switch off his emotions and detach himself mentally from the physical activity by treating his clients as depersonalised objects.'

'Yuk!' said Val with a shudder. 'Those poor clients!'

'Well, if they go to a prostitute,' said Lewis, 'what else can they expect?'

'Thank you, Lewis,' said Nicholas. 'Thank you, Val. Robin, have you anything else to add?'

'Only the obvious comment that the man's probably deep in denial about his self-destructive behaviour.'

Nicholas turned to the rest of us. 'Questions, anyone?'

'Yes,' said Lewis, never backward in coming forward. 'Robin, what's your opinion of Gavin's fixation with Carta?'

'I'd favour the simple explanation: as soon as he saw her, Gavin made the decision to seduce her to boost his fragile ego, and when Carta persistently turned him down her power to say no made her all the more alluring.'

'How does his hetero promiscuity square with his devotion to pseudo-mother Elizabeth?' Val said confused.

'In his eyes Elizabeth's the one who's noble enough to love him. He can't hope for love from anyone else (so he thinks) but at least he can boost his self-esteem by indulging in recreational sex with attractive women.'

'Pathetic!' muttered Val.

I said to Robin: 'Your explanation about Gavin's fixation with me doesn't take into account the almost mystical significance Gavin attaches to being a friend of Richard's,' and Nicholas added: 'My theory is that Carta and Richard are both symbols to Gavin of the world he's left behind.'

'The relationship with Richard interests me very much,' said Robin quickly as if fearing we thought he had missed a trick. 'If Gavin's built a wall around himself by depersonalising his clients, then one can say that Richard breached that wall. But how was it done?'

'Richard took him sailing,' I said at once. 'Gavin said he learned to sail when he was a child – presumably his father taught him.'

'In that case, I wonder if we're looking at someone whom Gavin came to see as a substitute father? Forget the sexual angle for a moment – I'm not suggesting Gavin's father abused him. But if Gavin was prepared to see this client as a person instead of an object, a person from the world he'd lost—'

'—then maybe that's when he began to wish himself back in that lost world,' concluded Nicholas. 'Maybe what we're seeing here is a beaten-up traveller who's regaining consciousness but who's still too weak to help himself. And we know who rescued the beaten-up traveller in the parable.'

'Well, before we all rush off to play the Good Samaritan,' said Lewis sardonically, 'let's just remind ourselves that although we're required to help this young man if possible, we're not required to smash ourselves up for him – and that leads us back to the ethics of taking morally tainted money and the tabloids going to town.'

Nicholas said: 'Fair enough. We've taken a look at the main

issues, we've got Robin's psychological portrait to help us and now we've reached the point where we can have a general discussion about all the problems, moral or otherwise, which this case presents. Lewis, do you want to start the ball rolling?'

'Fasten your seat belts, chaps!' murmured Val good-naturedly. 'We're in for a bumpy ride . . .'

XII

We talked and talked. Some people think Christians have an easy time deciding what's right and what's wrong, but those are usually the people who think Christianity is a monolith, all Christians are fundamentalists and the Bible is like an ethical phone directory, listing every correct response in black and white. The reality is that there are many Christianities and numerous Christians who shy away from fundamentalism, while the Bible is capable of many different interpretations, even by scholars who have devoted their lives to studying it. Besides, we all bring our own agenda to ethical questions, and no matter how far we try to adopt objective positions we can never completely eradicate our subjective opinions. All we can do is to be as aware as possible of our prejudices so that they can be allowed for and discounted; fair, balanced judgements are not beyond achievement, but a great deal of hard work has to be done before they can emerge.

We slogged on. Nicholas, who had kept us on a tight rein during the preliminary discussion, now allowed the conversation to sprawl as if he felt he should give every opportunity for an unexpected insight to surface, but no blinding revelation occurred, and after we had covered the same ground from a variety of different angles, he embarked on the task of establishing a group resolution.

'Let's go back to the specific issues and see if there's been any change of mind,' he said. 'The questions are: should we return the money already received, and should we refuse to accept any further money? I'd now like to pose a third question as well: what should we do about Gavin himself? Okay, short answers, please. Lewis?'

Lewis said promptly: 'Return the money we have. Refuse the money to come. Invite Gavin to the Healing Centre to assure him that although we're unable to accept the donations we've been very impressed by his efforts and we'd like to know him better.'

'Val?'

'We should keep the money we already have,' said Val firmly. 'We took it in good faith and we've no way of proving the donors acted under duress. But I don't think we should touch a penny more now we know the donations are being generated by a prostitute in the course of his work. As for Gavin, yes, let's invite him here, take an interest, affirm him as best we can.'

'Robin?'

'Honestly, Nick, I still think we should keep the money we already have. I admire the consistency of Lewis's position, but I'm with Val on this one.'

'And any future donations?'

'I can't make up my mind without first talking to Gavin – so yes, I'm all for inviting him to the Healing Centre. Let's boost that rock-bottom self-esteem of his by treating him as a friend of Richard's, someone well worthy of our attention.'

Nicholas turned to me: 'Carta?'

'I'm still totally opposed to returning the money we have,' I said strongly. 'Sorry, Lewis, but sometimes I think the Church really does get too hung up on sex, and whether Gavin's achieved his fundraising miracles in bed or out of it just isn't important as far as I'm concerned.'

'Is it really of no importance to you,' demanded Lewis, 'that he may well have consistently taken advantage of unhappy, vulnerable people in order to impress you with his fundraising skills?'

Instantly I knew this was a killer question which pulled the rug from under my feet and put me in the wrong. Yet instantly I also knew that I had to stand by Gavin. I never paused to analyse this decision. I merely knew what I had to do and I did it.

'Listen,' I said. 'Gavin's behaviour's abominable. His language is filthy. He's caused me a lot of trouble and aggravation. But let me tell you as your fundraiser that he's done a terrific thing for us, and it couldn't have been easy for him. These clients of his aren't sad-sack losers – they're big-time businessmen who aren't going to hand over their money easily, least of all when prompted by someone they pay for sex. I'm convinced that to achieve this level of success Gavin must have targeted the donors with great care, designed a psychologically apt approach for each one of them and then played them along with the maximum of subtlety and skill. He deserves all the praise we can throw at him, and that's why I say now that affirming him is yet another reason why we should not only keep the past donations but accept the donation in the pipeline as well. Never mind Gavin's motivation – he's doing enormous good! Never mind the donors – they're tough enough to look after themselves! Never mind the tabloids – no one's going to talk to them! We should stop agonising over the moral issues and instead go down on our knees to thank God for this totally miraculous windfall!'

'And should we invite Gavin to the Healing Centre?' asked Nicholas in a neutral voice but he was smiling at me.

'You bet – and we should tell him we're damn grateful!' I suddenly felt so exhausted that I leaned forward over the table and buried my face in my forearms.

'Well, that was certainly spoken from the heart!' said Lewis in his kindest voice, and Robin and Val also murmured words of encouragement.

Hauling myself upright again I said: 'Nicholas is waiting to outdo me. Go on, Nicholas, for God's sake get us sorted before we all start climbing the walls . . .'

XIII

'What we're all united on,' said Nicholas, 'is the need to invite Gavin to the Healing Centre. I certainly believe we should do this, and I also believe our attempts to affirm him as a person when he comes here would be much more effective if we didn't return the money we've already received. What's done is done, and I don't think we can undo it without causing more problems than we solve. As for the donation in the pipeline, there's no doubt that if we refuse it we'd be in a position to give ourselves a moral pat on the back, but are we really in business simply to bestow moral pats? I seem to remember Jesus made some stringent comments on those who played religion strictly by the book and were over-preoccupied with saving themselves from some dire fate . . .

'I think this is one of those cases where we have to acknowledge the conventional rules and then summon the courage to step outside them. My father used to say that only by wholeheartedly embracing the monastic framework could a monk know when it was safe to step outside that framework in order to serve God in a situation where an orthodox response seemed inadequate. I believe we're in a similar situation now.

'It's Gavin who's at the heart of this discussion, isn't it? Not the money. Not St Benet's. But Gavin. He's tugging at our sleeves like a little child who wants to be noticed, and bearing in mind our call to serve others we have to ask: how can we best help him? How can we best respond to his persistent tugs at our sleeves?

'Lewis made a valid point earlier when he said we must beware of becoming co-dependents, enabling Gavin to continue his life as a prostitute by acting as if we go along with what he does. We must leave him in no doubt that we can't condone his exploitation of homosexuals and his abuse of his own body, but we can and must encourage him by recognising the efforts he's made for a good cause, and that's why, like Carta, I think we should also accept the donation in the pipeline. But after that we should end the moral ambiguity of the situation by suggesting he stops tapping his clients for donations and embarks on some orthodox fundraising for us instead – he could work part-time, join the volunteers. By inviting him to do that we build up his self-esteem and give him a prepaid ticket into the world of Richard Slaney, but we'll never get that far if we reject any of the donations, because Gavin's ego is too fragile to allow him to bear the rejections without running away. So we've got to accept the donations in order to reach him – we've got to step outside our conventional ethical framework and be unorthodox, because only by moving away from the well-lit highway are we ever going to rescue this beaten-up traveller who's been left for dead in the dark.'

He stopped speaking.

My voice said: 'I'd cheer but I'm so banjaxed that only a squeak would come out.'

'That's a powerful image, Nick,' said Robin, and Val said: 'You've got it right.'

'Okay, Lewis,' said Nicholas wryly without waiting for further comments. 'You can fire both barrels now.'

Without hesitation Lewis launched himself into the attack.

XIV

'My dear Nicholas,' said Lewis, 'of course I admire your liberal idealism and your sincere desire to help this dangerous and destructive young man whom you so romantically picture as a victimised traveller. But I'd be failing in my duty to you as your colleague if I didn't say that I think you're gravely mistaken. By accepting the donations, you *are* condoning his prostitution. The plain fact of the matter is that none of these donations would exist unless Gavin Blake had been financially rewarded for having sex with the donors. Naturally I share your desire to heal Gavin's self-esteem and help him build a new life, but believe me, going along with his prostitution by accepting the fruits of it isn't the way to achieve this worthy aim. So stop trying to play God, Nicholas, with all this addled talk of stepping outside the rules, and leave God in charge here! I assure you he can run things rather better than you can.'

As I fought the urge to grab a banana from the fruit bowl and hit Lewis over the head, Nicholas said levelly: 'Fair enough. No one knows better than I do that I can get things wrong, but those are my views and since we're all currently trying to be as honest as possible, these are the views I must express. However, they could change when I meet Gavin again – in fact all our views should be open to amendment then as he'll be providing us with a lot of new information.'

Mollified by this good-natured response Lewis had the grace to backtrack a little. 'I don't wish to give the impression I'm completely inflexible,' he said, 'but I do feel I'm the only one here who's looking at the case with his eyes wide open.'

'There's something else I'd like to say,' I intervened, anxious to move on from Lewis's traditionalist spiel. 'Sorry, Nicholas, but I've just got to say this no matter how nutty I sound.' And to the others I announced: 'I think Gavin's Elizabeth is Mrs Mayfield.'

The meeting roared back to life as everyone rushed to embrace the diversion.

XV

Naturally the verdict on my theory was 'not proven', but there was a lively interest in the possibility that our enemy had resurfaced.

'Wicked old witch!' said Val robustly. 'Evil old fraud! But how did she manage to enslave Gavin? I thought she was a middle-aged frump with crinkly grey hair!'

'You think she's not clever enough to give herself a total makeover? Anyway the grey hair was a wig and the downmarket clothes were just part of the persona she was pushing at the time!'

'But if she's going for radical change, why keep the name Elizabeth?'

Robin was unimpressed by this objection. 'People who move from alias to alias often do keep their first names,' he said. 'From a practical point of view it means you never slip up by failing to respond when someone addresses you, and from a psychological point of view, retaining the first name provides a thread of continuity in what may be a very disjointed life.'

'Talking of disjointed lives brings us back to Gavin,' said Nicholas, who had listened without comment as I had aired my obsession. 'Perhaps we should now move into the final stage of the meeting and consider how we should handle his visit to the Healing Centre.'

Val said: 'What makes you so sure he'll accept our invitation?'

'Carta will be delivering it.'

'Oh yes?' I said, trying not to sound steamrollered.

'When are we going to schedule the visit?' asked Robin cautiously. 'My timetable next week is . . .'

Everyone promptly started clamouring about how busy they were, but Nicholas said the meeting had to be on Monday, while our discussion was still fresh in our minds, and it had to take place after Gavin had finished work at six-thirty.

There then followed a not particularly productive discussion of how Gavin should be questioned about his fundraising, but we soon realised that it would be better to rely on a friendly spontaneity than a detailed plan. At this point, just as we were all about to go cross-eyed with exhaustion, Nicholas called a halt and summarised what had been agreed: we had decided by a majority vote to keep the past donations, although to appease Lewis Nicholas said we should keep an open mind about the donation in the pipeline until we had talked to Gavin.

Having completed this summary Nicholas closed the meeting by thanking us all for giving up our Saturday afternoon, but just as I was thinking how much I was looking forward to the rest of my weekend he added: 'Let's get together tomorrow, Carta, and plan exactly how you're going to deliver this invitation to Gavin.'

Telling myself crossly that there was no slave-driver to equal a clergyman once he slipped into a workaholic mode, I agreed to meet him on the following afternoon.

XVI

I was far from happy about adopting the role of the siren who would lure Gavin to St Benet's, and as I automatically started to review the meeting, it occurred to me that no one had asked if I found Gavin a threat to my peace of mind. I supposed they were all confident that I could deal with him as efficiently as I dealt with everyone else, but I knew their confidence was unjustified. It was the sheer irrationality of the sexual attraction which was so deeply threatening to me. Reason, logic, rational analysis – these were my survivor skills, giving me control over my life, and after my disastrous marriage I was frightened of losing that control.

On an impulse I avoided returning home directly and hurried instead to Eric's studio. I wanted to blot out Gavin by saying to Eric: 'I love you, I need you, I'm sorry everything's been such a mess,' but when I rang his doorbell no one answered. My spirits rose as I assumed he was waiting for me at home, but when I reached my house I found only a letter. He had written: 'Darling, I decided I had to make that second research trip to Norway right now to try to break my worsening case of writer's block. I'm sorry for not giving you more warning of this, but to be honest I feel that our meetings have become such a minefield that it seemed best just to take off for the airport and hope that absence really does make the heart grow fonder. Why do smart women so often get mixed up with absolute bastards? I know I used to be a bastard too in my gigolo days before we met, but at least I got my act together and grew up. However, maybe you have a psychological need to minister to men who have cosmic problems. Is it just a coincidence, I ask myself, that you allowed Gavin Blake to slither into your life so soon after your father died and you could no longer slave away trying to solve his gambling addiction? Okay, I'll stop there. Let me know when you finally ditch that hustler. All my love, ERIC.'

I sank down on the stairs.

Eventually I was able to wipe my eyes, clamber up to the living-room and pour myself some scotch. In despair I wanted to grab a transatlantic flight – nail a high-powered job in New York – start out all over again – but even while I was thinking these frantic thoughts I knew I would solve nothing by physically removing myself from this mess in London. I would merely take my problems with me and wind up despising myself for running away.

Dredging up all my willpower, I began to plan my crucial meeting with Gavin on Monday morning.

XVII

In the moment before he saw me Gavin appeared to be deep in thought, his eyes downcast, his face empty of expression as he wandered away from the Dutch church which stood in Austin Friars. Without the gloss of his professional persona he seemed younger, almost like a hard-working student focusing dutifully on his approaching exams, and suddenly, in a moment of revelation, the scales fell from my eyes so that for the first time I saw him as vulnerable. The voices of the Rectory meeting echoed in my head and I thought: yes, this is the beaten-up traveller who's been left for dead in the dark, and what he needs now isn't rejection but a lifeline.

The next moment he saw me and instantly slipped behind the mask of hypersexuality.

'Carta!' he breathed, all smoochy innuendo, but I was determined not to be alienated.

Calmly I said: 'Hi. Look, hold the stud-act for a moment, could you? I'm here to deliver a message from my boss . . .' And using a friendly, courteous tone of voice – a tone I had practised beforehand – I issued the invitation which Nicholas had drafted on my return to the Rectory on Sunday. This speech too I had rehearsed. I was surprised to find that even though I had taken such care to prepare for the meeting I was very nervous. I did not want to let down either St Benet's or Gavin himself.

209

But the speech made its mark. Astonishment flickered in Gavin's eyes but this was followed closely by delight. Then came other emotions not so easy to identify. Alarm, perhaps? Suspicion? I was unable to decide and Gavin was not about to enlighten me.

Smoothly he said: 'Churches aren't my scene, Gorgeous, but if you're going to be there I'll turn up.'

At once I knew he needed reassurance and encouragement. 'I'm going to be there. Definitely.'

'Phwoar! Then nothing could keep me away!'

'Everyone'll be so glad to see you – they think you've done something really amazing!'

'Who's everyone?'

'Nicholas and I. Lewis, the retired priest who assists at the church. Robin, the Healing Centre's psychologist. Val, the doctor who works with Nicholas.'

'All these people think I've done something really amazing?'

'Absolutely! We can't wait to offer you a glass of wine and say congratulations!'

'Sounds like you've all gone mental. What time's this rave?'

'Six-forty-five. I'll wait in the main reception area of the Healing Centre – just come down the steps from the churchyard and you'll see me beyond the glass doors.'

He sighed in the manner of a rock star anxious to avoid his adoring fans but knowing it would be good PR to appear gracious. 'Okay,' he said. 'No problem. But now if you'll excuse me, sweetie, I gotta run – a top-of-the-market leisure-worker like me never keeps a client waiting!' And with a ravishing smile he blew me a kiss before disappearing into the house.

The rush from the sexual charge which then slugged me kicked to pieces any notion I had been harbouring that my new understanding of Gavin as vulnerable would defuse the chemistry between us. I had been congratulating myself on behaving impeccably while giving reassurance to a damaged man, but now I felt I'd just been giving the maximum encouragement to a wrecker whom I still – *still*, despite all my determination to play my cards right for St Benet's – found much too attractive.

Just how on earth was I going to get a grip on this situation?

Maybe a head transplant wasn't such a bad idea after all . . .

CHAPTER FOUR

Gavin

'The healing ministry is available for everyone; there is no place
for discrimination of any kind. The common humanity and
uniqueness of each individual must be respected and valued.'

A Time to Heal
A report for the House of Bishops on the Healing Ministry

I'm going to meet Mr Charisma again. Carta's issued his invitation
to the St Benet's Healing Centre where I'm going to be slobbered
over by Mr Charisma and his myrmidons. (I like that word 'myrmidons'. Shakespeare uses it, but in which play? Can't remember.)

Of course I'm a severe embarrassment to Mr Charisma and the
myrmidons, but they've put their heads together and Mr Charisma's
said: 'Here's this piece of shit, chums. How do we make him smell
of roses so nobody can blame us for taking his money?' and some
bright myrmidon's piped up: 'We'll save him for The Bloke! That'll
make everything brilliant!' So they plan to convert me, but think
again, you snotty bastards, because I'm going to kick that idea right
up your collective arse where it belongs.

But the hell with them – all that matters is that I've achieved my
goal of dazzling Carta. Bed in a month, did I say? No, make that
two weeks! I'm on a roll here, doing great, and soon life'll be more
terrific than ever . . .

But meanwhile it's Monday morning and I've got to psych myself
up to face my first blow-job.

I go through my regular meditation routine but all the way
through the wake-up shift I'm thinking, thinking, thinking, and the
strange thing is it's not Gavin Blake Superstud powering the

thoughts. It's not Gavin Blake Ordinary Bloke either, the one who drinks lager and says 'nah' to Nigel and goes mad on the couch with the zapper. There's someone else on the scene now, and it's Gavin Blake Fundraiser Supremo, plotting his dynamic next move.

I've got to wear the right clothes for this slobber-fest at St Benet's. That's important. I may be shit but I'm going to be well-dressed shit. Mr Charisma will probably offer me his hand again because that's the Christian thing to do, but there's no need to make him feel he has to wash it afterwards. He doesn't really feel friendly towards me, of course. He's just going through the motions in order to be a good clergyman.

When the shift finishes I shunt back to Lambeth and pick a char-coal-grey suit ordered for me by an ancient client. It was his old-world, Savile Row wet dream of what every nice young man should wear. For luck I take the white shirt I wore to Richard's funeral, and I select a tie that's dark blue with a pale blue stripe: the Oxbridge colours. I'm going to look respectable enough to sell bibles.

After the last client of the lunch-time shift has been shoehorned out of the flat, I rest but sleep's impossible. The truth is I'm nervous about this visit to St Benet's. It's the thought of seeing two clergy-men, a doctor and a psychologist all at once – God, it's like being interviewed for a place in a bloody rehab programme! What are they going to say to me? What am I going to say to them? What *can* they say to me? What *can* I say to them?

I need to figure out the right role, the role through which Gavin Blake Fundraiser Supremo can most effectively display himself. How about 'Idealistic Young Executive'? No, that won't wash, leisure-workers don't have ideals. But wait a moment, I've got it, how about 'Post-Yuppie Supporter of the Arts', a bloke who's bored with banking and bonking and now only wants to listen to opera in between reading Shakespeare? Yeah, that'll go down well, that'll impress the hell out of them, problem solved.

Somehow I get through the late-shift. One client even asks me if I'm feeling unwell and I have to bust a gut to prove I'm in prime condition for the routine he likes but what a bore all that fake wrestling is! It's not just physically tiring – it's mentally exhausting having to dream up an erotic choreography which will ring the client's macho bells and allow him to kid himself we meet as phys-ical equals. What a fantasist! Silly plonker.

As soon as the last client leaves I shower and dress at top speed.

No time to straighten out the flat. I'll have to arrive early tomorrow to tidy up. Before I go I have a swig of wine from the bottle in the fridge, but that's a stupid thing to do because it means I have to wash my mouth out all over again. Mustn't turn up smelling of booze. Mustn't let them guess how bloody nervous I am. If Carta wasn't going to be there I wouldn't bother to show. I mean, I've got better things to do with my time, right? Course I have.

But I stick to the plan. Mustn't wreck my sizzling new relationship with Carta. Off I go along the part of Austin Friars which leads into Throgmorton Avenue, and then I beetle on west, crossing Moorgate and diving into Great Bell Alley. In and out of the backstreets I skim like a mouse in a maze as I take short cut after short cut until I hit Egg Street. The church is ahead of me now. I shudder but whisk up some courage by thinking of Carta waiting for me by the glass doors of the crypt where the Healing Centre's located. I tell myself she probably feels like Joseph Cotten waiting for Orson Welles in my father's favourite movie *The Third Man*. All we need now is some zither music.

Carta's waiting, just as she promised. She's wearing a trouser suit, which is a big mistake because it covers her legs, but I can still see her feet which are slinkily shod in skintight black leather. I try to joke to myself about chiropody but I'm too tense.

'Hiya, Frosty-Puss!' I say, breezing in as confidently as if I visited healing centres every day. 'Lead me to Mr Charisma and his myrmidons!'

'His *what*?'

'Myrmidons. Shakespeare. *Coriolanus*, act two, scene five.'

She looks suspicious, as well she might since I invented the entire reference and even (I discover later) named the wrong play, but she just gives me a tight little smile before saying carefully: 'Thanks for coming. Everyone's here.'

I'm too stressed out to take much notice of my surroundings, but we're in a brightly lit reception area, similar to the waiting-room of a doctor's surgery, and Carta's leading me over to a door marked CONSULTING ROOM ONE. The door's ajar. I can hear a voice murmuring beyond, but the sound ceases as Carta pushes open the door.

I expected a boardroom with everyone sitting at a long table. I pictured them all lolling in their chairs and snottily looking me up and down as I walked in. But the room's small and the occupants are perching on some old stacking chairs which have been arranged in a ragged circle. There's a desk but it's been pushed back against the waist-high bookcase which runs along one wall. Above the bookcase is the global corporate logo of The Bloke: a wooden cross with the metal image of a man fixed to it.

I nerve myself to face the two clergymen, the doctor and the psychologist who have assembled to look down on me. But simultaneously Carta's saying in an upbeat voice: 'Here's Gavin!' – and the next moment every single person in that room stands up as if The Bloke himself had walked into their midst.

'Welcome to St Benet's, Gavin,' says Nicholas Darrow, smiling at me.

* * *

Can't speak. Not sure why. I remember I have to play a role but I can't recall what it should be. I only know that these people stood up before I'd begun to play any role which would have made me socially acceptable. They stood up before I could open my mouth.

I'm being introduced but the words don't register. Each myrmidon offers me its hand to shake. I nod. I suppose I smile a little, the way one does at such times. The familiar reflexes carry me through.

I'm being offered a glass of wine. Soave or Valpolicella? The Healing Centre's been sent a case of each as a gift.

I choose the Soave but I forget to add 'please'. I'm still all over the place, trying to slip into a role but no longer sure what the role should be. I don't think I could carry off 'Post-Yuppie Supporter of the Arts' after all. In fact I doubt if I could carry off anything. But I can't be me. So I'll just have to hack it as a low-IQ City worker with a speech impediment – a fair enough description of my present performance.

'Why don't you take that chair next to Carta?' suggests Mr Charisma, and Carta gives me an encouraging smile.

I sink down on the stacking chair with the glass of chilled Soave in my sweating hand. Carta sits down too, slim ankles peeping out of those stupid trousers, but I can't think erotic thoughts any more. I can only take a sip of Soave and listen to the thumping of my heart.

Mr Charisma, very laid-back and appearing one hundred per cent sincere, starts to thank me on behalf of everyone at St Benet's for my hard work which has been so outstandingly successful.

* * *

Gradually I get my act together. I've realised the scene's a little like those Sunday morning drinks parties my parents used to throw in the days before Hugo became ill. A bunch of chums, not many, would turn up at noon and swill for an hour or so while the men chatted about sport and how the socialists were ruining the country, and the women nattered about children and schools and how to teach the au pair to make a decent cup of tea. In other words you talked of things which couldn't possibly upset people, even though you might be worried sick about your bank balance or your sex life or who was within an inch of a nervous breakdown.

The St Benet's gang too are all bent on saying nothing upsetting while they bust a gut to be friendly, and soon Robin the psychologist's gushing: 'Of course what I'm dying to know is how you approached this project from a *psychological* point of view. You must have selected your targets with *enormous* care.'

'Sure.' I can't quite figure this bloke out. He's a stick-thin, camp piece who's wrapped in a violet shirt and a wedding ring, and he's got the trick of emphasising certain words as if to brainwash you into believing how sincere he is. He looks gay, but as I know so well appearances can be deceptive. I speculate that he could be a bi who's decided he'd flourish best in a marriage, but no, if that was the case he'd probably opt to look dead straight, crafting his appearance to kill all bi rumours for the sake of his family. I decide this bloke's just a straight with a passion for kinky colours and a total indifference about whether or not people think he's gay. He must be very secure.

'Perhaps you'd like to tell us a little about your fundraising strategies,' says Mr Charisma, egging me on, and Carta says admiringly: 'I'm longing to hear how you did it!'

This is the moment to die for. Carta Graham, Golden Girl, is looking at me with genuine interest and respect *yet I'm not playing a role*. But of course I now have to vault into a role, no choice. If I have to talk about how Gavin Blake Superstud became Gavin Blake Fundraising Supremo, I can't be Gavin Blake Me telling the truth. That's because all the sex stuff has to be omitted. I spent a lot of time plotting each physical move which would send each donor to his own private version of gay heaven, and I used all my energy and skill to see the donors were swept through the pearly gates on a tide of orgasmic glory, but of course I could never admit that to a bunch of Christians. It would just reinforce their private opinion that I'm scum.

215

In panic I realise everyone's gazing at me with rapture as they wait for the explanation of my brilliant success. Why didn't I guess they'd want some details? Maybe I thought they'd be too priggish to want to know. Or maybe I was too busy deciding what to wear and enjoying the thought of being slobbered over by a load of do-gooders.

'Yeah well,' I mumble, clearing my throat to play for time, but then I'm launching myself into an ultra-cool performance of Gavin Blake Fundraising Supremo. 'Some of these blokes I see have a company policy about giving to charity, preferably a City charity, at least once a year,' I say. 'So, well, I picked one of those, researched his company, know-what-I-mean, talked to the client, figured out which approach would be best.' In an inspired moment I remember one of my non-sexual ploys. 'I mugged up the Appeal literature so that I could answer any questions right off, and then I designed a spiel for each client.'

'Terrific!' exclaims Carta encouragingly. 'I try to do that, but it's hard to get the spiel right, isn't it, and one never quite knows how it's going to go down.'

I think I'll be okay if I focus on Carta and pretend the others aren't there. 'Right!' I say warmly. 'It's risky stuff! Well, like I say, I picked a bloke who had a company policy about giving to charity. Then I see blokes who are running for some kind of City office, know-what-I-mean, and they like to look involved with charity stuff, so I picked one of those. And then I see blokes who have so much money they don't know what to do with it and they don't even have time to, you know, ferret away trying to find a good cause, so if I name a good cause they're going to say: "Hell, why not?" and write a cheque because it stops them feeling guilty that normally they never get around to giving much away. So I picked one of these blokes too. And to all the blokes my approach was like: "Hey, I'm going to do you a favour – here's a big opportunity for you!" because although these blokes hate being pressured for money, they love any opportunity to make themselves look clever, and the fact is they all truly appreciated my tip about St Benet's which is a great City cause, very respectable but very cutting-edge. Touches a lot of, you know, like, bases. It's very today, very now.'

As I finally dare to glance around the room again I see everyone's looking deeply impressed – except for the creepy cleric in the corner, what's-his-face, Lewis Hall, the oldie with the silver hair and black eyes and whiplash-thin mouth. Maybe *he's* gay. Repressed, of course. One of those celibate numbers who flagellates himself in secret to relieve the tension. He's looking at me as if he knows too bloody well I'm being economical with the truth. Shall I test him out, give him a hot look which would make him think all his forbidden fantasies were springing to glorious life? No, better not risk it. It might wreck my new role which I'm playing so cleverly: the leisure-worker with the heart of gold – the one who's lying in the gutter but looking up at the stars with a sheaf of charity cheques in his hand.

'That's great psychology!' Camp-stick Robin's saying with enthusiasm. 'Well done!' And the doctor next to him says brightly: 'You've tackled this like a real professional – have you done any fundraising before?' The doctor's called Val and she's a jolly-hockey-sticks type, plain but fun. No wedding ring. Could *she* be gay? Nah. Too nice, too normal. Impossible to think of her itching to finger-creep someone like bloody awful Norah.

'No, I'm a novice here,' I tell her modestly, awash with relief that everyone's much too Christian even to think of the sex details, let alone ask about them. 'But I admit I've found fundraising rewarding. It's been sort of, you know, a challenge, know-what-I-mean, something worthwhile.'

'I think you've shown a real talent!' says my loyal and extra-special friend Carta. 'In fact I think you're much more talented at fundraising than I am. I'm just a hard worker with good connections.'

I give her my best shy smile. 'Suppose that depends how you define talent,' I murmur, but the next moment the smile's wiped off my face as the old cleric in the corner jumps into the conversation.

'A talent's a gift from God,' he announces, and his voice startles me because it's so like my father's. As the old boy said nothing when we were introduced this is the first time I've heard him speak. 'A talent,' he adds, 'enables us to work hard at a task and not only enjoy it but find it uniquely fulfilling.' And he gives me a look as if his favourite hobby's blasting through bullshit.

But Mr Charisma spins the conversation into a different channel, like a sailor tacking to avoid a buoy in the water. 'Talking of your talent, Gavin,' he says, 'can you tell us more about the donation in the pipeline?'

My heart sinks. I really have decided that it's just too dangerous

217

to milk Colin. Best to switch off this line of enquiry and let everyone down gently later.

'I'd rather not go into detail right at this moment,' I say glibly. 'Don't want to jinx the project by talking too much about it! Specially as negotiations are at such an early stage.' The words are out of my mouth before I realise I've slipped up. I've almost invited them to ask what the word 'negotiations' means in this context, but even as I hope feverishly that everyone will be too Christian to push me further, the old bloke in the corner dives back into the conversation with the impact of a ton of bricks landing on glass.

'I'd like to hear a little more about these negotiations you're conducting,' he says in his old-fashioned public school voice. 'I think there's a dimension to all this you haven't mentioned, Mr Blake.'

I'm aware of Carta freezing as Mr Charisma shifts slightly in his chair. I glance at Robin but he's just looking blandly attentive. I glance at Val but she's busy adjusting one of her earrings. Shit! They're all hanging tough. Forget that delusion about Christians being pure-minded pushovers – it's showdown time at St Benet's for leisure-workers and no one's riding to my rescue. What the triple-fuck do I say next?

'It's okay,' says Carta rapidly in a low voice. 'But we've got to know about the bad stuff as well as the good stuff in order to figure out how we can best help.'

Only one answer's possible. 'What bad stuff?'

'We're talking about the way you earn your living, Mr Blake,' says the Reverend Lewis Hall, sex-fixated old creep.

'Oh that!' I say airily. 'You mean my business as a leisure-worker, performing a much-needed and much-appreciated service to stressed-out high flyers.'

There's an absolute silence.

I can't explain just how terrible that silence is. I only know I can't stand it. I want them to go back to talking about my talent as a fundraiser and saying how amazing I am.

At last I realise everyone's looking at Robin. This is where the psychologist has to be wheeled on to handle me with kid gloves. Shit, how humiliating. Sod these people, sod them—

'It's often difficult to talk about sex, isn't it?' Robin's stopped putting words in italics. His voice sounds smoother, quieter, far more subtly sympathetic. 'I expect even leisure-workers find it difficult sometimes.'

Screw him. 'I'll talk about any kind of sex you like!' I slam back.

'It doesn't bother me one fucking bit!' But no one gasps at my language. No one squirms.

Robin just says: 'I'm sure we all appreciate your offer to be frank. I wonder if I could just ask this: do you take special trouble – professionally, I mean – with someone you've marked as a donor?'

At once I see how I can counter-attack. Top leisure-workers don't discuss their clients. Who do these St Benet's people think I am, for God's sake? Some cheap rent boy smirking in Leicester Square?

'Do you seriously believe,' I say scandalised, 'that I'm going to breach my clients' trust by talking in detail about the exact nature of their transactions with me? Well, forget it! I've built my reputation on total discretion. I observe strict protocol here.' I love that word protocol. I'm talking style now, I'm talking class, and the conversation's soared upmarket. I'm winning.

'Let me reassure you that we don't need to know the details of the transactions,' says Robin in a mild voice as he cuts the ground from beneath my feet. 'We only want to know if the donors get free benefits in return for their generosity.'

'Certainly not!' I say indignantly, but Old Toughie now crashes back into the conversation.

'Mr Blake,' he says, 'are you trying to tell us that these donors received no special sexual favours from you in return for their donations?'

I raise an eyebrow. 'You got a problem with that?'

'Yes, I find it implausible. If I were to donate thousands of pounds to a good cause promoted by the person I was paying for sex, I'd certainly expect some gilt on the gingerbread!'

You've got to hand it to him. Isn't he a love? There's something brilliantly unstuffy about this murderous determination to call a spade a spade, and the nickname 'Old Toughie' doesn't even begin to do him justice. This bloke's nothing less than an Exocet missile in a clerical collar.

'My clients always get gilt on the gingerbread!' I snarl. 'They don't have to give to the charity of their choice in order to get that – total satisfaction's always built into the deal!'

Mr Charisma intervenes. He says calmly: 'Let's get one thing quite clear: we accept and welcome your talent for fundraising, Gavin. Be in no doubt of that. But the problem for us is that your talent for fundraising is set in the context of one of your other talents, and this other talent is a talent you abuse.'

219

I stare at him. 'What other talent?'

'Didn't you tell me at Richard's funeral that you had a talent for sex?'

He's bowled me a googly. I can't deny I said this (and what a bloody stupid thing it was to say to a clergyman!) but if I admit it, he'll start to work his way around to saying that my business as a leisure-worker taints the talent for sex which in turn taints the talent for fundraising which in turn taints the donations and makes them unacceptable – and this brutal Christian logic, I now see so clearly, is what this fucking charade's all about: they praise me to the skies for being so wonderful but then they say up yours, mate, stuff it, it's dirty money and we're sending it back to the donors. But that's not fair, that's not right, that's not—

'We want to be fair about this,' says Mr Charisma calmly, cutting across my agonised thoughts. 'We want to get this right. We can't condone the abuse of a talent. But we want to affirm the talent itself and also affirm you for all your hard work on our behalf.'

I struggle to understand. 'You mean – what you're saying is—'

'What I'm saying is we want to encourage every God-given talent you have and the good results they produce. But you see our dilemma, don't you? We can't sanction any fundraising that exploits the donors, but we do admire your imaginative use of your inter-personal skills in working for a good cause – it's a real challenge for us, I promise you, to work out a way forward here which does you justice without doing violence to what we believe to be right for St Benet's.'

I get a grip on my fury and frustration. I get a grip because I can see he really is trying to be fair. The leisure-working's shit but I'm not necessarily shit too – that's what he's saying. If I can convince him there was no exploitation, just me and my talents trying to serve St Benet's as honestly as I could despite the dodginess of the context—

I say firmly: 'There was no exploitation.' And as I speak I know this is true. 'These blokes are tough,' I insist. 'They make up their own minds. If I put pressure on them to donate, they'd soon come to resent it and then I'd be minus a client. All I can do is offer them a window of opportunity, but I make sure the view they see through that window is as attractive as I can possibly make it.'

I pause. Mr Charisma nods. He's sympathetic, still willing to listen.

'Okay, so this is where the talent for sex comes in,' I say, skating in a muck sweat across the thin moral ice. 'Okay, so a lot of people would think a talent for sex is a pretty paltry kind of talent whether it's being abused or not. And okay, so leisure-working's not the ideal context for that talent to be exercised. But it was the only talent and the only context I had when I started fundraising, and you can only work with what you have.' A memory hits me and I grab it. It's as if someone's thrown me a lifeline.

'My mother raised money for a cancer charity after my brother died,' I say rapidly, and there's no role-playing now, I've no energy to spare, it's all focused on putting across this deep truth and saving the donations. 'My father said to her: "How do you know you've got any talent for fundraising?" and she said: "I don't. But I know I've got a talent for being sociable." And she organised coffee mornings and drinks parties and bridge drives – all very ordinary stuff, but she planned every detail so carefully that each event was a big success and the money came flowing in . . . Yet a talent for being sociable's not much, is it? And the context she had to work in was very ordinary – I mean, she didn't have a career or an upper-crust social life. It was so easy for my father to look down on her longing to raise money, but in the end she reached the target she'd set herself and the cancer charity wrote a special letter to say how grateful they were. So even a paltry talent in a non-ideal context can be a force for the good, can't it? And why should a non-ideal context mean you can't offer up the paltry talent, specially if the paltry talent's all you've got to offer? Surely a good intention's got to be worth *something*! That's only right! That's only fair!'

I stop. No one says a word. They just look. Mr Charisma's eyes are luminous. Dr Val's high-gloss lush-lips are slightly parted as if she's caught her breath at the sight of something startling. Mr Pass-for-Gay Robin takes off his glasses as if he no longer trusts them and gazes at me wide-eyed. And Carta? Carta's smiling at me as if I'm truly special. Obviously I've hit some kind of jackpot but the stupid thing is I'm not sure how I've done it. Could it really just be by talking about Mum? I was hoping for at best a grudgingly conceded victory. I never visualised a knock-out triumph.

'That's a splendid story!' exclaims Mr Charisma at last, but the word 'story' rings alarm bells in my head. Frantically I protest: 'It was all true!'

'Yes, I know. It's hard not to recognise the ring of truth when it arrives with a deafening peal of bells. Now listen, Gavin, I want to make you an offer which I hope you'll consider very seriously. How would you like to work part-time for us at the Healing Centre?'

I nearly plummet right off my chair.

* * *

'The thing is,' Mr Charisma's saying as I take time out to marvel that I'm still upright, 'we'd like you to go on fundraising for us. Of course we'd have to change the context where you do the work, but that wouldn't be a problem if you came here as one of our volunteer helpers.'

At first all I can think is: he's joking. Then I realise no one's laughing. Wondering if I'm going mental I manage to mutter something which reveals total non-comprehension.

'We have a number of volunteers like Carta who work here, offering their special talents to St Benet's,' explains Mr Charisma placidly. 'Now, we can't use your talent for sex—' He slips me a smile '—but we can certainly use your talent for fundraising. Think what you have to offer! A willingness to work hard and take trouble, an ability to be good with people, clever at sussing them out and winning their liking, a tenacity which enables you to keep going when the going gets tough – all admirable qualities! So if you could spare us a few hours a week we'd be more than happy to have you on board.'

I swallow, clear my throat. Words eventually come out of my mouth. I say: 'You don't really want me here. You couldn't. You just want to – quote – "save" me to make yourself look good, but what makes you think I want to be "saved", Mr Taking-one-hell-of-a-lot-for-granted Darrow?'

Mr Charisma nods gravely as if he knows he sometimes takes one hell of a lot for granted and isn't this an aggravating fault to have, he knows he really should be able to do better. Then having somehow permeated the air with an apology without even opening his mouth, he says with a kind of knock-out seriousness: 'I'm not sure how you're using that word "saved", but I'll say this: I don't like seeing people's talents blighted. I don't like seeing people fail to realise their potential. And yes, I do want these people to be saved – saved from frustration and despair – but I wouldn't use the word "save" here. I'd say I want them to be *liberated* to become the people God designed them to be. I'd say I want them to be *empowered* to achieve fulfilment and a lasting happiness.'

Panic nibbles the pit of my stomach. In a fuck-you voice I insist obstinately: 'I'm liberated and empowered already, thanks very much! And anyway as far as your job offer goes, my manager wouldn't let me work for anyone but her, she'd forbid it right away.'

Oh my God, I've blown it. I tell him I don't need liberation and a second later I'm admitting my manager calls the shots. And now that silence is back again, the terrible silence which I know I've just got to break.

In a rush I say: 'My manager's wonderful to me, wonderful, and that's why I always choose – *choose* – to do what she wants. Okay, I'm not doing what she wants right now, she wouldn't want me to be here, but I made an exception tonight to my rule about always choosing to do what she wants. I came here because Carta asked me. I came here because she and I were both friends of Richard Slaney. And that means something. That's special. That's *real*.' Suddenly I find myself thrusting my right hand sideways towards Carta. I don't look at her. I just stretch out my hand and she takes it in hers, she never hesitates, because she knows that what I'm saying is true.

I know now why that silence was so unbearable. It's the silence of truth, the silence people keep when they've no option but to listen to lies. I lied earlier when I described my job in upbeat euphemisms, and the silence dropped on me like a lead weight. I lied just now about being liberated, and back came the silence to crush me to pulp. But when I told the truth about my mother Nicholas Darrow had plenty to say, and when I told the truth about how important Richard's friendship was to me, Carta grasped my hand without hesitation.

I see now that these people are all focused on the truth of my situation, and when I lie they react like musicians with perfect pitch who are forced to listen to someone singing flat. These people see my life as it really is, while I . . . well, I never quite face it, do I? And why the fuck should I, I'd like to know? Their truth doesn't have to be my truth! God, how do I get out of this, how do I retreat with dignity, it's role-playing time again, got to be, can't retreat with dignity while I'm being Gavin Blake Me, the stupid plonker who's finally fucked up this scene, so—

'What you all fail to understand,' drawls Gavin Blake Superstud as Carta's hand and mine slip apart, 'is that I've got a great life and the last thing I want is to be "liberated" from it! I make loadsa

223

money. I've got a nice home, a fantastic car, sharp clothes in the closet – shit, I've even got a valet who cooks for me and does my chores! I'm proud of what I do, I tell you! I've got everything I could possibly want!'

In the crippling silence which follows, someone stands up. It's Mr Exocet-Missile. I might have known that in the end he'd be the one to blast me to pieces. Of course he hates me, despises me, thinks I'm the lowest of the low.

He walks across the room and plants himself on a spot twelve inches from my shoes. Then he stoops over, puts his hand gently on my shoulder and says in such a kind voice that my head swims: 'But Gavin, where's your freedom to be yourself?'

I'm slaughtered.

*   *   *

I do a runner, bolting from the room and blundering up the steps towards the churchyard, but before I can reach the top Carta calls my name.

I stop. I wouldn't have stopped for anyone else, but I stop for her and she joins me. She's breathing quickly but otherwise she's cool. She offers me her business card for the first time, and as I take it I see her mobile phone number's printed below the number of her office. I look at the numbers dumbly but I know this is all to do with the way we clasped hands after I mentioned Richard, all to do with me talking about my mum, all to do with truth and me being me and getting treated as a real person instead of a load of shit.

Carta's saying: 'You ought to have all my numbers so that we can keep in touch about the donation in the pipeline.'

I'm confused. *All* the numbers? There are only two: the office and the mobile. Then I turn over the card and see the handwritten number she's scrawled on the back. 'Home' she's written after it. So I've scored – but not in any way that's remotely familiar. I've won a gesture of trust and I mustn't abuse it. That means any call I make has to be strictly business, but since I've decided not to go through with my plan to soak Colin there won't be any business to call about. Unless . . .

'Keep me posted,' says Carta with an edgy little smile, but she hides her nervousness by adding warmly: 'Thanks for coming – you were a big help to me.'

'I was?'

'Yes, I needed you to confirm your clients were tough guys who made their own decisions . . . And of course we all loved the story about your mother. It was like one of those parables, I forget which one, I'm not very good on the Bible yet, but it was definitely theological.' Turning away she says over her shoulder: 'Thanks again for making the effort to come here. We all really appreciated it.'

She click-clacks back down the steps and I stagger on up into the churchyard.

Then I hit Egg Street and start running to the car park near Austin Friars.

*   *   *

Falling into the car I jam a CD into the slot and Verdi's music begins to pour out, big, brash, lush and plush, a lavish wall of sound. I turn up the volume until it's head-splitting, chopping up all unwanted thoughts about the kind of life I lead and flattening the memory of how I so totally lost the plot at the end of my gala performance for the rehab crew. But the memory doesn't stay flat. It springs up again. Why did I make such a bloody pathetic balls-up? Because I was brain-damaged after being clobbered by that job offer, that's why. I still can't believe the offer was made. The Rector of St Benet's offered *me* a job! Maybe I should have accepted. Would I have worked alongside Carta? God! No, wake up, you dork, and stop fantasising. If I chose to work openly for St Benet's I'd have a death wish.

I tell myself I wish I'd never gone to the meeting but that's a lie. It was good to be thanked and praised and offered a job. And something happened between me and Carta, though I'm still not sure what it was. We held hands but it had nothing to do with sex. Weird. Almost pervy. Shit, my head's totally done in, that bunch have punched my lights out and it's a wonder I can even remember what happened . . .

But I'm remembering. I'm remembering Nicholas. Can't call him Mr Charisma any more as if he were a client who could be nicknamed and treated as meat. This is Mr Darrow who offered me a job, and when we met at Richard's funeral he said I could call him Nicholas or Nick. Carta calls him Nicholas so I shall too.

I go on remembering. I remember that throughout the interview no one used the P-word to describe my profession. That was a mark

225

of respect, wasn't it? And they didn't sneer when they said 'leisure-worker' either.

Elizabeth says there's never any need to mention the P-word because it's only used by narrow-minded people who can't accept that leisure-workers perform such a useful social service. The word 'sex-worker' is misleading too, conjuring up images of drugged-up trash in massage parlours. It's just not good enough for the kind of top-quality service I provide.

Elizabeth's a great one for using alternative vocabulary. It's not just the P-word which is taboo. 'Evil', 'decadent' and 'degrading' become 'naughty', 'pervy' and 'avant-garde'. Perversions are called 'speciali-ties' and given bright little names like 'water sports'. She does use the conventional four-letter words but only when conducting busi-ness. Once she's in a domestic setting the euphemisms rule supreme.

'I like to leave professional language at the office door,' she said to me once, although thank God she's never attempted to impose this preference on me. I need to use four-letter words to relieve the tension of my daily life, and I'd burst a blood vessel if I always had to talk like a Victorian maiden – or like a classic shady lady hooked on a dream of naff respectability.

'Professional language'! In the office, where sex is treated as a commodity, Elizabeth says 'fucking' as easily as some people say 'marketing' or 'sales'. The one four-letter word she never utters is 'love'. 'You do love me, don't you?' I said to her recently and she answered at once: 'Of course I do, pet,' but the word 'love' never passed her lips, and sometimes I think that if she really loved me she wouldn't want me to work in the leisure industry. But on the other hand, it's all I'm good for and she did spot my talent for it, so . . .

So I mustn't be too demanding. Instead of nagging her about love I should try remembering that *she's* the one who 'liberated' and 'empowered' me, converting a dead-eyed wreck into a mega-success.

But where's your freedom to be yourself, chum? And where's your liberation and empowerment now?

Oh, shit, shit, shit . . .

But it's no use cursing. What I have to do is pull myself together before I make a fatal slip, and that means no more double-life as a fundraiser and no more visits to St Benet's.

And Carta? Well, if I know what's good for me I'll give her up too, and I know what's good for me, don't I?

Punching off the Verdi I drive the last mile home in the deadest of dead silences.

* * *

Earlier in the day, to cover up my visit to St Benet's, I left a message for Elizabeth with Susanne to say that I was having a drink after work with Serena. I figured Elizabeth wouldn't mind if I spent an hour after work with the approved girlfriend, but when I get home she's irritated.

'Serena's for weekends, pet,' she says. 'I don't want you wearing yourself out during the week with after-work activities.' But then she relents and says she's glad I'm getting on well with Serena, such a nice girl and such good quality. She makes Serena sound like a stack of expensive bed linen.

By this time I'm exhausted but as soon as I'm upstairs I take the time to memorise Carta's home and mobile numbers until I'm confident enough to tear up her business card and flush it down the bog. (The office number's already memorised, and anyway that's recoverable from the Telecom totty.) Even though I've taken the sane, rational decision that it's too risky to see anyone from lifestyle-threatening, brain-blitzing St Benet's again I still can't bear to pass up Carta's personal numbers. I tell myself I just want them engraved on my heart as a souvenir. Am I nuts? No, I can argue that this move to memorise is actually crafty psychology. If I bin the numbers I'll immediately want to call her, but if I have the numbers available I won't feel so driven to do something risky. I can just live with the option to get in touch until the urge to call has faded.

Well anyway, that's my story and I'm sticking to it.

I flop into bed and crash out.

* * *

Despite the stress I wake the next morning feeling ready for anything – until I remember that at eight o'clock I have to screw Gilbert Tucker. Elizabeth even reminds me about this before I leave the house.

'Try and get some good angles for the cameras, pet, and make sure the full trick's turned. Asherton wants to see more than just you and Mr Tucker playing with each other's equipment.'

I drive to the City in a black mood which gets blacker when I

227

arrive. I've forgotten that I didn't clean up before leaving the flat yesterday, and now I have to rush around at top speed because I haven't allowed extra time for the chores.

When Gil arrives he asks for coffee, which is an unusual request for a client at that hour. I always do have coffee available for the early shift, but most of the time I'm the only one who takes a sip – in the intervals between appointments. The clients don't like to waste time coffee-drinking when they're paying big money for something else, but this lost clerical innocent actually expects to sit on the kitchen barstool and socialise! He says he 'just wants to talk' because 'sex isn't so important as building a relationship'. Why he can't admit he wants to fuck I don't know, but perhaps he feels he has to go through the motions of 'saving me' before he lets it all hang out.

'Look, mate,' I say good-naturedly, knowing we have to get a move on, 'I'm not an escort, paid to chat with you! You'll have to go elsewhere if you want one of those.'

'I've bought the time,' he says. 'Can't I do what I like with it?'

He's got to be seduced – and at eight o'clock in the bloody morning when I'm supposed to be doing routine stuff on automatic pilot! I want to opt out but when I think of Asherton's face if I wind up with no viewable tape I set to work. It takes less than five minutes to get Gil upstairs but I grudge every second of them.

At the top of the stairs outside the door of the main bedroom I pause, just as I always do, to usher the client across the threshold ahead of me. Then as Gil passes by I flick the switch that turns on the hidden cameras. It looks like a light switch. Nobody ever glances twice at it and nobody ever sees me turn it on. Although at the beginning of my career I recorded every session in case a client turned violent, nowadays I pick and choose. There's no point in recording if the client's a sexual non-event (no market for our porn sideline) and if we already have a performance of his on tape to protect ourselves if he ever tries to make trouble, so I suppose on average I film no more than half the sessions a day. There's a camera hidden in the fake smoke alarm, a camera hidden behind the collage of nude photos along one wall and, sneakiest of all, a camera tucked into one of the metal knobs on the ornate iron bedframe. That's for close-ups. The cameras are wired to transmit pictures directly onto videotape which is activated by the electronic equipment in the second bedroom. Tommy has a great time cutting and splicing the

228

film from the three cameras so that the viewer gets a jolt every twelve minutes, just as the porn industry recommends. Porn's very scientific and well researched nowadays. Boring.

I'm not expecting much from Gil. When we did the freebie he was kind of pathetic as he was so out of practice, and this time he's not much better but I can see he's got some kind of mild potential. It helps that I've done him before and know that provided I take care he's not going to seize up at the crucial moment, but I must say I'm relieved when I get past the tricky zone.

I glance at my watch but surreptitiously so that the gesture doesn't show on camera. The fuck's going to be a quickie but I can't coast home, I've got to build to an erotic designer climax in three minutes flat. And all this before eight-thirty in the morning! God, I don't know how those downmarket leisure-workers can do it for peanuts. At least I get well paid.

We finish at eight-twenty sharp. That gives him five minutes to clean up before leaving and it gives me five minutes on my own to prepare for the next client. Gil knows he's allowed a shower provided he takes no more than two minutes, but he shyly asks if I'll have a shower with him. No way, mate! You just want another jolt but time's up and out you go. I don't put it to him as frankly as that, of course. I'm all rueful regret but I don't back down. Why am I being so brutally professional with this nice bloke? Because I can't afford to get involved. Because I don't like to think I'm shafting him towards Asherton. Because this session's a nightmare, that's the truth of it, and I've got to stay detached to keep sane.

'Hey, listen!' I say casually, following my instructions from Elizabeth as I lead the way downstairs. 'I know I'm out of your price range, but I like you a hell of a lot and I'm sure now we could have a great time together. Why don't I fix it with my manager so that you get a big discount? She always allows me one client I see just for pleasure.'

I wonder if he can possibly be stupid enough to swallow this, but he does. It's all that romantic idealism which is slopping around in his head – plus his recent eighteen months on a no-sex diet which is enough to drive any normal man up the wall. Gil may be a clergyman but he wasn't designed to be a celibate saint. He was designed to be a good man in a one-to-one committed relationship with the companion of his dreams. It's just his bad luck that his dreams are the Church's nightmares, but I suppose these gay clergymen hope the Church will redefine the term 'unnatural sex' so that everyone can live happily ever after. Well, a new definition's certainly needed, considering that we now know men have an erogenous zone by the prostate which can only be accessed via the anus. What can be more natural than wanting to tickle an erogenous zone? But I can't quite see the dog-collared straights ever debating that one in the Church of England's General Synod.

I suddenly realise Gil's saying: 'I really shouldn't see you any more.'

Shit, I have to run the seduction line again and we're clean out of time.

I do my best. Physical contact. Gooey words. A real melting moment. He backs down, says he'll call Elizabeth.

'You'll find her very understanding!' I say, smiling, as I open the front door wide, but still he doesn't go. He's giving me a flyer – something about gay Christians and how they all need to look after one another.

Big deal! Who's looking after Gil?

'I thought the Christian view was that all human beings should look after one another,' I say, somehow keeping my voice casual although I'm ripe to yell with impatience. 'Why should caring be allocated according to what people get up to in bed?' And as he opens his mouth to deliver some pathetic activist spiel I say with a laugh: 'No, don't tell me! We'll talk about it next time.'

I finally succeed in shoehorning him out of the flat. Then I go to the kitchen and toss the flyer in the garbage.

*　　*　　*

'That was very nice, dear,' says Elizabeth to me that evening after viewing the take of the third camera. Following orders I've brought back the tapes myself instead of leaving them to be collected by Tommy. 'Very professional.' She glances at Asherton who's looking like a food junkie after a thousand-calorie hit: all wet lips and bright eyes and a tongue that can't stay still. 'But personally,' she adds, 'I'm still not with you on this one, Ash. Tucker's looks are pretty run-of-the-mill if you ask me, and Gavin had to work ever so hard to make him look interesting.'

'I'm sure Gavin can help Gilbert become more accomplished! How long do you think it would take, Gavin my dear, to buff him to a high lustre?'

230

Asherton's insisted that I should be present while the tapes are being played so that I can see for myself what improvements need to be made. I'm loathing every minute of this scene, although I keep my face expressionless. I don't mind seeing myself on tape. I stopped being self-conscious about my performances a long time ago and in fact it does me good to see how professional I am at my job. But I just hate to see that mega-perv drooling over Gil.

Answering his question I say: 'If I could see him a couple of times a week for a month, I'm sure I could produce a big improvement. Basically he just needs practice.'

'Plus a little instruction, I think . . .' Asherton gets technical. I'm handed paper and a pen and told to take notes.

Eventually Elizabeth reins him in. 'My boy doesn't do SM, as you well know.'

'But this is merely exploring the boundaries!'

'Yes, but your boundaries are on bloody roller skates!'

They haggle away about pervy sex and I listen like a zombie as I wait for the chance to escape.

'. . . all right, my boy'll do that but he won't do . . .'

'. . . yes, yes, of course I want to keep the boy happy, but I don't see why he can't get Gilbert to—'

I suddenly remember Nicholas offering me a job as if I counted, I mattered, I was special, and the next moment my voice says: 'I'm nobody's "boy". I'm a twenty-nine-year-old man.'

Neither of them takes any notice. I'm not a person to them at that moment. I'm just interactive bait for the fish.

Finally Elizabeth says: 'What exactly are you after here, Ash? I don't see how we can discuss Tucker's training properly if you don't tell me what you plan to do with him at the GOLD meeting.'

'*Pas devant le garçon, ma chère.*'

This is a power-play. Elizabeth doesn't speak French though she does speak German, the result of working for a year in Bonn when she was young. (Something to do with providing British girls for the army of occupation, but the Germans got very pissed off and Elizabeth's been xenophobic ever since.) However, when Asherton spouts his French she outmanoeuvres him by guessing what he wants. In-depth discussions about GOLD are always top secret. 'Gavin,' she says colourlessly, and jerks her head towards the door.

Obediently I jump to my feet, but seconds later I'm hiding behind the half-open door of the office across the hall. It's evening. Susanne's

231

gone. The room's in darkness. I peer through the space between the hinges, and sure enough Asherton opens the living-room door to check that I'm not eavesdropping. When it closes again I give him another twenty seconds either to resettle himself or to be paranoid enough to take a second peep, and then I'm gliding back across the hall to put my ear to the panel.

Elizabeth's exclaiming: 'You're joking! A tableau? If you're worried about the members getting jaded, the answer is to overhaul the standard rituals, not to stage a weird one-off where people stand around like statues!'

'You're making too narrow an interpretation of the word "tableau", my love. Naturally what I have in mind is a *tableau vivant*—'

'Oh, stop showing off your bloody French!'

'—by which I mean an exciting happening (as we used to say in the sixties) with minimal dialogue. We lead up to it by putting on a full-blooded version of the black mass to get everyone in the mood – all the trimmings, lots of incense, Gilbert swathed in yards of heavenly Anglo-Catholic lace—'

'Well, pardon my laughter, I'm sure! As I said only the other day, this is just *so* old hat—'

'Do you want to know my plan or don't you?'

'All right, dear, go on. You do ever such a nice version of the black mass for a warm-up. And then?'

'Then we stage the first tableau. I'm designing a graded series of four, each one more stimulating than the last and all of them on the theme of the dominator dominated.' Asherton hesitates for a second before adding smoothly: 'Of course I would have consulted you at the start about the tableaux, but they don't involve any occult practice. I was hoping you'd design the black mass, but if you now feel such a rite's beneath you—'

'You can rejig the last one I designed. What happens in the first tableau?'

'Gilbert, who of course has dominated the mass, now becomes the victim on the altar table. The girl who played the quasi-deflowered pseudo-virgin in the mass is temporarily set aside, and—'

'Wait a mo, you've lost me. How do you get Tucker to fuck the girl in the mass?' Elizabeth's gone into professional mode. This is Business with a capital B. 'You can't get away with fakery!' she says. 'The audience would never stand for it, and anyway Tucker's not an actor, he'd never be convincing.'

232

'This is where Gavin comes in.'

'Oh no he doesn't!'

'Let me explain. In the mass Gavin is the acolyte, doing the deflowering on Gilbert's behalf. Then in the first tableau he has a struggle with Gilbert and emerges dominant. The struggle, of course, can be made to look *deliciously* stimulating, particularly if Gilbert's taught the right wrestling moves.'

'And what happens next?'

'Gavin then fucks Gilbert while the girl watches, and after that, in the second tableau, the girl adopts the role of dominatrix and we can have a most thought-provoking threesome in which—'

'You're trying to cram in too much, and if you take my advice you'll simplify – cut out the straight stuff and make the whole show one hundred per cent gay. Don't worry about the straights in the audience – work in a lesbian duet somewhere and both sexes'll be more than happy. In fact if the choreography's done right even an all-male duet will have everyone panting to join in.'

'Yes, but—'

'Get the Big Boys to pick up a rent boy to play the virgin at the mass – or better still a resting actor who can ham it up. The acolyte can still do the mock-deflowering – I can't see Tucker playing the lead there even when the pseudo-virgin's a man – but make sure the acolyte's attractive and competent, and no, you're *not* using Gavin! My boy doesn't do party work, he doesn't do any stuff which strays across criminal boundaries and he certainly doesn't go poncing around in a series of fucking tableaus!'

'The word is "tableaux", my love. There's no "s" – the French put an "x" on the end and pronounce the word as if it were still in the singular.'

'Oh, bugger the frigging French! Ash, I mean what I say about Gavin.'

'But he'll only be required for the mass and the first two tableaux! He won't feature in the last two when the Big Boys take over and stage the hard stuff!'

'How hard is hard?'

'Well, if you bear in mind dear Gilbert's calling, what could be more wonderously compelling than a climax involving a high, wide, wooden cross?'

'Something that doesn't run the risk of you being banged up for murder! Supposing he dies?'

'Of course he won't die! It takes hours to kill someone that way!'

'But he could go into shock, have a stroke—'

'My dear, I know exactly what I'm doing and I assure you Gilbert will survive!'

'Yes – to tell the police everything! Ash, you simply haven't thought this through!'

'What do you mean?'

'You don't have enough leverage to shut him up. I agree you probably have enough leverage to get him to perform the mass – a video of him with Gavin ought to do the trick, no problem. But if he's a victim on the scale you have in mind he's going to need more than the threat of embarrassment and humiliation to stop him talking. Don't forget that according to Gavin, Tucker's an activist. In other words, it's no secret that he's gay, and to get blackmail to act as a gobstopper where GBH is involved you *must* be able to expose a secret, preferably a criminal act which is more than just a run-of-the-mill party threesome and preferably a criminal act which doesn't incriminate anyone else—'

'My dear, I'm finding your relentless scepticism distinctly tiresome. Did you seriously think I hadn't thought of all that?'

'So what's the plan?'

'In the third tableau he'll take part in a criminal act in which no other people are involved. Do you remember Bugsy, Bonzo's Great Dane?'

'Oh God, not that silly mutt who tried to eat Norah's chihuahuas!' Elizabeth's laughing. She's actually laughing. Then before Asherton can finally lose his temper with her she says pleasantly: 'Well, you're certainly doing your best to ginger up GOLD, dear, and you can be sure I wish you well – if I'm giving you a hard time it's only because I'm worried about what would happen to you if anything went wrong.'

'You mean you're worried about what would happen to *you* if anything went wrong!'

'Now who's being sceptical! No, I'm not worried about myself. If Gavin doesn't participate, I'm not involved . . . But don't let's quarrel, there's a pet, life's too short. How about another gin and tonic?'

Stiff with horror I creep away.

* * *

234

'Hey, Junk-Hunk.'

'Piss off, Trash-Tart.'

After spending a lousy night and an even lousier day agonising about Gilbert Tucker it's a relief to get home and start baring my teeth at Susanne. In times of stress there's comfort in a familiar routine.

Taking no notice of my half-hearted order to piss off, Susanne demands: 'Why's everyone so hyped up over this Gilbert creature? I've had Tommy bellyaching about having to splice the Gilbert tapes in a rush for the Cobra. I've had Elizabeth oozing into the phone to the Gilbert that he's going to get a jumbo discount in the future. And now I've had to bump the Greek geek off the Thursday late-shift so that the Gilbert can get a prime slot! What's going on?'

'Ask Elizabeth.'

'You joking? She doesn't employ me to ask the wrong questions when there's something weird going on, and anyone can see this Gilbert business is totally weirdissimo. Why's the Cobra frothing over like this?'

'Overloaded with venom. Wants the multiple orgasm of the big bite.'

'Don't we all, pet, as Elizabeth would say . . . Hey, you're looking flaky, you know that? Dark circles under the eyes, skin too pale, hairline looking more moth-eaten—'

'Shut it, slag!'

'You'd better perk up before Friday when Sir Colin takes you to the opera! Is he planning to grope your bits in his box?'

'So what if he is? At least my bits aren't pervy, like those bowling-ball boobs you lug around!'

'At least my bits are mine to do what I like with, which is more than you can say for any of your bits!'

'I have a whole army of people queueing up for my bits because they think they're great! Who's queueing up for yours?'

'God, you are *so* pathetic—'

I slam the door of the office and hurl myself upstairs.

*   *   *

Somehow I get through the rest of the working week, but on Friday night I can't relax because I have to do this bloody escort duty with Colin. It should make a difference that I'm going to Covent Garden, but I know he'll make it impossible for me to concentrate on the music, and to make matters worse the opera is *Die Frau Ohne Schatten*, which is definitely not some schmaltzy concoction which one can take in while dozing. Although I'm not too keen on the music of Richard Strauss I always feel it's worth making an effort to be keener, but this new production of *DFOS* is hardly about to mark a breakthrough for me.

Haitink's the conductor, emphasising the chamber-music quality which infiltrates the score, and yes, I can see he's doing a good job, but I don't go for chamber music. Anna Tomowa-Sintao plays the shadowless woman of the title, and yes, she sings well and yes, she looks even better, but she doesn't make me want to grab her. And as for those David Hockney sets . . . No, no, no, as far as I'm concerned the whole junket's off-key, blah, a disappointment . . . but maybe I'd have felt differently if I wasn't being forced to accept it as a prelude to gay sex.

In the interval we're just sipping champagne, the way one does at those sort of plush raves for the snobs who know their *opéra bouffe* from their *bel canto*, when there's an interruption. A slim bloke, fiftyish, well dressed, a little above medium height, with pale eyes, pointy features and pin-thin lips, drifts past us idly before doing an elaborate double take and wheeling back.

'Sir Colin Broune?' he croons. 'What a coincidence! I was just talking about you the other day with my friends—' He reels off two big names in the City, both former clients of mine who wound up members of GOLD '—and we were all saying how much we admired your takeover of United Sulphides. May I introduce myself? The name's Asherton.'

Colin's in an expansive mood, willing to be courteous, and after they've shaken hands he asks him if he too works in the City. Asherton says he does, he has a number of directorships and of course follows the fortunes of the most distinguished captains of industry very closely.

'Oh yes?' says Colin blandly, but I'm sure he's preening himself after this smooth little tribute. 'By the way, may I introduce my friend Gavin Blake?'

'How do you do, Mr Blake.'

'How do you do, sir.'

Colin enquires how Asherton met those two former clients of mine.

'Ah, it's interesting that you should ask me that! We all met – but perhaps this isn't quite the moment to discuss the occasion.

May I buy you a drink some time at—' He names one of Colin's clubs in St James's.

'I'm a member there!' says Colin, all benevolence.

'Then I trust it's all right if our secretaries talk to arrange a date? Let me give you my card . . .'

As Colin takes the card I feel as if I'm watching a healthy man swallow a mouthful of food riddled with E coli.

'And now, if you'll excuse me . . .' Asherton glides away, mission accomplished.

'Smooth sort of chap,' comments Colin, 'but he seems to move in the right circles. What did you think of him?'

'Not my type.'

Colin laughs and gives me a leer which is meant to signify excited affection.

The evening drags drearily on.

* * *

Colin takes me afterwards to some stuffy swill-palace for the rich which is dead boring for anyone under thirty but which allows him to display me as his latest high-gloss accessory. Poor deluded bastard. I'm aware of people staring at us, just as they did in the opera house, and I know they're thinking: oh God, look at that fat old fart with the smooth young leisure-worker, what a pathetic sight. Or at least . . . No, that's not what they're thinking. They're telling themselves: oh God, look at that ugly old bugger with the upmarket *sex-worker*, what a laugh. But no, I've got it wrong again. Face it, Gavin, face it, what they're really thinking is: oh God, look at that sad old man who's being taken to the cleaners by that despicable money-guzzling PROSTITUTE – pass the sickbag, please.

'What's the matter, Gavin?'

The forbidden P-word is still corroding my mind like acid on metal. 'Nothing. Sorry, I'm not used to escort work.'

'But you know me! You're not talking to a stranger!'

I think: you're the one who's talking to a stranger, chum, and you don't even know it.

I spend the whole dinner longing for it to end.

* * *

I'm so exhausted that I oversleep the next morning and only wake up when Elizabeth buzzes me on the intercom. 'I don't like being stood up, pet. How long are you going to keep me waiting in my negligée?'

My brain retrieves the fact that it's Saturday. Bolting out of bed I don't stop to shave. I just rush down to her kitchen to make the early morning tea, but that turns out to be a case of more haste less speed.

'I'm not having my face scraped!' says Elizabeth crossly after I've arrived with the tea and given her a kiss, so I rush upstairs to my razor, but when I hotfoot it back again my coordination's askew and my control's shot.

'You deliberately drank too much to pay me back for insisting you did escort work for once!'

'No, I didn't, I swear I didn't—' I somehow manage to appease her, and by the time I bring her breakfast in bed my multiple apologies have been accepted.

She gives me a peck on the cheek. 'Did you enjoy the opera?'

'No.'

'Oh, what a shame! How did the pick-up go?'

'Dead smoothly, but I still can't see Colin falling for GOLD. If Asherton laces it with pervy stuff, Colin won't stand it for a moment.'

'Oh, neophytes are always handled with care, dear! Don't be misled by all this ridiculous attention Asherton's paying to Gilbert Tucker. That romp's just for the senior hierarchies.'

'Hierarchies?'

'People work their way up to different levels, according to their rate of spiritual progress. It's only when you're fairly advanced that you learn how to satiate the body so that the spirit can be fully liberated.'

'Well, I can't see Colin ever getting beyond the first level!'

'Nonsense, he'll be longing to ascend! The truth is that although the GOLD rituals need a complete makeover, we're still promoting a version of an ancient Gnostic tradition which has always been attractive to spiritual seekers. And what's wrong with being a spiritual seeker?'

'Seeking in pseuds' corner.'

'Really, Gavin, I don't know what's got into you this morning! First you oversleep, then you come down unshaven, then you lose the erection, then you get the erection but come too soon—'

'I'm sorry, I'm sorry—'

'—and finally you behave like a stupid little boy by being cheeky

238

about matters you're much too young to understand! Well, I'm very put out, dear, I really am. I don't see why *I* should have to suffer just because you're out of sorts – run off and take some Alka-Seltzer, for God's sake, and don't come near me again until you've remembered how to behave!'

In shame I slink away.

*　*　*

I go to the local health club to work out and get my body functioning properly. I'm thinking how braindead I was to criticise GOLD. Elizabeth may have made up her mind to kiss GOLD goodbye, but she's still got an emotional stake in that fake religion she's hatched, and if I knock it she's always going to take the sneer personally. And while on the subject of GOLD, don't let's forget that I'll be asking for trouble if I start to whinge about how bored I am with GOLD's current Great White Financial Hope, Sir Colin Broune. If Colin fails to join GOLD, a furious Elizabeth might think I was to blame because I didn't try hard enough to keep him happy – and when Elizabeth's really furious with me anything can happen.

I found that out right at the beginning. It was when Tommy was training me and I decided I couldn't stand it any more. I'd fluffed a move and Tommy had taken the opportunity to hurt me. Bloody sadist. Anyway, I lost my temper, knocked him out and disappeared for the weekend to Amsterdam where I drugged and drank till I dropped. When I ran out of money I came back – couldn't live without Elizabeth, my only hope of getting a life – but I found the Big Boys were waiting to take me to the Pain-Palace.

Never again.

God, how did I ever dare do any fundraising for St Benet's? I must have been out of my skull. Carta's just a beautiful dream, I can see that now. She'll never go to bed with me. She's prepared to be friendly because of the fundraising but deep down she still thinks I'm scum. Well, I am, aren't I? I can't even protect myself now by using the word 'leisure-worker', and that's because something's happened in my mind. Hugo's still yelling out the P-word from his crevice, but I'm used to muzzling Hugo and this new shift of consciousness has nothing to do with him. It's as if being offered a job – being treated as a real person – forces me at last to face the truth about the work where I'm treated as meat.

I feel I want to say to myself in the manner of a recovering alcoholic: my name's Gavin Blake and I'm a prostitute. But of course, unlike a recovering alcoholic, I could never say such a thing out loud. The P-word's so putrid. It makes me feel I don't count, I don't matter, I'm just filth.

When I return home from the gym Elizabeth says she'll give me a second chance, and in bed I find I'm fully recovered. Thank God. Crisis over.

Now at last I can relax in the knowledge that I'm completely safe . . .

*　　*　　*

I'm in excruciating danger and I feel as if I'm travelling in a plane that's just been hijacked.

It happens on Tuesday when Colin has his next session with me. I'm just wasting another kilo of baby oil on massaging the blubber when he murmurs: 'By the way, I made a decision about that charity of yours.'

The plastic bottle slips out of my hand and thumps him between the shoulder blades, but luckily it's almost empty. Scooping it up I say in a casual voice: 'Oh yeah?'

'Yes, I decided I liked the idea.'

'Ah . . . I thought as you hadn't said any more about it—'

'You came to the opera with me, didn't you?'

'Yes, but I wasn't dumb enough to think that guaranteed—'

'It guaranteed I read the brochure. Then this morning I made the decision to explore the situation further so I rang them up and demanded to speak to the Rector. He was very civil, said we should meet.'

I've stopped massaging. As I watch my hands I notice with fascination that they're unsteady.

'So,' says Colin, still unaware that I'm in shock, 'I've asked him to come down to the Hall on the weekend after next, and I thought it would be an excellent idea if you were there too.'

I panic. 'No, that's not possible – Elizabeth would never allow it – don't even think of approaching her—'

'I phoned her this morning,' says Colin.

*　　*　　*

I nearly pass out. I have to squeeze my eyes shut for a moment before I can ask: 'What did she say?'

'Oh, she went through all that rigmarole about you not doing escort work at weekends, but I took no notice. I said it would do you good to have a little holiday in the country, and finally she agreed.'

'Colin . . . did you mention Mr Darrow?'

'No, Darrow's visit's none of her business.'

'And you didn't mention that I'd given you that tip about the Appeal?'

'Of course not! What we say in the privacy of this room is confidential – I rely on your discretion and you can certainly rely on mine. Besides, while I'm exploring the possibility of making this donation I want to treat the entire matter as top secret.'

I start to breathe evenly again. 'Thanks . . . The truth is Elizabeth's very anti-Church and she'd be furious if she knew I was championing St Benet's.'

'Of course she would! She's against the Church because she's a thoroughly corrupt woman, and I won't rest until I've persuaded you to leave her and come to live with me . . . You'd like to see my country house, wouldn't you?'

'Uh—'

'Then that's settled. I don't care what I pay. It'll be worth it.'

I restart the massage, thank my lucky stars for Colin's discretion and wonder if there's any way I can avoid not only the stupefying boredom of forty-eight hours in his company but the insane risk of another encounter with Nicholas Darrow.

*   *   *

When the late-shift ends I recall the numbers engraved on my heart and call Carta on her mobile.

I've decided it's best to keep quiet about my own invitation to Colin's country house. If Nicholas knew Colin's prostitute was going to be there he might feel he had to cancel, and if Colin really is going to give money to St Benet's without any further effort on my part, I don't want to queer the pitch. Anyway, I hope to wriggle out of this bloody invitation. Elizabeth knows I need to recuperate at weekends and she knows the last thing I need right now is more escort work.

'Hullo?' says Carta suddenly in my ear.

'It's Gavin. Sorry I haven't been in touch. How are you doing?'

'Fine . . . Gavin, is this really you?'

'Think so. Let me check. Yep, it's me. Why?'

'You're not calling me dumb sex-names. I think this is a hoax call!' she says joking. 'Say something to convince me you are who you say you are!'

'We held hands during a special moment in a church crypt last week. Listen, friend. The big fish is on the line and he tells me he and Nicholas are planning to meet.'

'Oh wow – you mean—'

'Yeah. Him. The one with the place in the country and the invitation for the weekend after next. Check it out with Nicholas.'

'He's already told me. Can't wait to see the lavish Wiltshire mansion!'

My heart gives a great thud. 'You're going with him?'

'Of course! This is major fundraising!'

'Cool!' I breathe, reeling from the testosterone surge. 'Keep me posted, huh? Take care.'

As I sign off, my equipment feels ready to bust out of my trousers. What a wimp I've been, saying I'm scum and wallowing in the P-word! The truth is I can still play the superstud like no other bloke in this town, and if Frosty-Puss and I spend the night under the same roof I'll score. After all, do I or do I not have a talent for sex? And is she the Golden Girl of my dreams or isn't she? If this were a book, I tell myself fiercely, *of course* the hero and heroine would finally get together and shag themselves senseless in an orgy of you-name-it-we-do-it stud/babe gymnastics.

And the chore of doing escort work on a weekend? No problem! In fact now I know Carta's plans I can hardly wait for that nice little holiday in the country . . .

CHAPTER FIVE

Carta

'The challenge in pastoral care here is to identify with suffering people and to offer companionship on their journey . . .'

A Time to Heal
A report for the House of Bishops on the Healing Ministry

I

'Nicholas,' said Lewis, 'you shouldn't touch this invitation with a bargepole.'

We were at the Rectory after Gavin had called to tell me that my latest hot prospect was none other than the client he had marked as the major donor-to-be. Lewis, Nicholas and I had agreed to meet immediately and were now closeted in Nicholas's study.

'I don't understand,' I said to Lewis, making a huge effort to cling to my patience. 'Why do we have to handicap ourselves by keeping this donor at arm's length?'

'I'm not saying we have to do that. I'm saying that all negotiations should be conducted at St Benet's. That's because once you and Nicholas cross Sir Colin's threshold you step into his private life and run the risk of condoning the relationship with Gavin.'

'But we can't go around offending potential donors by refusing their invitations!' I cried. 'We just can't!'

'Hold it,' said Nicholas soothingly. 'Let's get this quite straight. I don't think that accepting the invitation does involve me in Sir Colin's private life except in a purely formal sense, and I certainly don't believe it would involve me in that private life's seamy side. A lot of tycoons do business by entertaining people at their country houses, and the private life on display there is inevitably acceptable because

243

anything else might wreck the business under discussion.'

'Everything I've heard about Sir Colin supports this,' I added before Lewis could speak. 'The word is that he lived for many years with a man who recently died, but Sir Colin has the reputation of being very discreet about his private life. He'll never even mention Gavin to us, I'm sure of that.'

'So he's recently been bereaved?' said Nicholas interested. 'Maybe what we're seeing here is an unhappy man, very lonely, missing his partner and looking for love in entirely the wrong place. From a pastoral point of view—'

Lewis made another strong intervention. 'Nicholas you mustn't get pastorally involved with this man – or if you do, you can't take his money. Get back on course and face the fact that this donor is one of Gavin's clients and that you're up to your neck in a situation riddled with moral ambiguity!'

'Can I just make a practical point?' I said, trying to extricate us from the metaphysical mire by beaming in on the big issue. 'As Gavin's not going to be present when we meet Sir Colin, does it really matter whether the meeting takes place in the country or the City? Surely all that matters is that Gavin's not there.'

'I agree,' said Nicholas abruptly. 'We should accept the invitation to Wiltshire and we should explore what's on offer – and we can go forward secure in the knowledge that Gavin will be both absent and unmentioned.'

The conversation closed.

II

I had been relieved to hear from Gavin because it had worried me when he had stayed out of touch even though I had given him all my phone numbers. What an irony that I should now be keen to hear from him! But something had happened to our relationship during that fraught meeting at the Healing Centre. It was as if, for a few disorientating seconds, someone had switched off the sexual current which flared between us so that we saw each other in a radically altered light. When he had reached out trustingly during that pathetic final monologue I had clasped his hand without a second thought and known myself to be linked with

244

him in some way impossible to describe. But I had said nothing about my feelings afterwards. I was embarrassed because they seemed to fall so far short of the professional detachment achieved by my colleagues, who were ruthless in their analysis of him after he had fled.

'A nasty piece of work,' said Val as we held the post-mortem on the meeting. 'Very manipulative, a skilled liar and totally untrustworthy. Of course he got under our skin when he reworked the parable of the talents, but how do we know a single word of that story about his mother was true?'

'I hate to say this,' remarked Robin to Nicholas, 'but Val's right to be sceptical. That's a very disturbed young man, and I don't think he can be reached simply by offering him a part-time job – or indeed by any conventional method of befriending. He needs psychiatric help.'

Neutrally Nicholas said: 'A hysteric personality, do you think? Someone with a borderline personality disorder?'

'Not necessarily. I was wondering if he'd ever had an untreated breakdown or endured some serious trauma.'

'The death of the brother?'

'I was thinking more of rape or some other form of assault. The shock can result in manifestations of inappropriate behaviour coupled with dissociation and denial . . . What was your own opinion, Nick?'

'Well, obviously he's a manipulative liar but then his lifestyle hardly encourages him to be anything else. And obviously he's profoundly disturbed, but then one would hardly expect him to be otherwise. But I believed the story about his mother.'

'Why?' I said, believing it too but needing to have a solid reason for doing so.

'He was astonished by the effect that the story had on us. I concede he probably came across the parable of the talents during his education, but I don't think he was consciously adapting it.'

'So is the parable a sign?' I said rapidly. 'Does it mean the situation's from God and not from . . . well, not from something that's not God?'

Nicholas smiled at me and said: 'Possibly. But we must still be cautious.'

There was a pause while we all came to realise that one of us had so far said nothing.

'Lewis?' said Nicholas at last.

'Oh, the situation's quite obviously from God,' said Lewis gloomily, 'and we must do our very best for Gavin no matter what the cost to ourselves.'

III

As we all boggled at him, Lewis laughed and added: 'I'm still not saying we should take unacceptable risks. I'm just saying that we shouldn't spare ourselves in doing what we can to help this boy – and he's a lost boy if ever there was one. Forget personality disorders, post-traumatic shock and all that modern guff! He's lost, that's all that needs to be said, and what he needs is the chance to come home – to come home, as the mystics would say, to his true self. And yes, of course the story about his mother was true, and yes, of course it was extraordinary that in his grossly disabled spiritual state he should borrow a narrative framework from Our Lord Jesus Christ, and yes, of course it was a sign from God that we're to do our best to release the boy from his prison! Although having said all that, I'd like to add that for me the most extraordinary part of the entire extraordinary interview wasn't the story about his mother. It was the moment when he held out his hand to Carta.'

'Surely that was just a sex play to win her sympathy?' said Val unimpressed.

I opened my mouth and shut it again. At that point I was so worried that my sexual attraction to Gavin was clouding my judgement that I decided any comment could only be a mistake.

'I think the handclasp was an instinctive gesture made when he realised he was skirting a psychological abyss,' Robin was saying, 'and we probably shouldn't read too much into it. Gavin's denial was crumbling and he got frightened – which reminds me, Lewis, I did think you went too far at the end. Gavin had resurrected his defences to protect himself, and you shouldn't have tried to tear them down again.'

'Nonsense!' said Lewis robustly. 'I was throwing him a lifeline, expressing care and concern!'

I was unable to stop myself asking: 'But will he be all right?'

'I don't think you need worry, Carta,' said Robin, adopting his most soothing professional manner. 'The odds are that Gavin managed to slip back into denial after he left the Healing Centre, and this'll protect him from the truths he can't face – and shouldn't face without psychiatric help.'

Lewis made no comment on this but said to Nicholas: 'I'll put Gavin on the prayer list straight away. I've been praying for him myself, but I haven't yet put his name before the group.'

'So what happens next?' I said confused. 'What should my next move be?'

'You wait,' said Nicholas promptly. 'You've given him your numbers. He'll be in touch.'

Robin agreed. 'He won't be able to resist another trip into the world of Richard Slaney,' he said, 'particularly now he knows he'll be treated with respect here.'

'Poor bastard!' said Val impulsively. 'I didn't mean to be too hard on him, but he's such a walking disaster – look how he keeps stirring us up!'

Nobody argued with her.

Nicholas urged us all to pray for Gavin, and the post-mortem on the interview finally closed.

IV

There had been another notable conclusion which had emerged from the post-mortem: we were now all certain that the donation in the pipeline should be accepted.

'Here's someone with a very fragile personality,' had been the comment from Robin, 'someone who needs every possible affirmation and support. We can't refuse the donation now.'

'Much as I disliked Gavin,' Val had said, 'I think we have to give him whatever support we can,' and Lewis had added: 'Accepting this future donation is certainly risky but I feel we have to do it.'

After marvelling that we were now of one mind on this subject despite the variety of opinions about Gavin himself, I decided to linger at the Rectory after the post-mortem in order to have a private word with Lewis. I wanted to talk to him about the handclasp. I also knew it was time to admit I needed help with the chaotic knot which Gavin constantly created and recreated in my head.

'You seem to be advancing in your quest to see Gavin as a multi-dimensional person instead of a two-dimensional stereotype,' commented Lewis after I had uttered the magic words 'I can't cope' and spewed out the muddle I was in. 'Your ability to see him as vulnerable when you met in Austin Friars this morning was definitely a big step forward, particularly since that took place before the meeting which exposed his vulnerability.'

'But the problem is I can't seem to shake off *my* vulnerability! I keep thinking I'll toughen up but I don't.'

'Maybe you're trying to toughen up in the wrong way.'

'What do you mean?'

'Before I try to answer that, let's just do a survey of the invisible landscape here so that we can work out what's going on between the two of you on the psychical and spiritual level. I think Nicholas's original idea has been proved right and that you and Gavin are currently travelling together on a journey. We can't tell yet what this is ultimately going to mean for you, but if things go right the journey should lead to healing, redemption and renewal.'

'And if it goes wrong?'

'Then we're talking of damage, disintegration, even destruction . . . But better not dwell on that. Be like a tightrope walker and don't look down.'

'So what did the handclasp mean in this context?'

'It meant you're both up there on the high wire, each with the potential to save the other from the long drop. Gavin wobbled, reached out to you – and you were there, no question about it, no hesitation.'

'But what about my relationship with Eric?' I burst out. 'Gavin's creating havoc in my personal life!'

'Maybe the relationship with Eric needed a shake-up.'

'But—'

'I suspect the relationship with Gavin and the relationship with Eric aren't mutually exclusive. It just seems as if they are because Eric's been behaving foolishly and you've been unsettled by Gavin's sex appeal.'

'*Unsettled?*'

'All right, how about sandbagged? Carta, the challenge – and this is where we get to the problem of how you toughen yourself up – the challenge is to think of Gavin in a radically different way. Think of him as an abused child who wants desperately to be loved. If you have sex with him you merely join the list of his abusers and wind up abused in your turn when he discards you, so try thinking of yourself as his older sister, fed up with his outrageous behaviour but knowing you've got to be there for him. The fact is that what Gavin requires of you up there on the high wire is neither sex nor romance nor even a sentimental affection, but a clear-eyed, no-nonsense sisterly love that he can trust.'

'And Eric?'

'Oh, Eric requires everything but a sisterly love! You see? The two relationships aren't designed to impinge on each other. Now listen carefully, Carta. I know you've taken in what I've just said. But I also know that within minutes of leaving this room, you're going to look back on my advice and think: dear old Lewis, how kind he was, but of course his older-sister line had no relation to reality, he's forgotten what it's like to be in the grip of a powerful sexual attraction—'

'Lewis, I'd never think—'

'Yes, you would, but listen. The notion that strong sexual attraction can't possibly be withstood is one of the most fashionable fairy tales of our present culture. The reality is we can say no as well as yes – God gives us free will, not biological slavery.'

'Well sure, I do realise—'

'Now we've reached the heart of what I want to say about toughening up. I'm not suggesting you should repress your feelings. I'm suggesting you should sublimate them. That's crucially different. If you repress them by pretending they're not there, they won't go away – they'll merely control you unconsciously before breaking out later just as violently, if not more violently, than before. And I suspect this is where you've been going wrong in trying to toughen up. You've been opting for repression instead of sublimation.'

'Okay,' I said cautiously. 'Okay . . . But what does sublimation involve?'

'You don't try and blot the feelings out. You face them and you use the energy they generate in a productive and meaningful way. Sublimation, unlike repression, means *you're* the one in charge.'

'Examples?'

'Well, suppose you really were an acrobat up there on the high wire with Gavin. You notice he's looking supremely attractive and the next moment you're so overcome that all your energy has to be spent on keeping your balance. You try not to look at him, but the more you try the worse you wobble and finally you fall.'

'Repression.'

'Exactly. But now listen to this. Once again you're up there on the high wire with Gavin. Once again you notice that he's looking supremely attractive, but because you know he's very sick you're also aware he's in great danger. Suddenly he starts to wobble and at once all your energy is channelled into saving him. Part of that energy would automatically be used to make sure you kept your own balance, but you wouldn't be thinking of yourself. You'd shut right down on the self-centredness in order to keep him alive, and the sexual attraction at that moment would be irrelevant, set aside as non-essential for survival.'

There was a silence as I recognised this sublimation script, but finally I puffed out my cheeks as if I'd just climbed a steep flight of stairs and said: 'That reminds me of the moment when Gavin and I clasped hands. All I could think of was helping him get through that meeting without breaking down – I didn't think of myself, only of him, and sex definitely wasn't on the agenda at all.'

'I rest my case . . . And now a final word about Eric. Maybe that brother of his could help him be wiser here. Eric always listens to Gilbert, doesn't he?'

'Yes, but Gil's been so busy with his Aids ministry that they haven't met for ages.'

After a pause Lewis said: 'Gilbert should take care he doesn't suffer burn-out.'

'Oh, I'm sure he's all right,' I said automatically. 'He's not the kind of clergyman who breaks down.' And I began to worry again about Eric in Norway . . .

V

After talking to Lewis I did feel better, and although I still found it hard to visualise how I could keep pushing the right sublimation button, I knew he had given me a useful idea to explore. I was not in the least bothered by the fact that he had broken so many of the rules of modern spiritual direction, the rules which required today's spiritual director to be more of a non-directing 'soul-friend' than an authoritarian adviser. The last thing I ever seemed to want was a non-directive 'soul-friend' shyly fostering insights. I always wanted a clerical buccaneer who would take charge and tell me what to do, and although I did realise that Lewis was able enough to adopt other styles with other people, I found this thought unsettled me. It made me wonder if his decision to serve up the style I preferred was because he felt I was too spiritually stupid to respond to a more sophisticated approach, and this suspicion made me feel more spiritually stupid than ever.

My conversation with Lewis concluded the important discussions resulting from Gavin's visit to the Healing Centre. There followed an interval of several days during which Gavin remained out of sight, but eventually he phoned to identify my new hot prospect, Sir Colin Broune, as his client, and the coming weekend in Wiltshire took on an entirely different dimension.

I did wonder whether to call Eric to keep him abreast of the news.

But in the end, unable to face another row, I did nothing.

VI

My ploughed-up private life explains why I was not only willing and able to work through the weekend but was actually looking forward to the visit to Sir Colin's country house near Devizes. Despite Gavin's participation, I knew it would be a mistake to regard the donation as in the bag and I was stimulated by the challenge Sir Colin represented. I had already worked out that it was Nicholas who would have to take the fundraising lead; after further research I had pegged Sir Colin as a man who was not just indifferent to women but averse to them, and who would always prefer to do business with his own sex. His big interest outside his work was music, but neither Nicholas nor I were experts in this field.

'The topic that we all have in common is the City,' Nicholas had said when we brainstormed our approach to this big fish. 'You can talk money and business to him and I can talk the livery companies, the Lord Mayor and the Corporation hierarchy. Is he interested in cars? I wouldn't mind chatting about his latest Rolls.'

Although Nicholas had a private income and could well have afforded a smart car he always chose to avoid extravagance and demanded no more of a car than that it should get him from A to B without a fuss. On the journey down to Wiltshire that Saturday he drove his white Peugeot which contained no tape deck, no phone and, most amazing of all, no radio. This should have made the journey restful, but I could have used some soothing music. I had never before spent a weekend in a grand country house, and my working-class Glaswegian roots were twitching.

Nicholas, on the other hand, seemed wholly relaxed about the inevitable grandeur to come, but his roots were rather different from mine; he actually owned a small country house, his mother's family home, which had been let for years to an Anglican religious order. Alice said he wanted to retire there eventually, but I couldn't quite imagine Nicholas being content to loaf around in the country being uncharismatic.

We drove on. It was a cool November day with strong gusts of wind and big fleecy clouds which moved at a brisk pace across the sky. Once we left the motorway the Wiltshire countryside was all smooth green hills dotted with sheep and garnished with the occasional clump of trees. It was an ancient landscape. Megalithic stones standing in a nearby field contrasted oddly with the warning notice of the Ministry of Defence that the area beyond the fence was an army shooting range.

'It's good to get out of London,' Nicholas commented as we approached our journey's end. 'Despite Lewis's misgivings I think this trip's going to be a success.'

'Is that a psychic prediction?'

'Let's hope so!'

As we laughed we reached a village where the cottages were built of stone and roofed with dark thatch. There was no village green but a stream ran alongside the main street, and beyond the church a signpost marked THE HALL pointed across the bridge into the woods.

A minute later we saw the house. The car swerved as Nicholas's hands slipped on the wheel and I gave a gasp of astonishment.

An enormous Gothic pile, towered, turreted and teased into fantastical shapes, was glowering at us beyond the gates by the lodge. There was even a gatekeeper who sprang out and checked who we were before opening the gates with the flick of a remote control. As I glanced up the drive again I felt that the architectural corpse, mummified for twentieth-century living, looked both utterly surreal and deeply unpleasant. I had never seen anything like it except in horror films, the kind where the heroine runs screaming down the grand staircase only to trip over a severed head in the hall.

'Roll out your ghost-busting skills, Nicholas!' I said, trying to make a joke of my uneasiness, and he smiled, but as soon as he had parked the car on the gravel sweep in front of the house his mood changed. He said abruptly: 'I'm getting very bad vibes.'

'Because of the architecture?'

'Because of the symbolism. We both expected a pleasant country house and we've been handed a Gothic horror.'

'Sorry, you've lost me. Are you implying—'

'Something frightful's going to hit us. Lewis got it right. We should never have come.'

'But Nicholas, the situation hasn't changed just because we now find Sir Colin lives in a Gothic mansion! What frightful thing could possibly happen?'

The front door of the house opened and out walked Gavin.

VII

I said: 'Oh my God.' I tried closing my eyes and opening them again but Gavin was still there. 'Nicholas,' I said weakly, 'Nicholas—'

'Yes. Disaster.'

'What on earth do we do?'

'Be normal. Betray nothing.'

We crawled out of the car just as Gavin surged up to us. He was wearing a mixture of smart casualwear, plenty of blue and palest grey with a subtle dash of creamy white, and looked like a film star taking time out on the set of his latest multi-million-dollar movie. I tried to think of him as my younger brother. Nothing happened.

'Hi!' he said, smiling radiantly. 'Surprise!'

'Surprise!' I echoed, smiling radiantly back as the chaotic knot began to re-form in my head.

'Welcome to the modern version of Hellfire Hall! Did you ever see such a perfect location for a horror film?'

'Can't wait for the buckets of blood. When did you get down here?'

'Last night . . . Hi, Nicholas!'

Nicholas casually gave him a hand to shake before saying: 'I thought you didn't do escort work?'

'Bloody right I don't but – hold it, here's Colin. I'll have to brief you later . . .'

A middle-aged man, well over six feet tall and built like an American refrigerator, was now watching us from the vast doorway of his home. His baldness was alleviated by a few strands of greying hair. His plain face was scored by a set of harsh lines which suggested belligerence, cunning and a vile temper when crossed. I immediately took a deep dislike to him.

'Mr Darrow,' he said, rudely looking Nicholas up and down, but if he had thought Nicholas was a limp-wristed pushover, he was now disillusioned.

'Sir Colin? How do you do,' Nicholas said effortlessly, quite unintimidated. 'May I introduce my colleague, Carta Graham?'

A fleshy paw was shoved at me. I slipped my hand into it and had my bones crunched.

'Come in,' said Sir Colin, still not bothering to waste energy on a smile, and as soon as he turned to lead the way across the threshold Gavin gave me a sultry look as he allowed his arm to brush against mine. To my horror I realised he was not only deep in denial again but still fixated on playing the stud. That mystical clasp of the hands might never have happened, and as the weekend's gruesome potential for disaster flashed before my eyes I had to fight the urge to slug him in what he coyly referred to as his 'equipment'.

Or at least that was what I told myself as the physical contact seared my arm like a burn.

'As it was Gavin who aroused my interest in your cause,' Sir Colin was saying to Nicholas, 'I thought it would be appropriate if he joined us this weekend. I understand he met you at the funeral of Richard Slaney.'

'That's correct.'

Sir Colin said no more on that subject but suggested that Nicholas should give his car keys to a hovering flunkey (footman?) who had been told to retrieve the luggage. A much grander person (definitely the butler) was lurking in the triple-height hall to show us to our rooms.

Up the grand staircase we toiled and down a picture-studded

gallery we trailed. Acres of soft rich carpet ensured our footfalls were noiseless, and yards of dark oak-panelled walls enhanced the atmosphere of somnolent gloom. Eventually the butler stopped and opened a door. 'This is your room, sir. The lady's room is at the end of the passage.'

Nicholas thanked him and added to me: 'I'll call for you in ten minutes.'

The butler moved on. Following him to the end of the corridor I found myself in a large round room set in one of the many turrets. Beyond the four-poster bed there were views across a striking garden, beautiful even in November, to the woods which surrounded the village.

My suitcase arrived within moments of the butler's departure, and Nicholas soon followed.

'Time for an emergency conference,' he said as I let him in. 'Can we or can't we believe that the discreet Sir Colin Broune's deliberately flaunting his male prostitute?'

'We can't. He's either gone fruity-loops or—'

'—or he has no idea we know Gavin's a prostitute.'

'Sane but ignorant?'

'That's the most likely explanation, but it needn't be the right one. Okay, while we're waiting for Gavin's briefing, let's just do a reality check to try to get our heads round this mess. We know for a fact that Gavin tipped off Sir Colin about St Benet's, and we know for a fact that Sir Colin's Gavin's client, but that's about all we do know. We've been assuming Sir Colin's more than capable of making his own independent decision about whether to support us, but if he's infatuated with Gavin – infatuated enough to invite him to be present this weekend – that may not be the case at all.'

'You're saying the prostitution could be crucial here.'

'Well, what do you think? What are the odds that Sir Colin's said to Gavin: "I'll give to your cause but I want you for a weekend in the country"? Gavin doesn't do escort work and doesn't work on weekends, so it's a safe bet he's here to provide the sweetener that'll open the chequebook. That means that if we accept the resulting donation—'

'—we'd be not only accepting the fruits of prostitution but condoning Gavin's lifestyle—'

'—and that's something which we can't and mustn't do. It was different with the other three donors, when we took the money in good faith, but this time we're hopelessly compromised.'

'Nicholas, I agree with every word you've said, but how on earth do we get out of this disaster?'

We had been standing by the window during this fraught conversation but now, as if to reflect the fact that we were mentally shifting gears, we both sat down on the wide window seat and racked our brains for inspiration.

'I could make a secret call to Lewis,' I said at last, 'and get him to phone you here with news of an emergency which requires your immediate return.'

'No, I can't lie my way out of a tight corner. We've somehow got to survive the weekend here without nailing the donation.'

Another twinge of inspiration flared. 'Hang on,' I said, 'you're making the assumption that the donation's now inevitable, but that still needn't be true. Supposing Sir Colin actually has no intention of giving to St Benet's. Supposing he's just been stringing Gavin along in order to get him to do the escort work he never normally undertakes. If Sir Colin has no intention of giving, we're off the hook.'

'No, we're not. I'm still left condoning a wrong relationship which is being played out under my nose.'

'But don't you see? If you're not profiting from the situation, the weekend becomes viable! Where's the Church law that forbids Christians to follow Jesus' example of mingling with prostitutes and other lowlife?'

Nicholas mulled this over. 'Okay, but I still ought to be upfront with Sir Colin. I have to say right from the start that I can't take his money.'

'But he may not offer us any! Look, Nicholas. If you go downstairs now and say to Sir Colin: "I'm sorry, I can't take your money because of its association with your prostitute," I think that would be pretty damn crude and unkind. We'd do much better to wait until he actually offers the money because (a) it may never happen, and (b) at least the truth would then be a required response and not just an unsolicited verbal mugging.'

Nicholas was silent, thinking.

I pushed on. 'It's unlikely anyway that Sir Colin will make a decision about the donation this weekend,' I said. 'Remember that we've been invited here only to allow him to explore the option. Of course if he admits the prostitution you'll have to make your position clear, but I'm certain that'll never happen – he won't even admit the homosexual relationship! Gavin will have a cover story to explain how they know each other.'

'But what do I do when Sir Colin asks about the Appeal?'

'Tell him about it. Why not? Downplay the financial angle, of course, but talk up the ministry of healing and all the good work done at the Healing Centre.'

Nicholas made up his mind. 'Fair enough,' he said, 'we'll tough it out, but Carta, can I now give you some advice about how to survive this weekend? One: do your best to have no time alone with Gavin, who's clearly back in denial and panting for a sexathon. Two: if a tête-à-tête proves unavoidable, make sure you're nowhere near a bedroom. And three: lock your door tonight *and* wedge it shut. The keys on this floor could be interchangeable.'

'Message received and understood!'

'Sorry to play the Victorian paterfamilias—'

'Relax! You're well within your rights as my boss to give me advice on how to avoid wrecking myself, and I promise not to behave like an airhead.'

Brave words. But what was the reality beneath the tough talk? I tried to think of Lewis's image of the high wire, but the conversation seemed remote and I was unable to connect with it on an emotional level.

With growing uneasiness I followed Nicholas downstairs.

VIII

The butler, on the look-out for us in the hall, led the way into a reception room where a fire flickered beneath a marble chimney-piece. Sir Colin was just asking what we wanted to drink when he received word that a call he had been expecting had come through; excusing himself, he left the room, and the butler followed him after distributing some champagne.

'Thank God!' exclaimed Gavin as soon as the three of us were alone together. 'Now I can talk! Listen, I sell gym equipment to health clubs – remember, Carta? That was my line at Richard's funeral and that's the line I told Colin I'd take this weekend. Colin doesn't know you know I'm a leisure-worker. He's going to present me as his second cousin's son who's interested in a new sales career in one of the divisions of RCPP. He thinks I met you both – *both*, Carta – for the first time at Richard's funeral, and he thinks you believe the flat in Austin Friars is my home.'

Confronted by so many lies stacked up like a house of cards it was hard to know what to say which wasn't judgemental, but I tried quoting: '"O, what a tangled web we weave!"' and made sure my smile was chilly.

However, Nicholas was not prepared to accept this multiple deception with any kind of smile, and despite all the talk of affirming Gavin he now had no hesitation in being critical.

'I dislike lies, Gavin,' he said strongly, 'and I'll go along with these only because I've no wish to be unkind to our host by exposing the deception. And while we're on the subject of deception, why didn't you tell Carta you'd be here? You did us no favours by failing to let us know.'

Gavin took a gulp of champagne and tried to be truculent. 'What does it matter to you,' he said, 'whether I'm here or not?'

'Think about it. You're an intelligent man. Just think.'

I saw how Gavin was affirmed by the word 'intelligent' even as his behaviour was condemned, but before I could find the words which would place me in the same frame, Gavin said rapidly: 'Okay, I'm sorry, but I thought that if I told you I was coming you'd cancel and that might affect the donation.'

At once Nicholas said: 'Why exactly *are* you here? Your manager never normally insists on weekend escort work, does she?'

'Colin's paying a lot of money.'

'No doubt, but since I'm sure he's not the first millionaire who's been prepared to shell out for weekend escort duty, I still want to know why he's the one who gets what he wants. Come on, Gavin! After landing us in all these lies, don't you think you owe us a slice of truth?'

Gavin hesitated but only for a second. 'A friend of my manager's wants Colin to join a private club which needs a financial boost. So when Colin invites me here Elizabeth says he has to be humoured.'

'What's this club called?'

'Dunno.'

'Who's your manager's friend?'

'Some suit or other. Hey, don't mention this to Colin whatever you do! He may not know about the club yet and if he finds out ahead of time Elizabeth'll know I've grassed and then I'll be in deep shit.'

Nicholas suddenly gave him a warm smile. 'You remind me of a character in a John Le Carré novel,' he said. 'One of those spies who gets himself tied up in such a knot that he can't work out how to come in from the cold.'

I saw Gavin smile back, basking in the sympathy Nicholas was projecting, but all he said was: 'My dad liked John Le Carré's books.'

At that point Sir Colin returned to the room and we were obliged to sink into half an hour's small-talk before lunch, but my thoughts were skimming round and round in my brain like racing greyhounds. I was thinking: so Elizabeth's using Gavin to hook for a private club. And Kim was lured into a secret, pseudo-religious society by Mrs Mayfield, although that particular group wasn't just for gays. If I could somehow prove the organisations were one and the same . . . but how could I, when I had never known the name of Kim's corrupt society which had peddled a perverted form of Gnosticism?

Pushing aside my obsession with the past, I willed myself to focus on the present.

IX

I thought Sir Colin might ask Nicholas questions about St Benet's during lunch, but he merely talked at mind-numbing length about the recession, the ERM disaster and the impact on the City of the latest bombing strikes by the IRA. By the time lunch ended I was exhausted by the effort of being a good listener, and glancing at Gavin, who had long since sunk into a bored silence, I saw he was obviously wishing he was back in London.

'Now!' said Sir Colin as we drank our coffee in yet another vast reception room. 'I thought I'd give you a tour of the estate in my new four-wheel-drive Mercedes – a marvellous car, drives straight up a cliff without pausing for breath and I shouldn't be surprised if it swims too, although I confess I've never used it to ford a river. We'll be back in time for tea, of course – can't miss tea, can we? –

and then I'm sure you'd like time to relax in your rooms before dinner. I've invited a few people to join us tonight, not many, can't bear big dinner parties so there'll only be nine of us altogether. The local parson's coming, plus one of the local doctors – oh, and their wives, of course. Didn't want Carta to be all alone when we gentlemen get to the port! There's also another person who'll be joining us, but he's not a local man. The fact is, Nicholas, I want the doctor and the parson to hear you talk of your ministry so that they can give me their professional opinions afterwards. Hope you've no objection.'

'None at all,' responded Nicholas courteously as my heart sank at the prospect of trial by jury.

'Colin,' drawled Gavin, rousing himself from his stupor of boredom, 'did you just imply the ladies wouldn't be drinking port with us? For God's sake, which end of the century are you living in?'

'It's all right, Gavin,' I said quickly. 'This is Colin's house and he's entitled to make the rules.'

'Gavin,' said Sir Colin, 'you're behaving like some immature rebel student. Stop it.'

'Sure – on condition I skip the port-drinking tonight and keep the ladies company, like a eunuch in the Ottoman Empire!'

I immediately laughed in the hope of easing the tension. 'You'd make a rotten eunuch, Gavin!' I said lightly, but my heart sank when he gave me his hottest smile.

Keeping his face expressionless Sir Colin rose to his feet. 'I suggest we all meet in the hall in ten minutes,' he said, and Nicholas and I, both anxious to smooth over the awkwardness, took care to respond with enthusiasm.

As we moved towards the door Gavin tried to follow us, but Sir Colin called him back.

'I can see why Gavin normally does no escort work,' murmured Nicholas to me as we emerged into the hall on our own. 'He's hopeless at it. Carta, no more remarks, please, about how Gavin would make a rotten eunuch – yes, I know you were only trying to defuse the tension, but Colin didn't like it. If he and Gavin have another spat, stay relentlessly neutral.'

I hastily promised I would before adding: 'Of course Gavin was right about all that port rubbish.'

'Of course he was, but as you yourself said, it's Colin's house and he's entitled to make the rules.'

We trudged on up the grand staircase to retrieve our coats for the drive.

X

Contrary to all my expectations the weekend then started to be enjoyable. The Mercedes romped off the road onto cart-tracks and off the cart-tracks into territory where there was no track of any kind. Up and down the valleys we plunged, in and out of the fields, around the spinneys, past clusters of megalithic stones and along flat-topped hills where amazing views stretched on all sides of us. Sir Colin, enraptured with his new toy, was as gleeful as a child on a roller coaster. Even Gavin, who started the trip slumped in the front seat, soon became animated, while Nicholas and I, side by side in the back, found ourselves reacting with a genuine enthusiasm. At four o'clock we all returned to the Hall in good spirits.

When tea was served Gavin behaved immaculately, passing around the plates of triangular sandwiches and the two varieties of cake. Betraying nothing of their relationship by so much as a flicker of an eyelash, Sir Colin largely ignored him in order to reminisce with Nicholas about the 1960s. I could see Sir Colin becoming less intimidating as they shared their middle-aged memories.

At the end of the meal he reminded us that we were now allowed time in our rooms before the next bout of socialising. 'Drinks at seven,' were his parting words. 'We'll dine at quarter to eight.'

'So far so good,' muttered Nicholas to me as we once more toiled up the grand staircase. 'I'll come to see you at six-forty-five, if I may, to have a quick review of our dinner-party strategy.'

'Fine,' I agreed before we went our separate ways.

After I had had a bath I put on my robe and lounged for a while on the bed with a book which I never managed to open; my mind was too busy roaming around the past again as I tried to avoid thinking of Gavin, but at last I clambered off the bed and wedged myself into my smartest, newest, little black dress. I had just finished reapplying my make-up when I heard the knock on the door.

I glanced at my watch. Nicholas was five minutes early, but that was good. The more time we had to discuss strategy the better.

'Come in!' I called without a second thought.

The door opened.

'Hiya, Gorgeous,' said Gavin.

XI

I kept outwardly calm even though I felt as if the floor were disintegrating beneath my feet. 'Oh, it's you,' I said offhandedly, at once trying to treat him as a younger brother with tiresome habits. 'I thought you were Nicholas. He'll be here any moment for a conference.'

'Nice work if you can get it!' he teased. 'How about you and I having a conference later?'

Struggling to get a grip on myself I moved sideways in order to put the armchair between us. 'I don't think you and I have anything to confer about,' I said but my voice was stiff with dread and I knew he was still in control. In despair I silently screamed to myself: younger brother, *younger brother*, YOUNGER BROTHER! But nothing, not even Lewis's advice, switched off that erotic charge which was powering its way through my guts.

I struggled on. 'Listen, sonny—' That sounded more confident. Maybe the trick was to talk to him as if he was fourteen '—if you think I'm panting to go to bed with you—' I broke off. It was because the corners of his mouth had curved fractionally, suggesting humour, heat and havoc, and as the erotic charge powered through my guts again I panicked. 'Gavin—'

'Okay, Golden Girl, no need to get stressed out – I'm not going to rip your sexy dress off just yet! I'll come back later when the old fart's snoring loud enough to bust a window. Oh, and don't get stressed out about Aids either! I've got some wonderful condoms specially for the occasion, feather-light, ultra-top-quality—'

The scene fell apart and I was saved.

XII

Emotional revulsion suddenly met my mindless desire head on. I could almost hear the crash echoing through my skull. Without hesitation I stopped cowering behind the chair, walked right up to him and slapped his face. 'You *bloody* rent boy!' I yelled at him. 'How many more times do I have to tell you to get real? How dare you treat me as if I were a slag with no self-respect! And how dare you speak with such contempt of that repulsive client of yours who's so starved of love that he has to pay scum like you to create the lousiest possible imitation of it! You may think of sex as being no more important than a cup of tea, but people get *hurt* by what you do, they get torn up and broken – and no, don't try to deny it, I saw what you did to Moira, she visited me, she was vilely humiliated and unhappy – and I saw what you did to Richard too! You really messed him up, he was on the rack, he was almost crying with the pain of it all. *You*, a friend of Richard Slaney's? Don't make me laugh! A real friend wouldn't have trashed him like that, and the truth is you abused him just as you abused Moira – but you're bloody well not going to abuse me! In fact you can be very sure I'm never going to bed with a PROSTITUTE either now or at any other time!'

I stopped speaking. Silence fell. Gavin was no longer looking at me, no longer even rubbing his face where I had hit him. I noticed how his perfect cheekbones seemed more prominent when his skin was pale with shock, but at that moment his looks meant nothing to me. I was too busy watching his vulnerability surface, and the instant I at last stopped worrying about my own vulnerability and focused on his with my eyes wide open, I realised with horror that he was reeling with the pain I had inflicted. I saw then that his destructive behaviour called forth destructive behaviour in others; he was constantly offering himself up for punishment, constantly trashing himself as ruthlessly as he trashed his victims.

I thought: you stupid, stupid little boy, can't you see you're right out there on the edge?

And in a flash – in a crackling shift of consciousness which seemed to churn the very centre of my brain – I was up there on the high wire with my damaged younger brother, and my whole being was focused on snatching him back from the abyss.

XIII

'Wait.'

That was my voice. It wasn't loud and it wasn't panicky. One has to keep cool up on the high wire; one has to keep calm.

'Wait,' I said again, and another silent moment slipped by while we both remained motionless. I knew I had to reach out to steady him, but the wire was so unstable that I was reluctant to make any physical movement. I had to concentrate on staying balanced while I used words to restore his confidence, but I knew that with the right words I could stop him falling.

I said: 'Sorry. I shouldn't have spoken to you like that, but I just hate what you do for a living. If only you'd be the Gavin who showed himself at the Healing Centre! I liked that Gavin so much, and when we held hands . . .' I hesitated but managed to say: 'We were real friends then, no play-acting. Everything was so real.'

I saw him swallow before he tried to speak. Then he said in a voice barely louder than a whisper: 'I didn't mean to hurt Richard.'

'I know you didn't, Gavin.' As the wire ceased to swing, I made my voice as gentle as I possibly could. 'I know how much he meant to you.'

Impulsively he said: 'I'm getting out of leisure-working soon. My manager has plans. I'm going into films.'

'What kind of films?'

He said nothing.

'Gavin, ditch her. Listen, I spent a lot of my life crucifying myself with the need to make big money, but now I realise I'd have been far happier earning less and enjoying a lifestyle which reflected the kind of person I really am.'

'It's not just the money. I love her,' he said, finally looking at me. His eyes were a grave, clear blue. 'I was nothing before I met Elizabeth, but she had faith in me, she believed I had talent. I owe her everything.'

'But if she loves you,' I said, speaking gently again, 'how can she encourage you to live like this?'

He backed off, reaching for the door handle. It was as if he had finally been able to move from the high wire to the platform at the far end; for the time being, at least, he was safe.

As I stepped onto the platform to join him, relief made my focus slip, and I started to think again about myself. The mention of the name Elizabeth deflected me into the past.

'Gavin,' I said as the mood altered between us, 'have you ever heard of a man called Kim Betz?'

He paused. 'What was that last name again?'

'Betz. B-E-T-Z.'

'No, who's he?'

'He was my husband. He was a City lawyer who got drawn into a vile way of life which included membership of an occult society, and he was introduced to the society by this woman Elizabeth Mayfield whom I mentioned to you the other day . . . Has your Elizabeth ever operated as a psychic healer or had connections with the occult?' But even as I spoke I knew it was useless to question him. If he loved her he would lie for her. I would learn nothing here.

Gavin said firmly: 'That kind of rubbish just isn't her scene.'

'So this private club you recruit for—'

'God knows what that's about, but if Elizabeth's involved you can bet it's got nothing to do with religion.'

There was a knock on the door as Nicholas arrived for our conference.

XIV

'Boss, I'm sorry, it was a mistake, I let him in because—'

'Glad to see you're still in one piece. Or are you?'

I sank down on the bed with a groan.

As soon as Nicholas had arrived Gavin had excused himself and vanished, leaving me to try to explain the situation as best I could. I omitted all mention of the high wire; I wanted to keep that for my next talk with Lewis, but I told Nicholas what had been said and I added that I knew I had been wrong to lose my temper.

To my relief Nicholas was supportive. 'The trick is to know when to handle Gavin with kid gloves and when to chuck the gloves in the bin,' he said. 'It was actually vital to disabuse him of his sexathon fantasy. Okay, maybe you were too outspoken, maybe Robin would have had palpitations, but you put everything right when you apologised. I think you handled the scene rather well.'

I was enormously relieved. 'But I shouldn't have called him a prostitute instead of a leisure-worker, should I?'

'By now he's probably edited it from his memory to protect himself. He'll do that so long as he can't admit out loud what he is — and the day he does admit it out loud, of course, will be the day he takes a major step forward towards healing.'

'And talking of healing—'

'Yes, let's focus on our performance at this dinner party.'

Once more we sank down on the window seat as the conversation changed gears.

XV

'I'm certainly not keen on Colin's proposal that we should do a performing-seal act before his hand-picked jury,' said Nicholas dryly after we had spent a few minutes adapting our standard presentation, 'but we can cheer ourselves up with the fact that no matter what the doctor and the priest think of the ministry of healing, they're bound to give us a fair hearing out of deference to our host. There's no way we can be heading for one of those blood-on-the-carpet debates the media love to stage.'

I heard myself say: 'I wonder.'

Nicholas did a double take. 'You're sceptical?'

'Well, having now spent some time in Colin's company I have a clearer idea of his tycoon type. He's what I call a boardroom barracuda and I don't trust him an inch.'

'For heaven's sake! What do you think he's going to do?'

'Take a big bite. He could well be the kind of man who'd get a charge out of playing power-games with a priest in front of an audience — he'd enjoy playing devil's advocate to see if you go flaky.'

'Are you sure you're not being too influenced by your memories of blood and thunder at Curtis, Towers?'

'Of course I'm being influenced by them! That's why I can recognise Colin as a boardroom barracuda!'

'Okay,' said Nicholas, still doubtful but willing now to plan for the possibility I had outlined. 'Okay. But if you're right and Colin turns bloodthirsty, for heaven's sake don't ride to my rescue! You might commit the cardinal sin of wiping the floor with him in debate, and then we'd have to cope with his wounded ego, his anti-women prejudices and God knows what else.'

I laughed and promised to curb my forensic skills.

When we went downstairs a maid waiting in the hall directed us to yet another reception room, this one adjacent to a huge conservatory full of ancient palms and lush vegetation. The glass doors that separated the two areas were closed, but the lighting ensured that the conservatory's interior appeared not only beautiful but exotic.

'I feel like Eve in the Garden of Eden!' I whispered to Nicholas.

'In that case watch out for the serpent.'

Sir Colin came to meet us. Gavin had yet to appear, but there was someone else present and belatedly I remembered Sir Colin mentioning a guest who was 'not a local man'. The stranger, who looked like a Whitehall mandarin, was formally kitted out in a well-tailored black suit. I was certain I had never met him, but when he looked startled to see Nicholas I assumed they knew each other.

I was wrong.

'My dear Colin!' the stranger exclaimed as he swivelled to face his host. 'You didn't tell me you'd be entertaining a clergyman!' but Sir Colin only said with his most deadpan expression: 'I thought it would be an interesting surprise for you.' And that was when I realised this boardroom barracuda was busy outplaying not just Nicholas and me but all his guests in a game I had insufficient information to understand.

Meanwhile Nicholas was saying to the stranger: 'I've got a feeling we've met before although I can't recall where it was.'

'No,' said the man smoothly as I heard footsteps behind me in the corridor, 'we've never met, but allow me to introduce myself. My name's Asherton.'

The footsteps instantly halted, and spinning round I saw Gavin, shocked to the core, in the doorway.

CHAPTER SIX

Gavin

'Emotional dis-ease lies behind many illnesses. The breakdown of relationships in marriages, families and other human groups strains the well-being of those involved. Drug addiction and alcoholism, the abuse of the human body and mind, and the prevalence of crime, violence and racism are signs of a deep-rooted sickness in our local and national life.'

A Time to Heal
A report for the House of Bishops on the Healing Ministry

It's nightmare time at Hellfire Hall. Asherton's popped up without warning, like the genie in a Christmas panto who erupts onstage as soon as Aladdin rubs his magic lamp. But this genie's no cute pantomime demon. He's all smarmed down and brushed up in a Savile Row suit and looking respectable enough to cringe at the word 'vice'. I'm so shattered that I stand in the doorway like a statue someone's tried to deliver to the wrong address.

'We met at the opera, didn't we?' says Asherton with a curve of his pin-thin lips. 'Good evening, Mr Blake.'

'Good evening, sir.' I finally get my feet working again and move forward to accept the routine glass of champagne from Old Toffee-Nose, the butler. What I really want is a double brandy with a pint of lager on the side. Or a double lager with a pint of brandy on the side. Anything but another round of that plug-awful Froggy-Pop.

Meanwhile as I think these frenzied thoughts about booze, my self-preservation instinct kicks in and I realise I've got to remind myself who knows what because if I make one slip now I'll be heading for the Pain-Palace in no time flat. Let me think, let me think, let me think . . .

Right, here we go. One: nobody's aware that Asherton and I are long-standing acquaintances. Two: Asherton doesn't know I've met either Nicholas or Carta prior to this weekend. Three: Colin thinks I met both Nicholas *and* Carta for the first time at Richard's funeral, and he thinks I first heard about the Appeal there, but although he learned about the Appeal through me he's not going to tell either Asherton or anyone else that I've done a full-blooded fundraising number in the bedroom. And four: Nicholas and Carta won't breathe a word to Asherton about any of my fundraising activities because the subject's confidential, and they also won't breathe a word about any other confidential conversation I've had with them, particularly the one involving my braindead admission that Elizabeth's interested in recruiting Colin for a 'club' run by a friend of hers who's a suit. So . . . if everyone acts in character and keeps quiet about the facts which could sink me, I might just survive this nightmare intact.

Meanwhile, as I'm trying not to shit bricks, the life-saving cavalry arrives in the form of the other guests, the innocent ones: Mr and Mrs Local Doctor and Mr and Mrs Local Parson – all middle-aged, middle-class, middle-brow, middle-everything, the dead norm of magnificent British decency which still flourishes outside that crude Thames-side cesspit which calls itself London and kids itself it speaks for England. But before I can heave a sigh of relief I notice Asherton boggling at the sight of another clerical collar, and suddenly I wonder what Colin's playing at. Just how far has Asherton got with reeling in this big fish? I told Nicholas that Colin knew nothing about GOLD yet, but it looks as if I was wrong. The obvious explanation for Asherton's presence here is that he's already played the GOLD card and won a favourable response, but supposing the big fish now turns out to be Jaws, ready to chomp up everything in sight?

Grappling with these apocalyptic thoughts, I shelter by Mr and Mrs Local Doctor and act as if I'm too shy to do more than speak when spoken to.

'And what's *your* connection with Sir Colin?' says Mrs Local Doctor kindly.

Lady, if only you knew. 'I'm his second cousin's son,' I murmur almost inaudibly. 'I'm contemplating a career change and I'm hoping Colin will point me in the right direction.'

Asherton's approaching. He's slithered away from both clerics, sidestepped Carta and he could be closing in on me – but no, he's fastened on the doctor, who turns to talk to him. That means I can

269

go on sheltering in the lee of the doctor's wife. The clerics are busy chatting. Carta's looking at me as if she's longing to find out why I'm being so self-effacing, but any conversation with her could be dangerous – it might look to Asherton as if I know her well, and besides I'm so churned up at present about Carta that I don't want to talk to her. My glorious bed-dream's been wiped. She used the P-word. I'm really upset. But at the same time I'm riveted because she says she likes me, the real me, not Gavin Blake Superstud, not Gavin Blake Fundraiser Supremo, not even Gavin Blake Ordinary Bloke, but Gavin Blake *Me*, the load of rubbish that's no use to anyone. I wouldn't believe this but I do because she mentioned the magic moment when our hands clasped. I was no one else then but myself, but if she liked me at that moment the liking just has to be real because the handclasp was all about a very deep reality, I know that now. But what exactly is this deep reality, and what are Carta and I supposed to do with each other if we can't fuck?

I suddenly realise Mrs Local Parson's glided alongside me to ask what part of the world I come from and we go through the rigma-role of where I went to school and what my father's profession was. But this lady's smarter than Mrs Local Doctor. She never asks how I know Colin.

After an interval which seems more like thirty years than thirty minutes dinner's announced and in an effort to avoid Asherton I decide to be the last one to leave the room. Bad decision. He falls into step by my side as soon as I move into the hall and by this time the others are too far ahead to hear us.

'Did you know Darrow was going to be present?'

'No, sir.'

'What the hell's going on?'

'Colin heard about St Benet's and thinks it might be good PR to donate to their Appeal.'

'Why didn't you tell Elizabeth this?'

'I've only just found out.'

The opportunity for private conversation ceases as we enter the dining-room and wander around scanning the place cards. Colin's put Nicholas and Asherton facing each other in the middle of the table and they're flanked on either side by the four innocents: Asherton's sitting between the doctor and Mrs Local Parson, Nicholas between the parson and Mrs Local Doctor. Both women are on either side of Colin, who's at the head of the table. Carta and I are seated opposite each other, she next to the parson and I next to the doctor, but as there are an uneven number of guests Colin has no one facing him at our end of the table.

Dinner begins with a mush-ball on rabbit food, the kind of knick-knack cuisine which one can toss off in two bites and be even hungrier afterwards than one was before. I'm still recovering from my brush with Asherton, but when I start thinking clearly I realise there's been no announcement that Nicholas and Carta are going to do a St Benet's number.

'Do tell us about your ministry, Nicholas!' one of the innocents is saying warmly, and Nicholas answers: 'I believe I'm going to be encouraged to do so later,' but Colin neither looks at him nor comments. What the hell's he playing at? Meanwhile my neighbour the doctor is talking to Asherton about the rising levels of teenage drug abuse in rural areas. Asherton's looking wonderfully shocked. I sip some wine and decide it tastes poisonous. I wish to hell someone would wheel on a trolley groaning with all the drugs anyone would need to get totally freaked out and beamed up.

'. . . and of course the young are encouraged by the absence of good role models to regard drug-taking as normal,' the doctor's saying, and adds to me: 'You must be under thirty – what do you think?'

'I'm not interested in drugs, sir. I'm into keep-fit. Minimum alcohol, regular work-outs, no junk food.'

'Splendid!' exclaims the doctor heartily. 'How encouraging!'

'A perfect role model for the young!' agrees Asherton creamily, and the sound of that sugar-and-cyanide voice makes me toss back the rest of my dud wine.

After the starter comes the fish course, a sliver of lemon sole in a slimy sauce with a shrimp stuck on top. Another bottle of wine appears but I turn up my glass because I can't afford to get seriously trolleyed, particularly since the doctor zeroes in on me again during the next course (beef Wellington, duchesse potatoes, mixed veg) and I'm kept busy explaining my fictitious job as a gym equipment salesman. By the time we've all finished pudding I'm knackered, but there's no respite because after the cheese and fruit have circulated Colin drops his H-bomb.

'Now we come to the climax of the party!' he declares, beaming at us. 'We're going to have a debate. On the one hand—' He gestures to Nicholas '—we have a representative of the Church of England who is at present engaged in a fundraising drive for his ministry

271

of healing at St Benet's-by-the-Wall in the City of London. And on the other—' He gestures to Asherton '—we have a representative of a religious society, the Guild of Light and Darkness, which is a form of the ancient Gnostic tradition, and he too clearly has hopes that I might contribute to his cause. Two religious men – and both after my money! Whom should I favour? Well, gentlemen, let's see how well you perform before a jury of your peers who will decide the winner of the debate! Do you want me to toss a coin to decide who goes first?'

Everyone gapes, gobsmacked.

*   *   *

I've never seen Asherton look so rattled.

'My dear Colin,' he says rapidly, 'I'm afraid you entirely misunderstand the nature of my metaphysical interests! My society is, as I thought I'd made clear to you, entirely private and can't possibly be the subject of a dinner-party discussion!'

'What a pity!' says Nicholas at once, staging a speed-of-light recovery from the H-bomb's blast. 'But never mind – my metaphysical interests are open to all, not merely to a privileged few, and I'm more than happy to discuss them with anyone anywhere!'

'Surely it's not quite *comme il faut* to discuss religion at dinner parties?' says Mrs Local Doctor, too nervous to realise she's shafting her host by implying he doesn't know how to behave.

'Quite right!' exclaims Asherton, more than willing to slam a backhander at his host after Colin's not only ignored the fact that GOLD's top secret but has even blasted its full name around the table. 'Religion is essentially a private matter, far from the reality of public affairs and normal social engagements.'

'Do you really think so?' says Nicholas politely, subtly conveying an impression of amused astonishment – as if Asherton's opinion was almost too quaint to be taken seriously. 'Surely the idea that religion should be locked away from everyday existence implies, if you'll forgive me saying so, a failure to understand what religion is all about. A great religion's a world-view and a way of life, and if it doesn't address itself to the realities of day-to-day living then it's of no use to those seeking meaning and value in their daily lives.'

'Oh come, come, Mr Darrow!' oozes Asherton. 'Isn't Christianity really only about "pie in the sky when you die"?'

'If that were true everyone would be queueing up to commit suicide, but as we all know, that kind of mass exit is confined to phoney cults and perverted religion.'

(I think: nice one, mate. Cheers.)

'But nevertheless,' persists Asherton, still slimeballing away, 'think of the Sermon on the Mount! Aren't so many Christian concepts just an escape from reality?'

'How strange you should believe that!' says Nicholas, wide-eyed as if with innocent wonder. 'I always understood that it was the Gnostics who sought to evade reality with their themes of escaping into other worlds! Surely it's Christianity, in the person of its crucified leader, which confronts the blood, sweat and tears of reality head on?'

(I think: another nice one, mate! Let no one say you haven't gone down fighting.)

Asherton says sardonically, easing up on the charm: 'Ah, but such an exaltation of death and suffering surely risks being seen as an exercise in sado-masochism!'

'Confronting the reality of death and suffering isn't the same as exalting it. You're forgetting that Christ preached life in abundance and the primacy of love, not multiple destruction and the triumph of hate.'

(I suck in my breath at this third whack in succession and think astonished: POW!)

'Life in abundance!' exclaims Asherton with a little designer-sniggle of a laugh. 'But everyone knows that Christianity has a record of dealing out death and destruction second to none!'

'How about those death-dealing atheists Mao Tse-tung, Pol Pot and Stalin?' enquires Nicholas instantly. 'The truth, surely, Mr Asherton, is that all religions can be corrupted – take Gnosticism, for instance. Gnosticism should be about a collection of beautiful fictions containing profound spiritual truths, but how much of that tradition is incorporated in your Guild of Light and Darkness? Just what kind of Gnosticism are you actually promoting here?'

'I read such an interesting article on Gnosticism the other day,' chips in Mr Local Parson, trying to pour oil on the troubled waters as the temperature of the debate rises. 'It referred to that splendidly readable book by—' He says a name that sounds like Inane Bagels, but I realise it's probably Elaine Bagels – or maybe Elaine Pagels, since the 'b' sound was more of a pop than a blast – but Mr Local

Doctor, not listening, says irritably: 'I don't understand this Gnostic stuff. What's the core premiss?'

'The importance of spiritual liberation,' says Asherton, very hushed, very reverent.

Nicholas says crisply in a down-to-earth voice: 'There were different strands of Gnosticism in the old days, some close to Christianity, some far removed from it – the nearest equivalent today would be the New Age Movement – but generally speaking it centred on the belief that you can attain salvation by secret knowledge, occult knowledge, given only to an elite. Christianity, on the other hand, believes that salvation – wholeness of body, mind and spirit leading to liberation and empowerment – is available to all through the example, power and grace of Jesus Christ.'

'That's all very well,' says Asherton, barely able to hide his contempt, 'but you don't practise what you preach, do you? Christians aren't interested in the wholeness of body, mind and spirit! How can they be, when the body is something they despise?'

'On the contrary, it would be heresy for us to despise the body when we believe God became flesh and blood in order to embrace his creation to the full. But how does your Guild of Light and Darkness treat the subject? I hope you haven't fallen into the old Gnostic error of splitting the body off from the spirit and behaving as if the body's of no importance! Or have you rejected the practice of satiating the body with physical excesses to keep it quiet while the spirit supposedly soars towards salvation?'

'Why how exciting you make it sound!'

'You find physical abuse exciting, Mr Asherton?'

'I didn't say that!'

'Didn't you? In that case are you agreeing with me that mind, body and spirit are one, and that if we downgrade any of these things we downgrade our humanity?'

'No, I'm not saying that either!' snaps Asherton, voice suddenly all cyanide and no sugar. 'That's just naive nonsense. Spiritually the body's only an encumbrance, and that's why an exaggerated veneration of the body's so wrong – it's the reason why Christianity's so against sex—'

'Christianity's against the abuse of sex, not sex itself. How could Christianity – genuine Christianity – be against sex when sex is such an important function of the body, the body which Christianity says should be treated with dignity and respect? But of course if your society is following a strand of Gnosticism which says the body is of so little account that sexual abuse is actually encouraged—'

'I deny that charge absolutely!' explodes Asherton, rigid with fury as he hypes up his lies. 'What the Gnostics seek to do – by various ancient practices which I'm not allowed to disclose – is to work on setting the body aside so that the spirit can flourish. What can be more religiously desirable than that?'

'A religion which believes body, mind and spirit should work together instead of against one another,' said Nicholas immediately. 'A religion which says body, mind and spirit shouldn't be divided by anyone seeking the health and healing which underpin salvation.'

(Dazed by the sight of Asherton being continually walloped I can only think: game, set, match . . .)

But of course I'm fantasising. He'll come back and win in the end, just as he always does, and meanwhile he's saying patronisingly: 'I think we should leave health and healing to the medical gentlemen – don't you agree, Doctor?'

'Quite so,' says this dumb old git. 'A terrible lot of quackery goes on outside orthodox medicine.'

I want to leap to my feet and shout furiously: 'Let him have it, Mr Charisma!' but of course I stay welded to my chair and anyway Nicholas doesn't need me bawling out encouragement like a football hooligan. He says shortly to Dinosaur-Doc: 'Are your patients simply bodies to you? Do you take no account of their individual personalities?'

'Well, of course I didn't mean to imply—'

Nicholas doesn't wait for him to finish. Back he swings to Asherton. 'I think you'd agree with me,' he says, 'that we live in a culture unhealthily obsessed by the body, a culture where the spirit is greatly neglected. But the solution, surely, is not to say the body's so unimportant that people can trash it in any way they like. The solution's to say that the body's so important that it should never be trashed either by starvation or gluttony or sexual abuse or any other kind of tormented behaviour.'

'Wait a minute!' says Asherton, snaking back into the attack. 'You're being very dictatorial here! What about the freedom of the individual? Why shouldn't people have the right to choose what to do with their own bodies?'

'For people caught up in the trap of abusing the body, there *is* no freedom – it's as if they're locked up in jail. Take prostitutes, for instance, who spend their time splitting off their bodies from their minds in order to survive the abuse and degradation—'

'Please!' cries Mrs Local Doctor, all pink cheeks and heaving bosom. 'This truly can't be a suitable subject for a clergyman to discuss!'

'Nonsense, Dorothy!' says Mrs Local Parson, magnificently robust. 'Christians don't have no-go areas! It's all God's world, isn't it?'

'Go on, Nicholas,' orders Colin, ignoring the women.

'My point is that sometimes people are so impoverished that they have to sell themselves to survive – they're imprisoned by material deprivation. And sometimes people are so damaged by psychological wounds that they too feel they've no choice but to sell themselves – they're the ones imprisoned by emotional deprivation. But whatever the source of the deprivation, freedom of choice isn't there.'

(I think – no, I don't think – can't—)

'But my dear sir!' purrs Asherton, slithering onto the warpath again. 'A lot of prostitutes, especially the ones at the top of the market, enjoy what they do! How dare you want to deprive them of their pleasure as well as their livelihood!'

'I thought it was an open secret that prostitutes soon come to despise their clients. What kind of pleasure do you get from having sex with someone you despise? And what kind of pleasure do the clients get from paying for such a travesty of love?'

'A great deal of physical satisfaction! We're not all after love, you know!'

'Oh, but I think we are,' says Nicholas at once. 'We all need to love and be loved, and that's why prostitution's such a rip-off. Love is the great reality, and no substitute bought and sold in the market-place can ever begin to equal it.'

The words hit my head like flying nails.

'Ah, you old-fashioned romantic!' mocks Asherton, beside himself with the desire to gut this lethal shit-buster once and for all. 'But as every sophisticated person knows, it isn't love that makes the world go round! It's money and power!'

And suddenly I find I'm sitting bolt upright in my chair. I've just realised that Nicholas is paying out the rope so that Asherton can hang himself. By this time Asherton's in such a lather of fury and loathing that he's forgotten where he is and who's listening. He's now so totally focused on wiping Nicholas off the map that he's been lured into insisting a deep-sleaze profession's just a free-market lifestyle choice and love's just a four-letter word. I can almost feel the representatives of Middle England vibrating with repulsion. Their legendary decency and honesty, their fabled kindness and humanity, are all outraged. Asherton's losing this battle, he's losing it – he's not invincible – he doesn't always have the last word—

'You puzzle me, Mr Asherton!' says Nicholas Darrow Mega-Hero as he moves in so smoothly for the kill. 'For a religious man, you seem to have a very low opinion of human beings! But I myself believe in the dignity and worth of each individual, even a prosti-tute, because I believe that each one of us is precious in God's sight. Do I take it that you'd just regard this as further evidence that I'm a hopeless romantic?'

'But of course!' exclaims Asherton pityingly. 'Let's face it, my friend! Certain groups in the human race are little better than animals, and the idea that each individual is someone special is merely sentimental claptrap put out by soft-hearted idealists!'

Nicholas doesn't bother to reply. He just looks up the table to his host, but Colin's already leaning forward to complete the demo-lition job.

'And I'm sure all of us around this table,' he says flatly, 'will recognise that last sentence as the philosophy which led the Germans to Auschwitz. Thank you, gentlemen. As we hardly need to vote on who won that debate, may I now invite the ladies to retire to the drawing-room?'

In a silence louder than a thunderclap, the three women slowly stand up and walk away.

* * *

Immediately Asherton excuses himself and leaves. I'm just thankful he's not staying at the Hall, but Colin didn't invite him, did he? I think he sussed Asherton right from the start and fingered Nicholas to fillet him. No flies on this captain of industry when he's dealing with villains who pitch assaults on his wealth.

'I'm so glad we had the chance to talk,' he says poker-faced to Asherton as Old Toffee-Nose the butler prepares to spirit the guest away.

Asherton oozes gratitude for the hospitality, purrs goodbye to

277

one and all, and glides off without looking back. I'm still worrying about the fact that I've witnessed his humiliation when Colin says: 'Nicholas, can I now ask you to speak for five minutes about your ministry?'

How ruthless can you get? Not content with delegating the job of cobra-gutting to Nicholas, Colin expects the poor bloke to do a fundraising number – and without any help from his fundraiser, now shut away in the drawing-room like a second-class citizen! Not surprisingly Nicholas's spiel's more than a little ragged, and he barely mentions either the Appeal or his plans for the future. Talk about underplaying a hand! I wonder if I should do another pitch to Colin later tonight, but I decide it's probably best to leave the subject of the Appeal well alone.

That's because my relationship with Colin isn't exactly all sweetness and light at the moment. The trouble is I've been so bored with the escort work that I've been what he calls 'impertinent'. He even said I was asking to be 'disciplined'. Shit, that's all I need – a hulking great client lumbering out of the S&M closet! I'll have to remind him my menu doesn't include him beating me up – and let's hope there are no handcuffs in his *objets d'art* collection.

I now find I have to have a big hit of port in order to face the fun and games in the bedroom. Of course I want to think about what Nicholas said – about the words which seemed to drill holes in my head so that the truth could roar straight into my mind like a white-hot lava flow – but I don't dare. That's because if I start rerunning the debate I may not be able to get through the rest of the evening. I might vomit when Colin starts slobbering over me. I might seize up in the wrong place if he wants to practise his buggery-for-beginners lesson. I might do a runner, get sacked like Jason and Tony, never see Elizabeth again . . .

So I mustn't think of Nicholas.

I have to split that scene off now, cut it loose, stay totally focused on my job in order to survive . . .

*   *   *

As soon as we're alone in his room Colin demands: 'Does Darrow know the truth about how you earn your living?'

I've been in such a sweat about the sex that I failed to anticipate this question, but I see now that for Colin this is the big issue.

A gay relationship can be discreetly indulged, he thinks, provided nothing's done to scare the servants, but no one under any circumstances must know he pays. People would pity him. All that money and no one'll do him for free! Sad, they'd think, sad. I can almost smell Colin's blood curdling as he recoils from such a humiliating vision.

I say firmly: 'Colin, I always practise total discretion. No one here knows about the money.'

He believes me. Or does he? 'I know the subject of prostitution did come up naturally,' he says, 'but nevertheless I was wondering . . . well, what do you think of Darrow? He's attractive, isn't he?' And he stares, challenging me to deny I'm nuts about Nicholas.

'Oh, for God's sake, Colin!' I exclaim. 'That man's so straight he'd make the Leaning Tower of Pisa look horizontal!'

'You might still find him attractive!'

'Why would I waste my time?'

Colin says with a roughness which makes me freeze: 'Can't you see that I was asking myself why you supported St Benet's and the obvious answer was that you were in love with someone there?'

I keep my nerve. 'I support St Benet's because I admire their approach to illness. When my brother was dying I didn't notice the medical profession making much effort to treat *his* mind and spirit as well as his body.'

Colin at once backs down. 'My darling, I'm sorry, I'd forgotten Hugo,' he says, and his remorse seems genuine, but a second later he's trying to ambush me again. 'What were you and Asherton talking about on the way into dinner?'

This jolts me but instantly I groan: 'Oh God, can't you guess? He wanted my phone number!'

'I thought as much!' Colin takes a moment to curse Asherton before demanding: 'What did you say?'

'I said: "Excuse me, sir, but that's currently privileged information." And I thought: you creep, get lost!'

Colin laughs and grabs me. But before the inevitable slobbery smooch arrives he mumbles in a voice thick with emotion: 'What about Darrow's comment that prostitutes despise their clients? Is it true?'

I don't just give him a quick 'no'. Instead I say seriously: 'Maybe a low-grade rent boy would despise his clients because the odds are his clients would be scum. But as an upmarket leisure-worker

I respect my clients because I know they're all successful men.'

'So you respect me?'

'Course I do! You're big and strong and tough and I think you're terrific!'

He believes me.

Silly old sod.

Pathetic.

*   *   *

Luckily the sex doesn't require all my professional skills, which is just as well since the port has left me several grunts short of a porno-symphony. Colin's had far more to drink than I have and he's far older, so all he's capable of is some semi-conscious kissing and pretend-biting. He doesn't require me to do anything but fake rapture. Then he's out for the count. Removing the condoms I crawl out of bed and use his bathroom as I shower off the saliva.

Back in my own room at last, I find that the relief of being alone hits me with such a wallop that I have to lie down for five minutes to recover. Again I want to think, to review the debate, but my brain's past it. I get to the en-suite bathroom to use my toothbrush and mouthwash and then take another shower, a longer one. I'm starting to feel sick, not as the result of the alcohol – I'm still outside the hangover zone – but as the result of all that slimy rich food. Just thinking of the food revolts me so much that I return to the bathroom to make myself throw up.

That's better. I finally feel in control.

I knock back a glass of water and pass out.

*   *   *

I wake at six and at once my rested brain starts to work at the double. I review the debate. I think of Nicholas. Huge emotions stir in me and have to be slapped down. Can't deny they're there, but at the same time I have to ensure they don't seize control and wreck me. What I must concentrate on is this: before breakfast I have the chance to see Nicholas without Colin lumbering around, and whatever happens I must grab this chance because there's something I have to do.

Retrieving Richard's cuff links which I wore last night I slot them carefully back into their little Tiffany box, but before I close the lid I gaze at them for a long moment. I'm thinking how I never appreciated Richard's love when he was alive. I wrote it off as just a typical client infatuation, but I know better now. He might have started out by being infatuated with Gavin Blake Superstud, but in the end on that boat it was *me* he cared about, the me Carta likes, the me Nicholas always addresses.

'Love is the great reality,' Nicholas said, telling the truth right up to the end, the truth which blew Asherton away. And now I can see that when I meet Nicholas this morning I have to stand in that truth, I have to be Gavin Blake Me, no one else. Then by some mysterious process which I still don't understand, he'll accept me as I am and I won't be shit any more and I won't be junk either. I'll count, I'll matter, I'll be special.

When I'm dressed I slip the little box into my pocket and pad downstairs to wait in the room nearest the front door. The time's twenty to eight.

Five minutes later I hear Nicholas and Carta come downstairs. They're going to church. Last night they asked Mr Local Parson the time of the early Communion service.

Having given my friends a head start I follow them to the village, sit in the churchyard and breathe loads of clean country air as I savour being alone. I figure that's *my* way of being spiritual on a Sunday morning.

At eight-twenty-five the door of the church opens and people begin to trickle away. There are three old biddies, one old tosser and the St Benet's Two. Mr Local Parson's reluctant to let them go but at last he retreats into the church and it's time for me to step out from the tombstones like an updated version of Magwitch in *Great Expectations*.

'Hi,' I say.

They're both surprised but in no way hostile. Nicholas even smiles, and when I see that smile I know I won't be able to deliver the speech I planned. In fact the huge emotions I'm experiencing again mean that I can't say anything at all. I can only pull out the Tiffany box and offer it to him.

'This is for me?' says Nicholas startled.

I nod, watching the box as it passes into his hands.

He opens the lid. The silver links glitter. They're so beautiful that my throat aches to look at them.

'Good God!' says Carta staggered. 'Those are Richard's, aren't they? The ones Moira gave you after the funeral!'

I hear her but she's in another dimension. All I can see is the silver, ravishing, radiant – and now redeemed.

'Don't you want them any more?' says Carta baffled. 'In that case why don't you sell them and give the money to a good cause?'

She doesn't understand. But Nicholas says firmly to her: 'Good causes are always with us, and Gavin can give to one whenever he pleases. But this is a special gift for a special occasion, and it's a gift which he's perfectly entitled to make if he chooses. Thank you, Gavin.'

I find I have to sit down. Sinking onto the bench nearby I cover my face with my hands.

'Carta,' says Nicholas, 'give us a moment, would you?' and he sits down at my side. He doesn't touch me. He simply waits. The box is still in his right hand, still open. The outline of the cuff links are just a blur now but I can see the silver shining.

At last I'm able to say: 'I'm sorry I made Richard so unhappy.' That sentence is true, all of it. I try another. 'It's not right that I should have those cuff links.' That sentence is true too. I'm exhausted already by all this truth-telling, but I'm winning. I'm doing wonderfully well. 'Moira would never have given them to me anyway,' I say in a new burst of confidence, 'if she'd realised I was a—'

And then the silence falls, smothering me.

I think: I can't say it. I can't.

But I know I must. Right now this minute with this man I have to stand in the truth.

I try again. 'Moira would never have given them to me,' I say, 'if she'd realised I was a—'

I break off but this time I'm sweating, even gasping with the effort to complete the sentence. And I do complete it. I win the fight, I say the word, and of course it's PROSTITUTE.

No big deal, right? Wrong. To hear other people say the word isn't so bad – I can block that out. To think the word to myself in a fit of depression isn't so bad either – it winds up as just a memory which can be wiped. But to speak the word, to name the slime – and to someone respected and admired – no, that's pulling the plaster off an open wound and shoving salt in the gash.

Uttering those three syllables takes all my strength and I slump back on the bench, but Nicholas doesn't go away. He still doesn't touch me and I still can't look at him but he's still there.

Then he says: 'That was brave.'

I have to scrub my eyes with my hand, but the wound's closing over and I know now that if I look at him I'll see no contempt. In a rush I say: 'I don't just want you to have the cuff links to make good what I did by taking them. I want you to have them because you beat that bastard last night.'

'He was rather more than just someone you'd met once at the opera, wasn't he? I saw your face when you walked into that room and found him there.'

I manage to nod.

'He's your manager's friend who runs the "private club" you mentioned.'

I nod again. 'I've known him for years,' I say, the words cascading out of my mouth. 'He's so bloody powerful and everyone's so bloody terrified of him that he does what he likes, but you beat him, you did it, you won – and I want to say thanks not just for that but for everything else, for treating me like a real person, for respecting me, for practising what you preach. I shan't see you again because it's too dangerous, but I want you to know I'll never forget how you touched my life, never as long as I live.'

Speaking clearly to make sure I understand and remember, Nicholas leans forward and says: 'If the danger escalates to unacceptable levels, you can always get help from St Benet's. We've had plenty of experience in dealing with people who want to escape from evil cults.' And when he sees I've taken this on board he adds: 'How far are you involved with the Guild of Light and Darkness?'

'I'm not a member and I don't go to meetings. I'm just involved in the recruiting process.'

'Is the club for gays only?'

'No, my manager's part-owner of an escort agency, and there's a girl there who trawls for straights just like I trawl for gays.'

'Any women members?'

'A few, I think, but I don't know how they get recruited. Maybe the woman who runs the escort agency has some kind of grapevine that identifies possible members – or maybe they just get introduced by the hetero membership. The truth is I don't know much about GOLD because it's top secret.'

'Gold? Ah, GOLD, yes, the acronym . . . How far is your manager connected with it? Can you tell me a little more about her?'

'I can't tell you more about anything. If they find out I've grassed—' A shudder hits me.

'I understand, but now listen carefully, Gavin. GOLD may be a legal organisation but that doesn't mean its activities stay within the law. Because these cults need an escalating level of thrills to keep their members satisfied, people like Asherton nearly always wind up going too far, so don't make the mistake of thinking he's beyond the law, and don't make the mistake of thinking you've no option but to play along with him. When you're caught in a trap it's easy to be paralysed by your powerlessness, but traps can be sprung and the victims can walk free.'

Of course he doesn't know I can't live without Elizabeth. In the end I just say: 'Maybe life in the trap's all I'm good for.'

'Are you sorry for the life you've led since you fell into the trap? And would you truly want to do better if you were set free?'

'Well, sure, but—'

'Then you qualify for a fresh start.'

After a pause I say: 'That's the line The Bloke took, isn't it?'

'That's the line The Bloke took, yes.'

After another pause I say: 'In the church at Compton Beeches, there's a stained-glass window of The Bloke doing the shepherd number.'

'I noticed. Lots of sheep looking as if their fleeces had been shampooed and blow-dried ready for an upmarket agricultural show . . . except for the sheep he was carrying back on his shoulder. That little sheep was in poor shape.'

'But it was coming home.'

'Yes,' says Nicholas, 'it was coming home.'

I scrub my eyes again with the back of my hand and stand up. 'Better get back,' I mutter. 'You go ahead. I don't want Colin to know I've been talking to you.'

'Remember: you'll always be welcome at St Benet's and you can always turn to us for help.' And he moves away at last to the churchyard gate where Carta's waiting.

*   *   *

I feel as if I've been stretched on Asherton's rack at the Pain-Palace, but by a huge effort of will I get a grip on all the searing emotions and survive the rest of the morning. Colin gives us a tour of the garden after we've lolled around reading the Sunday papers. It's low-key activity and my stress levels get a chance to dip.

The party breaks up after a traditional Sunday lunch with other local guests, but when everyone's gone, even Nicholas and Carta, Colin refuses to tell me whether he plans to make the donation. Sod him! I can't wait to get away now but Colin's booked me till six so that I can bring his weekend to a mouthwatering climax.

I try to be Gavin Blake Superstud, but it's not so easy away from Austin Friars. At the flat I have my routine to help me slide into the right personality, but here I'm adrift, desperately trying to programme my brain so that my body can deliver the goods.

'What's the matter, Gavin?'

I say I'm fine, and kill the urge to bolt.

Then I slither into position to be screwed.

*　*　*

I travel back to London feeling like used toilet paper, but by the time I reach the suburbs I've practised a dozen possible versions of my opening dialogue with Elizabeth. I haven't called her. That might look panicky, suggesting I was hellbent on smoothing over the mess for any number of guilty reasons. Let Asherton be the one who sounds off to her about the St Benet's Two. It's much safer if I just play the pretty-boy in a sulk, unable to think of anything except how much I hate escort work.

'Never again!' I declare as I tramp into Elizabeth's presence at last. 'Never, never, never again will I spend the weekend with such a drop-dead boring old—'

She blasts the whining aside. 'What the hell's all this about St Benet's?'

'Oh God, yes, that really was the cherry on the parfait!'

'Did you really have no idea – *no idea at all* – that Darrow and the Graham bitch had been invited?'

'Well, of course not! I'd have told you, wouldn't I?'

'You didn't tell me something Sir Colin told Asherton – that you met both that bitch AND DARROW at Richard Slaney's funeral!'

I get such a fright that my stomach seems to do a double somersault.

'Why didn't you tell me?' shouts Elizabeth in fury.

'It was sheer panic. I thought that if you knew you'd go ballistic, but listen, darling, listen, the meeting was all over in a flash, I swear it! Darrow was hauled away almost at once by Bridget Slaney so I never got to talk to him at all, and Carta got kidnapped a couple of minutes later by some people who worked at Richard's firm. She used to work there too, so they all knew one another.'

There's a taut silence while I listen to my heart banging but at last Elizabeth says, still furious: 'The worst mistake I've made for a long time was to let you go to that funeral!' Then miraculously her mood changes. 'All right, pet,' she says in a resigned but not hostile voice. 'Get yourself a drink and sit down. I need to know exactly what happened at Sir Colin's house.'

She believes me. Weak with relief I retrieve a bottle of Slimline tonic from her kitchen and slump down beside her on the sofa to deliver my censored account of the weekend.

*   *   *

'What a way for a gentleman to behave!' says Elizabeth scandalised when I've finished. 'Imagine Sir Colin trotting out all that stuff about GOLD despite having been told it was confidential! No wonder Asherton felt hurt and betrayed, poor love! And imagine trotting it out to Darrow, of all people! And as for that debate . . . well, words almost fail me, but I'm not surprised it was a disaster. Asherton doesn't do debates. He tells people what to think and they don't talk back – well, naturally they don't, they're just so relieved to be spared all the worry of thinking for themselves.'

'What's Asherton going to do?'

'There's nothing he *can* do except forget Sir Colin and move on. But the important thing from our point of view is that Sir Colin still doesn't know of your connection with Asherton and he's still keen on you.'

'I'm not doing any more escort work with him!'

'It's never a good idea to have a closed mind, dear, particularly when one's dealing with a multi-millionaire, but meanwhile we've got a far more urgent problem to deal with and that's this: Asherton thinks you're playing some kind of double game.'

'Oh God!' I groan, all outraged innocence even though my stomach's double-somersaulting again. 'I knew it! I knew he'd take a swipe at me! It's all because I witnessed Darrow wiping the floor with him!'

'That may well be true, but he's certainly come up with a very nasty theory. He thinks you made a play for Carta Graham at the funeral by boasting you could get a multi-millionaire to contribute to her Appeal. He thinks you're bored with all the gays, and now you're no more reliable than Jason and Tony were when I had to give them the boot, but I don't believe that theory and I'll tell you why: you're very much cleverer than Jason and Tony, and I just can't believe you'd be quite such a bloody fool.'

I have to be dead careful. If I keep playing the outraged innocent she could decide a guilty conscience is making me bluster. So what should my primary reaction be here, bearing in mind that Asherton's spewing venom all over me? Terror, of course. I'd be terrified even though Elizabeth's signalling that she's on my side. I wouldn't trust that signal if I was innocent and I certainly don't trust it right now when I'm guilty. It could be just a trick to lure me into a confession. Although she denies it she may well believe every word of Asherton's theory.

Keeping my eyes lowered I try a frightened gulp and fractionally increase my breathing rate. Feels good. I gulp again and it finally dawns on me that I'm not acting. I really am scared shitless.

'Well, pet,' says Elizabeth, voice very dulcet and maternal, 'I may not share Asherton's suspicions, but I do think you might have been telling a fib or two. So why don't you now tell me just exactly what's been going on between you and Carta Graham?'

*   *   *

I decide a hint of truth's needed to help my lies along. A full-scale denial would be worse than useless.

'Okay,' I mumble, 'I'll admit it. I flirted with her at the funeral. But I didn't shag her.'

'Convince me.'

I put on my most serious expression. 'There were three reasons why the shag was a non-starter. One: it was Moira Slaney who made the play for me after the funeral and she didn't give me the chance to chase anyone else. Two: I quickly found out Carta had a fiancé and wasn't interested in a pre-wedding shaglet. And three: yeah, you're right, I'm not such a bloody fool as to mess up big-time – and that means, of course, that I never said to Carta I could milk Colin for St Benet's. I never even mentioned Colin to her.'

Elizabeth considers this speech calmly before asking: 'What happened with Mrs Slaney?'

287

Have to lie about Moira now. If I once admit I did shag someone after the funeral, Elizabeth will never believe it wasn't Carta. 'The shag with Moira was a non-starter too,' I say. 'I could see she was emotionally up the creek and bound to be more trouble than she was worth.'

'Smart boy! I'm impressed . . . Who's Carta Graham's fiancé?'

'That bloke you mentioned the other day when you and Asherton were discussing the Betz fiasco.'

'Eric Tucker? Now, that's interesting – I wonder if he's related to Gilbert after all? Since Gilbert was at that funeral along with the Graham bitch—'

'They weren't together. I never saw Carta with anyone but Darrow.'

'Yes, but if Mrs Slaney was keeping you so busy—'

'Oh right, yes, I certainly wasn't watching Carta all the time . . . Could it be important if Eric and Gilbert were related?'

'Well, if Gilbert not only knows Darrow through his job but also has a relation who's engaged to Darrow's fundraiser, Asherton might finally be persuaded to abandon his bloody stupid plan to make Gilbert perform for GOLD . . . No, half a mo, I haven't got that right, have I? Asherton's mad for revenge. Having been trounced by one priest he'll be even keener to drag another through the mud, and the more Gilbert's connected to Darrow, the better Asherton'll like it. Oh, bugger Asherton! I'm ever so put out with him!'

I detect a ring of truth here, and decide that Elizabeth really is on my side. Better still, I think she's swallowed my brilliant mix of fact and fiction, but I can't afford to pat myself on the back just yet. Over-confidence could be fatal.

'There's one thing I'm still not clear about,' she's saying, veering away from the subject of Asherton to zero in again on my story. 'Did Sir Colin really never mention to you that he was seriously interested in St Benet's?'

'Never, but is that so surprising? Why should he think I'd be interested in RCPP's charitable-giving programme?'

'Because on this occasion you knew the people involved!'

'Yes, I did, but Colin didn't realise that until he told me Darrow and Carta would be staying at the Hall.'

'When was that?'

'Friday. The evening before they arrived.'

'In that case why on earth didn't you phone me on Friday night with the news? I didn't know about Asherton's dinner-date in advance but I'd have certainly passed on the news about Darrow immediately and then Asherton would have cancelled!'

'Hey, you weren't the only one to have no access to Asherton's engagement diary! How was I to know he was planning to parachute in for dinner? Colin played that card totally squashed to his chest!'

'Yes, but—'

'Okay, I'll come clean. The reason I didn't call you on Friday night was because I was hoping you'd never have to know about the St Benet's invasion, just as I hoped you'd never have to know I'd met those two at Richard's funeral. But for God's sake, Elizabeth, is that so hard to understand? I didn't want you to go ballistic – I couldn't face that, sorry, but I just couldn't. I always so hate the thought of upsetting you, darling—' I allow my voice to sink to a whisper '—I love you so much.' I'm sort of pretending yet not pretending here. I'm hyping it up like an actor, but it's the truth I'm hyping, and I know I sound one hundred per cent sincere.

'Poor pet!' says Elizabeth indulgently. 'What a pickle you got yourself into, didn't you? Very well, we'll say no more about it, but in future I must know *everything*, no matter how panicky you may feel about telling me.'

I promise fervently to keep her fully informed.

*   *   *

I'm prickling all over with sweat as I survive this high-risk inter-rogation, but I can't relax yet. 'How do we convince Asherton I'm innocent?' I ask nervously.

'Don't worry, dear. I won't let him take it out on you and anyway he needs you to train up Gilbert Tucker.'

'God, I wish you could just kiss Asherton goodbye!'

'That makes two of us, pet. Now that Darrow's found out about GOLD, it's more important than ever that I stage a strategic with-drawal, but the trouble is I can't do it while Asherton's in this humil-iated and furious state. It's too dangerous. If he thinks I'm going cool on him he's going to get paranoid, and believe me, a paranoid Asherton isn't on the list of people I'm dying to meet.'

'But isn't it more dangerous to stay in his orbit than to leave it?'

'Not quite, dear. That's because Darrow has no evidence that Asherton's involved in anything illegal. Darrow certainly has the potential to whip up police interest, but we're still a long way from being obliged to take the next plane to Brazil. In fact the most pressing danger at present actually comes not from Darrow but from Asherton himself, refusing to back down from staging this idiotic romp with Gilbert Tucker.'

Idiotic romp! What a euphemism! Feeling uneasier than ever I say: 'I think we should definitely have a holiday in Rio until after the GOLD meeting.'

'And how do you think *that* would look to Mr Paranoia? If he pulls off this romp – and I reckon the odds are still just about in his favour – he'll never forgive me for not having enough faith in him to stay put and he'll start trying to think of nasty little ways to pay me back. No, we've got to hope for the best and carry on as usual – which reminds me, I've got some nice news for you. You'll get your two days off now, just as I promised, and guess who's got the next two days off as well! Serena! I've specially arranged it with Norah to compensate you for working through the weekend!'

I fake delight.

'Oh, and bring me the early morning tea tomorrow, pet, and we'll pretend it's Saturday!'

Perking up I thank her profusely for her generosity and then stagger upstairs to savour my survival.

*   *   *

I'm so relieved the interrogation's over that I binge as soon as I get upstairs to my kitchen. I know the last thing I need is an overdose of calories but I just can't resist the nervous urge to stuff my face. Unfortunately Nigel then comes downstairs from his attic to welcome me back and finds me throwing up noisily in the bathroom.

'Too much rich food,' I say as he hovers over me in concern, but I know he'll notice the ransacked interior of the fridge.

The next morning after breakfast in bed with Elizabeth I call Serena and arrange to take her out to dinner. I know I've got to do all I can now to make Elizabeth think I'd never dream of dumping my authorised girlfriend. If I did, Elizabeth would think I was still hankering for Carta.

After a quick meal at a Pimlico trat I take Serena to a West End cinema. That avoids the chore of talking to her. I wish I could

290

dump her after the film but I know I have to whisk her over to Austin Friars for a shag. Well, at least she's not a man. That has to rank as some kind of plus.

The next day I decide to concentrate on the shag so within minutes of hitting Austin Friars at noon we're screwing our brains out. Lunch gets kind of lost in the shuffle, but later we stop off at a pub for some basic nosh. I know it's cheap of me not to take her to a decent restaurant, but I can't face spending a long time talking to her. It makes me think of the vile months I spent working for Norah and meeting all those pathetic needy women who used to upset me so much by reminding me of – but no, it's better not to think of Mum. Better to say I hate getting involved with women like that because it just reminds me how useless I am, unable to help the poor cows in any way that really matters.

Finally I drop Serena at Norah's house and the date ends. Thank God. On my way home I halt the car on Horseferry Road and reach for my phone to call Carta. Well, why shouldn't I have a treat after following orders so obediently for hours and hours? It's early evening and she should be home from work, so after surveying the numbers engraved on my heart I phone her on her mobile. That should stop Sad Eric picking up the call.

'Yes?' says Carta cautiously a moment later.

'Just checking in,' I say, feeling happier than I've felt all day. 'How are you doing?'

'Gavin!' She doesn't sound as if she feels I'm harrassing her, and the fact that she's used my name suggests Sad Eric's not around. 'Has something happened?' she adds tensely, no doubt thinking of the mega-donation.

'No, nothing – I just got through two days off and I'm not due to see Colin again till Friday afternoon. Heard anything from him?'

'Not a tweet. I'm beginning to suspect he has no intention of giving to anyone.'

'Don't give up hope!'

'Easier said than done! Listen, I'm glad you've called. I wanted to say how sorry I was about my mistakes last weekend – not just hitting you and bawling you out, but being so dumb about those cuff links. Giving them away was a great gesture. I really admired it.'

'Ah.' I start to glow.

'I was just wondering,' she adds. 'Would you like to come to my office after work one day this week to try to figure out the Colin situation?'

I kill the impulse to shout: 'Yes, *yes*, YES!' and say instead: 'I'd really like that, but it's too risky. I've got to keep clear of St Benet's now.'

'Maybe we could meet somewhere else. The thing is I don't just want to talk about Colin. I want to tell you the whole story about what happened to me in 1990.'

My heart sinks. '1990?'

'When my husband died. You see, I think if you knew what happened you'd want to help me, and all I want is proof that your Elizabeth isn't my Mrs Mayfield—'

'But I've told you she's not!'

'Yes, but . . . Gavin, all I'm asking you to do is listen!'

'But what good would that do when I know I can't help? Look, I gotta run—'

'No, wait! There's something crucial you have to know. Nicholas and Lewis both think you and I have been brought together to help one another. We're travellers on a journey, they say, and—'

'What? Sorry, the connection's breaking up, I can't hear you,' I lie, but she just keeps right on talking.

'—and I can see the journey produces a special kind of friend-ship – life-saving—' Her voice breaks. She gives a muffled sob.

I'm horrified.

*　　*　　*

I'm horrified not just because cool, clever Carta's been talking like a mystical nutter. I'm horrified because she's revealed herself to be an emotional mess, yet another one of the needy women who churn me up deep down. It just reminds me again of Mum after Hugo died. Mum held herself together while he was dying but afterwards she went to pieces and I couldn't help her – I wanted to, I tried to but I was useless, she told me so.

That's why I can now only get close to strong non-needy women who don't get emotional. That way I don't let anyone down, and besides . . . I need all my strength just to survive, don't I? I'm not in a position to go around helping people. I'm not my brother's keeper, and I'm sorry but I can't be my sister's keeper either.

'Hey, lighten up!' I urge glibly, fighting back the panic. 'We'll meet again soon, I promise – call you later – take care—' I cut the connection and collapse with relief.

But then I start to think. I don't want to. I want to switch off and drive the rest of the way home on auto-pilot, but I go on sitting in the stationary car while I rerun the conversation. Over and over again I tell myself: I can't help her. There's nothing I can do.

Yet there's someone in my head saying I can. I'm not sure which of my personalities this voice belongs to, but he's speaking with authority. He's saying that I'm the one man who has the power to help this very special woman in this particular situation, and I now have the power to prove I'm not just a waste of space when it comes to helping a woman in need. I'm not a waste of space anyway, he says. I'm special, I count, I matter.

I say to him out loud: 'I can't betray Elizabeth.'

But he just tells me that I can at least listen when Carta talks. I can hold out my hand to her, he says, just like she held out her hand to me at St Benet's.

I don't know who the hell I am when I'm talking to myself like this because this character doesn't chime with any of my familiar roles. In fact he can't be one of my personalities at all because none of them would behave in this way. So he must be some kind of delusion.

Isn't it weird the tricks your mind can play when you're stressed almost out of your skull?

*   *   *

As I arrive home Elizabeth calls out from the living-room, but although my nerves lurch there's no crisis. She just wants to give me some information about Gil.

'We don't have as much time to train him as we thought,' she says when I'm sitting down beside her on the sofa. 'Asherton phoned to tell me that the date for the GOLD romp's been set for Saturday week. Apparently the stars are in an interesting conjunction that weekend and he's determined to cash in on the Zodiac angle.'

'So what did you say?'

'Naturally I played along and said Gilbert would be grade A by then, but am I promising more than we can deliver? I've been so busy starting up my new group that I haven't had time to view the most recent tapes.'

I wonder if I can save Gil by talking down his performance – yet at the same time I know I can't lie because the tapes are there to show exactly what grade he's reached. Cautiously I say: 'He's improved, but let's face it, he's never going to set the fruit on fire. He's just a nice bloke who likes some conventional gay fun, so if Asherton's hoping for a porn-star-is-born performance he's going to be disappointed.'

'Luckily all we promised Asherton was an improvement, but let's try and make Gilbert as improved as possible in the time we've got left. Why don't I slip him a couple of extra sessions? If you were to see him next weekend—'

'Forget it! This weekend's a gay-free zone!'

'It's all very well for you to get huffy, pet, but our best hope of keeping on good terms with Asherton and defusing his nasty suspicions of you is to deliver Gilbert to him as prime meat!'

'I'm not saying I won't do the extra sessions. I'm just saying I'd rather do overtime next week than have gay sex this weekend,' I argue, and she lets me have my way, but I'm feeling polar-cold at the thought of Gil being delivered to Asherton as prime meat. How can I possibly serve up Gil like this? But I've got to, haven't I? Otherwise *I'll* be the one who winds up at the Pain-Palace. Unless . . .

I suddenly get the glimmer of an idea.

* * *

The key factor is that Gil's a clergyman, and everyone knows that clergymen aren't supposed to hang out with people like me. So if Gil were to say his God's come through on the spiritual mobile and told him to give me up, no one would think it odd. It's the kind of thing that would happen to a straying clergyman with a conscience, and best of all I'd be blameless, specially as I've already promised to improve him by doing overtime.

So what I've got to do is pick a quarrel and lay so much guilt on him that he snaps. I know I'm going to hurt him, but I've no choice. He's got to be saved.

Wednesday morning arrives. Elizabeth's decreed that six of the clients who had to be cancelled during my past two days off have to be fitted in during the rest of the week, so I'm doing two extra sessions a day. With one exception these punters are the important clients, the rich ones who slip me expensive presents and lavish tips to show how easily they can pay my fees. The exception is Gil, who probably has trouble affording me even at a heavy discount, but since he's the most important client of all at present he's up there among the high rollers. He's due at three, normally the end of the lunch-time shift.

The fact that I'm doing more work than usual means I have to pace myself very carefully to cope with the extra stress. We're talking loads of sexual fakery here, and to guard against a disaster with Gil I've filled a syringe with the drug that guarantees an erection.

The worst thing, psychologically, is the fact that the performance with Gil has to be filmed. I can get away with not bothering to film anyone else today – there are no newcomers and all the punters are already on tape. So if I have a failure with anyone else it won't matter, I can offer them plenty of other fun routines and make sure they leave satisfied. But if I fail with Gil and the cameras are turning I'm in deep shit. Better the needle than that.

The crucial problem is when to inject myself. The stuff takes time to work so ideally I should inject it halfway through the previous appointment, but if I already have an erection then I could be injecting myself into a nightmare. On the other hand if I leave the shot until just before Gil arrives I might be limp as a wimp for far too long. In the end I decide to wait to see what kind of state my equipment's in halfway through the prior appointment, and in fact it looks as if it's been nuked – the stress has taken its toll. Fortunately this isn't crucial as this client likes to do all the work, but unfortunately he's going so strong that I can't escape to the bathroom to jab myself. I try every trick I know to get him to finish but he just yowls and dribbles and keeps juddering. God, sex is bloody hell sometimes, it really is – and that's the great state secret of our sex-berserk culture. Sex can be absolutely – bloody—

The client finally finishes. I scoot to the bathroom and stick the needle in my equipment. Revolting. Everything's revolting. Why the fuck am I leading this bloody revolting life? Because it's all I'm good for, that's why. Yet when I went to St Benet's they treated me as if—

No, wipe all thought of St Benet's. Just focus on the present. Focus and survive.

Off goes the bugger with the climax problem. In comes the clergyman offering himself up to be trashed.

'Gavin!' He's so pleased to see me. If he were a puppy he'd be wagging his tail so fast it'd be invisible.

Out of sheer biological perverseness my equipment stages a recovery even before the drug starts to work – which means that once the drug kicks in I'm in a good deal of discomfort. Fucking hell! I can hardly wait to lock myself in the bathroom and cool off. The relief, when I finally turn off the cameras, is cosmic.

Five minutes later we're sitting on the barstools at the kitchen counter and sipping Chardonnay – or at least he is. I'm OD-ing on OJ as I prepare to pick the quarrel which'll save him.

But before I can get stroppy he says: 'Gavin, I hate to ask, but . . .'

He's run out of money. Could I have a word with my manager and persuade her to allow him credit?

With another surge of cosmic relief I realise I've been presented with an alternative way to save him.

'Sorry, mate,' I say. 'No credit ever allowed except via regular credit cards,' but to my horror the silly bloke says: 'Okay, I'll borrow the money from a friend. She won't ask any questions.'

Oh my God. He can't mean – he couldn't mean—

'Shit, Gil, are you talking about Carta?'

He looks embarrassed. 'That needn't concern you,' he says, trying to stand on his dignity, but the trouble is he's got no dignity left. I've shredded it.

'Look, chum,' I say, even forgetting the ache in my equipment, 'are you out of your clerical mind? Carta's my friend and I'm not having her ripped off by an out-of-control cleric who's deep into a mid-life crisis!'

'It's not like that!'

'Oh yes it is! Look, if you want to screw around good luck to you, I'm no puritan, but stop being a clergyman first, okay? You're paid to be a moral leader, someone in this filthy, putrid world who *isn't* wallowing around in the shit, and people don't like it when their moral leaders smash their hope that life's not quite such a dump as it seems to be!'

He looks stricken. Brilliant! This quarrel's going really well.

'Okay,' he mutters. 'I won't borrow from Carta. But I'll find the money somehow.'

Horror slugs me all over again. 'What about your job?' I yell in a last-ditch attempt to blast him back to sanity.

'That's between me and God.'

'*God?* Shit, what kind of god can you possibly worship? What kind of god gives you a green light to get fucked by a leisure-worker – A PROSTITUTE – and pretend it's some kind of romantic affair?'

'Gavin—'

'You know what I think? I think all this gay rights crap has done your head in! You're floating along in an idealistic dream which is totally unconnected with reality!'

But now Gil starts to fight back. He's no pushover, I'll say that for him, and although he's allowed me to bad-mouth him, I'm not to be allowed to slag off his sacred cause.

'Nothing can be more realistic,' he says strongly, 'than working to ensure gays are treated as human beings and accepted into mainstream society.'

I decide I've no choice but to keep the quarrel stoked up. I've got to save this heroic idiot, got to. 'Oh, puh-leeze!' I exclaim offensively. 'The reality is that even if gays are formally accepted into the mainstream, people will still pity them as handicapped or reject them as revolting – and if you weren't gorging yourself on gay dreams in the gay ghetto, you'd see that as clearly as I do!'

'But things do change eventually as mankind's moral and religious sense evolves! A civilised society now accepts that discrimination's wrong, whether it's against women or Jews or blacks or gays or any other group, and we have to make sure our society practises what it preaches!'

'By bouncing around being an activist? Oh, grow up!'

'That's the kind of put-down men used to use when dealing with the suffragettes, but look where women are today!'

'Yeah, just look at them – overworked, underpaid and still getting slagged off by men! Do you seriously think anything really changes deep down? Anyway you're kidding yourself if you're equating the women's cause with the gays—'

'I don't think so, not on the most fundamental human level. The fact is that gays, like women, are oppressed and made to suffer—'

'Oh, stuff that victim spiel! Take responsibility for your actions, for God's sake, and stop whingeing around boring everyone rigid! If gay activists would spend more time keeping their bloody mouths shut—'

'If gay activists spent more time keeping their bloody mouths shut, the same old prejudice and discrimination would just keep going! Don't you understand, Gavin? *Someone's* got to speak up! How can the world ever progress if we all accept the status quo and do nothing? How can we live in this broken, suffering world, which is still in the process of creation, without busting a gut to help our Creator redeem it all so that everything finally comes right?'

I open my mouth. But then I shut it again.

I find I've nothing to say.

* * *

So much for the quarrel I'm supposed to be picking. I'm still beating my brains out to dream up a new way to save him when he says: 'I think I know why you're so cynical. It's because you're a gay man who's oppressed and made to suffer but no one comes to your rescue.'

Genuine rage floods through me. 'Oh, sod off about the fucking gays, for God's sake, and stop implying the fucking straights can't have it just as difficult as they do! I'm a straight and life's been bloody hell and don't you ever, *ever* tell me I've had it easier than any gay!'

He stares at me. 'You're not straight,' he insists, obstinate as ever. 'You're just saying that to put me off.' Then some kind of penny drops. 'You've staged this whole quarrel because you think you'd be doing me a favour by breaking up our relationship!'

'Oh, piss off!'

He slips away without another word, but I know he'll be back. Disaster.

* * *

I get home to be greeted with the news that Gil's credit card's been negged. Susanne tried to run it to cover his next session which this week has been scheduled for Friday.

'That's a complication we certainly don't need,' says Elizabeth crossly. 'I don't want him to miss a session, but we can't keep him on when there's no money. It would look too suspicious.'

'Maybe now he's broke he'll quit.'

'Oh, I don't think he'll do that, pet! He's well and truly hooked . . . No, what I've got to do is encourage him to find the cash. I'll have a word with him tomorrow, say Friday's slot will have to be cancelled but we'll fit him in on Monday if he can wire the money before the weekend.'

'Any word from Colin?'

'None, so I'm sure we're safe, but when you see him on Friday take care to lull any suspicions he might have – dole out the ecstasy in cartloads.'

I begin to worry again about my equipment going on strike. Life's suddenly nothing but a nightmare . . .

*　*　*

The next day's Thursday and after the wake-up shift I call Carta. I've spent half of last night working out that I have to make this call. I know I let her down by backing off when we last spoke. It's true I can't give her the information she wants, but she's got to know I'm not just a shit who doesn't give a damn.

'Hey, it's me,' I say when she picks up. 'Just to say I'm sorry I flaked out on you like that. I'm not good when women get upset but that's not because I don't care. It's because I care so much I can't handle it.'

She seems stunned by this admission and I'm not surprised. I'm stunned by it myself. I rehearsed it over and over again while I was lying awake last night, but I wasn't sure I'd have the nerve to say it to her. It makes me sound a real wimp, but I feel only the truth has a hope of working here.

And it does work. She says slowly: 'I'm sorry too, sorry I got upset. I shouldn't have tried to download all that stuff over the phone.'

She says nothing else on the subject and neither do I, but I know everything's been put right and we're still friends. Hurrying on in a rush of relief I ask: 'Any word from Colin?'

'Zilch.'

'Shit.' But suddenly I see how I can make amends to her for my broken-reed performance the other night. 'Look, Colin's got a visit to Austin Friars booked for tomorrow at the end of the day. Stop by at six-thirty and I should be able to tell you more about what's going on.'

She's delighted. 'Great! I'd really appreciate that!'

'On second thoughts make that six-forty. I don't want the two of you meeting on the doorstep,' I say, and blow a kiss into the phone. 'That's platonic,' I add hastily before ending the call.

Then I sigh and start fantasising again about the magic shag. It's

299

a waste of time, I know it is, but I need a fantasy or two to keep me going at present when life's such a bloody nightmare.

If only there was some way of saving Gil. But there's no way now. No way at all.

*   *   *

I'm so stressed out that on Friday morning I eat too much cooked breakfast after the wake-up shift and start to worry seriously about my weight. I can't afford to put on a single pound. Got to look perfect. I have no control over so much of my life at present but at least I can control my body.

Later, as I flush away the vomit in the lavatory bowl, I remember Nicholas talking of wholeness, of how body, mind and spirit should be one. My body's in perfect health but the rest of me's cut off from it and strung out on a rack. What's my spirit anyway? I suppose it's got to be my real self, Gavin Blake Me, but is the spirit just the fundamental "I" of personality or does it exist above and beyond all that? And most baffling of all, who's that mysterious Other, the one who's not "I", the one who's not any of my roles, the one who keeps whispering through the closed doors of my mind: 'Help Carta. Save Gil. Help Carta. Save Gil . . .'

The buzzer sounds. I'm still standing stark naked in front of the bathroom mirror where I planted myself for a fat-cell check. Wiping all dotty thoughts about an Other from my mind, I vault into my jeans and sprint off to face the next client who wants to use me.

*   *   *

Colin fails to arrive on time for his double-slot which concludes the late-shift. I wait and wait, fearful that he's sussed the link with Asherton, yet when I finally call Elizabeth she's still sure he'll show.

At six o'clock, just when I've written him off, the buzzer sounds and I let him in.

'Hi!' I say concerned as he stumps out of the lift. 'You okay? I was worried.'

He grunts, offering neither an apology nor an explanation, and suddenly I'm remembering our first meeting when he was upset but concealing his feelings behind a mask of bad temper.

'Can I get you a drink?' I ask, keeping calm.

300

He shakes his head, hangs up his coat with a savage swipe of his arm and starts to plod upstairs.

If he wants to unnerve me he's succeeded. In fact I'm so unnerved that I activate the cameras. There's no need to record the scene now Asherton's no longer interested in him, but if there's trouble I can at least film it so that Elizabeth can see I wasn't at fault in any way.

I decide to tackle the problem head on. 'Hey!' I say, closing in behind him as he stands staring out of the window. 'What's up?'

Swinging round he slaps me so hard on the cheek that I reel backwards and sprawl across the bed. Adrenaline floods through me. I'm on my feet in a flash, every muscle tensed, all my self-defence lessons slotting into sequence in my brain. Thank God I switched on the cameras! Although he's never been violent before, his buttoned-up emotions and filthy temper make him a prime candidate for the meltdown scenario – but what's triggered this meltdown? He's got to have uncovered the connection with Asherton, there's no other explanation.

'Okay,' I say rapidly as he stands panting and glaring at me. 'Okay, okay, okay, whatever I've done I'm sorry, but can you tell me what it is? Honestly, Colin, I'm in the dark here—' I'm in pain too. My face is still throbbing.

'You've lied to me!' he says, his voice shaking with rage. 'You've deceived me about a most fundamental aspect of your true nature!'

'Huh?' I'm so relieved that he hasn't uncovered the Asherton link that I'm not as quick on the uptake as I should be.

'You fuck women!'

Oh my God. How did he—

'No, don't you deny it – I've had enough of your bloody lies! I know you've been seeing a woman! I've had you watched!'

'*Watched?* But for God's sake why?'

'I didn't like the way you looked at that woman last weekend. I suppose you thought I was so infatuated with you that I wouldn't notice!'

'Well, I may have flirted mildly with her but that was nothing, just a bit of social role-playing—'

'You *bloody* liar, you were having an affair with her and she asked you to help her get money out of me for St Benet's!'

'Colin, I have never – repeat, *never* – had an affair with Carta Graham! Why should you think—'

'I engaged the private detectives first thing on Monday morning so I know all about that slim blonde woman you took to Austin Friars!'

'Shit, Colin, that wasn't Carta!'

'I know it wasn't – my men took pictures! Obviously you'd either finished with Miss Graham or else you were running the two affairs simultaneously!'

'I'VE NEVER HAD AN AFFAIR WITH CARTA!'

'Well, what about the other girl? Don't tell me you brought her here just to admire the view!'

'Okay, that's my friend Serena, but it's all platonic, I've known her for years, and the reason I brought her here was because I didn't want to take her to Lambeth. Elizabeth doesn't approve of her.'

'You mean she's jealous! You and Mrs Delamere are lovers, aren't you?'

'Absolutely not! Colin, Elizabeth's over fifty years old! If I was straight – which I'm not – I'd be into chicks, not mother hens!'

'I wasn't born yesterday, Gavin. You've made the mistake of thinking that just because I don't know as much about sex as you do I know equally little about human nature, but I know corruption when I see the evidence for it! There's a connection, isn't there, between Mrs Delamere and Asherton? I'm sure now it was no coincidence that we met him at the opera that night. I think he uses you to recruit for that perverted society of his.'

'Oh, for God's sake! Give your imagination a rest!' I exclaim, but of course I'm shocked rigid and Colin takes no notice of this routine denial.

'If you'd never set eyes on Asherton before that night at the opera,' he says, 'why did you look so stunned when you saw he'd turned up at the Hall? Obviously there was some kind of deep connection there, and at first I just wrote him off as one of your former clients, particularly when you told me later that he'd asked for your phone number. Refreshing his memory, I thought! But then I started to wonder. I'd already seen you looking at the woman as if you were a heterosexual, and I thought: if he could lie about the sex he could lie about anything – and now I realise you've told me lie after lie, but you can stop lying now because we're finished – it's over – I never want to see you again!'

I lose it. That's because deep down I'm scared about how I've screwed up. I suppose I'm thinking something like: what the hell, since I've already screwed up so badly, let's bloody well screw up all the way.

'I never want to see you again either, you ugly old fart!' I yell. 'And if you ever thought I enjoyed heaving your bloated old body around, maybe you were born yesterday after all! Get the fuck out and good riddance!'

Then all hell breaks loose as he goes for me.

I curse myself for the loss of temper but it's too late. Of course I can get the better of him in a fight, but if I hurt him he might call the police and although we'd have him on film as the aggressor, the police could be much too interested in someone who can connect Elizabeth and Asherton.

I weave and dodge – and finally decide to bolt downstairs. If I can grab a knife from the kitchen I reckon I can threaten him to his senses.

So I hurtle out of the bedroom onto the landing, but then the hell of a thing happens: the world tilts as if London's been hit by an earthquake, and losing my balance I start to tumble down the stairs. I break my fall by clutching the rail, but in doing so I bang my head and that's the last thing I remember for a while.

I lose consciousness.

* * *

When I open my eyes again the buzzer's rasping above my head. Dimly I realise I'm lying in a heap on the hall floor. The clock on the wall says six-thirty, which is an odd time for a client to be arriving, but no, wait a minute, this week I've been fitting in bumped VIPs, so . . . no, wait again, this is Friday, one VIP was fitted in at three o'clock, the other picked up a cancellation earlier and Colin was definitely my last punter of the day.

Colin . . .

I remember, but even as I gasp the buzzer goes again – two short toots and a long blast. The noise goes right through my aching head and out the other side. Dragging myself onto my knees I reach for the receiver. 'Yep?'

'Gavin! I thought you'd forgotten about me and gone home!'

It's Carta. Can't remember why she's here but never mind, she can make me a cup of tea. I press the button to let her in and then I slump back into a sitting position. My brain's still off-colour but

303

otherwise I'm in one piece. Bruised but unbroken. I've been worse.

'What's happened?' she exclaims as soon as she sees me.

'Fell downstairs. Row with client.'

'Colin?'

'Oh right, I told you he was coming, didn't I? That's why you're here.' I peer into the mirror by the front door, but to my relief I find the marks left by Colin's slam have faded. Lucky it was his palm he used and not his fist . . . I lurch against the wall as the wuzziness returns.

'Sorry,' I mutter. 'Got to be horizontal. Please could you make me some tea?' I seem to be fixated on the idea of Carta making tea. It must be because tea-making's so domestic, so absolutely the favour one friend would do for another in a crisis.

'Leave it to me,' she says, taking charge. 'You go and lie down.'

I clamber upstairs and plop down on the bed as the memory of the row hits me again. Elizabeth's going to be furious that Mr Moneybags has gone down the drain and horrified that he's linked us to Asherton. I start to sweat.

'Try some of this.' Carta's arrived and she's handing me a mug of dark tea. 'I put some sugar in it to counter the effects of shock.'

'Thanks.' I hitch myself up on the pillows and take a swig while she draws up a chair, the wooden one which I scrub down after it's been used for sex games. It's wonderful to see her sitting on it. I feel it's been cleansed at the deepest level, just as the cuff links were cleansed when I handed them to Nicholas.

'You should see a doctor,' she's saying. 'Shall I call Val? I'm sure you don't want to go to hospital and wait hours in Casualty.'

It occurs to me that sending for Dr Lush-Lips could be a wise idea. I'm still feeling floaty, keen to stay horizontal. 'Okay,' I say, and Carta goes downstairs to retrieve Val's number from her bag.

Back in the bedroom after making the call she asks: 'Can you tell me about the row with Colin?'

The short answer is no, not entirely. That's because I don't want to tell her about Serena. However I get my battered brain to do a little editing, omit mentioning the detectives and just say Colin became suspicious after seeing how well Carta and I got on last weekend, so suspicious that he eventually decided I was a closet hetero.

'He must be paranoid!' exclaims Carta, justifiably amazed that Colin should leap to this conclusion on the strength of a couple of hot looks.

'Sure he's paranoid!' I say. 'He's one of the misogynists who think any man who does a chick chat-up can never be trusted gay-wise.' I then tell her how I lost my temper and he lost his marbles. 'So I'm afraid the donation's gone down the tubes,' I conclude, genuinely depressed. 'I blew it. I'm really sorry.'

But she's wonderfully forgiving and good about it.

'It's not your fault,' she says. 'You're not to blame for the fact that he's irrational about women, and he may well have had no intention of donating anyway.'

'True. But all the same—'

'Gavin, don't feel badly – please! You've still raised an amazing amount of money for us and we're still enormously grateful.'

I feel better when she says this. In fact I even haul the extension phone out of the bedside table's cupboard to call Elizabeth and warn her I'll be late back.

'Did Sir Colin show up?' she demands at once.

'Yeah – I'll tell you everything later,' I stall and hang up before the buzzer blares. Val's been visiting a patient in Bow, just outside the Square Mile, so she hasn't had far to come.

Carta hurries downstairs to let her in.

*   *   *

'The good news is there's no serious damage,' says Val after examining my eyes with an ophthalmoscope. 'You've got a small bump on your head where you hit the wall, but the skin's not broken and I don't think the blow itself could have been hard enough to make you unconscious. Did you say you felt dizzy before you fell?'

'Yes, but—' I break off. A horrific thought's hit me. Maybe I'm ill. Maybe I've finally picked up HIV. Maybe in ten years' time I'll be dead. And as this terrible prospect erupts in my mind I want to shout: 'But I haven't had the chance to live!' and I know that has to be the real me talking, the Gavin Blake whose spirit's been so crushed for so long that he's not even sure what his spirit is.

'Let's just take your blood pressure,' Val's saying as she fishes in her medical bag for the right contraption, but even when the procedure's finished her expression remains impassive. Nothing for me to read there, not even a flicker of sexual interest. 'You a lesbian?' I demand at last in a feeble attempt to divert myself from my panic.

Val doesn't bother to reply, just tucks the blood-pressure bondage

305

gear back into her bag. Then she asks neutrally: 'Have you been feeling unwell lately?'

'Nope.'

'Eating properly?'

My sentence of death is abruptly lifted as I realise what's wrong with me. 'Maybe not,' I mumble, so relieved I can hardly speak.

'When did you last eat?'

'I had a big breakfast mid-morning but I couldn't keep it down. Same thing happened yesterday too.'

'Lunch?'

'Skipped it.' I smile at her. 'No wonder I'm feeling wuzzy! It's a stomach upset plus lack of food.'

But apparently Val doesn't think this is the end of the consultation. Turning to Carta, who's been hovering nearby like an anxious older sister, she says: 'I'd better have a word with him on his own.'

Carta slips away, beautiful feet tapping on the stairs, and immediately Val turns up the heat.

'How often have you been vomiting?'

'Oh, not often at all! Just after meals.'

'How long's this been going on for?'

'Few days.'

'Open your mouth, please.'

'My *mouth*? But there's nothing wrong there – I don't even have a sore throat!'

'I want to look at your teeth.'

I'm so astonished that I open my mouth wide without any further protest and Dr Lush-Lips peers inside. I do recover enough to say 'Aaah!' in a suggestive way, but when there's no reaction I know she just has to be a dyke. The reason why I failed to realise this sooner is because she's so different from Nightmare Norah.

Val snaps off the torch. 'Does the vomiting take you by surprise or are you able to choose when to do it?'

'What are you talking about?'

'Oh, come on, Gavin!'

'I don't know what you mean!' I protest, but I do know. And what's more I know that she knows that I know. Okay, I think, what the hell – it's no big deal. So long as I don't have Aids, what do I care?

'Well, as a matter of fact,' I say casually, 'I've been choosing to do it. I've been worried about getting fat, but I'm not being neurotic

306

here, just professional. I've got to look perfect for my job.'

'Sure.' To my surprise she stops playing the dominatrix and looks sympathetic. 'But Gavin, you don't want to get into the habit of throwing up, you really don't. The stomach acids rot the teeth and it's not good for your throat either. Maybe you need to talk this problem through with someone.'

'What problem?' I say. 'It's not a problem. I'm just temporarily off my food.'

'That's the problem. Best to take care of it before it gets a real grip on you.'

'But it's nothing to get excited about! I mean, blokes don't get bulimia, do they? That kind of stuff's just for chicks.'

Val waits for a moment before saying gently: 'At the Healing Centre I keep a file of articles from medical journals about eating disorders in men.'

I make some flip remark about sexual equality having gone too far, but she just says: 'Are you registered with a GP where you live?'

'No, I go to my manager's private doctor.'

'Okay, can you ask him to test you for anaemia?'

I hesitate. Dr Filth tells Elizabeth everything. 'Can't you yourself do the test?' I say to Val.

'I could, yes – you're certainly in the catchment area of my practice by having this flat in Austin Friars, but I'll need your National Health number to get you on my books.'

'Fine. I'll dig that out and come to see you.'

'Don't leave it too long . . . Have you got any food here?'

'Biscuits.'

'Milk?'

'Yep.'

'Have a glass of milk and some biscuits before you try to go home, and drink a glass of water too – more if you can manage it. And as a precaution don't drive. Take a taxi home, and when you get back do please eat a good meal which goes in one end of you and in due course comes out the other.'

I say meekly: 'Yes, doctor,' and wink at her as she leaves, but when I'm alone I sag back on the pillows.

I'm rattled.

*   *   *

307

'I'll call you,' I say later to Carta when we part. After the milk, biscuits and water I'm feeling much sharper – which is just as well, since I only have the cab ride to Lambeth in which to prepare my story.

Of course Elizabeth hits the roof when she hears I've been dumped, but when I swear I did my best to avoid the disaster she calms down and demands the details.

I start to inch my way through the minefield. 'He arrived in a filthy temper,' I say. 'It turned out he'd got it into his head that I fancied Nicholas Darrow last weekend.'

'Darrow! Well, he's certainly the type that can switch both sexes on, but I wouldn't have pegged him as having any gay interest. How could Sir Colin have thought—'

'I'm not saying he thought Darrow was responding – he just thought I was smitten. Anyway on Monday he puts PIs on my trail, and they come up with the evidence that I'm shagging Serena – a far worse crime than melting over Darrow. So jealousy runs rampant and before you can say "melodrama" he's crashing around like a rhino on uppers. Finally he belts me across the face, yells that he never wants to see me again and stalks out. The reason why I'm late back is that I was so zapped by the whole fiasco that I just had to sit down for a while with a glass of wine to recover.'

'I'm not surprised! But maybe he'll backtrack once he calms down.'

'No chance.' This is the truly tricky part, trickier than avoiding all mention of Carta, throwing in the Nicholas rigmarole and omitting my wimpish fall downstairs. 'Colin suspects you and Asherton are connected,' I say rapidly, 'and he's guessed I recruit for GOLD.'

Elizabeth's language slips. 'Shit.' After taking a large gulp of her drink she says in her flattest voice: 'Then that's that.'

'Darling, I'm sorry – I know how disappointed you must be—'

'All that money gone to waste! But how the *fuck* could it have happened? Why should that bugger suspect—'

'Well, of course,' I say acidly, 'this is entirely Asherton's fault – and I'm not just referring to the way he blew the debate. On our way into dinner that night he was stupid enough to collar me for a private interrogation about Darrow, and Colin looked back and noticed. I tried to defuse Colin's suspicions by saying Asherton'd been making a pass, but Colin's no fool and I bet it was then he started to wonder about a conspiracy.'

'You think that was the real reason he had you watched?'

'I'm sure he was getting jealous twinges as well, but yes, basically he distrusted me on every front and wanted to know just what the hell was going on.'

Elizabeth knocks back the rest of her drink and holds out her glass. 'Get me another, would you, pet?' she says abruptly, but although she's still furious, the word 'pet' signals the fury's not directed at me.

I'm so relieved I nearly make a mess of refilling her glass, but luckily I have my back to her and she can't see how unsteady my hand is. My big problem now is that Asherton'll tell her *I* was the one who revealed the conspiracy by looking so horrified when I first saw him at Hellfire Hall – a dead giveaway of our secret connection, as both Nicholas and Colin instantly realised. But I'll worry about that later. My prime task right now is to pass Elizabeth's glass back to her without puking into it. Elizabeth has a revolting taste in drinks. It's all sweet sherry and saccharine cocktails and treacly liqueurs, and at present she's treating herself to that thick creamy stuff which looks like whisked sewage.

'All right,' says Elizabeth when I'm sitting down beside her again, 'this is the way we'll play it. We don't tell Asherton that you and Sir Colin are finished. It's just too complicated, and now that Sir Colin's not a candidate for GOLD Asherton doesn't need to know his latest moves anyway. And we certainly don't tell Asherton that Sir Colin's sussed the conspiracy. That would make Asherton a tad nervous in case Sir Colin goes to the P-O-L-I-C-E, and it's never a good idea to give someone like Asherton extra worries, particularly when paranoia's already his middle name.'

I'm dead relieved again. If Asherton does try to dump the responsibility for the Colin disaster on me, he'll get nowhere because this is a subject Elizabeth no longer wants to discuss, specially as she now believes my version of who's to blame. She'll just write off Asherton's attack as paranoia and move on.

However I can't relax yet – this reference to the P-O-L-I-C-E at once has me sitting forward on the edge of my chair. 'God, do you really think Colin'll go to the police about me?'

'No, in my opinion caution will triumph and Sir Colin will do nothing that'd reveal he's been seeing a leisure-worker. That's why you were so clever not to punch him up. If there'd been a fight his injured pride might have lured him into doing something silly, but as it is . . . No, on that score you're safe enough and so am I.'

I hear the unspoken 'but'. 'What's the other score?'

'This is where we get back to Asherton and last weekend's dinner-party fiasco. Remember I told you that the danger from Darrow wasn't actually pressing because there was no hard evidence against GOLD?'

'So what's changed?'

'Well, there's still no hard evidence. But what now worries me is that this scene at Austin Friars today could get both Darrow and the police involved.'

'But you just said—'

'I said Sir Colin wouldn't complain to the police about you, and I'm sure I've got that right. But I think he could complain to them about Asherton, and Darrow would back him up. All that outrage Sir Colin feels about Asherton and me and you and the conspiracy – it's all got to be dumped somewhere, and he'll see Asherton as the only dumping ground.'

'But if there's no hard evidence—'

'You're missing the point, dear. The point is that when a wealthy, powerful man like Sir Colin Broune makes an allegation, the police can't just sit on their derrières and do nothing, and what we don't need, absolutely *don't* need, is the police breathing down Asherton's neck in the run-up to the romp with Gilbert Tucker. If the romp gets rumbled and GOLD goes up in smoke—'

'—Gil's evidence of how he came to be there would link us both to the disaster.' I try to think coherently. 'Do you think the vice squad already have their eye on Asherton?'

'Must do, but the question is what, if anything, they can see. Ash is just one of a load of porn operators, and the Act is so flabby and useless the police can't do much about them – unless, of course, the Vice get lucky and turn up stuff that's totally unacceptable.'

'I'd have thought Asherton was swimming in stuff that's totally unacceptable.'

'Well, up till now I reckon he's been all right on GOLD. The secrecy's been well maintained and the goings-on haven't been too iffy. But that SM group is in a different league altogether. The Vice must have heard rumours.'

'I thought no one ever talked!'

'No one directly grasses him up, but word gets around on the street and the police snouts are paid to pick up rumours. Asherton's been safe so far because in practice members of SM groups are allowed to do anything short of killing one another, but the trouble is times seem to be changing.'

I remember a report which recently caught my eye in *The Times*. Elizabeth heard the news from Asherton who, she said, was 'ever so shocked'. 'You're referring to that S&M group which was arrested en masse the other day.'

'Exactly. All adults, all consenting and all nicked! Now put that new persecution policy from the Vice together with a possible complaint from Sir Colin, and you'll see where I'm going.'

'The police will hit Asherton where he's vulnerable.'

'Yes, they'll try to infiltrate the SM group, and once they do that they could pick up information about GOLD, since there's a crossover between the two groups—'

'—and that puts us in the frame!'

'Wait a mo, pet, it gets worse. If we're now seeing the result of the police's decision to get tough on SM groups, that decision must have been taken some time ago. So supposing the police have *already* infiltrated Asherton's SM group and crossed over into GOLD? If a cop from the Vice is in the audience when the Tucker romp takes off—'

'—it's coronary time. But Elizabeth, this is all supposition, isn't it? Do you really think—'

'I'm thinking that the best way to survive serious trouble is always to prepare for the worst. For instance, supposing we eventually do find ourselves being questioned by the police. We say that as far as you and I knew, Gilbert was just another client. We say that Tommy showed the videos to Asherton and Asherton decided to close in on Gilbert without consulting us. We say that not only were neither of us present at the romp but we knew absolutely nothing about it.'

'Okay, but—'

'That should buy us some time. Then of course we skip to Rio before the police can take GOLD apart and Darrow crashes around trying to identify GOLD as the society Kim Betz belonged to – and as soon as Darrow hears about the mysterious "Madame Elizabeth"—'

'But could either Darrow or Carta actually identify you now you've had the surgery?'

311

'They might not be able to make a positive identification from a photo, but if they saw me in the flesh . . . Well, I won't be hanging around for a police line-up, but let me tell you, pet, a forced emigration is *the* last thing I want, and that's why I'm so bloody livid with Asherton for putting everything at risk.'

This last speech underlines to me that I have to wipe the fantasy of saving Gil by giving the police an anonymous tip-off about the romp. Of course I'd love to be on a plane to Rio with Elizabeth, but Elizabeth would hate it – *she* has to be the one who picks the time to retire and the place to retire to, and if she's on the run, furious and bitter, she might start to suspect I blew the whistle. Or even if she doesn't, she might decide to dump me out of sheer rage that I wasn't finally able to keep Colin sweet and harmless, forever showering us with money while finding physical bliss with me and spiritual bliss through her beloved GOLD.

Meanwhile Elizabeth's still slamming Asherton. '. . . and I just don't understand why he should be so obsessed with Gilbert Tucker! All right, I know there's all that idealism begging to be smashed, but the man's not young, he's not a stunner and he's no satyr in the sack. I mean, I ask you! What's the point?'

Gut-twisting concern for Gil drives me into wanting to know more details of the romp in the hope that there's a weak spot I could exploit. Reminding myself that Elizabeth has no idea I eavesdropped when Asherton first revealed his revolting plan, I say idly: 'I suppose there's no chance Gil will fail to turn up?'

'None. You're forgetting the two of them already know each other after meeting at Bonzo's Aids hospice. Ash will simply invite Gilbert over for a drink and say you're going to be there as well.'

My heart sinks. I know she's right and this is an invitation Gil wouldn't refuse. 'Okay, so what happens after the drink? I suppose he gets shown the video – is Tommy going to offer a composite of the best session?'

'No, no, he'll do a composite of the composites to make sure the video's really mouthwatering.'

'And then?'

'That idiot Asherton's determined to stage a black mass as a warm-up, but that's not the problem. Gilbert'll do that once he's seen the video. But after that he's not going to be willing to do anything, and once they use him in the SM games we're talking assault, GBH, the works. Asherton's mad, absolutely certifiable, to involve a non-

312

consenting adult who isn't a waif and stray, but no one's going to stop him, are they? He'll get his way, just as he always does.'

In despair I say frivolously: 'Maybe he'll fall under a bus.'

'How can he when he rides around all the time in that show-off Rolls-Royce?' Elizabeth heaves a sigh. 'I keep hoping someone'll murder him,' she says, 'but no one ever does. Typical, isn't it? Nice, law-abiding people get murdered every day, but a really awkward gentleman like Asherton bounces along without a scratch.'

I can think of several ways to describe Asherton but 'awkward gentleman' isn't one of them. Elizabeth's talent for euphemisms has reached a new high.

I want to ask her what they plan to do with Gil after the romp's over, but I just don't have the stomach to frame the question.

'You'd better run off and have your dinner, pet,' Elizabeth's saying, 'but I'll see you first thing tomorrow for our Saturday fun.' And she gives me a steamy kiss to signal that I'm forgiven for the disaster of losing Mr Moneybags.

I stagger upstairs.

*　　*　　*

Nigel serves up veal marsala and hovers around as if he's afraid I'll bin it, but I clean my plate and although I hesitate outside the bathroom later I move on into my room. I can't afford to make a habit of passing out in front of clients and I certainly want to keep myself fit for Elizabeth. I'll pick up some iron pills to take care of the anaemia – if I have it – and stop acting weird over food. It's no big deal.

I've just hit the sack after taking paracetamol for the dull ache in my head when I have such a shock that I nearly levitate. I'm still agonising about Gil, and suddenly a fragment of my conversation with Elizabeth this evening reruns itself in that beat-up junk heap between my ears. It's the bit about the Tucker videos – generated, of course, by the hidden cameras – and now I'm finally remembering that although I switched on the cameras when Colin and I entered the bedroom, I never switched them off.

I leap out of bed and stand shuddering in the dark as I think of the cameras recording Carta bringing me tea and Val doing her doctor number.

I try to work out what to do. The big question is whether Tommy's already picked up the tapes. On any other weekday night he would have done, but Friday is when he often goes out drinking with his mates and the routine checking of the Austin Friars technology gets left until Saturday or Sunday. With any luck those videotapes will still be sitting in their machines, and all I'll have to do is replace them with blanks. Tommy won't query them. He knows a non-recording day does sometimes happen.

I'm recovering from the shock. The only difficulty now is that because Val insisted I took a taxi home my car's still in the City. Inconvenient. But not a problem.

I dress and slip silently out of the house.

* * *

Another disaster. My luck's gone walkabout. I manage to pick up a cab but when I get to the flat I find Tommy's already collected the tapes. I know this without even having to examine the machines because we have a system to signal that everything's ready for my next working day: he leaves a playing card face up on top of the cabinet where the blank videos are stored.

As soon as I enter the second bedroom I see the upturned ace of diamonds and spew out some bad language. Then I try to think some problem-solving thoughts.

If Tommy's made the effort to come here on a Friday night, it probably means he's got something special lined up for the weekend and he could well be going away. Tommy's a football fan who treks all over the place to see his team's beautiful male bodies bounding around. So what I now have to do is take three blank tapes from the stock in the cabinet and swap them sometime over the weekend during his absence for the three tapes he's collected. If anything goes wrong – if, for instance, he noticed tonight that the tapes had been used but finds them blank when he comes to view them on Monday – I'll admit to the swap but explain it by saying Colin got the better of me in a fight and I didn't want Elizabeth to know. But the odds are Tommy wouldn't have examined the tapes closely when he picked them up. He'd have popped them straight into a bag while daydreaming of his weekend footy-fest.

As I leave the flat I wonder whether to pick up my car, but I decide that would be risky. Elizabeth might have noticed this evening after we parted that my car wasn't sitting on its slot. If she then sees tomorrow morning that it's there she'll want to know

314

when and why I retrieved it. I can explain its absence by saying it had to be workshopped, but I can't say it drove itself home.

The City's a graveyard at this hour, no cabs, but on Ludgate Hill I get a night-bus to Westminster, and from there it's not so far to walk over the river to Lambeth.

Arriving home exhausted I sleep as soon as my head thumps painfully against the pillows.

*　*　*

The next morning I'm up well before my early shag with Elizabeth because I need to find out Tommy's plans for the weekend and I reckon that if he really is going away he'll be aiming for an early departure. Jogging down the wooden steps which lead from Elizabeth's raised ground floor to the back garden at basement level, I take a look into Tommy's flat and see him ambling around the kitchen like a shaven-headed gorilla.

He sees me and opens his patio door. 'What are you up to, Sunshine?'

'Filling in the time before I shag Elizabeth. You're up early, aren't you?'

'Off to Amsterdam for the weekend.'

'Football?'

'Among other things.' He leers at me. 'Know what I mean?'

'I think I can just about get the gist. Enjoy yourself!' I say politely before wandering away to inspect a flowerbed.

I idle away another couple of minutes in the garden to convince him I'm just marking time and have no interest whatever in where he spends the weekend. Then I return indoors to make tea for Elizabeth.

*　*　*

The next stage of the retrieval operation ought to be simple but it won't be. In an ideal world I'd wait for Tommy to leave and then slip down to his flat via the basement stairs inside the house, but the door which opens onto those basement stairs in Elizabeth's hall is always kept locked and I don't know where the keys are. Yet I've got no other way to access Tommy's flat. Tommy has all the keys for the basement's front door and for the patio door at the back, while the windows which face the street are not only locked but tarted up with steel shutters which get used when he's away. Everything's wired to the hilt, and above the front door's a smart little burglar alarm box which is supposed to make would-be thieves burst into tears and move on.

Elizabeth approves of this external security glitz, but Locksmith Tommy's expertise makes her all the more determined to win the internal battle of the basement stairs. After all, Elizabeth's the house-owner and she needs to call the shots with this slimeball tenant – she doesn't want him trotting upstairs for a snoop when she's out. So she keeps her door to the stairs locked and bolted and she keeps the kitchen door which leads to the wooden steps and the garden locked and bolted too. Of course Tommy could pick the locks and she'd be none the wiser, but if he cuts or busts the bolts she'd know and then she'd borrow a couple of Asherton's Big Boys to sort him out. Knowing this, Tommy leaves both doors well alone.

So my problem's this: how do I get hold of the keys to the basement stairs? (There are two locks.) The first thing I have to do, obviously, is find out where the hell the keys are. Elizabeth keeps a spare set of her house keys and car keys on a hookboard in her kitchen, and the key to the kitchen door hangs there as well, but there's no ring holding the keys to that vital hall door. If Elizabeth's the only one who knows where they are I'm in trouble, but my guess is she'll have told Nigel. It's the kind of detail a housekeeper should know in case of an emergency.

When I return to my duplex after the shag with Elizabeth I find Nigel reading the *Sun* and eating cereal. I plonk myself down opposite him. 'Where does Elizabeth keep the keys to the basement stairs?'

'In the safe,' he says, crunching away on his Frosties, and then does a double take. 'Why?'

'Crisis. You know I told you last night I'd been ditched by Mr Moneybags? Well, it was worse than I let on. There was a punch-up and he knocked me out.'

'Gav! Why didn't you say?'

'Too proud to admit the truth even to you, mate, but listen, it gets worse: I forget about the cameras recording the whole scene, Tommy's now got the videos and unless I retrieve them this weekend when he's in Amsterdam I'm flapjacked. What's the combination of the safe?'

Nigel stares at me in concern. 'Dunno. That's not the kind of information Elizabeth trusts me with.'

I stare back, even more concerned than he is. 'Nige, are you saying Elizabeth's the only one who can get at those keys?'

'No, I'm just saying I don't know the safe combination. But Susanne does.'

My heart sinks to the soles of my feet as I realise my fate's now in the false-nailed talons of a Barbie-doll lookalike with bowling-ball breasts. 'Shit!' I'm close to panic.

'What are you going to do?' says Nigel, empathising so hard with me that he sounds as agonised as I do.

'Well, there's no choice, is there, mate?' I say, resigning myself to the inevitable. 'I've got to talk to Susanne.'

*   *   *

Over to the City I trek again to rescue my car. Then I drive to Norah's house in Pimlico where Susanne roosts in the basement flat. On the way I remember that although Serena has a business date for this evening, we've agreed to meet in the afternoon, an agreement I now decide to cancel. Can't face Serena at the moment. Can't cope with all that pretending.

Parking down the street from Norah's house I put through the necessary call to Serena and emerge from the car. The next bit's tricky. I don't want anyone from Norah's ménage to see me as I zip down to Susanne's flat, but I suppose that if anyone pulls up a window and yells: 'Hiyu!' I can always say I'm delivering something for Elizabeth.

I pad past the black railings, angle through the little gate and trot down the steps. No window gets heaved up. No one yells 'Hiya!' or 'Yo!' or even 'Yoo-hoo!' Luck's finally starting to run my way and not a moment too soon because I'll need all the luck I can get once I'm face to face with Susanne.

I press the doorbell.

I'm still not sure what to say, and my indecision's because I've never found the knack of lying successfully to her. She sees straight through me with those feral black eyes of hers. Unlike Norah's current crop of well-educated girls, Susanne's worked the streets. Nothing I say or do could ever shock her, because as far as prostitution's concerned she's been there, done that and got the T-shirt – or in other words, she's been beaten up, banged up and buggered up and she's had the nervous breakdown to prove it. But she's survived, and now she has this flat all to herself and a regular pay cheque which has nothing to do with renting out her private parts. She's escaped from the system, but I'm still trapped in it, and suddenly I know why I can't stand the sight of her. It's because she's got a life and I haven't. She's got the freedom to be herself, while I—

The door opens. She's there, staring at me in astonishment. Her long black hair, which she usually wears scrunched up and tartily draped, is loose, curtaining her pointy face and making her look like a wannabe witch. She hasn't coated herself with make-up yet so she looks pale and spotty. Odd to see her without false eyelashes, but otherwise her eyes are all too familiar: pitch-black, sullen, hostile.

'Shit, look at this!' she says, passing up the five-star welcome. 'What the hell do *you* want?'

'I'm in a mess and I need your help. Can I come in, please?'

She's more astonished than ever but she's impressed by the 'please'. This really must be serious, she's thinking. He's being well-behaved enough to stifle himself and he's spoken two sentences without calling me some slaggish nickname.

Opening the door wider she says severely: 'Don't step on the cat and don't be snotty about the décor.'

I follow her through the hall to the eat-in kitchen at the back of the house. The basement flat's at ground level here, just like Tommy's, and the windows look out on Norah's garden where a tiny lawn is framed by shrubs. A tree screens the garden from the house behind on the parallel street, and a white wrought-iron spiral staircase, much more arty than the wooden steps at Elizabeth's house, curls from the patio to the balcony outside Norah's kitchen above us.

In Susanne's kitchen I see herby-looking things in pots, dirty dishes in the sink and Alexis the cat sitting unhygienically on the table. I offer my index finger to see if the mog's mean enough to try a bite, but my flesh only rates a disdainful sniff.

'You watch it,' says Susanne to the cat. 'You don't know where he's been.' To me she adds: 'Suppose you want coffee.'

I spot some over-boiled dregs in a glass jug. 'No, thanks. Just your help.'

'I don't like you being so nice,' she says, slitty-eyed with suspicion. 'What's the story?'

Psyching myself up I sit down with her at the kitchen table. The cat gets removed to Susanne's lap where it purrs and tries to head-butt her breasts. It's a wonder it doesn't knock itself out.

'So?' says Susanne impatiently.

'Had a disaster last night. Colin arrives and goes mental. The jealous perv suspected me of hetero-bonking and hired some PIs who uncovered my dates with Serena.'

'And?'

'I made a balls-up of the self-defence and got knocked out. Didn't tell Elizabeth – it was bad enough having to tell her that Colin had ditched me. Then late last night my beaten-up brain remembers the whole scene's on tape.' I pause for air.

'And?' says Susanne again without expression.

'I shoot off to Austin Friars but Tommy's already retrieved the tapes. He's now gone to Amsterdam for the weekend and I've got to get into his flat to substitute blanks – but of course I need the hall door keys from the safe, and I was hoping we could do a deal about the combination.'

Susanne sighs before crooning to the cat: 'What do you think, loveliness? What do you think of that funny little story Mr Blake's been spinning us? Isn't it just the cutest little story you ever heard?' Then she dumps the cat on the floor, leans forward with her elbows on the table and snarls: 'Wise up, Junk-Hunk! Tell me the truth or get lost! What's on that tape which makes you shit bricks at the thought of Elizabeth seeing it?'

Dry-mouthed with fright I realise I have to come a little cleaner.

ʬ ✝ ♠

'The whole disaster dates back to last weekend,' I say, prepared to edge closer to the truth but still editing carefully as I go along. 'I was so bored that I flirted with Elizabeth's *bête noire*.'

'Bate what?'

'Elizabeth's enemy, the girl who's currently running the St Benet's fundraising campaign.'

'Oh, her. Cartwheel-something.' Naturally Elizabeth's been moaning to her right-hand woman about Colin's house party.

'Carta Graham. I was just so pissed off with everything that I couldn't resist a little flutter to cheer myself up. I mean, it was nothing serious, just a few hot looks—'

'Pass me the sickbag! Okay, you were nutso enough to give the Cartwheel a whirl. Then what?'

'Colin intercepts one of my hot looks and later dumps the PIs

319

on my trail. When he finds out I've conned him sex-wise he figures I've got the con-power to be part of a wider scam involving Asherton and GOLD.'

'Bad news. Okay, I can see why he wants to beat you up, but—'

'Colin was my last appointment yesterday, right? Well, Carta was dead keen to know if he was planning to donate to her Appeal so I told her to come to Austin Friars at six-forty—'

'Oh yeah, I get it. The Cartwheel gets on tape when you take her up to the bedroom for a—'

'Wrong. I mean, right – she gets on tape, but shagging isn't on the menu, I feel like shit and have to be horizontal. Carta brings me a cup of tea and summons the St Benet's doctor who also gets taped—'

'Okay, this is beginning to hang together, but it's still not right. Come on, pinhead! Do you really expect me to believe that Moneybags decked you?'

'Well, he . . . well, I . . . Okay, this is the way it was. He charges at me to beat me up. I want to avoid a fight because I don't want to be videoed winning it – much better if he's just shown as the aggressor. So I get off camera and try to bolt but then I lose my footing and fall down the stairs, knocking myself out – here, you can feel the bump on my head if you don't believe me!'

'Okay, I'm convinced – I still don't believe you've told me the whole truth, mind, but I believe enough to accept you have a big problem with those tapes. Now tell me why I should help you and risk getting into deep shit.'

I slide my tongue around my dry lips. 'I'll pay.'

'What kind of price are we talking about?'

'Name it.'

There's a silence which lasts seven seconds. I'm counting. Then she says: 'I don't want cash. I want drinks at the Ritz and dinner at the Savoy. Tonight.'

'Done. What's the combination of the safe?'

'Hold it! If you seriously think I'm going to hand over the safe combination and sit back while you go merrily on your way, you've made a very big mistake!'

I nerve myself for the next round of negotiations.

* * *

Susanne gnaws her thumbnail before saying: 'Elizabeth keeps a record of the safe combination in her en-suite bathroom, behind the porno-pic over the toilet. If she ever finds out about all this, you're to tell her you found the number by accident when you took down the pic for a closer look. She's never to know I've grassed.'

'Fair enough.'

There's a pause, probably because we're both thinking of Elizabeth's bathroom pictures, but finally I ask: 'What exactly's in that safe?'

'No need to get excited – all the top-secret stuff's in a locked steel box, and no, I don't have the key to it. If Elizabeth's ever arrested my instructions are to chuck the box in the river and take my final bonus. There's five hundred quid in an envelope which is also kept in the safe along with various papers, some jewellery and the keys to the basement stairs.'

'I can't understand why she keeps those keys in the safe! What's wrong with the kitchen hook-board?'

'She keeps them in the safe for the same reason that she has two fancy locks on the basement stairs door even though Tommy's a locksmith and could pick them. She wants to make sure that if any burglar gets into the main part of the house it'll be more trouble than it's worth for him to get into the basement. Why do you think Tommy's flat's like a fortress? It's because of the hard-core porn he produces for Asherton when the S&M group's filmed.'

I suspected Tommy did this. When he was training me in his flat I was never left on my own to explore, but I knew one room was set aside for his film-work even before he started dealing with the tapes from Austin Friars.

'Tommy's put in a new alarm system since you were trained,' Susanne's saying, 'but Elizabeth made him put the control panel on the wall just by the stairs. That way she just punches in the switch-off code when she makes an unscheduled visit to the flat and punches in the switch-on code when she leaves.'

'You know the codes?'

'There's a note of them in the safe along with the keys, and Tommy's forbidden to change any number without telling her. Weird, isn't it? Like some nutty version of the dominatrix game . . . Hey, are you going to change your mind about coffee? Because I'm going to throw out those dregs and make myself something drinkable.'

321

I decide this offer's worth accepting, and when she produces some expensive individual filters I feel we're approaching a state which could be described as an *entente cordiale*.

'So you see the problems, don't you?' she says after we've finished mulling over the pervy relationship between Tommy and Elizabeth. 'Retrieving those tapes is so tricky that I've got to be on hand to stop you making a balls-up. Have you ever opened a safe?'

I have to admit this is still on my list of things to do.

'You might make a muddle opening it. Or you might open it and make a mess inside so that Elizabeth would know she'd been raided. Or you might make a mess of the alarm system – oh, there's no end to the messes a pinhead like you could make, specially if you're in a dozy state after banging your head! You need supervision.'

I don't argue. In fact deep down I'm pleased to have help after so much time spent battling away on my own. I say: 'I'd appreciate the back-up. Thanks,' and at that point she orders me to book the table at the Savoy.

We move into the living-room, which has a long sofa sprinkled with cushions and cat hairs. On the self-assembly shelving beyond the jumbo TV stand a herd of china pigs, a couple of candles which stink and a load of Mills and Boon paperbacks.

'If you make some snotty comment about anything in this room I'll hit you,' she says as I check out the titles.

'I think it's great you read books,' I say seriously. 'Most people don't.' The *entente* shudders but survives.

I'm handed a phone directory, and when I make the call I'm told that the Savoy's currently holding dinner-dances in the main restaurant on Saturday nights. 'You want dancing?' I ask Susanne, my hand over the mouthpiece. 'It'll only be wrinkly stuff. Not like going clubbing.'

'What do you think I am – some poor cow of a teenager who only wants to get pissed, stoned and shagged out of her skull? I'm twenty-bloody-six, for God's sake! I've got *aspirations*!'

I remove my hand from the mouthpiece and book a table for two in the River Room.

* * *

Once we've got the evening sorted, we plan our assault on Tommy's flat.

322

As the result of breakfasting with Elizabeth I know her plans for the day: she's shopping in Oxford Street before meeting Norah for a matinée. Nigel's plans I also know, since they're the same every week: after buffing up the Austin Friars flat, he shunts off to the pub for lunch with the weekend regulars. So the house is going to be empty when we begin our raid at one.

Eventually we prepare to leave her flat. She pulls on a black leather coat over her lime-green spangled blouse and black stretch-pants, and exchanges her fluffy pink slippers for a pair of high-heeled boots. By this time she's caked herself in make-up, flounced up her hair and shovelled on the cheapo jewellery. Suddenly I realise that the make-up and the tacky trimmings are her equiv-alent of my Armani suits: something to hide behind, something to generate courage, something to boost a morale which always seems to need pumping up. But I notice that unlike me Susanne never glances at her reflection when we pass the mirror in the hall. She's confident now the armour's in place. In her world, the world where she has the freedom to be herself, she's more secure than I am.

When we get to Lambeth I park in the nearest side street and go ahead to make sure everyone really is out. Once Susanne joins me the raid begins.

We retrieve the number from the back of the porno-pic in Elizabeth's bathroom and return downstairs to the living-room where the safe lives behind an oil painting of a virginal girl who's clasping a bunch of lilies.

Susanne says idly as I remove the picture from the wall: 'I had a pervy punter once who could only get it up if I drenched myself in lilies-of-the-valley perfume. Turned out he was a convicted rapist.'

'Nasty.' I watch as she opens the safe. As soon as the door swings open I see the locked steel box, but the next moment Susanne's grabbed the little Jiffy bag containing the keys, and the door swings shut.

Having unlocked and unbolted the door to the basement, I allow Susanne to go ahead of me to fix the alarms. She punches in the codes. The infra-red eye fades. We've penetrated the fortress.

As I move forward I shudder at the memory of my training sessions. Suddenly I say: 'I hate Tommy.'

'Yeah, he's filth.' Her voice is as matter-of-fact as it was when she was talking of the disgusting punter, and her face is as expressionless as it was when we were surrounded by the bathroom porno-pics. This is the way things are, she's thinking. You don't throw a fit and waste vital energy. You grit your teeth and accept what you can't change, but this isn't condoning the filth. It's surviving it.

The three tapes, one for each camera, are easy to spot as soon as we enter Tommy's workroom. They're bound together with a rubber band on one of the counters, and beneath the band is a card bearing yesterday's date. Elizabeth rents space in a warehouse for the tape archives, so only the current videos get stored in the basement flat.

Setting the used tapes aside I slip the rubber band around the three blanks and tuck in the card. I've just put them back on the counter when I notice another stack of tapes at the far end and I move over to take a closer look. These tapes are also bound together with a rubber band, but this time the card reads TUCKER.

'What's the matter?' demands Susanne as I freeze.

'These are the spliced versions of my sessions with Gil Tucker. Look – Tommy's written "edited" and dated each one—'

'Careful! Don't mess them around or Tommy'll know they've been handled!'

I straighten the rubber band but find it hard to tear myself away. 'Wish I could nick them. This bloke just shouldn't be mixed up in this kind of crap.'

'Yeah? Personally I think punters deserve all the crap that's going – and if you nick those tapes you risk winding up as dog-food for Bonzo's Great Dane.'

I'm diverted. 'You've heard about that dog?'

'Elizabeth was talking about it the other day and saying it would be unreliable now Bonzo's dead. She said Alsatians are better at sex tricks than Great Danes anyway.'

Leaving Susanne to reset the alarm I return to Elizabeth's living-room and check my tapes out on the video. The scene with Colin comes up from three different angles. We're in business.

I take Susanne home, thank her profusely for her help and promise to pick her up at six-thirty. Out of Pimlico I drive and over the river, but on the far side I park the car by the entrance to Lambeth Palace and walk to the middle of the bridge. Here I chuck into the river the three tapes recording my Friday night activities with Colin, Carta and Val.

I'm safe.

Awash with relief I head home to recharge my batteries for the mega-glam evening ahead.

*　　*　　*

We're both worried in case Norah or one of the girls sees us together, so we've worked out a plan: I'll drive down the quiet Pimlico back-water and toot twice on the horn as I pass Norah's house. Susanne will count to fifty, leave the flat and teeter round the corner into the next street where I'll be waiting.

The plan unfolds without a hitch. Susanne's wrapped in a big black cloak and I daren't guess what's underneath it. Her thick black hair is swept up and skewered with diamanté clasps and her long legs are encased in shiny tights and her large feet are stuffed into high-heeled silver shoes which have a strap across the instep to ensure they stay on while she's dancing. She's also wearing false eyelashes and false fingernails in addition to the shovelled-on make-up. I sympathise with her desire to wear morale-boosting armour, but how can I walk into the Ritz with such a trashy piece? God, I sound like my mother, constantly worrying about what people will think. Hey Mum, look at my new girlfriend! Instant stroke.

Opposite the Ritz's Palm Court, there's a place where we leave our coats, and as soon as Susanne removes her cloak my jaw sags. She's wearing a hot-pink dress with a short skirt, and her deep, deep cleavage is guaranteed to stop dead any heterosexual male from nine to ninety within a radius of fifty yards. The bowling-ball breasts are like marble sculpted by Michelangelo or some other gay artist with enormous talent but only an approximate idea of what women look like. It's pseud but it's great pseud. Extraordinary.

We close in on the Palm Court. Two waiters converge to offer us a choice table by the gold statue. All the male punters at the other tables are ogling Susanne and all their female friends are ogling me. We're a maximum-impact couple. Everyone thinks we're sensational.

'What do you want to drink?' I drawl in a suitably languid voice as if we do this kind of stuff every night. Automatically I use an upmarket accent.

'Champagne!' rasps Ms Essex-Girl, heavy on the estuarine twang. 'And loads of it!'

I want to say to the waiter: 'Bring us a bottle of Krug,' but that's the kind of conspicuous consumption that's crude and would mean a discussion of vintages plus a wait while the bottle's being chilled. So I just say with restraint: 'Could we please have a bottle of your house champagne?' and before Susanne can demand something with a poncey label I murmur to her: 'The Ritz champagne's very famous.' That shuts her up.

As we swill the fizzy stuff, I think of the times I was brought here by sad rich elderly women during my career as an escort. Meanwhile Susanne's gazing and gazing and gazing, beady black eyes taking everything in. There's something touching about this wide-eyed childish absorption. She loves this place, *loves* it. She's like a priestess worshipping at a shrine.

Finally she says: 'It's like *Hello!* magazine come to life.'

I somehow doubt that the Ritz's PR team would welcome this comment. But on the other hand, perhaps they might. We all have to move with the times.

'Weren't you ever brought here when you did escort work?' I say.

She shakes her head. 'I never got the top punters. They went to the girls who spoke plummy.' She gulps some champagne before adding: 'I got taken to the Strand Palace once.'

The Strand Palace no doubt gets the thumbs-up approval it deserves in the AA Guide, but it's hardly sharing a five-star rating with the Ritz.

I don't laugh. I don't make some snotty remark. I just look polite and say nothing.

'I always dreamed I'd get to the Ritz one day,' says Susanne. 'I like dreams. It's dreams that keep you going.'

'Right. I dream of buying my own boat and sailing away into a golden sunset.'

We don't say much more, and finally we stream out, leaving behind a trail of open mouths, fractured conversations and an atmosphere humming with pushbutton lust. Outside we turn to look at each other and I know we're sharing the same amusement.

We giggle like a couple of schoolkids.

Then we set off for the Savoy.

*   *   *

Parking's tough in that area at night as the Strand's part of theatre-land, so I decide to leave the car in the Savoy's garage. I'm spending

326

money like water, but I tell myself I shouldn't grudge a penny of it. This girl's got me out of a very tight corner.

Into the hotel we glide and after the necessary visit to the cloak-rooms we're creaming our way through the huge lounge to the restaurant which overlooks the river. More heads swivel. More jowls quiver. More old men turn puce with the shock of unfamiliar erections. As I realise with astonishment that I'm enjoying myself I realise too that I'm having far more fun with trashy Susanne than I've ever had with upmarket Serena.

The dancing hasn't started so we have a quiet time to brood over our menus. Unfortunately Norah's lessons on menu-French aren't much use to Susanne here as the French is pretty impenetrable, even to someone like me who learnt menu-French when growing up.

'Why can't they use English?' says Susanne crossly. 'I mean, is this England or isn't it?'

I make a snap decision. Grandly I say: 'We'll get them to trans-late.'

'Won't they look down on us for not knowing?'

'I'd like to see them try!' I declare, and in fact the waiters all fall over themselves to be helpful. I pick a salad followed by grilled Dover sole, no veg. Susanne picks some lobster concoction followed by dolled-up duck. Veg galore. She even orders potatoes although the bird comes with rice. I hardly know where to look when she pops this request, but the waiter beams at her and writes it all down with a hand which never falters. I'm still recovering from the thought of potatoes nestling against rice when the wine waiter arrives.

'I want more champagne!' says Susanne, awash with greed, but I say firmly: 'More fun to sample something else,' and select a vintage Chablis tart enough to encourage sipping instead of swilling. I also order a large bottle of water.

'So what do you make of this place?' I ask her when we're finally shorn of flunkeys. 'Like it?'

'I don't mind.' She gazes avidly out of the long windows at the trees of the Embankment Gardens and the glittery ribbon of the river.

I don't ask her to explain what 'I don't mind' means in this context. I already know. 'I don't mind' is what socially deprived people say when they adore something but are terrified that if they admit it they'll be mocked. Or it's what they say when they're seething with excitement but want to seem ultra-cool. It's an infu-riating response, but I know that beneath those three syllables she's in ecstasy. We're only a few yards now from the Strand Palace Hotel, the apex of her ill-starred career as an escort girl, but we might as well be in another galaxy.

'Tell me about yourself,' I say to pass the time. 'Got any family?'

'Nah.'

'Parents dead?'

'Hope so.'

'What happened to your mum?'

'Dunno.'

'What did she do for a living?'

'Guess.'

'What about your dad?'

'Didn't have one.'

'Who brought you up?'

'Kiddie-home workers. Foster parents. Pervs.'

'How old were you when you went on the streets?'

'Thirteen. Then I was put in another home, but I met a pimp who helped me escape. Then I got to be sixteen so they couldn't force me to go back.'

'What happened next?'

'The usual. Drugs. Beatings. Prison – I got done for theft. Had to steal because of the habit but in prison I got the chance to straighten out. There was this prison visitor, a middle-class cow with a face like a pudding. She says: "You're a bright girl, I can tell. You'd enjoy learning things." And she says: "Once women are educated they get a better opinion of themselves and feel life should be more than slavery." I think of that lady sometimes. She made me feel special in spite of everything.'

'So you quit drugs?'

'Yeah. Went back on the streets, though. Well, how else was I going to live? Then my pimp got stamped on and I was grabbed by a new one who worked in a West End casino, and that's when things began to look up because I saw escort girls living a better class of life. So I chatted one up and found she worked for Norah, and then a couple of days later my pimp disappeared, his body was never found but I reckon they topped him, he was into all kinds of shit. Well, that was my chance, wasn't it, so before I could get grabbed by anyone else I went to Norah and . . . okay, I know that didn't work out, but I got my big break when Elizabeth decided I had potential. Happy ending.'

'That prison visitor . . . Was she religious?'

'Dunno, don't care. All I know is she gave me the will to get off drugs, the will to get a better life, the will to say in the end to Elizabeth: "What I want's an education." And that's when Elizabeth figured it was worth investing money in courses for me and training me to help run her businesses.'

We're silent for a while. The first course arrives and we chomp away until Susanne says: 'I bet you had a nice home with parents in it. So how come you threw it all away?'

'I didn't. I couldn't hang on to it, I wasn't good enough, I didn't measure up, so in the end I did my parents a favour by dropping out so that I wouldn't upset them any more.'

'Then what?'

'Drink, drugs, casual jobs. But one day I was looking up something in the Yellow Pages and I saw the ads for escort agencies and I thought escort work was an easy way to make a buck. (Yeah – don't laugh!) Well, I soon found I couldn't face it unless I was stoned – thank God Elizabeth picked me up when I got fired! She was my equivalent of your prison visitor. She thought I was special and she gave me the will to get my act together.'

Susanne says at once with fierce certainty: 'There's no way Elizabeth could ever be the equivalent of the Lady. The Lady would have looked at you and thought: he's a bright boy, he deserves better. Elizabeth would have looked at you and thought: here's a nice little earner, let's exploit him.'

'No, she cared about me right from the start, she really did—'

But at that point I'm interrupted by a blast on the trumpet which makes us jump nearly out of our skins. We've been so busy reminiscing about our putrid pasts that we've failed to notice the band setting itself up on the other side of the room.

'Dancing!' exclaims Susanne, black eyes shining like polished volcanic rock.

It was Norah who taught us both ballroom dancing. She always insists her escorts are good dancers of the old school because many of the clients are wrinklies who were young in the days when it was a social necessity to know how to foxtrot.

The band are still warming up when our main course is delivered. We shovel the food down, and the moment we're finally free to fling ourselves around, the band starts to play that sexy classic the wrinklies love: 'In the Mood'. Susanne and I look at each other.

We both know this one inside out. Norah used it for teaching. I can still remember it oomphing from her museum-piece record player in the corner of her living-room.

I jump to my feet. 'C'm'on!' I shout, and we're off, we're skimming onto the dance floor, we're showing all those wrinklies that not everyone under thirty thinks dancing means jigging up and down while zonked.

We swivel, we swoop, we sweat, we lunge, we twirl. We're wonderful and everyone knows it. The other couples melt away. The blokes in the band are smiling. The waiters have stopped serving. The punters are goggle-eyed. There's never been such a performance of 'In the Mood', never. It's Saturday night at the Savoy, it's Saturday night at one of the greatest hotels on earth, and Susanne and I are special, we count, we matter – and never more so than at this moment when we're living out something that's more than just our own truth. In an electrifying flash of understanding I know we're proving that the human spirit can triumph over anything – *anything* – even the most soul-destroying abuse, and that the final word on such wasting lies not with the abusers but with the abused.

'Encore!' comes a shout, and instantly more people bawl out: 'Encore, encore!' Everyone's clapping and cheering. We bow. I suddenly realise Susanne's not looking like a tart any more. She's looking like the last word in cosmopolitan chic. Her eyes are shining, her cheeks are pink, the breasts deserve an Oscar for special effects.

As the band strikes up again to respond to the demands for an encore, I know what ecstasy is and it's not a bloody pill. Ecstasy is me being not just myself but *all* of myself. My body, mind and spirit are finally working as one – but no, wait, it's better than that because I see now my spirit's not just one of a bunch of parts. It's the force which permeates every cell that's me and makes me *more* than just the sum of my parts. And the force isn't just pushing me to be myself now – it's pushing me to become the self I haven't yet got around to being, the self I was designed to be – yeah, that's it, *designed*, it's as if there's a blueprint situation going on and I'm a dream in the mind of the architect. He's got me down on paper, all the dimensions dovetailing, and he's breathed his spirit into his work the way creative people do, but the construction environment's been so tough that the builders couldn't cope so I'm still only a half-finished wreck. I need a big jolt to get the project back on course, and this is it, this is the big jolt, this is the architect grabbing the nearest blowtorch and turning on the power.

I'm being brought to life. Real life, not the life I had before. Maybe I've even been dead for a while without knowing it. Yeah, of course, that's it, I get it – I was dead but I'm being resurrected, like The Bloke. The Bloke's here now, obviously, putting that thought into my head. He was one of those people who called 'encore', and suddenly I see he's already been calling me to life – calling me through Richard, through Carta, through Nicholas, through all those St Benet's people who rose to their feet as I entered that room. Okay, I'm still lost, I'm still in a dark, dangerous place, but I'm going to be all right because The Bloke's determined to bring me back from the dead, he's determined to bring me home – and meanwhile he keeps sending people, like visions, to give me hope of better times to come. Even Susanne's a vision, drawing me into the dance which has raised my consciousness to the stars.

I understand about Carta now. She's a vision of a world that'll be waiting for me when I can finally come home. She's not just female fodder to be shagged and chucked. She's to be respected and valued, just as the St Benet's people respected and valued *me*. And why did they respect and value me? Because they tune in daily to The Bloke and he makes sure they see me not as filth but as a human being designed by God. Richard didn't tune in to The Bloke, but he treated me as special because he loved me, and love's all about treating people as special, isn't it? 'Love one another!' said The Bloke, and he knew what he was talking about. You can shag a thousand people but without love you're nothing. That's because the heart of the universe isn't exploitation and abuse and lies and cheating and wickedness and downright bloody evil. The heart of the universe is love.

'Gavin! *Gavin!* Wake up, pinhead! We're stars!'

I return to earth after my brief glide around eternity. The applause has exploded again and we bow some more but eventually the band drifts into an ancient waltz and other couples return to the floor. Leaving the wrinklies creaking, Susanne and I head for our table where the maître d' offers us complimentary glasses of – oh God – champagne.

The evening blazes on. The dessert cart cosies up to our table and I suddenly find I'm interested in eating (trifle with a spoonful of chocolate mousse). Later I order cheese, and with this final course I have a glass of port while Susanne has a farewell glass of champagne.

But as the result of hitting the water bottles we're still a long way from being legless. It would be criminal now, of course, to get trolleyed and ruin the golden impression we've created.

We stay until the band packs it in, and we dance the last waltz not exactly cheek to cheek but definitely chest to bowling-balls. Despite all the water-doses I'm not too happy about driving, but we purr back to Pimlico without smashing anything. We don't speak. We're still cocooned by our euphoria, and it's not until we reach Norah's street that I say: 'Do I get invited in? I mean, should I start looking for a parking space?'

'I want to crash out.'

'Ah. Okay, in that case—'

'Stop! There's a space!'

I stamp on the brake pedal but fluff the parking manoeuvre and wind up a meter from the curb.

'Not to worry,' says Susanne. 'You won't be staying long.'

Switching off the engine, I kill the lights and we look at each other in the pale glow of the streetlamp. Unexpectedly Susanne says: 'When I was in therapy after my breakdown I learned a thing or two. I learned what the word "co-dependent" means. Ever heard of it?'

'Sure.'

She doesn't believe me. 'Alcoholics have them, for instance. Co-dependents are the people who help the alcoholic cover up his way of life in the belief that they're doing him a favour. Co-dependents like to do favours because they themselves are hooked on being needed. Got it?'

'Got it. But what's all that to do with us?'

'Everything. Because I'm never going to be a co-dependent, never going to have a relationship with someone who earns his living from vice. By pretending a normal relationship's possible, I'd wind up going along with the Life, I'd wind up a co-dependent doing favours, and that's a guaranteed way to get trashed. So forget it. No one's ever, ever going to trash me again.'

After a pause I say: 'I'm getting out of the Life.'

'Oh yeah.' She smiles at me cynically, not believing a word I say. She doesn't even bother to inflect the words into a question. 'Well, so long, it's been great, I really enjoyed myself. Thanks.'

I shoot out a hand and grab her. 'What you've got to under-stand,' I say urgently, 'is that Elizabeth truly cares about me, always has, and that's why she gave me a home and a way of earning good money – okay, I know what I am, I'm not in denial, I'm a prostitute. *But not for much longer.* I'm just waiting till I've reached my financial target. Then Elizabeth's going to retire and we'll go away together and live respectably ever after.'

Susanne just looks at me. Then she says abruptly: 'You'd better come in for some coffee,' and seconds later I'm following her down the street to her flat.

*　*　*

'Okay, here's the deal,' says Susanne, closing the front door behind us. 'No shag of any kind, and if you start whingeing about being short-changed I'll belt you. You drink your coffee without being a pain and when I tell you to go you go.'

I don't bother to reply. I just pad along behind her and sit down, good as gold, at the kitchen table. I can cope with Susanne being combative. That's everyday stuff. What worries me is Susanne lecturing me earnestly in psycho-babble and shouting me down with pregnant pauses.

She makes coffee. Both of us opt to drink it black. When she finally sits down opposite me she wastes no more time but says in her flattest voice: 'You realise, of course, that Elizabeth and Norah still fuck each other.'

I've been expecting some anti-Elizabeth propaganda so I'm not too surprised by this remark. 'No, they don't,' I snap. 'Elizabeth's made herself very clear about that. Since their fling in the sixties they've been just good friends.'

'She's bullshitting you. Why do you think she's over at Norah's every weekend? Because when the girls are out on the town, she and Norah and those bloody chihuahuas are making it in the master bedroom!'

I'm disgusted by the bitchiness of this lie. 'How do you know?'

'I've seen it.'

I feel nothing for three seconds. Then I want to fall off my chair. But I can't. I'm frozen to it. 'What do you mean?'

'Just what I say. When I worked for Norah I was dumped by a punter one Saturday evening and when I got back early I heard the noises. So I crept up the stairs and watched through the hinges of the bedroom door. They hadn't even bothered to close it.'

333

'Okay – okay, but this was before I arrived on the scene, right? I mean, maybe they got together once for old time's sake but Elizabeth's not a lesbian, there's no way she could be seriously interested in—' I stop. I've suddenly realised I sound like Gil Tucker, refusing to believe I'm straight.

Meanwhile Susanne's saying: 'Don't be dumb, Elizabeth's beyond all that, she's not interested in being limited by any kind of sex category, she'd screw anything she fancied – oh, wake up, pinhead, wake up! This is a woman who has photos in her bathroom of people doing things with turds, for God's sake—'

'Yes, but—'

'You want the truth? You big enough to take it? Or are you just going to go on bleating about how much Elizabeth cares for you?'

'I—'

'Okay, let me tell it like it is. Elizabeth's psycho, Gavin. She's not running around with an axe and a nutso look, like in films, and you could talk to her for a long time before you realised something was off, but once the penny drops it's as if you see the word PSYCHO tattooed on her forehead. Know what I mean? No, you don't, do you – I'll have to spell it out. Basically she doesn't relate to people – relate normally, I mean. She understands the way they work but she's not emotionally into people, no way, she just uses them to make herself feel good. Elizabeth doesn't get her best kicks from sex – sex for her is just a fun way of passing the time, like watching game shows on telly. What turns her on – really, really turns her on – is power. That's why she's into businesses where she can OD on domination – sex groups, psychic healing, bogus counselling – yeah, you notice that when I had my breakdown and she wanted to make sure I got my head together properly she didn't attempt to treat me herself! Oh no! She wanted me up and running as soon as possible so that she could start a new line in domination by training me to be her PA. You name it, she'll try and dominate it: escort girls, a pretty-boy prostitute, a slimeball locksmith, even an old friend like Norah, poor cow, who's been in love with her for years—'

'But Norah likes young girls!'

'And Elizabeth likes young men! So what? That wouldn't stop Norah being in love with Elizabeth and Elizabeth trying to dominate her! And then, my God, there's the Cobra himself, there's bloody Asherton. Why do you think he and Elizabeth have been in each other's pockets all this time? No, sex doesn't come into it, and no, it's not just because they feed off each other's businesses. They're hooked on the rush they get out of knowing there's nothing the other won't do in a world where perviness rules okay and no bloody holds are barred! I'm telling you, she's got a major screw loose, she's sicko, and if you weren't so like a little boy who's lost his mum and clings to the first stranger who pats his head, you'd know that as well as I do!'

I know I have to assume an air of total calm. Glancing nonchalantly at my watch I say: 'Well, I can't expect you to understand. You don't know her like I do.' But my voice comes out more thinly than I intend and I sound strained.

'You're wrong,' she says at once. 'I know more about that woman than you've even begun to imagine.'

'Then tell me more!'

'No way! I'm not saying one single thing about her business interests to you!'

'You mean you're quite happy to keep your mouth shut for this – quote – psycho?'

'Well, look at it this way: I'm not the only PA in the world who has to keep her mouth zipped. Think of the people who work at MI5 or GCHQ!'

I hear what she's saying about confidentiality, but all my anxiety about Elizabeth's future business plan for me now flares up. I blurt out: 'Has Elizabeth ever mentioned to you that she wants to get me into porn movies – real movies, not just stuff like the Austin Friars edits?'

Susanne hesitates but decides a possible future project doesn't require the same discretion as a present going concern. 'Yeah,' she says, 'and I can see her point of view. You're getting to be an elderly pretty-boy, but you'd be good for at least another five years as a film stud. They could put make-up over your lines and you could wear a hairpiece if you have a big moult.'

I say unsteadily: 'I'm not doing another five years in the Life. I don't like being filmed when I fuck anyway, it's too bloody stressful, almost as stressful as escort work when you're expected to treat the punters as people instead of meat.' I know Susanne will understand this. That's why I'm tempted to add impulsively: 'I wouldn't mind retiring now – I haven't got as much money as I'd planned but I've got enough in my Cayman Islands account to buy a boat and get by for a while.'

An extreme stillness comes over Susanne. She's been fidgeting with her coffee-mug but now her fingers halt.

Clearing my throat I say: 'Of course you must know about the Cayman Islands accounts. I've only got one but Elizabeth's got several.'

'Sure,' says Susanne to the coffee-mug. 'I log the statements on the computer.'

I know I'll get nowhere if I ask a direct question. Instead I just keep talking in a casual voice as if we're discussing something trivial. 'As you open all Elizabeth's post,' I say, 'I expect you've wondered why my account statements go to her and not to me.'

Silence.

'It's because when she opened the account for me I was a new taxpayer and she knew the Revenue could take an interest in any mail I got from a tax haven. But as she'd already established her own accounts she reckoned her mail was safe from their snooping. So that's why my statements go to her and she passes them on to me.'

More silence.

I stand up before I can start hyperventilating. 'Well,' I say, 'I'd better be going before I outstay my welcome, but thanks for the coffee.' Then I sit down again with a thump. From a long way away my voice mutters: 'Okay, how's she screwing me?'

'I'm not saying a single bloody word! It was one thing to help you out of the stupid mess you got into with those tapes – it didn't involve her businesses and I could make sure the risk was non-existent, but the Cayman accounts are in a different league. You think I want to wind up in a cage at the Cobra's?'

I take another shallow breath. I sort of know what's happened but I can't believe it. The knowledge is so terrible that my brain just closes down whenever I try to put the knowledge into words.

The next moment I'm whispering: 'Please tell me. Please,' but Susanne's one step ahead of me. She must have realised I was going to beg. 'There's another reason why I can't talk,' she says, but she's stopped acting tough and her voice is far from unsympathetic. 'If I grassed I'd need to be taken care of in a safe place, but you couldn't take care of me because your Elizabeth fixation means you can't even take care of yourself. And you don't know a safe place anyway.'

At once I answer: 'You're wrong about that. The people at St Benet's would help us.'

336

'Oh, pull the other one! Pinhead, you're *such* a liar—'

'No, listen, *listen*, I'm coming clean with you, I swear it! I've got a connection with St Benet's that Elizabeth knows nothing about – it's the missing dimension of the story I told you about the tapes—'

'Shit, I knew you were keeping something back! What the hell have you been getting up to?'

My nerve fails. I'm exhausted, I'm shocked and I'm almost paralysed with fear. Time to back off before I make some catastrophic mistake – but maybe the mistake's already been made. If Susanne now goes to Elizabeth and says—

'Wait a sec,' says Susanne sharply as if sensing I'm about to cut and run, 'how about this for an idea? You tell me about St Benet's and I'll tell you about the Cayman accounts. Then we're safe because if one of us snitches on the other, the other can snitch back, so snitching's no longer an option.'

I try to get my head round this. I feel it's probably the solution but I'm in such a state I can't cope. 'Sounds good,' I say, 'but I'm knackered. Let me grab some sleep and come back here at nine.'

She doesn't argue. It's probably obvious that I'm past it. And maybe she too wants a breather. 'Okay,' she says, 'but do me a favour on your way here later and pick up a copy of the *Sunday Times*. I never miss their business section.'

We stand in the little hall by the front door like two nerdy teenagers uncertain how to end their first date. Eventually I bend my head to give her a peck on the cheek, but in the end I don't kiss her. Our faces glide past each other and the next thing I know we're having a comradely hug. Funny thing is her breasts don't remind me of bowling balls any more. They remind me of top-quality pillows, the kind you long to bury your face in after a bloody awful day at work.

I hug her harder than ever. Then I'm outside, groping my way up the steps into the street, and the front door's closing noiselessly behind me.

I'm alone in a violently altered landscape.

The big nightmare's begun.

*   *   *

Elizabeth's waiting up for me when I arrive home. This surprises me because I'm very late. Of course I have a cover story prepared,

337

but I'm in such a state that the last thing I want to do is deliver it. When she calls my name I stop trying to creep noiselessly up the stairs and pause to psych myself up. I've already seen that her door's ajar and there's a light on in her room, but I was hoping she'd fallen asleep while reading a magazine.

'Come here, pet,' she orders, and when I trail over the threshold she exclaims benignly: 'You're looking very smart! What have you been doing?'

'Had a second look at that opera Colin took me to – I couldn't concentrate the first time around when he was pawing me.'

'And since when has the Opera House closed down in the early hours of the morning?'

'Well, I got talking to a very classy American babe, and—'

'You and your Americans! I suppose I'll have to allow you one every now and then, but I really do wish you'd grow out of them!'

By this time she's smiling at me. She's wearing a peach-coloured silk nightdress, smart, with a yellow woolly bed jacket, dire, and she's propped up on a mound of cream-coloured pillows. Her brass-gold hair, wavy and unfastened, is frothing around her shoulders, and the taut skin of her face is so smooth in the soft light that it's obvious she's had the slack hitched up behind her ears. Tonight I'm more aware than I've ever been of her altered, mask-like face which makes it easy for her to conceal her secrets.

'Well, never mind,' she's saying placidly, 'forget the American. Norah's invited us for Sunday lunch tomorrow – or rather, today – so you'll be able to see Serena.'

'I'm not going.' The words escape before I can stop them, but luckily this is no big disaster. Elizabeth knows I hate lunching at Norah's.

'But afterwards you and Serena can slip upstairs for a while!'

Gavin Blake Toy-Boy opens his mouth to say obediently: 'Okay, darling, you win!' but someone muscles in ahead of him and shoots straight back: 'Shagging that boring chick while you and that dreary old dyke are gossiping in the living-room would be like a teenager trying to grope his first date while his parents were downstairs chatting about the church fete!'

It's Gavin Blake Me talking. He's finally slipped his leash. His resurrection's so far advanced that he just won't play dead any more.

Elizabeth stares at me. A blankness descends on her taut-skinned face and her blue eyes go dead. In my head I hear Susanne saying:

'Once the penny drops it's as if you see the word PSYCHO tattooed on her forehead.'

Fear finally overwhelms me. It's Gavin Blake Toy-Boy who stammers: 'Sorry, sorry, I didn't mean that, I take it all back—'

'You've had too much to drink, my lad, that's your problem! Well, all I can say is you'd better pull yourself together PDQ – and you can start by making no more snotty remarks about Norah!'

But the next moment Gavin Blake Toy-Boy's keeling over again, decked by this reckless chancer who just won't play dead. 'You're still shagging her, aren't you?' says Mr Unstoppable acidly.

* * *

In the dead silence which follows, words flash through my head. They are: Elizabeth, just in case you can't figure it out, love, your correct answer is: 'Oh, don't be so silly!' You're not seriously angry. You're just annoyed that I'm behaving like a drunk and making ludicrous accusations.

I wait. I see her take a sharp, deep breath. Then I hear her demand in fury: 'Who says I'm still shagging her?'

Queasiness hits me but automatically I protect Susanne. 'I do,' I say. 'I've been thinking and thinking about why you palmed me off on Serena and why you're always seeing Norah. It's the only explanation that makes sense.'

More words flash through my head. They are: Elizabeth love, this is where you exclaim: 'What utter nonsense!' and pick up your bedside magazine in a huff. You don't embark on elaborate denials and you don't attempt to justify shoving me at Serena.

But again, the correct response isn't the response that I get.

'Of course Norah and I are always seeing each other!' Elizabeth says, sounding both hurt and amazed. 'We have our business to run! And of course I've been keen for you to date an attractive, well-educated, superior girl like Serena! I have your best interests at heart! So how dare you twist these facts into a rabid accusation which is totally and utterly untrue? But I think I see what all this is about – you still feel miffed that we don't get together more than once a week. Well, I'm flattered – flattered enough to forgive you for your malicious accusation about my relationship with Norah and your nasty attitude to Norah herself. So as a special treat, why don't you take off those smart clothes of yours and get into bed?

But go to the bathroom first, please, to wash out your mouth. I don't want to be asphyxiated by alcohol fumes.'

I can't think what to do. I know this is some kind of test and I've got to shag her, but at the same time I know I won't be able to do it. Why? It's the word PSYCHO tattooed on her forehead. It's the false responses given as she slithers away from the truth. It's the horror of knowing something's wrong with my savings account. It's the real Gavin Blake coming alive at last and seeing how he's been manipulated when he was dead.

But if I don't shag her I'm in big, big trouble. She'll start to think I've had enough. She'll start to think I'm turning against her. She'll start to think I'm capable of double-crossing her in the worst possible way.

Feeling as if I'm being split by a meat-cleaver I obey her order to go to the bathroom, but I never get as far as washing out my mouth. As soon as I see the pictures on the walls the queasiness hits me again and I recognise the one way I can control this situation. Grabbing a towel I kneel down by the lavatory and ram a finger down my throat to help the nausea along.

*　*　*

She hears the vomiting and comes to watch.

'Sorry,' I mutter when it's over. 'Feel terrible.'

'All right, get upstairs. I don't want you near me when you're like this. Come back tomorrow at nine o'clock sharp.'

'Right. Nine. I'll be here,' I lie, and finally escape upstairs. I pause only to set the alarm on my bedside clock. Then I strip and crash out.

The clock shrills at six and instantly I'm wide awake, every nerve jangling as I remember what's happened. The Elizabeth crisis is mega but I can't face it till I find out about the money. Later I'll shag her, I'll even inject my equipment if I have to, but right now—

Right now I'm doing a runner.

I don't shower. I'm afraid the noise of the water in the wastepipe might wake Elizabeth. And I don't shave either. I'm tired of grooming Gavin Blake Prostitute to be a drop-dead stunner. I want to wear an old sweatshirt and shabby chinos and the beat-up jacket which Elizabeth says should be thrown away.

When I'm dressed I find paper and a pen and write: 'Darling

340

— Sorry, but I promised myself I'd drive down to Surrey today to visit Hugo's grave. I've been thinking of him lately. Please tell Norah I appreciate her invitation and I apologise for not accepting it. Sorry about all the crap I talked when I was pissed. Big love, GAVIN.'

I'm just padding through the living-room of my flat when Nigel comes downstairs from the attic.

'Gavin! You okay, mate? I've been so worried! When you weren't back by one last night, Elizabeth woke me up and started interrogating me and—'

'What did you tell her?'

'Nothing! Well, I did tell her you weren't eating right, but I felt I had to tell her *something* when she wanted to know what I thought was going on with you—'

'Did you tell her about the tapes?'

'Course not!' Nigel's shocked. 'Gav, I wouldn't let you down on something like that, I swear it – hey, did you get them back? Did Susanne help you about the safe?'

Again I move to protect Susanne. 'Didn't need to go to her in the end, thank God – I caught Tommy just before he left and said I'd been decked by Colin and didn't want Elizabeth to know. He gave me the tapes on condition we have a shag when he comes back from Amsterdam.'

'Oh, I'm so glad – I mean, I'm so glad you've got the tapes—'

'Forget that, just listen for a moment. You haven't seen me now, right? I've snuck off early but you don't discover that till later. You know *nothing*.'

'Okay, but what's going on? Why's Elizabeth so—'

'I'm having girl trouble. Elizabeth wants me to shag Serena. Serena's a big yawn. I want to shag a luscious stunner I've got my eye on. Elizabeth suspects I'm being a naughty boy, not doing what I'm told, so she's stomping around playing Mummy. It'll all blow over, it's not crucial, just concentrate on knowing nothing.'

I slip away, padding noiselessly down the stairs, and leave my note on the floor of the landing outside Elizabeth's door. I listen but hear nothing. On the ground floor I glide outside, closing the front door with the smallest possible click.

I'm on my way.

*   *   *

Leaving the house before Elizabeth wakes up means I'm much too early to arrive at Susanne's flat and I'm not sure what to do. London's comatose at this hour on a Sunday morning, so in the end I drive to Victoria Station and get a coffee from a vending machine.

Sitting on a platform bench I sip from my Styrofoam cup and decide there's a certain ruthless inevitability about my disintegrating life, as if someone's methodically smashing it up with a hammer. I feel I'm being steered through a series of interlocking situations which are all leading to one *Götterdämmerung*-type conclusion – but no, 'steered' isn't the word that describes what's happening to me, it's too gentle. I feel as if I've been lassoed and now I'm being dragged along the ground in a cloud of dust – but no, that's not right either. It conveys the idea of being captured but not the idea of being rescued. Someone's lassoed me, but with a lifebelt attached to a rope – yes, that's it. I was drowning in the sea but now the lifebelt's plopped over my head, the rope's snapped tight and a life-guard on the distant beach is tugging me through the shark-infested waters to safety.

The rescuer's got to be The Bloke. He's not a shepherd any more. Shepherds are passé. He's a lifeguard like in *Baywatch*. Cool. Okay, haul away, mate, and give my love to Mary Magdalene, patron saint of prostitutes, who of course is standing by looking just like Pamela Anderson. Phwoar! *Ultra*-cool.

Thinking of Pammy's cleavage reminds me of Susanne. What was it she said in her kitchen? 'If you weren't so like a little boy who's lost his mum and clings to the first stranger who pats his head . . .' That was a terrible thing to say, and so was that other remark of hers: 'You couldn't take care of me because your Elizabeth fixation means you can't even take care of yourself.' Bloody cow, insulting me like that! How could she have said such shitty things about me? How could she?

Because they're true, is the answer. And they're truths I have to face to survive.

So this is what it's like to follow Nigel's advice and come out of denial! I'm sitting unshaven, unwashed and dressed like a Welfare creep in Victoria Station and realising in despair that I may be too bloody vulnerable to reach the shore where my new life's waiting to begin. The Bloke may be reeling me in but supposing Jaws closes in for the big chomp? Disasters do happen. It's that kind of world, and there's nothing I can do except wait in a stupor of dread.

But then I remember something Gil Tucker said at the end of that row I engineered. I can't recall the clerical language he used but he definitely argued that you've got to be active, not passive, when dealing with the world's messes. So I can't just cling to the lifebelt and freeze at the thought of being chewed up. I've got to swim as hard as possible to relieve the strain on the lifeline, I've got to do all I can to help the lifeguard, I've got to *work* at being rescued.

I'm still thinking of the lifeguard when he beams me a telepathic message. He says: 'Forget Jaws. Concentrate on me.' Which is sensible advice because you function a lot better when you're not scared shitless.

I feel I ought to say something now he's made direct contact, but what words can I use? Can't connect with all that religious stuff. But if I think of him as a bloke only a little older than I am but a billion times more streetwise . . . 'Hey man,' I say in my head, 'I know you're the boss, I know you can make everything pan out, I'm sorry for all the bad stuff I've done, I want to start over, save me from the psychos, help me get out of this jam in one piece, you're a superstar and I know you can do it. Thanks, mate. Cheers.' And The Bloke says: 'Hang in there, chum. We'll get the sickos sorted. And whatever you do, don't lose hope.'

So I sit there, clutching on to hope with both hands. But at last I stand up. It's time to be active. It's time to work at my own rescue. It's time to start swimming in the shark-infested sea.

Having bought the *Sunday Times* for Susanne I drive to Norah's house five minutes away.

* * *

'Trouble with Elizabeth,' I say to Susanne as soon as I cross her threshold, and I tell her about the scene after my return home. Susanne's wearing a magenta-coloured wrap with matching high-heeled slippers, and she looks pasty-faced, hungover and cross.

'God, that's all we need – you going nuts!' she says. 'Listen, pinhead. Unless you brush up your talent as a liar we'll both be up shit creek. What's Elizabeth going to think now you're suddenly convinced she's shagging Norah? She'll figure that either Serena's been gossiping or I have, and let me tell you, you'd better bloody well pin it on Serena!'

'I protected you. I said—'

343

'Yeah, yeah, yeah, it's too early for all this, my brain's not working yet.' Grabbing the *Times* from my arms she tramps off to her bedroom. 'Why don't you have a shower?' she adds, confirming my suspicions that I reek.

Muzzling my impatience, which by this time has reached agonizing levels, I sluice off last night's sweat and emerge, fully dressed, to find the situation looks more promising. Susanne's wearing a sweatshirt and jeans and cooking scrambled eggs. I smell bread browning in the toaster and spot a large jug of coffee on the counter.

'I wasn't going to cook you anything,' says Susanne, 'because I was feeling mean, freaked out by your flakiness. And I don't mind telling you I'm scared too of this information exchange we agreed to have. But then I thought of the Savoy and felt more forgiving. Now sit down and don't get under my feet.'

I sit down instantly and concentrate on the task of being well-behaved. Now I know fear's at the bottom of her bad temper, it's not so hard to control my impatience but I still want to pace up and down the room like a tiger at the zoo.

Susanne plonks down in front of me a glass of orange juice, a cup of coffee and a plate of scrambled eggs on toast. I say a fervent 'thank you' and we eat in a silence broken only by the sound of the cat-flap as Alexis goes out. Susanne's pulled the blinds down so that no one strolling in Norah's garden can see us, but the blinds are pale so we don't need artificial light. The scrambled eggs are perfect. Despite my extreme tension I wolf everything down and wish there was more.

'I like cooking,' says Susanne when I take care to praise the eggs. 'I'm going to do a cookery course one day if the sickos don't punch my lights out.'

'Talking of the sickos—'

'Yeah, let's get down to business. You go first and tell me about St Benet's.'

I long to insist that she goes first, but I can't risk making her bad-tempered again.

When I finish explaining how my fascination with Carta lured me into fundraising, Susanne's only comment is: 'All I know about Christians is that they wear crosses with a man on them and do funny things on Sundays with a bloke that cross-dresses.'

So much for the Church. 'Okay,' I say, unable to control my impatience a second longer. 'Your turn. Tell me about—'

'Seeing as how you were in so deep with St Benet's you must have really freaked out when the Cobra turned up at that dinner party! Hey, this Sir Colin sounds a real go-er, punchy and ballsy with a wacky sense of humour – I like the way he knocked everyone's heads together before walking away with his moneybags intact!'

By this time I'm fit to burst a blood vessel. 'You should try having sex with him. Look, unless you tell me right now this minute about my Cayman account, I'll—'

'You don't have a Cayman account,' says Susanne abruptly. 'The money's there all right, but the account's in Elizabeth's name, not yours.'

*   *   *

When I can speak I say: 'But I've got the statements. Every month Elizabeth passes me the statement from the bank and the account's always in my name.'

'She gets me to forge it. It's easy with a computer. You lift the heading and the lay-out and type in what you want.'

'But how did she explain why this had to be done?'

'Said it was all for your own good and she was just looking after your money for you. Said young men could be stupid moneywise and she didn't want you going on a binge and blowing it all.'

'And you believed her?'

'Course not, but she was giving me a proper job, wasn't she? I wasn't going to rock the boat.'

I try to justify myself so that I'm not written off as a complete prat. 'She was very convincing when I was starting out. She said there was no need for me to declare all my earnings because as a new taxpayer I was in a situation where I was establishing a profile, a pattern which the Revenue could refer to in the years ahead. 'Start as you mean to go on,' she said, and told me I could get away with an undeclared offshore account. Then she slipped in the bit I told you yesterday, the bit about how it'd be safer if the correspondence went to her and not to me—'

'That's the point where she conned you. If the Revenue's allowed to grab letters from offshore banks, loads more people would be done for tax evasion.'

'I just assumed she knew what she was talking about. After all, she'd had her own Cayman accounts for years.'

345

'Yeah, Asherton set them up for her, didn't he? Funny to think of him being in banking before he diversified.' Susanne collects the coffee-jug and tops up our cups, but by this time I'm beyond speech. I just sit there at the kitchen table like a boxer who's successfully gone the full fifteen rounds only to be deprived of his prize on account of a technicality.

'I can understand why you were so dead keen to build up a retirement fund in double-quick time,' Susanne's saying, 'but of course it gave her a golden opportunity to control you long-term. You know what I think? I think she's reckoned all along that you'd do a burn-out eventually on the Austin Friars number, and I think she's had this porn-film idea simmering for some time. There's nothing on paper yet, I can tell you that, but she had lunch the other day with a producer Asherton knows, so I'll bet the project's now a priority.'

I get my tongue working again. 'But how could she think I'd ever—'

'She's sure you'll adapt, no problem. After all, you adapted to gay piecework, and she probably figures that if you can do that you can do anything.'

'Yes, but my plan was always to quit the Life when I had enough money, and she agreed to that!'

'Of course she agreed! She'd have agreed to anything to keep you sweet, but you can be sure she never intended to let you quit – why kiss a goldmine goodbye? Her only problem now is getting you into the film business at the highest level. Only the top porn actors pull down loadsamoney, but with your looks and experience you should be one of the big winners provided she can get the right deal with the right outfit . . . Yeah, by this time she'll have it all sussed out, and by controlling that Cayman account she's got you by the balls.'

Without a word I grope my way to the bathroom and lock the door.

*   *   *

Back in the kitchen after the elected throw-up I say: 'You've got to prove to me there's been forgery. I believe you but I've got to see proof.'

'Sure. I'll show you the blank bank statement forms I've produced.

346

I'll show you all Elizabeth's Cayman accounts on the computer, even the one you've been thinking is yours.'

'When?'

We pause to figure this out, but no great brainpower's required. The only reason why I can't answer my own question straight away is because I'm still traumatised.

Susanne says: 'Didn't you tell me you had a row with her about lunch at Norah's today?' and we agree to hit the office at one o'clock when Elizabeth will be in Pimlico.

But the biggest question of all still has to be asked. Speaking rapidly before my voice can crack I say: 'And now just tell me this: how the hell do I get hold of that money?' To prevent her slamming back a negative reply such as 'God knows' or 'Get real', I manage to keep talking, giving her some essential background. 'I've had minimal contact with that bank. Elizabeth always handled the deposits because they had to go via Switzerland, and I've never withdrawn a single penny because I've been so focused on saving. Elizabeth did give me a password for transferring the money out by phone, but since she knew I wouldn't use it—'

'It'll be a fake – the bank would just warn her that someone was trying to access her account.' Susanne pauses but I'm sure now she's sympathetic. She's pausing only because she's reached the crossroads and needs to review her decision one last time. Then she says: 'I can get you the money. I know all the right info to pass the security checks. But once I do that I won't just need a safe house – I'll need money to start over as well.'

'How much?'

'Ten per cent of your account. This is my chance to go totally legit and say goodbye to the Life once and for all. I don't want to blow it for lack of cash.'

Since she's got me over a barrel, I'm just glad she doesn't ask for more. Still, ten per cent of four hundred thousand quid isn't exactly peanuts.

I think of my savings. That sum represents the gifts received by Gavin Blake Superstud (less the cuts to Elizabeth, of course). The donors were all so rich they could afford to be insanely generous, and so infatuated with me that they didn't realise how mental they were. I had rules about the form the gifts took – for instance, I wouldn't accept stocks and shares, which would have been difficult to dispose of without involving the Revenue, and I told the clients to give me the cash instead. But I did take the jewellery, the classic cars (fun to drive but too expensive to run), the porcelain, the antique silver and the Picasso. All these objects were turned over to a very useful bloke who was a member of GOLD, a Bond Street dealer and an old chum of Elizabeth's, and he always got me good prices on the quiet with no questions asked.

Once I had the cash, it was easy to send it along the well-worn path to the Caymans because Elizabeth had established the route years ago. Asherton had his route to the Caymans, but Elizabeth, not trusting him too far, soon went her own way after he had helped her set up her first account. There was another useful bloke who belonged to GOLD, this one a Swiss banker who worked in the City but spent two days a week in Geneva where GOLD had a numbered account. The bloke took the cash there and popped it in GOLD's bank. Elizabeth then made a phone call to GOLD's treasurer in London, and before you could say 'tax evasion' the money would be wired out of the GOLD account and off across the Atlantic to that loyal outpost of Great Britain, the Cayman Islands.

My money always made the journey safely, and after a while I stopped having nightmares of the useful Swiss bloke disappearing into the blue with a suitcase of my cash. So much for my savings. Meanwhile I was living comfortably on my declared-to-the-Revenue earnings. Of course in addition to the taxman I had to pay Elizabeth's percentage and Nigel's wages and the Austin Friars expenses, but in another world I'd have been paying a mortgage, wouldn't I, and supporting a family, so although my outgoings were heavy they were no big deal. I still had plenty of money to spend on clothes and CDs and grazing in Covent Garden – in fact I even managed to send some of this after-tax money regularly to the Caymans to join the non-taxed stuff in the account which had never been mine . . .

'Wake up, pinhead! You're not listening!'

With a jolt I return from the affluent past to the bankrupt present. 'You want ten per cent of my account, yes—'

'—and I must come with you to St Benet's, but you'd better make sure they really can keep us safe.'

'I know it'll be okay.'

'What makes you so sure?'

'Nicholas Darrow's helped other people escape from bad scenes.

Also he knows just what Asherton's like and he won't underestimate him. And don't forget he's dealt with Elizabeth before and he won't underestimate her either.'

'So once we get to St Benet's—'

'—we gain the upper hand. Elizabeth'll be too busy doing her disappearing act to come after us, and Asherton'll be in a pink funk destroying the worst of his hard-core porn and pretending the S&M group members just get together for tea and biscuits.'

'Okay, that's the rainbow's end. Let's just hope we can arrive there – and with your pot of gold intact.'

We sit in silence for a moment, both overwhelmed by the nightmare ahead. A creepy, Asherton-like voice purrs in my brain: 'What are you going to do without Elizabeth looking after you and giving you a reason to stay alive?' But I don't answer that question because it's addressed to Gavin Blake Prostitute who's such a wimp that he has to have a Mummy-figure in order to function. Instead I say silently to the creepy voice: 'I want my money. I'll not be cheated out of what's mine.' This is the right non-wimpish reply. This is my real self, wanting justice and determined to tell Mummy Rip-Off goodbye. And yet . . .

The emotional reaction slugs me at last. My vision blurs as I stare down at the table.

Susanne's talking about moving her possessions into storage but I'm barely listening. I feel as if a black pit's opened in front of me and I'm standing with my feet half over the edge.

'Hey!' says Susanne sharply. 'You dying or something? You'd better lie down on my bed before you pass out.'

I escape to the bedroom and lie staring at the ceiling. I want to go on feeling angry with Elizabeth but I don't. I just feel worthless. My whole life's been justified by the belief that Elizabeth genuinely cared about me and thought I was wonderful. I ought to have known right from the start that this belief was nothing but a grand illusion. I'm not worth caring about, never was. I'm useless, a failure, a total waste of space. What's the point of trying to get my savings back? Even if I have the money to start a new life, I'm bound to mess everything up. Better to jump into the black pit right now and make an end of it. Then I won't need anything any more, least of all love.

'I can cook you some more scrambled eggs,' says Susanne from the doorway, 'but will you keep them down? I'm not slaving over a hot stove just to give you a second innings at the toilet.'

I roll over on my front and bury my face in the pillow. I did so love Elizabeth. I can tell myself till I'm blue in the face that I've been bloody stupid and totally pathetic, but it makes no difference. I hate myself for not being good enough for her to love me. I really did think that at last there was someone who cared.

The bed jolts as Susanne sits down on it. 'Listen, pinhead. Don't let your brain go on the blink and serve up a major depression – that's the surest way to get wiped. Just focus on how bloody LUCKY you are, having friends at St Benet's who care whether you're dead or alive. I've got no one but that cat, but am I puking into a toilet? Am I sobbing into a pillow? Am I considering topping myself because I'll never dance at the Savoy again? No, I'm bloody not! I'm saying thank God I'm still alive and thank God for this new chance to move on!'

I remove my face from the pillow, prop myself groggily on one elbow and demand: 'Who says you'll never dance at the Savoy again?'

'I do!'

'Well, you're wrong. One day I'll take you back.'

'Yah! Expect me to believe that? You won't want to see me again after all this is over – I'd just remind you of stuff you'll want to forget!'

'I'll never want to forget how we danced to "In the Mood".'

But she still doesn't believe me. 'You revving yourself up to ask for a shag?'

'No point. You'd never agree.'

'Well, I suppose it might be a laugh to see what all the fuss is about, but no, I'm not into bonking right now and you look too beat up to get it up anyway. I'd better do some more eggs, but if you toilet them I'll slap you.'

She disappears. I go to the bathroom and stare at the mirror. My eyes are bloodshot and I look about forty but I'm better. I've been yanked away from the black pit by Susanne wiring me the image of the dance, the memory of those precious moments when I was my whole self, infused with life and hope. I know now I want to feel like that again. I want to live. I want to reach that distant shore where the lifeguard stands, sweating blood to reel me in as I flounder past the sharks of depression and despair.

Trudging back to the kitchen I eat more scrambled eggs but this

350

time I keep them down, and not long afterwards Susanne and I leave for Lambeth where the Cayman accounts are waiting for me on the computer.

* * *

The house is empty, and we move straight to the office. The computer takes a while to get its wits together but eventually it responds to Susanne's orders and the Cayman accounts start to come up on the screen. I spot the figures in my last statement and call a halt. Even though I've had time to adjust to the bad news it's still a shock to see the account in Elizabeth's name. Silently Susanne unlocks a file cabinet and produces a bunch of blank bank statements ready for future forgeries.

'I know now why Elizabeth didn't want me to have a numbered account,' is the only comment I can make. 'It was important for the scam that I could see the account was apparently in my name.' Then suddenly I say: 'Show me the other Cayman accounts.'

Susanne returns to the computer and scrolls back so that I can take a proper look. There's an account in the name of Elizabeth Delamere, a joint account held with Norah, and an account in the name of Elizabeth Tremayne.

'What's this?' I demand. 'Part of a new identity?'

'Maybe, but as far as I know it's just a bank account title. I've seen no other documents in that name.'

'What's the point of it?'

'It's all to do with GOLD and the payments she gets for being a consultant. Apparently the Betz bloke, who used to be the treasurer, only knew her in her Mayfield identity so the payments used to go to Elizabeth Mayfield. Then after the Betz bloke topped himself the Mayfield identity had to go and she told GOLD's new treasurer to substitute this new name and bank account when he made her payments.'

'Why not just use the Delamere name?'

'Safety precaution. If Asherton ever goes down the tubes she wants no written evidence tying Elizabeth Delamere to GOLD and through GOLD to what's-his-face Betz.'

I ask her to print the most recent statements of all the Cayman accounts, and when I've pocketed them I say: 'Got anything incriminating on Asherton?'

351

'You're joking!'

'He ought to be nailed.'

'Forget it! No one would ever testify.'

'*I'd* testify if ever I got the chance.'

Her eyes widen. 'What did he do to you?'

'You don't want to know.'

'I don't remember this—'

'Elizabeth told you I was in a car crash. I was shut up in my room for two weeks while I recovered.'

I see the horror in her eyes. 'And Elizabeth let it happen?'

'She said I had to learn the lesson for my own good.'

'Shit, that's—' She breaks off, unable to think of the right word.

But I can. 'Evil,' I say, feeling as if I'm speaking an ancient language discarded long ago, and suddenly my anger turns outward at last instead of turning inward to lacerate me with self-hatred. 'Someone ought to stop her,' says my voice, 'and someone ought to stop him. I don't want any other kid to go through what I've gone through.' In a burst of energy I head for the door. 'I'm going to talk to Nicholas Darrow.'

'No, wait! If you grass to that Darrow thing-y now he'll want to barge in straight away and phone the police but we've *got to sort out your money first* or it'll get lost. I need at least three days.'

'Three days! But can't you just—'

'I want to play safe and switch the money through different accounts to avoid suspicion. I'll set up a new account in your name and Elizabeth's and transfer the money into that – I don't think the bank will query a joint account as she's already got one with Norah. Then I'll set up two more Cayman accounts, one in your name only, one in mine, for the next round of transfers, and finally I'll switch the money in both those new accounts to our own high-street bank accounts in London. It's just too risky to cut corners and try to do it all at once.'

I can see the sense of this. I calm down.

'There are other things to take care of too,' she's adding. 'For instance, I'll need those three days to sort out my stuff. And you need to talk to the Darrow thing-y to make sure he can give us a safe place to hole up in, but don't go into detail about Asherton and Elizabeth – save all that for later. Just say you want out of the Life and I'm coming with you.'

I nod but I'm barely listening. I'm thinking what *I* need to do before we make our break for freedom, and the next moment I announce: 'I'm going to save Gil Tucker.'

'Oh my God! Haven't we got enough on our plates without you messing around with the Gilbert? What's he to you anyway – just another punter! I mean, it's not as if he's your brother, is it?'

'Yes, it is. Before I leave this house for good,' I say firmly, 'I'm making another raid on Tommy's flat to nick the Tucker tapes.' And before she can argue I tell her what Asherton has in store for Gil at the next meeting of GOLD.

*   *   *

When I stop speaking Susanne just says: 'Asherton's lost it.'

'That's what Elizabeth thinks. She wants to distance herself now from Asherton, and she's going to do it by saying my movie career leaves her no time for GOLD.'

'Clever old bitch! It'll break her heart to kiss GOLD goodbye, but of course if Asherton's gone mega-nuts she's got no choice.'

I'm still focused on Gil Tucker. 'I've thought of tipping off the Vice about this coming GOLD event,' I say, 'but—'

'Good idea. Once you're at St Benet's you won't have to worry about being suspected of grassing.'

'Yes, but the trouble is a police raid would boot Gil out of the frying pan into the fire – he'd be eaten alive by the media, and those tapes would be used as evidence of how he got hijacked. He'll only be completely saved if I nick the tapes to make sure there's no comeback and then tell him to avoid Asherton like the plague.'

'But the nicking's so dangerous! It was one thing to break into that flat when Tommy was away but it'll be quite another to break in when he's at home!'

'I'll do it when he's asleep.'

'Supposing he wakes up?'

'No problem. I'm younger and fitter than he is. I'd knock him out and lock him up.'

'God, men are so *boring* when they do the macho number—'

'Okay, okay, I know you think I couldn't fight my way out of a paper bag, I know you think I'm just shit and of course you're right, I am, but if I can save Gil Tucker I'll be better than shit, I'll—'

'STOP!' she shrieks, making me jump. She's furious, livid. I've done her head in by bleating on about Gil – or so I think, but I'm

353

wrong. She walks right up to me, grabs me by the shoulders and starts shaking them. She looks about to kill me. She's literally panting with rage. 'Never,' she yells, '*never* again tell me you're shit! You're a total screw-up and you can be bloody dumb but *you're not shit*. Say that again and I'll pull out so much of your hair you'll need a wig!'

'Okay, okay—' I'm shattered but I've grasped that she's paying me a compliment so I don't bother to shrug myself loose. I just slide my arms around her waist and give her a hug, my chest meshing with the silicone hills, and although I have an erection she doesn't slap my face, she just turns aside, switches off the computer and says abruptly. 'We'd better get out of here before Elizabeth comes home.'

We leave.

* * *

We don't want to risk returning to Pimlico while there's a chance Elizabeth's still at Norah's house, so to pass the time we drive across the river, dump the car and go into St James's Park. It's not warm enough to lie on the grass but we sit on a bench by the lake and after a while I drum up the courage to hold her hand. She doesn't pull it away. She just says: 'If you're thinking you can treat me like all the other girls, forget it.'

'What do you mean?'

'Oh puh-*leeze*! You know bloody well you treat Norah's current crop as if they were all inflatable dolls – shit, if they weren't such a bunch of silly cows they'd be lining up to kick you in the balls, but no such luck, everyone's panting so hard to get done by you that they never even get a foot in the nearest pair of Doc Martens. And Elizabeth says you graze – *graze*, for God's sake! – in Covent Garden on American girls. Just what the hell do you think you're playing at?'

'Well, I—'

'Okay, I can see that after doing gays all week you need some kind of compensation, but bullshitting around in an Armani suit isn't compensation, it's crap. Real compensation would be trying to have a relationship which lasts longer than a weekend, but you can't do relationships, can you, and *that's* what you're trying to cover up with all this multi-shagging rubbish . . . I don't count the

354

Elizabeth relationship, of course. That's just some kind of weird kiddie-crush.'

'I don't want to talk about—'

'Okay, forget her, just listen while I tell you something else: the reason you're no good at real relationships is because you think you're shit. That's why I scragged you back at the house when you moaned how shitty you were. You've got to get some self-respect so that you stop living in terror of women telling you you're shit and trashing you before you can trash them – no, don't tell me I'm just a stupid ex-tom who doesn't know what she's talking about! I've had therapy! *And* I read all the psychology articles in *Cosmo*!'

We're still holding hands. Looking down at our intertwined fingers I say: 'But you're talking to me now as if I'm shit.'

'It's your shitty behaviour I'm talking about, pinhead! But you don't have to behave shittily.'

'You mean I'm okay but—'

'—but you shouldn't go around smashing people up. Even that airhead Serena deserves better.'

'Well, I never mean to break hearts, but the girls do sort of ask for it—'

'God, I thought only rapists came out with that line! Maybe you're shit after all.'

'No, no, no, I didn't mean—'

'Okay, so when you and your Armani suit light up like a thousand-watt bulb, the girls are going to pant for it. But "it" shouldn't mean having their hearts smashed, and having sex shouldn't mean leaving behind a trail of bloody corpses!'

'I do always try to be kind—'

'—as the euthanasia freak says before he murders his next wrinkly! Oh, stop making stupid remarks and just think for a moment, would you? Just try to imagine what it feels like to get trashed by someone you care about!'

But I only say: 'I don't have to imagine. I know.'

*   *   *

I fully expect Susanne to make some cutting remark about Elizabeth in response to this statement but she doesn't. She just holds my hand more tightly than ever.

We go on sitting on the bench and watching all the families go by as they enjoy their Sunday afternoon in the park. It's amazing to be reminded that there are normal people out there, people who don't sell themselves for money, people who only know about psychos from reading the newspapers.

'I like this place,' I say to Susanne. 'It's as if we're normal here.' And I watch the nearest normal family drifting by. There's a small child, sex male, who wants to feed the ducks. There's a baby, sex indeterminate, in a buggy. The adults have that vague look which comes from being pleasantly relaxed, and the little boy's beaming, blissfully unaware of how horrific life can be. I think: I was like that once, long ago.

But I don't want to think of the past, particularly since in the present Susanne and I have been holding hands for so long that they've practically fused. Dimly I realise that despite all the horrors I'm feeling good.

Eventually we return to Pimlico. No sign of Elizabeth's car outside Norah's house. With elaborate care we sneak separately down the basement steps and sag against each other with relief when we're reunited in the hall.

I kiss her on the cheek and she doesn't seem to mind. But then the cat arrives, yowling for food, so I'm put on hold while Susanne goes off to open a tin. This is what family life must be like when the baby demands attention. It's all normal, normal, normal . . . I think: my life's going to be normal one day. I'm going to be so normal that no one'll look at me twice as I walk around St James's Park on a Sunday afternoon with my wife and kids. I'll have a house with a dock for the boat. I'll do gardening and DIY. I'll—

'Okay, that takes care of the cat,' says Susanne. 'What shall we do next?'

I wait for her to add: 'And don't even think of shagging,' but she doesn't. This should be an electrifying go-ahead signal, but I'm so worried she might dismiss my behaviour as mere grazing that I can't think how to steam forward. Supposing I've misread her and she slaps my face? Supposing deep down she thinks I'm shit after all? At least I'm not wearing an Armani suit and lighting up like a thousand-watt bulb, but if I don't play the stud, how do I operate?

'I'd sort of like to get sort of closer, know-what-I-mean?' I mumble. 'But of course it all depends on what you want.'

'Yeah. Got a condom?'

I always carry condoms. That way I never have to pass up an opportunity to graze.

'Okay,' says Susanne when I give a dazed nod. 'Here's the deal: I don't want any kind of "performance" – what Elizabeth calls "choreography". I don't want anything fancy – no bloody frills. I want minimal foreplay, in for ten minutes max, then out with no fuss. Whether you climax is your business and whether I climax is mine. Got it?'

'Got it.'

'And no bloody drivel about how marvellous it all is, because I can spot your lies a mile off. In fact don't talk at all.'

'Can I grunt occasionally?'

'Only if you have to. No fake ecstasy.'

'But supposing I genuinely—'

'Look, do you want to shag me or don't you?'

'I do.'

'Then for God's sake get a move on!'

'Right . . . Do you have a timer I could set for ten minutes? I'm afraid I might overrun.'

'Oh no you're not! All prostitutes have a timer built into their brains when it comes to doing sex!'

'But we're not being prostitutes now, are we?' I say. 'This is you and me being friends.'

Susanne slumps down on the sofa and quietly sheds a tear.

*   *   *

It's her legacy from the Life. I understand that straight away and straight away I say urgently: 'You don't have to do this. It's okay. We'll still be friends.'

She wipes her eyes. 'I haven't done it since my last punter.'

My mouth drops open. 'You mean you've been all this time—'

'I vowed I'd never do it again unless I really wanted to.'

'That's wonderful! I wish I had that much control over my life!'

'It's been lonely,' she says, wiping her eyes again, 'but there are worse things than being alone.'

'You bet. Pervs. Uglies. Punters with bad breath—'

'Anyway I'm not alone because I've got my cat. I don't mind if I never do it again with anyone, and I'd rather top myself than go back to the Life.'

'I think you're brilliant, getting free of it all—'

'I wouldn't dream of doing it with you if it wasn't for that dance. But don't expect anything much because I'll be useless.'

Firmly I say: 'Even if you just act like a sack of potatoes I'll still think you're the best dancing partner in the world and we'll still be friends.'

'Screw-up!' she says, smiling at me through her tears, and that turns out to be the last word spoken in that flat for some time.

After the allotted ten minutes I ask: 'Okay if I go on a bit?' and she says: 'I don't mind.' After a further five I ask: 'Okay if I come now?' and she says: 'Might as well.'

Later when I return from the bathroom she says: 'I feel bloody sore, worse than a virgin of sixty who's done it for the first time. Did I feel like a load of old leather?' But I don't answer her with words. I just slide back into bed and hold her in my arms and kiss her as I'd kiss the best girl in the world, and she kisses me back and snuggles closer to me than ever and I know we're both happy.

Well, in one way it was just a run-of-the-mill shag, which is why I'm not wasting time going into porno-detail, but in another way, the way that mattered, it was a very special shag because we were being ourselves, both accepting each other as we were. Also – and I know this sounds pathetic but it's true – I was proud she'd decided I was good enough to do it with, even though she was so choosy. I felt afterwards too that I could look after her in bed even though she might have to look after me out of it. The real me needs a bit of looking after, I can see that now. Deep down I'm all dreams and unpractical ideas, which is why I'm comfiest with a tough, street-wise woman who can keep me organised.

After the shag Susanne keeps me organised by telling me I've got to eat some more, and she fixes what she calls a 'fry-tartar', a jumbo omelette stuffed with onions, peppers, tomatoes and pota-toes. We have to have eggs again because she's run out of every-thing else, but the frittata's so good I don't care. We drink Italian wine with it and the cat goes in and out through the cat-flap, just as it would in a normal home. I feel so happy being normal, but of course the rest of my life's not normal yet, not by a long chalk, and eventually I have to go.

We snog for a long time in the hall because we don't want the evening to end. Neither of us try to put our feelings into words. No point. Over dinner we've worked out our plan of action in

358

detail, so there's no need to say more about that either, and finally after one last kiss I leave.

I arrive home to find Elizabeth waiting for me, and at once I see she's in the foulest of tempers.

* * *

'You're going from strength to strength!' she says angrily, coming out of the living-room as I step into the hall. 'You stand me up, stand Norah up, stand Serena up – and all to go and moon over a grave! I don't know how you have the nerve to make such a feeble excuse! What have you really been up to?'

'Nothing! I just felt I needed to go for a drive to get my head together, that's all. I've been upset over the Colin disaster, and—'

'So how's your head now? You want Asherton to glue it together again?'

I start sweating but say levelly: 'I'm okay. Promise. All set for the punters tomorrow.'

'Come here.'

I force myself to step right up to her.

'Kiss me.'

I kiss her. I know what all this is about but I've anticipated it. I showered long and hard after the shag.

Drawing back, Elizabeth looks me straight in the eyes and says: 'You've been with someone,' but I know she has to be bluffing.

I look straight back and say: 'No I bloody haven't!'

'I warn you, Gavin, if you're lying to me in any way whatsoever—'

'No lies. Honestly. And I'm sorry about today, I really am, but I did write the note explaining and apologising – it wasn't as if I disappeared without a word—'

I'm cut off. She's gone back into the living-room and shut the door in my face.

Backing off I run upstairs. Nigel's home but he's on his way to his room so we just say hi. Then immediately he's out of sight the penny drops. I told him earlier that I didn't want to shag Serena because I had someone else in my sights. No wonder Elizabeth was so sure I'd been with someone! She wasn't being psychic, just well-informed.

I want to rush up to the attic and bang Nigel's head against the wall till he confesses, but I manage to calm myself down. I see the best way forward is to say nothing and let Elizabeth think her mole is still unsuspected. I never normally confide in Nigel anyway. I don't have to change my behaviour towards him.

I get to my room and wonder if it's been searched but nothing strikes me as suspicious. I pause, thinking. Since I started playing my double-game I've never regarded my bedroom as a safe place, so a search would be no big disaster. My safe place is in the attic junk-room where Elizabeth hoards various stuff and I keep the suitcases which I need for our holidays together. Underneath the spot where the suitcases are stacked I've taken up a floorboard and hidden the St Benet's brochures which I snitched from the church at the start of my fundraising career. I nearly hid them at Austin Friars, but both Tommy and Nigel have the run of that place and they'd have noticed a suspicious floorboard in a flat with no carpets. The attic junk-room at Lambeth seemed the ideal solution, but now I'm not so happy with it. If Elizabeth stays as suspicious as she was tonight she might decide to search my suitcases. I doubt if she'd shift them far enough to see that one of the short boards running into the eaves has less ingrained dirt around it than its neighbour, but the risk is still unacceptable, and since I'm doing no more fundraising I don't need those brochures anyway. I must get rid of them, and the sooner the better.

But right now I've got to wait. I don't want Nigel to hear me rooting around, and the best thing to do is return home tomorrow after the wake-up session. On Monday morning Nigel goes food-shopping at Sainsbury's and Elizabeth will either be out or she'll be busy in the office with Susanne. I can say I've forgotten some-thing – the American condoms Iowa Jerry has to have, the leather pouch the Greek geek fancies, another sex-pillow to replace the one that got dumped on by mistake – yeah, I'll think of something, anything, and then I can nip up to the attic to grab the brochures.

I go to bed and dream of Thursday, which is when the new life will begin – after Susanne's spent three days channelling the money, and I've nicked the Tucker tapes on Wednesday night. But then I wake up and know I'm in trouble. It's Monday morning and I have to go to work. It's Monday morning and I have to face the drop-dead frightfulness of my daily life. It's Monday morning and after hours spent dreaming of heaven I'm right back descending into hell.

Can't eat breakfast. At least I do, to stop Nigel telling Elizabeth about my poor appetite, but I throw the meal up, deliberately, five minutes later. Off I go to Austin Friars but by the time I reach the flat I'm good for nothing. I can't meditate, can't focus, can't get my act together. All the stress has done my head in. I sit on a stool, elbows on the kitchen counter, and shudder. Huge tears splash down my cheeks. I start to sob. Can't stop, not for a full thirty seconds. Then because I'm scared shitless and don't know what else to do I call Susanne.

'Right,' she says at once when I blurt out I can't go on – and all my life I'll remember how she was there for me when the crunch finally came. 'It's okay, I've been where you are now and I understand. Now listen. Don't answer the doorbell. You're stuck in traffic and you're not there.'

'Okay, but—'

'I'll be with you as soon as I can but I'm not dressed yet so you'll have to hang on for at least another three quarters of an hour. Can you do that?'

I say I can.

'When I arrive I'll give three short buzzes and three long ones so you'll know it's me. Okay? We'll work our way round this, Gavin, try not to worry, all it needs is extra planning.' She hangs up.

The doorbell rings seconds later but I don't answer it. Covering my face with my hands I feel as if the sharks have scented blood in the water and are closing in to tear me apart

* * *

By the time she arrives I'm red-eyed but tearless. I've drunk a couple of glasses of wine to calm me down. Three or four glasses, in fact. I feel muzzy but not wuzzy. I could be worse.

She's got to be smelling the alcohol on my breath but all she says is: 'Somebody ought to abolish the Tube. It's not even fit for animals.'

The buzzer blares again as she speaks. It's been blaring and blaring. Clients are always instructed that if there's no response when they first ring they're to wait five minutes before ringing again. That covers a situation where the schedule backs up, but normally this never happens because I never overrun. Clients come up by the lift, go down by the stairs and never meet, least of all on the landing outside my front door. I mean, I'm a top-class professional, right? I never mess my clients around or put them in awkward social situations or—

'Gavin!'

'Sorry, yes, I'm listening . . .' I tune back into the scene to find Susanne's put some coffee on and we're sitting side by side at the kitchen counter. 'Okay, this is what happens,' she's saying briskly. 'We have to accelerate the plan we made – do it all today. It'll be riskier but there are advantages – less time for anything to go wrong, for instance, less time having to play-act for Elizabeth.'

I nod. She puts her hand over mine and lets it rest there as she adds: 'The first thing we've got to do is stop Elizabeth finding out you can't work, but I can fix that. The early-shift clients will be leaving messages on the answerphone, but Elizabeth never goes into the office before I arrive and today she won't even be there at eleven because she's arranged to meet someone in Battersea at ten-thirty. So I can call all the clients scheduled for today and arrange refunds to keep them quiet.'

I manage to whisper: 'What about my money?'

'The Caymans are several hours behind us so I can't do anything till the afternoon, but that's okay, Elizabeth's got a two o'clock meeting with the escort agency accountant, so the coast'll be clear. I'll set up a joint account in your name and Elizabeth's, just as I planned, and transfer the money to it. Then I'll wait a couple of hours and transfer the lot to your account in London – and you'd better not go back on your promise to give me ten per cent! But if we're going for speed it's best to keep the deal simple. One new account to bring you onto the scene. One transfer to the UK – and on second thoughts, maybe I should leave a bit of money in the new Cayman account to avoid suspicion. Maybe I should leave some money in the old account too.'

'Just do whatever you think's best. If only it wasn't all so risky—'

'Maybe it's not so risky as it seems – I bet those Cayman banks are used to pushing money around all over the place with the minimum of questions asked! But I'll try and work late tonight in case the bank does a check-up.'

'God! Supposing Elizabeth's in the room when they phone?'

'Look, that's *my* problem and if it happens I'll deal with it somehow. What you've got to do is forget all that and concentrate on holing up here for the rest of the day without freaking out – by which I mean that if you get drunk tossing off all the clients' booze I'll bloody kill you.'

'What happens after I've holed up here all day?'

'Go home and pretend everything's normal. You wouldn't normally spend time with Elizabeth on a Monday evening, would you? Okay, so just say hi to her and then go upstairs, have dinner, chat to Nigel – only for God's sake watch what you say. I know you and Nigel are good mates but he's dependent on Elizabeth for a job and you can bet Asherton's got him on film doing something horrible. He's not to be trusted.'

I tell her my own suspicions about Nigel, and she's alarmed. 'Shit, the last thing we need is him playing supergrass!'

I remember Nigel saying he loves me but I don't repeat this to Susanne. She'd just laugh. Instead I say: 'He wouldn't want to harm me. But he's just no good at standing up to Elizabeth.'

'Little rat! Make sure he's in his room before you start packing!'

'Talking of packing—'

'It's essentials only for both of us. I'm going to have to leave most of my stuff behind.'

'What about the cat?'

'I'll pop her in a cattery this evening. Best if she's out of the way for a couple of days . . . Are you still planning to nick the Tucker tapes?'

I feel shivery but say I am. 'I'll wait till one in the morning to make sure Tommy's asleep.'

'Okay, I'll expect you around one-thirty – call me as soon as you're driving away and I'll be waiting for you down the street from Norah's – I'll be sheltering in the newsagent's doorway. Then we'll go to St Benet's, and let's hope they can deal.'

'Should I call Nicholas to warn him?'

'Better not. If he doesn't know anything, he can't cause complications.'

The coffee finishes percolating and Susanne pours each of us a mug. No milk. We're into serious caffeine-toking here.

We go over the plan again, and by the time the coffee's finished we're wired.

'One thing more,' I say as she prepares to leave. 'Wipe Gil's name from the client files before you leave tonight.'

'That Gilbert's going to wind up the luckiest gay in London by the time you've finished with him.'

363

We embrace for a long moment by the front door.

'Think of "In the Mood",' she says after I've given her a final kiss, 'and remember we've got a lot of dancing still to do.'

She leaves. In the kitchen I pour away the rest of the wine in the bottle I opened earlier, and switch to orange juice.

I've recovered my nerve.

*   *   *

Between shifts I stay in the flat. I haven't forgotten that I need to get rid of the St Benet's brochures, but they don't seem so dangerous now I know I'll be leaving that house for good tonight. I'll collect them this evening when I bring down my suitcase from the junk-room.

The day drags on while I watch daytime TV like a zombie. For lunch I eat some biscuits and drink some milk. Must take in some kind of fuel.

Finally, at six-thirty, I leave. It's such a relief to escape from that place. It's such a relief to know I'll never have to go there again.

When I arrive home I stop at the office and Susanne gives me a lacklustre 'hi' as if nothing's happened between us. Elizabeth's there too, and when she turns her back on Susanne to look at me, Susanne gives me the thumbs-up sign to let me know the plan's on track.

'Hullo, pet,' says Elizabeth casually. 'Everything all right?'

'Fine. Sorry about yesterday. I feel really bad about that now.'

'So you should!' But she's smiling at me. 'By the way, Nigel won't be in tonight. There's a party down at the pub for one of his friends and I said he could take the evening off on condition he left a nice cold supper for you.'

'Okay.' I will myself to linger in order to appear normal. 'How was your day?'

'Oh, busy, busy, busy . . . And I'm going out to dinner with Eva tonight – do you remember my friend Eva who had that very high-class business for Arabs near the Edgware Road a couple of years ago?'

'The silver-blonde with the accent?'

'That's the one. Well, she's off Arabs now, says the next big trend's Russians . . . You're looking a little peaky, pet! Perhaps I should take you on a mini-break before Christmas so that you can have some nice sea air.'

I smile at her. 'Bournemouth?'

'No, Bournemouth's no fun in winter except at Christmas. Perhaps Brighton. Brighton's always fun.'

'Let's make it soon,' I say, giving her a kiss before adding: 'Remember me to Eva.'

She says she will and we part very fondly, but as I force myself to dawdle up the stairs it's hard to repress the biggest possible shudder.

* * *

Nigel's already left for the pub. Good news. Tommy's car's absent from its parking slot and that probably means he's gone early to Austin Friars to pick up the tapes and check the equipment. Too bad he couldn't have gone later, after Elizabeth's departure. Then I'd have had the perfect opportunity to nick the Tucker tapes – but no, I'm wrong, Tommy might notice they were missing if I nicked them earlier than planned. The retrieval has to wait till he's asleep.

On an impulse I pad down to the first-floor landing and glance into the hall below. Susanne and Elizabeth are still in the office, but Elizabeth's telling her not to work late. Shit! If the Cayman bank phones while Elizabeth's still here . . . Closing my mind against this nightmare I make a mental note to check the fax machine and answerphone later in the evening.

After picking at the cold salmon salad Nigel's left for me I go to my bedroom to start selecting clothes. I decide to restrict myself to one suit – a conventional number, not some fuck-me designer two-piece – and a few items of casual gear. I thought I'd be upset when the time came to abandon my wardrobe, but when I look at the clothes I've used for my hustler's life I just want to puke. I mind more about leaving my books, and even more than that I mind leaving my CDs. I decide to take three of each with me. But which three? The problem absorbs me while I wait for Elizabeth to leave for her date with vice-queen Eva who got on the wrong side of the law two years ago but is now out of jail and beavering away to start up a call-girl racket that'll service the new Russian mafia. Elizabeth doesn't like Russians. She says she can never forget the Cuban Missile Crisis. Must be weird to be able to remember that kind of stuff.

She goes at quarter to eight. I shelter behind a curtain as I watch her drive away, but she doesn't look up. That's the last I'll see of Elizabeth in our present life, although I hope that one day in my new life I'll see her again – in the dock of a criminal court. But I probably won't. There'll be no evidence and she'll slither away again, doing her disappearing act.

I feel so churned up by these thoughts that I have to lose the few shreds of salmon salad which I've allowed into my stomach, but even after that the mental pain's so excruciating that I still feel out of control. So I go to the kitchen, find a steak-knife and cut myself on the forearm. Now I feel better. I'm conscious of an exquisite relief as I watch the blood trickle over the skin. I'm in control again. The pain of thinking how Elizabeth's trashed me is still there but I can feel other pain, such as the soreness of my throat after the vomiting and the rawness of my forearm after the cut, and the physical pain eclipses the mental agony.

My mobile rings. I've brought it in from the car, just as I do every night to outplay the Lambeth thieves, and it's lying on a table in the living-room.

'Check the office while she's out,' says Susanne the moment I take the call. 'Check the fax and the answerphone. We need to know if the transfer hasn't gone through.'

'Right. Shall I call you if everything's okay?'

'No, only if there's a hitch, and if I don't answer keep trying. Remember, I've got to take the cat to the cattery.'

She ends the call and I set down the mobile by the regular phone, the one that I'd never use for private calls because I'm sure Tommy's bugged it for Elizabeth. I discussed this communication hazard with Susanne earlier and made sure she had my mobile number.

Leaving my section of the house I retrieve the vital number sequence from the porno-pic in Elizabeth's bathroom and head downstairs to raid the safe for the basement keys. On my way I check the office but the machines are clear. So far so good.

Leaving the office I move into the living-room and remove the cheapo pastiche of an oil painting which conceals Elizabeth's safe.

* * *

As soon as the safe door swings open, my brain zips into top gear. I've been so wrapped up in my puking and cutting that I've failed to anticipate this dazzling window of opportunity, but now I see that this is when I finally uncover Elizabeth's secrets. Brilliant.

Having slipped the basement keys into my pocket I check the

366

documents in the safe, but they're only legal and insurance papers relating to the house and contents. I then take a quick look at the jewellery collection, which is tucked up in a pink velvety box, and alongside this treasure trove I find the Jiffy bag containing five hundred pounds: Susanne's pay-off if the police move in and she has to dump the steel box in the river.

I gaze at the steel box at the back of the safe. Then I unearth a screwdriver from the toolkit which lives beneath the kitchen sink and have a go at jimmying the lock.

Once I open the lid I see a nice new passport, crisp and shiny, in the name of Elizabeth Tremayne and with Elizabeth's picture in the photo-slot. Attached to the passport are various credit cards issued in the new name plus details of the Cayman account which I've already seen on the computer, the account designed to finance the new identity. Delamere, Mayfield, Tremayne . . . Funny how she gives herself names which suggest the spotless heroine of a romantic novel. I wonder what her real name is.

Returning to the box I excavate the next item. It's a folder labelled G.O.L.D. RITUALS, and inside there are several closely typed sheets of paper with diagrams which are about as interesting to me as a book on Church liturgy. There are also several packets of photos, but they just show the rituals being enacted. There's nothing particularly porno there except that in the last batch everyone gets to be naked. No, wait a minute, the last one of all shows a bloke wearing a fake phallus and there's a bunch of silly gits, male and female, kneeling down with their bottoms in the air as they wait to be done. Even so, this is hardly going to give the Vice Squad a coronary (no children, no animals), but I think I understand the point of this folder. It's a souvenir of Elizabeth's favourite project, something she can sigh over with nostalgia in her old age.

I turn over the photos, but nothing's written on the backs, not even a date. I was hoping to see the word BETZ, but no, Elizabeth wouldn't have wanted to keep a photo of him after he caused her so much trouble. So I haven't found a smoking gun here, but I still put the folder on my takeaway pile. At least the stuff links her to GOLD.

Then I see there's another folder in the box. This contains some copies of bank statements for the Guild of Light and Darkness, and I learn that GOLD has two banks, one a normal London high-street bank and the other the Swiss bank I already know about. Both sets of statements are dated 1989 and they're clipped to a copy of a

GOLD tax return. This is when I discover that only the high-street bank income gets reported to the Revenue. This is the bank which receives the membership subscriptions (called 'tithes' to make them sound religious). All the extra gifts go to Switzerland, which I now realise is the account used for any number of off-colour dealings, not necessarily confined to GOLD.

This has to be Elizabeth's insurance. This is the evidence that can sink Asherton for tax evasion if ever the two of them fall out – the evidence that'll allow the police to turn over Asherton's affairs. But how did Elizabeth get hold of this lethal weapon? Although she was a VIP in GOLD from the beginning, she wouldn't have handled the money. I flip through the tax return to the end and finally discover it's been signed by Asherton, as managing director – and by the treasurer, a certain Joachim Betz.

I think: GOTCHA!

This is the cast-iron proof that Carta wanted – the proof that GOLD was the scam which hooked her husband. It's also the cast-iron proof that GOLD employed 'Elizabeth Mayfield', referred to in the accounts as a 'consultant on religious ritual' who received quarterly payments for her expertise.

Obviously Elizabeth had a hold over Betz and got him to disgorge copies of these papers. Equally obviously she wouldn't want her connection with Betz to be known now, but as there's no mention of the Delamere name she could still tip off the Revenue by sending the evidence anonymously – she still has the power to make Asherton back off without putting herself in danger.

I put the folder on the takeaway pile. It's nice to think of the police having a whole new area to explore.

There's only one item in the steel box now and that's a chunky envelope. What's this? Lifting the unsealed flap I pull out a video, and as soon as I see the label on the spine my eyes go spherical. Elizabeth's written: (1) JASON (2) TONY.

My predecessors. The boys who got sacked after failing to stay the course. What the hell's all this about? Is Elizabeth really so sentimental about them that she keeps a video of their best gay moments with the punters? No way!

Crossing the living-room I shove the video into the machine below the television, and the next moment the horrors begin.

* * *

At first I don't take in what's happening. I just stare dumbly. Then understanding hits me and I nearly drop dead with shock, my heart-beat's missing for God knows how many seconds before starting up again. Then I think: no, no, I'm not seeing this, I've freaked out, I'm hallucinating. But I'm not. I see Asherton drooling on-screen as he starts to cut up living limbs.

I can't watch for much longer. I fast-forward to the end before backtracking and playing the last few seconds. In an ocean of gore a heap of skinned flesh twitches and lies still. That must be Tony. Jason would have met an identical end in the first half of the spliced tape. Two blokes like me, drop-outs, drifters, with no one to care enough to ask questions if they disappeared. Fingers shaking on the remote control, I press the stop button and rewind. I'm so shattered I can only think of all the times Nigel and I cracked black-humour jokes about Asherton making snuff movies. Of course we never thought he'd actually done it. I mean, that kind of thing always happens some-where else among people you don't know. Sure Asherton's a sadist, sure he's a creep and a perv, and yes, of course he's nuts, but—

Struggling to be calm I ask myself if this tape too was kept as evidence against Asherton, but I know it wasn't. Just possessing the tape converts Elizabeth into an accessory to murder, and that makes it much too dangerous to use in any power struggle. So why has she kept it? Well, for her it must be all about seeing villains get what they deserve. Jason and Tony became villains, not doing what they were told, maybe trying to go their own way, perhaps even being dumb enough to stop calling her darling and start accusing her of being a nasty old bag. Well, they got their comeuppance, didn't they? The horrific truth is that Elizabeth's kept this home movie because she finds it emotionally satisfying.

Hardly knowing what I'm doing I slip the tape into its case, switch off the machine and cram all the takeaway items back into the steel box. I also cram in Susanne's five hundred pounds before I close the safe.

Back upstairs I dump the box on my bed and try to take deep breaths to stop myself shivering, but it's no good, I have to go to the kitchen, pour myself a glass of wine and drink it straight off. Only then do I start to breathe normally. But I don't drink more than one glass. When you're travelling along the edge of the abyss and you've just looked down you don't start tap-dancing if you want to avoid the long drop. You chill out and refocus.

With the drink finished I make a crucial decision: I'm not going to nick the Tucker tapes. Susanne was right to disapprove of this scheme and of course I can see now it was crazy. I'll call Gil tomorrow, I'll make sure he never goes to Asherton's house, but I'm not retrieving those tapes – sorry, mate, but I can't risk getting caught, can't risk Tommy pulling a knife on me, can't risk winding up at the Pain-Palace. Gavin Blake Dead Martyr is a role I'm just not gasping to play.

Having made this decision I glance at the steel box. No reason why that can't go in my car straight away. I tie the lid down with string to compensate for the busted lock, and run downstairs but in the hall I hesitate. Better check on Tommy who by this time could be back from Austin Friars or wherever he went earlier. I open the front door a crack. Yes, his car's back on its slot. Out on the front doorstep I glance down at the windows but all the blinds are drawn so I'm safe. I look quickly up and down the street to check for would-be car thieves, but although traffic's thundering along the road, no one's walking along the pavement. Darting to my car I stash the box in the boot and zip back into the house.

Upstairs again I make a big effort not to panic, not to rush as I continue the task of gathering together all I want to take with me. I've put on a CD to soothe my nerves, but I'm not playing opera. I don't want to be reminded how Gavin Blake Prostitute used to anaesthetise himself, but on the other hand I know I need beautiful music, so I've chosen a piece which sounds like opera but isn't. It's become popular recently but so far nobody's desecrated it by turning it into a chart-buster fit only for *Top of the Pops*. It's a Mozart number, it's Wolfgang Amadeus talking directly to The Bloke, it's that nape-tingling church piece known as the *Laudate Dominum*.

The famous lady's singing. After a while I find myself singing along with her, can't stop myself, each sequence of notes is so bloody beautiful, and suddenly it strikes me as miraculous that amidst all the filth I'm wading through tonight something beautiful should be alongside me, not blotted out by the filth but towering above it, and as I sing those Latin words it at last occurs to me to translate them. *Laudate Dominum*: Praise the Lord.

I tell myself this is one of the CDs I have to take with me. 'Amen!' sings the famous lady as I make this decision. 'Amen, ah-ah-ah-ah-ah-ah-ahhh . . .' The final amen spans an amazing number of notes but at last the music finishes and there's silence.

I pause. The silence is unbroken, as my bedroom's not on the side of the house which faces the road. Opening the window I lean out and see that no light's shining from the basement into the back garden. Tommy must have gone out again. Or maybe he's in his workroom. Or maybe he's just having an early night after his orgies in Amsterdam. Anyway I don't have to worry about him any more.

Up I go to the junk-room to retrieve a suitcase and the St Benet's fundraising brochures. No sense in leaving the brochures behind to provide Elizabeth with a big clue about where I might have gone. I don't want her running away before the police can collar her. Let her just think I've beetled off into the blue with Susanne.

I've decided to take my large suitcase rather than the medium-sized one because this'll enable me to pack more books and CDs. But when I reach the suitcases my scalp crawls. The large one isn't quite covering the crucial floorboard. It's been moved.

Okay, so Elizabeth's now so suspicious that she's searched my luggage for clues, but that needn't mean . . . I drop to my knees, shove the case aside and lever up the floorboard.

The St Benet's brochures are still in a neatly stacked pile but they're no longer exactly parallel to the pipe which runs under the floor. I always leave them exactly parallel to the pipe, always, so that I'll know if—

Well, I know now.

She's found them.

*   *   *

For the second time that evening I feel fit to drop dead. It doesn't take me long to piece together the probable sequence of events. When I told Nigel yesterday that I was bored with Serena and there was a special someone I wanted to shag, I wasn't thinking of anyone in particular, not even Susanne. I was just trying to turn off the conversation so that I could escape from the house. But when Nigel found himself forced to repeat the conversation to Elizabeth, she'd have jumped to the conclusion I was referring to Carta. Elizabeth's chronic paranoia about St Benet's would have ensured she then searched for evidence – and once she started messing around in the junk-room with my suitcases she must have noticed the floor-board. Proof at last, she thinks after uncovering the brochures. She now knows I've been disobedient on the grand scale and lying to the back teeth as I double-cross her in the biggest possible way. This has to be worse than anything Jason and Tony ever did. And look what happened to them.

I lurch to my feet as my thoughts skitter on, driven by a rising tide of panic. Forget the stories about Elizabeth meeting Eva and Nigel going to a party. All I really know is that Elizabeth's decided to be out, she's given Nigel the evening off and she's even taken care to shoo Susanne from the premises. And why? Because something's going to happen here tonight. The talent scouts are going to come recruiting for the new snuff movie.

I'm tiptoeing to the door of the junk-room. Why am I tiptoeing? Because the house is so quiet that even my muffled footsteps sound creepy. Shit, I'm scared! Supposing someone's hiding in Nigel's room?

I take a deep breath and shove open his door but the room's empty. I'm about to relax when I notice a strange thing. All the surfaces are bare. There's nothing lying around. I open the doors of the closet. That's bare too.

Nigel's gone. Sacked. Wiped. Whatever. Somebody's said Gavin won't be needing him any more.

The next thing I know I've grabbed a case – the smaller of the two, no time to pack the larger one – and I'm in my room hurling the essential stuff into it. Somehow I remember to add my mobile from the living-room. Then I lock the case and pull out my house keys so that I can slot the key on the same ring, but no, this is dumb because I don't need the house keys any more. Abandoning them on the chest of drawers I slip the suitcase key into my pocket.

I switch off the lights but switch them on again. Let the talent scouts think I'm still up here. Skimming downstairs with my suit-case to the landing outside Elizabeth's bedroom, I pause. The house is totally quiet, totally still as I edge to the banisters and look down into the hall.

Everything's exactly as it should be. I relax in relief, but before I can skim on down the staircase, something happens which once more brings me to the brink of heart failure.

The door at the top of the basement stairs, the one Elizabeth always keeps locked and bolted, slowly starts to open.

*   *   *

372

I don't wait to see who or what comes out. I shoot into Elizabeth's bedroom and stand panting in the dark. As I wait I realise that Elizabeth must have left the door to the basement stairs unbolted and unlocked before she left. I never noticed the drawn bolts on my journeys through the hall that evening, but that's not so surprising since the door's just part of the hall furniture, not the kind of thing one would normally look at.

The intruders are on the next staircase now, the one that connects the ground floor to the first. Someone mutters a couple of words but someone else hisses: 'Shhh!' and the voice ceases. But the stairs creak. Those Big Boys weigh a lot, all bulging grotesquely as the result of steroid abuse. Wondering how many of them have come I watch through the crack above the door hinge, and I'm hardly breathing as the procession comes into view. Tommy's leading, showing everyone the way. He's followed by three of the Big Boys, shaven-headed, black-clad, loaded with earrings, nose rings, all kinds of rings – two of the scumbags, I know, even have rings through their equipment. And behind the Big Boys prowls Asherton.

To ease the abduction along, the Big Boys are carrying a whip, a pair of handcuffs and a large roll of duct tape. They've probably got knives too, hidden in their leather jackets. Asherton's so keen on knives.

Tommy opens the door onto the stairs that lead up to my flat, and the light from the second floor hallway illuminates all their faces. Asherton's wet-lipped, bright-eyed, hardly able to wait for the joys of the sadism to come.

Up the stairs they go, quiet as rats in silk slippers. As soon as Asherton's disappeared from view out I slip with the case and shoot down into the hall – but here's the hell of a twist: the front door won't open. It opened earlier when I dumped the steel box in the car, but now it's stuck fast. Asherton must have borrowed Elizabeth's keys and activated the Chubb lock as he came through the hall a moment ago. He'd have wanted to ensure that if I broke loose and made a run for it, I'd wind up either trapped in the house or else fatally delayed by pausing to use my house keys.

Well, I don't have my house keys, do I? I abandoned them in my room.

So I'm trapped.

Sounds indicate that my absence from the lower part of my flat's been discovered, but the bastards'll check the attic before they double back. Still gripping my case I streak down the basement stairs to Tommy's flat but fucking hell, the front door there's locked too – well, yes, it would be, wouldn't it, since Asherton's been busy closing down my options. I glance in Tommy's bedroom nearby and see the steel shutters are now masking the windows.

I start thinking of the back of the house – of the French windows opening onto the patio – but any escape I try to make through the garden would be doomed because the back gardens of all the houses in the block are surrounded by the houses themselves – it's a no-exit scene. But I could smash those windows – no steel shutters at the back – I could create a diversion, make the buggers *think* I've gone out into the garden. Then I could double back upstairs to get my keys – no, wait, there's a spare set in Elizabeth's kitchen – but no, you can bet the spare set won't be there now.

I dump my suitcase behind the door of Tommy's bedroom and head for the back of the flat, but as I pass his workroom a memory hits me and I flick on the light. The Tucker tapes are still sitting on the counter. Instantly I grab them. In the kitchen I snaffle a supermarket bag from a pile by the swingbin and shove the tapes inside. Then I snag a saucepan from the stove and start bashing the French windows – and let's hope to God the bust is audible at the top of the house.

The glass is still falling as I drop the saucepan, grab the bag of tapes and dive back to the front of the house where I rejoin my suitcase behind Tommy's bedroom door. Have the scumbags heard or haven't they? And if they haven't—

They have. Down they come, crashing like a herd of elephants. Tommy charges past and the Big Boys pound along behind him. I wait till they've rushed outside, footsteps crunching on the broken glass, and then I'm tearing up the stairs again on the journey to retrieve my keys.

I burst into the main hall.

Too late I realise that something's wrong. The light's on in the living-room and it shouldn't be on because when I came downstairs it was off. I suddenly realise – too late again – that in the basement I only saw Tommy and the Big Boys. Someone else has chosen to wait in comfort while the riff-raff go milling around in the gardens. Someone else is busy helping himself to Elizabeth's scotch. Someone else has a perfect view of me through the wide open living-room door.

It's Asherton.

* * *

I never hesitate. I'm so hyped up, so wired with panic, terror and the absolute determination to survive that I'm no longer creeping along the edge of the abyss – I'm surfing it on a giant wave of adrenaline.

As the glass jerks from his hands with shock I dump the suitcase, dump the shopping bag and streak into the room to knock the shit out of him.

'PAYBACK TIME, MOTHERFUCKER!' I yell, and he's terrified, so terrified that he beetles gasping behind the sofa. At that perfect moment, stripped of his musclemen, he's just another middle-aged suit who doesn't bother to keep fit. I can punch his lights out in seconds and he knows it. I can almost hear his filthy brain screeching as he tries to figure out what the fuck he can do.

He screams for the Big Boys, the Devil shrieking for his demons, but they're not here, they're long gone. It's just him and me. He cowers, he slavers, he whimpers – could be he's even shitting himself with fright, he's disgusting, I want to kill him, but no, that would mean he'd dragged me down to his own filthy level, that would mean he'd won. I just need him out of action so that I can retrieve the keys, but by God I'm going to make him sweat blood first.

In a flash I've heaved the sofa aside and I'm diving for him, but sheer terror makes him agile and he darts away. I jump up and close in on him again but he flings a vase at me, and as I duck I lose my footing and crash to the carpet. Up I spring with only a couple of seconds lost and I see he's backed against the wall at an odd angle, one arm curving behind his back, the other bent upwards to protect his face. Coward! Rage rushes through me as I remember all I suffered in his house, and I blast forward to grab him.

But the swine's outplayed me. He's faked the fear which lures me on, and the moment I'm poised for the big grab, the arm behind his back whips around me with the knife he must have whisked from his pocket when I was carpeted.

He stabs me between the shoulder blades.

* * *

I feel only a slight prick so I know I'm okay. Thank God I'm wearing a thick jacket. The nick's a shock but I recover pretty damn quick – have to, because the bastard's all set to cut me again.

This time I make no mistake. I punch him squarely on the jaw. Brilliant! He collapses, passes out. I kick him to make sure he's stopped faking, and then I kick him again, bloody hard, to relieve my feelings. But after that it's time to retrieve the keys. I'm about to shoot up to my room when I remember how he must have Chubb-locked the front door, and on searching his pockets I turn up Elizabeth's keys. Bingo! Yet with the Chubb lock cracked I hesitate. That knife of Asherton's is evidence and I've still got time to bag it – Tommy and the Big Boys will be galumphing around all the gardens in the block for some while yet.

Darting into the kitchen I draw a rubber glove over my right hand, tear off a strip of paper towel and return to the knife which I then wrap and drop in the shopping bag along with the Tucker tapes.

Time to leave.

Into the boot of the car go the suitcase and the shopping bag. Into the ignition goes the key. I'm off, I've done it, I've won.

I'm so awash with euphoria that I don't at first notice the odd crawling sensation in my back where I've been pinked. I'm also too busy trying to work out what to do next. It would be crazy to join Susanne right now at Norah's house – Elizabeth's probably waiting there. She won't want to be present at the Pain-Palace when the snuff movie's shot, too risky, but she'll be looking forward to a fun time later with the video. I can just see her relaxing on the sofa with an open box of chocolates beside her as she sips one of those liqueurs which look like sewage.

Once I'm over Lambeth Bridge I park on Horseferry Road, transfer my mobile from my suitcase to the driver's seat and call Susanne to tell her what's happened, but as the bell rings unanswered I remember her plan to leave Alexis at the cattery. Bloody hell. As I abandon the phone pain shoots through my shoulder and my shirt feels as if it's glued to my skin. I twist my other arm behind my back to try to get a fix on the damage and my fingers come back red. Bugger it! The bastard's knife must have gone deeper than I thought. Funny how I barely felt it.

The next thing I know I'm starting to feel wuzzy. God, that's all I need! But the odds are the wuzziness isn't the result of the pinking but of poor nutrition. What I need to do now is drive to the shops on Warwick Way and buy a takeaway to boost my energy levels.

But when I switch on the engine again I know I'm too wuzzy to drive even up the road into Pimlico. I'll have to get a cab, but I hate to leave a Jaguar on the street at night in an area full of low-income housing. I don't want a thief nicking the steel box once he's popped the boot.

Then I have a bright idea. I'm not far from the Houses of Parliament, an area brimming with security cameras. If I could somehow . . .

I get there. By making an enormous effort I reach Great College Street, which runs alongside a patch of lawn known as College Green. It's where the TV news people interview all those politicians. There's even an NCP car park underneath it – nice for the Jaguar, but I decide I have to stick to my plan to park on the street. If I go underground I might be too wuzzy to walk back up again.

It's too late for the parking restrictions to be operating so I drop the Jag on a yellow line right by the lawn. Great. But when I try to get out of the car I see to my horror that blood's been pooling in the driving seat. I do manage to stand upright, but when I nearly black out I slump back into the seat again. What do I do? There are no people around. The tourists are all bobbing around the West End rip-off joints by this time, and there are no TV cameras operating tonight on College Green.

I pick up my mobile again. What I've got to do is keep calling Susanne, but I'm having difficulty pushing the buttons. Bad news. My situation's getting trickier by the second. I wish I had some water. My mouth's gone bone-dry.

I manage to dial Susanne's number again but she's still not there.

I'm not doing at all well now. Breathing hurts. God, if that swine winds up killing me I'll – but no, I've got to live, there's so much to live for, I must think of dancing with Susanne, I must think of The Bloke busting a gut to reel me in after my searing encounter with the mega-shark.

Remembering that I have to *work* at being rescued I say urgently: 'What shall I do?' and straight away The Bloke snaps back: 'Call Nicholas.' This is a smart response, but there's a snag: I don't know the Rectory number. I try to remember how to get hold of Directory Enquiries, but I can't. Never mind, doesn't matter, The Bloke's yelling at me to call Carta instead. He knows I never forget any of *her* numbers. He's made sure they're all engraved on my heart.

I go for her mobile and she picks up at once.

'Carta!' I say, trying to sound loud and clear, but my voice comes out as a whisper.

'Who's this?'

'Gavin. Emergency. Asherton's stabbed me. Listen, take down this number—' I name the figures, using all my mental strength to get them in the right sequence. 'It's my friend Susanne's number,' I say. 'I'm getting out of the Life tonight and she's coming with me to St Benet's. Tell her – tell her—'

'Yes, yes – go on, Gavin, go on—'

'Tell her I'm parked on College Green – the grassy bit – opposite the Houses of Parliament – she'll sort everything out—'

'College Green – Parliament—'

'And Carta – one more thing in case I don't make it—'

'Yes, I'm here, I'm here—'

'My Elizabeth . . . Your Elizabeth . . . One and the same,' I whisper, and then the phone slides sideways against the steering wheel as I pass out.

*　*　*

The next thing I know I'm in one of those weird white vans, the ones which wail as they swoop through the streets, they have a special name but I can't think what it is. I want to open my eyes again but someone's just put lead weights on them – or so it seems – and when I remember the old custom of putting coins on the eyes of people who have died I suppose I have to be dead too – and I want to be angry that Asherton's killed me, but anger takes energy and I've no energy left to do anything but breathe.

Later the swaying and the wailing stop and I'm borne into a very bright building – I still can't open my eyes but I'm aware of the change in temperature as I go indoors and I'm aware of the light beyond my eyelids and I'm aware of running footsteps and the buzz of voices and the drone of a public address system, though I can't understand what's being said. Someone starts to manhandle me and I get the idea it's a punter – I'm so worried that I won't have the strength to tell him I'm not seeing clients today, but this is no punter, his hands are kind, and when I at last manage to open my eyes a fraction I see everything's white, there are white walls and white lights and people in white coats, and I'm hooked up to a line, it looks so weird, particularly as I can't remember what happened, I'm so disorientated . . . But suddenly I understand. This is the last stage of the journey to the shore. I've got past the shark-infested waters, and now all The Bloke's people have run into the surf to help pull me the last yards to the beach.

Finally one of The Bloke's people, the leader of the surfers, says: 'He'll do. But keep the police out, he can't be questioned yet.' And a woman asks: 'What about that clergyman?'

'Clergyman!' I shout – or I think I shout but in fact I can't speak and all I can do is listen to the leader saying briefly: 'No visitors till tomorrow.' Then I'm whisked away somewhere not so bright. 'Clergyman!' I shout again in my head. 'Clergyman!' but still the word doesn't get spoken aloud so no one takes any notice.

At that point I'm borne down a long corridor – or maybe it's a tunnel, and my spirits rise because at the end of it I can see a brilliant white light, far more brilliant than any light I've ever seen. I think: this has to be The Bloke, has to be. And I'm so excited. But the next moment the light's fading into a mist and the walls of the tunnel are melting away and I know it isn't the time to see The Bloke as he really is. 'But I'm with you always,' he says to me. 'I'll come to meet you again and again through other people.' And I know this'll be true because this is what he's already been doing. Then I see not only Richard, his eyes bright with love as we sail past the Needles, not only Carta, symbolising a world I long to recapture, not only the St Benet's people all rising to their feet as I enter the room, but Nigel telling me to come out of denial and Susanne showing me the power of the human spirit when we dance at the Savoy. And as I think of Susanne and me, somehow being enabled to care for each other despite the soul-destroying abuse we've endured, I see the giant forces of joy, truth, beauty and love merge in a huge blaze of colour which blots out the dark yet draws all the blackness back into itself so that everything is finally subsumed in that triumphant blaze and redeemed.

I say to The Bloke: 'If you're with me always, why haven't I seen you before?' and he answers: 'You always overlooked my footprints in the sand.' Then I realise I'm back on the shore, the shore of the life I was designed to live, the shore I left behind when I went swimming in the dark and dangerous sea, but now the sand's all

scuffed up from the surfers and although I look for the special footprints I can't find them. So I say: 'Where are the footprints you
made when you stood on the beach just now and watched your
people rescue me?' and he answers: 'I wasn't standing on the beach
then. I was in the sea alongside you, I was with the others as we
finally rescued you, and we all struggled together up the beach as
we carried you to safety.'

I open my eyes. I want to know what safety looks like. I want
to see the dawn of my new life.

I discover I'm in a small room with various tubes connecting me
to machines. Sunlight's streaming through the window and falling
on the man sitting at my bedside.

The stranger's a policeman, yawning over his notebook, but before
I can speak to him the door opens and The Bloke walks in. He's
dressed up as Nicholas Darrow but of course it's The Bloke,
performing his usual trick of manifesting himself through someone
else.

'You found me,' I say. 'I was so lost but you never stopped
looking.'

The Bloke smiles and asks me how I feel.

'Pretty beat up,' I confess. 'I'm not sure I can walk yet.'

In another dimension of reality The Bloke smooths my bedraggled fleece before tucking me up on his shoulder and reaching for
his shepherd's crook. But in this dimension of reality The Bloke just
takes my hand in his and says: 'You're going to be all right, Gavin.
You're coming home.'

PART THREE

Coming Home

'Destructive memories frequently stem from repressed
unresolved anger about emotional hurts in the past . . .
The healing of memories does not erase the memories,
indeed it commonly serves to bring them into consciousness, but their meaning is changed and their sting withdrawn. The memories become accepted and integrated
into the person's total life. The basis of this healing is
forgiveness – forgiving the person responsible for the
hurts . . .'

Mud and Stars
A report of a working party consisting mainly of
doctors, nurses and clergy

CHAPTER ONE

Carta

'For many people a sense of closure is very important.'

A Time to Heal
A report for the House of Bishops on the Healing Ministry

'People attack in others the faults which they suppress in themselves . . . Therefore conflict has a voice. We learn most from the people who threaten us most, and from the things which we abhor and reject.'

Mud and Stars
A report of a working party consisting mainly of
doctors, nurses and clergy

I

Gavin survived his stabbing. In my relief I thought his troubles would now be over, but I was wrong. His physical recovery might have been under way but mentally, emotionally and spiritually he was still crippled, and the next stage of his journey towards healing was in many ways even more hair-raising than those final days of his old life. Why didn't I realise this would be so? Because, as usual, I was too spiritually stupid to see the situation in all its dimensions. And also because at the time of the stabbing I was so euphoric at the thought of Mrs Mayfield finally being brought to justice . . .

II

Mrs Mayfield was at first not to be found, but the police arrested Asherton on the night Gavin was stabbed, and they searched his house before all the evidence of his criminal activities could be destroyed. I made sure of that; I told the police exactly what Gavin had said to me before he passed out.

As for Gavin himself, he remained in intensive care for several hours after the stabbing, and apart from the police only Nicholas, pushing his special status as a clergyman, was allowed to see him. But on the following afternoon the ban on visitors was lifted and Nicholas suggested to me that we went together to the hospital after work. By that time I was incapable of working anyway. Quite apart from the fact that I was beside myself in case Gavin had a relapse and died, I was also in a frenzy about Mrs Mayfield. The police had searched both her Lambeth house and the Pimlico house that belonged to her close friend, but to my horror she once again appeared to have vanished without trace.

On reaching the ward we learned that Gavin was only allowed one visitor at a time, and Nicholas, who had seen Gavin that morning, suggested that I should be the one who went in first. I had bought a small bunch of flowers, nothing overpowering, but as soon as I entered the room I realised they would be almost invisible beside the enormous cluster of chrysanthemums which were glowering in a corner. This lavish display had obviously been organised by the mysterious Susanne, Mrs Mayfield's secretary, whom Gavin was now claiming as a friend. I had not yet met this female. Lewis had collected her in his car on the previous evening and she was now staying at the Rectory, but when I had arrived at my office that morning I was told she had already departed for the hospital. I was now braced to meet her, but a nurse informed us that 'Gavin's girlfriend' had gone down to the cafeteria to get some food.

I was unsure what the word 'girlfriend' meant in this situation, and I found it strange he had never mentioned her. I had questioned Nicholas but he had been vague. However, Alice had been more forthcoming, and when she had told me Susanne liked cats and seemed a little shy, I had at once pictured a mousey little fluffette with a crush which Gavin had been able to manipulate to his own advantage.

'In you go, Carta,' Nicholas was saying as we reached the small side-ward where Gavin was recuperating. 'Remember, don't press him for information – he'll have had enough of that from the police.'

In I went. Immediately Gavin, ashen-faced and hooked up to various lines, opened his eyes and drawled: 'So what kept you?'

We laughed, but then I found I had nothing to say. A shaft of emotion converted me into the dumbest of dumb blondes, and the next moment I saw that he too could find no words to express his feelings. The mask of the debonair hero slipped and I saw only his fragility. There were shadows like bruises below his eyes.

He stretched out his hand and I clasped it as I set aside my flowers and sat down on the bedside chair. 'In the end,' he said after a while, 'yours were the only phone numbers I remembered – and you wouldn't have given them to me, would you, if I hadn't done the fundraising . . . Yeah, it's all been part of the journey, hasn't it, that journey you mentioned when I didn't want to listen. Look, I'm sorry I just treated you as shag-meat in the beginning, I didn't realise you were a gift – a life-saving gift, as it turns out—'

'You were a gift too, Gavin, identifying Mrs Delamere as Mrs Mayfield.'

'Mrs Mayfield!' he said with scorn, but I noticed how he looked away as if fearful he might betray the complexity of his emotions. 'Hey, did they nick her yet?'

'Not yet, no.'

'I'm sorry I lied to you about her, but I loved her and I thought she loved me.'

'I understand,' I said, but I didn't. I couldn't imagine him loving Mrs Mayfield, and to distract myself I asked: 'Why did you never mention Susanne?'

'We hated each other till last weekend. I hated her because unconsciously I was jealous – she'd got out of prostitution and I hadn't. And she hated me because unconsciously I reminded her of the way she used to be.'

From some distant corner of the past I remembered Nicholas – or was it Lewis? – saying to me: 'We hate and fear in others the faults we unconsciously hate and fear in ourselves.' Enlightenment overpowered me. I think I even gasped.

'What's the matter?' said Gavin at once.

'I've had a revelation. About Eric.'

'Oh him! You know, you could do better for yourself, you really could – you should marry someone truly amazing, like Nicholas.'

I got a grip on my cosmic thoughts. 'Nicholas?' I yelped. 'A clerical workaholic long on charisma but short on spare time? No, thanks!'

Nicholas chose that moment to look into the room. 'The nurse says keep it brief, Carta.'

'I'm out of here.' I gave Gavin's hand another squeeze. 'Take care of yourself. I'll be back,' I said, and blowing him a kiss I slipped away into the corridor.

III

I was still waiting for Nicholas to finish his visit when I heard the clack-slap of high-heeled boots ploughing purposefully down the corridor, and the next moment a tall, tarty-looking piece had planted herself in front of me. 'You Carta Graham?'

'Uh—'

'You the one who dragged Gavin into all that fundraising crap and nearly got him killed?'

'I—'

'Well, great! He needed a wake-up call to get him out of the Life. Nice to meet you.'

'Nice to meet you too,' I said, silently cursing Alice for making me expect a shy little fluffette, and added in my politest voice: 'You must be Susanne.'

IV

She had pouty orange lips, black eyes and also black hair which was twisted and skewered into a topknot. Her surgically deformed figure consisted of enormous breasts, a tiny waist, androgynous hips and very long legs. Wearing black tights, a short mauve skirt and a silver-spangled sweater under a fake-fur jacket, she was flaunting junk jewellery so copious that she clinked in time to the clacking of her high-heeled boots.

Hiding my horror as best I could I said in a heroic effort to be sociable: 'Any enemy of Elizabeth's is a friend of mine!'

'Fuck Elizabeth,' said Susanne. 'It's that pinhead in there we gotta talk about. You shagged him?'

I realised honey-voiced diplomacy was a waste of time. 'Never.'

'Just checking. Seen the mums?'

'Excuse me?'

'The chrysanthemums! In his room!'

'Oh yes, very nice—'

'I brought them earlier. I've been here all day. In fact I'm going to be around in his life more and more from now on. Got it?'

'Yep. Great. Good luck.'

'You don't mind?'

'He's all yours.'

Susanne still looked suspicious. 'You do realise he's got a thing about you? Says that no matter who he shags in future you'll always be his Beatrice.'

'Who?'

'Some cow in a book. The hero's lost in a dark wood and remembers this Beatrice who represents things.' She looked me up and down as if I'd missed a trick. 'I'm surprised you don't know about the book,' she said severely, 'seeing as how you've been educated.'

'Well, I—'

'I'm getting educated right now, as it happens. Computers today, law tomorrow. Got to have a career because Gavin's not the career type, he just likes opera and boats.'

'Maybe later when he's recovered—'

'Nah. But I don't mind. Career-crazed men are usually swine – which is why I think you were smart to hook up with a bloke who just writes stories. Going to marry him?'

'Well—'

'Everyone says marriage is going out of fashion but as far as I can see people keep doing it.'

'True, but I think a lot of people are justifiably nervous about making a long-term commitment in view of the fact that—'

'*Nervous?* God, how wimpish can you get? Can't those people recognise happiness even when it stands up on its hind legs and kicks them in the teeth? Fuck all the fear-of-commitment rubbish, this is real life, for God's sake, it's not a bloody rehearsal! Well—' She turned away '—I'd better go and see what that pinhead's

387

dreamed up next. Glad to have met you, I'm sure, and I suppose we'll meet again once Gav's with me at the Rectory, but if you so much as think of shagging him you're dead, know what I mean, and don't think I'm not serious because I am.'

'I assure you—' I began, but yet again I was not allowed to complete a sentence.

She turned her back on me and clip-clopped away.

V

'Nicholas,' I said crossly as we left the hospital, 'why on earth didn't you warn me about Susanne? She's frightful! And how could Alice possibly have described her as shy?'

'She was shy when she arrived at the Rectory last night. Or perhaps "overwhelmed" would be a better word to use.'

Realising that a traumatised Susanne might have acted out of character, I said no more on that score but merely commented: 'The sooner Gavin ditches her the better.'

Nicholas looked politely interested. I knew that look. It meant he had a devastating reply to make but had decided now was not the time to offer it.

'Okay!' I exclaimed, feeling crosser than ever. 'Okay, okay, okay! I'm jealous of her because she's got him and I haven't – but this is ridiculous because (a) I hate jealous people and (b) I don't want him anyway and (c) I'm much too sensible to be so irrational, and the fact that I'm being so irrational makes me *absolutely furious!*'

'Well done!' said Nicholas amused. 'Keep going!'

'I only want to add that despite all this I'm not totally fruity-loops. I'm still capable of deciding – in a rational manner quite unconnected with jealousy – that Susanne's not nearly good enough for Gavin!'

'Fair enough, but look at it this way, Carta: even when Gavin's physically recovered, he's going to need all the support he can get when he grapples with the reality of his new life, and Susanne's presence could well be crucial.'

I saw I could not argue with this, but I was still cross enough to ask: 'What are the Healing Centre's trustees going to say when you tell them two ex-tarts are sharing the attic flat of your rectory?'

'Should anyone complain,' said Nicholas, very steely, 'I shall tell them that I'm not the bedroom police, monitoring my guests on CCTV, and that there's no reason why the Christian tradition of hospitality shouldn't be extended to two former prostitutes who want to lead a better life.'

After a pause I said: 'Right.'

'And besides,' said Nicholas, moving in for the kill, 'although marriage is the ideal for couples, I'm not about to turn my back on two people who have a valuable one-to-one relationship. As you well know.'

At that point I did ask myself why the thought of an unmarried couple should now be arousing such strong feelings in me, but unfortunately the answer seemed only too obvious: the stress of my relationship with Eric had to be twanging some very discordant strings in my unconscious mind.

I felt mortified.

VI

The news I had been longing for came twenty-four hours later. Lewis rang me at home.

'They've got her,' he said.

The whole world paused on its axis, tilted, then began to revolve at an entirely different angle.

My voice said: 'Where – when – how—'

'It was just as Gavin suspected. She waited until the police had searched her friend's Pimlico house and then she hid in the basement flat where Susanne had been living. The police made a second raid early this morning.'

Hot tears burnt my eyes and scorched my cheeks.

'Carta, are you all right? Would you like me to come over?'

But I just wanted to be alone to digest the fact that my unfinished business was finally finishing. It was as if the year 1990 – *my* 1990 – was ending twenty-three months late, and I was set free to move forward into the future. I said to Kim, whom I still thought of so often: 'You can rest in peace now,' and the moment the words reverberated in my mind the peace enfolded me so tightly that I could no longer cry.

I thought about Kim then with great clarity. It had been a rotten marriage but for a brief time we had been happy. He had been a damaged man, but he had had a good side as well as a bad side, and I had loved that good side before the bad side, nurtured by Mrs Mayfield, had destroyed him. He was part of my past, an important part of my past, but he no longer had to exist in my present as an unavenged ghost nagging for retribution and making sure I was unable to make a full commitment to anyone else. Now I no longer had to look at an unmarried couple and feel subconscious guilt and shame about my inability to cut myself loose from someone so corrupt. With the 'good' Kim avenged, the 'bad' Kim would be free to wither away, and suddenly I caught a glimpse of him existing as a benign pattern in my mind, a catalyst in a dynamic process which in 1990 had led me to St Benet's and revolutionised my life.

I stayed with my memories for a long time but at last I felt strong enough to call Eric in Norway. I had been unable to talk to him about Gavin's stabbing, and in fact it was several days since our last conversation, but I was sure I could talk to him now.

And I did talk. I talked and I wept and I got in a muddle and I apologised and I repeated myself and I thought in despair how very unlike a cool rational lawyer I was being, but in the end none of that mattered; in the end all he said was:

'I'm coming home.'

VII

After I had wasted time shedding still more tears, I said shakily, trying to strike a lighter note: 'I was afraid you might play hard to get!' I was standing at my living-room window, and below me the strip of water, which separated the Wallside houses from St Giles Cripplegate, was glinting in the moonlight. 'In fact,' I added, 'I was afraid you might finally ditch me and I'd feel compelled to take a suicidal leap into the moat here like a latter-day Lady of Shalott.'

'The Lady of Shalott didn't actually jump into a moat. She—'

'Oh God, why can't I ever get a literary reference right? What with you lecturing me on Byron—'

'Tennyson.'

'—and Gavin comparing me with Beatrice, who I suppose was someone in a Shakespeare play—'

'Which Beatrice?'

'The one who was loved by some guy who got lost in a dark wood.'

'Ah, you mean Bay-ah-*tree*-chay!' said Eric, rolling out the Italian pronunciation. 'That's not Shakespeare, that's Dante!'

'Well, whoever it was I can report that Gavin's moved on – you should just see this new girlfriend of his! She's an ex-tart called Susanne who has breasts like footballs, and she wears black leather boots with six-inch heels.'

'Anything else?'

'Dream on, pal!'

'Does she actually talk or is there a string you pull to get a pre-recorded greeting?'

'Well, as a matter of fact she made a great speech today about fear of commitment being strictly for wimps.'

'I definitely want to meet this goddess! Can we invite her to dinner?'

'Gavin would have to come too—'

'I'd be too busy ogling Susanne's cleavage to notice. Incidentally, can I finally say something rational on the subject of Gavin Blake?'

'Yes, but let me just say that I've had a blinding revelation about your past attitude to him.'

'That makes two of us.'

'You had a blinding revelation as well? Does it relate to your sexy past?'

'What a polite way to allude to my career as a toy-boy, living off women to finance my career as a novelist!'

'Well, what I was thinking was—'

'Let me tell you. I looked at Gavin, didn't I, and hated what I saw, and what I saw was the self I'd been when I was young and stupid and hurt a lot of people who shouldn't have been hurt at all . . . God, I can't believe how long it's taken me to work that out! How can I apologise enough for being so dumb?'

'I wasn't exactly the last word in intelligence myself, was I? I shouldn't have got so involved with Gavin. But on the other hand—'

'—on the other hand, you wound up saving his life and he wound up delivering Mayfield – and Susanne! Can't wait to see those foot-balls!'

'Should I get my breasts enlarged before we meet at the altar?'

'If you do, you'll be left at it. Okay, put the champagne on ice and I'll call you as soon as I reach Heathrow tomorrow.'

'I love you!' I shouted, but he had gone.

After I had mopped myself up I found I was remembering how Gavin's words had enabled me to understand Eric's behaviour, and suddenly I thought: the journey continues. I supposed that we would stay close until after the trial, at which point the road we were travelling would peter out, bringing the journey to a quiet, undramatic close.

Blissfully unaware of my total failure to predict the future, I started to wonder how Gavin was coping with the news of his Elizabeth's capture.

CHAPTER TWO

Gavin

'Yet at the same time these are the people for whom Jesus had the greatest compassion – the poor in spirit, outcasts . . . People with crippling low self-esteem, with no value or regard for themselves nor, therefore, for others; deprived, disadvantaged and damaged in their development, maybe as much victims themselves as they are perpetrators of an offence against others; prisoners within their own minds . . . locked into self-defeating patterns . . .'

A Time to Heal
A report for the House of Bishops on the Healing Ministry

'Healing is never just cure. What else it is may be either good (e.g. a sign of new life) or bad (e.g. return to function in an unchanged situation). Some people would argue for a third category, indifferent; but that is to forget that there is no neutrality within the dynamic of salvation. We are always either being saved or perishing, whether cured or not. That is the knife-edge on which we live.'

Mud and Stars
A report of a working party consisting mainly of
doctors, nurses and clergy

So they've nicked her.

Of course I knew she couldn't have got far after I removed the passport and credit cards of her new identity, but I'm told she'd already filled out a passport application for Edith Binns, which turned out to be her real name. She'd also found time to dye her hair red and take her wardrobe downmarket (beige twinset, brown skirt and granny-shoes, according to my cop-totty mole). Let no one say she wasn't resourceful when under pressure from the P-O-L-I-C-E.

Well, so much for Elizabeth. I don't want to have anything to do with her now. I just want to get on with my life. But I can't. Dimly I realise I'm in limbo till after the trial. I can't move on. But on the other hand there's no way I'll back down from giving evidence. There's got to be justice here. Not just vengeance, which is personal payback time, but justice, which rights the record for all victims everywhere. I want not only justice for myself but for Jason and Tony as well.

I know I have to focus on holding myself together, but I start feeling nervous in case Elizabeth does a sicko-psycho number. She told me once it was possible to will someone to death, and although I thought at the time this was rubbish I now find I'm taking it seriously, particularly when the St Benet's team starts to take it seriously too. Old Mr Exocet-Missile, aka the Reverend Lewis Hall, says the special prayer-group's praying to repel any psychic attack she may make, but although this is supposed to reassure me, I feel more shitbrickish than ever.

The police identify Elizabeth from the fingerprints they have on file. I never knew she'd done time, but it turns out she was jailed years ago for minor vice charges plus indecent assault on some fifteen-year-old kid. It also turns out that Asherton was fired from his former job in banking, although he never went to prison. I won't rest until he's banged up for bloody life, even though the police explain it'll be tough to convict him of the assault that put me in hospital. That's because even though I gave them the knife which had his fingerprints on the handle and my blood on the blade, he can always claim he wounded me in self-defence.

But sod that. They'll get him for multiple murder, and if I have my way they'll get Elizabeth for commissioning it. My evidence is going to be crucial in showing how the Elizabeth–Asherton axis worked. It can't be proved conclusively that she turned Jason and Tony over to him for disposal once she tired of them and/or they failed to live up to her expectations as prostitutes, but I can bear witness to the probable sequence of events. And if they can't prove she commissioned the murders, at least they can show she went along with them. She made a bad mistake when she kept that snuff movie, the video and its case both plastered with her fingerprints.

Now and then I try to imagine the trial when I get to play Gavin

Blake Star Witness, but each time my stomach lurches and I have to stop. Sorry, Mum, wherever you are, but at least you're no longer Mrs Blake now you've remarried and perhaps you can pretend to your new friends that we're not related. Thank God Dad's dead and out of it all.

Nicholas and old Mr Hall — who now tells me to call him Lewis — have asked about Mum, but I don't want to talk. Robin, the straight psychologist whom I've privately labelled Mr Pass-for-Gay, has invited me to have a chat sometime about my current situation — no delving into the past, just a survey of present hot-spots — but I'm not playing. Sorry, mates, but I've got to focus on holding myself together and I'll do it my way, not yours.

In some ways I'm not doing too badly. I've got my money — Susanne's emergency wheeze worked. I'm out of hospital and convalescing in a brilliant safe house, a large flat at the top of the St Benet's Rectory. The house itself has a full security system plus a panic-button which connects directly with the nearest police station so I feel I can relax, and soon I realise no one's coming after me anyway. With Asherton's arrest his empire's collapsed.

On my arrival at the Rectory I'm introduced to Nicholas's young second wife, Alice, a curvy piece with a nice nature. It turns out she was originally an outsider, just like Carta and me, someone who was lassoed by The Bloke and drawn into the St Benet's circle. Alice, Carta and I — we're all outsiders whom The Bloke scooped up, a tiny fraction of all the millions he scoops up globally in the daily grind of making the world come right, and so when I look at Alice I see someone special, like Carta — another companion for me on the journey.

Alice has done her duty as a clergyman's wife by making up beds in two bedrooms of the safe house, but I say to Susanne: 'Okay if we save on laundry bedwise?' and she says: 'I don't mind.' So that's all right. Being without sex in hospital has done my head in so as soon as I'm no longer one big flop I do some catching up on lost time.

It's bliss without the paid sex but weird without all the sexual activity. Even though I've got Susanne my body doesn't know what to do with itself when I'm not shagging her. It's so used to being revved up — I suppose I'm hooked on my own adrenaline, and what I'm missing now isn't the sex but the adrenaline rush. I start drinking more to calm myself down, but Susanne watches me like a cat eyeballing a mouse so I know she'll pounce if I overdo it – and I don't want to overdo it, I want to get fit and look good again, not just for my own sake but for her sake too. She deserves more than just a pathetic bloke with eating problems who turns himself into a lush.

Curvy Alice, who's a cordon bleu cook, brings me some delicious snacks to help my convalescence along, but although Susanne and I are invited down for meals in the main part of the house, I always say no. Can't face anyone except Susanne for longer than five minutes. Can't even face Carta (now reunited with Sad Eric, yuk, don't want to think of him). It takes all my energy to face the police. Have to see *them* for more than five minutes at a stretch, no choice, they keep dropping in when their investigation reveals new facts they need to talk to me about – and their investigation has just turned up a new fact which sends the media into overdrive.

The forensic teams have been digging up the floor of Asherton's S&M dungeon, and they discover that Jason and Tony weren't the only blokes he snuffed.

*　　*　　*

I suppose I should have anticipated this. I knew about the 'chickens' who were recruited for the S&M games, but I assumed they'd been released afterwards, too terrified to talk. And maybe for most of them this really did happen. But maybe others died during the games, and that was when Asherton realised making snuff movies gave him the biggest buzz of all.

Horrendous. *Horrendous.* I'm shocked to pieces all over again, and this time I feel as if someone's saying to me: 'What are you doing walking around when all these other blokes have died?' Susanne says this is survivor's guilt and I should get counselling. But I can't face that. I just blot it out by heading for a high-stress interview which I can no longer avoid.

It's time to see the Reverend Gilbert Tucker at his vicarage near Blackfriars Bridge.

*　　*　　*

I'd called Gil from hospital to say I was out of action but I'd phone him later to fix a date when we could meet. (Since Asherton had been arrested by then there was no longer any need to worry about the romp.) That took care of Gil for the time being.

When I finally make the promised phone call I cut off all his questions and just say: 'Can I come to your place at six tonight?' and when he says 'yes' I hang up. I know I'm being a coward, but in view of what I've got to do to him I can't just chat away about nothing.

I've worked out I've got to tell him everything, but I'm not being driven by sadism, I'm being driven by a desire to ensure there are some mistakes he never makes again. I've got to shock him rigid. I've got to drill it into that romantic, idealistic head of his that clergymen are too vulnerable to mess around with prostitutes, and as for falling in love with one . . . No, Gil needs to wise up fast, poor sod, but who would have thought saving him would be so painful? I feel I'm sweating blood before I even arrive on his doorstep.

Susanne comes too, just in case the trip proves too much for me in my weakened state. We take a cab to Fleetside, where the vicarage stands next to St Eadred's church, and we arrive at one minute past six. I'm carrying the shopping bag of tapes and looking as if I've just come from the supermarket.

Gil joyfully flings open the door.

He looks at me, looks at Susanne, looks back at me again. His shining eyes go dead. His smile fades. If he were a puppy his tail would stop its whizzy-wag and slump deep between his legs.

'Sorry, Gil,' I mutter. 'Sorry, but I'll try and keep it brief. Can we come in?'

When he nods, unable to speak, I add over my shoulder as I pass him: 'This is my girlfriend Susanne. Is there a place where she can wait while we talk?'

This practical question helps him get his act together. He shows Susanne into a little sitting-room by the front door and takes me across the hall into a room which is clearly his study. As soon as the door's closed I hand over the videos. He takes them out of the shopping bag one by one and when they're all on his desk he stands staring at the pile.

Then I lay the facts on the line.

When I finish he's frozen with horror and his pallor has a greenish tinge. Great. Just what I wanted. But you poor sod, I'm so sorry.

What's he going to do? If he breaks down I won't be able to stand it, I'll have to cut and run, but that'll be terrible because afterwards I'll hate myself. If only we can somehow end this with dignity—

'It's hard to find the words to thank you,' he says, bringing the agonising silence to an end. 'You were a real hero, thinking of those tapes even when you were in such danger. I'll always be in your debt.'

'No. I got you into this mess so it was right I got you out of it. You owe me nothing.'

We go on sitting in that quiet clerical study with the tapes stacked between us, the remembrance of pornographic times past, but at last he says: 'The best thing of all here is that you've stopped selling yourself. That's what I've prayed for ever since we met.' He hesitates but manages to add in a firm voice: 'I'll keep praying for you, of course, and I wish you every success in your new life. I hope you'll be very happy.'

I don't even try to comment on this. Worried about him breaking down, was I? Shit, *I'm* the one on the verge of being the water-fairy here. Standing up I mumble idiotically: 'Thanks, mate. Good luck. Cheers.'

Then I'm out of that study, I'm collecting Susanne, I'm leaving that house in double-quick time before Gil can reduce me to rubble.

'You were right,' I say to Susanne as we collapse into a cab. 'Breaking hearts is a shitty activity.' I feel as if someone ruthless has handed me a pair of spectacles which makes it impossible for me now to see people as mere lumps of meat. My capacity for empathy's been stretched so hard I could yell with the pain.

'I suppose that so long as I was denying my own pain I was denying other people's,' I say. 'Or was I trying to take my pain out on those other people? But perhaps that's just saying the same thing in a different way.'

'Huh?'

'Nothing. I just wish I could talk to Nicholas about Gil but I can't, it would be a breach of confidence.'

'Oh, stop worrying about that stupid Gilbert! He'll wake up, realise how bloody lucky he's been and make sure he gives all tarts a wide berth in future. Happy ending.'

I suppose she's right. But I still wish Nicholas could learn about Gil's mess somehow and give the poor bastard a helping hand . . .

*   *   *

The next day I receive a letter addressed to Mr Gavin Blake, St Benet's Church, London EC2, and at the bottom of the envelope someone's printed PLEASE FORWARD, as if the writer has no idea I'm living at the Rectory.

Unfolding the letter I read: 'Hi Gav – I read the news in the papers, oh God all those bodies, who'd have thought he really did do snuffies, I nearly barfed all over my newspaper – listen, I didn't grass you up, I swear it, I never even found those brochures under the floorboard, I swear that too – well, I swore it to Elizabeth, but oh God that made her crosser than ever – she screamed at me to get out before she got Asherton to fix me, so I packed up, but when I was leaving I heard her on the phone, she was in her bedroom, nowhere near the office where Susanne was, she – Elizabeth, I mean – she was talking to Asherton, telling him to come and get you, saying you had to go the same way as Jason and Tony, and oh God of course I tried to call you, but you must of switched off the phone at Austin Friars or maybe you weren't picking up, and when I tried to call the house later, the line was dead, I suppose Tommy did something to it to stop you dialling 999, and oh God I never had your mobile number, did I, so there was no way I could get in touch, but Gav I was in agony, truly I was – maybe I should of gone to the police but I'm so nervous of being fitted up – I did call them anonymous but they probably thought it was a crank call and anyway by that time it was probably too late – oh God the relief later when I found out you'd survived, I just broke down and sobbed until my mate at the pub, the one I'm staying with, threatened to throw me out, and I didn't want that, specially as I don't know how I'll ever get another job, but never mind, all that matters is you're safe, but Gav I just want to say one thing more and that's this – I know you thought Elizabeth loved you but she didn't, I was the one who loved you and always will for ever but you don't have to see me again, that's okay, though if you want to write me a line to my mate's address (see above) I'd be ever so happy to hear from you and maybe we could have a drink sometime because you're a great bloke, the best, and don't let anyone tell you otherwise, take care, NIGEL.'

I sigh, remembering those cosseted days when my clothes were always clean in the closet and nutritious meals were always waiting for me at the right time in the kitchen. I remember too how Nigel nobly let me have charge of the zapper when we watched mindless TV together. I'll miss him.

But the information he provides is too important not to pass on to the police. Sorry, Nige, I know you've got a police phobia, but they've got nothing on you this time and you're not about to be banged up again in the perv-wing of a horror jail. Showing the letter to Susanne I say: 'Here's a witness who heard Elizabeth ordering my murder.'

'You'll never get that silly little shit to testify!'

'He'll do it for me if he's sure the police won't fit him up for kiddie-fiddling.'

'If I had my way I'd see he was fitted up for life!'

'But he put all the paedo stuff aside! He fell in love with me instead!'

'Only because he knew you'd never want to have sex with him.'

I have an uncomfortable feeling this is a shrewd insight, but I don't pursue it. Instead I write back to Nigel: 'Dear old friend, thanks for your letter. Good to know you're safe. It's okay, I did realise you told Elizabeth as little as possible and wouldn't have grassed me up over the brochures. About the job: don't sell yourself short. You're a great valet. Go to a top domestic agency. I'll give you a knock-out reference.

'Now listen, Nige. It's all very well you saying you love me, but do you love me enough to testify about that phone conversation you overheard? And the answer had better be yes. Think of all those bodies at the Pain-Palace. And remember: I was nearly one of them.

'Please help, mate. I'm counting on you. Love GAVIN.'

Then I pick up the phone.

*   *   *

I'm not so good after Nigel's reminded me of my old life. To calm myself I play my favourite tenor aria from *The Magic Flute* and yes, it's still beautiful and yes, one day I'll enjoy listening to it again, but I can't enjoy it now, it just splits my head open to reveal the black pit of unwanted memories. To try to get relief from my excruciating tension I avoid the booze but find I can't stop myself sneaking into the kitchen and cutting my forearm with a paring knife.

Disaster. Susanne catches me with the blood flowing and the knife in my hand. She knows just what it means and she's furious. 'If you ever do that again I'll walk out!' she shouts, and I'm so rattled I have to throw up my dinner but I do it very quietly and she doesn't hear.

I make a new effort to hold myself together. As soon as my body can take it I start going to the gym – not my old gym but another one on the northern edge of the Barbican. This improves me physically but mentally I'm still so clobbered that when I'm home I can hardly do anything but watch TV. Dimly I begin to realise that this is what I want – it stops me thinking. I get nervous, thinking of the future. I get sick, thinking of the past. All I've got is this weird, idle present, but at least Susanne's here to share it with me.

Susanne's got a job manhandling a computer for some outfit in the City and she comes home for lunch to make sure I eat. I can't even think about getting a job until the trial's over. I need all my strength to stay in one piece.

In contrast Susanne's not only got a job but she's developing a hobby – she's asked Curvy Alice to teach her how to cook. Susanne approves of both Alice and Nicholas, but she doesn't like Lewis. Interestingly she doesn't think he's a repressed gay, but she says he reminds her of some of the punters she knew – lots of interest in hetero stuff but no real empathy with women.

I'm just thinking I'm doing better, successfully holding myself together as I drift towards Christmas, when the bomb drops. Nicholas stops by one evening and tells me Carta's getting married in January.

*　　*　　*

'That's wonderful!' I exclaim, smiling radiantly as soon as I'm told the news.

But it's not. I feel churned up. I don't want her to marry that red-headed tosser. To tell the truth, I don't want her to marry anyone. I've faced up to the fact that she's not for me but I don't want anyone else to have her either. I want her to be sacred, precious, set aside like a sort of nun, someone whom I can visit every now and then, someone I can rely on to be constantly there for me at all times.

Of course I can't disclose any of these headbanger's thoughts, but I feel sad. Well, more than sad. I feel angry with myself for not being a better man, the kind of man who could hook a golden girl like Carta.

I haven't seen much of her lately. Not her fault. I still can't cope with the fact that she got back together with Sad Eric – now Cool Eric, Eric the Winner – and I can cope even less with the prospect of her marrying him. In fact the whole situation makes me want to run around smashing things. But I don't. I binge and throw up instead.

To my horror I now find I'm missing the Life. Of course I never tell anyone this. But I feel so powerless now, whereas in the Life I had power by the cartload – the power to make a lot of money, the power to control those poor sods who paid me, the power to walk into glitzy shops and buy top-of-the-range clothes. I miss all the boosts to my self-esteem too – the boost of hearing my clients gasp that I'm drop-dead sexy, the boost of being told I'm bloody good at what I do, the thrill of hearing Elizabeth croon that I'm wonderful, adorable, the apple of her eye. Okay, I know this is all pathetic, but the trouble is I haven't yet figured out a substitute for this crap and meanwhile I'm feeling I'm nothing any more, just a sad-sack loser who does little else but watch TV because he's so shit-scared of falling apart.

I know I ought to talk to someone about this, but I'm too frightened of how the conversation might go. Supposing prostitution's all I'm good for? Supposing I have to go back to it to earn a living but can't hack it and go nuts? Supposing—

'How are you doing now?' says Nicholas when I've finished lying about Carta, and I know he's giving me the opportunity to talk if I want to. But I can't.

'I'm fine,' I say. 'Brilliant. Better every day.'

But I'm not. I'm getting worse. Eventually Susanne catches me vomiting and I swear I won't do it again but she says I've got to see Dr Val. Val says it might possibly help if I have a chat with Robin, but I say no, no, I'm fine, and everyone backs off again.

'I'll be better after the trial,' I insist to Susanne. 'After the trial I'll finally be able to relax and then everything will be terrific, just as it should be.'

Susanne says nothing.

I start to panic. Supposing she leaves me? How would I survive? Even as I pine for Carta, I know I can't live without Susanne, the girl who tells me I'm not shit – although by this time she must be thinking I am.

In a frenzy of insecurity I start to worry about sex. Am I shagging her too often? Is she secretly thinking oh God, not another fuck? Is she longing to be shot of me altogether?

In agony I mutter: 'This okay for you?'

'What?'

'Me wanting sex.'

'I don't mind.'

'Because if I'm being a pain—'

'I'd say so.'

'You really don't mind?'

'Oh, stop twittering and start shagging!'

This is hardly rapture, but on the other hand Susanne isn't the rapturous type. I decide she's not on the point of walking out but she needs to be encouraged to stay, so the next morning I sneak off to Hatton Garden, where all the jewellers hang out, and buy her a gold ring with a diamond attached.

'What's this for?' she says suspiciously.

'Just saying thanks for putting up with me when I'm such a nerd. Thought a diamond might compensate.'

'You mean it's real?' She takes the ring from the finger of her right hand where she rammed it a moment ago, and stares reverently at the stone. 'Or have you gone back to your lie-a-minute routine?'

I show her the receipt. She nearly passes out when she sees the price.

'That's ever so nice,' she says dazed. 'I've never had such a present. Ta.' Then she pulls herself together. 'But don't do it again till you're earning,' she says sternly. 'We need to be able to afford the right property when the time comes to buy a home.'

I note the 'we' with enormous relief. I'm safe for a while yet, but at that point I start to worry in earnest about how the hell I'm going to earn a living, and half an hour later I'm throwing up again.

God, what a mess I am! Maybe it's time to ask the St Benet's people for help, but no I can't, I can't – if they take me apart how do I know they can put me back together again? And I've got to be in one piece for that trial.

In despair I finally ask The Bloke for help. I hate asking him for another favour when he's already saved my life, but if he could only ease the stress somehow I'd be so grateful . . . I ask for a little extra piece of hope to take the edge off the intolerable despair.

*　　*　　*

Susanne has a brilliant idea. She looks up from studying the property pages in the *Sunday Times* and says: 'I don't think we should wait till spring before buying our home. The housing market might

403

start to recover and right now there are real bargains to be had in Docklands at rock-bottom prices.' So we drive east out of the City to Docklands to take a look.

It's still little more than a giant building site, abandoned when the recession hit, but some of the blocks of flats on the river are finished and the views are stunning. Then Susanne reveals she has a bigger vision than a mere flat on the river. 'There are new houses,' she says, 'just off the river on one of the old docks, and each house comes with a mooring space. You could have your boat.'

I'm electrified. I've been handed a dream which could come true. I feel as if I'm standing in a desert after the rains have arrived for the first time in years, and I know the tap marked HOPE has been turned all the way on.

I'm going to survive, I know I am. I mustn't give up, mustn't despair. Everything'll be okay in the end, everything's going to work out . . .

*   *   *

No one's keen on my plan to move out of the Rectory in the new year, but Nicholas promises he does understand that working on the house will be more fun for me than watching daytime TV, and I can hardly wait now to get my own place.

London's about to close down for the Christmas/New Year skive-off, but Susanne says we'll make an offer on the house now in case the builders hike their prices on January the first. I leave the nego-tiating to her and she drives a hard bargain with the terrified estate agent. The house has four bedrooms, two bathrooms, a large living dining-room, a back garden the size of a tablecloth, and the mooring space. I stand on the edge of the dock and gaze at the water and dream till I'm dizzy.

Then I have to come down to earth and make decisions about Christmas. I'm tempted to accept the invitation from the Darrows to Christmas dinner, but in the end I turn it down. Can't face all the food. Too afraid of bingeing. I also feel that memories of past Christmas dinners at Elizabeth's favourite hotel in Bournemouth can only be blotted out by watching mindless TV non-stop.

So Susanne stocks up with chilled food from Marks and Spencer, I stock up with some videos of recent movies, and we prepare to spend the holiday on our own.

But next Christmas, of course, it'll be different. Next Christmas I'll be normal – I'll have 'come home to my true self,' as Nicholas puts it. Next Christmas will be after the trial, and after the trial my new life will finally begin . . .

Or will I freak out tomorrow and fuck up my life all over again?

No, don't think of that, don't think of it, don't think, *don't think*, DON'T THINK—

CHAPTER THREE

Carta

'Everyone knows the harsh reality of suffering . . . It is that part of the human condition, as philosophers might say, which unites everyone in knowledge and understanding, sympathy and commitment . . .'

A Time to Heal
A report for the House of Bishops on the Healing Ministry

'Words like "healthy" and "healing" are always limited by their contexts. For example, healing may refer to the mending of a physical wound or of a relationship. Something is healthy if it is functioning as intended. A healing is the removal of an obstacle to health.'

Mud and Stars
A report of a working party consisting mainly of doctors, nurses and clergy

I

By the time Christmas arrived I was so worried about Gavin that I found it hard to concentrate on the tasks of sending cards and buying presents. After he had turned down the invitation to Nicholas's birthday party on Christmas Eve, I said urgently to Lewis: 'You and Nicholas have got to do something about Gavin! You must help him – you absolutely must!'

'But Carta, he has to want us to help him. Until that moment comes all we can do is be there for him and give him every possible support – which naturally includes prayer.'

'Yes, yes, yes, but isn't there something active we can do?'

'Prayer is not a passive activity.'

I wanted to shriek with frustration.

Since prayer was something I found difficult I decided I should focus instead on supporting Gavin by being friendly and encouraging. This was harder than it might seem because he was living as a recluse, and although I had made several suggestions that we should meet, he had turned the invitations down. I had concluded that Susanne was being jealous, determined to cut me out of his life.

However, Christmas afforded a new opportunity to be friendly. Since I now knew who 'Beatrice' was I bought him the latest paperback edition, complete with scholarly introduction, of Dante's *Divine Comedy*, and in order to enter fully into the spirit of Christmas I even bought a Santa Claus coffee-mug for that impossible cow Susanne. Armed with the two gifts I arrived at the Rectory flat after work on Christmas Eve, but Susanne opened the door and I was not asked to come in. Even though Gavin had turned down the invitation to the party that evening, I thought he would at least be prepared to see me for five minutes if I arrived with gifts.

'Sorry,' said Susanne flatly. 'He's resting.' As an afterthought she added: 'Thanks for the prezzies but we haven't got you anything because we weren't expecting anything.'

I opened my mouth to say that didn't matter, but the door was already closing noisily in my face.

I retired fuming to Wallside.

II

'I was talking to Lewis about Gavin's current predicament,' remarked Eric as, still fuming, I changed into a smart outfit for the buffet supper which was to mark Nicholas's fiftieth birthday. 'As Lewis sees it, Gavin's undergoing such an enormous and stressful change after giving up prostitution that he's got no energy left over for socialising – all his strength goes into beating back the new dangers. Lewis reminded me of the story about the man who had a demon cast out only to find that seven new demons had jumped in to fill the empty space.'

'Sounds familiar. Who was the storyteller?'

'Jesus Christ.'

I uttered a gargling sound to indicate self-disgust. 'God, I must do some serious studying – what a rotten Christian I am—'

'You know something? You seem to think that if you say that often enough it lets you off the hook of trying to be better informed!'

'Rubbish! I just feel that no matter how hard I study I'll still be spiritually stupid – I'll never be a whizz at prayer, never do anything fantastic in church, never be a spiritual genius—' I decided I had chosen the wrong dress to wear. In exasperation I peeled it off and flung open the wardrobe doors again.

'No problem!' Eric was saying, his amusement making me feel more exasperated than ever. 'I enjoy you pretending to be a dumb blonde – it revives my macho side!'

'Since when has it needed reviving? Damn it, what am I going to wear for this party?'

'The sexy ice-blue number with the cleavage.'

'My push-up bra shrank in the wash . . . Oh, how I wish Gavin was going to be there in his best Armani suit!'

'What's wrong with me in my best Top Shop number?'

'Nothing, you fruity-loop! All I meant was—'

'Wait a minute, I never finished that story about the seven demons and its relevance to Gavin's current situation. What the story's doing, you see, is stating in old-fashioned religious language a well-known psychological truth: if you cure an addict of one addiction, he'll immediately get addicted to something else unless you get at the root of why he needed to get addicted to anything in the first place.'

I forgot the rival merits of Top Shop and Armani. 'You can't be saying Gavin's addicted to prostitution!'

'No, just the money and the big high from all the endorphins generated as the result of over-exercising. (That's sex to you and me, sweet pea.)'

'My goodness, I'd never have guessed!' I said sweetly. 'Thanks for explaining!'

'Well, as you're so keen to play the dumb blonde—'

'Ugh! I feel a scream coming on—'

'Okay, here's the bottom line: the cash and the buzz create a powerful anaesthetic for Gavin, and once there's no more prostitution there's no more anaesthetic either – which means—'

'—there's a big hole in his life—'

'—and nature abhors a vacuum. Ideally his true self should now take charge and push him towards a better life, but since this true self is probably still as damaged as ever, another distorted way of life and another anaesthetic may well take him over. He could start to hit the bottle or do drugs – or he might even be tempted to go back to prostitution. The real problem hasn't been solved, you see. The damage which has caused all this mess and pain hasn't been healed.'

'He's got to get into therapy!'

'Maybe. But don't forget that when I was washed up as a toy-boy Gil saved me not with psychotherapy but just by being there, caring for me without being sentimental and allowing me to recover my self-respect.'

I thought about this for a long moment before saying, 'In that case I wish I could see how to play the Gil-role here.'

'Maybe you just have to keep travelling on the journey so that Gavin can know where the path is. Then perhaps one day you'll find he's travelling alongside you again after his detour in the dark wood.'

'You mean I'm to be a sort of ambulating streetlamp?'

'Well, I agree it's not the last word in glamour, but—'

'Even a small torch can be life-saving.' I retrieved the black dress which I had jammed back in the wardrobe. 'I think I'm going to wear this after all . . . Or shall I?'

'Why not just go in your underwear and say you're practising for your honeymoon? Incidentally, talking of the honeymoon, did that travel agent call you back yet?'

The conversation veered abruptly from Gavin's trauma to our own. Getting married this time around, I had decided, was nothing less than an endurance test designed to drive even the sanest couple up the wall.

III

The problem was that this second wedding of mine was much more like a normal wedding than the first one had been. Kim had had no family, and my own family, for various reasons which had seemed sensible at the time, had not been invited. We had had no one to please but ourselves and had kept the event as brief as possible. This time around, both sets of families were not only attending the ceremony but were ruthlessly giving us advice on everything from the guest list to the choice of hymns. I had now reached the stage where I wanted a quick ceremony at St Benet's with a couple of witnesses in the dead of night followed by a long honeymoon on the other side of the world.

However, Christmas is no time for feuding, and early on Christmas Day Eric and I drove down to Winchester to spend two days at his parents' house. Fortunately Gil was also going to be there; his Guild church was closed over the holiday. Indispensable at family gatherings, he soothed his tiresome mother, played with his young nephews and niece, and even managed to talk to his boring brother Athel, the oldest of the three sons, about the pros and cons of the single currency. He could also chat to his formidably intellectual father about early English history, discuss Tuscan recipes with Athel's dreary wife, neutralise any outrageous remark which Eric made out of sheer nervous tension, and clear up any wreckage which resulted when the children got into fights.

'You're amazing, Gil!' I said to this paragon at the end of the afternoon on Christmas Day when I entered the kitchen to help myself to some more coffee and found him vigorously cleaning the stove. Everyone else had either passed out after eating too much or was watching television in a stupefied silence. 'A real Christian role model!'

He gave a brief smile but said nothing, and once I had refilled my coffee-cup I looked back at him. He was cleaning the stove as if his life depended on it.

Suddenly I found myself saying: 'Is anything wrong?'

'Just my whole life. But never mind, we all go through bad times.'

I was shattered. In a very discreet, very private way I hero-worshipped Gil. I thought he was the ideal gay priest and I admired him so much for having the courage to stand up for his convictions. I knew very well that clergymen were not plaster-cast saints but ordinary people with their own problems, but it was still a shock to be told his life had taken a wrong turn.

Uncertainly I said: 'Is there anything I can do?'

'You can pour me some of that coffee.'

I found a clean mug and as I filled it he said:

'It's all my own fault, a self-inflicted mess.'

'How do you mean?'

'Not sure I can talk about it. I don't think I have the right to ask you not to tell Eric.'

410

'Gil, I'm a lawyer. A confidence is a confidence. If you don't want me to tell anyone, even Eric, then of course I won't.'

We sat down at the kitchen table with our coffee. I was so disturbed, wondering what he was going to disclose, that I barely heard his indistinct opening sentence.

'I made a fool of myself with the wrong man,' he said. 'I was in debt before I met him, and he was the kind of man . . . the kind of man you want to spend money on. But even now the affair's over I'm so far in debt that I'm going to have to ask Dad to bail me out – not the best of situations, but my credit's exhausted, I've been borrowing from church funds and unless I get two thousand pounds in double-quick time I'm going to be in serious trouble.'

Without hesitation I said: 'No need for your father to know. I'll put up the money.'

'My dear Carta, I didn't mean – you mustn't think—'

'No, I did realise you weren't fishing.'

'But—'

'Listen, I'm going to be your sister-in-law. I've money to spare. I'd be happy to help. What's the problem?'

He was unable to speak. Leaning forward with his elbows on the table he shaded his eyes with his hands.

I remembered how inadequate I had felt trying to help Moira in her fraught emotional situation. I felt equally inadequate now. Awkwardly I asked: 'Have you talked to your spiritual director yet?'

'I sacked him when I chucked celibacy. Maybe I should now sack myself by chucking the priesthood.'

'Gil!' I was horrified.

'I feel such a failure, such a sham—'

'But you mustn't feel that way, you mustn't!' Reaching across the table I grabbed his hands as he let them fall from his face. 'The fact that you've had a disaster doesn't mean you're not still a good priest!' I said rapidly. 'And if you leave the priesthood you'll be compounding the disaster, it'll be a victory for the powers of darkness – oh God, how melodramatic that sounds, how hard it is to find the right words to express such a crucial reality—'

'No, the words are right but I'm beyond responding to them. I can't go on, I'm finished.'

'You must talk to Nicholas. He likes you, he respects you, I know he'd want to help—'

'If he knew what I'd done he'd never respect me again.'

'Okay, don't tell him, but at least get him to recommend a spiritual director! Why don't you go and see that marvellous nun of his?'

'She's a Roman Catholic. She'd be anti-gay. She'd just push the celibate line at me.'

'Nicholas wouldn't think so highly of her if she were that inflexible! Gil, you can't drop out without at least trying to get help! Please – do it for my sake if not for your own!'

He swallowed, and when I saw the tears in his eyes I realised he needed privacy. 'Let me just get my chequebook,' I said. 'At least I can solve your financial problems even if I can't sort out your spiritual ones.' And I went upstairs to my room.

When I returned he was still slumped at the table in front of his mug of coffee, and as I sat down again opposite him he said in despair: 'I can't accept a loan from you, I really can't. It'll allow me to straighten out the church funds, but I've got so many other debts – it would take forever to pay you back—'

'I don't give loans. That's the quickest way to ruin a relationship. This'll be an extra Christmas gift.' I wrote a cheque for the amount he had mentioned, handed it to him and said firmly: 'Happy Christmas, Gil.'

He tried to speak but it was too difficult. He had to wait a moment and try again. 'The words "thank you" have never seemed so inadequate.'

'But they're all that needs to be said.' In an effort to divert him from the cheque I asked: 'How did you meet this guy who proved to be such bad news?'

'Through a mutual friend.' The cheque was still trembling between his fingers but as I watched he folded the paper and slipped it into his pocket. 'The trouble was,' he said, 'he wasn't just some run-of-the-mill hunk with no table manners. He was an absolute stunner – so sexy, so handsome, so smart, so amusing – but he was also a five-star heartbreaker incapable of loving me in any way that could have made a real relationship possible. God, how I despise myself for being pathetic enough to fall for him! I've never felt so horribly humiliated.'

And as I heard this uncanny echo of Richard Slaney's suffering I knew exactly who the heartbreaker was and why Gil's debts had spiralled out of control.

IV

At once I saw I had to stop him realising I had guessed the truth. It was bad enough for him that I knew he had picked the wrong man. If he realised I knew the man was a prostitute, this repulsive fact would lie like a corpse between us and putrefy our relationship. At that moment I could not have explained why this should be so; I only knew instinctively that my assessment of the situation was right. It seemed there was an invisible line marking off how much I was prepared to tolerate when I was faced with a clerical aberration – and yet the line upset me because I felt it shouldn't exist. I was a liberal, benign towards gay priests and more than ready to declare that the Church was being unrealistic in its expectation that they should be celibate. So, logically, I could only call myself a hypocrite as I now recoiled from the mess Gil had made of his private life.

This time I could not even convict myself of jealousy because he had been to bed with Gavin and I hadn't. When Moira had been trashed I had still been in the grip of my sexual attraction to Gavin, but I now found Gavin's extreme vulnerability was the very reverse of a sexual turn-on. The strong feelings he aroused in me – compassion, protectiveness, empathy with his sufferings and a burning desire to help – were by this time so extensive and so deep that lust, whether repressed or sublimated, barely got the chance to flicker.

But if lust wasn't colouring my negative response to Gil, what was? I thought the answer to this question would emerge as I digested the disaster, but no rational explanation presented itself. I also found I was increasingly worried about Gil as he struggled on, battered and burned out, with no one to help him. I had no intention of ever betraying his secret, but one day early in the new year I was disturbed enough to seek an interview with Nicholas after work, and when we met in his study at the Rectory I said: 'Can we talk about Richard Slaney?'

Naturally Nicholas was surprised by my request, but after raising an eyebrow for a second he said: 'Of course!' and invited me to continue.

'I've been bothered by one of the issues Richard raised,' I said. I had been planning this opening manoeuvre very carefully. 'Not the gay issue – that was no problem. It was his humiliating infatuation with Gavin that was the chiller, but why? We're all capable of making bad choices in our relationships, so as a rational, logical, thoroughly modern liberal, why can't I accept Richard's rotten choice without automatically thinking "yuk"?'

'Because what you're actually saying to yourself is: "Screwing people for money is wrong", and you're entitled to say that, it's an acceptable moral position. Just because you're a liberal doesn't mean you have to throw all your moral values out of the window.'

'True.' The next manoeuvre was tricky; I had to turn the subject from straying laymen to straying priests, but the switch had to look unpremeditated. Carefully I said: 'I do realise I shouldn't be judgemental about Richard. After all, it's not as if he set himself up as a role model for leading an integrated life, is it? He wasn't, for example, a schoolmaster – or a priest. I know I'd find it very difficult not to be judgemental about a priest who wound up in the kind of mess Richard was in.'

Nicholas said without batting an eyelash at this transition: 'Any priest, heterosexual or homosexual, who uses a prostitute is certainly behaving unacceptably and needs help.'

'But even if I found out a priest had been using a prostitute, I shouldn't be judgemental, should I?'

'Ideally no, but you'd be only human if you felt angry and disillusioned. Priests have a responsibility to practise what they preach. Of course we all fail in some way or other and we all need forgiveness, but none of us should be surprised if laymen get upset by clerical behaviour which is just plain wrong.'

My nails were digging into the palms of my hands by this time but I made an immense effort to sound casual and detached. 'Well, this isn't really relevant to Richard,' I said, 'but you've got me interested in this clerical angle. Supposing there's a hypothetical gay priest, and supposing this hypothetical gay priest goes off the rails and gets involved with a hypothetical male prostitute. Is that the fault of the priest's spiritual director?'

'No, it's the fault of the priest. The first thing someone who goes off the rails has to do is face up to what he's done and not blame it on anyone else.'

'Ah,' I said, and with dread realised I was unsure what to say next.

'Unfortunately once a priest starts going off the rails he may well ditch his spiritual director out of guilt and try to go it alone,' added Nicholas to help me along, 'and that's usually a recipe for disaster.'

'I can imagine.'

We sat thinking about hypothetical gay priests having hypothetical disasters with hypothetical male prostitutes. I was still desperately trying to work out how I could move from the hypothetical to the actual, but much as I longed to blurt out: 'Gil's in desperate trouble – please help,' I knew I could never do it.

I suddenly became aware that my clasped hands were white-knuckled, but before I could eliminate this giveaway body language Nicholas murmured vaguely: 'Gay priests are under a lot of pressure these days, and the stress makes disasters easier to happen. In fact I know a gay priest,' said Nicholas, picking up a pen and beginning to draw on the A4 pad in front of him, 'who worries me very much. He has a demanding ministry and an unsatisfactory private life and he works too hard. It's a classic recipe for burn-out.'

I held my breath.

'Too many vulnerable priests like him wind up in trouble . . . but that needn't mean they're bad priests. Often they've just been sliced up by the cutting edge of reality – and that can happen to any of us, can't it? It happened to me in 1988 when my first marriage broke up. It happened to you in 1990. One gets sliced up and stressed out and then the disasters start to multiply.'

I slowly expelled my breath. A few feet away Nicholas was close to finishing his quick sketch and I saw he had drawn a cat. Nicholas was very fond of cats.

'If Richard Slaney had been a priest,' he said, 'you'd have a right to feel angry when you learned he'd been using a prostitute. But after a while, perhaps, you'd come to see this stress-related behaviour was the result of deep unhappiness, and although you'd still want to say "yuk" you might well remember your own experience of being mangled by the cutting edge of reality – and having got that far, you might also find to your surprise that the forgiveness you want to feel is then possible because you'd have the empathy and understanding to put the painful situation in the right perspective.'

We sat in silence while Nicholas put whiskers on the cat. Then I said: 'That's helpful. Thanks.' And having counted to five I added very, very tentatively: 'This gay priest you're so worried about—'

'As a matter of fact I've been meaning to talk to him for some time but I never got around to it. I'll give him a call.'

'He ought to see your nun. But as she's a Roman Catholic he probably thinks she's inflexible about gays.'

'I'll put him straight.' Setting down his pen he smiled at the unintentional pun and at last looked at me directly. 'I'm glad your hypothetical case reminded me of him.'

I nearly passed out with relief.

But the moment I was able to set aside my anxiety about Gil I found I was free to start worrying again about Gavin.

VI

Soon after Christmas I heard that Gavin had paid a deposit on a house in Docklands, the area of London worst hit by the collapse of the property market. I could understand his desire for a place of his own but I thought it was unwise of him to commit himself to buying a house when his situation was so far from settled, and I blamed the witch-bitch for egging him on to shell out his money. I was now more consumed than ever by the conviction that she was determined to cut me out of his life and that his removal from the Rectory was the next step in her master plan.

I was just wondering if Susanne was keeping him locked up, like some character in a horror novel, when I caught him slinking through the main hall of the Rectory one morning on his way to the gym; I had deliberately left the door of my office open so that I would see him if he flitted past. Shooting out of my chair I reached the hall before he could open the front door.

I wasted no time on casual chat. 'Did you know that Susanne's been refusing to let me speak to you?'

He looked embarrassed. 'I'm not much good with people at the moment,' he said unhappily, eyes averted, and at once I felt stricken. So the decision not to see me had been his and not hers. I felt guilty for pestering him and furious with myself for feeling as rejected as if we had been lovers.

'Sorry,' I mumbled, 'I only wanted to help but I see now I'm doing the opposite.'

He said, oddly shy: 'I'm always glad to see you. It's just that I don't have the energy for socialising, but of course after the trial it'll be different.'

'After the trial,' I said. 'Yes.'

There was an awkward pause before he asked: 'How are the wedding plans going?'

'Stickily. Eric says it might be better to run away and get married on a beach in the Caribbean, but neither of us can bear to give up St Benet's.'

'Susanne and I are getting married,' said Gavin casually, 'but don't tell anyone – it's not official yet.'

'Great! Happy ending.'

'Yeah, brilliant!'

We exchanged delighted smiles.

'Well,' said Gavin, opening the door, 'I'll be on my way. Gotta keep fit.'

'Flex those pecs!'

'You bet!' He slipped out.

The door closed.

Sinking down on the nearest chair I wondered when I had last felt so depressed.

CHAPTER FOUR

Gavin

'Life is lived as if in a dream because reality is hell, and the face smiles as if to prove nothing is wrong.'

A Time to Heal
A report for the House of Bishops on the Healing Ministry

'We perceive evil differently as a child, as an adolescent and as an adult . . . Not only individuals but whole societies may grow or regress in their understanding of evil.'

Mud and Stars
A report of a working party consisting mainly of
doctors, nurses and clergy

I don't know when I've last felt so depressed. Why did I tell that braindead lie to Carta about getting married to Susanne? Because I don't want Carta to know how much I mind her getting married to that flabby heap of red curls. Because I want her to think I'm a normal bloke, capable of coping with a wife-scene. Because . . . oh stuff it, stop being so pathetic.

Of course I want to marry Susanne and at least try to be a normal bloke, but she'd never agree to it. She's got plans which don't include me. She must have. That's why, when I gave her the ring, she never brought up the subject of why blokes give girls diamond rings, and I certainly wasn't going to bring it up when it was plain she wanted to pass the ring off as just a piece of extravagance. I'm useful to Susanne at the moment, that's all. I'm good for free board and lodging plus a sex life, and the cat doesn't have to worry about where its next bowl of Whiskas is coming from. But after the trial they'll both be off. Susanne doesn't really want to live in Docklands with a loser

418

like me. That's just a fantasy she's created to help me along.

'What's up with you?' she demands the evening after my conversation with Carta. We've just watched *EastEnders* and I'm still staring like a zombie at the screen.

'Saw Carta today.' I zap the volume to mute.

'Oh, bugger that wonder-woman! Why can't she leave you alone? Every time you see her you get upset!'

'She says she and Eric are tempted to get married on a beach in the Caribbean.'

'So what's stopping them? What does it matter how you get married so long as you do it? I'd do it anywhere!'

I perk up. 'Didn't know you were interested in marriage.'

'Why the hell shouldn't I be? I suppose you think an ex-tom's not good enough to be married, but let me tell you, Mr Middle-Class-Surrey-Snotty-Snob, I want the lot – husband, kids and a nice home with a Jacuzzi and one of those oak kitchens with a whatsit in it!'

'What's a whatsit?'

'The big thing that's always hot.'

'Sounds like a randy husband.'

'It cooks as well as it heats and it's on all the time—'

'A useful randy husband.'

'Oh, stop clowning around and tell me what it's called!'

'An Aga,' I answer obediently, but I'm hardly aware of what I'm saying. I'm hypnotised by the thought of Susanne seeing a husband in her long-term future. But of course she's not thinking of me, can't be. She'll be angling for one of those filthy-rich Essex men, dripping with gold medallions and draped in naff leisurewear and drenched in putrid aftershave.

'Women have to slave to get a man to marry them,' she's saying as I morosely picture Del or Tel or whatever her future husband's likely to be called. 'If a man can get away with a live-in shag he will, but if a girl's got a line on her face or if she looks like a pig she never even gets to do a live-in. It's bloody unfair.'

'Well, you can't blame a bloke for not wanting to shag something pig-like, and lots of blokes do get married, don't they, I mean it still happens—'

'You'd never do it!'

'Oh yes I would, but who's going to look at me now and see a potential husband?'

419

'You serious? You have the bloody nerve to sit there, looking like a film star, and say—'

'But I want someone who understands what goes on beneath the looks!'

'Oh, women love doing that, they'll be falling over themselves to understand you, you'll find some cream-and-peaches, college-educated, middle-class—'

'You're totally hung up on class, you know that? But the class system's dead as a dodo!'

'God, another of your fantasies! Listen, I'm a realist. You'll marry Peaches and I'll have to make do with some East End git who's migrated to Chigwell—'

'I'd fight him off.'

'Not if you were married to Peaches you wouldn't!'

'I'm not marrying Peaches! How could she ever understand what I've gone through?'

'You won't want to think about what you've gone through!'

'But how could I ever forget? No, my wife's got to be someone who can accept both me and my memories, someone who's always going to understand, someone who's brave and tough and smart and sexy and dances to "In the Mood" better than any other girl on earth—'

Susanne screeches: 'How dare you wind me up like this? I'll kill you!'

I zap the picture, roll over on the couch and grab her to show I mean what I say.

*   *   *

'We'll do it after the trial,' I say as soon as we come up for air, 'and preferably on a beach.'

'Okay, but it's got to be a real wedding, just like in films and on telly, and on second thoughts, forget that beach rubbish. I want a church, I want a long white dress, I want flowers, I want music—'

'Hey, wait a minute, this is all getting much too complicated—'

'Typical man – shitting bricks at the idea of a decent wedding! Okay, forget it, I never thought you were serious anyway.'

I promise her a white wedding in church – after the trial – and an Aga in the kitchen.

*   *   *

I'm so dazzled by all these plans for the future that I barely notice when Carta marries Eric and sets off on her honeymoon. They did invite us to the wedding but of course we didn't go.

By this time I'm longing to do some preliminary shopping around for my boat, but I decide to rein myself in. I need to keep the remainder of my capital intact until I figure out how I'm going to earn my living. I tell myself I'll make a decision on my future career after the trial. Everything's on hold till after the trial, everything. After the trial I'll do this, after the trial I'll do that, after the trial I'll—

And suddenly the trial's upon us.

My eating habits have been better but now they go to pieces again. We moved into our house in March as soon as the builders had finished it, and I've kept my anxieties at bay by embarking on a demanding DIY programme – bookshelves, fun lighting, a little office for the computer – but now everything comes to a halt. I feel as if I've been breathing clean pure air on a mountain-top but someone's just sneaked up behind me and pulled a black bag over my head.

The trial's going to take place in the number one court at the Old Bailey, and if you're talking criminal law you can't get more mega than that. Visiting the courthouse beforehand, I stand outside and look up at the golden statue on top. It's Justice – or rather Justice Personified. Decked out primly in classical draperies she's blindfolded as if she's taking part in some sinister S&M game, but she's got a sword in one hand and a pair of scales in the other so you know she's no pushover. She gleams in the sun, like the gold cross on top of St Paul's Cathedral, a stone's throw away, and she dominates this side of Ludgate Hill. Old Bailey is the name of the street where the courthouse stands, but a lot of people don't know that. You say 'Old Bailey' and everyone thinks: criminal courts, the ones where the big horrors get aired.

Asherton's been charged after all in relation to my stabbing, even though there were no witnesses and even though he's bound to say he stabbed me in self-defence. But the Crown Prosecution Service is much more interested in nailing him for that incident when I was starting out with Elizabeth and had to be taught the lesson in obedience. It turns out that this lesson was recorded on tape, although I never knew it. (I was blindfolded a lot of the time or else granted only limited vision.) Anyway, the tape was neatly filed under BLAKE in Asherton's S&M library. Brilliant! Of course Asherton will counter-charge that I was into S&M and consenting to everything, but the tape will be so revolting no one will believe him, particularly when the prosecution points out I had no connection with his S&M group and never did S&M parties when I was a prostitute. At least the tape will show how Asherton tortured waifs and strays – it'll be a big nail in his coffin as he tries to wriggle out of the charge of murdering Jason and Tony and the other poor bastards who wound up buried in his dungeon.

I can't wait to testify about what that villain did to me. Put me on that witness stand and he'll be totally fucked. And so will those Big Boys who carried out the 'choreography' of sadism he 'designed' for me. They're all talking now, all betraying him and betraying Tommy in their desperation to avoid murder charges. Tommy's still insisting he was never involved in the filming, but there are too many witnesses to say he was, and he'll go down for a long, long time. He'll never say a word against Elizabeth, though, because she owns him body and soul. *I'm* the one who's going to nail Elizabeth as I testify to the Asherton–Delamere axis. Nigel will be backing me up, but he's a fragile witness, and it'll be left to me to make sure the prison door slams shut.

Carta would like to testify too, but there's no hard evidence now which would prove Elizabeth was implicated in the criminal mess which destroyed Kim Betz. My evidence from the safe that she was involved with GOLD was certainly helpful to the police, but it wasn't enough for them to reopen the Betz file. Luckily Carta accepts this. She says at least I came up with answers to the questions which had been tormenting her, and at least Elizabeth's being brought to justice.

When I look back now at my life with Elizabeth I see it all with abnormal clarity, as if I'm a bystander watching this woman for the first time. I hear all her cosy little endearments and her relentless stream of euphemisms which translate the vile into the acceptable. I see her making shopping lists for Nigel and trundling off to the hairdresser, I see her wearing frothy negligées, odes to conventional femininity, I see the gleam in her eyes as she plays bingo at that arch-conventional hotel in Bournemouth. I'm even watching her chatting idly with Norah over Sunday lunch about the Royal Family. It all seems so normal – normal to the point of banality. Who would have thought that evil would present itself in such a banal way?

Even Asherton looked like a typical City suit. More creepy still, he knew all the right people – he slithered in and out of those smart clubs and houses and was always judged, as old Mrs Thatcher used to say, 'one of us'.

It makes me realise that evil's not just something out there in another country. It's crawling all over everywhere, constantly, but most of the time we don't see it, can't see it, don't dare see it because it's too bloody frightening. Not everyone has the balls to look evil straight in the eye and name it, as Colin did. But Colin always saw the wood from the trees, didn't he? He only faltered with me, but he didn't falter for long. Once he realised I was conning him he kicked me out of his life. I know now I never saw Colin as he truly was – I just saw him as meat to be manipulated and mocked. But he had his principles and he saw the truth. He was one of the good guys.

The trial, blitzing into the media like a comet colliding with the Earth, catches up all our hidden fear of evil and exposes the dreaded darkness to the light. It dawns on me that this is part of justice. You bring in the light and the darkness recedes. The more light you bring in the less dark there is. The Bloke's the light, and he wants everything that's now dark to be made light – he wants everything to be healed and redeemed, yes, I see what he's getting at – or at least I think I do – it's a sort of vision where reality is both now and not-yet . . . And meanwhile here we all are at the Old Bailey, and Ms Justice, with her sword and scales, is finally on the loose.

My hour's come. I feel like a French aristocrat two hundred years ago. Up I walk to the guillotine – and there's Madame Defarge, longing for my head to bounce into the basket.

But I'm going to be all right. It's Madame Defarge's head that's going to roll. Walking into the witness box with The Bloke right behind me, I finally turn my back on all the years of lying and swear to tell the truth, the whole truth and nothing but the truth.

And I do.

*   *   *

The part I'm ashamed about now is how I secretly loved being the centre of attention as Gavin Blake Star Witness. I hated myself for loving it, but you see, it made me feel powerful again, it was like taking a holiday from being a worthless drop-out. In my temporary fairy tale, crafted and hyped up by the slavering media, I was still high-octane sex personified, the superstud who shagged men for outrageous sums of money by day and shagged gorgeous girls for free by night. The conservative wrinklies were writing disgusted letters to the *Daily Telegraph*, the middle-aged liberals were simpering in the *Guardian* that I was a 'free spirit' (yeah, pull the other one, you silly wetsies) and the voices of Yoof Culture (a bunch of dorks brain-mangled, obviously, by E) were gabbling incoherently on TV that I was cool. Looking back I can see clearly how unreal all this hype was, but the escape it offered enabled me to get through my ordeal without cracking up.

Did I ever feel a twinge of sentimental nostalgia when Elizabeth and I were together in that courtroom? No. To get through that trial I had to shut out all the emotions she roused in me, even the most trivial – I even avoided the risk of being overwhelmed by taking care never to look her in the eyes. It was Nicholas who gave me this tip. He said she had such a powerful and malevolent personality that she would try to hypnotise me and break my will if I gave her half a chance. So I just sneaked glances at her now and then when she was looking the other way.

Although I knew she'd changed her appearance, it was still a shock when I saw this grey-haired, dowdy-looking woman who looked as if she was the pillar of her local church. I just couldn't connect this run-of-the-mill granny-figure with my steamy, curvy, ageless, blonde *femme fatale* – and this was good. It made it easier for me to shut down the emotions which might have slaughtered me on the witness stand.

Carta made things easier for me too. She was always there, her presence giving me courage, and as our paths merged again after the months of separation I thought: I'm finally ending that unfinished business of hers. She's been crucially important to me and now I'm being crucially important to her.

So the trial achieved its purposes, both the obvious ones and the private, hidden ones, but it's all in the past now. It's over.

Asherton and Elizabeth go down for life for multiple murder, for the attempted murder of me at the end of my Lambeth life and for that bloody assault on me at the beginning of it – and 'life' is going to mean life and not a fifteen-year stretch with full remission for good conduct. Asherton's judged guilty but nuts, so he winds up at Broadmoor, the top-security hospital for the criminally insane. It's Elizabeth who goes to prison, though of course she's not sane either, can't be. However, apparently you've got to be more than just a psychopath to get a meal-ticket for life in a place like Broadmoor.

For three days after the end of Elizabeth's long career as Mrs Pass-for-Normal, I'm badgered by the media but I give no interviews. I know it's time to fade into obscurity, the male Cinderella who's heard the chimes at midnight and has to pad home in his sweatshirt and jeans from the ball. The tabloid press froth at the thought of my memoirs and a famous PR man offers to handle the negotiations, but I turn down all the amazing sums of money I'm being offered. I can no longer be the person these vampires think I am, and anyway the word 'vampire' hardly does justice to their pervy greed. They even expect me to reveal the names of my clients! Don't these slimeballs understand that I was always famous for my discretion? No, I'm having nothing to do with them. I know better than anyone else by this time that when you sup with the Devil you need more than just a long spoon to survive.

Luckily the media monsters soon move on to their next vat of blood and they stop camping outside the Rectory where Susanne and I and the cat have been staying during the trial. We're finally free from all the hysterical scrutiny. It's celebration time. After we've moved back home to Docklands, Susanne and I knock off a bottle of champagne, make love for hours and wake up still in ecstasy.

'This is the start of my new life!' I yell, bounding out of bed and flinging back the curtains. 'I'm going to get married, buy a boat and live happily ever after!'

An hour later I'm having a complete nervous breakdown.

CHAPTER FIVE

Carta

'Furthermore, at some points of Christian growth people can find themselves 'blocked' . . . (perhaps) with a deepening awareness of the need to address an event, maybe from years previously.'

A Time to Heal
A report for the House of Bishops on the Healing Ministry

'The essence of sin is "other people telling me who I am and I believing them". Collusion with inauthentic images of myself can only be a denial of the irreducible originality of the given self, and thus an offence to God. In this sense sin is linked to a great deal of ill-health; for to believe and to enact a lie about myself, however unconsciously or for whatever noble motives, can only be conducive to sickness.'

Mud and Stars
A report of a working party consisting mainly of doctors, nurses and clergy

I

I first heard something had gone wrong with Gavin in the summer of 1993. I had survived my wedding (unexpectedly enjoyable), my honeymoon (well up to expectations) and the initial weeks of married life (not much different from unmarried life as Eric was on a creative binge and spending most of his time at the studio). I had also survived the trial. What I was having trouble surviving was the last lap of the St Benet's Appeal. We needed another fifty thousand to cope with rising costs and unforeseen extras, but I was suffering from fundraising fatigue and felt exhausted by the thought of this extra mountain to climb.

On the morning Gavin became ill I was sagging in my office swivel chair and wondering again how I could restart my campaign. Having done almost no work during the trial I was feeling oppressed by guilt, and the buzz of the Rectory intercom came as a welcome diversion.

'Susanne's just phoned,' said Alice upstairs. 'Gavin's had some sort of collapse. Nicholas and Val are on their way out to him.'

I was stunned because this was the last thing I would have predicted. At the onset of the trial Gavin had become a peculiarly sanitised version of his old self: charming, confident and extroverted but with his language cleaned up and his hypersexual aggressiveness tuned out. I had assumed he was finally on the mend and that the trial would be as much a catharsis for him as it was for me.

I had wanted to be at the Old Bailey every day, and through the Crown Prosecution Service team I had managed to arrange that two seats were reserved for me in the public gallery. Realising how traumatic it would be for me to see Mrs Mayfield again, Nicholas had insisted that someone should always come with me, and in fact he himself was at my side at the end. When Mrs Mayfield stood in the dock for sentencing, he reached out and took my hand.

I saw judgement passed upon her for her crimes.

Her smooth, surgically altered face was eerily expressionless, but she looked up at the public gallery and stared not at me but at Nicholas. He stared back, and she was the first to look away. Then she glanced at me but her time in the dock had run out and she was taken away, taken out of my life for ever. When Gavin and I met up afterwards we flew into each other's arms and wept, like the survivors of some huge disaster.

Yet now he had collapsed. As Alice told me this latest news I began to realise that although I was home and dry at last after my long ordeal, Gavin's ordeal had merely moved into a different phase.

'What exactly happened?' I demanded.

'I'm not sure. Susanne didn't say much, just asked Nicholas to come over as soon as possible.'

I called the house in Docklands.

'Oh, it's you,' said Susanne, sounding neither friendly nor unfriendly but merely businesslike, as if she were making one of Gavin's appointments. 'He's not available, he's gone unsociable again. Sorry.'

'Alice tells me that Nicholas—'

'He just left. All that praying stuff's weird – imagine talking to

God as if it's a person! It's almost as creepy as Gavin talking about that Jesus thing-y as if he lived just down the street.'

'*Does he?* I mean, does Gavin—'

'Yeah, mental . . .'

Since the traumatic events surrounding Kim's death I had actually thought long and hard about Jesus Christ, although of course I had never said so. One hardly wanted to be mistaken for some fanatical born-again, and anyway I had always felt that actions spoke louder than words; embarking on a totally new life had, for me, said all there was to say. But now I wondered if my reticence was further evidence of my spiritual inadequacy. If even Gavin could chat away about—

'. . . so Val wants to get him to a hospital . . .'

Abruptly I tuned in again to the rasping in my ear.

'. . . but Gav says he won't go, he's afraid of being zombified and his head rearranged without his permission.'

'For God's sake! How did all this come about?'

Susanne's willingness to explain probably indicated how rattled she still was. 'I'd taken another day off so that we could get settled back at the house,' she began, 'and we were in the supermarket doing a big shop when suddenly some bloke bumps into him by accident, nothing major, just a short brush-past, but the next moment Gav's white as frigging snow and starting to pant. Off he runs, and when I follow I find he's flung himself into the car and he's doubled up in the passenger seat with his hands over his face and he's sobbing and shaking like he's totally lost it. Which he has. Course I could see it coming a mile off. He was so hyped up fighting evil and seeing justice was done that now the trial's over he's crashed.'

'But this is a catastrophe!'

'No, it's a nervous breakdown, I know, I had one. They take between six to nine months usually, maybe even a year. Then you're okay.'

'Yes, but—'

'In the meantime Val's given him some tranx – good ones, not head-shredders, and—'

'But he must see Robin and have therapy!'

'Nah, forget it. Gavin says he can only see men who are ultra-straight and even then they mustn't be allowed to touch him. All the gays have done his head in, poor bastard, and now he can't bear to think of anything connected with the Life – the reaction's hit him with a mega-thwack and he's zapped.'

428

I was so appalled that I could only mumble how sorry I was. But although later I wrote to Gavin to send sympathy and offer support, he was apparently too ill to reply.

II

He was ill all that summer, unable to leave his house, unable to socialise, unable to do anything except watch television in his bedroom with the blinds drawn. Val found him a good local doctor, a woman who, like Val herself, at first recommended a short period of hospitalisation so that his case could be assessed and a more sophisticated drug therapy prescribed, but Gavin remained deter-mined not to leave his house and as he was non-violent and non suicidal there was no question of compelling him.

Lewis eventually took over from Nicholas as Gavin's primary carer from St Benet's. Nicholas was overwhelmed that summer by his private life; his ex-wife was pestering him for help because their elder son had fallen in love with a lap-dancer while the younger one had dropped out of a legal training in order to start up an alternative comedy magazine called *Bog*. Eric said soothingly to Nicholas that this was very normal behaviour for two well-brought-up males who were under twenty-five, but I could hardly blame Nicholas for looking harassed. Alice, who was still not pregnant, confided to me that she thought Nicholas ought to change jobs and move well away from London before he too had a nervous break-down, and I found he was heaving nostalgic sighs at the thought of his family manor house in the south-west. But I couldn't see him stepping down from St Benet's when he was still in his prime.

Meanwhile, as Nicholas floundered around with his family, over-worked as usual at the Healing Centre and indulged in escapist dreams of his old home, Lewis had the time, the freedom and the single-minded dedication to attend to Gavin. He started to visit the Docklands house twice a week, and soon after this visiting pattern had been established he reported that Gavin wanted to see me.

This was fortunate as I now had a special reason for wanting to see him.

I had just had an extraordinary interview with Sir Colin Broune.

III

The return of Sir Colin Broune to the St Benet's scene began with a phone call from his secretary.

'The St Benet's Appeal office,' I droned as I sat slumped at my desk in front of the morning's post, but before I could go on to identify myself, an acid-voiced contralto was enquiring if I were Carta Graham.

I confirmed that I was. My new marriage had not altered my decision to retain my maiden name at work.

'Sir Colin Broune will see you at five o'clock today at his office at number sixty-three, Old Jewry.'

'Excuse me?'

The sentence was repeated with a robotic precision which left no room for argument. I agreed to present myself, hung up and raced over to the Healing Centre.

'He must be thinking again of a donation,' I said feverishly after grabbing Nicholas between appointments, 'and we can take the money now, can't we? I mean, at this stage we know Gavin can't be pressuring him.'

'Right!' Nicholas was as enthralled as I was, but he added: 'I'm surprised he asked to see you and not me. Remember how he prefers to deal with men if he has the choice?'

'Maybe he's mellowed!' I was enraptured by the possibility that Sir Colin might end my anxiety about the final stretch of the Appeal, and in fact I even wondered if he would donate the whole fifty thousand pounds outstanding. 'In your dreams!' I muttered to myself as I returned to the office, but the vision of a monster cheque refused to go away.

Having arrived at RCPP's towering headquarters at two minutes before five I was directed to a lift which rocketed me straight to the top floor. Here I spent a restful ten minutes while I watched the acid-voiced contralto toying with her latest computer behind a wraparound desk suitable for controlling the universe.

At last I was escorted to the chairman's office, the ultimate corporate status symbol. Floor-to-ceiling windows faced the dense architectural jungle of the City where modern skyscrapers crowded around the elderly fortress of the Bank of England. Classical paintings, all no doubt of breathtaking value, clung glumly to the walls.

An oak desk, huge, plain and square like its owner, stood marooned amidst an ocean of pale gold carpet. The top of the desk was bare, signalling that the chairman was so perfectly in control of his empire that clutter was something which could only happen in the offices of other people, far away on a distant floor.

'Good afternoon, Miss Graham,' said Gavin's former client, drawing a veil over the memory of that weekend at his country house when we had addressed each other informally.

'Good afternoon, Sir Colin,' I said, taking care to look respectful but not intimidated.

He mangled my hand and invited me to sit down but I was not offered any refreshment. Nor did he indulge in small-talk. When we were seated, I in a wing chair uncomfortable for anyone under six feet tall, he in a swivel chair which plainly hoped to be a throne when it grew up, he simply said: 'The events of the trial reminded me of that famous saying attributed to Edmund Burke: "All that is required for evil to triumph is for good men to do nothing." I did nothing after that weekend house party, even though I realised Asherton was pushing views that should be opposed by all right-thinking men no matter whether they believe in God or not. But in the weeks since the trial I've been thinking about what I can do to put right my omission.'

He paused. I thought: my God, this is it, he's going to give.

'While meditating on the situation,' pursued Sir Colin, 'it occurred to me that at the trial Gavin Blake showed a great deal of courage. It also occurred to me that in the end it was the people of St Benet's who helped him, while I merely washed my hands and moved on. There's a message for me there, I feel, Miss Graham, and I trust I'm not so deficient in honesty that I'm unable to read it.'

As he opened a drawer of his desk and took out an envelope, my heart banged so loudly that I was sure he must have heard it. The numbers five and zero were trying to mate in my brain, a triumph of hope over cynicism.

'You were a personal friend of Gavin's, I remember,' he said abruptly. 'You met him through Richard Slaney, who was one of your fellow partners at Curtis, Towers.'

I somehow achieved a nod.

'That's why I asked to see you and not Darrow. As a personal friend of Gavin's you will, I hope, agree to deliver this letter to him – and don't put it in the post, it's too important, I want to make sure it's delivered into his hands. If you could do this for me, Miss Graham, at the earliest opportunity, I'd be extremely grateful.'

The golden rule for all fundraisers is never offend a millionaire, not even when all you want to do is fling back your head and scream with disappointment.

'Yes, of course, Sir Colin,' I said smoothly. 'I'll go to his house as soon as I can.'

That closed the interview. Not only was there no stunning donation but there was not even a morale-boosting token gift. I was merely a convenient minion selected to deliver his special mail. Perhaps I could get a job as a post-person when I finally flaked out of fundraising.

Poker-faced I offered my hand for re-mangling and abandoned him to his empty desktop.

IV

It was on the evening after my interview with Sir Colin that Lewis rang to say Gavin had asked to see me, and when I mentioned Sir Colin's letter Lewis suggested we should go together to the house in Docklands.

'If the letter were to upset Gavin it might be better if I was there,' he said, and we agreed to make the journey on the following afternoon.

I had not been to Gavin's home before. It was one of twelve houses in a terrace which faced a narrow strip of water, and a few boats were already bobbing at their moorings. The area was bleak, but I could see the gulls wheeling over the nearby river, and not far away loomed the massive tower of Canary Wharf, symbolising the regeneration and transformation of this eastern swathe of the capital.

'It's London,' I commented wryly, 'but not as we know it,' and before Lewis could reply, Susanne was opening the front door.

'He's only just got himself out of bed,' she said without wasting time on preliminaries. 'You'll have to wait.' I was reminded of Sir Colin's contemptuous indifference to small talk.

The house was larger than it looked from the outside, and the living-room with its dining-area, open-plan kitchen and view over the water, had the potential to be attractive. The furniture looked as if it had been ordered from a Habitat catalogue: modern lines, primary colours, each piece simple and functional. A number of plants added splashes of greenery to the windowsills.

We sat down at the dining-table. Lewis had told me that he always conducted conversations with Gavin there so that the table could act as a protective barrier; Gavin was still deeply phobic about being touched by men.

'Gav!' yelled Susanne after she had made us tea. 'You still alive?' She dumped our mugs in front of us, and as she did so Gavin came down the stairs.

He was rail-thin and there were dark shadows beneath his eyes. His hair was longer and shaggier, suggesting that being a barber would never be Susanne's métier, but he had taken time to shave, and his sweatshirt and jeans both looked freshly laundered. I realised he had made a big effort to appear well for me.

'Gavin!' I exclaimed warmly, but found I was unsure what to do next. I knew that as a woman I was allowed to touch him, but clasping his hand in that context seemed too formal and hugging him might have been more than he wanted, particularly as Susanne was standing by.

'Hi,' he said with a fleeting smile. 'Don't get up. Hullo, Lewis.'

'Well, I'm off,' said Susanne, plonking a mug of tea in front of him as he sat down opposite me. 'Back in an hour, Gav. Cheers.' She grabbed her bag and clip-clopped out. The door banged noisily.

My instant reaction was: how does he stand it? But I repressed that thought in order to concentrate on making the right moves. I felt I had fluffed the greeting by being too tentative. 'How are you doing?' I said, trying to sound sympathetic without being oppressively caring.

'Still breathing.' He gave me another quick smile but said nothing else, and it was a relief when Lewis intervened.

'Carta's brought a letter from Sir Colin Broune, Gavin,' he said, 'and I think it must be important because he wanted it delivered by hand. Carta, tell Gavin what happened.'

I did my best but I was very conscious that Gavin was unable to look at me, and as I pushed the letter across the table towards him I was unnerved when he shrank back as if it were contaminated. To my distress I saw his eyes fill with tears.

'I'll tell you what I could do,' said Lewis crisply, exuding both kindness and common sense. 'I could read the letter aloud but slowly, so that you could easily interrupt if you wanted me to stop. The trouble is that if you don't know what Sir Colin's written, you might start to wonder about it later and that could make you anxious, particularly if you don't want to read the letter yourself.'

Gavin hesitated, nervously revolving the mug of tea between his hands, but when he at last nodded, Lewis read with numerous pauses: '"My dear Gavin, I regret the manner of our parting and I apologise for my anger. You were very brave during the trial. In fact your courage made me see not only how deeply I failed you but how all your clients should feel guilty about what happened. The truth is we colluded with Mrs Delamere. The fact that I unwittingly became entangled with Asherton is, I feel, symbolic of how easy it is to allow evil to enter one's life, and how hard it often is to recognise and reject it.

'"I understand from various reports in the newspapers that you have now abandoned your occupation. Should this be true, and naturally I hope it is, you will be looking for a job. I write to say that a place could be found for you in one of the divisions of RCPP, and I can ask the head of personnel to assess you to decide where you would flourish best. Even if you later decide the job doesn't suit you, it will at least be a beginning, a stepping-stone to a job you prefer. You and I need never meet again. My organisation is extremely large and I seldom see employees below a certain level, particularly if they are not employed at my headquarters in Old Jewry.

'"I wish to say one thing more. You were kind to me when we first met. I hope that now you will allow me to be kind in return. Yours sincerely, COLIN."'

Lewis stopped reading. Then after a long silence Gavin leaned forward and buried his face in his hands as he wept.

V

Lewis instantly turned to me but I needed no prompting. Springing to my feet I shot around the table, stooped over Gavin and hugged him. How self-centred I had been, merely seeing Sir Colin as a walking chequebook! 'This is better than any donation Colin could make,' I said strongly as I sat down at Gavin's side. 'A good job

434

with a good company – it'll be just what you need once you're well!'

Gavin wiped his eyes on the cuff of his sweatshirt and whispered: 'I could never accept it.'

I was shocked. 'But he obviously wants to help!'

He turned to Lewis. 'Explain to her.'

'It would be as if Gavin were continuing to profit from a client,' said Lewis evenly, and added before I could protest: 'But it's an interesting letter, isn't it, Gavin? Sir Colin, it seems, is rather more than just a run-of-the-mill City hatchet-man.'

Gavin managed to say: 'I'll read the letter now. But I can't touch it.' So I spread both sheets of paper in front of him on the table.

After he had stared at the handwriting for some time he said: 'It was good of him to apologise, good of him to say nice things about me, good of him to try to help. But he's got it wrong about colluding with Elizabeth. It wasn't my clients' fault that all I could do to make a living was sell myself.'

'It's right that you should want to take responsibility for your actions,' said Lewis, 'but it's right too that Sir Colin wants to take responsibility for the part he played in keeping you in business. And it's especially right that he should now want to make amends by stressing that you're brave, that you deserve better in future and that you're worthy of support and encouragement.'

But Gavin could only comment: 'I still can't accept his offer.'

I opened my mouth to argue but Lewis pushed my foot to shut me up.

'Very well,' he said to Gavin, 'but would you like me to write to him that you're not well and won't be job-hunting for a while? You might feel the letter requires some kind of response.'

'Yes, but I'm the one who's got to respond – he'd be furious if he knew someone other than me had read all that.' Retrieving a pad of notepaper and a pen from the nearby desk he sat down again at the dining-table and eventually, after several false starts, he produced a note which read: 'Dear Colin, I appreciated your generous letter. Thanks. But I'm ill now and not job-hunting and I feel RCPP wouldn't be viable anyway. Sorry. GAVIN.' At that point he paused, chewing the top of his pen for several seconds before adding rapidly: 'PS. It's not Aids.'

'That's thoughtful,' I said.

435

'They all worry about it. I worried about it.' As he looked at me directly I saw all the emotional damage reflected in his eyes. If the damage had been physical, the eyes would have been bruised and bloodied. It was eerie how a person could be so hurt yet have no scars to show for it, just the haunted expression of extreme pain stoically endured. 'I've had my final Aids test,' he said to me. 'It was clear. I'm all right. I'm going to live.' Tears spilled down his cheeks again as he turned his head sharply away. 'I was so afraid of getting it,' he said. 'So afraid. All the time.'

I hugged him again, and as he leaned trustfully towards me I thought how we had clasped hands at the Healing Centre, I thought how we had clung to each other after Mrs Mayfield's sentencing, I thought of all our nerve-jangling encounters when we had been exploring our relationship as fellow travellers, deeply and mysteriously connected, on a journey neither of us could have foreseen.

He said: 'Please don't wash your hands of me.'

And I said: 'Never. I'm here for you and I'll go on being here for you.'

'The people I loved in the past either went away or never loved me back.'

'I love you, Gavin. I won't let you down, I promise.'

We sat there at the table in that quiet room, and Lewis, utterly still, sat opposite us. Outside the sun was shining and seagulls wheeled across the flat landscape in a flicker of arcs bleach-white against the blue sky.

'I often wondered what it would be like to have a sister,' said Gavin, 'but of course I only had a brother.' Releasing my hand he rubbed his eyes and began to fold the letter he had written. 'Lewis wants me to talk about my family,' he added, 'but it's hard.'

'I sympathise – I always find it hard to talk about my family too. My father was a compulsive gambler and that created endless problems when I was small.'

'Then I feel lucky,' said Gavin, 'because when I was small I had no problems.' He sighed before adding painfully: 'Hugo was the most wonderful brother to me. I had wonderful parents and a wonderful home. Everything was wonderful, but the trouble was I couldn't hold on to it, I wasn't good enough, it all just slipped through my fingers.'

'But why didn't someone hold on to you?'

'What do you mean?'

'Well, my mother held on to me. She kept me from being taken into care when my father made a mess of our life in Glasgow. She married again and moved to Newcastle because she saw that as the chance to give me a decent home. I would have slipped through her fingers if she hadn't hung on so tightly, and if I *had* slipped it wouldn't have been my fault. It would have been hers.'

Gavin thought about this but finally shook his head and said: 'You were probably a terrific kid and worthy of all those efforts your mum made. But I wasn't. I just couldn't measure up.'

'To Hugo?'

'To everyone.'

'All those wonderful people who weren't wonderful enough to see you were slipping through their fingers? Ugh! Pardon me if I puke! If they left you feeling that everything was your fault, there's something seriously wrong with your definition of "wonderful"!'

Gavin's expression was at first shocked but then, reluctantly, enchanted. With amusement he said to Lewis: 'She's not like a therapist, is she? No therapist would be that outspoken.'

'I can almost hear the mewing as Robin has kittens.'

We all laughed before Gavin said carefully to me: 'As you're not a therapist, you won't try to rearrange my head, will you?'

'No, I just want to rearrange the heads of all those wonderful people. Preferably by banging them together.'

'Then I'll talk to you,' he said. 'I'll tell you about my family.' And at last, often pausing to fumble for the right word, he began to speak of the past.

VI

'Let me make one thing clear from the start,' said Gavin. 'This story isn't about sibling rivalry. Hugo was the best of brothers to me. We got on. I idolised him.'

He hesitated so I nodded to show him I had taken this information on board without wanting to swing a hatchet at it. Across the table Lewis was so motionless that I wondered if he was still breathing.

'In fact,' said Gavin, 'I loved Hugo so much that when he was dying I promised to live his life for him once he was dead – and I did try to do that, I really did, but I just wasn't up to it. So I broke my promise to him and I failed to compensate my parents for his loss. That was when I knew I had to go. I had to spare them any further grief.'

'Wait a minute,' I said. 'I'm not quite with you. How did you try to "be" him, as you put it?'

'I tried to read medicine. Hugo was going to be a doctor, but not just an ordinary GP like Dad. Hugo was going to be a surgeon, a Harley Street specialist, a real high flyer. Mum and Dad were so proud of him.'

'But what did you really want to do?'

'Be an architect, but Dad said I wasn't pushy enough to hustle for commissions. He said I'd be happier teaching in a private school where there were no discipline problems – and maybe he got that right. I could have spent those long school holidays sailing.'

'Why didn't you go into the Navy?'

'Dad said I was too much of a loner to make a go of it.'

'Your dad seems to have been – no, sorry, let's not get diverted. You made this doomed decision to be a doctor, you said—'

'—but it was so boring, I couldn't get interested, I failed all my early exams—'

'Well, of course you did! How could you do well at something you had no aptitude for?'

'Ah, but Hugo couldn't accept that. I'd invited him into my head so that he could enjoy me living his life for him, but when I reneged on the deal he turned hostile, and every day since then he's told me I'm shit. In fact sometimes I think he hates me so much that he'll never rest till I'm as dead as he is.'

At once I knew I could carry the conversation no further, but simultaneously Lewis commented: 'I can understand Hugo's disappointment, but he's very wrong to vent his anger on you.'

'But he refuses to accept he's doing anything wrong!'

'That's because he's not being approached in the right way.' Lewis leaned forward in his chair. 'Maybe I can help here. I've come across this kind of case before, and I know that the unquiet dead can cause a lot of problems for the living.'

'That's what Elizabeth said.'

There was a deep silence before Lewis asked sharply: 'You're saying she helped you in some way?'

'She called it psychic healing,' said Gavin in a bleak voice as I shuddered from head to toe.

VII

'I believed in it at the time,' said Gavin, 'because I was so desperate, but later I came to see it didn't work, and after that I hated all that psychic rubbish.'

Lewis said: 'I understand, but can you tell me exactly what happened?'

'I told Elizabeth about Hugo and said: "I've tried drink, I've tried drugs but nothing shuts him up for long, nothing," and Elizabeth just said: "Leave him to me." I think she hypnotised me then although she never used the word "hypnotism" and it was all very subtle, not like the hypnotist stuff you see on TV. After we'd made love she'd massage my head and say she was smoothing away Hugo so that he wouldn't bother me any more. And it worked for a while. But in the end the effect wore off and that approach never worked again . . . I didn't tell Elizabeth, though. I was afraid she'd be angry and say it was all my fault that I'd failed to stay cured.'

I shuddered again, but Lewis was saying evenly: 'People who are sick should never be made to feel guilty if a cure isn't forthcoming. A wonder-worker on an ego trip may want to preserve his self-esteem by laying the burden of failure on the patient, but a healer working to serve God shouldn't be worrying about his self-esteem.'

Cautiously Gavin said: 'You're saying it's integrity that separates the good healers from the bad.'

'Yes, but let me stress that all healing comes from God, and God can use anyone or anything to achieve his healing purposes. However, because the ministry of healing deals with exerting power over others, it's immensely vulnerable to corruption. And if the patient puts his faith in a corrupt healer, the risk of adverse consequences is very great.'

Gavin mulled this over before asking: 'Do you think that beneath all the corruption Elizabeth had a genuine healing gift?'

'Possibly, but there's a sense in which any gift is neutral – it's what you do with it that counts. For instance, take Elizabeth's psychic gift, which she used in order to boost the healing gift she had – or which she used in order to make people think she had a healing gift. The words "psychic powers" often appear in a sinister context, but in fact there's no reason why they should be associated with evil rather than good – the powers themselves are neutral. If Elizabeth had chosen to offer her psychic gift to God so that he could use it as a force for the good, I'm sure a great many people would have been spared a great amount of unhappiness.'

Gavin did some more mulling but finally said: 'You're a St Benet's healer. You do healing right. But how do I know you'll be any more successful than Elizabeth was at fixing Hugo?'

'You don't. And I can't guarantee success. But if you want me to try to help you, I'd be very willing to give it a go.'

Gavin gave a great sigh, and when he said simply: 'Where do we begin?' I knew his journey had restarted again after the crisis which had brought him to a halt.

VIII

'The first thing to understand,' said Lewis, 'is that compulsion won't work here. In other words, we can't just say to Hugo: "Get lost!" Instead we have to establish a situation where he can see his journey back to God as a homecoming rather than an undeserved journey into exile.'

'But how—'

'Let me take a little time to think and pray about this. Then I can come up with a plan of action, but meanwhile there are some questions I need to ask. First of all, did Hugo have any other ideas about life after death apart from existing as a spirit in your head?'

'No, neither of us believed the Christian stuff about the resurrection of the body. That's just contrary to common sense.'

'So is much of the world revealed by modern physics! But let me merely say that St Paul didn't think resurrection involved the flesh. It all depends how you define "body" and in this case the word "body" is probably a codeword for the whole person, a pattern

440

produced by a certain mind, spirit and body all working together. This pattern – a pattern of information, you could call it – would be capable of being lifted from its original context and replayed in another environment. Like written music which gets to be played in the concert hall.'

I could see this intrigued Gavin but his only comment was: 'Hugo says he's more than just a pattern of information.'

'Tell Hugo that all analogies ultimately break down but they're useful if not pushed too far . . . Now, here's my next question: what did your parents think about this idea that you should live Hugo's life for him after he died?'

'Oh, I never discussed it with them! But obviously they must have been glad to see that I was doing all I could to make amends for the fact that I was the one left alive.'

I wanted to cry out in protest but I knew I had to leave the response to Lewis. Calmly he said: 'Did your parents ever come right out and say they wished you'd died instead of Hugo?'

'No, of course not! But I knew that was how they felt. Hugo was so special.'

'You never thought they might be thankful to have one son left?'

'No, not after I failed my medical exams and it was obvious I couldn't take Hugo's place. I did think of killing myself,' said Gavin as an afterthought, 'but I decided it would mean so much hassle for them, and as I'd caused them so much trouble already I didn't want to cause them any more. Disappearing seemed cleaner somehow – more considerate.'

'I understand . . . And what did Elizabeth have to say about your parents?'

'She said I was well rid of them,' said Gavin, but I could see he was barely concentrating on what he was saying. It was obvious a terrible thought had occurred to him. 'Talking of Elizabeth . . . do you think it's likely – do you suppose – could Elizabeth have decided to join forces with Hugo now to will me into total insanity, the kind you don't recover from? Am I ill because I'm being possessed by Hugo's evil spirit?'

'Absolutely not!' said Lewis robustly. 'For one thing, you show none of the signs of possession, and for another, Hugo is not an evil spirit. He's an unhappy, angry, immature spirit who's got himself stuck in the wrong place – your head – and now needs help in going home.'

Gavin sagged back in his chair but still looked shattered.

'Courage!' said Lewis, smiling at him. 'We have an interesting task in front of us! We have to help the dead rest in peace and we have to ensure the living move on towards the life they're called to lead, but meanwhile I'd like to congratulate you on taking this enormous step forward and talking of these very difficult matters. Well done! I'm extremely impressed!'

Gavin gazed at him with an expression in which hope and trust mingled with fear and dread. 'You really think Hugo will forgive me in the end?'

'We'll work at helping him understand that neither of you can be blamed here. You were both too young to know better.'

'You mean that when Hugo and I agreed I should live his life for him—'

'You picked the wrong form of healing. The promise to live his life was a magnificent gesture on your part, but it didn't heal the spiritual wounds caused by the knowledge that he was dying before his time. It only anaesthetised them by promising a future that could never have worked out.'

Gavin's face crumpled.

'We'll stop there,' said Lewis, standing up. 'I'll come back on Monday with my plan of action – unless, of course, you want to cancel. Don't forget you're never under any obligation to see me.'

Gavin nodded. Tears were streaming down his face, but before I could embrace him again he was gone, rushing upstairs to his room as if finally overwhelmed by all his pulverising memories.

IX

We waited until Susanne returned. Lewis forbade any comment on the scene while we were still in the house, but as soon as we had set off in his car I exclaimed in fury: 'Those parents of his! How could they have made him feel so unloved and unwanted?'

'That's the big question. I suspect they got bogged down in the bereavement process, but—'

'That's no excuse!'

'—but there has to be more going on than that.'

'I blame the father, browbeating Gavin out of his career choice

442

and then making no effort to stop Gavin doing medicine when he was obviously unsuited to it!'

'But maybe Dr Blake was right to think Gavin was unsuited to be an architect, and maybe he honestly believed Gavin was capable of being a doctor.'

'But—'

'Anyway, fathers often try to throw their weight around like that, it's not unusual. Far more significant, I felt, was that Gavin never mentioned his mother.'

'Obviously she was hopeless, and I still think both of those parents must have behaved monstrously!'

'Well, if that's true, he's certainly made them pay.'

'By disappearing, you mean? But that wasn't revenge! He disappeared because he couldn't go on!'

'True. But a disappearance is like a suicide. There can be a lot of hidden aggression going on.'

'Well, I think in this case the aggression was deserved! Why did they never try to trace him?'

'Maybe they did.'

'But they could trace him now as the result of the trial!'

'You mean his mother could. His father's dead.'

'All right, forget the father, but why isn't the mother beating a path to his door?'

'Perhaps she needs a little time to recover from hearing what her son actually did choose to do with his life.'

That silenced me. It took me a full minute before I was able to say: 'Sorry, I'm rushing to judgement, let's move on to something else. What did you make of all the Hugo stuff? Did you think Gavin was behaving like a nutter?'

'On the contrary, I thought he was making an excellent attempt to describe an unusual reality which is hard to put into words.'

I made another big effort to rein myself in. 'I hear what you're saying,' I said, 'and thanks to your help in 1990 I know ghosts are a psychological phenomenon often generated by guilt and grief – I know they should be accepted as a form of reality not normally accessible to us – but you don't seriously believe, do you, that Hugo's ghost has now taken up residence in Gavin's head?'

'If Hugo's ghost represents a psychological phenomenon, where else is it going to exist?'

'Yes, but—'

'Carta, we have to accept Hugo's reality here. He's very real for Gavin and therefore he should be very real for us as we try to help. My guess, based on experience, is that he'll also be very real when I pray with Gavin later and help Hugo relax his grip on Gavin's psyche. It'll be as if a real person departs and Gavin will be changed.'

We drove on in silence as I considered this assessment but finally I asked: 'How long will it take to separate them?'

'A couple of months, perhaps. It's a question of how easily Hugo can be brought to consciousness after being a repressed memory for so long, but thanks to you I think Gavin will now feel encouraged to recall him.'

'Thanks to *me*? But all I did was build a bridge which you could scramble across to begin the healing!'

'My dear,' said Lewis, 'it was you who began the healing. You enfolded him in unconditional love so that he trusted you enough to want to confide. You succeeded where Nicholas, Val, Robin and I had all been failing.'

I stared at him. 'You're saying I was accidentally lined up just right with God so that he was able to use me even though I'm spiritually stupid?'

'No, I'm saying that God is love and that you were able to present that fact to Gavin in a way that was crucially meaningful to him. Carta, isn't it time to abandon your spiritual inferiority complex?'

Not for the first time I thought how kind he was to pretend my spiritual side was other than minuscule, but I made no attempt to argue with him. After my success with Gavin – all due, of course, to the accident of my being in the right place at the right time and somehow managing to say the right thing – I didn't want Lewis to feel his flattering words had been a mistake.

Crossing the border into the City at last we headed for my house on Wallside.

X

As I opened my front door Eric emerged from the upstairs living-room to greet me. 'Not working?' I said delighted, hoping that his current draft of the new novel was complete. I was much looking forward to his next lucid interval.

'I had an important phone call,' he answered, smiling at me as he clattered down the stairs into the hall, 'and I knew I had to be at home when you got back.'

I was intrigued. 'Good news?'

'The best!' He swung me off my feet, spun me around and kissed me very smoochily on the mouth. When I came up for air I said: 'Snog-heaven. Mad about it,' and kissed him very smoochily back. I felt as if I were in the final reel of a Hitchcock film, the one where the cool blonde melts into the arms of the sexy hero and the train thunders into the heavily symbolic tunnel.

'The latest trend in high-powered eroticism: Marriage is the new Cohabitation!' declared Eric, quoting imaginary headlines. 'But don't you want to hear my stunning news?'

'I've guessed it!' I said, rapidly updating Hitchcock to the late twentieth-century world of potential scientific horrors. 'You're pregnant!'

'Help! Do I have that radiant oestrogen look?'

'Don't worry, darling, I'll take care of you. But seriously—'

'Seriously, there's terrific news and it's waiting for you in the living-room.'

'What form does it take?'

'It's six feet tall and wears a clerical collar.'

'Nicholas? Oh my God, *Alice* must be pregnant! How absolutely—'

'No, it's better than that.'

'It couldn't be.' I pounded up the stairs and erupted into the living-room with such speed that Nicholas jumped. He had been standing by the window but now he drifted towards me as if determined to appear the last word in nonchalance. Only his eyes betrayed him. They were a brilliant grey-blue, signalling that he was bursting with excitement. In his hand were two slips of paper.

'These arrived by special messenger at the Healing Centre an hour ago,' he said casually. 'I thought you'd like to see them straight away.'

I took the two slips of paper.

One was a cheque drawn on the charities fund of RCPP, and the other was a cheque drawn on the personal account of Sir Colin Broune.

Each one was for fifty thousand pounds.

CHAPTER SIX

Gavin

'Some clergy have also found the study of a family tree to be a useful means of discovering broken relationships, traumatic events and family traits as well as disowned, lost, forgotten and unmourned relatives . . . Many have found that such prayer for the healing of the past and for the peace of (the) departed . . . can bring a sense of release from oppressive influences.'

A Time to Heal
A report for the House of Bishops on the Healing Ministry

'A psychiatrist once suggested that healing involved a "restoration of the capacity to love". He might have added, the capacity to receive and accept love.'

Mud and Stars
A report of a working party consisting mainly of
doctors, nurses and clergy

Colin's finally coughed up. Talk about being anally retentive! What's that kind of money to him? Small change.

I'm not taking that job he's offered me, and Susanne's not surprised. 'Imagine old Moneybags saying you need never meet him again!' she comments. 'Once you were in RCPP he'd take a peek and once he'd taken a peek he'd want to go all the way down memory lane!'

As it happens I'm not at all sure she's right, but I do know that if I worked for Colin I'd always be dreading this scenario. Playing devil's advocate I say: 'It'd solve the job problem,' but she answers: 'What's the point of solving one problem only to end up with a bigger one?' and she reminds me that at present I don't need to worry about being unemployed. Her own job means there's money

446

coming in to boost the income from what's left of my savings. We can tick over if we live quietly, and at present living quietly is all I can do. 'You have to wait till the nervous breakdown's finished,' says Susanne, making it sound like an unmissable show on TV.

The wonderful thing about Susanne is that she never doubts that I'll get better. She did, so she figures I will. Another wonderful thing is that she never complains. When I'm first unable to go out she just says: 'Thank God I had time to get a driving licence. I wouldn't fancy doing the shopping by bus,' and when the final horror of the breakdown slugs me – impotence – she only remarks: 'Well, I suppose it's not surprising that your cock decided it needed a rest.' But the impotence crushes me. Sex is the only thing I'm good at, and now the main routine's been taken away.

'I could do injections,' I say, but I know I can't. I can't do any of those things I did in the Life, I can't, I can't, I can't . . .

I'm panicking. I know there's more to sex than just getting it up and sticking it in, but I panic anyway. That's what happens when your brain goes on the breakdown blink. It's all anxiety, fear and despair.

'How can you take this so calmly?' I yell at Susanne, but she wipes the panic off the map by shrieking: 'Because I know life can be a bloody sight worse!' In a normal voice she adds firmly: 'Now think, pinhead, *think*. We've got our own home, all paid for, we've got enough to eat and we don't have to have sex with smelly, revolting people in order to make a living. We're the luckiest ex-hookers in London! So why don't you stop whingeing and start being grateful for this fantastic new life we've got?'

I make a mental note to talk to Lewis about this insight. Trust Susanne to cut through all the crap and see the situation as it really is.

*   *   *

Some time before Carta's Great Visit, Lewis starts turning up at the house twice a week and staying for fifty minutes. Susanne says this is like a therapist's appointment where an hour is set aside but five minutes is allocated at each end for arriving and departing. He says straight away at the start of this routine that we don't have to make conversation. He likes silence, feels at ease with it, and if I can't talk he won't mind. So at first we just loaf around listening to music and nothing much gets said. He makes it clear I don't have to see him, but I always do. He's my link with the real world which I hope to get back to one day. And soon I find out he knows a lot about music. He brings me little pieces of Bach's cantatas on tape like a parent-bird producing food for the oversized fledgeling who can't bring himself to leave the nest.

After a while I find I'm talking about my nest, the house. I explain that the furniture's just a load of flatpack specials to tide us over till we can choose something better. I tell him how much I liked fixing up the house before I got ill, and how depressed I feel because I can't face doing anything now. I even tell him that when I was a kid I used to design houses which I planned to build when I grew up. Of course I wouldn't want to be an architect now because I'd probably wind up having to design things like offices, but I still like the idea of designing and building a house – or a boat. I loved my father's boat. I loved the way every inch of precious space was used so creatively. I do mention to Lewis how crazy my father was about his boat, but at this point – and it's before Carta's Great Visit – I don't want to talk about my family so I quickly change the subject back to music.

It occurs to me early on during my sessions with Lewis that he's the same age as my father would have been if he'd lived. They were both born in 1921, over seventy years ago. I'm also reminded how like my father Lewis sounds. That old-fashioned public school accent's identical and so's the timbre of his voice.

Every time Lewis visits me we take great care to avoid all possibility of physical contact. The thought of even an accidental brush with a male body reminds me of the Life and I can't bear it, I can't – if I think of what I allowed those blokes to do to me all that time I'll go mad, I'll cut myself and cut myself, I'll slice off my equipment, I'll—

Mental. I know I'm being mental, and that means I'm not so bad, doesn't it? If I was really ill I wouldn't know how mental I was. So I can tell myself it's no big deal, it's just a breakdown and I'll get better. I haven't got a mental illness where the prognosis is poor.

But sometimes it feels as if I have. Sometimes I wonder if I'll ever get better. Sometimes—

'You'll get better,' says Lewis on one of his early visits. When he was young he was a chaplain at a mental hospital so he knows about mental illness. It doesn't faze him. *I* don't faze him, even at our first session when I say straight out: 'I don't want to talk about religion.' I'm afraid he might go all fundamentalist on me and spout stuff about the blood of the Lamb, but as soon as the sentence is out of my mouth I panic. Supposing Lewis decides I'm not worth visiting? Supposing the St Benet's team loses interest? Supposing my one link with Carta gets wiped? (Can't ask her to visit when I'm such a mess.)

But Lewis puts everything right. He says: 'We don't need to talk about anything you don't want to talk about. I haven't come here to dictate to you. I'm here to serve. That means listening when you want to talk, responding when you require a response and praying with you if you should wish me to do so. I'm not a doctor, I'm not a therapist, I'm a priest.'

I'm reassured. I don't want a doctor and I don't want a therapist. I'm too scared they'll say I'm mad and need to be locked up so that my head can be rearranged and the real me destroyed. But Lewis is non-threatening. And beyond Lewis, as I gradually realise, is The Bloke, a positive force battling with the negative forces which are keeping me sick.

'I don't believe in dogma,' I say to Lewis as I try to explain how negative I feel about religion. 'I just believe in The Bloke because he actually lived and made a difference.'

Lewis says that maybe I'm a mystic. They tend to sit lightly to doctrine, he says, and illustrate that there are all sorts of ways to be religious. A great religion, he says, is never a monolith but a bunch of diverse groups catering for different psychological temperaments. Christianity caters well for mystics, although too often people in the West behave as if mysticism's only available in Eastern religions. Mysticism, I learn, means a direct knowledge of God – or a direct experience of The Bloke – or it can mean an experience, impossible to describe concisely, of the splendour of the world despite all the suffering, a sense of the overarching unity of all things. Anyone can have a mystical experience, says Lewis, even people who pride themselves on their rational, analytical minds (I think of Carta) but those more inclined to approach religion as mystics are less likely to suppress their mystical experiences and are more drawn to the challenge of exploring them.

'If mystics can tune in without any help from the Church,' I say, 'why bother with the Church at all?'

'Good question!' says Lewis approvingly as if I'd displayed a dazzling intelligence instead of a basic curiosity. 'And the answer is we need the Church as a framework to stop us getting so pleased with ourselves that we go over the top into egomania and start thinking we ourselves are God. That attitude's characteristic of religious corruption, and the dangers of corrupt religion, as Mr Asherton showed us, are very great.'

I shudder at the memory of Asherton, but to my surprise I feel better after this conversation. I feel I've got a new interest, particularly when Lewis (who's obviously a mystic himself) begins to talk of meditation. In a burst of optimism I even decide I'm well enough not to make Carta recoil in horror, and when I tell Lewis I want to see her he reports back that by coincidence she has a pressing reason for wanting to see me. He discloses no details on the phone, but it turns out she wants to deliver Colin's letter offering me a job.

* * *

Carta creams in for Her Great Visit, the goddess from another dimension. I'm pleased to see her because I know then she really cares about what's been happening to me, but at first the scene goes badly wrong because I wind up crying in front of her. Pa*thet*ic! But she was sweet and hugged me. I loathe that word 'sweet' but that's what she was – and shit, I never even got an erection! Hugged by a goddess and my equipment stays deader than chopped wood! But here's the truly amazing part – I mean, more amazing than the hug: despite the water-fairy stuff, she even . . . no, skip that. No wait a minute, I'll say it. She *even* – yes, I know this sounds like a fantasy, but I swear it's true – *she even said she loved me*. Of course she doesn't really, how could she, but she cared enough to want me to believe she does, and that's almost as good. I wanted to shout: 'I LOVE YOU TOO!' but of course I couldn't, it would have turned her off, she'd never have come near me again.

Anyway, the bottom line was that she was sweet and she cared – and yes, I know that sounds sick-making but, as I now realise, it's a miracle. It led directly to the next miracle: I began to talk about my family at last, and this marked the beginning of my big effort to get sorted.

So Carta's alongside me again. The journey continues. But surely she herself has 'come home' now? If coming home to your true self

450

means being set free to realise your full potential, what can possibly be restricting her freedom now she's finally come to terms with the past? Can't imagine, she seems so together – together enough to make her Great Visit, although I don't want to see her again until I'm sure I won't cry in her presence.

Meanwhile Nicholas has been to see me, and I appreciate this as I know how busy he is, but I'm happy so long as I have Lewis. As the result of the Great Visit, Lewis is developing a plan that'll evict Hugo from that crevice in my mind which he's occupied for so long. It's all part of my rehab, part of ensuring that I'm no longer just an unintegrated mess, lying, role-playing and brutalising myself.

I think about rehab. This, says Lewis, is The Bloke's primary job – The Bloke's not only a symbol of integration but he *is* integration, the force working to make everything whole in a world of broken fragments. God's fighting away in the chaos to bring his creation under control, says Lewis, and The Bloke is God's way of manifesting himself to show us he's not just sitting on his backside drinking Australian lager (as I've suggested) while the work-in-progress is such an unfinished junk-heap.

Eventually everything will be made good, says Lewis, even the dark vile bits, but meanwhile (as I've already worked out) it's important to line yourself up with The Bloke, the integrating force, so that you can give him a helping hand instead of being just a waste of space and/or a dark vile bit. That's where prayer and meditation come in. You've got to be lined up right with the force, you've got to journey inwards to find the right position, you've got to find the centre of yourself – your real self – because that's where God exists as a spark, and then once you're hooked up to that spark within, says Lewis, you can connect with the God without – you can turn outwards to face the world and live dynamically as part of the integrating force: a worker on the rehab job, a soldier on the Operation Redemption front, a contributor to the make-it-all-come-right side of God's huge creative splurge.

That's why it's so important to be your true self. How can you find the centre of yourself if you're busy being someone else? And even if you're trying to be your true self, how can you make progress if your mind's littered with a series of roadblocks? No, you've got to get yourself sorted – *I've* got to get myself sorted – which is why I've agreed to tackle Hugo again even though the prospect makes me shit-scared.

451

Supposing Hugo gets murderous? Supposing he decides to drive me totally insane? Supposing he makes me top myself?

I want to bang my head against the wall.

*   *   *

Lewis calms me down. He says I can forget all the blood and thunder because we're just not moving into an adversarial situation. We have to put Hugo in the right frame of mind by befriending him. That's not going to be easy because Hugo's so angry, but it's hard to stay angry for ever, particularly if one's approached with sympathy and respect.

Lewis says we should start by reviewing the happy memories of the past, so slowly I pluck them out and hold them up to Hugo for inspection. Hugo likes this. He's surprised, of course, and suspicious too but he soon gets interested. In the end he doesn't even mind when I recall the childhood memories which aren't so good, because Lewis helps me set these in a friendly context. So when I recall Hugo clobbering me in the nursery for overworking his fire engine, Hugo refusing to let me ride his new bike, Hugo yelling at me when I forgot to feed his guinea pig, Lewis and I take a moment to reflect that possessiveness about toys is common, little kids shouldn't mess with bikes that are too big for them, failing to feed guinea pigs is unacceptably absent-minded. Hugo finds these judgements very fair. 'In other words,' I say to him, 'you could be a bruiser sometimes but it wasn't often and you were never a bruiser without provocation.' And he finds this a reasonable judgement. As I say to Lewis, Hugo was basically a good bloke and the older he got the nicer he was to me. We usually played together without fighting, although that was probably because I'd discovered that the way to have a quiet life was always to let him take the lead. But then he was older and knew how.

Every time Lewis and I review memories of Hugo we pray for him. We offer the memories to God, all of them, good and not so good, and we say thanks for Hugo's life, he counted, he made a difference, the pattern he made on those early years of mine was important. I tell Lewis I'm glad I know what it was like to have a brother, and he says he envies me. He never had one. He tells me he had a weird childhood and after misbehaving on the grand scale he wound up living in a Church of England monastery run by his

452

great-uncle. I get the impression Lewis was a teenage tearaway before the word 'teenager' was invented.

'But Great-Uncle Cuthbert saved me,' says Lewis nostalgically. 'Great-Uncle Cuthbert was a monastic masterpiece.'

I'm interested in this Cuthbert bloke, but right now . . .

Right now I can only think of Hugo.

* * *

We're like archaeologists uncovering a valuable artefact. We have to expose it little by little, brushing away the earth so carefully that nothing gets damaged. And Hugo's now emerging steadily, the Hugo who was the best of brothers, generous-natured, exuberant, fun. I used to patter along in his wake, not so clever, not so sporty, paler, more serious, more introverted. 'Why can't you be more like Hugo?' my mother would exclaim when I didn't want to go to the neighbourhood kiddie-parties, but my father would say: 'Let him be. Not everyone likes to be sociable.' My mother hated any dig he made about being sociable. 'Just because you're so dull, you can't see why anyone should want to have a good time!' she'd cry, but he'd never argue with her, he'd just go into his study and close the door.

'It sounds as if your parents weren't so happy even before Hugo died,' says Lewis one day, but at once I tell him how despite the age difference they were famous for being happily married.

'He was a lot older,' I add. 'He'd been married before but his first wife was an invalid and they had no children. When she died he was chased by hordes of women, Granny said, because he was a doctor and good-looking and as the result of the invalid wife and the busy medical practice he had a sort of harassed, exhausted air which made women long to spoil him rotten. He didn't mean to break hearts, Granny said, but he couldn't seem to work out how not to. He was basically just a quiet, shy type.'

'And how did your mother capture this lethal blushing violet?'

'She was the bright extrovert who had the chutzpah to go after what she wanted and get it.'

'Did she enjoy sailing?'

'No, but Hugo and I loved it.'

'Who was the better sailor?'

'I was,' I say without hesitation. 'Hugo preferred sports that involved a ball, so I became the sailor and the swimmer. That way there was no competition.'

'Your talent for sailing must have created a strong bond with your father.'

'Yes, it did. He and I liked the parts of sailing which Hugo never seemed to notice.'

This intrigues Lewis. 'Such as?'

'The beauty of the seascapes. The feeling of being at one with nature . . . Dad talked about it once to me when we were sailing without Hugo – we were sailing down the Solent towards the Needles . . . You know the Needles, those spectacular cliffs at one end of the Isle of Wight?'

'I've seen them, yes.'

'They were looking wonderful that day. The weather was very fine, but there was a stiff breeze so we were sailing in optimum conditions, and everywhere seemed to me so beautiful. I said to Dad: "This is paradise – I'm so happy!" and when he smiled at me and said: "So am I!" everything was perfect, perfect, perfect . . . I remember that day because it was the last happy time I had with any member of my family. Hugo was diagnosed two days later. That was why he hadn't come sailing with us. He was already ill.'

Lewis offered no comment, but I could feel the strength of his sympathy.

'And I'll tell you something else,' I hear myself say, 'something extraordinary. The last time I went sailing with Richard Slaney, we sailed along that same stretch of water under identical conditions, and suddenly, just for a second, I looked at Richard and saw my father looking back – and that was so unexpected because usually the person Richard reminded me of was Hugo.'

'Ah!' says Lewis as if I've suddenly pulled a white rabbit out of a hat, and I see I've dealt him a big surprise.

* * *

'We all realised Richard was special for you,' explains Lewis, 'but we all fell into the trap of thinking you saw him as a father-figure. Can you tell me why he reminded you of Hugo?'

This was easy. 'Richard was clever and fun with lots of style,' I say, 'and so was Hugo. They didn't look alike and Hugo certainly wasn't gay, but there was still a resemblance in personality.' I pause to remember them both before adding: 'I didn't see the resemblance straight away. At first Richard was just another client. But when we were on his boat together the resemblance to Hugo hit me between the eyes – it was like having the old Hugo back again.'

'Was that when you started to hanker for the world you'd left behind?'

'Maybe.' I try to see the truth but I feel as if I'm standing in sunlight while peering back into a fog. 'Even before I met Richard,' I say, 'I used to drive down to Surrey and coast around the area where I used to live, so I suppose I was like an emigrant who gets homesick, but I never seriously thought of going back. I couldn't imagine living without Elizabeth.'

'But after you went sailing with Richard—'

'Yeah, you're right, that *was* when I began to want to go back even though I still couldn't imagine living without Elizabeth.' As I pause to peer again through the fog I find it's floating away and I can see the past more clearly. 'The point about Richard,' I say finally, 'is that by reminding me of Hugo – the good Hugo, not the angry Hugo in my head – he reminded me of all the happy times I'd had when I was younger, the times all the later misery had blotted out.'

'So Richard rearranged the past for you. He reminded you of a world where you didn't have to live a life so at odds with your true self.'

I nod as I watch the last of the fog disperse. 'When I was sailing with Richard it was as if I was back in that world,' I say, 'and Richard saw me then as I really was. Maybe that was when he fell in love with me. Before that he'd just been infatuated.'

'But what were your feelings for Richard by then? How did you feel about having sex with someone who reminded you of your brother?'

I sigh as I search for the words which will finally bury Gavin Blake Leisure-Worker, that caring bloke who performed a valuable social service. 'When I worked,' I say, 'Richard wasn't Hugo. Richard wasn't even Richard. He was just another lump of meat on the block, someone – no, something – I could manipulate for money by doing a set of routines I'd been trained to perform. It was like being an animal. Or possibly a robot. But it wasn't like being human and doing something called "making love".' I run out of steam but

Lewis nods and doesn't press me with another question. I'm not being judged here. He's still on my side, still understanding.

'Even when Richard reminded me of Hugo,' I say, 'he was still just a client when we got to the bedroom. I mean, how could it have been otherwise? Fundamentally I wasn't into gay sex and Richard wasn't sexually attractive to me. In fact even if I'd been gay I can't imagine him turning me on – he was overweight, he didn't work out and he wasn't up to much in the sack, those heavy drinkers never are. Because I liked him I did make the extra effort to give him a good time, but I was still working, still acting and performing for money. So when we were together I was never having a loving relationship with a brother. I was always just ripping off a bloke who reminded me of my brother.' I stop, feeling ready to collapse. Is there anything more exhausting than telling a string of shitty truths you'd rather not face? But the paradox is I know I'm going to feel better now. Lewis still accepts me. It's going to be all right.

With a huge effort I drum up the energy to blurt out: 'I wish Richard was still alive. I wish I could tell him how sorry I am that I hurt him.'

'That, of course, is very commendable,' says Lewis at once, 'but I think you should beware of turning Richard into a Victim with a capital V.'

I look up. 'What do you mean?'

'Well, it occurred to me while you were talking that my Great-Uncle Cuthbert would have taken a tough line here, and he would have taken it with Richard, not with you. He would have said that a sophisticated man who consorted with a prostitute would have known exactly what he was doing and would have deserved every-thing he got . . . But then Great-Uncle Cuthbert was always very severe on the subject of immorality and particularly when the immorality was homosexual.'

I'm hooked on Great-Uncle Cuthbert. I just love the way he's so politically incorrect. 'Was he a closet gay, Lewis?'

'I was never able to decide and he gave no clues, but I'm quite sure he believed that his sexual preferences were between him and God and as such were in no way a subject for general discussion. In fact he would have said that modern society's obsession with sex was unhealthy, immature and idolatrous, and created a severe distor-tion of reality.'

'Wow!' I'm enthralled by the sheer subversive magnificence of this fearless alternative vision.

Lewis smiles, and prepares to tell me more.

* * *

Our talks continue with this format: we discuss me for as long as I can stand it, and then as a reward Lewis gives me another instalment of his monastic soap opera. Cool. I like hearing about all the monks Great-Uncle Cuthbert ruled with a rod of iron, and I'm spherical-eyed to learn there was no homosexuality in his all-male roost. No overt homosexuality anyway. Lewis says the main sin was gluttony. But there was no anorexia or bulimia, not in Great-Uncle Cuthbert's monastery. Great-Uncle Cuthbert would have called them spiritual illnesses, a sign that the soul wasn't lined up right with God and in consequence was writhing in agony. Great-Uncle Cuthbert didn't mince his words. He lived in a less wimpish age and never pulled the punches when he was speaking about God, religion and the spiritual.

I like hearing about all these blokes who did without sex, and that's not because I'm thinking of entering a monastery. It's because I like hearing about a lifestyle that's totally different from the one that's nearly finished me. Dimly it dawns on me why Lewis is keen to spin me these stories. He's saying you don't have to have a sicko lifestyle selling yourself for money. You don't even have to have a conventional mainstream lifestyle, trotting off to work each day in an office and being a couch potato with your wife in the evenings as you snooze in front of the TV. And you certainly don't have to live an isolated-bubble lifestyle, thinking only of yourself. There are other options, other ways of living – and other ways too of looking at the things you feel you can't do without.

'Human beings love idols,' says Lewis, 'because human beings love to worship, but if you worship the wrong gods, you risk being seriously cut off from reality.'

Anything can become an idol, he says: a nation, a political party, a head of state – drink, drugs, food – football, rock music, pop stars – cars, boats, designer clothes – sex, exercise, loadsamoney – you name it. All these things may be good in themselves, but once they become an obsession you squander time and energy on illusions, your priorities get rearranged, your balanced lifestyle goes down the tubes and your true self gets stomped on. Or in other words, getting cut off from reality can make you physically, mentally and spiritually ill.

I pick out my past idols from his list, the addictions I used in order to fill the worship-space in my head. What I now have to do is fill the worship-space in my head with the right stuff, the stuff that's codenamed God, but I'm not going to be interested in the souped-up father-figure who gets wheeled out to bore for religion, and you can forget the nursery-rhyme old man in the sky. I still like the idea of God as a fraught artist, and Lewis says fine, it's a passable image because art is about reality and God is Ultimate Reality itself – line yourself up with Ultimate Reality, Lewis says, and you become real in your turn, playing your part in the scheme of things and feeling fulfilled as your real self has the chance to flourish. But—

'—but,' warns Lewis, 'remember that no image of God can give more than a glimpse of him, and that projecting images on to God can be very dangerous.' And he points out that God can be converted into an idol too, and when God becomes a false god bad religion breaks out. That's why The Bloke's so important, I see that now. He knows what the real God is and he can point the way to him.

I mosey around in all this spiritual stuff like a dog circling a deeply relevant lamp-post but finally I ask: 'Why doesn't The Bloke just fix me?'

'He's not a magician, Gavin. He operates through love, not through a magic wand.'

'That's all very well, but I want him to come along and—' I break off as I remember. He's already here, working through Lewis. All I've got to do is work hard in return, but it's so emotionally exhausting and I'm still so sick.

'You'll get better,' says Lewis. 'I'm sure of it.'

I don't know whether I believe him or not. But I do know I'm being given the strength to stagger on.

* * *

Hugo's fully excavated now and ready for a serious one-to-one talk, but we're putting him on ice for a short while in order to excavate the surrounding areas more fully. We talk some more about my parents. We talk about my father's own brother Hugo who was killed in the war, and about my mother's awful sisters: Pansy, who eloped with an American soldier, and Marigold, who married a millionaire and lived at St George's Hill in Weybridge and looked down on my mother for getting stuck with a mere country doctor.

Then I talk about Granny, Mum's mother, who loved to gossip and who was a colossal snob, and about Other Granny, Dad's mother, who played Edwardian songs on the piano and whom Granny called 'common' just because Other Granny had once had to earn her living teaching music. Then I talk about Grandfather, Mum's dad, who liked cricket, and about Grandad the Other Grandfather, who grew prize tomatoes in his greenhouse, and about the various cousins, all of whom had been either snotty or weird.

But we start praying for all my family, even the snotty or weird members, and at that point I tell Lewis I'd like to pray for my father, I'd like to say how grateful I am to him for teaching me to sail and how precious the memory is of that day we sailed past the Needles. And after these prayers I think I might be able to talk at last about what Hugo's death did to my parents, but although I tell Lewis I want to try, the words still refuse to come.

So Lewis diverts me again by playing Scheherazade, and at last he goes further back than his teenage days at the monastery. He tells me his childhood was spent with an uncle and aunt at their Sussex mansion because his widowed mother was too busy having affairs to care for him. He says he loved her anyway but hated the uncle and aunt, so he got himself expelled from school in the hope that he could go and live in Paris with his mother and her current lover.

'Naturally they were horrified,' says Lewis dryly, 'and in fact after that no one wanted to give me a home, but at least Great-Uncle Cuthbert believed that my salvation was his moral duty. However, he was a tough old man and overt affection wasn't his strong suit. Life was hardly a bed of roses,' Lewis adds, finally revealing the dark side of the monastic soap opera, and of course I can identify with the pain of not being wanted.

I know I can tell him everything now.

He'll understand.

*   *   *

I start by saying how after Hugo died my father withdrew from me to immerse himself in his work and my mother sank fathoms deep

459

in depression and neither had anything to say either to me or to each other.

'But there was nothing particularly new about any of that,' I say casually, as if the memories are really not too bad once you get used to them. 'Dad was always immersing himself in his work and Mum had had depressions before and neither of them had had much to say to each other for years. It was just that Hugo's death magnified all this crap to an unbearable degree.'

'You're saying they couldn't cope with the loss.'

'Right . . . They'd had so much invested in him.'

'The Harley Street dream?'

'Yes, you see, Mum would have liked Dad to have been a Harley Street specialist because that would have put her on a level with Aunt Marigold in St George's Hill. So Hugo being a Harley Street specialist would have been the next best thing.'

'And your father wanted this for Hugo too.'

'To be fair to Dad, I have to say he wouldn't have minded if Hugo had just wound up a GP, but he definitely wanted him to be a doctor. Dad himself had followed in his father's footsteps – in fact in Dad's world, the world he grew up in, elder sons followed in their father's footsteps, no question, and if the elder son died the next son would step up to fill his shoes. That was why it was so awful when—'

'—you couldn't fill them. I understand . . . So Hugo was sustaining your father's world-view and compensating your mother for the fact that your father hadn't lived up to her expectations.'

'Hugo compensated Mum in other ways as well. He was everything Dad wasn't – outgoing, gregarious, open, straightforward . . . Dad was always working or feeling tired or going sailing or shutting himself up in his study.'

'Not the easiest of husbands, perhaps – and this wasn't the happiest of marriages, was it, even though everyone thought it was such a success.'

'True, but Hugo made everything okay,' I say. 'He kept the marriage stitched together.'

'But there must have been other crucial stitches, surely, or your parents would have separated after he died. Was it you, do you think, who then kept the marriage from disintegrating?'

'Oh no,' I say at once. 'No, it wasn't me. Couldn't have been.'

'Why not?'

I give a little shrug, fidget with my watchstrap.

'You mentioned your mother was prone to depression,' says Lewis, moving on – or is he only moving sideways? 'Was this clinical depression treated by a doctor?'

'Suppose so. She got pills. Dad said she was fine.'

'And when was this?'

'After I joined Hugo at boarding school and she was left on her own at home. But Granny the Gossip – Mum's mum – told us Mum wasn't nearly as bad as she was the previous time.'

'What happened the previous time?'

'Post-partum blues. Suicide attempt. Granny shouldn't have let that slip out, naughty old girl.'

'The post-partum blues were after you were born?'

My throat starts to tighten. 'Yep.'

Lewis waits. I wait. Eventually Gavin Blake Debonair Survivor cruises in and says languidly: 'Mum didn't want another baby.'

'Is that what your grandmother said?'

'No, no, no!' I sound shocked. 'Granny would never have said anything like that.'

'Then who did?'

I think of all the millions of women in the world and wish I could pick one at random and lie about her. But of course I can't. No more lies. I have to tell the truth, and the truth here is that the woman was none other than—

'Mum,' I say casually to Lewis, and smother a fake yawn as I glance away.

* * *

'Ah,' says Lewis, keeping the world turning.

'Yeah.' I try to stop fidgeting with my watchstrap before I break it. 'Mum told me after I was chucked out of medical school,' I say nonchalantly. 'It was when I could no longer cope with trying to be Hugo. She lost her temper and shouted: "You're hopeless, you'll never get anywhere, never achieve anything, I wish I'd never had you, I wish I'd had that abortion I wanted," and then she burst into tears and started screaming she wanted to kill herself, and Dad came out of his study to see what all the fuss was about and he said: "For God's sake, what is it now? Shut up, the bloody pair of you!" he said, and after my mother ran off sobbing I tried to explain

461

to him she was disappointed I hadn't made the grade as Hugo would have done but he just said: "Well, how do you think *I* feel? It's a tragedy you haven't the brains to be a doctor," and that was when I knew both of them were wishing I was dead and Hugo was alive. I left home that same day.'

'I'm not surprised.'

Gavin Blake Debonair Survivor begins to fragment. 'I suppose you'll want to excuse Mum by saying she was just suffering from another bout of her clinical depression,' I say defiantly, unable to fake nonchalance a second longer, 'but I say fuck her clinical depressions, fuck them, she treated me as if I barely existed after Hugo died – and even before that it was all Hugo, Hugo, Hugo, she didn't give a shit for me ever, she just pretended she did. Elizabeth was the one who gave a shit,' I say violently as the emotion swamps me, but then I have to squeeze my eyes tight shut to ward off the pain. Elizabeth the mummy-substitute and *femme fatale* – my grand illusion. Elizabeth hadn't given a shit either. Elizabeth had wanted me dead.

Just like my mother.

'Oh God,' I say, 'oh God—'

'Okay, we'll stop there.'

'*No!*' I shout, making him jump. I tell myself I'm not going to be weak and wet and wimpish, I'm not, I'm so fucking tired of being such a fucking mess. Peeling my fingers from my face I say strongly: 'My mother was a stupid bitch. She spoilt Hugo rotten, she slobbered over him endlessly, but at the end when he was dying she was no bloody use at all. He wanted to talk about death but she refused to listen, she always insisted he'd get well, she failed him totally—'

'And your father?'

'In denial! Worse than Mum! Do you hear that, Lewis? This man was a doctor, for God's sake, a *doctor*, and he couldn't cope with someone who was dying! He failed Hugo as well. That's why I had to step in. I was fifteen years old and yet I had to bear the whole back-breaking burden. *I* was the one who had to talk to Hugo about death, *I* was the one who had to make that terrible promise to ensure he died in peace, *I* was the one who let him into my head and wrecked my life – *I suffered far more than they did!* And I tried so hard to make it up to them for being alive when he was dead, so *hard* I tried—'

'It was hell, wasn't it? No wonder you're angry—'

'*Angry?* Fucking hell, that word doesn't even begin to describe how I feel!' I yell, and then suddenly I'm sobbing. Fucking hell again. But I'm not stopping now. Can't. My heart's banging, my eyes are streaming, my breath's coming in shudders, but somehow I'm still talking, still spewing out these godawful shitty truths – only this time they're worse than shitty, they're so dreadful they're sort of cosmic, like Medea killing her children or Oedipus killing his father, they're the kind of truths that make you want to die when you're speaking them, but at the same time you know you're speaking them to survive.

'I hated them all,' I say in between gasps as the tears burn my face. 'I hated Mum and Dad for leaving me to cope alone and making me feel so guilty that I was alive. I hated Hugo for dying and then for taking over my life. And worst of all I hated myself for not being able to become Hugo, for letting down not just my brother but the parents I loved – and I did love them, I loved them all the time I was hating them, I loved Mum and Dad, I loved Hugo, and the more Mum and Dad grieved for him and ignored me the more I wanted their love and despised myself for not being good enough to get it. It made me feel so worthless, such a failure, so absolutely undeserving of any love at all—' I break off, too awash to go on.

Lewis wants to touch me but he knows he can't. He wants to put his arm around my shoulders and comfort me, but he knows he has to keep his distance. I can feel all this compassion but I'm blocked off from it behind the glass walls that my sickness has built to separate me from normality. But he takes off his pectoral cross and he slides it to the middle of the table.

When he withdraws his hand I pick up the cross and wrap my fingers around the Bloke-image. Can't see it. Too many tears. But I stop sobbing and shuddering. I feel as if I've been trampled into the mud by a herd of elephants, but at least I'm quiet and still.

Lewis says: 'You were very courageous, offering Hugo hope no matter what the cost to yourself, and as I made clear earlier, it certainly wasn't your fault that your way of helping him could never have worked out. Nor was it your fault, let me now add, that your parents were so overwhelmed by the tragedy that they couldn't love you as you deserved.'

I want to break down all over again but I don't. I keep myself together somehow, and after a long pause I manage to whisper: 'But if it's not my fault . . . are Mum and Dad to blame for everything that went wrong?'

463

Lewis's voice stays firm. 'Obviously they made some very big mistakes, but before we unload our blame we need to ask ourselves if we know the whole story. For instance, were there any mitigating factors? I always wish,' he adds, 'that I'd had the chance to ask my mother if there were any mitigating circumstances which explained why *she* rejected me when I was young.'

I digest this. More seconds slip by but finally I say: 'Can I just shovel all the blame on God for allowing this to happen?'

'You've certainly got cause to complain to him, but make sure you listen afterwards for his answer. Every mess has to be redeemed and put right – that's just as much a part of the creative process as the waste and mess. So in his answer you'll see the path to redemption, and then you can work out how you can best give him a helping hand.'

I bin the idea of skiving off or collapsing in a useless heap. Obviously my first task in giving God a helping hand has to be to keep on keeping on, clearing the roadblocks from my mind no matter how painful that process is.

So where have I got to? The area around Hugo's now been fully excavated. He's ready. I'm ready. No more delays.

Taking a deep breath I say: 'I think it's time for Hugo to go home.'

* * *

The anniversary of Hugo's death falls this month, and I tell Lewis on his next visit that I want to lay flowers on the grave and say goodbye.

Lewis asks how I feel about leaving the house, but I'm confident I can do it. 'I've got a mission,' I tell him. 'I really want to get to that grave.' But I don't explain just why the visit to the grave's so vital.

I'm very aware of Hugo at the moment. He's now calm, silent, waiting, no longer hanging around my neck like a lead weight but lying peacefully on my chest like a heavy gold medallion – something valuable but not something you want to lug around twenty-four hours a day. How light I'll feel when he's gone! But he may not want to let go. We've been sharing a body for so long that we're like Siamese twins.

I feel clearer now about the tragedy. I'm seeing us all as victims who got mown down in one of God's messier creative splurges and mangled by the splurge's dark vile bits, the bits which haven't yet come right. But I know now that God's not just out there lolling idly in front of his canvas. He's in a muck sweat, painting away to save the picture, and although my family was blasted apart by the thwack of the creative process, the creator himself can't rest until he's brought us back into the right pattern.

Mum, Dad, Hugo and I are all waiting to be reintegrated in the design – we're all waiting to come home to our allotted places – and as I realise this, I find the other members of my family are crowding into my head as if hoping for a big reunion. Grandfather, Grandad and Other Granny all died before I left home, but death doesn't matter in this context, the important thing is that they're alive in my head – in psychic reality, as Lewis puts it – and right now they're busy milling around with all my memories of the living. God, whatever happened to arch-bitch Aunt Pansy in Los Angeles and rich-bitch Aunt Marigold in St George's Hill? What happened to snotty cousins Arabella, Charlotte and Jeremy in England and weird cousins Rick, Mary-Elizabeth and Ham (short for Hamilton) in America? All those lost people . . . But they helped create the pattern of my childhood, the pattern which now has to be retrieved so that my old life can be integrated at last with the new.

Yes, it's going to be okay this time, Hugo, I promise . . . It's as if we're in one of those old-world dances where you have to go through a whole chain of set moves before you finally come home down the finishing strait. Our dance was ripped up in our youth because an earthquake struck the ballroom, but I've cleared away the fallen debris, the band's come back and now we can return to the floor to pick up the dance where we left off – we're going back to the point where we danced the wrong steps because we were too young to know the right ones. It wasn't our fault we danced the wrong steps, Hugo, and in this scenario it wasn't your fault either, Mum and Dad. And although the four of us wound up wasted we don't have to stay that way, we're being given a second chance, we're being led back to the ballroom floor. What makes me so certain? Well, I'll tell you. It's because we're being led back by The Bloke himself – yes, we are, Hugo, yes, we are! He wants us back and he'll go to any lengths to get us there because he's the *Healer*, he's the *Leader*, he's LORD OF THE DANCE, and this time we're *all* coming home . . .

* * *

When Lewis and I plan the graveside visit, I express my deepest fear: I tell him Hugo might not want to leave, but this time for the best of motives – he might want to stay to look after me just as he did when we were young. Worse still he might be hurt if he's asked to go.

Lewis is pretty sure Hugo will be keen to go once all's finally straight between us. Am I, perhaps, the one who feels ambivalent about Hugo's departure? I have to admit I'm scared of the vacuum Hugo's departure will create in my mind, but Lewis says that as Hugo will always be with me now as a cherished memory, there can't be a vacuum in my mind when his after-death self departs. And suddenly I see it all: the good memories will pour into the vacuum, the light will triumph over the dark, and Hugo will ride the light like a surfer, creaming away across the bluest of seas to his new life – not the life he would have had if he'd lived but a redeemed life in a healed creation, the creation which exists in God's head as he tries to bring his messy canvas into line with the shimmering dream which drives him.

I'm more frightened than I thought I would be at the prospect of leaving home, but Susanne and I experiment successfully with driving round and round the block until I'm relaxed. I know now I can do the trip to Surrey. I know I can.

I tell Susanne to buy white carnations, one for each of the birthdays Hugo never had, and she's made the florist arrange them in a spray. She's also made sure there's a card but I don't show her what I write on it. I've got a plan for that card, but I'm not telling anyone yet what it is.

Finally Lewis drives me down into Surrey in his beat-up Volksie which looks as if it should have been MOT'd off the road a long time ago. It roars and bounces and screams down the A3. Lewis is quite a driver. Other drivers stare at him in disbelief as they swerve to let us pass.

I'm in the back seat so there's no risk of us touching. I don't want to ruin everything by freaking out as the result of a collision. I don't even want to think about it so I focus instead on fighting the agoraphobia. But I'm okay. Eventually I'm even able to notice that the countryside's looking beautiful in the autumn sunshine. We've made an early start, although I haven't told Lewis why this is so important. It's part of the secret plan I have, and I'll only disclose it later if it bears fruit.

To my huge relief I find I'm still okay once we're parked at the church and I have to leave the car. No panic attacks. I'm totally focused on getting to that grave, and when I reach it I'm so overcome that Lewis suggests we sit down for a moment. But I don't want that. I stand by the grave and read the headstone and say Hugo Hugo Hugo over and over again to myself as I think of him.

Eventually I nod to Lewis, and standing six feet apart we quietly say the Lord's Prayer. I can't finish it – too much emotion – but Lewis is there to finish it for me. Then I talk to Hugo. I say I'm sorry for not being able to fulfil the promise I made to let him live my life, but it was a promise I shouldn't have made because it was wrong. He had a better life waiting for him instead of this second-rate existence locked up in my head, and I say I'm sorry I didn't understand this at the time but thanks to Lewis I understand it now.

Then I say to Hugo what a great brother he was and what joy he gave everyone, specially Mum and Dad and me, and although he wasn't around for long he certainly transformed our lives by being so special. I say I'll always remember the pattern he made on my life before he got ill, it was a great pattern, a wonderful pattern, and it'll stay with me for ever – which means he'll always be part of my life whatever happens, but part of it in the best possible way.

'I'm sorry I kept you so long by sticking to that dumb plan and then junking it in a way that stopped you moving on,' I say finally. 'What a mess! Can you ever forgive me?'

And Hugo answers: 'Lighten up, chum! I was just as dumb as you were – why couldn't I see the plan was a load of balls? No wonder everything went wrong!' and when I ask him again to forgive me he says: 'No sweat, but it's me who needs forgiveness for screwing up your head like that. In fact how can I possibly move on until I'm sure you're all right?'

I'm glad Lewis and I prepared for this reaction. Trying not to sound anxious I answer: 'My friends will see I'm all right. You don't have to worry,' but still Hugo hates to leave me unprotected.

This is when Lewis intervenes. He tells Hugo kindly but firmly that now's the time to go, and Hugo doesn't argue. That's when I know he's secretly longing to leave.

In a rush I say to him: ''Bye, mate. Remember, you were special, you counted, you—' but he interrupts before I can say 'mattered'. He's laughing. 'Okay, okay!' he protests. 'I get the message! But make sure you get your head together soon because your new life's going to be the best memorial I could ever have.'

Those are the last words of his I hear. My eyes are burning but I'm all right. I put the spray of carnations on the grave and tell Lewis I need a little time alone. As he retreats I stoop to make sure the florist's card's fully visible in the little plastic bag which will protect it from the rain. I've written: 'In loving memory of HUGO, best of brothers. GAVIN', and below this I've printed my address.

I stay a while longer. It's very quiet in the churchyard, very peaceful. 'Hugo?' I say softly at last, but there's no reply. He's gone, slipping away across the sea to the distant horizon, journeying at last from darkness into light. I call to The Bloke: 'He's coming home!' but The Bloke calls back: 'He's already here!' So I know the return was instant. That's because there's no time there and no space either – it's all beyond time and space, Lewis says, but our brains aren't wired to imagine such a world so it's no use trying to visualise it.

I walk over to Lewis and say: 'He's home.' I'm aware of a huge lightness buoying me up and I know I don't want to grieve. 'I'm free to be me now.'

Lewis smiles. 'Sailing off into the golden sunset?'

'No, I think that's turning out to be a sort of metaphor, know-what-I-mean, like, kind of . . .' I get bogged down but Lewis makes no attempt to rush me. Eventually I say: 'Sailing away from everything was an escape-dream created when I was unhappy. I still want to sail but I don't want to sail away into the blue any more – if you run away you just take your problems with you.'

Lewis smiles again and exclaims encouragingly: 'That's a valuable insight – excellent! I'm very proud of you for all you've accomplished today!'

I feel good when he says that. And I feel good about Hugo. As we leave the churchyard I stop to look back, and I see how quiet it is, how peaceful, how absolutely as an English country churchyard should be. It always seemed so lonely and desolate before.

I resolve to come back next year with more flowers.

Hugo'll like that.

*   *   *

Off Lewis and I drive back to London. By this time I'm feeling so grateful that I start thinking about how I can best reward him for all his help, and as we reach the outskirts of London I think back to his first visit to my house when he arrived with his portable Communion gear in case I wanted one of the special wafers plus a hit of the special wine. When I said I didn't, he asked me if I'd been christened and confirmed and I said yes, christening was a must-have social occasion where I came from, and my Church-of-England-foundation school had ensured, even in the 1970s, that I got 'done' when confirmation time came around. (Of course these are pathetic reasons for getting christened and confirmed, but they didn't alter the fact that I'm now entitled to take part in the wafer-wine number in any Communion gig.) Lewis made no comment on this classic example of the English converting religious ritual into a couple of middle-class tribal rites. He just said: 'I always think Communion's about healing,' and then he changed the subject.

But now I think I see how I can reward him for all the help he's been giving me. I say: 'I'd like to take Communion again one day soon.'

I think I've pitched this just right – I sound winningly respectful and serious – but he gives me a sharp, streetwise look in the driving-mirror. 'Gavin,' he says, 'there's no need to take Communion just out of a desire to please me. It's very important that you wait until the time's right, and there must be no outside pressure hurrying you along.'

After a pause I say. 'I just wanted to give you a present to say thank you.'

'That's not necessary but it's a very kind thought and I'd be most ungracious if I were to pour cold water on it. How about a bottle of wine from your local supermarket?'

I immediately decide to call up Fortnum's and order an insanely expensive claret, but within minutes I've figured out he really doesn't want me spending a lot of money. And what am I trying to buy here anyway? The trouble is that the more Lewis praises me the more nervous I feel that I may wind up disappointing him, and if I disappoint him he might reject me just as my father did.

'It's all a question of trust, isn't it?' he says to me gently when I confess these thoughts to him. 'You find it hard to trust people not to reject you, and you're willing to live a lie to please them, just as you lived a lie in order to please Elizabeth, but as you should know by now, you don't have to live a lie to please me. Quite the reverse. I want you to live in the truth.'

469

I at once decide I can trust him enough to cancel my plan to blow three hundred quid on a bottle of claret from Fortnum's.

But I'll tell Susanne to buy the very best of the Australian reds when she next goes to the supermarket.

* * *

Because Lewis refuses to pressure me, I think some more about taking Communion. I've stopped considering it as a way of repaying him and now I'm speculating that it might help to line me up better with The Bloke.

But after a while I know deep down I can't face Communion. Not yet anyway.

'Is it because of the risk of physical contact with the priest?' says Lewis when I broach the subject with him later.

'It's more than that. It's the whole business of kneeling down before a man and—'

'Ah, I see.'

'Sorry. Don't mean to be blasphemous.'

'I know.' Of course Lewis understands. He always does. 'It won't make any difference, will it,' he says, 'if I tell you that you don't have to kneel down.'

'It'd make some difference but not enough. The idea of being that close to a man while he offers something that represents a body—'

'Yes.' He thinks for a moment and comes up with a bright idea. 'Nicholas could arrange for a woman to bring you the sacrament at home. How would you feel about that?'

'One of those new women priests, you mean?'

'I was thinking of a deaconess I know. Once the elements have been consecrated by a priest, a deaconess is allowed to—'

I say flatly: 'I don't want a man anywhere near that sacrament. He'd pollute it. The priest's got to be a woman.'

For the first time I see Lewis at a loss for words. He clears his throat. He scratches his head. He's stunned.

'So what's the big deal?' I demand. 'Do you really think The Bloke would give a shit whether it's a man or a woman doing the priest-stuff when somebody's ill and needs help?'

Lewis stages an overdue recovery. 'Quite so,' he says soothingly. 'Quite so. We must see what Nicholas can do – he knows most of the first batch of women priests, and meanwhile maybe one of our non-Communion healing services might be more suitable anyway.'

I'm interested in the idea of a healing service. Carta's told me there's one every week at Friday lunch-time. Apparently a healing service did wonders for her when she went through her crisis in 1990.

'Maybe a bit later,' I say, 'when I'm more used to going out. And no Communion, not yet, not till I've done a healing service.'

'That's fine, but let me just make it clear that you don't have to come to St Benet's to receive the laying-on of hands, and the laying-on of hands doesn't require a priest. This deaconess I mentioned would make a house call.'

But the home option doesn't feel right. The idea of some strange revvy-totty cavorting around laying on hands in my own home rings no bells for me at all. In fact Susanne would probably be cross and call it pervy.

'I'll have to think about this,' I say to Lewis, and he nods willingly, keen to make amends for dropping the ball earlier.

Funny old bloke! Imagine him being wobbly about women priests!

It's time he did some serious updating.

*　　*　　*

My mother arrives two days later on a Saturday morning when Susanne's out at the supermarket. Susanne and I have kept ourselves to ourselves so I know, when the doorbell rings, that the caller won't be a well-meaning neighbour. It won't be any of our friends either. They always call first before arriving on our doorstep.

Leaving my room I go downstairs and open the front door.

Outside is this slim woman, beautifully dressed and made up, every grey hair dyed a classy walnut colour to make her look forty instead of fifty-three. No face-lift, though. Hair-dyeing's acceptable nowadays but face-lifts are still vulgar. The lack of creases is probably because she dabbles in HRT, like Elizabeth.

Of course I knew Mum would go to the churchyard to lay flowers on Hugo's grave on the anniversary of his death. That's why I made sure I was there early. I had to get my carnations in first so that she would see them and find my address on the card.

Never thought she'd visit me like this, though. I was expecting

471

a letter. Or, in my more pessimistic moments, nothing. But now I feel as if The Bloke's slammed us together with such force that we're totally winded.

I'm the one who gets his lungs inflated first. 'Hullo, Mum,' I say as if we met only last week. But I find I can say nothing else, and talking's still beyond her.

We can't think what to do with each other. In the end I open the door wide and she tiptoes in, clutching her smart Gucci handbag. No wild emotion here, of course. That would be vulgar. And no wild speeches either.

'My girlfriend's out,' I say. 'You've got me all to yourself.'

She hears the magic word 'girlfriend' but she can't make sense of it despite my hetero write-ups in the tabloids. (Serena sold her story to the *News of the World* and was last seen heading for Heathrow in a very long limo.) The problem is Mum's convinced no man could be a prostitute unless he himself was gay. One doesn't normally encounter such people, of course. One doesn't have any homosexuals where one lives. One doesn't mix with that sort of person at all.

I show her into the living-room and offer her coffee. She nods, looking at the cheap furniture as if she's deep in some Third World country which isn't coloured pink in the atlas any more.

I make the coffee while she sits on the sofa, and when I return I find she's crying quietly into a very classy lace handkerchief.

'It's okay,' I say. 'I'm on a new course now. No need to dwell on anything the papers said. That's all over.'

She can't even take a sip of coffee. All she can do is weep but eventually she manages to whisper one word. It's: 'Darling.'

She's gone nuts. The trial's unhinged her. She sees this despised second son, the one she wanted to abort, the one she said was useless, the one she wanted dead instead of Hugo, the one who's just shocked her and shamed her for life, and yet all she can say is: 'Darling.'

'There, there,' I say awkwardly, knowing I mustn't display any emotion by touching her. 'Don't cry, not when you're looking so terrific!'

But she's not listening. She's checked the tears and she's dredged up all her strength and the next moment she's blurting out: 'Forgive me. Please. Forgive me.' And when she reaches out to me as she's never reached out to me before, I do touch her after all – I take her in my arms, and as we cling to each other, the two survivors

472

of that terrible earthquake, The Bloke draws silently back to give us the space we need.

* * *

It turns out she was stricken with remorse after I disappeared. Dad was too, she says. They did try to trace me. They registered me as a missing person and private detectives were hired, but as I was floating around doing casual labour I wasn't plugged in to any system which would have made me traceable. I also used aliases for a while and only returned to my real name when I took the escort job with Norah who, running a legal business, wanted my national insurance number for her records. But by that time my parents had abandoned the search.

'I always felt you were alive,' says Mum, 'but losing you was like a second death. First Hugo, then you.'

I explain how I felt I was doing them a favour by disappearing. I explain how I hated myself for failing to be a Hugo-clone. I explain—

But she can't bear it. With tears streaming down her face she whispers: 'The further we travelled from your disappearance, the more clearly we saw how you'd been harmed. Then *we* were the ones eaten up by self-hatred.' And the next moment she was saying it was all her fault, everything was her fault, she wished she'd been the one to die of a heart attack instead of Dad.

I'm reminded of how I used to say to myself: 'Everything's my fault, I wish I'd been the one to die instead of Hugo.' But I'm wiser now. I've been able to see this attitude is destructive and wrong. So I say to Mum: 'You made big mistakes, sure, but we all did. What matters now is that you're sorry and I'm sorry and Dad and Hugo would be sorry too if they were here, and if only I can now find out why you and Dad made your mistakes, maybe you and I can draw a line under the past and make a fresh start.'

But she's still locked away with her guilt and grief and she can't grasp this at all so in the end I just plunge right to the heart of the pain to try to lance it. I ask: 'Why did you want to abort me?'

She's stunned. 'What makes you think I did?'

'You let the information slip once when you lost your temper.'

'I couldn't have done! I couldn't possibly have told you such a terrible thing! I couldn't have been so cruel!'

473

'You mean you don't remember?' I forget about forgiveness. She dropped this information on me all those years ago, information that slaughtered me, and now the silly bitch doesn't even—

'It wasn't true!' she cries desperately. 'I lied!'

'No you fucking didn't! It was the fucking truth!'

She blanches at my language, shrinks back from my anger. We're into reality big-time here, and this reality isn't going to be swept back under the Surrey rug.

'I *couldn't* have told you!' she insists, still crying. 'Only a bad mother would say such a terrible thing!'

I spot the problem. She's always consoled herself with the belief that she's a good mother, and if I take that belief away from her she'll have nothing.

I get my anger under control and make a new effort to reach her. 'You weren't a bad mother,' I say carefully, 'but as I just said, you made mistakes and I need to know how you came to make them. Why didn't you want me when you got pregnant?'

'Oh, but I did, I did—'

She's still not getting it. 'Mum, the neighbours aren't listening, the family aren't here, the Mothers' Union hasn't bugged the room and there's no need to keep up appearances any more! Talk to me, for God's sake! Tell me what happened or I'll wash my hands of you!'

She sobs and sobs but finally whispers in despair: 'I couldn't cope. I shouldn't have married so young. I shouldn't have married a man who was so much older and so wrapped up in his dead wife . . .'

It all comes out. Apparently Dad was a far more complex character than I ever imagined. Everyone felt so sorry for him, chained for years to his invalid first wife who had been unable to give him children, but this mass-sympathy was totally misplaced. Dad secretly loved having a frail wife, the last word in adoring dependence, and he secretly thrived on the quiet, orderly home life with no kids. After his wife died he was so traumatised that he slid straight away into a mid-life crisis and fell violently in love with a twenty-year-old babe (Mum). After they were married he fell violently in love again, this time with the idea of chucking up his job and sailing off into the golden sunset, but of course this escape-fantasy had to be abandoned when Mum got pregnant with Hugo. However Dad did get a new boat and soon sailing played a bigger part in his life than ever. All his spare income was poured into the boat. Mum was given a stingy allowance and only the minimum of hired help. He wouldn't even employ an au pair girl, a fact which just about sums up his interest in women once his boat-obsession took over. You'd think a chic French girl might have perked up his domestic life, but no, all he wanted was to worship the boat, his idol.

'He was never around,' says poor Mum desolately. 'He worked all hours attending to those ghastly patients and then on his time off he was always heading for the coast. I did try to get interested in sailing, but once I'd had a baby—'

'Did he really want children?'

'God knows what he wanted. He told me once he was bored with being a doctor, but when I asked him what he wanted to do instead he didn't know. He just said he'd never considered doing anything else because he'd wanted to please his father, and now he was too old to change professions.'

'He sounds seriously unhappy!'

'Oh, but he covered it up beautifully and no one ever guessed! The patients worshipped him and he liked that – I think he was a good doctor in spite of everything, and he loved you and Hugo even though he never gave me any help when you were young. Well, men didn't in those days, it was a different world, and I was too young myself to cope single-handed with all that responsibility – I didn't understand adult life, I was so overwhelmed by the hard reality of marriage and so disillusioned when he turned out not to be the romantic husband I thought he would be—'

'No wonder you got depressed!'

'The depressions were terrible. The pills I had to take were terrible. Everything was terrible. It was like living all the time in a black fog.'

'But surely Dad was sympathetic?'

'Yes, but he was so busy with his patients, the ones who were really ill.'

'You were really ill! Listen, if you were struggling to cope, why did Dad let you get pregnant again before Hugo was old enough to start nursery school?'

'I don't know. We never talked about contraception. I didn't know anything about it. Then after you were born he had a vasectomy – without consulting me, of course – and that was that, but I felt so sad later. I'd have loved another baby when you and Hugo were both at boarding school.'

'But Mum, this was the 1960s! Surely you must have known something about birth control?'

'The early sixties were just like the fifties, and people stayed ignorant and innocent for longer then . . . Oh, how I wished I was one of that small London minority who created "Swinging London"! I loved parties, I loved to dance—'

'I like to dance too. Mum, why on earth did you stay with this bloke?'

'Oh, I couldn't have left, not possibly! What would everyone have thought? Divorce was so different in those days – deserting wives lost custody of their children and I couldn't have borne that.'

'You could have gone later after Hugo died!'

'How could I? I had no money of my own and I'd never had a job. Where would I have gone? What would I have done? Besides, I still had you – until you vanished. Oh God, that was terrible, *terrible*—'

'Well, you've got me back now,' I say briskly, hoping to avert another tear-storm. 'I know I'm not Hugo but at least I'm not dead.'

The magic name diverts her and she does a classic slide into Hugomania as she says with a passion worthy of Jocasta how handsome and clever and charming he was. I somehow keep my mouth shut. Hugo, of course, was all those things, but he could also be arrogant, pig-headed and snobbish. He wasn't a saint. In fact he was sex-mad enough to shag a local waitress when he was only fifteen. (Mum and Dad never found out.) But it's no good trying to argue with Mum here. If she needs to cling to a fantasy of St Hugo, maybe I should respect the fact that she's still unhappy enough to need a fantasy to cling to, but my God, I can see how all this gooey sentimental drivel drove poor old Dad straight to the boat.

I decide to interrupt her. 'Mum, is Granny still alive?' I ask, but I learn that Granny the Gossip, the last of my grandparents, died in 1991. I feel sad. Her favourite daughter, rich-bitch Aunt Marigold, used to keep her in a plush granny-flat over the multiple garage of the mansion at St George's Hill, so snotty cousins Arabella, Charlotte and Jeremy saw far more of her than Hugo and I did, but Granny doted on all her grandchildren, even cousins Rick, Mary-Elizabeth and Ham, weird offspring of arch-bitch Aunt Pansy in Los Angeles. How could I have been so warped that I dismissed Nigel's talk of unconditional love as rubbish? How could I have been so fixated on my parents that I told Carta the people I loved never loved me in return? Welcome back to my life as a cherished memory, Granny

476

– sorry for all the pain I must have caused you by disappearing, but I know you've forgiven me. Unconditional love was your speciality.

As I sigh I realise Mum's returned to earth after her trip to fantasy-heaven where she keeps her best airbrushed memories. 'But it's no good getting emotional about Hugo,' she says hastily. 'The only thing that matters now is that you're alive – oh, I'm so happy to have found you! And how happy your father would be too if he were here!'

'What's your present husband like?'

But she's cagey. She doesn't want to talk about him. 'He doesn't know I've come to see you,' she says, not looking at me. 'After the trial he said it was just as well you and I weren't in touch. Of course I wanted to get in touch, but I was so afraid you'd reject me, just as you did when you went away, and I was still trying to summon up the courage to write to that clergyman, the one the papers said sheltered you, when—'

'—when you went to Hugo's grave and found my card.'

'Exactly! Oh darling, I cried and cried, I was so . . .'

I tune out. I'm busy thinking that I'm not going to like Step-Dad. But poor old Mum's not so bad when you get to know her. I'll take her dancing somewhere when I'm well and I'll give her a little fun – I'll send her flowers on Mother's Day and give her a nice present at Christmas and maybe I might even take her to the theatre around the time she has her birthday. Do I still bear her a grudge? No, what's the point? She was just a victim of her class, her times, her marriage to that peculiar bloke, my father. Lethal old Dad, playing Dr Heartbreaker and effortlessly creating havoc! I can almost hear the sighs of his lovelorn patients (both sexes) mingling with Mum's sobs as he buckets around in the wrong walk of life and never manages to get himself sorted.

I can't wait to discuss him again with Lewis.

'It's so wonderful to see you, darling!' Mum's saying dewy-eyed. 'How handsome you've become, even more handsome than Hugo!'

Watch it, Jocasta! I'm not auditioning for Oedipus.

Fortunately Susanne chooses that moment to return home from the supermarket.

*　*　*

Of course Mum's appalled by Susanne. And Susanne's appalled by Mum. They stare at each other in the manner of two animals from different species prepared to fight over a choice piece of meat, but within seconds I'm realising that this situation could work to my advantage. Susanne won't let Mum convert me into Oedipus, and Mum won't let Susanne into her home too often – which means I'll only have to face Step-Dad on a very occasional basis.

Mum soon takes herself off. We've exchanged phone numbers and we've agreed to have lunch at Fortnum's when I'm feeling less agoraphobic. Another tear's shed as she lingers on the doorstep out of sight of Susanne. She whispers that she can't find the words to express all her feelings. Have I truly forgiven her? She loves me so much and if I can somehow manage to love her a little in spite of everything—

'Of course I can – don't be soppy, Mum!' I say, instantly converted into a shining example of repressed middle-class behaviour complete with antique vocabulary, but I give her a big hug so I think she does drive away happy in the end.

'That's a very funny sort of lady,' says Susanne, busy unpacking the groceries when I return indoors. 'You glad she turned up?'

'I don't mind,' I say, borrowing her favourite act-laid-back phrase.

'Did you tell her you're getting married once you're well?'

'Sorry, I only had time to tell her you existed.'

'What do you think she'll say about our plans?'

'"Thank God." She'll take it as cast-iron proof that I'm straight.'

Susanne muses pityingly: 'I suppose she hasn't been around much.'

'Just to hell and back. Turns out my dad was in love with a boat.'

'Pervy! If you ever started preferring a boat to me I'd beat you up!'

'I bet. Hey, what would you do if you knew nothing about contraception and I hit you for two kids in three years before running off to have a vasectomy without your permission?'

'I'd castrate you, walk out with the kids and never look back.'

'Luckily for Dad, Mum wasn't programmed to think along those lines.'

'Poor cow! I'll try to be nice to her whenever we meet in future.'

I tell her this is a generous offer, and try not to imagine how Mum would be looking if she'd overheard this conversation . . .

* * *

Carta enjoys hearing about my mum. Carta visits me regularly now I'm getting better but Susanne doesn't object. That's because she's figured Carta's a useful role model, someone from a socially deprived background who became a high flyer in the City jungle. The two of them discuss the stockmarket together while I potter around making coffee. Talk about role reversal! I must have turned into one of those 'Caring Nineties' New Men, the sad sods who share the housework, love to cook and think nothing of cleaning up the baby-poop. The sooner I get back to good mental health the better! I'm feeling an urgent need to down beer, kick ass, pump iron and stomp on every New Man in sight.

I know I'm on the mend, since I can now go outside for short spells and can even drive the car, but I still have nightmares that if I touch another man I'll freak out, mutilate myself with the nearest knife and be carted off to the brain-factory for a neuron reassignment which'll not only destroy my true self but zombify me into a domestic accessory for feminists – except that my Essex feminist wouldn't keep me, she'd walk out and I'd never see her again.

'Shit, you're still so mental!' says Susanne exasperated.

'You mean you'd stay even if I was zombified?'

'I'd stay even if you were an embalmed corpse!'

I'm so encouraged by this reassurance that my impotence comes to a sensational end. 'Hey, look at that!' I shout, like Christopher Columbus discovering America.

'God, that's pervy! I say "embalmed corpse." and you get stiff enough to drill concrete!'

'Do you think it'll peg out if I put it in?'

'Well, don't just lie there asking, pinhead – give it a go!'

I keep the erection. I'm ecstatic but terrified. 'It'll peg out. It's bound to peg out. Or it'll pop off. It's bound to pop off. Shit, I can't believe I'm actually doing this—'

'Oh, stop wittering and get on with it! Didn't I always tell you your cock would perk up once it'd had a good rest?'

I keep going for two whole minutes. I know that sounds pathetic, but two minutes is a long time when you've been unable to do it for weeks. Afterwards I wallow in euphoria – only to be slugged by post-coital tristesse. I've taken a big step back to normality, but I'm still nowhere near cured of my phobia about touching men.

*   *   *

479

I decide an assault has to be made on this phobia. Waiting for it to go away won't do. This is because I can't bear the thought that I may soon be fully recovered from agoraphobia and bulimia but still be unable to lead a normal life, mingling with other people.

Lewis and I agree that now's the time for me to attend one of the St Benet's healing services, but having made this bold decision I go wobbly and back down from fixing a date. Supposing the healing doesn't work?

'You can try again later. It's not an all-or-nothing situation,' says Lewis soothingly, and reminds me of the difference the St Benet's team makes between a healing and a cure: a complete cure can never be guaranteed, but a healing, an improvement in the quality of life, is always possible. 'One should think of health as a journey towards a cure, a journey punctuated by healings,' says Lewis. 'And anyway one can argue that a complete cure is never possible because no one can be completely well in mind, body and spirit – such perfection simply doesn't exist in this life. It's the journey towards the cure that's so vital.'

'I feel my journey's grinding to a halt again,' I say, still bogged down in pessimism.

'Then it's all the more important to keep praying for progress.'

'But nothing happens!' I've already prayed myself puce, begging The Bloke to shatter the glass walls that the phobia's built around me, and now I just want to yowl with frustration.

'You mean nothing's happened yet,' says Lewis, 'but to continue to pray is in itself a gesture of faith, signalling that we trust God to heal you when the time's right.'

'But why isn't the time right now?'

'There's clearly another block on the road, but I'm sure you'll get past it once you work out what it is.'

I think I'm just afraid of failure, and it's the thought that I'll fail to be healed which is doing my head in.

I'm in despair.

*   *   *

Lewis cheers me up. He points out what a success I've been, achieving the difficult reconciliations with Hugo and my mother, and now overcoming the nightmare of impotence. (I waited a while to tell him in case I had a relapse, but no, I'm okay.)

Lewis says we should have a drink to celebrate these successes, so we swill some red wine and I show him the letter I've just received from Mum. She says we don't ever have to talk of my London life before the trial. I want to tear my hair at this attempt to sweep my career as a prostitute under the rug, but Lewis suggests that she should be allowed to assimilate the past at her own pace and that I should try to be patient, resisting the urge to fling the truth at her.

I know he's right. Do I really want to talk to Mum about my life as a shag-star? Do I need to? Mum knows what I was, so my nervous urge to parade my past in lurid detail's not only OTT but possibly a revenge-impulse disguised as honesty. Yuk! No, I've got to be kind to the old girl and rein myself in.

'Excellent!' says Lewis, pleased that I've produced this insight. 'Well, at least you're being very clear-eyed about your relationship with your mother.'

I'm just about to preen myself when I realise this is a loaded sentence and we're now in the middle of a pregnant pause. This is because Lewis has laid the emphasis not on the phrase 'very clear-eyed' but on the word 'mother'.

'Hey!' I say. 'What other relationship do I have to be clear-eyed about now I've got both Mum and Hugo explored, explained and sorted?'

But of course I know.

*   *   *

'If you're thinking of Dad,' I say to Lewis, 'you can forget him. He's not a problem – he was just a boat-freak who got his stethoscope in a twist. I've got no hard feelings about him now.'

But the instant these words get uttered I know my feelings are hard as granite.

Dr Heartbreaker. The bloke who was so screwed up he wasn't there for any of his family when it mattered most.

What a shit.

*   *   *

'He was no use when Hugo was dying,' I say ferociously to Lewis later. 'He was no use to my mother when she was so ill with depression. And he was no use to me after Hugo died. He never stopped

481

me trying to become a doctor although he knew I'd never had any interest in medicine.'

'Maybe he simply told himself that if he could become a doctor to please his father, you could too.'

'But he shouldn't have been so angry when I failed!'

'Maybe you weren't the one he was really angry with.'

I stare. 'Meaning?'

'Perhaps he was angry with himself. Perhaps he was wishing *he'd* failed those exams when he was young. Perhaps your escape from medicine reminded him of how he was still imprisoned in it.'

I chew this over but wind up saying: 'He still shouldn't have taken it out on me.'

'No, he shouldn't. It was a very painful rejection, wasn't it, even worse than his emotional withdrawal after Hugo died.'

'Bastard.' I'm shuddering. I try to stop myself but I say the word again. *'Bastard.'* This time I sound violent. A huge rage fills me as I think of him being bored by his doting patients, oppressed by his marriage, indifferent to everyone and everything but his boat. I can still hear the click of that lock as he withdrew to his study and shut the door in my face.

'He hurt people,' I say. I'm breathing really hard now. My lungs feel as if they could burst. 'He *hurt* people. Think how he treated my mother! He broke her heart!'

'Ah yes,' said Lewis without expression, 'but heartbreaking's a symptom of profound unhappiness, isn't it? Anyone who systematically hurts other people is usually carrying a load of unhealed pain.'

All the violence drains from my body, and I cover my face with my hands.

* * *

Seconds slip by. Nothing else happens except that I try to swallow and find there's some kind of football lodged in my gullet.

'Your father was an angry man, trapped in the wrong life,' says Lewis at last. 'It's painful to be trapped in the wrong life, as you yourself well know. It stifles the spirit when you lead an inauthentic existence, out of tune with the person you really are. Indeed, the person you really are becomes crushed and maimed.' He paused before adding: 'This was what happened to your father. But luckily — even, one's tempted to say, miraculously — alongside all the sad memories of his distorted self, you have this magnificent memory of him as he really was. Think of that voyage past the Needles! Your father loved you then, didn't he? He loved you, he loved the sailing, he loved the beauty of the seascape – he was at one with himself, and *that's* the father you want to remember.'

More seconds drift past. I want to retreat to my room and close the door and sit in silence as I yell in my head for the pain to stop—

Or in other words, I want to behave just like my dad.

Trying to give myself a break I mumble: 'Well, it's no use beating myself up over this. He's dead now.'

'Yes, but he's still alive in your head, isn't he? The only reason you haven't noticed him until now is that Hugo was making so much noise.'

That's true. I know it's true. In my head Dad's been another angry, disapproving presence, forever critical and hostile.

'I can forgive him for being a heartbreaker,' I say at last, 'but he'll never forgive me for what I've done with my life. I know he must have forgiven me for not becoming a doctor – Mum said he was keen to find me when I disappeared – but he'll never forgive me for becoming a prostitute.'

'But you're no longer a prostitute, are you? Don't you think that your father, who loved you, would forgive you now you're trying to lead a new life?'

All I can say is. 'I won't believe it until he tells me himself.' How irrational can you get? But fortunately Lewis, as usual, never turns a hair.

'Maybe it'll be easier than you think for your father to forgive you,' he suggests. 'After all, he contributed to your lost years, didn't he? Maybe he now feels guilty.'

'I could never work out what he was feeling.'

'But you knew exactly what he was feeling when you sailed together past the Needles!'

'He'll never come back to me as he was then.'

'Never's a long time, Gavin. Don't give up hope of receiving word that forgiveness has taken place.'

'Well, I'm not waiting for *that* before I go to a healing service!'

'Fair enough, I agree there's no need to hang about, particularly now you've looked at your father with your eyes wide open. Do you want to fix a date?'

But I can't. Supposing I do get healed and can finally live like a normal person? Then I'd have no choice but to ask myself how I'm going to earn my living, and I still can't face the massive anxiety that question raises – just thinking of it makes me want to binge and throw up, even though my bulimia's been so much better lately.

'You need a rest,' says Lewis comfortingly. 'You've gone a long way very fast and now it's time to catch your breath. So let's forget about your father for a moment, and I'll tell you about mine.'

I perk up and prepare to be entertained.

*   *   *

'He was a serial killer,' says Lewis poker-faced. 'You name it, he murdered it: tigers, lions, elephants, birds, rabbits, foxes – oh, and Germans. Naturally he survived the First World War.' And as I laugh, relaxing just as he intended, he adds: 'He died when I was very young so at least I was spared the task of trying to please him by following in his footsteps.'

'I suppose Great-Uncle Cuthbert was a father to you instead,' I say, still smiling, but Lewis answers seriously: 'Great-Uncle Cuthbert was my mentor, and that's not the same thing. All young men growing up need older men who can be mentors, but unfortunately not all fathers have the mentor mentality.'

At once I'm deeply interested. 'You're my mentor even though I'm grown up, aren't you, Lewis?'

'That's for you to say. My job's to be useful to you. If you care to define that as being a mentor, so be it, but it's not something I have the right to name and impose.'

'Could you still be my mentor even after I'm well?' I ask, worried by this self-effacing reply, but Lewis assures me that mentors are useful at any stage of life and even if one's fighting fit. Mentors in matters of the spirit are particularly important in adult life, he says, and if I want him to be my mentor in the future he'd be more than happy to oblige.

Instantly I feel more secure. Even when I'm well Lewis will be there as I struggle to lead a normal life again. And talking of leading a normal life—

I resolve to disclose to him my massive anxiety about getting a job.

*   *   *

'I just don't know what to do,' I say on his next visit. I've now been trying to review this employment problem intelligently instead of freaking out and running to the fridge, but my brain just behaves as if it's mislaid fifty points of IQ. 'I don't want to be an architect any more. Don't want any long expensive training. I could be a builder, but how would I learn? Anyway, stacking bricks all day long could be boring. I'd rather build boats, but how could I do that with no qualifications?'

Round the mulberry bush I go for the umpteenth time. I'm such a dreamer, Susanne says, and there's always such a gap between my dreams and reality. But what *is* the reality here, and what *have* I been designed to do at this particular stage of my life?

'Well, I can think of one thing you already do very successfully,' says Lewis without hesitation.

I'm sunk in gloom. 'Yeah. Prostitution.'

'Raise your sights a little higher.'

'You mean . . .' God, I'm beginning to be seriously worried about my brain. How could the idea of fundraising never occur to me? Because I associated it with the Life, that's why, but if I now uncouple it . . .

'I can't imagine fundraising in a non-prostitution setting,' I say, going defeatist out of sheer nervous fright that there might actually be a job out there I could do. (How do I get an interview when I've no CV? How do I explain that my big experience in raising money is to screw for it?) In panic I retreat into fantasy. 'Maybe I could be a mentor like you, Lewis,' I say, picturing myself rescuing some pint-sized shitlet who thinks turning tricks at Piccadilly Circus is the last word in sophistication.

'You'd have a lot to offer as a mentor,' says Lewis, stunning me. 'You've been around, learning about life the hard way, and there are plenty of people out there who could benefit from your wisdom and experience.'

Maybe the image of the shitlet wasn't such a fantasy after all. 'Runaways, you mean?' I say. 'Kids who wind up penniless in London, like I did, and get involved in drugs and prostitution?' I think about this but can't visualise the route to getting involved. Would I need to become a social worker? A policeman? A – no, scrub the word 'priest'. I'd never be good enough for that.

'There are organisations which help these young people, of course,' says Lewis, 'and a good fundraiser is always in demand. I

485

realise the problem of having no CV, but Nicholas would give you a reference.'

I'm stunned all over again as the word 'fundraising' uncouples itself from the word 'prostitution' and floats alluringly before my eyes. I've glimpsed the future and I like it. And most important of all, it's do-able – it's not just a dream which could never come true.

Telling myself exuberantly that all I have to do now is get healed, I decide to fix a date when I can attend the healing service.

* * *

Bloody hell, I've backed away from fixing a date again, but I can't help it, I'm in a flat spin.

My brand-new anxiety creeps up on me unawares and is innocently triggered by Nicholas, who drops in for a chat. He thinks the fundraising-for-runaways plan is brilliant and he says of course he'll give me a reference. He makes me feel very happy, but when Lewis next visits I'm horrified to hear that Nicholas is thinking of leaving St Benet's.

'But he can't!' I protest. 'It's not possible!'

Lewis smiles and says: 'He thinks it's time he went home.'

'Home' is home in a literal sense this time. Lewis is referring to that old manor house where Nicholas grew up. But surely he's much too young to retire?

Lewis starts to explain. Nicholas has now been at St Benet's for twelve years, and once the expansion of the Healing Centre's completed it could well be the right time for him to change direction, depending on what God has in mind. No one's indispensable, Lewis points out briskly, and even the most successful healing teams can become fossilised and lose their cutting edge. Better to make the change before this happens and leave on a high note. The Holy Spirit blows in all kinds of directions, says Lewis, and the trick is to recognise which way the wind's gusting so that one can go with the flow.

The flow is currently making Nicholas take a hard look at this country house he inherited from his mother. It's been let for years to an Order of Anglican Benedictines – Great-Uncle Cuthbert's Order – but the monks are getting old now, and the retreat-house they established must come to an end.

'Nicholas has been thinking of starting a different kind of healing centre there,' says Lewis. 'It would be modelled on Burrswood in Kent and would be like a small hospital with convalescent facilities where doctors and priests could work together, just as they do at St Benet's. There's a very beautiful chapel in the grounds, rather like the chapel at Little Gidding . . .'

I stop listening. The panic's slugged me. If Nicholas is going home not to retire but to found St Benet's Mark Two, surely he'll need the help of the greatest oldie of all time, the mentor I can't possibly afford to lose?

'What about you?' I say, nearly passing out with the effort to sound casual. 'He'll want you to go with him, won't he?'

'Nicholas and Alice have indeed invited me to continue living with them,' agrees Lewis, 'and that's most kind of them, but I've cluttered up their home quite long enough and besides, living in the country wouldn't suit me. I'd miss the concerts and the art exhibitions.'

The relief's cosmic. 'You'll stay on at St Benet's?'

'That wouldn't be fair on the new rector. And besides, without Nicholas . . . no, I must move on. I'm not sure yet where I should move to, but I'm sure God will make his wishes clear in due course.'

Panic slugs me again. Supposing God decides to send him to his family? His daughter's married to one of the northern bishops, and their vibrant city has both a concert hall and an art gallery . . . But I don't like to ask him any more questions. I'd look such a wimp if he realised I was freaking out at the thought of him being a long-distance mentor.

The result of all this panic is that I look at my future plans much more nervously. And this may be no bad thing, because in my nervousness I sense I'm becoming more realistic. Even when I'm well I don't think I'll have the confidence to plunge straight away into a high-powered fundraising job (always assuming I'm offered one). I need something to bridge the gap, some modest job which will allow me to get office experience and build up my confidence. But how do I go about it? And what the hell would I be capable of doing in an office anyway?

I'm in such a state that I phone Carta to pour out these new employment problems, and she promises she'll help me solve them.

She's the best sister a man never had. I still think she's megashaggable, but so what? A man can have a megashaggable sister and realise shagging's a total non-starter – that's what the incest taboo's all about. There's a sort of plastic side to the brain, as I worked out long ago when I was meditating on sexual orientation, and that's why the brain can adapt to all kinds of peculiar circumstances. My brain's now been moulded by the journey to think of Carta as the best kind of older sister, the kind who escorts you to kindergarten and holds your hand so tightly you can't wriggle free to run under a bus, the kind who doesn't just dump you when you reach the school playground, the kind who takes you to your classroom and tells the local bully that if you're beaten up there'll be hell to pay.

I think Carta and Susanne are both aware now that they're like sisters-in-law, and that's why they can finally get on. Their relationships with me don't impinge on each other, they dovetail.

Weird. But then maybe miracles always are . . .

*   *   *

The very next weekend Carta visits me, and with her comes Eric Tucker who used to be Mr Over-the-Hill but who's now Mr Prime-of-Life, bursting with health and vitality after the success of his last book. Instantly I decide I don't want to see him, but Carta goes off to the kitchen area to waffle with Susanne while coffee's being made so I wind up alone with this bloke who's got a golden career. I hate him and feel a mega-failure. Major relapse.

'Carta says you're worried about how to ease your way into the job market,' he says, 'and I wanted to give you a tip: get the basic office skills. It won't take too long and it won't cost too much. Then you can always earn money temping as a secretary.'

I'm just thinking I hate him worse than ever for underlining what an unqualified mess I am, when I realise he's dangled a good idea in front of me. Even a modest proper-job would build my CV and boost my morale – and maybe I could even have fun hanging around the water cooler with all those gorgeous . . . no, I couldn't. Gavin Blake Office Shag-Star isn't a role I want to audition for. Susanne would castrate me and walk out.

My thoughts skitter on but Eric interrupts them. To my amazement he says: 'I was a mess in my twenties. I lived off women so that I could write my books, and I wound up ploughed under. But my brother Gilbert made me get office skills and eventually I got my life back on track.' He stops, clears his throat. 'Well, that's it,' he says airily as if he's been talking about nothing instead of doing something cool and brave. 'That's all I came to say. Thanks for listening.' And he joins Susanne and Carta who are still chatting about the stock market.

That evening I write him a letter. It reads: 'Hey, thanks for the tip. Thanks for giving a shit. Thanks for telling me how you got sorted. GAVIN.' I chew the end of my pen for five whole minutes before adding: 'PS. I hope you and Carta will be very happy.'

The funny thing is it's much easier to accept that marriage now I know he was a bit like me once but busted a gut to put himself right. He's earned her, he's worthy of her. Okay, good luck, mate, I think as I seal the envelope, and the next moment I realise I'm feeling less anxious about my future employment. If he can turn his life around with the aid of a modest proper-job, then I can too.

*　　*　　*

The St Benet's future's publicly unfolding: Nicholas announces his decision to leave in six months' time. Carta will stay on to manage the office and continue supervising the conversion of the new building, but eventually, she says, she'll get a job as a lawyer in the voluntary sector. She's enjoyed the fundraising but she feels it's not quite her métier.

Val and Robin will be remaining at St Benet's to support the new rector, but Lewis sticks to his decision to leave. His son-in-law the bishop has just received a big promotion to a glamorous southern diocese, but just when I'm telling myself that Lewis won't be able to resist going there to be cared for by his daughter in his old age, he tells me he's determined not to live on his son-in-law's doorstep. He never says so, but I reckon this son-in-law isn't his kind of clergyman.

Seizing the chance to ask him directly about his future at last without making him think I'm obsessed with staying close to him, I blurt out: 'So which city will you be living in?'

'Why, this one, of course!' says Lewis, astonished that I should be in any doubt.

'But you did mention moving—'

'Yes, but to another borough! I was asking myself whether I should move from the City to Westminster or to Kensington and Chelsea or—'

'But that's wonderful!' I shout. Then I get a grip, can the hysteria and say with the necessary seriousness: 'You mean this is okay with God? He doesn't want you to leave London?'

'Naturally God's aware that I'm much too old for such a radical change!' says Lewis, smiling at me, 'and if I stay in London it'll be easier for him to find a place where I can be useful.'

However it seems a short holiday in Cambridge could be on the cards. Lewis says he has a ladyfriend there and although he knows his destiny's to be an unmarried mentor like Great-Uncle Cuthbert, he always enjoys her company. This lady, who's also uninterested in marriage, is a theology graduate currently campaigning for cathedral reform. 'She's rather eccentric,' says Lewis fondly. Talk about the pot calling the kettle black! Maybe they'll get together one day at the altar after all.

I decide I wouldn't mind if Lewis were to produce an interesting wife, but he seems pretty sure he'll get a flat on his own. He's looking for one in Bayswater, where Great-Uncle Cuthbert's Anglican–Benedictine Order still has its headquarters not far from Marble Arch. This house was where Lewis spent his adolescence after being rescued, the house which now seems closest to his idea of 'home'. He couldn't possibly be a monk, he says, but if he lives nearby he can visit often and perhaps be useful to the community in various ways.

Meanwhile everyone's saying: 'How's poor old Lewis going to manage without Nick and Alice?' but he'll be fine. He's not strapped for cash, he'll find the right flat and he'll stuff it with all his music gear and his books and his icons. He'll visit his monks for the daily services in their chapel. He'll keep on working, seeing the people who come to him for spiritual direction. And best of all he'll keep on seeing me.

I'll look after him.

But at present he's busy looking after me, busy being my mentor. He says I have real spiritual gifts. *Me!* Imagine that! What's so great about Lewis is that he's always so encouraging, so sympathetic, so approachable . . . all the things poor old Dad never was. I'm thinking of Dad a lot at the moment – no doubt because he represents unfinished business – and sometimes when Lewis speaks with that same old-fashioned accent I'm enthralled because I recognise him as a healed version of my father.

Thinking of healing resurrects the subject of the weekly healing service, and now that my fear of losing Lewis has been terminated, I find my anxiety levels are low enough to allow me to commit to a date.

It's time to beam in on St Benet's.

* * *

The healers at the services vary, I've learned, because they're drawn from all those who work at St Benet's plus anyone Nicholas chooses to invite, and as Lewis has already told me, they don't have to be priests and they don't have to be men. When Carta received her crucial healing, it was Val, Dr Lush-Lips, who did the laying-on of hands. The healer puts his/her hands on your head – or slightly above your head – and says a prayer. You can even tell him/her what to pray for. The theory is that the healer's lined up so accurately with The Bloke at that moment that The Bloke's power just whooshes straight through to the person who needs healing. This sounds weird, even iffy, but Carta swears the whole process as practised at St Benet's is very low-key, very safe, totally honest. There's no guru promising to walk on water before he drives off in his Rolls-Royce, no wonder-worker egging people on to screech and writhe before they reach for their chequebooks. There are just the healers working quietly and unobtrusively without payment, and beyond them all is The Bloke. Lewis says The Bloke's always there.

As I nervously mull over these reports of the healing service, I know I'll feel a lot less jittery if I can make up my mind who I want my healer to be. I don't have to choose Val. I don't even have to choose Lewis's deaconess. I—

'YOW!' I shout, punching the air with a clenched fist as the image of the ideal person smashes into my mind. Why didn't I think of her before? My IQ must be even more off than I thought it was, but on the other hand no one's put her name forward for consideration. Can't think why not, though. She's the obvious choice.

'*You* do it,' I say firmly to Carta.

* * *

She's shattered. Stunned. Obviously this idea's never occurred to her just as it's never occurred to anyone else. More weird still she

491

now behaves like a preschooler invited to sit A-level physics.

'Oh, but I'm not up to it,' she gabbles in panic. 'I'm just an administrator, not spiritually gifted at all. I'm just a beginner Christian.'

I stare at her, and seeing my astonishment she gabbles on, trying to sound rational but only seeming more nutso than ever. 'I want you to have the best person for the job,' she says, cheeks now a luscious creamy pink, 'and that can't be me, couldn't be. You need someone really special.'

'I can think of no one more special in this context than you. Can't you see? This is where the road's going! We're looking at journey's end!'

She starts to get it. 'You mean—'

'The Bloke's designed it and we've got to help him by rising to the occasion. It's meant to be a grand finale for winners, not a shiver-fest for a couple of wimps!'

Suddenly Carta's eyes fill with tears. She whispers: 'I'm so frightened of failing you.'

But I know all about fear of failure. I know how it can tear you up inside and maim your true self and stop you functioning at your best. Lewis says all spiritual problems are generated by fear of some kind. Fear of failure, fear of rejection, fear of abandonment, fear of loneliness, fear of dying . . .

But no fear's stronger than love. That's why I hug Carta tightly before releasing her and saying: 'Okay, tell me: what's the story?'

*　*　*

Of course she's only got an inferiority complex, but that's not the point. The point is it's a roadblock and has to go. How can you be your whole self when there's a part of your mind telling you that in one area at least you're no good, you're hopeless, you're rubbish? And this has nothing to do with humility. Lewis says genuine humility means being totally realistic about your strengths and limitations. An inferiority complex is about being unrealistic, about having a distorted view of yourself. It's not the same thing at all.

Golden Girl tries to outline her problem. She's always relied on her intelligence, she says. It's been the only thing that's never let her down. People you trust let you down, she says (what's the betting she's thinking of that father of hers, the compulsive

492

gambler?). People behave like absolute shits, she says (what's the betting she's thinking of husband number one, that swine Betz?). People try to stab you in the back, she says (what's the betting she's thinking of every woman-hating male in the City who's tried to wreck her past career as a high flyer?). But so long as you've got brains, she says, you can work out how to survive.

That was her philosophy until 1990 when her brains failed to save her and her world crashed. Then she found out that a load of the most important things in life such as truth, beauty and goodness – and of course love – the whole spiritual package – aren't always accessible through intellectual reasoning and streetwise brainpower. In fact although Christianity can be very intellectually high-powered indeed, spiritual stuff can never be fully sorted by the human intellect. It's too mysterious, and this makes intellect-dependent Carta baffled. How does she cope with this weird new world she's uncovered and make the most of her new raised consciousness? Answer: she doesn't. She's too nervous of failing. She's always equated survival with intellectual success, and she can't imagine surviving in a dimension where there are no exams to pass and you're required to function as the whole you and not just as a brain on legs.

Yes, she did manage to summon the nerve to work for St Benet's, she says, but she could only do the work because it was non-spiritual. She doesn't seem to realise that the deepest spirituality, as I've found out from observing Lewis, is essentially practical and thoroughly engaged with normal everyday life. In contrast Carta seems to think there's a little box in her head marked 'spiritual' which never gets opened unless she's trying to pray – and she's no good at prayer anyway, she says. She's very sorry, but she's sure God understands.

Instantly I picture God staring aggrieved at this flaky little fleck of paint which keeps wilting on the canvas and marring the pattern he's planned for this micro-area. 'You bet God understands!' I snap. 'He's probably saying: "What a load of bullshit!" and tearing his long white beard!'

She manages to laugh. 'I'm nuts, aren't I?'

'Welcome to the club. But we can get healed.'

'I suppose if I were to research healing thoroughly – study the techniques – equip myself with the right special knowledge—'

'You're wandering into the wrong religion! This isn't about special knowledge, as the Gnostics thought, so you can give the high IQ a rest before you blow a fuse. All you and I have to do here is love one another and trust The Bloke.'

She gazes at me as if I'm talking Sanskrit. Funny how people can learn a lot about Christianity and yet be unable to apply it to their daily lives. 'I'm not talking about love as airy-fairy guff or sentimental goo,' I say. 'I'm talking about love as creative dynamite, a force which can make a difference to everyday life and open up all kinds of opportunities which wouldn't otherwise be there. Healing opportunities, for instance.'

'Sure,' she says earnestly, but I know she's still at sea so I decide I have to hit the brain on legs with a flying tackle.

'What's your problem about love?' I demand. 'Why do you feel it has to be kept safe in your head in a little box marked "spiritual"?'

'What on earth do you mean?' she hits back hotly, but she's pulling down all the defences in double-quick time. 'I love Eric. I love you. I love my St Benet's friends. I even love my family when they're not driving me nuts. I don't have a problem about love, just about being spiritual.'

'But love's the most spiritual thing there is!'

'Yes, but . . .' Her eyes fill with tears again. I wait. She looks away. I wait some more, but finally she whispers: 'Love hurts when it goes out of control. It got so I couldn't stand the pain.'

I see it all.

*   *   *

'You're talking about Kim, aren't you?' I say.

'Yes, but I've got over him. I've integrated the good and bad memories. I'm happily married to someone else and my marriage to Kim is no longer unfinished business. I'm fine now.'

That's the way it ought to be, of course. And that's the rational response, the one Carta the Lawyer has drafted with the aid of her intellect and can spew out word-perfect on cue. But how far does this response connect with reality? Well, I know what I think, but I know too that I can't say it. She'd just deny she's still damaged, low on trust, high on suspicion, emotionally tight-arsed, struggling all the time to control love, only letting it out of that multiple-locked little box in her head when she's absolutely sure she won't get wasted.

Well, I'm sympathetic. Of course I am. I know all about loving and being trashed. But I also know, thanks to Susanne and Lewis and The Bloke, that trashing doesn't have to have the last word. You must never knuckle under to being trashed. That represents a failure to respect the worth of your true self, and it converts the trashing into a roadblock in no time flat.

Meanwhile Carta's insisting as she wipes away the tears: 'I'm fine. I just get emotional sometimes at the thought of Kim, that's all.' She scrunches up the Kleenex and gets herself together. 'What were we talking about before we nose-dived?'

'The healing service. You'll do it, won't you?'

'Do what?' The brain on legs must be still punch-drunk from all the spiritual chitchat.

'The laying on of hands, dum-dum!'

'Oh God, I'd quite forgotten—'

'Think of the journey!' I urge, egging her on. 'You're not going to fall by the wayside now, are you?'

'Certainly not!' she says, recovering fast.

'Then friend, I'm begging you: help me out here. If you really love me—'

'I'll do it,' she says, and the die's cast.

She's going to be in that church with me, and there's now no way I'm going to back off in a fit of panic. I need her to be there for me and *she needs me to be there for her* and I'm never going to let her down, never.

So off we go hand in hand at last into the final stretch of the finishing strait of our epic journey, but as I well know from my harrowing swim to shore through the shark-infested waters, there's still no guarantee of survival. It may be grand finale time, but it could also be the time I get blasted.

I'm terrified.

*　*　*

I wear a black tracksuit with a white trim. I never wear an ordinary suit nowadays or designer clothes. Susanne's chosen the tracksuit for me at an East End discount store. For the healing service I also make her buy me some glasses, fake ones which have plain lenses. Sunglasses in winter would look too Mafioso yet I must have something to hide behind as I venture out into the world to take

495

my place among a crowd. I've grown my hair longer for extra camouflage, and in the mirror I see this thin, bespectacled nerd in cheapo gear complete with scuffed trainers. No gay on the make would give me a second glance.

I'll be okay in church, I'm sure of it, but Susanne's going to be in the congregation with me in case anything goes wrong. I did ask her if she'd mind coming to the service but she just said: 'Why should I?' and looked aggressive, as if I was implying she wasn't good enough to attend.

I take some tranx because I can't risk freaking out before the service can even begin. Am I showing a lack of faith in The Bloke's power to heal? No, I'm just blocking off the chance that I'll go nuts before he arrives. I'm lacking faith in *me*, that's the problem. I've come a long way but I'm not healed yet and I'm only human. Of course I'm going to be stressed.

Susanne drives us to St Benet's and pops the car in the space we've been promised on the Rectory forecourt. She then fetches Alice, who's volunteered to be my other female bodyguard, making sure no man sits next to me. More role reversal! Tough women everywhere and a single terrified wuss who needs cocooning. My God, once I get through all this breakdown crap I'm going to open a bar for the macho and call it the Testosterone Club.

We sneak into the church well ahead of the main crowd and sit in the front so that no one has to push past us to get to the central aisle. Val arrives to say she'll be standing within reach when I receive the healing, but I'm not made to feel more of a wuss than ever because I know it's standard practice to have insiders nearby to help catch anyone who passes out. I'm not anticipating passing out. If I go nuts in a big way I'll be fully conscious – why waste the chance for a good primal scream?

When I'm seated I close my eyes, take deep breaths and listen to Mozart in my head. The famous lady's singing the *Laudate Dominum* and once more I'm sailing down the Solent towards the Needles.

'Dad?' I say in my head, but as always, there's no reply.

Susanne grabs my hand and I realise I'm trembling. I get a grip on myself as the organ starts to play, and when I glance at Alice she smiles back encouragingly. I can feel the warmth of her personality soothing me and helping me keep my breathing even.

There are plenty of people present. No shortage of people during the working week in the Square Mile of London's financial district when the City's population of a few thousand swells to over a quarter of a million daily. Conversations are humming behind me but at last everything starts. The healers appear. There's no procession, no drama. They just walk on. Carta's wearing a blue suit with a white blouse and looks paler than usual.

Needless to say, she's gone the whole intellectual hog. She's read the classic books on healing, she's made notes, she's memorised outstanding passages, she's drafted prayers which she's submitted to Lewis for approval, and she's even drafted alternative prayers in case she decides the first ones aren't appropriate after all. How do I know about this whirl of dedicated activity? Because she's told me on the phone, and I've thanked her for going to so much trouble. I'm sincere too, I'm not laughing at her. That's because the real message here is that she cares. For her it's the intellectual machinations that are important, but for me the important thing is the love that drives them.

I think of how Carta was there in the beginning when Richard had his coronary, and now she's with me at the end when I either get healed and found the Testosterone Club or get certified and submit to neuron reassignment. Lewis and I talked again yesterday about the journey, and he pointed out how beneficial it had been not just for me but for her. He said: 'She was compelled to undertake the painful but necessary task of reassessing her relationship with Eric which, when you entered her life, was going nowhere. She succeeded in raising the money for St Benet's even though fundraising's not her true métier. She saw Mrs Mayfield sentenced, an experience which enabled her to move out of the shadow of the past and marry again. And now she's taking a healer's role in this service – a very big step for her, and one which she would never have considered a short time ago. If she hadn't met you, how much of all that would have happened?'

I think now, after recalling this conversation, of all Carta's done for me. I wouldn't be here if I hadn't met her. She was my bridge to St Benet's, a bridge thrown together by The Bloke in a brilliant move which converted my routine sexual harassment into the kind of life-giving, life-saving relationship which I could never, in my dumb ignorance, have imagined. All I need to do now to kickstart the new life that's been opened up for me is to get reconciled with Dad and healed of my phobia, and instead of saying to myself in

497

panic: 'How do Carta and I bear it if this trip today's a bust?' I should be fixing my eyes on the way ahead in the belief that the last two of my roadblocks are about to be blown aside.

I clamp down on my anxiety as I realise everyone's standing up to sing a hymn. Alice sings away confidently on my left but I can't even manage one note, my vocal chords have gone on strike. I glance at Susanne. She's not singing either but she's fascinated, beady black eyes taking everything in, big mouth slightly open in amazement. Nothing like this has ever happened to her before. She's like an astronaut taking his first steps on the moon and I know she's thinking: weird, maybe pervy but maybe not, sort of creepy but sort of interesting, not exactly a barrel of laughs but they mean well, no one's getting hurt or ripped off, yes, it's okay, I'll go along with it, *I don't mind.*

I tighten my clasp on her hand. I love Susanne. And no, I'm not going to outgrow her when I'm better. And no, it doesn't matter that she's not religious. Lewis says religious people have a horrible tendency to write off people who aren't 'religious', but what does 'religious' in this narrow, judgemental sense mean anyway? You can be very 'religious' and yet miss the whole point of religion. The Bloke came for everyone, that's the truth of it. He didn't just come for 'the religious'. He came for me, a prostitute, someone who thought he had no religion at all. In the New Testament The Bloke's on record as being really kind to a prostitute. In fact the incident where The Bloke showed her she counted, she mattered, is so important that it's recorded in all four Gospels. All you 'religious' people out there who have been looking down your noses at me and wincing at my filthy language and filthy lifestyle should remember that The Bloke himself never flinched or turned away.

Oh my God, I must be psychic. Lewis is reading the first lesson, and—

Yes, here it comes. The woman sneaks in to a social gathering, she washes The Bloke's feet with some ultra-luxury stuff which has obviously cost her a bundle – and at once all the snotty onlookers are saying she should have given the money to the poor instead. But The Bloke puts them in their place just as Nicholas put Carta in her place when I gave him Richard's cuff links, the most beautiful and the most expensive present I could produce at that moment.

I think of that poor slag two thousand years ago. I think: I know how you felt, sister. You saw truth and goodness, such truth and such goodness that you wanted to offer up the most valuable thing you had as a token of your gratitude for being given such a vision – but the vision wasn't just a vision, and it wasn't taking place in some never-never land either. The truth and the goodness came out to meet you in reality right here on earth. It didn't matter that you were the lowest of the low. The truth and goodness encircled you, they made you feel you counted, you mattered, because beyond the truth and the goodness was love, and love is the great reality, the greatest reality any of us can ever know.

I suddenly realise that Lewis has stopped reading, and in the silence that follows, the hairs stand bolt upright on the nape of my neck.

The Bloke's arrived. He's sauntered through the closed doors, and now he's moving among the crowd.

Nicholas says some prayers but I can't hear a word because I'm so busy willing The Bloke to move in my direction. Then comes another hymn. The Bloke's moved up to the altar to join the healers, I think, but I'm not sure. I just know he's in the church.

Robin reads the second extract from the New Testament. St Paul's talking about how The Bloke appeared after his death to five hundred people at once. Mass hysteria? Mass hypnosis? No, just a psychic aspect of reality, the aspect that's normally difficult to access. I bet I'm not the only person right now in this church who knows The Bloke's here – and no, don't tell me this is all wishful thinking! I can't see him, I can't hear him, I can't touch him, I can't smell him, but reality is far, far wider and deeper and more mysterious than the stuff that's available to our senses, and I *know* he's with us now. That doesn't mean I'm not gobsmacked, though. When Lewis said The Bloke was always at the healing services, I thought he was indulging in clergy-speak. I never dreamed The Bloke would actually—

The healers are getting ready.

But I'm not nervous now because I'm so focused on this extraordinary presence. I wait, breathing deeply, until it's time for me to make my move.

We've decided that I should be the last one to go up because then there'll be no risk of me bumping into anyone. There are three healers at work – Nicholas, Lewis and Carta – and so when I go up to replace whoever's coming down at that moment, there'll be two other people up there with me receiving healing, but even if these other two are men it won't matter because we'll be standing several feet apart.

The moment comes. Susanne, as arranged, remains seated but Alice stands up with me and takes me to Carta. It's not standard practice to have an escort, but Alice is making a gesture of solidarity, and as we all draw together I'm again aware of us as the three outsiders, all originally alienated and lost, yet all led in the end to St Benet's and the alternative lifestyle on offer here. Alice began her journey before Carta, just as Carta began her journey before I began mine, but now all our paths are meeting as the dance moves into its final bars.

Alice takes a step back as I reach Carta.

I remove my glasses. I don't need to hide behind them any more, and at last Carta and I are face to face. She's standing on the chancel step, so although she's still shorter than I am she's more on a level with me.

She opens her mouth. Being Carta she's rehearsed her next words as carefully as she's researched them, and knowing approximately what they'll be I've framed my response. She's going to ask: 'Any special prayer you'd like me to say?' and I'm going to answer: 'Pray for you and me and our journey, and for all those who love and pray for us.'

But she doesn't say what she's planned to say, and I don't say what I've planned to say either. In the end we say nothing at all.

That's because in a flash we're beyond words. The greatest, the most profound truths are beyond words anyway. We look at each other and we love each other and that's enough. We don't need to do any more.

I see the tears fill her eyes as she finally understands. This is where all your books get closed, Carta. This is where you unplug the computer. 'Love one another,' said The Bloke all those years ago in one of the greatest of all commandments, and that's what we're doing, we're totally lined up with him, and as the line-up locks into place we're dead centre in the path of this colossal power.

I yell in my head: 'HEAL HER!' – yeah, I don't think of me, only of her – but the words are just an unnecessary reflex and it wouldn't have mattered if the plea had never zipped through my brain. He understands, he knows, he's here – and suddenly Carta's calm. She's one hundred per cent sure she's doing the right thing in the right place at the right time – and because of this she knows, just as I do, that nothing at all, neither storms, nor earthquakes, nor typhoons, nor tornados, nor rivers, nor mountains, nor shark-infested seas – nor phobias, nor complexes, nor hang-ups, nor freak-outs, nor fear in all its many destructive forms – *nothing*, NOTHING can block us both now from our journey's end and coming home.

She reaches up with confidence. She puts her hands gently on my head, and as I gasp for my next breath the colossal power scores a direct hit on my brain.

The Bloke's standing right behind her. He's streamed right through her and he's taken over her hands.

I'm zapped. I stagger – lose my footing – and before either Val or Alice can reach me from behind, the man who's just received healing on my right darts sideways to steady me.

'No!' cries Carta, grabbing me away from him as Val blocks him off, and at once the man falls back – but not before I've cringed as if I'm still unhealed.

With a vile jolt I realise there's no 'as if'. I'm not healed. Despite everything going dead right, I'm still dead phobic. The Bloke will have to have another go later. I feel terrible for letting everyone down. What a failure I am! How fucking bloody useless! It's a mega-relapse. I'm shredded.

I want to run all the way home, but I owe it to my friends to act my socks off and pretend everything's fine. And whatever happens Carta must never know. I can say the fatal cringeing was just a mindless reflex and meant nothing. So long as I pretend to be well now, I can always say in a couple of weeks' time that I've had a relapse for reasons which have nothing to do with her performance today.

I make a huge effort to calm myself by breathing evenly. The service is almost over, thank God. Just one more hymn to go.

Afterwards I wait for the crowds to disperse. Mustn't run the risk of being touched. I try to tune in to The Bloke but nothing happens so I figure he must have gone.

Alice says anxiously: 'Are you all right?' and that's when I realise I can't lie. I can't let my friends know what's happened, not yet, but I can't say one word that isn't true. So I answer her by saying: 'I'm pretty overwhelmed,' but I smile at her to signal she's not to worry.

Someone else appears. Carta. My heart sinks but then I see what

I have to do. I have to forget me and focus on her, just as I did before. That way I can be totally happy and totally truthful.

I leap to my feet and hug her. 'You were great!' I exclaim. '*Great!*' Well, that's no lie, is it? She was so brave to agree to take part in the service. She was so magnificent to love me enough to be there. The word 'great' hardly does her justice.

She hugs me too but she's waiting for me to say how I am and when I say nothing she looks up at me anxiously. 'How do you feel?'

'Shattered.'

'That man—'

'What man? Oh, him! Sorry, my brain's in pieces, I haven't reassembled it yet—'

'It's okay, don't worry!' she says at once. 'I've read all about this. Sometimes the healing doesn't kick in immediately. Sometimes—'

'Good to know all that research wasn't entirely wasted! Hey, shouldn't you be on the door with Nicholas and Lewis to say goodbye to all your new fans?'

We promise to talk later and away she skims with Alice, both convinced that the healing couldn't possibly have failed. Well, at least Carta got healed today even if I didn't.

I sink down in my seat again. Susanne and I are all alone now at the front of the church. She doesn't ask how I am. She knows. Well, I could never fool Susanne, could I? She always sees straight through me with those sharp black eyes of hers. But they're not sharp now. They're full of her special brand of no-bullshit love. Holding my hand again she waits as I dredge up the strength to leave.

And then something truly phenomenal happens, even more extraordinary than The Bloke taking over Carta's hands and scoring a direct hit on my brain.

I'm just slumped there, awash with misery and utter humiliation, when the colossal power streams back like a bomb smashing through the roof, and the next moment psychic reality's exploding all over everywhere.

'Well done, Gavin!' my father exclaims, and his voice is so loud and so clear that I almost jump out of my skin. '*Well done!* You've shown tremendous courage today – I'm *so proud* of you!'

At once I think: he's forgiven me. He still loves me. We're sailing once more past the Needles, we're together again at last.

I leap to my feet. I know it's my father who's there, and when I swing around and see only Lewis, I'm neither surprised nor disappointed. Lewis uttered the words but my father was speaking through him. The Bloke picked someone with an identical voice because he wanted to make quite sure I got the message, and the message is that Dad and I are finally reconciled.

Another bomb hits the scene as I realise what this means. The dance has ended – the dance has come right. The relationships are healed. Love's won out. The colossal power's not just zapped me and moved on – it's wheeled around and zoomed in to complete the job, it's encircled me, it's infused me, it's liberated me, and I know now beyond any shadow of doubt that this is the moment when my new life finally begins.

'I'm home,' I say stunned to Lewis. 'This is it. I've come home to my true self.' Then the wonder of it hits me between the eyes. 'JESUS CHRIST!' I shout, and at once the glass walls of my phobia shatter into a million pieces. 'I'M HOME, I'M HOME, I'M HOME!'

And simultaneously I'm hurtling forward into Lewis's outstretched arms.

Author's Note

The Heartbreaker is the third in a trilogy of novels about healing in modern London. Each book is designed to be read independently of the others, but the more books are read, the wider will be the perspective on the multi-sided reality which is being presented. The first book, *A Question of Integrity* (published in the USA and Canada as *The Wonder Worker*), is set in 1988 when Alice Fletcher meets Nicholas Darrow at a time when his marriage is under strain. The second book, *The High Flyer*, is set in 1990 when Carter Graham (before she became Carta) seeks help from Nicholas and his colleagues as the result of her marriage to Kim Betz and her encounters with Mrs Mayfield.

The Quotations

The Right Reverend Professor Richard Holloway, author of the books quoted at the beginning of the chapters in part one, was Bishop of Edinburgh from 1986 to 2000, Primus of the Scottish Episcopal Church from 1992 to 2000 and Gresham Professor of Divinity from 1997 to 2001.

Mud and Stars, the book quoted throughout *The Heartbreaker*, is subtitled: 'The Report of a Working Party on the Impact of Hospice Experience on the Church's Ministry of Healing'. Although dealing primarily with hospice care, the report also has much to say about the ministry of healing in general. The chairman of the working party, which consisted mainly of doctors, nurses and clergy, was Dr Robert Twycross, Clinical Reader in Palliative Medicine at the University of Oxford.

A Time to Heal, the book quoted at the beginning of the chapters in parts two and three, is subtitled: 'A Report for the House of Bishops on the Healing Ministry', and reviews the ministry of healing in the Church of England. The working party which produced this report consisted of priests, members of religious orders, doctors and lay-people, and the chairman was the Right Reverend John Perry, Bishop of Chelmsford.